T0146809

"Some of the top names in urban fantasy are joined by some of today's best historical mystery writers in this top-notch anthology . . . The rational and supernatural are perfectly blended in entries like Lisa Tuttle's remarkable 'The Curious Affair of the Deodand,' a Sherlockian homage that deserves sequels. [Laurie R.] King's versatility is demonstrated convincingly in 'Hellbender,' which is set in a future where human and salamander DNA have been combined and plotted in ways that Chandler would recognize." —*Publishers Weekly*

"Urban fantasy in a noirish vein . . . This is a pretty strong selection of longer stories . . . One masterwork like Bradley Denton's 'The Adakian Eagle,' one of the best stories of the year so far, would justify a book of duds, and *Down These Strange Streets* is not that. Stories by Carrie Vaughn, Laurie R. King, and Glen Cook, among others, justify the price of admission." —*Locus*

"There [are] lots [of stories], some in the past, some in the future, and all entertaining as you get to read old favorite characters or are introduced to new ones. I always enjoy anthologies for the variety in the stories, and this one provides plenty, but all with a paranormal detective bent." —NewsandSentinel.com

"This book boasts a stable full of star power . . . Grab this mystifying and chilling collection to start Halloween early this year." —*Shelf Awareness*

"Urban fantasy fans are sure to enjoy this latest compilation of sixteen short stories by several leading authors of the genre . . . 'The Bleeding Shadow' by Joe Lansdale is a satisfying, stand-alone little horror story about a struggling blues musician who signed away more than he realized in order to become a better player. Simon Green's 'Hungry Heart,' set in the Nightside of London, is [a] short tale about a witch who, in a bid for more power, gets everything she deserves. 'The Adakian Eagle' is an outstanding telling of a young soldier stationed in Alaska during World War II struggling to seek a balance between duty and morality while deciding whom to trust . . . This is a strong anthology."

—*Monsters and Critics*

Down These Strange Streets

Edited by

GEORGE R. R. MARTIN AND
GARDNER DOZOIS

ACE BOOKS, NEW YORK

THE BERKLEY PUBLISHING GROUP
Published by the Penguin Group
Penguin Group (USA) Inc.
375 Hudson Street, New York, New York 10014, USA
Penguin Group (Canada), 90 Eglinton Avenue East, Suite 700, Toronto, Ontario M4P 2Y3, Canada (a division of Pearson Penguin Canada Inc.) • Penguin Books Ltd., 80 Strand, London WC2R 0RL, England • Penguin Ireland, 25 St. Stephen's Green, Dublin 2, Ireland (a division of Penguin Books Ltd.) • Penguin Group (Australia), 707 Collins Street, Melbourne, Victoria 3008, Australia (a division of Pearson Australia Group Pty. Ltd.) • Penguin Books India Pvt. Ltd., 11 Community Centre, Panchsheel Park, New Delhi—110 017, India • Penguin Group (NZ), 67 Apollo Drive, Rosedale, Auckland 0632, New Zealand (a division of Pearson New Zealand Ltd.) • Penguin Books, Rosebank Office Park, 181 Jan Smuts Avenue, Parktown North 2193, South Africa • Penguin China, B7 Jaiming Center, 27 East Third Ring Road North, Chaoyang District, Beijing 100020, China

Penguin Books Ltd., Registered Offices: 80 Strand, London WC2R 0RL, England

Cover art by Larry Rostant.
Cover design by Lesley Worrell.
Text design by Tiffany Estreicher.

PUBLISHING HISTORY
Ace hardcover edition / October 2011
Ace trade paperback edition / December 2012

Ace trade paperback ISBN: 978-1-937007-91-1

The Library of Congress has cataloged the Ace hardcover edition as follows:

Down these strange streets / edited by George R. R. Martin and Gardner Dozois.—1st ed.
p. cm.
ISBN 978-0-441-02074-4
1. Fantasy fiction, American. 2. Mystery fiction, American.
I. Martin, George R. R. II. Dozois, Gardner R.
PS648.F3D59 2011
813'.0876608—dc23
2011027173

146122990

To our friend Jack Dann,
who has walked down some pretty strange streets himself

CONTENTS

THE BASTARD STEPCHILD

There's a new kid on the shelves in bookstores these days. Most often he can be found back in the science fiction and fantasy section, walking with a certain swagger among the epic fantasies, the space operas, the sword-and-sorcery yarns and cyberpunk dystopias. Sometimes he wanders up front, to hang out with the bestsellers. They call him "urban fantasy," and these past few years he's been the hottest subgenre in publishing.

The term "urban fantasy" isn't new, truth be told. There was another subgenre that went by that name back in the 1980s; it mostly seemed to involve elves playing in folk-rock bands and riding motorcycles through contemporary urban landscapes—usually in Minneapolis or Toronto, both of which are very nice towns.

The new urban fantasy may be some kin to that 1980s variety, but if so, the kinship is a distant one, for the new kid is a bastard through and through. He makes his home on streets altogether meaner and dirtier than those his cousin walked, in New York and Chicago and L.A. and nameless cities where blood runs in the gutters and the screams in the night drown out the music. Maybe a few elves are still around, but if so, they're likely to be hooked on horse or coke or stronger, stranger drugs, or maybe they're elf hookers being pimped out by a werewolf. Those bloody lycanthropes are everywhere, though it's the vampires who really run the town . . . And don't forget the zombies, the ghouls, the demons, the witches and warlocks, the incubi and succubi, and all the other nasty, narsty things that go bump in the night. (And worse, the ones that make no sound at all.)

Try being a cop in a town like that.

Try being a private eye.

The bastard subgenre that is today's urban fantasy is the offspring of two older genres.

Horror is the mother that gave it birth. (And that's *horror*, if you please, don't give me any of this "dark fantasy" claptrap, that's just a feeble attempt to pull a cloak of respectability down over the grinning skull of a genre that traces its own roots back to penny dreadfuls and Grand Guignol.) The vampires, werewolves, ghosts, and ghouls that roam the alleys of today's urban fantasy all started out in the horror ghetto originally, given form and voice by Bram Stoker, Edgar Allan Poe, H. P. Lovecraft, and the generations of writers who followed in their twisted, misshapen footsteps.

The father of today's urban fantasy, however, is the mystery story. And not just *any* old kind of mystery story. The so-called cozy story of detection, where little old ladies puzzle out who killed the curate in the snuggery with no weapon but a lace doily, is not part of its heritage. No, we're talking *noir* here, we're talking the strong stuff, raw and dirty. The ancestors of Harry Dresden, Anita Blake, Rachel Morgan, Mercy Thompson, Jayné Heller, and the rest of that hard gang of demon hunters and vampire killers who populate the alleys and byways of urban fantasy can be found in Sam Spade, Lew Archer, Travis McGee, Mike Hammer, and Race Williams . . . and, of course, Philip Marlowe, Raymond Chandler's iconic private eye.

In his classic essay in *Atlantic Monthly*, "The Simple Art of Murder," Chandler wrote:

> Down these mean streets a man must go who is not himself mean, who is neither tarnished nor afraid. The detective must be a complete man and a common man and yet an unusual man.

The heroes and heroines of urban fantasy fit Chandler's prescription perfectly . . . though I expect that even Marlowe himself would be surprised at just how unusual some of them can be. But maybe not.

Truth be told, the private eye of Chandler and Hammett and their hard-boiled successors has more in common with the vampires and werewolves of horror fiction than with most real-life private investigations. Whereas their fictional counterparts are solving murders, unraveling plots, and walking through the bad neighborhoods that even the cops dare not enter, the real-life PIs spend their days documenting adultery for sleazy divorce lawyers, dealing with corporate security and industrial espionage, and investigating fraudulent insurance claims. The urban fantasists are only taking the trope one step further. Sam Spade has more in common with Harry Dresden than either of them do with the people you'll find listed under "Private Investigators" in the yellow pages.

Raymond Chandler also wrote:

> The private detective of fiction is a fantastic creation who acts and speaks like a real man. He can be completely realistic in every sense but one, that one sense being that in life as we know it such a man would not be a private detective.

The heroes of urban fantasy come out of the hard-boiled mystery, while the villains, monsters, and antagonists have their own roots in classic horror . . . but it is the *combination* that gives this subgenre its juice. For these are two genres that are at heart antagonistic. Horror fiction is a fiction steeped in darkness and fear, and set in a hostile Lovecraftian universe impossible for men to comprehend, a world where, as Poe suggested, death in the end holds dominion over all. But detective fiction, even the grim, gritty, hard-boiled variety, is all about rationality; the world may be dark, but the detective is a bringer of light, an agent of order, and, yes, justice.

You would think this twain could never meet. But bastards can break all the rules, and that's half their charm. The chains of convention need not apply.

Consider, for example, a case wherein a dead body is found drained of all blood.

If a reader comes upon that scenario in a horror novel, he knows at once that there's a vampire lurking about somewhere. The cops may or may not twig to it, depending on the world the story is set in, but the reader knows the answer: the book says HORROR on the spine.

If a reader comes upon the identical scenario in a mystery novel, though . . . Well, now he knows it is definitely *not* a vampire, no matter what it looks like. Some psycho killer who thinks he's a vampire is about as far as any "realistic" mystery novel will go.

In both cases, genre expectations define and shape our reading experience and color the ways in which we will perceive the events of the story.

It is only when the bastard stepchild takes the stage that real uncertainty sets in. Now we're dealing with a hybrid form: part fantasy, part mystery. All the conventions must be called into question. Suddenly the puzzle is a puzzle again. Maybe it's a vampire, maybe it's a psycho, maybe neither, maybe both, maybe something else entirely. Better keep reading to find out.

"Better keep reading to find out" are the sweetest words any writer can hear.

Of course, today's urban fantasists are by no means the first to cross the classic private eye story with fantasy and horror. Poe himself did it, with those murders in the Rue Morgue. Arthur Conan Doyle confronted Sherlock Holmes with the Hound of the Baskervilles . . . and though, in the end, the hound proves no more supernatural than Lassie, the story's frisson all comes from the possibility that he may be something much darker and more frightening.

And then there is Robert A. Heinlein, the most unlikely proto–urban fantasist of all . . . but what else is one to make of my favorite Heinlein story, "The Unpleasant Profession of Jonathan Hoag," wherein the mousy Hoag hires a husband-and-wife team of private eyes to investigate what it is that he finds under his fingernails when he wakes up every morning. Is it blood, or . . . something else?

(I won't spoil the story by telling you. The Bird is Cruel.)

That's the great thing about this bastard stepchild. The streets he walks are just as mean as those that Spade and Marlowe walked, but considerably stranger . . . and they can take you most anywhere. As the book that you hold in your hand will show.

My partner in crime Gardner Dozois and I did not restrict ourselves to a single genre or subgenre when assembling this table of contents. Instead, we reached out to fantasists, mystery novelists, crime writers, romance authors . . . and some of the top names in contemporary urban fantasy. All we asked of them was that the story involve a private detective and a case with a fantastic slant, be it real or . . . less so. Whether you're a fan of mystery fiction, urban fantasy, horror, or science fiction, you should find some of your favorite writers in these pages . . . and other writers you may never have heard of who we think you'll enjoy just as much. So come walk these strange streets with us, and let's see where we'll end up.

George R. R. Martin
July 1, 2010

DEATH BY DAHLIA

by Charlaine Harris

New York Times bestseller Charlaine Harris is the author of the immensely popular Sookie Stackhouse series about the adventures of a telepathic waitress in a small Southern town, a series that includes *Dead Until Dark*, *Living Dead in Dallas*, *Club Dead*, *Dead to the World*, and seven others. The Sookie novels have now been adapted into a popular HBO television series called *True Blood* as well. To satisfy the curiosity of her fans, Harris has edited a guide to the Sookie series, *The Sookie Stackhouse Companion*. Harris is also the author of the four-volume Harper Connelly paranormal series (*Grave Sight*, *Grave Surprise*, and two others), as well as two straight mystery series, the eight-volume Aurora Teagarden series (consisting of *Real Murders*, *A Fool and His Honey*, *Last Scene Alive*, and five others, recently collected in *The Aurora Teagarden Mysteries Omnibus 1* and *The Aurora Teagarden Mysteries Omnibus 2*) and the five-volume Lily Bard series (consisting of *Shakespeare's Landlord*, *Shakespeare's Champion*, and three others, recently collected in *The Lily Bard Mysteries Omnibus*), as well as the stand-alone novels *Sweet and Deadly* and *A Secret Rage*. She's also edited the anthologies *Crimes by Moonlight*, and, with Toni L. P. Kelner, *Many Bloody Returns*, *Wolfsbane and Mistletoe*, *Death's Excellent Vacation*, and *Home Improvement: Undead Edition*. Her most recent novel is a new Sookie Stackhouse book, *Dead Reckoning*.

Here she takes us, in company with the powerful vampire Dahlia Lynley-Chivers, to a lavish party for various creatures of the night, where the festivities get a bit rougher and more deadly than even Dahlia might have anticipated.

Dahlia Lynley-Chivers had been a woman of average height in her day. Her day had been over for centuries, and in modern America she was considered a very short woman indeed. Since Dahlia was a vampire and was reputed to be a vicious fighter even among her own kind, she was usually treated with respect despite her lack of inches and her dainty build.

"You got a face like a rose," said her prospective blood donor, a handsome, husky human in his twenties. "Here, little lady, let me squat down so you can reach me! You want me to get you a stool to stand on?" He laughed, definitely in hardy-har-har mode.

If he hadn't preceded his "amusing" comment on Dahlia's height with a compliment, she would have broken his ribs and drained him dry; but Dahlia was fond of compliments. He did have to bear some consequence for the condescension, though.

Dahlia gave the young man a look of such ferocity that he blanched almost as white as Dahlia herself. Then she stepped pointedly to her left to approach the next unoccupied donor, a blond suburbanite not too much taller than Dahlia. The woman opened her arms to embrace the vampire, as if this were an assignation rather than a feeding. Dahlia would have sighed if she'd been a breather.

However, Dahlia was hungry, and she'd already been picky enough. This woman's neck was at the right height, and she was absolutely willing, since she'd registered with the donor agency. Dahlia bit. The woman jerked as Dahlia's fangs went in, so Dahlia considerately licked a little on the wound to anesthetize the area. She sucked hard, and the woman jerked in an entirely different way. Dahlia was a polite feeder, for the most part.

The blonde's arms squeezed Dahlia with surprising force, and she gripped a handful of Dahlia's thick, wavy, dark hair, which fell in a cascade reaching almost to Dahlia's waist. The blonde pulled Dahlia's hair a little, but she wasn't trying to pull Dahlia off . . . not at all.

At Dahlia's age, she didn't need to drink much at a sitting (or perhaps *at a biting* would be a more appropriate phrase). After a few pleasurable gulps, the vampire had had enough. Dahlia didn't want to be greedy, and she'd taken such a small amount that it would be safe for the woman to donate again on the spot.

Dahlia gave a final lick, and when the air hit the licked puncture marks, her natural coagulant set to work almost instantly. The blond woman seemed disappointed that the encounter was over and actually tried to hold on to Dahlia. With a stiff smile, Dahlia removed herself with a little more decision. The donor turned to the next vampire in line, who was Cedric. She would have to be stopped after that; most people who enjoyed being bitten enough to be listed with the donor agency simply weren't smart about when to stop.

"You could be a little nicer," Dahlia's best friend Taffy said reprovingly. "Would it have hurt to you tell the breather how good she was?" Dahlia would have ignored anyone else who ventured to give her advice on her manners, but Taffy was within two hundred years of being as old as Dahlia. They were the oldest vampires in the nest, and their friendship had survived many trials.

Taffy had been practically Amazonian during her lifetime, and she remained an impressive woman even now. She was five foot seven and busty; her light hair exploded in a tangled halo around her head and fell past her shoulders. Taffy's husband Don was one of the trials they'd survived, and it was because of Don's preference that Taffy went heavy on the makeup and tight on the clothes. Don thought that was a mighty fine look on Taffy.

Of course, Don was a werewolf. His taste was dubious, at best.

Taffy waved at Don, who was over by the food table. Werewolves were always hungry, and they could drink alcohol until the cows came home—and then the Weres would eat them. A party with an open bar and a buffet was like heaven to Don and his new enforcer, Bernie. The two Weres were making the most of the opportunity, since politics demanded they be in the vampire nest for Joaquin's ascension celebration.

Dahlia noticed Don and Bernie casting contemptuous glances at the group of blood donors. Werewolves thought humans who were willing to give blood to vampires were from the bottom of the barrel. Any self-respecting Were would rather have his fur shaved off. Dahlia was sure Don didn't mind giving Taffy a sip in private . . . at least she hoped that was the case. During Dahlia's own brief marriage to the previous enforcer, her husband had not been averse to a little nip.

The demons and half-demons huddled together in a corner, and just after a very skinny female said something, they all burst into laughter. Dahlia looked for one half-demon computer geek she knew better than the others. With a frisson of pleasure, she spotted Melponeus's reddish skin and chestnut curls in the cluster. Their eyes met. The half-demon and Dahlia exchanged personal smiles. They had had some memorable evenings together in Dahlia's bedroom on the lower level of the mansion. The glitter in Melponeus's pale eyes told Dahlia that the demon wouldn't mind a replay.

She might retrieve some pleasure from this dismal evening, after all.

A few creatures Dahlia didn't recognize were scattered through the crowd. No fairies, of course; vampires loved fairies to death, literally. But there were other creatures of the fae present, and a witch. Joaquin had a reputation as a liberal, and he'd made up the party list and presented it to Lakeisha, who'd retained her post as the executive assistant to the sheriff despite the change in regimes. Lakeisha had sniffed at some of the inclusions, but she had obeyed without a verbal comment. All the vampires were walking softly and carefully until they learned their new leader's character. Since he'd lived on his own, not in the nest, until his appointment as sheriff, Joaquin was a largely unknown element.

As Taffy took Dahlia's arm to steer her over to the buffet to join Don, Dahlia said, "I'm not enjoying myself, though I ought to be."

"Why not?" Taffy asked. "The humans will be gone soon, and we can be ourselves. It's not like we haven't seen this coming. Cedric has been getting more and more set in his ways. He's lazy. He's sloppy. A waistcoat every day. So dated! He can't even pretend to belong to this century."

Like all successful vampires, Dahlia knew that the key to surviving for centuries was adaptation. And the most conspicuous adaptation was following the trend in clothes and language. This had been essential when vampires existed in secret, so they could blend in with a crowd long enough to cut out their prey. Vampires were an increasingly familiar presence in business and politics, but they found that society still accepted them more easily if they mimicked modern Americans. It was true, too, that old habits died hard. It had been only six years since the undead had "come out," and to vampires that was less than the blink of an eye.

"I did see that Cedric would have to be replaced," Dahlia said. "I don't know Joaquin well, and maybe I'm worried about how he will rule, and how living in the nest will be with him in residence. At least he had a very conventional ascension."

"It couldn't have been more standard," Taffy agreed. "And soon the guests will be gone and we can amuse ourselves. I'm pleased with Joaquin's first steps. The mansion is looking beautiful, more beautiful than it did for my wedding." Taffy tapped the newly polished wooden floor with the toe of her boot. The reception room, which was large and full of dark leather furniture and scattered rugs, was at the back of the mansion and looked out onto the garden. Taffy had gotten married in that garden one memorable night. Though the night was chilly the fountain was splashing away in the dimly lit courtyard outside the French doors. The lights didn't need to be bright; vampires have excellent night vision.

Dahlia was proud that the mansion, which housed the vampire nest of Rhodes and was the area headquarters for all vampires, was polished and sparkling, clean and newly redecorated. However, Dahlia's pride had a certain nostalgic tinge. Though for decades they'd all tried to prod the old sheriff, Cedric, into installing new carpet and modernizing the bathrooms, she found that she missed the old fixtures. And she missed the former sheriff, too. Maybe he counted as an old fixture.

"I'm going to talk to Cedric," she said.

"Not the smartest move, homes," Taffy cautioned. Taffy always tried to use current slang, though sometimes she got it wrong or was off by five years . . . or ten.

"I know," Dahlia said. The new sheriff, Joaquin, was certainly keeping an eye open to see who approached Cedric; but Dahlia was not afraid of Joaquin, though she did regard him with a certain respect for his devious ways. The ousting of Cedric had been handled with a sort of ruthless finesse. Cedric, sunk into what he thought would always be his cushy job, had been foolishly complacent and unaware. "I'll join you later," she told Taffy. "Though I may stop to have a word with Melponeus, too."

"Playing with fire," Taffy said, grinning broadly.

"Yes, we did that last time." Even half-demons could produce fireballs. The memory caused Dahlia to have her own tight smile on her lips as she approached the former sheriff.

"Cedric," she said, inclining her head very slightly. Even Dahlia didn't care to provoke Joaquin by appearing to offer Cedric obeisance.

"Dahlia," he said, his voice laden with melancholy. "See how the peacock preens?"

Joaquin, in the center of a cluster of other vampires, was dressed to kill. Obviously Joaquin felt like the king of the world on his ascension night. In his thin, dark hand he held a goblet of Royalty (a blend of the blood of various European royals, who could keep their crumbling castles open with the money they made by tapping into their own veins). His favorite artiste, Jennifer Lopez, was playing in the background. He was wearing a very sharp dark gray suit with a pale gray silk shirt, and in his crimson tie was an antique pearl stickpin. Fawning all over Joaquin was Glenda, a flapper-era vamp who had never been Dahlia's favorite nest sister.

"You could use a little preening, Cedric," she observed. Cedric was wearing fawn-colored pants and a white linen shirt with a flowered waistcoat, his favorite ensemble. He had many near-duplicates of all three pieces hanging in his closet.

Cedric ignored her comment. "Glenda looks good," he said. In the past Glenda had slipped into Cedric's bedroom from time to time, more to keep the sheriff sweet than from any great affection. Dahlia had often seen the two clipping roses in the mansion garden at night. They'd both been ardent rose growers in life—or at least, Glenda said she had been.

Glenda, who was no more than ninety, did actually look very tempting this evening in a thin blue silk slip dress with absolutely no undergarments. She was smoothing Joaquin's shirt with the air of someone who knew what lay beneath the silk. Dahlia harbored a certain appreciation for Glenda's cleverness.

"You know she's trash," Dahlia told Cedric.

"But such delicious trash." After tossing his head to get his long pale hair out of his way, Cedric took a pull on his bottle of Red Stuff, a cheap brand of the synthetic blood vampires drank so they could pretend they didn't crave or require the real thing. This was sheer affectation; Dahlia had watched Cedric approach a donor.

Red Stuff was a far cry from Royalty in a crystal goblet. Cedric's mustache drooped, and even the golden flowers and vines in the pattern on his waistcoat looked withered.

Having served their purpose, the human donors were being ushered out of the large reception room by a smiling young vampire. They'd be taken to the kitchen and fed a snack, allowed to recover from their "donation," and returned to their collection point. This had been found to be the most efficient method of dealing with the humans the agency sent. If they weren't shepherded every step of the way, these humans showed a distressing tendency to want to hide in the mansion so they could donate again and again. Some vampires weren't strong-willed enough to resist, and then . . . dead donors and unwelcome attention from the police followed.

The only donor left in the room was the young man who'd irritated Dahlia. He seemed to be in the process of irritating Don, Taffy's husband, packmaster of Rhodes. That proved his stupidity. Dahlia turned back to Cedric.

"Will you stay in the nest?" Dahlia asked. She was genuinely curious. If she'd found herself in Cedric's position, she would have packed her bags the second the king chose Joaquin.

"I'll find an apartment elsewhere, sooner or later," Cedric said indifferently, and Dahlia thought that this perfectly illustrated Cedric's drawbacks as a leader.

Though he'd been a dynamic sheriff in his heyday, Cedric had gradually become slow . . . and that was the nicest way to put it. This indolence and complacency, creeping into Cedric's rulings and decisions over the decades, had been his downfall. It was no surprise to anyone but Cedric that he'd been challenged and ousted. To the newer vamps, the only surprise was that Cedric had ever been named to the position in the first place.

"The situation won't change," Dahlia said. Cedric would make himself a figure of fun if he gloomed around the mansion during Joaquin's reign. "I'm sure you've saved money during your time in office," she added, by way of encouragement. After all, all the vampires who lived in the nest contributed to their sheriff's bank account, and so did the other vampires of Rhodes who chose to live on their own.

"Not as much as you would think," Cedric said, and Dahlia could not restrain a tiny gesture of irritation. Her sympathy with the ex-sheriff was exhausted. She excused herself. "Melponeus has asked to speak to me," she lied.

Cedric waved a dismissive hand with a ghost of his former graciousness.

While Dahlia strode across the carpet to the cluster of demons, not the least hampered by her very high heels, she glanced back to see Cedric open the door to the hall leading to the kitchen. He stepped through at the same time as Taffy and Don. Glenda called, "Taffy!" and passed through after them.

Then Dahlia stopped in front of Melponeus, his fellow demons clearing the way for her with alacrity. Though Dahlia was a straightforward woman by nature, she was also incredibly conscious of her own dignity, and she didn't care for the leering element in the smiles the demon's buddies were giving her. Melponeus himself surely knew that. After the barest moment of conversation, he swept Dahlia away to an empty area.

"I apologize for my friends," he said instantly. Dahlia forced her rigid little face to relax and look a bit more welcoming. "They see a woman as lovely as you, they can't regulate their reactions."

"You can, apparently?" Dahlia said, just to watch Melponeus flounder. He knew her better than she'd thought, because after a moment's confused explanation, he laughed. For a few minutes, they had a wonderful time with verbal foreplay, and then they danced. "Perhaps later . . ." Melponeus began, but he was interrupted by a scream.

Screams were not such an unusual thing at the vampire nest, but since this one came in the middle of an important social occasion, it attracted universal attention. Every head whipped around to look east, to the wing occupied on the ground floor by the kitchen.

"Don't move," called Joaquin, to stem the surge of the crowd in the direction of the commotion. Somewhat to Dahlia's surprise, everyone obeyed him. She found that interesting.

Even more interesting was the fact that Joaquin searched the crowd until his eyes met hers. "Dahlia," he said, in lightly accented English, "take Katamori with you and find out what's happened." Katamori had been something of a policeman a couple of centuries ago.

Dahlia had to work to keep her face expressionless. "Yes, Sheriff," she said, and jerked her head at Matsuda Katamori, a vampire who had an apartment near Little Japan. Katamori, who appeared just as surprised as Dahlia at being singled out, immediately glided to her side. They moved quickly to the door to the passage leading to the mansion's kitchen.

It wasn't a wide space, and the carpet had been installed to deaden sound, not to beautify. Both the vampires were alert as they moved silently down the passage to the kitchen. The swinging door had been propped open.

When the mansion had been built in the early 1900s, the builder could not have imagined that the kitchen would be used by non-eaters. The white tile floors and the huge fixtures had been maintained, even updated, once or twice during the century that had passed. When Cedric had bought the mansion at a bargain price (glamour had been involved), he'd left the kitchen as though it would still be needed to prepare a banquet. Normally, the stainless steel fixtures shone in the overhead lights suspended from the high ceiling.

Now the stainless steel was splashed with red. The smell of blood was overwhelming.

From where they stood just inside the doorway, Dahlia and Katamori couldn't see the body because of the long wooden table running down the middle of the room, but a body was undoubtedly there. The only thing living in the kitchen was one of the half-demons, a skinny girl Dahlia hadn't met before. The girl was standing absolutely still, very close to the corpse, if Dahlia's nose was accurate, and her hands were up in the air. Smart.

Dahlia enjoyed the smell of blood, but she preferred her blood to be fresh and its source living, as did every vampire but the rare pervert. Once the blood had been out of the living body for more than a couple of minutes, it lost much of its enticing smell, at least to Dahlia's nose. From the delicate twitch of Katamori's nostrils, he felt much the same.

The girl's feet were hidden from view by the old wooden table, originally intended for staff meals and food preparation. But the blood smell was emanating from the area around her, and red had splashed the gleaming range and refrigerator on the south wall. She was standing squarely in front of the refrigerator.

The half-demon girl opened her mouth to speak, but Dahlia held up her hand. The girl closed her mouth instantly.

"Is any of this blood yours?" Dahlia asked.

The girl shook her head.

Dahlia and Katamori looked at each other. Dahlia didn't have to look up far to meet his eyes. He waited for her instructions. She was the senior vampire. She liked this silent acknowledgment a lot. Dahlia said, "I'll go right, you take left." She didn't know much about Katamori, but she did know that his reputation as a fighter was almost as formidable as her own.

Without a word, the slightly built Japanese vampire began working his way around the north side of the table, his eyes and ears and nose working overtime. The north wall featured huge windows, now black. The effect was unpleasant, as if the night were watching the scene in the kitchen, but Dahlia was not about to be distressed by any nighttime creepiness. She herself was the thing that went bump in the night.

She began circling the table to the south side. The stove tops and ovens, a stainless steel prep table with pots and pans on a shelf underneath, and an industrial refrigerator and a freezer filled the wall. A few steps revealed the crime scene. The half-demon girl was standing stock-still on the edge of the pool of blood that had flowed from the victim. Dahlia took in the whole picture, then began noting the details.

The corpse was that of the young man who had irritated her, the human donor she'd last observed having words with Don. The man's throat had been torn out. Dahlia had seen much worse in her long, long existence, but she was irritated at the waste of the blood.

The half-demon girl had not a speck of blood on her, except for her shoes, which were red Converse high-tops, now somewhat darker around the rubber soles. Dahlia raised her delicate black eyebrows and looked across the room.

"Katamori?" she said.

"Lots of people have been through," Katamori answered.

From this laconic response, Dahlia understood that he'd found nothing tangible on his side of the room, but that there were complex scent trails. That made sense. The north side of the kitchen was the natural route to take to get to the door on the far end of the long room. This door led into a mudroom with hooks for wet weather gear and gardening clothes. On the other side of the mudroom, a heavier door opened out onto the broad apron marking the end of the service driveway. All the humans who'd come to the mansion to donate earlier in the evening had both entered and left the mansion through that door.

"Please stay where you are for the moment," Dahlia said to the half-demon, who bobbed her head in a series of sharp nods. Since the blood pool and the body took up the whole of the floor between the appliances and the table, Dahlia bent her knees and leaped over the table, landing lightly on her amazing heels on the other side.

She met Katamori at the end of the table, and together they looked back at the body. There was a series of bloody footprints leading away from the corpse, footprints too large to be those of the half-demon girl. These prints led to the first exit door, the door to the mudroom. Together, they examined it. There were no bloody fingerprints on the knob or the glass panes. Dahlia bent over to sniff the knob, then shrugged. "A bloody hand touched it, but that tells us nothing," she said, and pushed the door open. Katamori tensed, ready for anything.

The mudroom was empty.

The two vampires stepped into the small space. The floor was covered with a rubber mat, and there was a bench running along each side. Underneath were stored a few pairs of boots, some of which had been there for forty years. A coat or two hung from the row of hooks mounted above the benches. At least one of the coats had been there for two decades, an elaborate black coat with a huge fur collar. "I don't think anyone will return to get this one," Katamori said, and pushed it with his finger. A cloud of dust rose up. Dahlia noticed that most of the hooks were similarly covered in dust. Only two of the hooks were shiny enough to indicate they'd been used recently.

The knob of the solid door that led to the outside was pristine to the eye, and when Dahlia bent to smell she got only a whiff of blood, a slightly weaker trace than that on the inner knob. "Left this way," she told Katamori. "Let's finish the kitchen, then we'll report."

They turned back into the kitchen.

Before they'd left, the humans had piled their plates and cups by the sink. Fainting humans were bad for business, so the agency had insisted the vampires take a tip from the blood bank in offering refreshments. Nothing to be found there; the victim hadn't approached that area.

"What do we have so far?" Katamori asked.

"There's a vampire smell in here, very recent," Dahlia said.

"Besides the half-demon, I'm getting humans, a werewolf, at least two vampires."

Werewolves. Dahlia's mouth twitched. But first of all, she had to interrogate the only living creature in the cavernous room. "Demon girl," she said, "explain yourself." Now that Dahlia spared a moment to take in the half-demon's ensemble, Dahlia's eyes widened. The skinny creature, whose short hair was dyed a brilliant lime green, was wearing black Under Armour from top to bottom. Her red sneakers were a fine clash with the lilac miniskirt and a buckskin vest lined with fleece.

"I'm Diantha," the girl said. And then she began a long sentence that was possibly in English.

"Stop," Katamori said. "Or I'll have to kill you."

Diantha stopped in midword, her mouth open. Dahlia could see how very sharp the half-demon's teeth were, and how many of them seemed to be crammed into her little mouth. Katamori would have quite a fight on his hands, and Dahlia found herself hoping it wouldn't come to that.

"Diantha, I'm Dahlia. Our names are similar, aren't they?" Dahlia said. She hadn't tried to sound soothing in a century or two, and it sat awkwardly on her. "You must speak so that we can understand you. Maybe it will help you to be calm if we tell you we know you didn't do this thing."

"We do?" Katamori knew the reason, but he wanted Dahlia to spell it out.

"No blood on her, except on her shoes." She didn't bother to lower her voice. Diantha's bright eyes were on her so intently that she knew the girl could read her lips.

"I'mtherunnerformyuncleinLouisiana," Diantha said. She didn't seem to need to breathe when she spoke, but at least this time she spoke slowly enough—at less than warp speed—that the vampires could understand her.

"And you are here at the ascension party because . . . ?"

"Rhodesdemonswereinvited, Iwasstayingthenightafterbringing—" And the rest of her sentence ran together in a hopeless tangle.

"Slower," Dahlia said, making sure she sounded like she meant it.

Diantha sighed noisily, looking as exasperated as the teenager she appeared to be. "Since I was here for the night, they invited me to come with them." She put an almost visible space between each word. "Nothing else to do, so I came with."

"You're visiting from Louisiana on a business errand, and you came to the mansion with the Rhodes demons because they were invited."

Diantha nodded, her green spikes bobbing almost comically. If Dahlia hadn't seen demons fight before, she might have laughed.

"How did you happen to enter the kitchen?" Katamori asked. During Dahlia and Diantha's conversation, he had circled the table to stand at Diantha's back. She had turned slightly so she could keep both vampires in view, since she was now bracketed between them. Despite Dahlia's assurances, the half-demon girl didn't like her situation at all. Her knees bent, and her hands fisted, ready for a challenge.

But when she spoke, her voice was steady enough. "I was going to the refrigerator," Diantha said, still making the effort to speak slowly. "You guys were out of Sprite, and I thought it would be all right if I checked to see if there was more in the refrigerator. Ismelledtheblood—"

Dahlia held up an admonishing hand, and Diantha slowed down. "I yelled because I smelled the blood as I stepped in it."

"Not before?" Most supernaturals had a very sharp sense of smell.

"Smell of vampire had deadened my nose," Diantha said.

That made sense to Dahlia. Though the scent of vampire was naturally delightful to her, she had been told many times that it was overwhelming to other supernaturals.

"Was the blood still running when you came in?" The thicker trickles from spurting arteries were barely moving down the shiny surface of the appliances, and the cast-off drops that had been slung away when the throat had come out were beginning to dry at the edges.

"Little," Diantha said.

"Was anyone else here?" Katamori said.

Diantha shook her head.

The two vampires glanced at each other, eyebrows raised in query. Dahlia couldn't think of any more questions to ask. Evidently Katamori couldn't, either.

"Diantha, in a second you can move." Dahlia and Katamori closed in on each side of the body. "All right," Dahlia said. "Step out of the blood. Take off your shoes and leave them."

The half-demon girl followed Dahlia's instructions to the letter. She perched on the wooden table to remove her red high-tops. She placed her stained shoes neatly side by side on the floor. "Stayorgo?" she asked, looking much more cheerful now that she wasn't so close to the corpse. Demons didn't often eat people, and proximity to the body hadn't been pleasant for her.

"I think you can go," Dahlia said, after a moment's thought. "Don't leave."

"Gobacktotheparty," the girl said, and did so.

By silent agreement, the two vampires bent to their task. With their excellent vision and sense of smell, they didn't need magnifying glasses or flashlights to help them analyze what they saw.

"The human donors came into the kitchen and ate and drank," Katamori began. "A vampire shepherded them."

"As always," Dahlia said absently. "And that's a vampire we need to talk to, because somehow this human got left behind, or he hid himself. Obviously, the shepherd should have noticed."

"A werewolf came through here, probably after the death. Perhaps more than one werewolf," Katamori continued. He was crouched near the floor, and he looked up at Dahlia, his dark eyes intent. His black braid fell forward as he bent back to examine the floor, and he tossed it back over his shoulder.

"I don't disagree," Dahlia said, making an effort to sound neutral. Any trouble that involved the werewolves would involve Taffy. "I think we should tell Joaquin that the shepherd needs to come here now, or as soon as he's returned."

Katamori said "Yes," but in an absent way. Dahlia went to the swinging door. As she'd expected, one of Joaquin's friends, a wispy brunette named Rachel, was waiting in the hall. Dahlia explained what she needed, and Rachel raced off. Cedric had forbidden the use of cell phones in the mansion, and Joaquin had not rescinded that rule yet, though Dahlia had heard that he would.

In two minutes Gerhard, the shepherd of the evening, came striding down the hall to join Dahlia. She could tell by the way he walked that he was angry, though he was smiling. That perpetual smile shone as hard as Gerhard's short corn-blond hair, which gleamed under the lights like polished silk. He'd lived in Rhodes for fifty years, but he and Dahlia had never become friends.

Dahlia didn't have many friends. She was quite all right with that.

"What would you like to know?" Gerhard asked. His German accent was pronounced despite his long years in the United States.

"Tell me about taking the humans out of here," Dahlia said. "How did you come to leave this one behind?"

Gerhard stiffened. "Are you saying I was derelict in my duties?"

"I'm trying to find out what happened," Dahlia said, not too patiently. "Your execution of your duties is not my concern, but Joaquin's. The man is here. He isn't supposed to be. How did that come about?"

Gerhard was obliged to reply. "I gathered the humans together to leave. We came to the kitchen. I followed procedure by showing them the food and drink provided. After ten minutes, I told them it was time to go. I counted as we left, and the number was correct."

"But here he is," Katamori said, straightening from his crouched position by the body. "So either your count was incorrect, you are lying, or an extra human took his place. What is your explanation?"

"I have none," Gerhard said, in a voice so stiff it might have been starched.

"Go to Joaquin and tell him that," Dahlia said, without an ounce of sympathy.

"Well, then." Gerhard became even more defensive. "This man and I had come to an arrangement. I left him here because upon my return we were to spend time together."

"Though he had already donated this evening," Dahlia said.

"His name was Arthur Allthorp. I have been with him before," Gerhard said. "He could take a lot of . . . donation. He loved it."

"A fangbanger," Katamori said. Fangbangers, extreme vampire groupies, were notorious for ignoring limits.

Gerhard gave an abrupt nod.

Neither Dahlia nor Katamori remarked on the fact that Gerhard had initially lied to them. They knew, as did Gerhard, that he would pay for that.

"He was my weakness," Gerhard said violently. "I am glad he is dead."

This sudden burst of passion startled Dahlia and disgusted Katamori, who let Gerhard read that in his face. Gerhard whirled around to leave the kitchen, but Dahlia said, "What time did you leave with the humans? Was anyone in here with the man Arthur when you took the others away?"

Gerhard thought for a second. "I bade them get into the vans at ten o'clock, since that was the time appointed by the agency that sent them. There was no one in here. But I could hear people coming down the hall as I waited for the other donors to exit. I'm sure one of them was Taffy."

Dahlia would have said something unpleasant if she'd been by herself. As it was, she was aware of Katamori's quick sideways glance. Everyone in the nest knew that Dahlia and Taffy were friends, despite Taffy's unfortunate marriage. Dahlia's own brief marriage to a werewolf had been forgiven, since it had lasted such a short time. But Taffy showed every sign of continuing her relationship with Don, and even of being happy in it, to the bafflement of the other vampires of Rhodes. "We'll have to find Taffy and Don and ask them some questions," she said. "Gerhard, would you request this of Joaquin?"

Gerhard gave a jerky nod and barged out the door, shoving it with such force that it was left to swing to and fro in an annoying way.

Dahlia turned her attention back to the spray of blood on the fixtures and the blood pooled on the floor, still wet. "In my experience," she said to Katamori, "it takes over an hour for blood to begin to dry. Given its tacky quality and the low temperature of this room, I believe the body has lain here for at least thirty minutes, give or take."

Katamori nodded. They were both experts on blood. They looked up at the clock on the kitchen wall. It read ten forty-five.

"If Gerhard did leave with the humans at ten o'clock . . . say it took him five minutes to encourage them to put their dishes by the sink, and to get them out the door . . . then this Arthur was left by himself at ten oh five or ten ten. I talked to Cedric, and then I danced with Melponeus." Dahlia was trying to figure out when the scream had brought the party to a halt.

"We heard Diantha at ten thirty," Katamori said. With some surprise, Dahlia saw that he was wearing a watch, an unusual accessory for a vampire. "And we were in here within a minute and a half of that. We've been investigating for perhaps twenty minutes. So someone entered the kitchen between ten minutes after ten and twenty-five minutes after ten, by the narrowest reckoning."

"And this Arthur died of his throat being ripped out," Katamori said.

"Yes. Though he may have been choked before that. Without the excised material it's hard to say."

"It's over here." Katamori pointed to a grisly little mound of skin and bone half-hidden under a chair.

Dahlia squatted to peer at the discarded handful. "This is so mangled, I still can't say whether he was choked. This tissue was tossed aside, not consumed."

Katamori made a moue of distaste.

Dahlia said, "I was thinking of the trace of werewolf, and all that that implies." Werewolves would eat human flesh, at least when they were in their wolf forms.

"Do you think we've seen everything there is to see, smelled everything there is to smell?" Katamori asked, tactfully bypassing the werewolf issue.

"Let's go through the human's pockets," Dahlia suggested, and Katamori squatted on the other side of the body. Dahlia had quick, light fingers, and she was thorough. Folded and stuck in a pocket on her side of the corpse, she found a sheet from the donor bureau containing a rendezvous point and a scheduled donation time for tonight. Just as Gerhard had said, the donors were to be picked up at eight, then returned to the pickup point at ten.

Dahlia wondered if Gerhard had told Arthur to make sure he was included on the donor list. It couldn't have been a coincidence that Gerhard's favorite banger had been included in the donor party. In the last four years it had become a regular practice for the hosts of parties to which vampires had been invited to hire donors from a registered donor bureau, so they could be sure that all the human snacks on offer had been examined for blood-borne diseases and psychoses. There was a disease vampires could catch from humans (Sino-AIDS), and donors had been checked for hidden agendas ever since a donor in Memphis brought a gun and opened fire on the assembled partygoers.

Dahlia opened Arthur Allthorp's wallet to get his donation card, which was perforated with seven holes. The card was punched every time the agency sent him out. After Dahlia had turned over the body to go through the other pants pocket, Katamori patted down Arthur's legs. To their surprise, he found a knife in an ankle sheath. *Very* careless. Gerhard's inefficiency was now a mountain rather than a molehill.

After a glance of silent agreement, the two stood, having gotten all the information from the body. They looked all around the vast kitchen for any clue they might have missed. The blackness continued to stare in through the big windows. The blood continued to cling wetly to the stainless steel surfaces. Arthur Allthorp, fangbanger, continued to be dead.

After Katamori deadbolted the outside door, he and Dahlia left the kitchen. Rachel had resumed her post in the hall, and Dahlia asked her to keep guard over the swinging door. "Let no one into the kitchen until we're sure we don't need it anymore," she said. "No one will be able to enter from the outside."

Rachel nodded, her expression intense. She was still proving herself as a vampire, and Dahlia felt sure Rachel would stand her ground against anyone who wanted to see the body.

Back in the reception room, Joaquin had resumed his seat in the throne-like chair reserved for the sheriff. His ascension party had taken a definite downturn in tone. The festive atmosphere had degenerated to uneasy apprehension. The partygoers were milling around anxiously. The demons and part-demons had established a tight knot in one corner with Diantha in its center, and the fae (an oread, a rare nix, and an elf) clustered close to them.

Bernie Feldman, Don's enforcer, was watching the French doors with unmistakable worry. Bernie was standing oddly, as if nursing a hurt in his stomach. Dahlia followed his eyes. Approaching, obviously disheveled, were Taffy and Don. Taffy had her shoes in her free hand. The other hand was holding Don's, and the two were looking at each other with what Dahlia could only describe as goo-goo eyes.

"Disgusting," she muttered, and Katamori glanced at the happy pair. "They went through the kitchen," he said. "We're going to have to question them."

"Better report to Joaquin first."

The two vampires went to stand in front of their new leader. Dahlia bowed her head to a carefully calibrated angle. Katamori's head was perhaps a centimeter lower than hers. Joaquin accepted their gesture and waited for them to report. He looked better in the chair than Cedric had. Joaquin was slim and tall, with thin dark hair and large brown eyes. The new sheriff hadn't been a vampire as long as Dahlia (only two of the Rhodes vampires had been), but jobs didn't always go to the oldest.

Glenda was draped over the back of the sheriff's seat as if being Joaquin's new fuck buddy gave her some special status. Dahlia eyed the vampire with no expression. Her dislike of Glenda went from vague to specific.

"What have you discovered?" Joaquin asked, giving the two investigators all his attention.

Dahlia was pleased with the mark of respect. "The human was named Arthur Allthorp. He was a pet of Gerhard's." Dahlia had already spotted the blond vampire, who was trying to look stoic but only managing gloomy. "Gerhard allowed Arthur Allthorp to remain in the kitchen while Gerhard took the other donors back to their rendezvous point. I see that he has told you that." Gerhard was flanked by Troy and Hazel, the vamps Joaquin had named as his punishers.

"Furthermore," Katamori said, "I found a knife strapped to the human's ankle."

Another nail in Gerhard's coffin, perhaps literally.

"He died very quickly when his throat was torn out," Dahlia said. "We know he died in a fifteen-minute window, give or take a minute or two, between ten ten and ten twenty-five."

Katamori said, "Passing through the kitchen close to the time of death were the human donors, Gerhard, another vampire or two I can't identify, and at least one werewolf."

All eyes went to Don and Bernie, who had been whispering furiously into Don's ear. Don looked shocked and grim. Taffy was the only vampire standing anywhere close to them, and she took her husband's arm. He patted her hand to show her he appreciated the support. Bernie stood to Don's other side, and he had an expression Dahlia had seen before. It meant, *I'm ready to die, but I'd rather not.*

"It won't make any difference to you, Joaquin, but I didn't do it," Don said in his deep voice. "I can't imagine why I'd have any reason to kill the poor bastard, though maybe motive doesn't interest you." If Dahlia had had a moment to do so, she might have advised Don that this was not the time for sarcasm.

"Don and I did go through the kitchen," Taffy said. "But we were on our way out into the garden to have a talk."

"What was that talk about?" Glenda asked.

"You were right on our ass, so you probably know already. But I don't answer to you," Taffy said, and the light of battle flashed into her eyes.

"Any vampire who spends time with a werewolf has degraded herself and has no status in the nest," Glenda said, straightening and taking a step away from the sheriff's chair.

Dahlia was instantly on the alert. If she let Taffy take on Glenda, Don would get involved, and the whole situation would get unnecessarily complicated. When Glenda took another step in Taffy's direction, Dahlia was ready. She leaped and kicked as hard as she could, and Glenda went flying through the air with her beautiful clinging dress whipping around her, as Dahlia landed gracefully and spun around to make sure Glenda was down. The crack of Glenda's ribs was audible as she met the wall. She slid down to collapse on the carpet, bleeding and whimpering.

Joaquin didn't move, but his eyes were blazing. From their positions flanking Gerhard, Troy and Hazel snarled. There was a long, tense moment with all eyes on Dahlia.

"Excuse my preemptive punishment of Glenda, Joaquin," she said calmly. "I acted without your permission, but I was incensed at her presumption. She has no right to make such a pronouncement with you sitting in front of us. You alone have the right to determine who belongs in our community and who doesn't. Glenda showed unforgivable disrespect."

Joaquin blinked. "Interesting interpretation of Glenda's words," he said.

No one went to help the fallen vampire. Possibly they were all afraid that Dahlia would consider them an enemy if they did so.

"She *was* presumptuous," Joaquin said after a moment's consideration, and the room relaxed. Dahlia could tell that more than one vampire would have enjoyed seeing her deal out even more damage to Glenda, but she'd made her point and interrupted Glenda's accusation.

Joaquin continued, "Do you know who the other vampires were who passed through the kitchen at the vital time?"

"One was Cedric," she said. "I know his scent too well to mistake it. And I witnessed Glenda following Taffy, Don, Bernie, and Cedric out of the room, but I'm not sure if she entered the kitchen or not."

Joaquin's heavy eyebrows flew up in surprise. He looked at his predecessor.

"I walked through the kitchen," Cedric said. He was leaning against the wall. "I was right on the heels of Taffy and her werewolf, but Glenda went out before me, not after. I wanted to talk to her."

"Why?" Joaquin said. He looked up at Cedric, whose blue-patterned waistcoat was rumpled up above his belly. Even Cedric's boots were scuffed, while Joaquin's loafers shone like mirrors. The contrast could not have been more unkind: Cedric the old catfish, Joaquin the sleek barracuda.

To the side of the room, Glenda moaned as she struggled to her knees to get to her feet. Very quietly, another vampire stepped over to let her drink from him. Dahlia noticed that he was looking as neutral as possible, as if his arm just happened to be in the right place in front of Glenda's mouth for her to have a healing draft. He even kept his eyes on the floor so Dahlia couldn't meet them. Dahlia smiled inside. It was good to be feared.

"Why?" Cedric said. "Because I wanted to go outside, and I hoped she would walk with me, for old times' sake. Because, in case you hadn't thought of it, this is a very awkward evening for me, and I needed friendship."

The demons looked amused, the Weres embarrassed, and the vampires all looked elsewhere. An open admission of weakness was not the vampire way. Only Dahlia looked thoughtful.

Joaquin said, "Taffy, what happened out in the garden?"

Taffy bowed her head to her sheriff. "Of course I'll answer, if my sheriff asks it," she said graciously, reinforcing Dahlia's point. "We talked to Bernie, my husband's enforcer, about his lack of courtesy to one of the demons." She nodded her head toward Diantha. "Bernie was . . . uncouth enough . . . to make fun of her speech patterns. Don felt the need to teach Bernie a lesson about diplomacy. As you can see, Don made his point."

Now that danger had passed, Bernie had resumed his hunched-over position. He was clearly uncomfortable. He bobbed his head in acknowledgment, straightened, and winced. "My leader did correct me," he said.

"While we were in the garden," Taffy continued, "We remembered it was the site of our wedding, and we celebrated in an appropriate way." She smiled brilliantly at Joaquin, pleased that she'd phrased it so diplomatically. Taffy had never been subtle.

Don grinned at her and slung his arm around her shoulders. "We had a *great* celebration back in the bushes," he said. "Even if it was colder than a witch's tit."

The only witch present opened her mouth to protest, but Dahlia whipped her head around to look at the woman in a significant way. The witch's mouth snapped shut.

"But none of this offers any proof that the human didn't die at your hands," Joaquin said in the most reasonable of voices.

"We haven't got a speck of blood on us, Sheriff," Taffy said, holding out her arms to invite inspection. "When Don gave Bernie his etiquette lesson, he didn't break the skin. My husband knows that the smell of blood is tough on vampire sensibilities."

"Would the killer be blood-spattered?" Joaquin asked Dahlia. "You saw the wound."

"I'll defer to Katamori," Dahlia said. "It's well-known that Taffy and I are friends."

"A vampire moving at top speed, a vampire who had performed this kill many times, might be able to avoid the blood," Katamori said. "Anyone else would have had to change clothes." He walked over to the couple and examined them with minute care. "I see and scent no blood on Taffy and Don."

Dahlia's shoulders might have relaxed a fraction.

Gerhard said quickly, "I'll smell like blood because I took some from a donor this evening." It was Dahlia's turn to work, and she looked Gerhard over from stem to stern. She straightened to tell Joaquin, "He does have a trace of blood scent, and one pinpoint of blood on his collar, but nothing out of the ordinary."

Cedric said, "You may examine me, Katamori," though no one had suggested this. Katamori glanced at Joaquin, got no signal either way, and moved over to Cedric. He'd give Cedric a thorough examination, Dahlia knew. Katamori had never been fond of Cedric.

"I can't find any on Cedric's clothes," Katamori said. "Though he does smell slightly of blood."

Cedric shrugged. "I partook of the donors," he said.

There was a pounding on the mansion's front door.

Dahlia looked at the clock on the wall, just as a precaution. It was now eleven fifteen. Arthur Allthorp had been dead around an hour. The front doorkeeper for the evening, a young vampire named Melvin, came into the reception room so quickly that he skidded on the parquet floor. "The police are here, Sheriff," he said to Joaquin. "They say they've had a report of a body on the premises."

"How long can you delay them?" Joaquin snapped.

"Ten minutes," said Melvin.

"We'll need it," Joaquin said. "Go."

Melvin began walking slowly through the archway on his way back to the front door. He was looking at his watch.

"Katamori and I will dispose of the body," Dahlia said, and she and Katamori took off at top speed. As they passed Rachel, still on guard at the swinging door, Dahlia said, "Cleanup crew, right now!" Rachel moved so fast you could hardly see her go, and Dahlia could hear her call a few names in the reception room.

It wasn't the first time a body had had to be disposed of quickly in the mansion.

While Katamori unlocked the mudroom door, Dahlia pulled an ancient tablecloth from the linen closet. Together, the two vampires wrapped the body in the yellowing linen to prevent drippage. Dahlia took the feet and

Katamori lifted the shoulders. They were carrying the body out while the cleaning crew swarmed through the swinging door. Conveniently, all the cleanup material was kept in the kitchen, and as Katamori and Dahlia took their burden through the mudroom and out the final door, she glimpsed the vampires on duty opening cabinets to pull out the bleach and turning the faucets in the sinks while others fetched the mops.

The dead man had been tall and heavy. Since Katamori and Dahlia were not too far apart in height they could bear the weight equally, and they were both immensely strong, so Arthur Allthorp's weight wasn't an issue. His bulk was. They carried the body through the landscaped garden to the huge, formal fountain, which splashed in the middle of a knee-deep pool. The statue in the middle of the fountain was a woman in flowing drapery. She was holding a tilted jug, out of which the running water splashed into the pool. At the side of the fountain farthest from the house, they laid down the body. Dahlia leaped up on the broad edge of the pool and craned over precariously to fish a key from the statue's drapery. It wasn't in the fold that usually held it, and she had a moment's severe jolt until she felt the metal edge in the next fold down. All the vamps in the house knew the key's location, and once or twice it had been misplaced. With a huge feeling of relief, Dahlia hopped down, a little wet from the experience.

She squatted to insert the key in the keyhole of a large panel in the base of the fountain. This panel looked as though it had been designed to give access to the plumbing and the fountain mechanism, but the vampires had designed it for another use. Though this body was somewhat bigger than most of the previous bodies that had been hidden there, and though the hole was partially obstructed, they had to make it work. Dahlia actually crawled into the space to pull on the body, while Katamori remained outside to stuff the legs in. Then Dahlia had to crawl out over the body, getting even more rumpled and a bit stained in the process.

By that time, she and Katamori could hear the police surging through the mansion.

"I can't be found like this," Dahlia said, disgusted, looking down at her dress.

"Then take it off," Katamori said, holding the maintenance panel open. "I have an idea."

When the police came out to search the garden, they found Katamori and Dahlia frolicking in the fountain stark naked. The sight froze them in their tracks. Not only was it fall and chilly, but in the moonlit garden Dahlia was white as marble.

"All over," said one of the cops, awestruck. "And he's just a shade darker."

"Did you need to talk to us?" Dahlia asked, as if she'd just noticed their presence. Katamori, at her back, wrapped his arms around her. "I hope not," he said. "We have other things to do."

"Cold hasn't affected *him* much," muttered Cop Two. He was trying to keep his eyes off the vampires, but he kept darting glances in their direction. Dahlia could feel Katamori's body shake with amusement. Humans were so silly about nudity.

"No, no, you two are okay. No bodies in that pool?" asked Cop One, smiling broadly.

"Only ours," Dahlia said, trying to purr. She did a credible job.

"Probably a prank call," said Cop One. "Sorry we're interrupting your evening. We would have been here twenty minutes ago if there hadn't been a wreck on our exit ramp."

That was interesting, but they had to stay in character. "You're not disturbing us at all," Katamori said, bending his head to kiss Dahlia's neck.

"Let's look through the bushes," said Cop Two, scandalized, and the two policemen dutifully searched the paths and parted the bushes, trying not to watch the activity in the waters of the fountain while checking any place a body could be concealed.

Except for the one place it was.

But they made a slow job of it because they kept looking back to watch Dahlia and Katamori, whose cavorting progressed from warm to simmer to boil.

"Oh my God," said Cop One. "They're actually . . ."

"Did you know how *fast* they could move?" muttered Cop Two. "Her boobs are shaking like maracas!"

By the time the two marched back to the mansion's French doors, the two vampires were perched on the edge of the fountain, Katamori's legs hanging over the maintenance door while Dahlia sat in his lap. They both looked pleased and were whispering to each other in a loverlike way.

Dahlia was saying, "I'm much refreshed. What a good idea, Katamori."

"I enjoyed that. I hope we can do it again. Even out here. Perhaps without an audience next time. How many police were lined up inside, watching?"

"At least five, plus the two out here. Did you see what I found in the hiding place?"

"Yes, I saw. Joaquin will be so pleased with us. Surely the humans will leave soon. I think we did an excellent job of distracting them. Thank you."

"Oh, it was my pleasure," Dahlia said sincerely.

In half an hour, Joaquin himself came into the garden to tell them that the police had left. He was only slightly startled to find them still naked.

"I'm glad you've enjoyed each other's company," he said. "Did you have any problems concealing the body?"

"Let me show you what we found under the fountain when we opened it," Dahlia said, and reopened the panel to pull a bundle of clothing out. It was not her clothing, or Katamori's. She shook out the garments and held them up for Joaquin's viewing. He was silent for a long moment.

"Well," he said. "That's settled, then. Bring them in when you've readied yourself. Later tonight, I'll send Troy and Hazel out here to dispose of the body for good. I regret this whole incident." The new sheriff seemed sincere, to Dahlia. He turned and went into the mansion.

The two pulled on their own garments, though Dahlia hated resuming her stained dress. It had been a gamble leaving the clothes in a heap by the fountain, but it had been the right touch. Katamori and Dahlia checked each other to make sure they were in order. She tucked his shirt in a little more neatly, and he buckled her very high heels for her. They followed Joaquin back in through the brightly lit French doors.

The crowd had thinned.

"Where are the demons?" Dahlia asked Taffy, who was sitting beside Don on a love seat.

"They left when the police did," Taffy said, running her fingers through her huge mane of hair. "They were smart to go while the going was good."

"There's no harm in that," Dahlia told her friend. "Diantha was the only one involved, and we know she didn't do it."

"Melponeus looked sorry to be leaving without seeing you again," Taffy said slyly. "He did a little looking out the windows when the police seemed so interested in the garden. I think it sparked a few memories he enjoyed very much."

"You've had the demon?" Katamori was intrigued.

"Yes," Dahlia said. "The heat and texture of his skin made the experience very interesting. Nothing compared to you, of course." Dahlia could be polite when it mattered.

Joaquin and his bodyguards were waiting for Dahlia and Katamori to present their findings. All the Rhodes vampires gathered around when they entered. Joaquin, who had resumed his seat in his massive chair, waited impassively for their report. Cedric was still drinking Red Stuff and seemed even more unhappy, and Glenda, now completely healed, glowered at Dahlia.

But they joined the throng with the rest. Even Don and his enforcer rose to join the crowd when Taffy did.

"That was an excellent strategy to distract the police," Joaquin said. "Now tell us what you've discovered."

"We found a bundle of bloody clothes hidden in the base of the fountain," Dahlia said, and a ripple ran through the crowd. "If we hadn't had to hide the body, if no one had called the police, we might never have found them. Since Arthur Allthorp's murderer was the one who called the police, hoping to get the nest in trouble, you might say he cut his own throat."

Joaquin held up the bloody bundle. The smell was really strong now, and the Weres' upper lips pulled up in a snarl of distaste. Even Weres liked their blood fresh. Joaquin, with a certain amount of drama, shook out the garments, one by one.

"Cedric, I believe these are yours," he said.

"That's not true," Cedric said calmly. He swept a hand down his chest. "Someone is trying to incriminate me. This is what I have been wearing all evening."

"Not so," retorted Dahlia. "The flowers on your vest were golden at the beginning of the evening. After the death of the human, the flowers were blue." She was almost sad to have to say the words, but out of spite Cedric had almost condemned the whole nest to hours in the police station, days of bad press, and the end of the regime of Joaquin before it had even really begun. "The clothes you have on now are your clothes you wear when you garden, the clothes you leave hanging on a peg outside. Including the boots."

Everyone looked down at Cedric's scruffy boots. They were certainly not footwear anyone would choose to wear to a reception, not even Cedric.

For a second, fear flashed in Cedric's blue eyes. Only for a second. Then he charged at Dahlia, a wild shriek coming from his lips.

She'd been expecting it for all of a couple of seconds. She stepped to the left quicker than the eye could track her, seized Cedric's right arm as he went past her, twisted it upward at a terrible angle, and when Cedric screamed she gripped his head and twisted.

Cedric's head came off.

There was silence for a moment.

"I'm so sorry," she said to Joaquin. "I didn't intend his decapitation. The mess . . ."

"He'll flake away and we'll get out the vacuum cleaner," Joaquin said, with a good approximation of calm. Before his elevation to the sheriff's position, Joaquin had been in body disposal, Dahlia recalled. "If the stain won't clean out of the rug, we'll buy another."

That was something Cedric would never have said, and Dahlia brightened. "Thank you, Sheriff. He almost surprised me," she said, and she could barely believe the words were coming from her lips. Perhaps she would miss Cedric more than she had realized.

"When the humans charge the police in order to be shot, they call it 'suicide by cop.'" Katamori bowed to his new friend. He said gallantly, "We will call it 'Death by Dahlia.'"

THE BLEEDING SHADOW

by Joe R. Lansdale

Music may have charms to soothe the savage breast, but as the down-on-his-luck private eye in the gritty story that follows learns, it also has charms that can open doors—including doors to places where nobody ought to go.

Prolific Texas writer Joe R. Lansdale has won the Edgar® Award, the British Fantasy Award, the American Horror Award, the American Mystery Award, the International Crime Writer's Award, and eight Bram Stoker Awards. Although perhaps best known for horror/thrillers such as *The Nightrunners, Bubba Ho-Tep, The Bottoms, The God of the Razor*, and *The Drive-In*, he also writes the popular Hap Collins and Leonard Pine mystery series—*Savage Season, Mucho Mojo, The Two-Bear Mambo, Bad Chili, Rumble Tumble, Captains Outrageous*—as well as Western novels such as *Texas Night Rider* and *Blooddance*, and totally unclassifiable cross-genre novels such as *Zeppelins West, The Magic Wagon*, and *Flaming London*. His other novels include *Dead in the West, The Big Blow, Sunset and Sawdust, Act of Love, Freezer Burn, Waltz of Shadows, The Drive-In 2: Not Just One of Them Sequels*, and *Leather Maiden*. He has also contributed novels to series such as *Batman* and *Tarzan*. His many short stories have been collected in *By Bizarre Hands*; *Tight Little Stitches in a Dead Man's Back*; *The Shadows Kith and Kin*; *The Long Ones*; *Stories by Mama Lansdale's Youngest Boy*; *Bestsellers Guaranteed*; *On the Far Side of the Cadillac Desert with the Dead Folks*; *Electric Gumbo*; *Writer of the Purple Rage*; *A Fist Full of Stories*; *Bumper Crop*; *The Good, the Bad, and the Indifferent*; *For a Few Stories More*; *Mad Dog Summer: And Other Stories*; *The King and Other Stories*; and *High Cotton: Selected Stories of Joe R. Lansdale*. As editor, he has produced the anthologies *The Best of the West, Retro Pulp Tales, Son of Retro Pulp Tales* (with his son, Keith Lansdale), *Razored Saddles* (with Pat LoBrutto), *Dark at Heart: All New Tales of Dark Suspense* (with his wife, Karen Lansdale), *The Horror Hall of Fame: The Stoker Winners*, and the Robert E. Howard tribute anthology *Cross Plains Universe* (with Scott A. Cupp). An anthology in tribute to Lansdale's work is *Lords of the Razor*. His most recent books are a new collection,

Deadman's Road; an omnibus, _Flaming Zeppelins: The Adventures of Ned the Seal_; and, as editor, a new anthology, _Crucified Dreams_. He lives with his family in Nacogdoches, Texas.

I WAS DOWN AT THE BLUE LIGHT JOINT THAT NIGHT, FINISHING OFF SOME ribs and listening to some blues, when in walked Alma May. She was looking good too. Had a dress on that fit her the way a dress ought to fit every woman in the world. She was wearing a little flat hat that leaned to one side, like an unbalanced plate on a waiter's palm. The high heels she had on made her legs look tight and way all right.

The light wasn't all that good in the joint, which is one of its appeals. It sometimes helps a man or woman get along in a way the daylight wouldn't stand, but I knew Alma May enough to know light didn't matter. She'd look good wearing a sack and a paper hat.

There was something about her face that showed me right off she was worried, that things weren't right. She was glancing left and right, like she was in some big city trying to cross a busy street and not get hit by a car.

I got my bottle of beer, left out from my table, and went over to her.

Then I knew why she'd been looking around like that. She said, "I was looking for you, Richard."

"Say you were," I said. "Well, you done found me."

The way she stared at me wiped the grin off my face.

"Something wrong, Alma May?"

"Maybe. I don't know. I got to talk, though. Thought you'd be here, and I was wondering you might want to come by my place."

"When?"

"Now."

"All right."

"But don't get no business in mind," she said. "This isn't like the old days. I need your help, and I need to know I can count on you."

"Well, I kind of like the kind of business we used to do, but all right, we're friends. It's cool."

"I hoped you'd say that."

"You got a car?" I said.

She shook her head. "No. I had a friend drop me off."

I thought, *Friend?* Sure.

"All right then," I said, "let's strut on out."

I GUESS YOU COULD SAY IT'S A SHAME ALMA MAY MAKES HER MONEY TURNing tricks, but when you're the one paying for the tricks, and you are one of her satisfied customers, you feel different. Right then, anyway. Later, you feel guilty. Like maybe you done peed on the *Mona Lisa*. Cause that gal, she was one fine dark-skin woman who should have got better than a thousand rides and enough money to buy some eats and make some coffee in the morning. She deserved something good. Should have found and married a man with a steady job that could have done all right by her.

But that hadn't happened. Me and her had a bit of something once, and it wasn't just business, money changing hands after she got me feeling good. No, it was more than that, but we couldn't work it out. She was in the life and didn't know how to get out. And as for deserving something better, that wasn't me. What I had were a couple of nice suits, some two-tone shoes, a hat, and a gun—.45-caliber automatic, like they'd used in the war a few years back.

Alma May got a little on the dope, too, and though she shook it, it had dropped her down deep. Way I figured, she wasn't never climbing out of that hole, and it didn't have nothing to do with dope now. What it had to do with was time. You get a window open now and again, and if you don't crawl through it, it closes. I know. My window had closed some time back. It made me mad all the time.

We were in my Chevy, a six-year-old car, a forty-eight model. I'd had it reworked a bit at a time: new tires, fresh windshield, nice seat covers, and so on. It was shiny and special.

We were driving along, making good time on the highway, the lights racing over the cement, making the recent rain in the ruts shine like the knees of old dress pants.

"What you need me for?" I asked.

"It's a little complicated," she said.

"Why me?"

"I don't know . . . You've always been good to me, and once we had a thing goin'."

"We did," I said.

"What happened to it?"

I shrugged. "It quit goin'."

"It did, didn't it? Sometimes I wish it hadn't."

"Sometimes I wish a lot of things," I said.

She leaned back in the seat and opened her purse and got out a cigarette and lit it, then rolled down the window. She remembered I didn't like cigarette smoke. I never had got on the tobacco. It took your wind and it stunk and it made your breath bad too. I hated when it got in my clothes.

"You're the only one I could tell this to," she said. "The only one that would listen to me and not think I been with the needle in my arm. You know what I'm sayin'?"

"Sure, baby, I know."

"I sound to you like I been bad?"

"Naw. You sound all right. I mean, you're talkin' a little odd, but not like you're out of your head."

"Drunk?"

"Nope. Just like you had a bad dream and want to tell someone."

"That's closer," she said. "That ain't it, but that's much closer than any needle or whiskey or wine."

Alma May's place is on the outskirts of town. It's the one thing she got out of life that ain't bad. It's not a mansion. It's small, but its tight and bright in the daylight, all painted up a canary yellow color with deep blue trim. It didn't look bad in the moonlight.

Alma May didn't work with a pimp. She didn't need one. She was well-known around town. She had her clientele. They were all safe, she told me once. About a third of them were white folks from on the other side of the tracks, up there in the proper part of Tyler Town. What she had besides them was a dead mother and a runaway father, and a brother, Tootie, who liked to travel around, play blues, and suck that bottle. He was always needing something, and Alma May, in spite of her own demons, had always managed to make sure he got it.

That was another reason me and her had to split the sheets. That brother of hers was a grown-ass man, and he lived with his mother and let her tote his water. When the mama died, he sort of went to pieces. Alma May took the mama's part over, keeping Tootie in whiskey and biscuits, even bought him a guitar. He lived off her whoring money, and it didn't bother him none. I didn't like him. But I will say this. That boy could play the blues.

When we were inside her house, she unpinned her hat from her hair and sailed it across the room and into a chair.

She said, "You want a drink?"

"I ain't gonna say no, long as it ain't too weak, and be sure to put it in a dirty glass."

She smiled. I watched from the living room doorway as she went and got a bottle out from under the kitchen sink, showing me how tight that dress fit across her bottom when she bent over. She pulled some glasses off a shelf, poured and brought me a stiff one. We drank a little of it, still standing, leaning against the door frame between living room and kitchen. We finally sat on the couch. She sat on the far end, just to make sure I remembered why we were there. She said, "It's Tootie."

I swigged down the drink real quick, said, "I'm gone."

As I went by the couch, she grabbed my hand. "Don't be that way, baby."

"Now I'm *baby*," I said.

"Hear me out, honey. Please. You don't owe me, but can you pretend you do?"

"Hell," I said, and went and sat down on the couch.

She moved, said, "I want you to listen."

"All right," I said.

"First off, I can't pay you. Except maybe in trade."

"Not that way," I said. "You and me, we do this, it ain't trade. Call it a favor."

I do a little detective stuff now and then for folks I know, folks that recommended me to others. I don't have a license. Black people couldn't get a license to shit broken glass in this town. But I was pretty good at what I did. I learned it the hard way. And not all of it was legal. I guess I'm a kind of private eye. Only I'm really private. I'm so private I might be more of a secret eye.

"Best thing to do is listen to this," she said. "It cuts back on some explanation."

There was a little record player on a table by the window, a stack of records. She went over and opened the player box and turned it on. The record she wanted was already on it. She lifted up the needle and set it right, stepped back, and looked at me.

She was oh so fine. I looked at her and thought maybe I should have stuck with her, brother or no brother. She could melt butter from ten feet away, way she looked.

And then the music started to play.

IT WAS TOOTIE'S VOICE. I RECOGNIZED THAT RIGHT AWAY. I HAD HEARD HIM plenty. Like I said, he wasn't much as a person, willing to do anything so he could lay back and play that guitar, slide a pocket knife along the strings to squeal out just the right sound, but he was good at the blues; of that, there ain't no denying.

His voice was high and lonesome, and the way he played that guitar, it was hard to imagine how he could get the sounds out of it he got.

"You brought me over here to listen to records?" I said.

She shook her head. She lifted up the needle, stopped the record, and took it off. She had another in a little paper cover, and she took it out and put it on, dropped the needle down.

"Now listen to this."

First lick or two, I could tell right off it was Tootie, but then there came a kind of turn in the music, where it got so strange the hair on the back of my neck stood up. And then Tootie started to sing, and the hair on the back of my hands and arms stood up. The air in the room got thick and the lights got dim, and shadows crawled out of the corners and sat on the couch with me. I ain't kidding about that part. The room was suddenly full of them, and I could hear what sounded like a bird, trapped at the ceiling, fluttering fast and hard, looking for a way out.

Then the music changed again, and it was like I had been dropped down a well, and it was a long drop, and then it was like those shadows were folding around me in a wash of dirty water. The room stunk of something foul. The guitar no longer sounded like a guitar, and Tootie's voice was no longer like a voice. It was like someone dragging a razor over concrete while trying to yodel with a throat full of glass. There was something inside the music; something that squished and scuttled and honked and raved, something unsettling, like a snake in a satin glove.

"Cut it off," I said.

But Alma May had already done it.

She said, "That's as far as I've ever let it go. It's all I can do to move to cut it off. It feels like it's getting more powerful the more it plays. I don't want to hear the rest of it. I don't know if I can take it. How can that be, Richard? How can that be with just sounds?"

I was actually feeling weak, like I'd just come back from a bout with the flu and someone had beat my ass. I said, "More powerful? How do you mean?"

"Ain't that what you think? Ain't that how it sounds? Like it's getting stronger?"

I nodded. "Yeah."

"And the room—"

"The shadows?" I said. "I didn't just imagine it?"

"No," she said. "Only every time I've heard it, it's been a little different. The notes get darker, the guitar licks, they cut something inside me, and each time it's something different and something deeper. I don't know if it makes me feel good or it makes me feel bad, but it sure makes me feel."

"Yeah," I said, because I couldn't find anything else to say.

"Tootie sent me that record. He sent a note that said: *Play it when you have to.* That's what it said. That's all it said. What's that mean?"

"I don't know, but I got to wonder why Tootie would send it to you in the first place. Why would he want you to hear something makes you almost sick . . . And how in hell could he do that, make that kind of sound, I mean?"

She shook her head. "I don't know. Someday, I'm gonna play it all the way through."

"I wouldn't," I said.

"Why?"

"You heard it. I figure it only gets worse. I don't understand it, but I know I don't like it."

"Yeah," she said, putting the record back in the paper sheath. "I know. But it's so strange. I've never heard anything like it."

"And I don't want to hear anything like it again."

"Still, you have to wonder."

"What I wonder is what I was wondering before. Why would he send this shit to you?"

"I think he's proud of it. There's nothing like it. It's . . . original."

"I'll give it that," I said. "So, what do you want with me?"

"I want you to find Tootie."

"Why?"

"Because I don't think he's right. I think he needs help. I mean, this . . . It makes me think he's somewhere he shouldn't be."

"But yet, you want to play it all the way through," I said.

"What I know is I don't like that. I don't like Tootie being associated with it, and I don't know why. Richard, I want you to find him."

"Where did the record come from?"

She got the sheaf and brought it to me. I could see through the little doughnut in the sheath where the label on the record ought to be. Nothing but disk. The package itself was like wrapping paper you put meat in. It was stained.

I said, "I think he paid some place to let him record," I said. "Question is, what place? You have an address where this came from?"

"I do." She went and got a large manila envelope and brought it to me. "It came in this."

I looked at the writing on the front. It had as a return address *The Hotel Champion*. She showed me the note. It was on a piece of really cheap stationery that said *The Hotel Champion* and had a phone number and an address in Dallas. The stationery looked old, and it was sun faded.

"I called them," she said, "but they didn't know anything about him. They had never heard of him. I could go look myself, but . . . I'm a little afraid. Besides, you know, I got clients, and I got to make the house payment."

I didn't like hearing about that, knowing what kind of clients she meant, and how she was going to make that money. I said, "All right. What you want me to do?"

"Find him."

"And then what?"

"Bring him home."

"And if he don't want to come back?"

"I've seen you work, bring him home to me. Just don't lose that temper of yours."

I turned the record around and around in my hands. I said, "I'll go take a look. I won't promise anything more than that. He wants to come, I'll bring him back. He doesn't, I might be inclined to break his leg and bring him back. You know I don't like him."

"I know. But don't hurt him."

"If he comes easy, I'll do that. If he doesn't, I'll let him stay, come back and tell you where he is and how he is. How about that?"

"That's good enough," she said. "Find out what this is all about. It's got me scared, Richard."

"It's just bad sounds," I said. "Tootie was probably high on something when he recorded it, thought it was good at the time, sent it to you because he thought he was the coolest thing since Robert Johnson."

"Who?"

"Never mind. But I figure when he got over his hop, he probably didn't even remember he mailed it."

"Don't try and tell me you've heard anything like this. That listening to it didn't make you feel like your skin was gonna pull off your bones, that some part of it made you want to dip in the dark and learn to like it. Tell me it wasn't like that. Tell me it wasn't like walking out in front of a car and the headlights in your face, and you just wanting to step out there even though it scared the hell out of you and you knew it was the devil or something even worse at the wheel. Tell me you didn't feel something like that."

I couldn't. So I didn't say anything. I just sat there and sweated, the sound of that music still shaking down deep in my bones, boiling my blood.

"Here's the thing," I said. "I'll do it, but you got to give me a photograph of Tootie, if you got one, and the record so you don't play it no more."

She studied me a moment. "I hate that thing," she said, nodding at the record in my hands, "but somehow I feel attached to it. Like getting rid of it is getting rid of a piece of me."

"That's the deal."

"All right," she said, "take it, but take it now."

MOTORING ALONG BY MYSELF IN THE CHEVY, THE MOON HIGH AND BRIGHT, all I could think of was that music, or whatever that sound was. It was stuck in my head like an ax. I had the record on the seat beside me, had Tootie's note and envelope, the photograph Alma May had given me.

Part of me wanted to drive back to Alma May and tell her no, and never mind. Here's the record back. But another part of me, the dumb part, wanted to know where and how and why that record had been made. Curiosity, it just about gets us all.

Where I live is a rickety third-floor walk-up. It's got the stairs on the outside, and they stop at each landing. I lived at the very top.

I tried not to rest my hand too heavy on the rail as I climbed, because it was about to come off. I unlocked my door and turned on the light and watched the roaches run for cover.

I put the record down, got a cold one out of the icebox. Well, actually it was a plug-in. A refrigerator. But I'd grown up with iceboxes, so calling it that was hard to break. I picked up the record again and took a seat.

Sitting in my old armchair with the stuffing leaking out like a busted cotton sack, holding the record again, looking at the dirty brown sleeve, I noticed the grooves were dark and scabby looking, like something had gotten poured in there and had dried tight. I tried to determine if that had something to do with that crazy sound. Could something in the grooves make that kind of noise? Didn't seem likely.

I thought about putting the record on, listening to it again, but I couldn't stomach the thought. The fact that I held it in my hand made me uncomfortable. It was like holding a bomb about to go off.

I had thought of it like a snake once. Alma May had thought of it like a hit-and-run car driven by the devil. And now I had thought of it like a bomb. That was some kind of feeling coming from a grooved-up circle of wax.

EARLY NEXT MORNING, WITH THE .45 IN THE GLOVE BOX, A RAZOR IN MY coat pocket, and the record up front on the seat beside me, I tooled out toward Dallas, and the Hotel Champion.

I got into Big D around noon, stopped at a café on the outskirts where there was colored, and went in where a big fat mama with a pretty face and a body that smelled real good made me a hamburger and sat and flirted with me all the while I ate it. That's all right. I like women, and I like them to flirt. They quit doing that, I might as well lay down and die.

While we was flirting, I asked her about the Hotel Champion, if she knew where it was. I had the street number, of course, but I needed tighter directions.

"Oh, yeah, honey, I know where it is, and you don't want to stay there. It's deep in the colored section, and not the good part, that's what I'm trying to tell you, and it don't matter you brown as a walnut yourself. There's folks down there will cut you and put your blood in a paper cup and mix it with whiskey and drink it. You too good-looking to get all cut up and such. There's better places to stay on the far other side."

I let her give me a few hotel names, like I might actually stay at one or the other, but I got the address for the Champion, paid up, giving her a good tip, and left out of there.

The part of town where the Hotel Champion was, was just as nasty as the lady had said. There were people hanging around on the streets, and leaning into corners, and there was trash everywhere. It wasn't exactly a place that fostered a lot of pride.

I found the Hotel Champion and parked out front. There was a couple fellas on the street eyeing my car. One was skinny. One was big. They were dressed up with nice hats and shoes, just like they had jobs. But if they did, they wouldn't have been standing around in the middle of the day eyeing my Chevy.

I pulled the .45 out of the glove box and stuck it in my pants, at the small of my back. My coat would cover it just right.

I got out and gave the hotel the gander. It was nice looking if you were blind in one eye and couldn't see out the other.

There wasn't any doorman, and the door was hanging on a hinge. Inside I saw a dusty stairway to my left, a scarred door to my right.

There was a desk in front of me. It had a glass hooked to it that went to the ceiling. There was a little hole in it low down on the counter that had a wooden stop behind it. There were flyspecks on the glass, and there was a man behind the glass, perched on a stool, like a frog on a lily pad. He was fat and colored and his hair had blue blanket wool in it. I didn't take it for decoration. He was just a nasty son of a bitch.

I could smell him when he moved the wooden stop. A stink like armpits and nasty underwear and rotting teeth. I could smell old cooking smells floating in from somewhere in back: boiled pigs' feet and pigs' tails that might have been good about the time the pig lost them, but now all that was left was a rancid stink. There was also a reek like cat piss.

I said, "Hey, man, I'm looking for somebody."

"You want a woman, you got to bring your own," the man said. "But I can give you a number or two. Course, I ain't guaranteeing anything about them being clean."

"Naw. I'm looking for somebody was staying here. His name is Tootie Johnson."

"I don't know no Tootie Johnson."

That was the same story Alma May had got.

"Well, all right, you know this fella?" I pulled out the photograph and pressed it against the glass.

"Well, he might look like someone got a room here. We don't sign in and we don't exchange names much."

"No? A class place like this."

"I said he might look like someone I seen," he said. "I didn't say he definitely did."

"You fishing for money?"

"Fishing ain't very certain," he said.

I sighed and put the photograph back inside my coat and got out my wallet and took out a five-dollar bill.

Frog Man saw himself as some kind of greasy high roller. "That's it? Five dollars for prime information?"

I made a slow and careful show of putting my five back in my wallet. "Then you don't get nothing," I said.

He leaned back on his stool and put his stubby fingers together and let them lay on his round belly. "And you don't get nothing neither, jackass."

I went to the door on my right and turned the knob. Locked. I stepped back and kicked it so hard I felt the jar all the way to the top of my head. The door flew back on its hinges, slammed into the wall. It sounded like someone firing a shot.

I went on through and behind the desk, grabbed Frog Man by the shirt, and slapped him hard enough he fell off the stool. I kicked him in the leg and he yelled. I picked up the stool and hit him with it across the chest, then threw the stool through a doorway that led into a kitchen. I heard something break in there and a cat made a screeching sound.

"I get mad easy," I said.

"Hell, I see that," he said, and held up a hand for protection. "Take it easy, man. You done hurt me."

"That was the plan."

The look in his eyes made me feel sorry for him. I also felt like an asshole. But that wouldn't keep me from hitting him again if he didn't answer my question. When I get perturbed, I'm not reasonable.

"Where is he?"

"Do I still get the five dollars?"

"No," I said, "now you get my best wishes. You want to lose that?"

"No. No, I don't."

"Then don't play me. Where is he, you toad?"

"He's up in room fifty-two, on the fifth floor."

"Spare key?"

He nodded at a rack of them. The keys were on nails and they all had little wooden pegs on the rings with the keys. Numbers were painted on the pegs. I found one that said 52, took it off the rack.

I said, "You better not be messing with me."

"I ain't. He's up there. He don't never come down. He's been up there a week. He makes noise up there. I don't like it. I run a respectable place."

"Yeah, it's really nice here. And you better not be jerking me."

"I ain't. I promise."

"Good. And, let me give you a tip. Take a bath. And get that shit out of your hair. And those teeth you got ain't looking too good. Pull them. And shoot that fucking cat, or at least get him some place better than the kitchen to piss. It stinks like a toilet in there."

I walked out from behind the desk, out in the hall, and up the flight of stairs in a hurry.

I RUSHED ALONG THE HALLWAY ON THE FIFTH FLOOR. IT WAS COVERED IN white linoleum with a gold pattern in it; it creaked and cracked as I walked along. The end of the hall had a window, and there was a stairwell on that end too. Room 52 was right across from it.

I heard movement on the far end of the stairs. I had an idea what that was all about. About that time, two of the boys I'd seen on the street showed themselves at the top of the stairs, all decked out in their nice hats and such, grinning.

One of them was about the size of a Cadillac, with a gold tooth that shone bright when he smiled. The guy behind him was skinny with his hand in his pocket.

I said, "Well, if it isn't the pimp squad."

"You funny, nigger," said the big man.

"Yeah, well, catch the act now. I'm going to be moving to a new locale."

"You bet you are," said the big man.

"Fat-ass behind the glass down there, he ain't paying you enough to mess with me," I said.

"Sometimes, cause we're bored, we just like messin'."

"Say you do?"

"Uh-huh," said the skinny one.

It was then I seen the skinny guy pull a razor out of his pocket. I had one too, but razor work, it's nasty. He kept it closed.

Big guy with the gold tooth flexed his fingers and made a fist. That made me figure he didn't have a gun or a razor; or maybe he just liked hitting people. I know I did.

They come along toward me then, and the skinny one with the razor flicked it open. I pulled the .45 out from under my coat, said, "You ought to put that back in your pocket," I said, "save it for shaving."

"Oh, I'm fixing to do some shaving right now," he said.

I pointed the .45 at him.

The big man said, "That's one gun for two men."

"It is," I said, "but I'm real quick with it. And frankly, I know one of you is gonna end up dead. I just ain't sure which one right yet."

"All right then," said the big man, smiling. "That'll be enough." He looked back at the skinny man with the razor. The skinny man put the razor back in his coat pocket and they turned and started down the stairs.

I went over and stood by the stairway and listened. I could hear them walking down, but then all of a sudden, they stopped on the stairs. That was the way I had it figured.

Then I could hear the morons rushing back up. They weren't near as sneaky as they thought they was. The big one was first out of the chute, so to speak; come rushing out of the stairwell and onto the landing. I brought the butt of the .45 down on the back of his head, right where the skull slopes down. He did a kind of frog hop and bounced across the hall and hit his head on the wall, and went down and laid there like his intent all along had been a quick leap and a nap.

Then the other one was there, and he had the razor. He flicked it, and then he saw the .45 in my hand.

"Where did you think this gun was gonna go?" I said. "On vacation?"

I kicked him in the groin hard enough he dropped the razor and went to his knees. I put the .45 back where I got it. I said, "You want some, man?"

He got up and come at me. I hit him with a right and knocked him clean through the window behind him. Glass sprinkled all over the hallway.

I went over and looked out. He was lying on the fire escape, his head against the railing. He looked right at me.

"You crazy, cocksucker. What if there hadn't been no fire escape?"

"You'd have your ass punched into the bricks. Still might."

He got up quick and clamored down the fire escape like a squirrel. I watched him till he got to the ground and went limping away down the alley between some overturned trash cans and a slinking dog.

I picked up his razor and put it in my pocket with the one I already had, then walked over and kicked the big man in the head just because I could.

I KNOCKED ON THE DOOR. NO ONE ANSWERED. I COULD HEAR SOUNDS FROM inside. It was similar to what I had heard on that record, but not quite, and it was faint, as if coming from a distance.

No one answered my knock, so I stuck the key in the door and opened it and went straight away inside.

I almost lost my breath when I did.

The air in the room was thick and it stunk of mildew and rot and things long dead. It made those boiled pigs' feet and that pissing cat and that rotten-tooth bastard downstairs smell like perfume.

Tootie was lying on the bed, on his back. His eyes were closed. He was a guy usually dressed to the top, baby, but his shirt was wrinkled and dirty and sweaty at the neck and armpits. His pants were nasty too. He had on his shoes, but no socks. He looked like someone had set him on fire and then beat out the flames with a two-by-four. His face was like a skull, he had lost so much flesh, and he was as bony under his clothes as a skeleton.

Where his hands lay on the sheet, there were bloodstains. His guitar was next to the bed, and there were stacks and stacks of composition notebooks lying on the floor. A couple of them were open and filled with writing. Hell, I didn't even know Tootie could write.

The wall on the far side was marked up in black and red paint; there were all manner of musical notes drawn on it, along with symbols I had never seen before; swiggles and circles and stick figure drawings. Blood was on the wall too, most likely from Tootie's bleeding fingers. Two open paint cans, the red and the black, were on the floor with brushes stuck up in them. Paint was splattered on the floor and had dried in humped-up blisters. The guitar had bloodstains all over it.

A record player, plugged in, sitting on a nightstand by the bed, was playing that strange music. I went to it right away and picked up the needle and set it aside. And let me tell you, just making my way across the room to get hold of the player was like wading through mud with my ankles tied together. It seemed to me as I got closer to the record, the louder it got, and the more ill I felt. My head throbbed. My heart pounded.

When I had the needle up and the music off, I went over and touched Tootie. He didn't move, but I could see his chest rising and falling. Except for his hands, he didn't seem hurt. He was in a deep sleep. I picked up his right hand and turned it over and looked at it. The fingers were cut deep, like someone had taken a razor to the tips. Right off, I figured that was from playing his guitar. Struck me, that to get the sounds he got out of it, he really had to dig in with those fingers. And from the looks of this room, he had been at it nonstop, until recent.

I shook him. His eyes fluttered and finally opened. They were bloodshot and had dark circles around them.

When he saw me, he startled, and his eyes rolled around in his head like those little games kids get where you try to shake the marbles into holes. After a moment, they got straight, and he said, "Ricky?"

That was another reason I hated him. I didn't like being called Ricky.

I said, "Hello, shithead. Your sister's worried sick."

"The music," he said. "Put the music back on."

"You call that music?" I said.

He took a deep breath, then rolled out of the bed, nearly knocking me aside. Then I saw him jerk, like he'd seen a truck coming right at him. I turned. I wished it had been a truck.

LET ME TRY AND TELL YOU WHAT I SAW. I NOT ONLY SAW IT, I FELT IT. IT WAS in the very air we were breathing, getting inside my chest like mice wearing barbed-wire coats. The wall Tootie had painted and drawn all that crap on shook.

And then the wall wasn't a wall at all. It was a long hallway, dark as original sin. There was something moving in there, something that slithered and slid and made smacking sounds like an anxious old drunk about to take his next drink. Stars popped up, greasy stars that didn't remind me of anything I had ever seen in the night sky; a moon the color of a bleeding fish eye was in the background, and it cast a light on something moving toward us.

"Jesus Christ," I said.

"No," Tootie said. "It's not him."

Tootie jumped to the record player, picked up the needle, and put it on. There came that rotten sound I had heard with Alma May, and I knew that what I had heard when I first came into the room was the tail end of that same record playing, the part I hadn't heard before.

The music screeched and howled. I bent over and threw up. I fell back against the bed, tried to get up, but my legs were like old pipe cleaners. That record had taken the juice out of me. And then I saw it.

There's no description that really fits. It was . . . a thing. All blanket-wrapped in shadow with sucker mouths and thrashing tentacles and centipede legs mounted on clicking hooves. A bulblike head plastered all over with red and yellow eyes that seemed to creep. All around it, shadows swirled like water. It had a beak. Well, beaks.

The thing was coming right out of the wall. Tentacles thrashed toward me. One touched me across the cheek. It was like being scalded with hot grease. A shadow come loose of the thing, fell onto the floorboards of the room, turned red, and raced across the floor like a gush of blood. Insects and maggots squirmed in the bleeding shadow, and the record hit a high spot so loud and so goddamn strange, I ground my teeth, felt as if my insides were being twisted up like wet wash. And then I passed out.

WHEN I CAME TO, THE MUSIC WAS STILL PLAYING. TOOTIE WAS BENT over me.

"That sound," I said.

"You get used to it," Tootie said, "but the thing can't. Or maybe it can, but just not yet."

I looked at the wall. There was no alleyway. It was just a wall plastered in paint designs and spots of blood.

"And if the music stops?" I said.

"I fall asleep," Tootie said. "Record quits playing, it starts coming."

For a moment I didn't know anything to say. I finally got off the floor and sat on the bed. I felt my cheek where the tentacle hit me. It throbbed and I could feel blisters. I also had a knot on my head where I had fallen.

"Almost got you," Tootie said. "I think you can leave and it won't come after you. Me, I can't. I leave, it follows. It'll finally find me. I guess here is as good as any place."

I was looking at him, listening, but not understanding a damn thing.

The record quit. Tootie started it again. I looked at the wall. Even that blank moment without sound scared me. I didn't want to see that thing again. I didn't even want to think about it.

"I haven't slept in days, until now," Tootie said, coming to sit on the bed. "You hadn't come in, it would have got me, carried me off, taken my soul. But you can leave. It's my lookout, not yours . . . I'm always in some kind of shit, ain't I, Ricky?"

"That's the truth."

"This, though, it's the corker. I got to stand up and be a man for once. I got to fight this thing back, and all I got is the music. Like I told you, you can go."

I shook my head. "Alma May sent me. I said I'd bring you back."

It was Tootie's turn to shake his head. "Nope. I ain't goin'. I ain't done nothin' but mess up Sis's life. I ain't gonna do it."

"First responsible thing I ever heard you say," I said.

"Go on," Tootie said. "Leave me to it. I can take care of myself."

"If you don't die of starvation, or pass out from lack of sleep or need of water, you'll be just fine."

Tootie smiled at me. "Yeah. That's all I got to worry about. I hope it is one of them other things kills me. 'Cause if it comes for me . . . Well, I don't want to think about it."

"Keep the record going, I'll get something to eat and drink, some coffee. You think you can stay awake a half hour or so?"

"I can, but you're coming back?"

"I'm coming back," I said.

Out in the hallway I saw the big guy was gone. I took the stairs.

WHEN I GOT BACK, TOOTIE HAD CLEANED UP THE VOMIT AND WAS LOOKING through the notebooks. He was sitting on the floor and had them stacked all around him. He was maybe six inches away from the record player. Now and again he'd reach up and start it all over.

Soon as I was in the room, and that sound from the record was snugged up around me, I felt sick. I had gone to a greasy spoon down the street, after I changed a flat tire. One of the boys I'd given a hard time had most likely knifed it. My bet was the lucky son of a bitch who had fallen on the fire escape.

Besides the tire, a half-dozen long scratches had been cut into the paint on the passenger side, and my windshield was knocked in. I got back from the café, parked what was left of my car behind the hotel, down the street a bit, and walked a block. Car looked so bad now, maybe nobody would want to steal it.

I sat one of the open sacks on the floor by Tootie.

"Both hamburgers are yours," I said. "I got coffee for the both of us here."

I took out a tall cardboard container of coffee and gave it to him, took the other one for myself. I sat on the bed and sipped. Nothing tasted good in that room with that smell and that sound. But Tootie, he ate like a wolf. He gulped those burgers and coffee like they were air.

When he finished with the second burger, he started up the record again, then leaned his back against the bed.

"Coffee or not," he said, "I don't know how long I can stay awake."

"So what you got to do is keep the record playing?" I said.

"Yeah."

"Lay up in bed, sleep for a few hours. I'll keep the record going. You're rested, you got to explain this thing to me, and then we'll figure something out."

"There's nothing to figure," he said. "But God, I'll take you up on that sleep."

He crawled up in the bed and was immediately out.

I started the record over.

I got up then, untied Tootie's shoes and pulled them off. Hell, like him or not, he was Alma May's brother. And another thing, I wouldn't wish that thing behind the wall on my worst enemy.

I SAT ON THE FLOOR WHERE TOOTIE HAD SAT AND KEPT RESTARTING THE record as I tried to figure things out, which wasn't easy with that music going. I got up from time to time and walked around the room, and then I'd end up back on the floor by the record player, where I could reach it easy.

Between changes, I looked through the composition notebooks. They were full of musical notes mixed with scribbles like the ones on the wall. It was hard to focus with that horrid sound. It was like the air was full of snakes and razors. Got the feeling the music was pushing at something behind that wall. Got the feeling too, there was something on the other side, pushing back.

IT WAS DARK WHEN TOOTIE WOKE UP. HE HAD SLEPT A GOOD TEN HOURS, and I was exhausted with all that record changing, that horrible sound. I had a headache from looking over those notebooks, and I didn't know any more about them than when I first started.

I went and bought more coffee, brought it back, and we sat on the bed, him changing the record from time to time, us sipping.

I said, "You sure you can't just walk away?"

I was avoiding the real question for some reason. Like, what in hell is that thing, and what is going on? Maybe I was afraid of the answer.

"You saw that thing. I can walk away, all right. And I can run. But wherever

I go, it'll find me. So, at some point, I got to face it. Sometimes I make that same record sound with my guitar, give the record a rest. Thing I fear most is the record wearing out."

I gestured at the notebooks on the floor. "What is all that?"

"My notes. My writings. I come here to write some lyrics, some new blues songs."

"Those aren't lyrics, those are notes."

"I know," he said.

"You don't have a music education. You just play."

"Because of the record, I can read music, and I can write things that don't make any sense to me unless it's when I'm writing them, when I'm listening to that music. All those marks, they are musical notes, and the other marks are other kinds of notes, notes for sounds that I couldn't make until a few days back. I didn't even know those sounds were possible. But now, my head is full of the sounds and those marks and all manner of things, and the only way I can rest is to write them down. I wrote on the wall 'cause I thought the marks, the notes themselves, might hold that thing back and I could run. Didn't work."

"None of this makes any sense to me," I said.

"All right," Tootie said. "This is the best I can explain something that's got no explanation. I had some blues boys tell me they once come to this place on the south side called Cross Road Records. It's a little record shop where the streets cross. It's got all manner of things in it, and it's got this big colored guy with a big white smile and bloodshot eyes that works the joint. They said they'd seen the place, poked their heads in, and even heard Robert Johnson's sounds coming from a player on the counter. There was a big man sitting behind the counter, and he waved them in, but the place didn't seem right, they said, so they didn't go in.

"But, you know me. That sounded like just the place I wanted to go. So, I went. It's where South Street crosses a street called Way South.

"I go in there, and I'm the only one in the store. There's records everywhere, in boxes, lying on tables. Some got labels, some don't. I'm looking, trying to figure out how you told about anything, and this big fella with the smile comes over to me and starts to talk. He had breath like an unwiped butt, and his face didn't seem so much like black skin as it did black rock.

"He said, 'I know what you're looking for.' He reached in a box and pulled out a record didn't have no label on it. Thing was, that whole box didn't have labels. I think he's just messing with me, trying to make a sale. I'm ready to go, 'cause he's starting to make my skin crawl. Way he moves ain't natural, you know. It's like he's got something wrong with his feet, but he's still able to move, and quick-like. Like he does it between the times you blink your eyes.

"He goes over and puts that record on a player, and it starts up, and it was Robert Johnson. I swear, it was him. Wasn't no one could play like him. It was him. And here's the thing. It wasn't a song I'd ever heard by him. And I thought I'd heard all the music he'd put on wax."

Tootie sipped at his coffee. He looked at the wall a moment, and then changed the player again.

I said, "Swap out spots, and I'll change it. You sip and talk. Tell me all of it."

We did that, and Tootie continued.

"Well, one thing comes to another, and he starts talking me up good, and I finally I ask him how much for the record. He looks at me, and he says, 'For you, all you got to give me is a little blue soul. And when you come back, you got to buy something with a bit more of it till it's all gone and I got it. 'Cause you will be back.'

"I figured he was talking about me playing my guitar for him, cause I'd told him I was a player, you know, while we was talking. I told him I had my guitar in a room I was renting, and I was on foot, and it would take me all day to get my guitar and get back, so I'd have to pass on that deal. Besides, I was about tapped out of money. I had a place I was supposed to play that evening, but until then, I had maybe three dollars and some change in my pocket. I had the rent on this room paid up all week, and I hadn't been there but two days. I tell him all that, and he says, 'Oh, that's all right. I know you can play. I can tell about things like that. What I mean is, you give me a drop of blood and a promise, and you can have that record.' Right then, I started to walk out, cause I'm thinking, this guy is nutty as fruitcake with an extra dose of nuts, but I want that record. So I tell him, sure, I'll give him a drop of blood. I won't lie none to you, Ricky, I was thinking about nabbing that record and making a run with it. I wanted it that bad. So a drop of blood, that didn't mean nothin'.

"He pulls a record needle out from behind the counter, and he comes over and pokes my finger with it, sudden-like, while I'm still trying to figure how he got over to me that fast, and he holds my hand and lets blood drip on—get this—the record. It flows into the grooves.

"He says, 'Now, you promise me your blues-playing soul is mine when you die.'

"I thought it was just talk, you know, so I told him he could have it. He says, 'When you hear it, you'll be able to play it. And when you play it, sometime when you're real good on it, it'll start to come, like a rat easing its nose into hot dead meat. It'll start to come.'

"'What will?' I said. 'What are you talking about?'

"He says, 'You'll know.'

"Next thing I know, he's over by the door, got it open, and he's smiling at me, and I swear, I thought for a moment I could see right through him. Could see his skull and bones. I've got the record in my hand, and I'm walking out, and as soon as I do, he shuts the door and I hear the lock turn.

"My first thought was, I got to get this blood out of the record grooves, cause that crazy bastard has just given me a lost Robert Johnson song for nothing. I took out a kerchief, pulled the record out of the sleeve, and went to wiping. The blood wouldn't come out. It was in the notches, you know.

"I went back to my room here, and I tried a bit of warm water on the blood in the grooves, but it still wouldn't come out. I was mad as hell, figured the record wouldn't play, way that blood had hardened in the grooves. I put it on and thought maybe the needle would wear the stuff out, but as soon as it was on the player and the needle hit it, it started sounding just the way it had in the store. I sat on the bed and listened to it, three or four times, and then I got my guitar and tried to play what was being played, knowing I couldn't do it, 'cause though I knew that sound wasn't electrified, it sounded like it was. But here's the thing. I could do it. I could play it. And I could see the notes in my head, and my head got filled up with them. I went out and bought those notebooks, and I wrote it all down just so my head wouldn't explode, 'cause every time I heard that record, and tried to play it, them notes would cricket-hop in my skull."

All the while we had been talking, I had been replaying the record.

"I forgot all about the gig that night," Tootie said. "I sat here until morning playing. By noon the next day, I sounded just like that record. By late afternoon, I started to get kind of sick. I can't explain it, but I was feeling that there was something trying to tear through somewhere, and it scared me and my insides knotted up.

"I don't know any better way of saying it than that. It was such a strong feeling. Then, while I was playing, the wall there, it come apart the way you seen it, and I seen that thing. It was just a wink of a look. But there it was. In all its terrible glory.

"I quit playing, and the wall wobbled back in place and closed up. I thought, *Damn, I need to eat or nap, or something.* And I did. Then I was back on that guitar. I could play like crazy, and I started going off on that song, adding here and there. It wasn't like it was coming from me, though. It was like I was getting help from somewhere.

"Finally, with my fingers bleeding and cramped and aching, and my voice gone raspy from singing, I quit. Still, I wanted to hear it, so I put on the record. And it wasn't the same no more. It was Johnson, but the words was strange, not English. Sounded like some kind of chant, and I knew then that Johnson was in that record, as sure as I was in this room, and that that chanting and that playing was opening up a hole for that thing in the wall. It was the way that fella had said. It was like a rat working its nose through red-hot meat, and now it felt like I was the meat. Next time I played the record, the voice on it wasn't Johnson's. It was mine.

"I had had enough, so I got the record and took it back to that shop. The place was the same as before, and like before, I was the only one in there. He looked at me, and comes over, and says, 'You already want to undo the deal. I can tell. They all do. But that ain't gonna happen.'

"I gave him a look like I was gonna jump on him and beat his ass, but he gave me a look back, and I went weak as a kitten.

"He smiled at me, and pulls out another record from that same box, and he takes the one I gave him and puts it back, and says, 'You done made a deal, but for a lick of your soul, I'll let you have this. See, you done opened the path. Now that rat's got to work on that meat. It don't take no more record or you playing for that to happen. Rat's gotta eat now, no matter what you do.'

"When he said that, he picks up my hand and looks at my cut-up fingers from playing, and he laughs so loud everything in the store shakes, and he squeezes my fingers until they start to bleed.

" 'A lick of my soul?' I asked.

"And then he pushed the record in my hand, and if I'm lying, I'm dying, he sticks out his tongue, and it's long as an old rat snake and black as a hole in the ground, and he licks me right around the neck. When he's had a taste, he smiles and shivers, like he's just had something cool to drink."

Tootie paused to unfasten his shirt and peel it down a little. There was a spot halfway around his neck like someone had worked him over with sandpaper.

" 'A taste,' he says, and then he shoves this record in my hand, which is bleeding from where he squeezed my fingers. Next thing I know, I'm looking at the record, and it's thick, and I touch it, and it's two records, back to back. He says, 'I give you that extra one cause you tasted mighty good, and maybe it'll let you get a little more rest that way, if you got a turntable drop. Call me generous and kind in my old age.'

"Wasn't nothing for it but to take the records and come back here. I didn't have no intention of playing it. I almost threw it away. But by then, that thing in the wall, wherever it is, was starting to stick through. Each time the hole was bigger and I could see more of it, and that red shadow was falling out on the floor. I thought about running, but I didn't want to just let it loose, and I knew, deep down, no matter where I went, it would come too.

"I started playing that record in self-defense. Pretty soon, I'm playing it on the guitar. When I got scared enough, got certain enough that thing was coming through, I played hard, and that hole would close, and that thing would go back where it come from. For a while.

"I figured, though, I ought to have some insurance. You see, I played both them records, and they was the same thing, and it was my voice, and I hadn't never recorded or even heard them songs before. I knew then, what was on those notes I had written, what had come to me was the countersong to the one I had been playing first. I don't know if that was just some kind of joke that record store fella had played on me, but I knew it was magic of a sort. He had give me a song to let it in and he had give me another song to hold it back. It was amusing to him, I'm sure.

"I thought I had the thing at bay, so I took that other copy, went to the post office, mailed it to Alma, case something happened to me. I guess I thought it was self-defense for her, but there was another part was proud of what I had done. What I was able to do. I could play anything now, and I didn't even need to think about it. Regular blues, it was a snap. Anything on that guitar was easy, even things you ought not to be able to play on one. Now, I realize it ain't me. It's something else out there.

"But when I come back from mailing, I brought me some paint and brushes, thought I'd write the notes and such on the wall. I did that, and I was ready to pack and go roaming some more, showing off my new skills, and all of a sudden, the thing, it's pushing through. It had gotten stronger 'cause I hadn't been playing the sounds, man. I put on the record, and I pretty much been at it ever since.

"It was all that record fella's game, you see. I got to figuring he was the devil, or something like him. He had me playing a game to keep that thing out, and to keep my soul. But it was a three-minute game, six if I'd have kept that second record and put it on the drop. If I was playing on the guitar, I could just work from the end of that record back to the front of it, playing it over and over. But it wore me down. Finally, I started playing the record nonstop. And I have for days.

"The fat man downstairs, he'd come up for the rent, but as soon as he'd use his key and crack that door, hear that music, he'd get gone. So here I am, still playing, with nothing left but to keep on playing, or get my soul sucked up by that thing and delivered to the record store man."

TOOTIE MINDED THE RECORD, AND I WENT OVER TO WHERE HE TOLD ME the record store was with the idea to put a boot up the guy's ass, or a .45 slug in his noggin. I found South Street, but not Way South. The other street that should have been Way South was called Back Water. There wasn't a store either, just an empty, unlocked building. I opened the door and went inside. There was dust everywhere, and I could see where some tables had been, 'cause their leg marks was in the dust. But anyone or anything that had been there was long gone.

I went back to the hotel, and when I got there, Tootie was just about asleep. The record was turning on the turntable without any sound. I looked at the wall, and I could see the beak of that thing, chewing at it. I put the record on, and this time, when it come to the end, the thing was still chewing. I played it another time, and another, and the thing finally went away. It was getting stronger.

I woke Tootie up, said, "You know, we're gonna find out if this thing can outrun my souped-up Chevy."

"Ain't no use," Tootie said.

"Then we ain't got nothing to lose," I said.

We grabbed up the record and his guitar, and we was downstairs and out on the street faster than you can snap your fingers. As we passed where the toad was, he saw me and got up quick and went into the kitchen and closed the door. If I'd had time, I'd have beat his ass on general principles.

When we walked to where I had parked my car, it was sitting on four flats and the side windows was knocked out and the aerial was snapped off. The record Alma May had given me was still there, lying on the seat. I got it and put it against the other one in my hand. It was all I could do.

As for the car, I was gonna drive that Chevy back to East Texas like I was gonna fly back on a sheet of wet newspaper.

Now, I got to smellin' that smell. One that was in the room. I looked at the sky. The sun was kind of hazy. Green even. The air around us trembled, like it was scared of something. It was heavy, like a blanket. I grabbed Tootie by the arm, pulled him down the street. I spied a car at a curb that I thought could run, a V-8 Ford. I kicked the back side window out, reached through, and got the latch.

I slid across the seat and got behind the wheel. Tootie climbed in on the passenger side. I bent down and worked some wires under the dash loose with my fingers and my razor, hot-wired the car. The motor throbbed and we was out of there.

It didn't make any kind of sense, but as we was cruising along, behind us it was getting dark. It was like chocolate pudding in a big wad rolling after us. Stars was popping up in it. They seemed more like eyes than stars. There was a bit of a moon, slightly covered over in what looked like a red fungus.

I drove that Ford fast as I could. I was hitting the needle at a hundred and ten. Didn't see a car on the highway. Not a highway cop, not an old lady on the way to the store. Where the hell was everybody? The highway looped up and down like the bottom was trying to fall out from under us.

To make it all short, I drove hard and fast, and stopped once for gas, having the man fill it quick. I gave him a bill that was more than the gas was worth, and he grinned at me as we burned rubber getting away. I don't think he could see what we could see—that dark sky with that thing in it. It was like you had to hear the music to see the thing existed, or for it to have any effect in your life. For him, it was daylight and fine and life was good.

By the time I hit East Texas, there was smoke coming from under that stolen Ford's hood. We came down a hill, and it was daylight in front of us, and behind us the dark was rolling in; it was splittin', making a kind of corridor, and there was that beaked thing, that . . . whatever it was. It was bigger than before and it was squirming its way out of the night sky like a weasel working its way under a fence. I tried to convince myself it was all in my head, but I wasn't convinced enough to stop and find out.

I made the bottom of the hill, in sight of the road that turned off to Alma May's. I don't know why I felt going there mattered, but it was something I had in my mind. Make it to Alma May's, and deliver on my agreement, bring her brother into the house. Course, I hadn't really thought that thing would or could follow us.

It was right then the car engine blew in an explosion that made the hood bunch up from the impact of thrown pistons.

The car died and coasted onto the road that led to Alma May's house. We could see the house, standing in daylight. But even that light was fading as the night behind us eased on in.

I jerked open the car door, snatched the records off the backseat, and yelled to Tootie to start running. He nabbed his guitar, and a moment later we were both making tracks for Alma May's.

Looking back, I saw there was a moon back there, and stars too, but mostly there was that thing, full of eyes and covered in sores and tentacles and legs and things I can't even describe. It was like someone had thrown critters and fish and bugs and beaks and all manner of disease into a bowl and whipped it together with a whipping spoon.

When we got to Alma May's, I beat on the door. She opened it, showing a face that told me she thought I was knocking too hard, but then she looked over my shoulder and went pale, almost as if her skin was white. She had heard the music, so she could see it too.

Slamming the door behind us, I went straight to the record player. Alma May was asking all kinds of questions, screaming them out. First to me, then to Tootie. I told her to shut up. I jerked one of the records out of its sheath, put it on the turntable, lifted the needle, and—the electricity crackled and it went dark. There was no playing anything on that player. Outside, the world was lit by that bloodred moon.

The door blew open. Tentacles flicked in, knocked over an end table. Some knickknacks fell and busted on the floor. Big as the monster was, it was squeezing through, causing the door frame to crack; the wood breaking sounded like someone cracking whips with both hands.

Me and Alma May, without even thinking about it, backed up. The red shadow, bright as a campfire, fled away from the monster and started flowing across the floor, bugs and worms squirming in it.

But not toward us.

It was running smooth as an oil spill toward the opposite side of the room. I got it then. It didn't just want through to this side. It wanted to finish off that deal Tootie had made with the record store owner. Tootie had said it all along, but it really hit me then. It didn't want me and Alma at all.

It had come for Tootie's soul.

There was a sound so sharp I threw my hands over my ears, and Alma May went to the floor. It was Tootie's guitar. He had hit it so hard, it sounded electrified. The pulse of that one hard chord made me weak in the knees. It was a hundred times louder than the record. It was beyond belief, and beyond human ability. But it was Tootie.

The red shadow stopped, rolled back like a tongue.

The guitar was going through its paces now. The thing at the doorway recoiled slightly, and then Tootie yelled, "Come get me. Come have me. Leave them alone."

I looked, and there in the faint glow of the red moonlight through the window, I saw Tootie's shadow lift that guitar high above his head by the neck, and down it came, smashing hard into the floor with an explosion of wood and a springing of strings.

The bleeding shadow came quickly then. Across the floor and onto Tootie.

He screamed. He screamed like someone having the flesh slowly burned off. Then the beast came through the door as if shot out of a cannon.

Tentacles slashed, a million feet scuttled, and those beaks came down, ripping at Tootie like a savage dog tearing apart a rag doll. Blood flew all over the room. It was like a huge strawberry exploded.

Then another thing happened. A blue mist floated up from the floor, from what was left of Tootie, and for just the briefest of moments, I saw Tootie's face in that blue mist; the face smiled a toothless kind of smile, showing nothing but a dark hole where his mouth was. Then, like someone sniffing steam off soup, the blue mist was sucked into the beaks of that thing, and Tootie and his soul were done with.

The thing turned its head and looked at us. It made a noise like a thousand rocks and broken automobiles tumbling down a cliff made of gravel and glass, and it began to suck back toward the door. It went out with a sound like a wet towel being popped. The bleeding shadow ran across the floor after it, eager to catch up; a lapdog hoping for a treat.

The door slammed as the thing and its shadow went out, and then the air got clean and the room got bright.

I looked where Tootie had been.

Nothing.

Not a bone.

Not a drop of blood.

I raised the window and looked out.

It was morning.

No clouds in the sky.

The sun looked like the sun.

Birds were singing.

The air smelled clean as a newborn's breath.

I turned back to Alma May. She was slowly getting up from where she had dropped to the floor.

"It just wanted him," I said, having a whole different kind of feeling about Tootie than I had before. "He gave himself to it. To save you, I think."

She ran into my arms and I hugged her tight. After a moment, I let go of her. I got the records and put them together. I was going to snap them across my knee. But I never got the chance. They went wet in my hands, came apart, and hit the floor and ran through the floorboards like black water, and that was all she wrote.

HUNGRY HEART

by Simon R. Green

New York Times bestseller Simon R. Green is the author of the eleven-volume Nightside paranormal series, which takes an intrepid PI to "the dark heart of London, where it's always three A.M." and monsters and creatures from myth and legend meet and mingle—and sometimes hire you to take on a dangerous job. The Nightside books include *Something from the Nightside*, *Agents of Light and Darkness*, *Hex and the City*, *Hell to Pay*, and seven others. Green has also written fantasy series such as the seven-volume Hawk and Fisher sequence (*No Haven for the Guilty*, *Devil Take the Hindmost*, *The God Killer*, and four others) and the three-volume Forest Kingdom sequence (*Blue Moon Rising*, *Blood and Honor*, *Down Among the Dead Men*), science fiction series such as the five-volume Deathstalker sequence (*Deathstalker: Being the First Part of the Life and Times of Owen Deathstalker*, *Deathstalker War*, and three others) and the related three-volume Deathstalker Legacy sequence (*Deathstalker Legacy*, *Deathstalker Return*, and *Deathstalker Coda*), and fantasy/spy story series such as the five-volume Secret Histories sequence (*The Man with the Golden Torc*, *Daemons Are Forever*, *The Spy Who Haunted Me*, *From Hell With Love*, and *For Heaven's Eyes Only*). He also has written stand-alone novels such as *Shadows Fall* and *Drinking Midnight Wine*, and he has started a new paranormal series, Ghost Finders, with *Ghost of a Chance* and his most recent book, *Ghost of a Smile*.

Here private detective John Taylor, long accustomed to dealing with ghosts and wizards and ghouls in the Nightside, takes on his strangest case, that of a witch who lost her heart—and wants it *back*.

THE CITY OF LONDON HAS A HIDDEN HEART; A DARK AND SECRET PLACE where gods and monsters go fist-fighting through alleyways, where wonders and marvels are two a penny, where everything and everyone is up for sale, and all your dreams can come true. Especially the ones where you wake up screaming. In London's Nightside it's always dark, always three o'clock in the morning, the hour that tries men's souls . . . and finds them wanting.

I WAS DRINKING WORMWOOD BRANDY IN THE OLDEST BAR IN THE WORLD when the femme fatale walked in. The bar was quiet, or at least as quiet as it ever gets. A bunch of female ghouls out on a hen night were getting tipsy on Mother's Ruin and complaining about the quality of the finger buffet. Ghouls just want to have fun. A pair of Neanderthals who'd put away so many smart drinks they were practically evolving before my eyes. And four Emissaries from the Outer Dark were playing cutthroat bridge and cheating each other blind. Just another night at Strangefellows—until she walked in.

She came striding between the tables with her head held high, as though she owned the place, or at the very least was planning a hostile takeover. She slammed to a halt before my table, gave me a big smile, and let me look her over. A tall, slender platinum blonde, late teens, Little Black Dress . . . big eyes, big smile, industrial-strength makeup. Attractive enough, in an intimidating sort of way. An English rose with more than her fair share of thorns. She introduced herself in a light breathy voice and sat down opposite me without waiting to be asked. She tried her smile on me again. On anyone else, it would probably have worked.

"You're John Taylor, private investigator," she said briskly. "I'm Holly Wylde, and I'm a witch. My ex stole my heart. I want you to find it, and get it back for me."

Not the strangest thing I've ever been asked to find, but I felt obliged to raise an eyebrow.

"I'm being quite literal," she said. "All witches learn how to remove their hearts, and keep them safe and secure in some private place, so that no one can ever fully kill us. As long as the heart stays safe, we always come back. Hardly sporting, I know, but if I believed in things like fair play I'd never have become a witch in the first place. My ex, bad cess to his diseased soul, used to be my mentor. Taught me all I know about magic, and rogered me breathless every evening at no extra cost. Gideon Brooks; perhaps you know the name?"

"No," I said. "Which is unusual. I know all the Major Players in the Nightside, all the real movers and shakers on the magical scene; but I don't know him."

She shrugged prettily. "When it comes to forbidden knowledge, Gideon is the reason why a lot of it is forbidden. A very powerful, very dangerous man, on the quiet. Anyway, I thought we were getting on splendidly. But when I decided I'd learned enough to leave Gideon and strike out on my own, he suddenly got all possessive on me. I thought we were just mentor and student, with benefits, but now he's all over me, declaring his undying love and how he can't live without me! Well. I was shocked, Mister Taylor. I don't do emotional entanglements. Not at this stage in my career. I tried to be graceful about it, but there's only so many ways a girl can say 'No!' in a loud and carrying voice. So. After a while he calmed down, apologized, and said he was just worried about me. Which was fair enough. But then he persuaded me to hand over my heart, so he could place some heavy-duty protections on it, to keep me safe once I was out on my own. And like a fool, I believed him. He has my heart, Mister Taylor, and he won't give it back! And whoever owns a witch's heart will always have power over her. I'll never be free of him."

She finally stopped for breath and gave me the big smile again, accompanied by the big, big eyes and a deep breath to show off her bosoms. I gave her a smile of my own, no more sincere than hers. For all her artless honesty and finishing-school accent, Holly was as phony as a banker's principles. All the time she'd been talking to me, her gaze had been darting all around the bar, hardly ever looking at me, and never making eye contact for more than a few seconds. Which is a pretty reliable sign that someone is lying to you. But that was okay; I'm used to clients lying to me, or at the very least being economical with the truth. My job is to find what the client asks for. The truth makes the job easier, but I can work around it if I have to.

"What kind of a witch are you, Holly?" I said. "Black, white, Wiccan, or gingerbread house?"

She bestowed a happy wink on me. "I never allow myself to be limited by other people's perceptions. I'm just a free spirit, Mister Taylor; or at least I was, until I met Gideon Brooks. Nasty man. Say you'll help me. Pretty please."

"I'll help you," I said. "For one thousand pounds a day, plus expenses. And don't plead poverty. That dress you're wearing costs more than I make in a year. And don't get me started on the shoes."

She didn't even blink. Just slapped an envelope down on the table before me. When I opened it, a thousand pounds in cash stared back. I gave Holly my best professional smile and made the envelope disappear about my person. Never put temptation in other people's way, especially in a bar like Strangefellows, where they'll steal your gold fillings if you fall asleep with your mouth open. Holly leaned forward across the table to fix me with what she thought was a serious look.

"They say you have a special gift for finding things, Mister Taylor; a magical inner eye that can See where everything is. But that won't help you find my heart. Gideon placed it inside a special protective rosewood box, called Heart's Ease. No one can pierce the magics surrounding that box—and only Gideon can open it. And you won't be able to find him or his house, either. Gideon lives inside his own private pocket dimension that only connects with our world when he feels like it. I only saw him when he let his house appear, at various places throughout the Nightside. And I haven't seen him since he stole my heart." She looked me right in the eye while she told me this, so I accepted most of it as provisionally true.

She leaned back in her chair and gave me her big smile again. It really was quite impressive. She must have spent a lot of time practicing it in front of a mirror.

"I know: Find a missing heart, and a missing man, in a missing house. But if finding them were easy I wouldn't need you, would I, Mister Taylor?"

She got up to leave. As entirely calm and composed as when she'd entered, despite her fascinating sob story.

"How will I find you?" I said.

"You won't, Mister Taylor. I'll find you. Toodles."

She waggled her fingers at me in a genteel good-bye, and was off, striding away with a straight back, ignoring her surroundings as though they were unworthy of her. Which they probably were. Strangefellows isn't exactly elite, and you couldn't drive it upmarket with a whip and a chair. I sipped thoughtfully at my wormwood brandy for a while, and then strolled over to the long mahogany bar to have a quiet word with Strangefellows' owner, bartender, and long-time pain in the neck, Alex Morrisey. Alex only wears black because no one has come up with a darker color, and he could gloom for the Olympics, with an honorable mention in existential angst. He started losing his hair while he was still in his early twenties, and I can't help feeling there's a connection. He was currently prodding the bar snacks with a stick, to see if they had any life left in them.

A bunch of spirits were hanging round the bar: shifting semitransparent shapes that blended in and out of each other as they drained the memories of old wines from long-empty bottles. Only Alex could sell the same bottle of wine several times over. I made the sign of the extremely cross at the spirits, and they drifted sulkily off down the bar so Alex and I could talk privately.

"Gideon Brooks," Alex said thoughtfully, after I'd filled him in on the necessary details. He cleaned a dirty glass with the same towel he used to mop up spills from the bartop, to give him time to think. "Not one of the big Names, but you know that as well as I do. Of course, the really powerful ones like to stay out of sight and under the radar. But the rosewood box, Heart's Ease . . . that name rings a bell. Some sort of priceless collectible; the kind that's worth so much it's rarely bought or sold, but more often prized from the dead fingers of its previous owner."

"Collectibles," I said. "Always more trouble than they're worth. And the Nightside is littered with those magic little shops that sell absolutely anything, no questions asked, and certainly no guarantees. Where the hell am I supposed to start?"

Alex smirked and slapped a cheap flyer down before me. ONCE AND FUTURE COLLECTIBLES, announced the ugly block lettering. I should have known. All kinds of rare and strange items turn up in the Nightside, from the past, the future, and any number of alternate earths. The jetsam and flotsam of the invisible world. And, this being the Nightside, there's always someone ready to make a profit out of it. The Once and Future Collectibles traveling show offered the largest selection of magical memorabilia and general weird shit to be found anywhere. Someone would know about the rosewood box. I made a note of the current address and looked up to find Alex grinning at me.

"You know who you need to talk to," he said. "The Queen of Hearts. She's bound to be there, and she knows everything there is to be known about heart-related collectibles. Big Bad Betty herself . . . I'm sure she'll be only too happy to renew your acquaintance . . ."

"Don't," I said. "The only good thing that woman ever taught me was to avoid mixing my drinks."

"I thought you made a lovely couple."

"You want a slap?"

I LEFT STRANGEFELLOWS AND HEADED OUT INTO THE NARROW RAIN-SLICK streets of the Nightside. The night was bustling with people, and some things very definitely not people, all in hot-eyed pursuit of things that were bad for them. Hot neon burned to every side, and cool music wafted out of the open doors of the kind of clubs that never close; where you can put on the red shoes and dance till you bleed. Exotic smells from a hundred different cuisines, barkers at open doors shilling thrills so exotic they don't even have a name in polite company, and, of course, the twilight daughters, patrolling every street corner; love for sale, or something very like it. You're never far from heaven or hell in the Nightside, though they're often the same place, under new management.

I was heading for the old Market Hall, where the Once and Future Collectibles were currently set up, when someone eased up alongside and made himself known to me. He was got up like a 1950s biker: all gleaming black leathers, polished steel chains, peaked leather cap, and an almost convincing Brando swagger. He couldn't have been more than sixteen, seventeen, with a corpse-pale face and thin colorless lips. His eyes were dark, his gaze hooded and malignant. He matched my pace exactly, his hands stuffed deep in the pockets of his leather jacket.

"The name's Gunboy," he said, in a calm, easy monotone, not even looking at me. "Mister Sweetman wants to talk with you. Now."

"All lines busy," I said. "Call back later."

"When Mister Sweetman wants to talk to someone, they talk to him."

"How nice for Mister Sweetman. But when I don't want to talk to people, I have a tendency to push them off the pavement and let them go play with the traffic."

Gunboy took one hand out of his jacket pocket and pointed it at me, the fingers shaped like a child's imaginary gun. He let me have a good look at it, and then pointed the single extended finger at a row of blazing neon bulbs set above the door to a Long Pigge franchise. His hand barely moved, but one by one the bulbs exploded, sparks flying wildly on the night air. A large man in a blood-soaked white overall came hurrying out to complain, took one look at Gunboy, and went straight back in again. Gunboy blew imaginary smoke from his finger and then stuck it casually in my ribs. He wasn't smiling, and his dark gaze was hot and compelling.

"Conceptual guns," he said, his lips barely moving. "Conceptual bullets. Real, because I believe they are. The power comes from me, and so do the dead bodies. Come with me, or I'll make real holes in you."

I considered him thoughtfully. Down the years, I've acquired several useful and really quite underhanded tricks for dealing with guns aimed in my direction, but they all depended on there being some kind of actual gun to deal with. So I gave Gunboy my best *I'm not in the least intimidated* smile, and allowed him to take me to his master. Gunboy was kind enough to put his hand back in his pocket as we walked along together. I'm not sure my pride would have survived otherwise.

MISTER SWEETMAN TURNED OUT TO BE STAYING AT THE HOTEL DES HEURES: a very upmarket, very pricey establishment, where all the rooms were individually time-coded. Stay as long as you like in your room, and not one moment will have passed when you step outside again. The ultimate in assured privacy—as long as you keep your door locked. You could spend your whole life in one of those rooms—though don't ask me how they manage room service.

Gunboy guided me to the right room, performed a special knock on the door, waited for it to open, and then pushed me inside. The single finger prodding me in my back was enough to keep me moving. Mister Sweetman was waiting for us. A very large Greek gentleman in a spotless white kaftan, he rose ponderously from an overstuffed chair and nodded easily to me. His head was shaved, he wore dark eye makeup, and he smiled only briefly as he gestured for me to take the chair opposite. We both sat down, looking each other over with open curiosity. Gunboy stayed by the door, his hands back in his jacket pockets, looking at nothing in particular.

"Mister Taylor!" said Sweetman, in a rich, happy voice. "An honor, my dear sir, I do assure you! One bumps into so many living legends in the Nightside that it is a positive treat to encounter the real thing! I am Elias Sweetman, a man of large appetites, always hungry for more. You and I, sir, have business to discuss. To our mutual benefit, I hope. You may talk candidly here, Mister Taylor; dear Gunboy will ensure that we are not interrupted."

Gunboy gave me a brief look, to indicate that I'd better behave myself, and then leaned back against the door. His eyes were immediately elsewhere, as he thought about whatever teenage thrill-killers think about. I was going to have to do something about Gunboy, for my pride's sake. I smiled easily at Sweetman while he arranged the folds of his kaftan for maximum comfort. He looked like a man who liked his comforts. He smiled on me like some favorite uncle who might bestow all manner of treats if he felt so inclined.

"Your reputation precedes you, Mister Taylor, indeed it does, so let us not beat about the bush. You are currently in pursuit of a certain prize that I have a special interest in; the box, Mister Taylor, the rosewood box. It has gone by many names, of course, inevitable for a treasure that has passed through so many hands down the centuries, but I believe you might know it as Heart's Ease."

"I know the name," I said, carefully noncommittal.

He let out a sharp bark of laughter. "I do admire a man who plays his cards close to his chest, indeed I do, Mister Taylor! But there's no need to be bashful here. I have pursued the rosewood box for many years, through many lands in many worlds, disputing with equally serious collectors along the way, but now . . . the box has come to the Nightside. So here we all are. Yes . . . I must ask you, Mister Taylor: what, precisely, is your interest in the box?"

I didn't see any good reason to conceal the truth, so I gave him the reader's-notes version of what Holly told me, concealing only her name. When I was finished, Sweetman gave his short bark of laughter again.

"Whatever the rosewood box may turn out to contain, Mister Taylor, I can assure you it is most definitely not the heart of some unimportant little witch. No, no . . . the box contains a source of great power. A great man's heart, perhaps even a god's . . . Some say the box contains the preserved heart of the great old god Lud, the original foundation stone for London. Others say the box contains the missing heart of that terrible old sorcerer, Merlin Satanspawn. Or perhaps the heart of Nikola Tesla, the broken and bitter saint of twentieth-century science. No one knows for sure; only that the box contains a power worth dying for. Or killing for . . . Certainly, the box has become so famous in its own right it has become a collectible in itself, whatever it might eventually prove to contain."

"So," I said, "a source of wealth, and possibly power. No wonder so many people want it."

"Passed from hand to hand down the years, acquiring blood and legends along the way, Mister Taylor. Priceless because there isn't enough money in the world to buy it. You have to be man enough to take it, and hold on to it."

He was leaning forward now, licking his lips, his eyes gleaming. He was so close to what he'd chased for so long he could almost taste it, and only his need to be sure that he knew everything I knew kept him from harsher methods of interrogation. And since he had no way of knowing how little I did know, I made a point of leaning back in my chair and stretching easily.

"What do *you* think is in the rosewood box?" I said.

He leaned back in his chair and studied me thoughtfully, taking his time before answering. "I have been given good reason to believe that the box contains the heart of William Shakespeare, Mister Taylor. The heart of England itself, some say."

"And what would you do with such a thing, once you got hold of it?"

Sweetman smiled widely. "I mean to eat it, Mister Taylor! Only the rarest and most exquisite gastronomic experiences can arouse my jaded palate these days, and this particular delicacy should prove most satisfying . . . You have a gift for finding things, Mister Taylor. Find the box for me. However much the little witch is paying you, I will double her offer."

"Sorry," I said. "But I have to be true to my clients."

"Even when they lie to you?"

"Perhaps especially then."

I got up to leave, and Sweetman immediately gestured to Gunboy at the door. He straightened up as I approached and brought one hand out of his leather jacket. I brought one hand out of my trench coat pocket, ripped open the sachet of coarse pepper I always keep with me, and threw the whole lot in his face. His head snapped back, startled, but it was already too late. He sneezed explosively, again and again, while shocked tears ran down his face from squeezed-shut eyes. He waved his finger back and forth, but it didn't worry me. With his nose and eyes full of pepper, there was no way Gunboy could concentrate enough to manifest his conceptual guns. Never leave home without condiments. Condiments are our friends. I easily sidestepped the weeping Gunboy and opened the door. I risked a quick look back, just in case Sweetman had his own hidden weapons, but he had lost all interest in me. He had his arm around Gunboy's shaking shoulders and was comforting him like a child. Or almost like a child.

I shut the door quietly behind me and left the Hotel des Heures. At least I hadn't wasted any time.

THE OLD MARKET HALL IS A GREAT OPEN BARN OF A PLACE, AND THE ONCE and Future Collectibles traveling show filled it from wall to wall with hundreds of stalls, large and small, offering more rare and unusual memorabilia in one place than the human mind could comfortably accommodate. I strolled up and down the aisles, glancing casually at this stall and that, carefully not showing too much interest in anything. Not that there was anything particularly exceptional on offer . . . An old Betamax video of Elvis starring as Captain Marvel, in some other world's 1969 movie *Shazam!* One of Dracula's coffins, complete with original grave dirt and a certificate of authenticity. The mummified head of Alfredo Garcia, smelling strongly of Mexican spices. And the mirror of Dorian Gray.

I finally wandered over to the Queen of Hearts' stall, as though I just happened to be heading in her general direction. Big Bad Betty was running the whole thing on her own, as usual: large as life and twice as imposing. A good six feet tall and strongly built, she wore a stylized gypsy outfit, complete with an obviously fake wig of long dark curls and a hell of a lot of clanking bracelets up and down her meaty arms. The fingers of her large hands were covered in enough heavy metal rings to qualify as knuckle-dusters, and she looked like she'd have no hesitation in using them. She was attractive enough, in a large, dark, and even swarthy kind of way. I gave her my best ingratiating smile, and her baleful glare didn't alter one iota.

I pretended to look over the contents of her stall, to give her time to realize the scowl wasn't going to be enough to scare me off. Big Bad Betty liked to style herself the Queen of Hearts because she specialized in heart-related collectibles. She was currently offering the carefully preserved heart of Giacomo Casanova (bigger than you'd think), a phial of heart's blood from Varney the Vampyre, and a pack of playing cards that once belonged to Lewis Carroll, with all the hearts painted in dried blood. Nothing special . . .

"You've got some nerve showing your face here, John Taylor," Betty said finally.

"Just looking," I said easily. "I do like a good browse."

"I hired you to find my missing husband!"

"I did find him. Not my fault he'd had his memory wiped and didn't remember you anymore. And not in any way my fault that he'd had his memory wiped to make sure he wouldn't be able to remember you. Maybe you should have tried counseling . . ."

She scowled at me. "You never called me afterward. Not once."

"That wasn't what you hired me for."

"What do you want here, Taylor? On the grounds that the sooner you're out of my sight, the better."

"What can you tell me about the rosewood box, called by some Heart's Ease?"

She couldn't resist telling me. She does so love to show off what she knows, and no one knows more about hearts than the Queen of Hearts.

"The box is centuries old, supposedly first put together in pre-Revolutionary France, designed to contain the suffering of a brokenhearted lover. He put it all in the box, so he could be free of it. Hence the name, Heart's Ease. How very French. Though there are other stories . . . that what the box contains has become something else, down the centuries. Something . . . darker. Hungrier. Making the box the perfect container for all kinds of magical and significant hearts. Which is why the box has had so many other names. Heartbreaker, the Hungry Heart, the Dark Heart; you pays your money, and you believes what you chooses. Far as I know, no one's dared open the box for years. Any collector with two working brain cells to bang together stays well clear of it.

"Now: Buy something, or get lost."

I nodded politely and moved away from her stall as quickly as possible without actually running. I'd gotten everything I needed from Betty, but I was still going to need a little specialized help if I was to find Gideon Brooks, his traveling house, and the rosewood box. So I concentrated and raised my special gift. My inner eye slowly opened, my third eye, my private eye; and I looked round the Market Hall with my raised Sight, searching for what I needed. A key that would unlock a traveling dimensional door. Something blazed up brightly, not too far away, glowing white-hot with mystical significance. I strode quickly down the aisles and finally stopped before a stall that offered nothing but keys, in all shapes and sizes. Skeleton keys to unlock any door, blessed silver keys to reveal hidden secrets, solid iron keys to undo chastity spells. Keys are very old symbols and can undo any number of symbolic magics.

One key stood out among all the ranks and rows of hanging keys, shining very brightly for my inner eye only. A simple brass key, marked with prehuman glyphs. I'd seen its kind before, in certain very restricted books. This was a summoning key, which could not only open any door, but actually bring the door to you. Just what I needed. Unfortunately, the key didn't have a price tag on it. And in a place like this, that could only mean that if you had to ask the price, you couldn't afford it. So, I used my gift to find the one moment when the stall-holder's attention was somewhere else, and I just reached out, took the key, and walked away.

I could always give it back later, when I was finished with it. When I found the time. The stall-holder really should have invested in some half-decent security spells.

I WAS HEADING CASUALLY FOR THE NEAREST EXIT, THE KEY TUCKED SAFELY away in an inside pocket, when Holly Wylde appeared suddenly out of the crowd to block my way. She smiled at me winningly.

"I had a feeling you'd be here. And so you are! Aren't you glad to see me again?"

"I don't know," I said. "I do prefer my clients to tell me the truth, whenever possible."

"I didn't exactly lie," she said, pouting. "All right, yes, there's a lot about the rosewood box I didn't tell you, but I was pretty sure you'd find that out on your own, once you started looking. I didn't want to scare you off, after all; and I do so want my heart back! I just don't know what I'll do without it."

I sighed. It was hard to stay mad at her. Though probably worth the effort.

"Why would Gideon Brooks put your heart in such a precious and important box?"

"Because it was the only thing he had that he knew I couldn't get into," she said artlessly.

"And all you want is your heart back?" I said. "You don't care about the priceless and important box?"

"Well," she said, "if it should happen to fall into our hands, that would be a nice bonus. Wouldn't it?"

"You're batting your eyelashes at me again," I said. "Stop it."

"Sorry. Force of habit."

"Other people are looking for the box," I said, shifting onto what I hoped was safer ground. I told her about Sweetman and Gunboy, and she stamped her little foot and said a few baby swear words.

"The fat man and his toy boy; I knew they were sniffing around, but I didn't know they were this close. We have to get to Gideon before they do! All they care about is that box. They wouldn't care about my poor little heart."

"Sweetman seemed very sure the box holds some famous or important heart," I said.

"Might do. Who knows?" said Holly, shrugging easily. "Who knows how many hearts have ended up inside that box, down the years? I only care about mine. What are you doing here, anyway? Such a tacky place, all full of tat and kitsch. I can feel my street cred slipping away just for being here."

"I have acquired a useful little toy that will bring Gideon's door right to us," I said.

She squeaked excitedly and did a happy dance right in front of me. "Yes! Yes! I knew you wouldn't let me down!"

"I tell my clients everything," I said pointedly. "Are you sure there isn't something more you should be telling me?"

"I don't think so," said Holly Wylde, her wide eyes full of an entirely unconvincing innocence.

We left the Market Hall together, and I found a reasonably calm and quiet place to raise my gift again. I sent my Sight shooting up out of my head into the night sky, speckled with more stars than the outside world ever dreams of, and then looked down at the Nightside streets turning slowly beneath me. All around I could See the subtle flashes and occasional flare-ups of magical workings, and the more openly dramatic radiations and detonations of mad scientists at play. Giant wispy forms marched up and down the streets, passing through buildings as though they weren't even there; just the ancient Awful Folk, going about their unknowable business. All kinds of traffic thundered through the streets, carrying all kinds of goods and people, and never ever stopping. And some buildings just disappeared from view, coming and going, replaced by other buildings following their own inscrutable journeys.

Everyone knows a moving target is hardest to hit.

Down in my own person, I held the summoning key firmly in my hand and focused my gift through it; and immediately one particular building jumped out at me with extra significance, as the key locked on to the one special door I needed to find. The building hopped and skipped around the Nightside, appearing and disappearing apparently at random; but more like a fish on the end of a line now I had the summoning key. I chased Gideon Brooks up and down the Nightside, sticking close no matter how many times he tried to throw me off, my mind soaring impossibly fast from one location to another, invisible and undetectable, until finally Gideon Brooks just gave up, and his home settled down in one place and stayed put. It materialized right before me, presenting a quite unremarkable door, and squeezed into place between two perfectly respectable establishments, which rather grudgingly budged up to make room for it. I dropped back inside my head and released my hold on the summoning key. The door before me looked entirely unthreatening, but I checked it over with my Sight anyway, just in case. Heavy-duty protective magics crawled all over the door, and spat and sparkled on the air round the building.

I held up the key, muttered the proper activating Words, and unlocked all the protections, one by one. It took quite a while. Holly squeaked excitedly and clapped her little hands together.

And that was when Sweetman and Gunboy turned up. They were just suddenly there, strolling down the street toward us, Sweetman in his great white kaftan rolling along like a ship under full sail, Gunboy swaggering at his side like an attack dog on a short leash. Holly actually hissed at the sight of them, like an affronted cat, and moved quickly to stand behind me. I carefully shut down my Sight so I could concentrate on the matter at hand.

"My dear Mister Taylor," said Sweetman, as he crashed to a halt before me. "Well done, sir, well done indeed! I knew I could rely on you to chase Gideon Brooks down, but I have to say, I never thought you'd be able to run his very special house to ground too. You shouldn't look so surprised to see me, my good fellow, really you shouldn't. Dear Gunboy and I have been following you ever since you left the hotel."

"No you haven't," I said flatly. "I'd have noticed."

"Well, not personally following, as such," Sweetman agreed. "I took the liberty of slipping a small but very powerful tracking device into your coat pocket while you were preoccupied with poor Gunboy. The dear boy does make for such marvelous misdirection."

I looked at Gunboy. "And how do you feel, being used like that?"

He took one hand out of his pocket and pointed it at me. "I do what Mister Sweetman says. And so will you."

"Are you going to let him talk to you like that?" said Holly, from behind me.

"As long as he's pointing that conceptual gun at me, yes," I said. "Mister Sweetman, as I understand it, and I'm perfectly prepared to be told I don't, it's been that kind of a case . . . You want the rosewood box, and the very important heart you believe it contains. You are not, I take it, interested in this young lady's heart, also inside the box?"

Sweetman inclined his large head judiciously. "No offense, young lady, but I would have no interest in your heart under any conditions."

"For someone who didn't want to offend," said Holly, "I'd have to say you came pretty damned close."

"The point being," I said quickly, "that since we all want different things from Gideon Brooks, we don't have to be at each other's throat. We can work together to acquire the box, and then each take what we want from it."

"Are you crazy?" said Holly, hurrying out from behind me so she could glare at me properly. "Give up on the box?"

"You hired me to find your stolen heart," I said. "Or are you now saying the box is more important?"

"No," said Holly. "It's all about the heart." She looked at Gunboy. "We could use some serious firepower, if we're going up against Gideon Brooks."

Gunboy looked at Sweetman, and then put his hand back in his pocket.

"Don't sulk, boy," said Sweetman. "It's very unattractive."

I smiled around me. "I love it when a compromise comes together."

AND THEN WE ALL LOOKED ROUND SHARPLY, AS THE DOOR BEFORE US opened on its own. I felt a little disappointed that I wouldn't get to show off what I could do with my gift and the summoning key. We all stood looking at the open door for a long moment, but nothing menacing emerged, and there was only an impenetrable gloom beyond. We looked at each other, and then I led the way forward—if only because I didn't trust any of the others to react responsibly to anything unexpected. Sweetman and Gunboy fell in behind me, and Holly brought up the rear.

Beyond the door lay a simple, dimly lit hallway, with no obvious magical trappings. It could have been any house, anywhere. The door closed quietly behind us, once we'd all entered. The four of us pretty much filled the narrow hallway. A door to our left swung slowly open, and I led the way into the adjoining room. When in doubt, act confident. The room was open and warmly lit, with no furnishings or fittings; just bare wooden floorboards, and one very ordinary-looking, casually dressed middle-aged man, sitting on a chair surrounded by a great pentacle burned right into the floorboards. He was holding a simple wooden box in his hands; perhaps a foot long and half as wide.

The lines of the pentacle flared up abruptly as Sweetman approached them, and he stopped short. The lines shone with a fierce blue-white light, blazing with supernatural energies. Sweetman stepped carefully back and gestured to Gunboy, who smiled slowly as he took both hands out of his jacket pockets. And then he stopped, looked almost abjectly at Sweetman, and put his hands away again. Apparently conceptual guns were no match for older and more established magics.

I looked at Holly. She was staring unblinkingly at Gideon, but I couldn't read the expression on her face. She didn't look angry, or scared; just utterly focused on the box in his hands.

"You're a witch," I said to her quietly. "Can't you do anything?"

She scowled suddenly as she looked at Gideon. It might just have been the scowl, but she didn't look pretty anymore. "If I could break his protections, I wouldn't have needed your help."

"You never did like having to depend on other people," the man on the chair said pleasantly. "And you really couldn't stand someone else having power over you, even when you came to them to learn the ways of magic. You were the best student I ever had, my dear—until you grew impatient, and tried to steal my secrets. And when that failed, you had to go looking for power in all sorts of unsuitable places." He looked at me. "Whatever she's told you, you can't trust it. She'll say anything, do anything, to get what she wants. She slept with demons so they'd teach her the magics I wouldn't, she stole grimoires and objects of power, and she would have stolen my heart . . . if I hadn't taken precautions."

"No one tells me what to do," said Holly. "With your heart in my hands, you'd have taught me everything I wanted. And as for the demons, every single one of them was better in the sack than you."

Women always fight dirty.

"I kept my place moving so you couldn't find me," said Gideon. "I should have known you'd go to the infamous John Taylor, the man who can find anything. What did she tell you, Mister Taylor? When she wasn't smiling her pretty smile at you?"

"She said you stole her heart," I said. "And put it in the rosewood box."

"Oh, Holly," said Gideon, and he actually laughed briefly. "It's *my* heart in the box, Mister Taylor. I put it there after she tried to steal it. Because she couldn't stand the idea of anyone having a hold over her."

"So . . . you don't have any feelings for her?" I said, just to be sure.

"Ah," said Gideon. "I should have known that would be the heart of the matter, so to speak. Is that why you're here, Holly?"

"You never loved me!" said Holly. She stood directly before him, just outside the pentacle, both her small hands clenched into fists. "I did everything right, and you still never loved me!"

"You never loved anyone," Gideon said calmly. "You always loved power more. I was just your mentor."

Holly turned suddenly to me. "You believe me, don't you, John? You'll get the box for me. And then we can make him do anything we want!"

"Sorry," I said. "But I never believed you, Holly. You hired me to find the rosewood box. Well, there it is."

"She was the one who let word get out that I had the box," said Gideon. "So that avaricious men from all over would come looking for it, and she could set them against me. Just in case you didn't work out, Mister Taylor. How does it feel, being used?"

I shrugged. "Comes with the job."

Gideon Brooks turned his attention to Sweetman and Gunboy. "It's really nothing more than a simple storage box, you know. Perhaps a little more famous than most. It may have contained any number of important or significant items, in its time, but the only heart it contains now is mine. Where Holly can't get at it."

Sweetman's brief bark of laughter held even less real humor than usual. "My dear sir, you don't really expect me to believe that? I have followed the box through unknown cities and blood-soaked streets, and I will have it. Gunboy, point those marvelous hands of yours at Mister Taylor and the little witch. Now, Mister Brooks. Give up the box, or everything my enthusiastic young associate does to these two young people will be your responsibility."

Holly looked at Gunboy, and then at Gideon. "You wouldn't really let him hurt me, would you, sweetie? You did say I was the best student you ever had . . ."

"I had students before you," said Gideon. "And there will be others after you. Though hopefully I'll choose a little more wisely next time. I am still quite fond of you, Holly, against all my better judgment. But not enough to put my heart at risk."

"What about me?" I said.

"What about you?" said Gideon.

"Fair enough," I said.

"Ah well," Holly said brightly. "Plan B." She turned her most charming smile on Gunboy and took a deep breath.

Sweetman chuckled. "Trust me, young lady; you have absolutely nothing that dear Gunboy desires."

"But he has something I want," said Holly. "I want his heart."

She made a sudden grasping gesture with one outstretched hand, and Gunboy screamed shrilly as his back arched and his chest exploded. His black leather jacket burst apart and the bare flesh beneath tore open, as his heart ripped itself from its bony setting and flew across the air to nestle into Holly's waiting hand. Blood ran thickly between her fingers as the heart continued to beat. Holly's pretty pink mouth moved in a brief moue of distaste, and then she closed her hand with sudden vicious strength, crushing the heart. Gunboy fell to the floor and lay still, eyes still staring in horror, his chest a bloody ruin. Sweetman let out a single cry of absolute pain and loss and knelt down beside Gunboy to cradle the dead body in his huge arms. Blood soaked his white kaftan as he rocked Gunboy back and forth, like a sleeping child. Silent tears ran down Sweetman's face.

"So," I said to Holly. "That's the kind of witch you are."

She dropped the crushed heart to the floor and flicked blood from her pale fingers. She smiled at me sweetly. "I'm the kind of witch you don't want to disappoint. I did tell you Gideon dealt in forbidden knowledge, and I was such a good listener. Now be a good boy, and go get the box for me. You can find a way past Gideon's defenses. It's what you do."

"Yes," I said. "But there's a limit to what I'll do."

She gave me a cold measuring look, and I met her gaze unflinchingly. Never let them see fear in your eyes.

"I bought your services, for a thousand pounds a day," Holly said finally. "And the day isn't over yet."

"I found the box for you," I said. "Not my fault your heart isn't in it. Still, after all my investigations, I probably know more about the box than you do. It was originally made to contain all the pain and horror of a man's broken heart; and it's still in there. Trapped inside the box for centuries, growing stronger and more frustrated. It's been alone so long, it must be very hungry for company by now. You may know the box as Heart's Ease, and perhaps it was, originally; but it has another name now. The Hungry Heart."

I raised my gift, found my way past Gideon's protections, and used my gift and the key to unlock the rosewood box. The lid snapped open, and the Hungry Heart within reached out and grabbed Holly and pulled her inside, all in a moment. It might have taken me too, if Gideon hadn't immediately forced the lid closed again. We looked at each other, in the suddenly quiet room.

"She wanted my heart," said Gideon. "Now she can keep it company . . . forever."

Sweetman looked up, still cradling the dead Gunboy. "What is that . . . What's really inside the box?"

"The stuff that screams are made of," I said.

STYX AND STONES

by Steven Saylor

Bestseller Steven Saylor is one of the brightest stars in the historical mystery subgenre, along with authors such as Lindsey Davis, John Maddox Roberts, and the late Ellis Peters. He is the author of the long-running Roma Sub Rosa series, which details the adventures of Gordianus the Finder, a detective in a vividly realized Ancient Rome, in such novels as *Roman Blood*, *Arms of Nemesis*, *Catilina's Riddle*, *The Venus Throw*, *A Murder on the Appian Way*, *Rubicon*, *Last Seen in Massilia*, *A Mist of Prophecies*, and *The Judgment of Caesar*. Gordianus's exploits at shorter lengths have been collected in *The House of the Vestals: The Investigations of Gordianus the Finder* and *A Gladiator Dies Only Once: The Further Investigations of Gordianus the Finder*. Saylor's other books include *A Twist at the End*, *Have You Seen Dawn?*, and a huge non-Gordianus historical novel, *Roma: The Novel of Ancient Rome*. His most recent books are a Gordianus novel, *The Triumph of Caesar*, and the big second volume in the Roma sequence, *Empire: The Novel of Imperial Rome*. He lives in Berkeley, California.

With the suspenseful story that follows, "Styx and Stones," he introduces a whole new series of tales that will take a teenaged Gordianus to visit the Seven Wonders of the World; his traveling companion is the elderly Greek poet Antipater of Sidon. The Seven Wonders stories take place in 92–90 B.C., and so serve as a prequel to the first novel in the Roma Sub Rosa series, *Roman Blood*, which is set in 80 B.C. Here, venturing far beyond the world of Rome and Greece, Gordianus and Antipater discover that the fabled city of Babylon is a mere ghost of its former glory, haunted—and menaced—by its wanton past.

IN BABYLON, WE SHALL SEE NOT ONE, BUT TWO OF THE GREAT WONDERS of the World," said Antipater. "Or at least, we shall see what remains of them."

We had spent the night at a dusty little inn beside the Euphrates River. My traveling companion had been quiet and grumpy from the moment he got out of bed that morning—travel is hard on old men—but as we drew closer to Babylon, traveling south on the ancient road that ran alongside the river, his spirits rose and little by little he became more animated.

The innkeeper had told us that the ancient city was not more than a few hours distant, even accounting for the slow progress of the asses we were riding, and all morning a smudge that suggested a city had loomed ahead of us on the low horizon, very gradually growing more pronounced. The land between the Tigris and Euphrates rivers and for miles around is absolutely flat, without even low hills to break the view. On such a vast, featureless plain, you might think that you could see forever, but the ripples of heat that rose from the earth distorted the view, so that objects near and far took on an uncertain, even uncanny appearance. A distant tower turned out to be a palm tree; a pile of strangely motionless—dead?—bodies suddenly resolved into a heap of gravel, apparently put there by whoever maintained the road.

For over an hour I tried to make sense of a northward-traveling party that seemed to be approaching us on the road. The shimmering heat waves by turns appeared to magnify the group, then make them grow smaller, then disappear altogether, then reappear. At first I thought it was a company of armed men, for I thought I saw sunlight glinting on their weapons. Then I decided I was seeing nothing more than a single man on horseback, perhaps wearing a helmet or some other piece of armor that reflected a bluish gleam. Then the person, or persons, or whatever it was that approached us, vanished in the blink of an eye, and I felt a shiver, wondering if we were about to encounter a company of phantoms.

At last we met our fellow travelers on the road. The party turned out to consist of several armed guards and two small carts pulled by asses and piled high with stacks of bricks, but not bricks of any sort I had seen before. These were large and variously shaped, most about a foot square, and covered on the outward-facing sides with a dazzling glaze, some yellow, some blue, some mixed. They were not newly made—uneven edges and bits of adhering mortar indicated they had been chiseled free from some existing structure—but except for a bit of dust, the colored glazes glimmered with a jewel-like brightness.

Antipater grew very excited. "Can it be?" he muttered. "Bricks from the fabled walls of Babylon!"

The old poet awkwardly dismounted and shuffled toward the nearest cart, where he reached out to touch one of the bricks, running his fingertips over the shimmering blue glaze.

The driver at first objected, and called to one of the armed guards, who drew his sword and stepped forward. Then the driver laughed, seeing Antipater's bright-eyed wonder, and waved the guard back. Speaking to Antipater, the driver said something in a language I didn't recognize. Apparently, neither did Antipater, who squinted up at the man and said, "Speakee Greekee?"

This was my first visit to a land where the majority of the population conversed in languages other than Latin and Greek. Antipater had a smattering of Parthian, but I had noticed that he preferred to address the natives in broken Greek, as if somehow this would be more comprehensible to them than the flawless Greek he usually spoke.

"I know Greek, yes, little bit," said the driver, holding his thumb close to his forefinger.

"You come from Babylon, no?" Antipater also tended to raise his voice when speaking to the natives, as if they might be deaf.

"From Babylon, yes."

"How far?" Antipater engaged in an elaborate bit of sign language to clarify his meaning.

"Babylon, from here? Oh, two hour. Maybe three," amended the driver, eyeing our weary-looking asses.

Antipater looked in the direction of the smudge on the horizon, which had grown decidedly larger but still held no promise of towering walls. He sighed. "I begin to fear, Gordianus, that nothing at all remains of the fabled walls of Babylon. Surely, if they were as large as legend asserts, and if any remnants still stand, we would see something of them by now."

"Bricks come from old walls, yes," said the driver, understanding only some of Antipater's comments and gesturing to his load. "My neighbor finds, buried behind his house. Very rare. Very valuable. He sell to rich merchant in Ctesiphon. Now my neighbor is rich man."

"Beautiful, aren't they, Gordianus?" Antipater ran his palm over a glazed surface, then lifted the brick to look at the bottom. "By Zeus, this one is actually stamped with the name of Nebuchadnezzar! It must date from his reign." For a moment I thought Antipater was about to break into verse—creating extemporaneous poems was his specialty—but his thoughts took a more practical turn. "These bricks would be worth a fortune back in Rome. My patron Quintus Lutatius Catulus owns a few, which he displays as specimens in his garden. I think he paid more for those five or six Babylonian bricks than he did for all the statues in his house put together. Ah well, let's push on."

Antipater gave the driver a coin for his trouble, then remounted, and we resumed our slow, steady progress toward the shimmering smudge on the horizon.

I cleared my throat. "What makes those old bricks so valuable? And why did the Babylonians build their walls from bricks in the first place? I should think any proper city wall would be made of stone."

The look Antipater shot at me made me feel nine years old rather than nineteen. "Look around you, Gordianus. Do you see any stones? There's not a quarry for miles. This part of the world is completely devoid of the kind of stones suitable for constructing temples and other buildings, much less walls that stretch for miles and are so wide that chariots can ride atop them. No, except for a few temples adorned with limestone and bitumen imported at great expense, the city of Nebuchadnezzar was constructed of bricks. They were made from clay mixed with finely chopped straw, then compressed in molds and hardened by fire. Amazingly, such bricks are very nearly as strong as stone, and in the ancient Chaldean language the word for *brick* and *stone* is the same. They can't be carved like stone, of course, but they can be decorated with colored glazes that never fade."

"So the famous walls of Babylon were built by—" I hesitated over the difficult name.

"King Nebuchadnezzar." Antipater made a point to enunciate carefully, as he had when speaking to the cart driver. "The city of Babylon itself was founded, at least in legend, by an Assyrian queen named Semiramis, who lived back in the age of Homer. But it was a much later king, of the Chaldean dynasty, who raised Babylon to the height of its glory. His name was Nebuchadnezzar and he reigned five hundred years ago. He rebuilt the whole city on a grid design, with long, straight avenues—quite different from the chaos you're accustomed to in Rome, Gordianus—and he adorned the city with magnificent temples to the Babylonian gods, chief among them Marduk and Ishtar. He constructed a huge temple complex called *Etemenanki*—the Foundation of Heaven and Earth—in the form of a towering, seven-tiered ziggurat; some say the ziggurat rivals the pyramids of Egypt in size and should itself be numbered among the Seven Wonders. For the delight of his Median queen, who was homesick for the mountain forests and flowery meadows of her distant homeland, Nebuchadnezzar built the Hanging Gardens, a paradise perched like a bird's nest high above the earth. And he encircled the whole city with a wall seventy-five feet high and thirty feet wide—wide enough for two chariots to meet and pass. The walls were fortified with crenellated battlements and towers that rose over a hundred feet, and the whole length was decorated with patterns and images in blue and yellow, so that from a distance the Babylon of Nebuchadnezzar shimmered like baubles of lapis strung upon a necklace of gold."

He gazed dubiously at the horizon. The smudge continued to grow, but looked more like a daub of mud than a jewel—though it seemed to me that I was beginning to glimpse a massive object that rose above the rest of the smudge and shone with various colors. Was it the ziggurat?

"What happened to Nebuchadnezzar's empire?" I said. "What happened to his walls?"

"Empires rise, empires fall—even the empire of Rome, someday . . ." This was not the first time Antipater had expressed his disdain for Rome's imperial power, but even here, far from Rome's influence, he spoke such words under his breath. "Just as the Assyrians had fallen to the Chaldeans, so the Chaldeans fell to the Persians. A hundred years after the death of Nebuchadnezzar, Babylon revolted against Xerxes, the same Persian monarch who foolishly imagined he could conquer Greece. Xerxes had more success with Babylon; he sacked the city and looted the temples, and some say he demolished the great walls, destroying them so completely that hardly a trace remained—only a multitude of glazed bricks, coveted by collectors across the world. A hundred years later, when Alexander advanced on the city, the Babylonians offered no resistance and came out to greet him, so perhaps indeed they no longer had walls adequate to defend them. They say Alexander intended to restore Babylon to its former glory and to make it the capital of the world, but instead he died there at the age of thirty-two. His successor built a new city nearby, on the Tigris, and named it for himself; the new capital of Seleucia claimed whatever wealth and power remained in Babylon, and the ancient city was largely forgotten—except by the scholars and sages who flocked there, attracted by the cheap rents, and by astrologers, who are said to find the ziggurat an ideal platform for stargazing."

"So we're likely to meet astrologers in Babylon?" I said.

"Without a doubt. Astrology originated with the Chaldeans. The science is still a novelty in Rome, I know, but it's been gaining in popularity among the Greeks ever since a Babylonian priest of Marduk named Berossus set up a school of astrology on the island of Cos, back in the days of Alexander."

We rode along in silence for a while. I became certain that the highest point of the ever-growing smudge must indeed be the multicolored ziggurat, dominating the skyline of Babylon. I could also make out something that appeared to be a wall, but it did not look very high, and in color it was a reddish brown, as if made of plain clay bricks, not of shimmering lapis and gold.

"What about the Hanging Gardens that Nebuchadnezzar built for his wife?" I said. "Do they still exist?" I said.

"Soon enough, we shall see for ourselves," said Antipater.

AT LAST THE WALLS OF BABYLON LOOMED BEFORE US. I COULD SEE THAT Antipater was profoundly disappointed.

"Ah, well, I was prepared for this," he said with a sigh, as we crossed a dry moat and rode through the gate. Had we encountered it anywhere else, the wall would have been reasonably impressive—it rose perhaps thirty feet and extended as far as I could see along the bank of the Euphrates—but it was made of common reddish-brown bricks. This wall was certainly not one of the Wonders of the World.

We passed though a lively marketplace, full of exotic smells and colorful characters; the place exuded a quaint provincial charm, but I didn't feel the unmistakable thrill of being in one of the world's great cities, like Rome or Ephesus.

Then, ahead of us, I saw the Ishtar Gate.

I didn't know what to call it at the time; I only knew that my jaw suddenly dropped and my heartbeat quickened. Bright sunlight glinted off the multicolored tiles, animating the amazing images of remarkable animals—magnificent horned aurochs, roaring lions, and terrifying dragons. Other patterns were more abstract, suggesting jewels and blossoms, but constructed on a gigantic scale. Blue predominated, and there were as many shades as one might see on the face of the sea in the course of a day, from the bright azure of noon to midnight indigo. There were also many shades of yellow and gold, and borders made of a dazzling green. The parapets that towered above us were crenellated with a pattern that delighted the eye. But the gate was only a fragment, standing in isolation; the wall extended only a short distance to either side, then abruptly ended.

A group of natives, seeing our astonishment, ran toward us and competed to engage us in conversation. At length Antipater nodded to the one who seemed to speak the best Greek.

"What is this?" said Antipater.

"The great wall!" declared the man, who had a scraggly beard and was missing several teeth.

"But this can't be all of it!" protested Antipater.

"All that remains," said the man. "When Xerxes pulled down the walls of Nebuchadnezzar, this gate he left, to show how great was the wall he destroyed. The Ishtar Gate, it is called, to the glory of the goddess." He held out his palm, into which Antipater obligingly pressed a coin.

"Think of it, Gordianus," Antipater whispered. "Alexander himself rode though this very gate when he entered the city in triumph."

"No wonder he wanted to make his capital here," I said, gazing straight up as we passed under the lofty archway. "I've never seen anything like it. It's truly magnificent."

"Imagine many such gates, connected by a wall no less magnificent that extended for miles and miles," said Antipater. He shook his head. "And now, all vanished, except for this."

As we rode on, the man followed after us.

"I show you everything," he offered. "I show you Hanging Gardens, yes?"

Antipater brightened. Was there some chance that the fabled gardens still existed, so many centuries after the time of Nebuchadnezzar and his Median queen?

"Not far, not far!" the man promised, leading the way. I asked his name. "Darius," he said, "like the great Persian king." He smiled, showing off his remaining teeth.

We passed through a shabby little square where merchants offered cheap trinkets—miniature aurochs and lions and dragons—to the tourists, of whom there were a great many, for we were not the only travelers who had come to Babylon that day in search of the fabled Wonders. Beyond a maze of dusty, winding alleys—surely this was not the grid city laid out by Nebuchadnezzar—we at last came to the foot of a great pile of ruins. Arguably, this structure reached to the sky, or once had done so, before time or man demolished it, so in a way it resembled a mountain, if only a small one.

Darius urged us to dismount and follow him. Before we could go farther, another fellow insisted that we each pay for the privilege; this fellow also promised to look after our asses. Antipater handed the gatekeeper the requested coinage, and Darius led us to a stairway with rubble on either side that ascended to a series of small landings. Along the way, someone had placed numerous potted plants, and on some of the landings spindly trees and thirsty-looking shrubs were actually growing from the debris. The dilapidated effect was more sad than spectacular. At last we came to an open area near the summit, where broken columns and ruptured paving bricks gave evidence of what once had been a magnificent terrace, now shaded by date palms and scented by small lemon and orange trees. The leaves of a knotty-limbed olive tree shimmered silver and green in the breeze.

"Hardly the mountain forest that Nebuchadnezzar built," muttered Antipater, catching his breath after the ascent. After the steady climb, I felt a bit light-headed myself.

"How do they water all these plants?" I said.

"Ah, you are wise, my young friend!" declared our guide. "You perceive the secret of the Hanging Gardens. Come, see!"

Darius led us to a brick-framed doorway nearby, which opened onto a shaft that ran downward at a sloping angle. Coming up the dimly lit passage toward us was a man with a yoke across his shoulders, with a bucket of water connected to each end. Huffing and puffing and covered with sweat, the water-bearer nonetheless flashed a weary grin as he emerged into the light and shambled past us.

"A good thing we're near the river, if men have to carry water up this shaft all day," I said.

Antipater raised his eyebrows. "Ah, but once upon a time, Gordianus, this shaft must have contained the mechanism that delivered a continuous flow of water for the gardens." He pointed to various mysterious bits of metal affixed to the surface of the shaft. "Onesicritus, who saw these gardens in the days of Alexander, speaks of a device like a gigantic screw that lifted great volumes of water as it turned. It seems that nothing of that remarkable mechanism remains, but the shaft is still here, leading down, we may presume, to a cistern fed by the river. Without the irrigation screw, the industrious citizens of Babylon have resorted to the labor of their own bodies to keep some semblance of the garden alive, from civic pride perhaps, and for the benefit of paying visitors like ourselves."

I nodded dubiously. The Hanging Gardens might once have been magnificent, but the decrepit remains could hardly compare to the other World Wonders we had seen on our journey.

Then I walked a few steps beyond the opening of the shaft, to a spot that afforded an unobstructed view of the ziggurat.

The walls of Babylon had been pulled down. The Hanging Gardens were in ruins. But the great ziggurat remained, rising mountainlike from the midst of the dun-colored city. Each of the seven stepped-back tiers had once been a different color. Almost all of the decorative work had been stripped away (by Xerxes when he sacked the city, and by subsequent looters), and the brick walls had begun to crumble, but enough of the original facade remained to indicate how the ziggurat must once have appeared. The first and largest tier was brick red, but the next had been dazzling white (faced with imported limestone and bitumen, I later learned), the next decorated with iridescent blue tiles, the next a riot of patterns in yellow and green, and so on. In the days of Nebuchadnezzar, the effect must have been unearthly. Amid the ziggurat's marred perfection I noticed tiny specks here and there on its surface. It was only when I saw that these specks moved—that they were, in fact, men—that I realized the true scale of the ziggurat. The thing was even larger than I had realized.

The sun was at last beginning to sink, casting its lowering rays across the dusty city and bathing the ziggurat in orange light. *Etemenanki* the Babylonians called it, the Foundation of Heaven and Earth. Truly, it seemed to me that so huge and strange a thing could scarcely have been created by human hands.

Antipater had similar thoughts. Standing next to me, he broke into verse:

What monstrous Cyclops built this vast mound for Assyrian Semiramis?
Or what giants, sons of Gaia, raised it in seven tiers
To scrape against the seven Pleiades?
Immovable, unshakable, a mass eternal,
Like lofty Mount Athos it weighs upon the earth.

Travel-weary and light-headed though I was, I caught Antipater's mistake. "You said Nebuchadnezzar built the ziggurat, not Semiramis," I said.

He gave me that look again, as if I were a child. "Poetic license, Gordianus! Semiramis scans better, and the name is far more euphonious. Who could compose a poem around a name as cumbersome as 'Nebuchadnezzar'?"

As darkness fell, Darius helped us find lodgings for the night. The little inn to which he guided us was near the river, he assured us, and though we could smell the river while we ate a frugal meal of flatbread and dates in the common room, our room upstairs had no view of it. Indeed, when I tried to open the shutters, they banged against an unsightly section of the city wall that stretched along the waterfront.

"Tomorrow you see Etemenanki," insisted Darius, who had shared our meal and followed us to the room. "What time do I meet you?"

"Tomorrow, we rest," said Antipater, collapsing on the narrow bed. "You don't mind sleeping on that mat on the floor, do you, Gordianus?"

"Actually, I was thinking of taking a walk," I said.

Antipater made no reply; he was already snoring. But Darius vigorously shook his head. "Not safe after dark," he said. "You stay inside."

I frowned. "You assured Antipater this was a good neighborhood, with no thieves or pickpockets."

"I tell the truth—no worry about robbers."

"What's the danger, then?"

Darius's expression was grave. "After dark, *she* comes out."

"She? Who are you talking about? Speak clearly!"

"I say too much already. But don't go out until daylight. I meet you then!" Without another word, he disappeared.

I dropped to the floor and reclined on the mat, thinking I would never get to sleep with Antipater snoring so loudly. The next thing I knew, sunlight was streaming in the open window.

By the time we went down to eat breakfast, the sun was already high. There was only one other guest in the common room. His costume was so outlandish, I almost laughed when I saw him. The only astrologers I had ever seen were on the stage, in comedies, and this man might have been one of them. He wore a high yellow hat that rose in tiers, not unlike those of the ziggurat, and a dark blue robe decorated with images of stars and constellations sewn in yellow. His shoes, encrusted with semiprecious stones, ended in spiral loops at the toes. His long black beard had been crimped and plaited and sprinkled with yellow powder so that it radiated from his jaw like solar rays.

Antipater invited the stranger to join us. He introduced himself as Mushezib, an astrologer visiting Babylon from his native city of Ecbatana. He had traveled widely and his Greek was excellent, probably better than mine.

"You've come to see the ziggurat," speculated Antipater.

"Or what remains of it," said Mushezib. "There's also a very fine school for astrologers here, where I hope to find a position as a teacher. And you?"

"We're simply here to see the city," said Antipater. "But not today. I'm too tired and my whole body aches from riding yesterday."

"But we can't just stay in all day," I said. "Perhaps there's something of interest close by."

"I'm told there's a small temple of Ishtar just up the street," said Mushezib. "It's mostly hidden from sight behind a high wall, and apparently it's in ruins; it was desecrated long ago by Xerxes and never reconsecrated or rebuilt. I don't suppose there's much to see—"

"But you can't go there," said the innkeeper, overhearing and joining the conversation. He, too, looked like a type who might have stepped out of a stage comedy. He was a big fellow with a round face and a ready smile. With his massive shoulders and burly arms, he looked quite capable of breaking up a fight and throwing the offenders onto the street, should such a disturbance ever occur in his sleepy tavern.

"Who forbids it?" said the astrologer.

The innkeeper shrugged. "No one *forbids* it. A deserted temple belongs to no one and everyone—common property, they say. But nobody goes there—because of *her*."

My ears pricked up. "Who are you talking about?"

Finding his Greek inadequate, the innkeeper addressed the astrologer in Parthian.

Mushezib's face grew long. "Our host says the temple is . . . haunted."

"Haunted?" I said.

"I forget the Greek word, but I think the Latin is *lemur*, yes?"

"Yes," I whispered. "A manifestation of the dead that lingers on earth. A thing that was mortal once, but no longer lives or breathes." Unready or unable to cross the river Styx to the realm of the dead, lemures stalked the earth, usually but not always appearing at night.

"The innkeeper says there is a lemur at this nearby temple," said Mushezib. "A woman dressed in moldering rags, with a hideous face. People fear to go there."

"Is she dangerous?" I said.

Mushezib conversed with the innkeeper. "Not just dangerous, but deadly. Only a few mornings ago, a man who had gone missing the night before was found dead on the temple steps, his neck broken. Now they lock the gate, which before was never locked."

So this was the nocturnal menace Darius had warned me about, fearing even to name the thing aloud.

"But surely in broad daylight—" began Antipater.

"No, no!" protested the innkeeper's wife, who suddenly joined us. She was almost as big as her husband, but had a scowling demeanor—another type suitable for the stage, I thought, the irascible innkeeper's wife. She spoke better Greek than her husband, and her thick Egyptian accent explained the Alexandrian delicacies among the Babylonian breakfast fare.

"Stay away from the old temple!" she cried. "Don't go there! You die if you go there!"

Her husband appeared to find this outburst unseemly. He laughed nervously and shrugged with his palms up, then took her aside, shaking his head and whispering to her. If he was trying to calm her, he failed. After a brief squabble, she threw up her hands and stalked off.

"It must be rather distressing, having a lemur so nearby," muttered

Antipater. "Bad for business, I should imagine. Do you think that's why there are so few people here at the inn? I'm surprised our host would even bring up the subject. Well, I'm done with my breakfast, so if you'll excuse me, I intend to return to our room and spend the whole day in bed. Oh, don't look so crestfallen, Gordianus! Go out and explore the city without me."

I felt some trepidation about venturing out in such an exotic city by myself, but I needn't have worried. The moment I stepped into the street I was accosted by our guide from the previous day.

"Where is your grandfather?" said Darius.

I laughed. "He's not my grandfather, just my traveling companion. He's too tired to go out."

"Ah, then I show you the city, eh? Just the two of us."

I frowned. "I'm afraid I haven't much money on me, Darius."

He shrugged. "What is money? It comes, it goes. But if I show you the ziggurat, you remember all your life."

"Actually, I'm rather curious about that temple of Ishtar just up the street."

He went pale. "No, no, no! We don't go there."

"We can at least walk by, can't we? Is it this way?" I said.

Next to the inn was a derelict structure that must once have been a competing tavern, but was now shuttered and boarded up; it looked rather haunted itself. Just beyond this abandoned property was a brick wall with a small wooden gate. The wall was not much higher than my head; beyond it, I could see what remained of the roof of the temple, which appeared to have collapsed. I pushed on the gate and found that it was locked. I ran my fingers over the wall, where much of the mortar between the bricks had worn away. The fissures would serve as excellent footholds. I stepped back, studying the wall to find the easiest place to scale it.

Darius read my thoughts. He gripped my arm. "No, no, no, young Roman! Are you mad?"

"Come now, Darius. The sun is shining. No lemur would dare to show its face on such a beautiful day. It will take me only a moment to climb over the wall and have a look. You can stay here and wait for me."

But Darius protested so vociferously, gesticulating and yammering in his native tongue, that I gave up my plan to see the temple and agreed to move on.

Darius showed me what he called the Royal District, where Semiramis and Nebuchadnezzar had built their palaces. As far as I could tell, nothing at all remained of the grandeur that had so impressed Alexander when he sojourned in Babylon. The once-resplendent complex, now stripped of every ornament, appeared to have been subdivided into private dwellings and crowded apartment buildings. The terraces were strewn with rubbish. The whole district smelled of stewing fish, soiled diapers, and cloying spices.

"They say that's the room where Alexander died." Darius pointed to an open window from which I could hear a couple arguing and a baby crying. The balcony was festooned with laundry hung out to dry.

If there had ever been an open square around the great ziggurat, it had long ago been filled in with ramshackle dwellings of brick and mud, so that we came upon the towering structure all at once as we rounded a corner. The ziggurat had seemed more mysterious when I had seen it the previous night, from a distance and by the beguiling light of sunset. Seen close up and in broad daylight, it looked to be in hardly better shape than the mound of rubble that had once been the Hanging Gardens. The surfaces of each tier were quite uneven, causing many of the swarming visitors to trip and stumble. Whole sections of the ramparts leaned outward at odd angles, looking as if they might tumble down at any moment.

Darius insisted we walk all the way to the top. To do so, we had to circle each tier, take a broad flight of steps up to the next tier, circle around, and do the same thing again. I noticed Darius pausing every so often to run his fingers over the walls. At first I thought he was simply admiring the scant remnants of decorative stonework or glazed brick, but then I realized he was tugging at various bits and pieces, seeing if anything would come loose. When he saw the expression on my face, he laughed.

"I look for mementos, young Roman," he explained. "Everyone does it. Anything of value that could be removed easily and without damage is already removed, long ago. But, every so often, you find a piece ready to come loose. So you take it. Everyone does it. Why do you frown at me like that?"

I was imagining the great temples of Rome being subjected to such impious treatment. Antipater claimed that the ancient gods of this land were essentially the same as those of the Greeks and Romans, just with different names and aspects; Marduk was Jupiter, Ishtar was Venus, and so on. To filch bits and pieces from a sacred structure that had been built to the glory of Jupiter was surely wrong, even if the structure was in disrepair. But I was a visitor, and I said nothing.

The way became more and more crowded as we ascended, for each tier was smaller than the last. All around us were travelers in many different types of costumes, chattering in many different languages. From their garb, I took one group to be from India, and judging by their saffron complexions and almond-shaped eyes, another group had come all the way from Serica, the land of silk. There were also a great many astrologers, some of them dressed as I had seen Mushezib that morning, and others in outfits even more outlandish, as if they were trying to outdo one another with absurdly tall hats, elaborately decorated robes, and bizarrely shaped beards.

On the sixth and next-to-last tier, I heard a voice speak my name, and turned to see Mushezib.

The astrologer acknowledged me with a nod. "We meet again."

"It would seem that every visitor in Babylon is here today," I said, jostled by a passing group of men in Egyptian headdresses. "Is that a queue?"

It appeared that one had to stand in line to ascend the final flight of steps to the uppermost tier; only when a certain number of visitors left were more allowed to go up. The queue stretched out of sight around the corner.

Mushezib smiled. "Shall we go up?" he said.

"I'm not sure I care to stand in that line for the next hour. And I'm not sure I have enough money," I added, for I saw that the line-keepers were charging admission.

"No need for that." With a dismissive wave to Darius, Mushezib took my arm and escorted me to the front of the line. The line-keepers deferred to him at once, bowing their heads and stepping back to let us pass.

"How do you merit such a privilege?" I asked.

"My costume," he explained. "Astrologers do not stand in line with tourists to ascend to the summit of Etemenanki."

A warm, dry wind blew constantly across the uppermost tier. The sun shone down without shadow. The view in every direction was limitless; below me I could see the whole city of Babylon, and to the north and south stretched the sinuous course of the Euphrates. Far to the east I could see the Tigris river, with sparkling cities along its bank, and in the uttermost distance loomed a range of snow-capped mountains.

Mushezib gazed at the horizon and spoke in a dreamlike voice. "Legend says that Alexander, when he entered Babylon and found Etemenanki in lamentable condition, gave gold to the astrologers and charged them with restoring the ziggurat to its former glory. 'The work must be done by the time I return from conquering India,' he said, and off he went. When he came back some years later, he saw that nothing had been done, and called the astrologers before him. 'Why is Etemenanki still in disrepair?' he asked. And the astrologers replied: 'Why have you not yet conquered India?' Alexander was furious. He ordered the whole structure to be demolished and the ground leveled, so that he could build a new ziggurat from scratch. But before that could happen, Alexander took ill and died, and Etemenanki remained as it was, like a mountain slowly crumbling to dust."

He gestured to the center of the tier. "This space is vacant now, but in the days of Nebuchadnezzar, upon this summit stood a small temple. Within the temple there was no statue or any other ornament, only a giant couch made of gold with pillows and coverlets of silk—a couch fit for the King of Gods to lie upon. Each night, a young virgin from a good family was selected by the priests to ascend alone to the top of Etemenanki, enter the temple, and climb upon the couch. There the virgin waited for Marduk to come down from the heavens and spend the night with her. When she descended the ziggurat the next day, the priests examined her. If her maidenhead was seen to be broken, then it was known that Marduk had found her worthy."

"And if she was still a virgin?" I asked.

"Then it was seen that Marduk had rejected her, to the eternal shame of the girl and her family." Mushezib smiled. "I see you raise an eyebrow, Gordianus. But is it not the same with your great god Jupiter? Does he not enjoy taking pleasure with mortals?"

"Yes, but in all the stories I've heard, Jupiter picks his own partners, and woos them a bit before the consummation. They're not lined up and delivered to him by priests to be deflowered, one after another. Jupiter's temples are for worship, not sexual assignations."

Mushezib shook his head. "You people of the West have always had different ideas about these things. Alas, for better or worse, Greek ways have triumphed here in Babylon, thanks to the influence of Alexander and his successors. The old customs are no longer practiced as they once were. Virgins no longer ascend the ziggurat to lie with Marduk, and women no longer go to the temples of Ishtar to give themselves to the first man who pays." He saw my reaction and laughed out loud. "You really must learn to exercise more control over your expressions, young man. How easily shocked you Romans are, even more so than Greeks."

"But what is this custom you speak of?"

"In the days of Nebuchadnezzar, it was mandatory that every woman, at least once in her life, should dress in special robes and place a special wreath upon her head, and then go to one of the temples of Ishtar at night and sit in a special chair in the holy enclosure. There she had to remain, until a stranger came and tossed a silver coin in her lap. With that man she was obliged to enter the temple, lie upon a couch, and make love. No man who was able to pay could be turned away. All women did this, rich and poor, beautiful and ugly, for the glory of Ishtar."

"And for the enjoyment of any man with a coin," I muttered. "I should imagine that the young, beautiful women were selected right away. But what if the woman was so ugly that no man would choose her?"

Mushezib nodded. "This was known to happen. There are stories of women who had to stay a very long time in the holy precinct—months, or even years. Of course, such an embarrassment brought shame upon her family. In such a case, sooner or later, by exchange of favors or outright bribery, some fellow was induced to go and offer the woman a coin and lie with her. Or, in the last resort, one of her male relatives was selected to do what had to be done. And at last the woman's duty to Ishtar was discharged."

I shook my head. "You're right, Mushezib—we Romans have a very different way of thinking about such things."

"Don't be so quick to judge the customs of others, my young friend. The so-called wanton nature of the Babylonian people was their salvation when Alexander entered the city. He might have destroyed this place, as he had so many other cities, but when the wives and daughters of Babylon gave themselves freely to Alexander and his men, the conquerors were not merely placated; they decided that Babylon was the finest city on earth."

I sighed. Truly, of all the places I had traveled with Antipater, this land and its people and their ways were the most foreign to me. Standing atop the so-called Foundation of Heaven and Earth, I felt how small I was, and how vast was the world around me.

Mushezib recognized some fellow astrologers nearby and excused himself, leaving me on my own. I lingered for a while atop the ziggurat, then descended the stairway to the lower tier, where Darius awaited me.

As we made our way down, level by level, I repeated to Darius my conversation with Mushezib, and asked him what he knew of the old custom of women offering themselves at the temples of Ishtar.

"Astrologer he may be, but Mushezib does not know everything," said Darius.

"What do you mean?"

"He tells you that sooner or later every woman satisfied a man at the temple and was released from her duty. Not true."

"Surely no woman was kept waiting at the temple forever."

"Some women had no family to rescue them. There they sat, day after day, year after year, until they became toothless old hags, with no chance that any man would ever pay to lie with them."

"What became of such women?"

"What do you think? Finally they died, never leaving the temple grounds, cursed by Ishtar for failing her."

"What a terrible story!" Suddenly, all that I had seen and heard that day connected in my thoughts, and I felt a quiver of apprehension. "The ruined temple of Ishtar near the inn, and the lemur who supposedly haunts it—do you think . . . ?"

Darius nodded gravely. "Now you understand! Imagine how bitter she must be, still to be trapped in the place of her shame and suffering. Is it any wonder that she killed a man who dared to enter the grounds a few nights ago?"

"Let me make sure I understand—"

"No, speak no more of it! To do so can only bring bad fortune. We talk of something else. And when we go back to the inn, we do not walk by the temple again!"

My curiosity about the ruined temple and its supernatural resident was more piqued than ever. Darius read my face.

"Do not go back there, young Roman!" he said, almost shouting. "What do you think would happen, if the old hag sees a virile young fellow like you, barely old enough to grow a beard? The sight of such as you would surely drive her to madness—to murder!"

Darius had become so agitated that I quickly changed the subject.

We spent the rest of the day walking all over Babylon, and I found myself growing more and more dispirited. All the proud structures that had once made the city great were in shambles, or else had vanished altogether. Many of the citizens were in a ruined state as well—I had never seen so many people crippled by lameness or deformity. Apparently these unfortunates flocked to Babylon to take advantage of the charitable institutions maintained by the astrologers and sages, whose academies were the main industry of the city, along with the thriving trade in tourism.

At last, as twilight fell, we wended our way back to the inn, with Darius leading the way. I noticed that our route was slightly different from the one we had taken heading out that morning; Darius deliberately avoided walking by the ruined temple of Ishtar. To reward him for serving as my guide all day, I could do no less than offer him dinner, but to my surprise Darius declined and hurried off, saying he would return the next morning, when Antipater would surely be rested and ready for his own tour of the city. Could it be that Darius feared to be even this close to the old temple after dark?

As soon as he was out of sight, I turned aside from the entrance to the inn and walked up the street, past the derelict building next door, to the low wall that surrounded the old temple. It was the dim, colorless hour when shadows grow long and merge together, swallowing the last faint light of dusk.

It was not as easy to study the wall as it had been earlier in the day, and the first place I chose to make my climb proved to be unscalable. But on my second attempt, I found a series of toeholds that allowed me to reach the top.

My feet secure in their niches, I rested my elbows on the top of the wall and peered over. The temple was indeed in ruins, with not much left of the roof and gaping holes in the walls. Any decorative tiles or statues appeared to have been removed. The wall of the derelict building next door and the city wall along the river enclosed the courtyard next to the temple, which was all in shadow; all I could see were some withered trees and fragments of building blocks and paving tiles. But amid this jumble, as my eyes adjusted to the dimness, I saw a row of waist-high objects that looked like the circular drums of a column. It occurred to me that these might be low-backed chairs carved from solid blocks of stone—too heavy for looters to carry off, I thought, or perhaps the ceremonial chairs had been left there because . . .

Seated on one of the chairs, almost lost in shadow, I saw an uncertain silhouette. It was impossible to tell whether the figure was facing me or had its back to me—until the figure rose from the chair and began walking very slowly toward me.

My heart sped up. All I could hear was the blood pounding in my head. The uncanny silence of the approaching figure unnerved me.

I opened my mouth. For a long moment, nothing came out, and then, my voice cracking and ascending an octave, I heard myself say: "Speakee Greekee?"

The figure at last made a sound—a hideous laugh more horrible than the crunching of broken bones. My blood turned cold. The figure reached up with clawlike hands and pushed pack the moldering wreath that obscured its face.

Had the thing once been a woman? It was revolting to look at, with hair like worms and eyes that glinted like bits of obsidian. Its pale, rotting flesh was covered with warts. Broken teeth protruded from the black hole of its gaping mouth. The thing drew closer to me, filling my nostrils with the stench of putrefaction. Its low cackle rose to a sudden shriek.

I scrambled back from the wall, desperate to get away. One of my feet slipped from its toehold and I tumbled backward.

The next thing I knew, I was coming to my senses, propped up in a chair in the common room of the inn.

"Gordianus, are you all right?" said Antipater, hovering over me. "What happened to you? Were you set upon by robbers?"

"No, I fell . . ."

"In the middle of the street? That's where Mushezib says he found you. It's a good thing he happened by, or you'd still be lying out there, at the mercy of any cutthroat who happened by."

Through bleary eyes, I saw that the astrologer stood nearby. Farther back, a few other guests were gathered around. The innkeeper was in their midst, standing a head taller than anyone else. He frowned and shook his head. Talk of robbers was bad for business.

"No one attacked me, Antipater. I simply . . . fell." I was too chagrined to confess that I had attempted to scale the temple wall.

"The lad must have the falling sickness. Common among Romans," said one of the guests, turning up his nose. This seemed to satisfy the others, who drew back and dispersed.

Antipater wrinkled his brow. "What really happened, Gordianus?"

Mushezib also remained. I saw no reason not to tell them both the truth. "I was curious. I wanted to have a look at the old temple of Ishtar, so I climbed to the top of the wall—"

"I knew it!" said Antipater. He scowled, then raised an eyebrow. "And? What did you see?"

"Ruins—there are only ruins left. And . . ."

"Go on," said Antipater. He and Mushezib both leaned closer.

"I saw the lemur," I whispered. "In the courtyard of the temple. She walked toward me—"

Mushezib made a scoffing sound. "Gordianus, you did not see a lemur."

"How do you know what I saw?"

"A young man with a powerful imagination, alone in the dark in a strange city, looking at a ruined courtyard, which he has been told is haunted by a lemur—it's not hard to understand how you came to think you saw such a thing."

"I trust the evidence of my own eyes," I said irritably. My head had begun to pound. "Don't you believe that lemures exist?"

"I do not," declared the astrologer. "The mechanisms of the stars, which rule all human action, do not allow the dead to remain among the living. It is scientifically impossible."

"Ah, here we see where Chaldean stargazing comes into conflict with Greek religion, not to mention common sense," said Antipater, ever ready to play the pedant, even with his young traveling companion still barely conscious after a dangerous fall. "As they rule supreme over the living, so the gods rule over the dead—"

"If one believes in these gods," said Mushezib.

"You astrologers worship stars instead!" said Antipater, throwing up his hands.

"We do not worship the stars," said Mushezib calmly. "We study them. Unlike your so-called gods, the vast interlocking mechanisms of the firmament do not care whether mortals make supplication to them or not. They do not watch over us or concern themselves with our behavior; their action is completely impersonal as they exert their rays of invisible force upon the earth. Just as the heavenly bodies control the tides and seasons, so they control the fates of mankind and of individual men. The gods, if they exist, may be more powerful than men, but they too are controlled by the sympathies and antipathies of the stars in conjunction—"

"What nonsense!" declared Antipater. "And you call this science?"

Mushezib drew a deep breath. "Let us not speak of matters about which our opinions are so divergent. Our concern now must be for your young friend. Are you feeling better, Gordianus?"

"I would be, if the two of you would stop squabbling."

Mushezib smiled. "For your sake, Gordianus, we will change the subject." He glanced at the innkeeper, who was serving some other guests, and lowered his voice. "Whatever you saw or did not see, it was good of you to calm the fears of the other guests—about the presence of robbers in the streets, I mean. Our poor host must hate all this talk of robbers, and of lemures, for that matter. He tells me he's negotiating to buy the empty building next door. By this time next year, he hopes to expand his business to fill both buildings."

Antipater surveyed the handful of guests in the room. "There hardly seems to be custom enough to fill this place, let alone an inn twice the size."

"Our host is an optimist," said Mushezib with a shrug. "One must be an optimist, I think, to live in Babylon."

THAT NIGHT I SLEPT FITFULLY, DISTURBED BY TERRIBLE DREAMS. AT SOME point I woke up to find myself drenched with sweat. It seemed to me that I had heard a distant scream—not a shriek such as the lemur had made, but the sound of a man crying out. I decided the sound must have been part of my nightmare. I closed my eyes and slept soundly until the first glimmer of daylight from the window woke me.

When Antipater and I descended the stairs, we found the common room completely deserted, except for Darius, who was waiting for us to appear. He rushed up to us, his eyes wide with excitement.

"Come see, come see!" he said.

"What's going on?" said Antipater.

"You must see for yourself. Something terrible—at the ruined temple of Ishtar!"

We followed him. A considerable crowd had gathered in the street. The gate in the wall stood wide open. People took turns peering inside, but no one dared to enter the courtyard.

"What on earth are they all looking at?" muttered Antipater. He pressed his way to the front of the crowd. I followed him, but Darius hung back.

"Oh dear!" whispered Antipater, peering through the gateway. He stepped aside so that I could have a better look.

The courtyard did not appear as frightening by morning light as it had the night before, but it was still a gloomy place, with weeds amid the broken paving blocks and the ugly reddish-brown wall looming behind it. I saw more clearly the stone chairs I had seen the night before—all empty now—and then I saw the body on the temple steps.

The man's face was turned away, with his neck twisted at an odd angle, but he was dressed in a familiar blue robe embroidered with yellow stars, with spiral-toed shoes on his feet. His ziggurat-shaped hat had fallen from his head and lay near him on the top step.

"Is it Mushezib?" I whispered.

"Perhaps it's another astrologer," said Antipater. He turned to the crowd behind us. "Is Mushezib here? Has anyone seen Mushezib this morning?"

People shook their heads and murmured.

I had to know. I strode through the gateway and crossed the courtyard. Behind me I heard gasps and cries from the others, including Darius, who shouted, "No, no, no, young Roman! Come back!"

I ascended the steps. The body lay chest down, with the arms folded beneath it. I looked down and saw in profile the face of Mushezib. His eyes were wide open. His teeth were bared in a grimace. The way his neck was bent, there could be no doubt that it was broken. I knelt and waved my hand to scatter the flies that had gathered on his lips and eyelashes.

A glint of reflected sunlight caught my eye. It came from something inside his fallen hat, which lay nearby. I reached out and found, nestled inside, a piece of glazed tile no bigger than the palm of my hand. Bits of mortar clung to the edges, but otherwise it was in perfect condition; the glaze was a very dark blue, almost black. Mushezib must have taken it from the ziggurat the previous day, I thought, breaking it off one of the walls. What had Darius said? "Everyone does it"—including godless astrologers, apparently, though Mushezib had not been proud of taking the memento if he had seen fit to conceal it inside his hat.

Looking up, I saw an image of Ishtar looming above me. Etched in low relief on a large panel of baked clay built into the front wall of the temple, the image had not been visible to me the night before. Could this really be Venus, as seen through the eyes of the Babylonians? She was completely naked, with voluptuous hips and enormous breasts, but the goddess struck me as more frightening than alluring, with a strange conical cap on her head, huge wings folded behind her, and legs that ended in claws like those of a giant bird of prey. She stood upon two lions, grasping them with her talons, and was flanked by huge, staring owls.

I heard a voice behind me—a woman's voice—issuing what had to be a command, though I could not understand the language. I turned to see that others had entered the courtyard—a group of priests, to judge by their pleated linen robes and exotic headdresses. Leading them was a woman past her first youth but still stunningly beautiful. It was she who spoke. At the sight of her my jaw dropped, for she was the very image of Ishtar, wearing the same conical cap, a golden cape fashioned to look like folded wings, and tall shoes that made her walk with an odd gait and mimicked the appearance of talons. At first, blinking in astonishment, I thought that she was as naked as the image of the goddess, but then a bit of sunlight shimmered across the gauzy, almost transparent gown that barely contained her breasts and ended at the top of her thighs. Her arms, crossed over her chest, did more to conceal her breasts than did the gown. In one hand she held a ceremonial ivory goad, and in the other a little whip.

Without pausing, the priestess strode forward. I stepped back to make way for her, concealing the small blue tile inside my tunic as I did so.

She gazed down at the body for a long moment, then briefly looked me up and down. "You are not Babylonian," she said, in perfect Greek.

"I'm from Rome."

She cocked her head. "That explains why you're foolish enough to enter this courtyard, while those who know better stay back. Do you not realize that an uneasy spirit haunts this place?"

"Actually . . ." I hesitated. I was a stranger in Babylon, and it behooved a stranger to keep his mouth shut. Then I looked down at Mushezib. Flies had returned to gather on his face. They skittered over his lips and his open eyes, which seemed to stare up at me. "I saw the thing with my own eyes, last night."

"You saw it?"

"The lemur—that's what we call such a creature in Latin. I climbed to the top of that wall, and I saw the lemur here in the courtyard. She was hideous."

The priestess gave me a reappraising glance. "Did you flee, young man?"

"Not exactly. I fell to the street and hit my head. That was the last I saw of her."

"What do you know about this?" She gestured to the corpse.

"His name is Mushezib, from Ecbatana. He was a fellow guest at the inn up the street."

"Why did he come here?"

"I don't know."

"Was it he who broke the lock we put on the gate?"

I shrugged and shook my head.

She turned and addressed the crowd that peered through the gateway. "This ruined temple is no longer sacred ground. Even so, the priesthood of Ishtar will take responsibility for this man's body, until his relatives can be found." She gestured to the priests. Looking nervous and reluctant, they stooped to lift the corpse and bear it away.

The priestess gave me a curious look. "All my life I've heard about the unquiet spirit that dwells here; the story must be centuries old. Some believe it, some do not. Never have I seen it with my own eyes. And never has violence been done here, until a man was killed a few days ago. That man died the same way, with his neck broken, and he was found on the same spot. Two deaths, in a matter of days! What could have stirred this lemur, as you call it, to commit murder? I must consult the goddess. Some way must be found to placate this restless spirit, before such a thing happens again." She gazed up at the relief of Ishtar, her mirror image, and then back at me. "Let me give you some advice, young Roman. Enjoy your visit to Babylon—but do not return to this place again."

She turned and followed the priests who were carrying away the body of Mushezib. I followed her, watching her wing-shaped cape shimmer in the morning sunlight. The cape was very sheer and supple, capturing the outline of her swaying buttocks. As soon as we were all in the street, the gate was pulled shut and men set to work repairing the broken lock. The priestess and her retinue departed. The murmuring crowd gradually dispersed.

ANTIPATER WANTED TO SEE THE ZIGGURAT. DARIUS, EAGER TO GET AWAY from the haunted temple, offered to show it to him, and I followed along. The visit took up much of the day. Antipater needed to rest before ascending to each successive tier, and without an astrologer to accompany us, we had to wait in line a long time to reach the uppermost platform.

From time to time, as we walked alongside the massive, crumbling walls,

I surreptitiously pulled out the little tile I had taken from Mushezib's hat. I was curious to see from what section of the ziggurat he had taken it. But though there were a number of places where bits of glazed tile remained, I could see no tiles that seemed to match exactly the deep, midnight-blue shade of the specimen I held in the palm of my hand.

An idea began to form in my mind, and other ideas began to revolve around it—rather as the stars revolve around the earth, I thought, and appropriately so, for at the center of these ideas was Mushezib the astrologer and his fate.

As we toured the city that day, I followed my companions in such a cloud that Antipater worried I was still dazed by the blow to my head. I told him not to worry, and explained that I was merely thinking.

"Daydreaming about that priestess of Ishtar, I'll wager!" said Darius with a laugh.

"As a matter of a fact, I may need to see her again," I said thoughtfully.

"Indeed!" Darius gave me a leer, then offered to show us the sacred precinct where the priestess resided. I took care to remember the location, so that I could find my way back.

We did not return to the inn until dusk. I wanted to have another look at the ruined temple, despite the priestess's warning, but I feared to go there after nightfall. Besides, I doubted that I could find what I was looking for in darkness.

The next morning, I woke early. While Antipater still snored, I slipped into my clothes and crept quietly down the stairs. I passed the open door to the kitchen next to the common room and saw, with some relief, that the innkeeper and his wife were already at work preparing breakfast.

Without a sound, I left the inn and hurried up the street. The gate was again securely locked, but I found the place where I had scaled the wall before. I climbed to the top, hesitated for just a moment, then scrambled over and dropped to the courtyard.

The dim morning light cast long shadows. I felt a quiver of dread. Every now and then, amid the shadows, I imagined I saw a movement, and I gave a start. But I was determined to do what I had come to do. My heart pounding, I walked all over the courtyard, paying special attention to the wall of the vacant tavern and also to the ground along the river wall, looking for any place where the earth might have been disturbed recently. It was not long before I found such a spot.

I knelt amid the uprooted weeds and began to dig.

THE SUN HAD RISEN CONSIDERABLY BEFORE I RETURNED TO THE INN.

"Gordianus! Where in Hades have you been?" cried Antipater. The other guests had all gone out for the day. Only Antipater and Darius were in the common room. "I've been terribly worried about you—"

He fell silent when he saw the company of armed men who entered the inn behind me, followed by the priestess of Ishtar.

Alarmed by the rumble of stamping feet, the innkeeper rushed into the room. His face turned pale. "What's this?" he cried.

Moving quickly, some of the men surrounded the innkeeper and seized his brawny arms. Others stormed the kitchen. A moment later they dragged the innkeeper's wife into the room, shrieking and cursing in Egyptian.

I sighed with relief. Until that moment, I had not been entirely certain of the accusation I had made against the innkeeper and his wife, but the looks on their faces assured me of their guilt.

The rest of the armed company dispersed to search the premises, beginning with the innkeeper's private quarters. Within moments, one of the men returned with a small but ornately decorated wooden box, which he opened for the inspection of the priestess. I peered over the man's shoulder. The box was filled with cosmetics and compounds and unguents, but the colors and textures were not of any common sort; this was the kit of someone who practiced disguise as a profession—an actor or street mime.

The most famous mime troupes, as even a Roman knew, came from Alexandria—as did the innkeeper's wife.

"Take your hands off that, you swine!" she cried, breaking free of the guard who held her and rushing at the man who held the box. He blanched at the sight of her and started back. So did I, for even without the horrifying makeup, the face of the hideous lemur I had seen in the courtyard of the temple was suddenly before me, and I heard again the shriek that had made my blood run cold.

Like a charging rhinoceros, she rushed headlong at the priestess, who stood her ground. I braced myself for the spectacle of the impact—then watched as the priestess raised her ceremonial goad and swung it, backhanded, with all her might, striking the innkeeper's wife squarely across the face. With a squeal that stabbed at my eardrums, the innkeeper's wife flailed and tumbled to one side, upsetting a great many small tables and chairs.

The guards swarmed over her and, after a considerable struggle, restrained her.

One of the men who had been searching the premises entered the room, stepping past the commotion to show something to the priestess. In his hand he held a lovely specimen of a glazed tile. Its color was midnight blue.

Gazing at the shambles of the common room, Antipater turned to me and blinked. "Gordianus—please explain!"

MUCH LATER THAT DAY, IN THE TAVERN OF ANOTHER ESTABLISHMENT—FOR the inn where we had been staying was no longer open for business—Antipater, Darius, and I raised three cups brimming with Babylonian beer and drank a toast to the departed Mushezib.

"Explain it all to me again," said Darius. He seemed unable to grasp that the lemur that had haunted the old temple had never been a lemur at all, so strong was his superstitious dread of the place.

I lubricated my throat with another swallow of beer, then proceeded. "At some point—we don't know exactly how or when, but not too long ago—the innkeeper or his wife went digging around the ruined temple grounds. Literally digging, I mean. And what should they discover, but a previously unknown cache of ancient glazed bricks, undoubtedly from the long-demolished wall of Nebuchadnezzar that used to run along the riverfront, where a newer, plainer wall now stands. They knew at once that those bricks must be worth a fortune. But their discovery was located in an old temple precinct; the land itself is common property and not for sale, and any artifacts or treasure found there would almost certainly belong to the priesthood of Ishtar. The innkeeper clearly had no right to the bricks, but he intended to get his hands on them nonetheless. The best way to do that, he decided, was to purchase the derelict property adjacent to the temple, from which he and his wife could gain access to the courtyard and the buried bricks without being observed. But negotiating to buy that property was taking time, and the innkeeper was fearful that someone else might go nosing about and find those buried bricks. The old tales about the place being haunted gave him a perfect way to frighten others away. The innkeeper's wife took on the task of playing the lemur. As we now know, in her younger days, she was part of an Egyptian mime troupe. She's an intimidating woman to start with; with the right makeup, and calling on her skills as an actress, she could be truly terrifying, as I experienced for myself. But the lemur didn't frighten everyone away; at least one man must have dared to enter the courtyard a few nights ago, perhaps out of simple curiosity, and he was the first to die."

"Was it the innkeeper's wife who broke the first victim's neck?" asked Antipater.

"She's probably strong enough, and we've seen what she's capable of doing when roused, but her husband confessed to the killing. Those brawny arms of his are quite capable of breaking any man's neck."

"And Mushezib? What was the astrologer doing in the courtyard in the middle of the night?" said Darius.

"I think it wasn't until after we all went to bed that night that Mushezib's thoughts led him to the same conclusion I reached, a day later. He had no belief in a lemur; what, then, had I actually seen? Perhaps someone pretending to be a lemur—but why? In the middle of the night, Mushezib broke the lock on the gate, slipped inside, and started snooping around. He even did a bit of digging, and found this, which he slipped under his hat." I held up the little tile. "If I'd seen his hands, and the dirt that must have been on his fingers, I might have realized the truth sooner, but his arms were folded beneath him, and the body was carried off by the priests before I could take a closer look."

"You were looking mostly at the priestess of Ishtar, I think," said Darius.

I cleared my throat. "Anyway, the innkeeper must have come upon Mushezib, there in the courtyard. There was a struggle—I heard Mushezib scream, but I thought I was dreaming—and the innkeeper broke his neck. As he had done with his previous victim, he left the body on the temple steps as a warning, and there we found poor Mushezib the next day.

"It wasn't until we went to the ziggurat, and I was unable to find any tiles that matched the one in Mushezib's hat, that I began to think he must have found that tile elsewhere. It occurred to me that he might have found it on the old temple grounds—and the rest of the tale unfolded in my mind. Early this morning I stole into the courtyard and found the spot where the bricks are buried. I also discovered a concealed and crudely made opening in the wall of the vacant building next to the temple. I went at once to the priestess of Ishtar to tell her of my suspicions. She gathered some armed men and followed me back to the inn. Along with the tiles the innkeeper had already dug up, the priestess's men also found a secret passage the innkeeper had made between his private quarters and the vacant building next door, which, as I had discovered, had its own concealed access to the temple courtyard, also made by the innkeeper. That was how he and his wife managed to enter the courtyard even when the gate was locked. By passing through the vacant building, the so-called lemur could appear and disappear—and the killer was able to surprise his victims and then vanish, never stepping into the street."

"What will become of that murderous innkeeper and his monster of a wife?" asked Antipater.

"The priestess says they must pay for their crimes with their lives."

"And what will become of all those lovely bricks?" asked Darius, his eyes twinkling at the thought of so much loot.

"The priesthood of Ishtar has claimed them. I imagine they're digging them up even now," I said.

"Too bad you didn't get to claim those bricks." Darius sighed. "You know, I hate to speak of such a thing, but not since the first day have I been given a single coin for the many excellent favors I have rendered to my new friends."

I laughed. "Never fear, Darius, you will be paid for your services!" I patted the heavy coin purse at my waist. That afternoon, after the arrest of the innkeeper and his wife, I had been called back to the sacred precinct of Ishtar for a private interview with the priestess. She warmly praised my perspicacity, and insisted that I accept a very generous reward.

Darius looked at the money bag, then raised an eyebrow. "Was that the only reward she gave you, young Roman?"

Antipater also looked at me intently.

My face turned hot. Was I blushing? "As a matter of fact, it was not," I said, but of whatever else took place between the priestess and me that afternoon, I chose to say no more.

PAIN AND SUFFERING

by S. M. Stirling

Considered by many to be the natural heir to Harry Turtledove's title of King of the Alternate History Novel, fast-rising science fiction star S. M. Stirling is the bestselling author of the Island in the Sea of Time trilogy (*Island in the Sea of Time*, *Against the Tide of Years*, *On the Ocean of Eternity*), in which Nantucket comes unstuck in time and is cast back to the year 1250, and the Draka series (including *Marching through Georgia*, *Under the Yoke*, *The Stone Dogs*, and *Drakon*, plus an anthology of Draka stories by other hands and edited by Stirling, *Drakas!*), in which Tories fleeing the American Revolution set up a militant society in South Africa and eventually end up conquering most of the earth. He's also produced the five-volume Fifth Millennium series and the seven-volume General series (with David Drake), as well as stand-alone novels such as *Conquistador*, *The Peshawar Lancers*, and *The Sky People*. Stirling has also written novels in collaboration with Raymond F. Feist, Jerry Pournelle, Holly Lisle, Shirley Meier, Karen Wehrstein, and *Star Trek* actor James Doohan, as well as contributing to the *Babylon 5*, *T2*, *Brainship*, *War World*, and *Man-Kzin War* series. His short fiction has been collected in *Ice, Iron and Gold*. Stirling's *New York Times* bestselling Emberverse postapocalyptic series (which is related to the Island in the Sea of Time novels) consists of the trilogy *Dies the Fire*, *The Protector's War*, and *A Meeting at Corvallis*, and the subsequent sequels *The Sunrise Lands*, *The Scourge of God*, *The Sword of the Lady*, *The High King of Montival*, and *The Tears of the Sun*. He has also written the Lords of Creation novels, *The Sky People* and *In the Courts of the Crimson Kings*. His most recent work, the Shadowspawn series, consists of *A Taint in the Blood* and *The Council of Shadows*. Born in France and raised in Europe, Africa, and Canada, he now lives in Santa Fe, New Mexico.

In the suspenseful story that follows, he takes us along with an ordinary cop who finds himself trying to deal with a most *un*ordinary criminal—one of extraordinary abilities, in fact, who seems impossible to beat.

I

Dream.

Eric Salvador always knew it was a dream; he just couldn't affect it or get out of it or do anything except watch and smell and taste and feel an overwhelming sick dread as it unfolded. There hadn't really been a burned-out MRAP at the end of the village street by the mosque. That had been somewhere else, that little shithole outside Kandahar he'd seen on his first tour, and it had only been there one day. It was a composite of all the bads, building up to the Big Bad itself.

A couple of other things are right for the day, he thought.

The way Olsen flicked the little Raven surveillance drone into the air, and the buzz of its engine as it climbed to circle above them, and the dopy little smiley-face button with fangs he'd glued to the nose of the Corps' thirty-five-thousand-dollar toy airplane. He'd tried to put little fake Hellfire missiles under the wings too, and Gunny had torn him a new asshole about it. The way the translator was sweating and his eyes were flicking here and there, you wondered if it was just the heat or generalized fear or if he knew something he wasn't saying.

Christ, I've had this fucking nightmare so many times I'm starting to sound like a movie critic.

Smith always went into the door of the compound the same way, the way he really had. Regulation, the two of them plastered on either side, Jackson taking out the lock on the gate with a doorknocker round, whump-*boom*, the warped old planks smacking inward as the slug blew the rusty lock into the courtyard, Smith following, his M-4 tucked into his shoulder and Jackson on his heels.

The explosion was always silent. Silent, slo-mo, the flames leaking around the fragments of wood and the two men flying and just enough time to realize *Oh, shit, this is a bad one* before a giant's hand picked him up and threw him backward until there was the impact and the pain.

Only this time was different. This time *something* walked out of the fire to where he lay with the broken ends of his ribs grating under the body armor that had saved his life.

The shape twisted and its wrongness made him want to scream out the bloody foam in his lungs, but the eyes were flecked yellow. And the voice *slithered* into his ears:

"Who's been a naughty boy, then?"

He began to sink into the dry dusty earth, and it flowed into his mouth and nose and eyes, the dust of ages and of empires.

"Naughty!"

"Christ!"

He lay panting in the darkness, smelling his own sweat and waiting to be sure he was awake—sometimes he dreamed he was, and then the whole thing started cycling through his head again. It was blurring away already, details fracturing like sunlight through a drop of water. His hand groped for the cigarettes on the bedside, and then he remembered he'd stopped.

"Go back to sleep," he told himself. "Dreaming's no worse than remembering, anyway."

Christ.

THE FIRE DEPARTMENT WERE TURNING OFF THEIR HOSES; DANK STEAM ROSE into the night, and chilly water dripped from the buildings to either side where they'd sprayed to keep the flames from spreading; there was a blank wall across the street. It was high-desert winter, cold, dry, moonlight visible on the white peaks of the Sangres floating off to the north.

"So what made it burn down, hey?" Salvador asked the investigator from the fire marshal's office.

"Arson," she said to the detective. "And it burned *up*."

"Yeah, arson. Some specifics would be nice, Alice," he said.

"That's the thing. I can't find any reason it *should* have burned. None of the usual indicators. It just did."

"Very much."

He ducked under the yellow police tape, a stocky man of thirty or so with a mustache and a blue jowl who'd put on a few pounds lately, not many, not enough to hide his hard outlines, with his coarse black hair still in a high-and-tight. There was a deep scar across one olive cheek, and he rubbed at it with a thumb; it hurt a little sometimes, where the flying metal of the IED had cracked the bone. The scar ran down under his mustache, giving a bit of a quirk to his mouth.

"One thing I can tell you," the investigator said. "This thing burned *hot*."

"Heavy accelerants? I can't smell anything."

"Right, gasoline or diesel you usually can. But damned if I can prove it yet, maybe with the lab work . . . I'd say yes, though. I've never seen anything like it. It's as if it *wanted* to burn. There's no sign it started in one place and spread. Everything capable of combining with oxygen just went up all at once, *whoosh*. The *cutlery* melted, and that's a lot hotter than your typical house fire."

The building had been a little two-story apartment house, one up and one down. This wasn't far off Canyon Road and the strip of galleries and was close to the Acequia Madre, the ancient irrigation canal, which meant it had been fairly expensive. But not close enough to be real adobe, which in Santa Fe meant *old* and *pricey.* Brown stucco pseudo-pueblo-Spanish-style originally over frame, like nearly everything in town that stayed on the right side of the building code.

Alice had worked with him before. She was a bit older than he—mid-thirties—and always looked tired, her blond hair short and disorderly. He liked the way she never let a detail slip by, no matter how hard she had to work at it.

"Santa Fe, where prestige is a mud house on a dirt road," she quoted. "So it's not likely an insurance torch. Not enough money here."

"Yeah. I couldn't afford *this* either. When it was still there. It must have gone up like a match head."

There wasn't enough left to tell any more details. There *was* a heavy wet-ash smell where bits and blackened pieces rested on the scorched concrete pad of the foundation. He blinked again. That smell, and the way the bullets had chewed at the mud brick below the window, flecking bits of adobe into his face. The way his armor had chafed, the fear as he made himself jerk up over the sill and aim the M-4, laying the red dot, the instant when the *mouj* had stared at him wide-eyed just before the burst tracked across his body in a row of black-red dots and made him dance like a jointed doll . . .

"Eric?" Alice said, jarring him out of the memory.

"Sorry," he said. "Deep thought."

She spared him any offensive sympathy and he nodded to her in silent gratitude, still feeling a little shaky. *Got to get over this. I can have flashbacks later.*

"Let me have the workup when you can," he said.

Of course, when I was on the rock pile I said I'd deal with it later, when it wouldn't screw the mission. This is *later, I suppose.*

"I'll zap it to your notepad," Alice said. "I've got to get some more samples now."

He turned away. Cesar Martinez was talking to the Lopez family, minus the three children who were with some neighbor or relative; the couple were sitting in one of the emergency vans, and someone had given them foam cups of coffee. His own nose twitched at the smell, though what he really wanted was a drink. Or a cigarette. He suppressed both urges and listened to his partner's gentle voice, calm and sympathetic. He was a hotshot, and he'd go far; he was *good* at making people want to help him, soothing them, never stepping on what they had to say.

"I was going to go back in. They were gone, and I was going to go back in and then—"

Cesar made a sympathetic noise. "You were having dinner when the man forced you out of the house?"

"Takeout Chinese, from Chow's," the wife said. Her husband took up the thread:

"And this man came in. He had a gun . . . a gun like a shotgun, but smaller, like a pistol," Anthony Lopez said. "It still looked pretty damn big. So was he."

He chuckled, and Salvador's opinion of him went up. It was never easy for civilians when reality crashed into what they thought had been their lives.

"How could you tell it was a shotgun?"

"Two barrels. Looked like tunnels."

"And the man?"

"He was older than me—fifty, sixty, gray hair cut short, but he was moving fast. He had blue eyes, sort of tanned skin but you could tell he was pink?"

"Anglo, but weathered?"

"Right. And he was dressed all in black, black leather. And he shouted at us, just *Go, go, go, get out, run, keep running.* We did."

"Exactly the right thing to do," Cesar said.

"But I was going to go back. Then it burned . . ." he whispered. "If I had—"

You'd be dead, Salvador thought. *On the other hand, if the guy hadn't run you all out, you'd all be dead. There's something screwy here. Arsonists don't care who gets hurt and they* certainly *don't risk getting made to warn people.*

Mrs. Lopez spoke again. "There was a younger man outside, when we ran out. He didn't do anything. He just *stood* there, with his hands in the air, almost like he was high or something. And there was a, a van or a truck over there."

She pointed to the wall of the compound across the street from what had been her house. Salvador made a note to see if they could get tire tracks.

"When we were across the street the younger man sort of, oh, collapsed. The older man with the gun, the one in black, helped him over to the van, not carrying him but nearly, sort of dragging him and putting him in the backseat. Then they drove off."

Cesar tapped at his notepad and called up the face-sketch program.

"The younger man looked like this?" he began, and patiently ran them through the process of adjustment.

Salvador stared, fascinated as always, watching the image shift, slowly morphing and changing and then switching into something that only an expert could tell from a photograph of a living person. He knew that in the old days you'd had to use a sketch artist for this, but now it was automatic. It would even check the final result against the databases with a face-recognition subsystem. When they'd given all the help they could, Cesar went on:

"Thank you, thank you both. We may have to talk to you again later."

He blew out a sigh and turned and leaned back against the end of the van, looking at the notepad in his hand. Salvador prompted him:

"Their stories were consistent?"

"Yeah, *jefe*. Right from the start, it wasn't just listening to each other and editing the memory."

He touched the screen. "Okay, sequence: When Mrs. Lopez got home with the kids, around five, Ellen Tarnowski's car, she's the upper-floor tenant, was there. Mr. Lopez, the husband, got home a little later and noticed it too. Because she's usually not back from work by then."

"They friends with her?"

"They know her to talk to, just in passing. Said she was nice, but they didn't have much in common."

The senior detective grunted and looked at *his* notepad, tapping for information; Mr. and Mrs. Lopez were a midlevel state government functionary and a dental hygienist respectively. Ellen Tarnowski . . .

Works at Hans & Demarcio Galleries. Okay, artsy. God knows we've got enough of them *around here.*

There were three-hundred-odd galleries in Santa Fe, plus every other diner and taco joint had original artwork on the walls and on sale. Half the waiters and checkout clerks in town were aspiring artists of one sort or another too, like the would-be actors in L.A. She looked out at him, a picture from some website or maybe the DMV: blond, midtwenties, full red lips, short straight nose, high cheekbones, wide blue eyes. Something in those eyes too, an odd look. Kind of haunted. The figure below . . .

"Jesus."

"Just what *I* said. Anyway, she comes downstairs just after Mr. Lopez arrives. Mrs. Lopez looks out the kitchen window and notices her because she's wearing—"

He checked his notes again.

"—a white silk sheath dress and a wrap. She knew it was Tarnowski's best fancy-occasion dress from a chat they'd had months ago. Another woman was with her. About Tarnowski's age, but shorter, slim, olive complexion or a tan, long dark hair, dark eyes . . ."

"Really going to stand out in *this* town."

"*Sí*, though if she's going around with *la Tarnowski* she will! I got a composite on her too, but it's not as definite. Mrs. Lopez said her clothes looked really expensive, and she was wearing a tanzanite necklace."

"What the fuck's tanzanite?"

The other thing we have hundreds of is jewelry stores.

"Like sapphire, but *expensive*. Here's what she looked like."

He showed a picture. The face was triangular, smiling slightly, framed by long straight black hair. Attractive too, but . . .

Reminds me of that mink I handled once. Pretty, and it bit like a bastard. Took three stitches and a tetanus shot.

"I don't think she's Latina, somehow," he said aloud, as his fingers caressed the slight scar at the base of his right thumb.

"Yeah, me too, but I can't put my finger on why. Incidentally, let's do a side-by-side with the composite on the man they saw standing still outside, when the old goatsucker with the gun ran them out past him. The one he shoved into the backseat later."

Salvador's eyebrows went up as the pictures appeared together. "Are they *sure* that's not the same person? It's an easy mistake to make, in the dark, with the right clothes."

His partner nodded; it was, surprisingly so under some circumstances.

"Looks a lot like Dark Mystery Woman, eh? But it was a guy, very certainly. Wearing a dark zippered jacket open with a tee underneath. Mrs. Lopez said he looked real fit. Not bulked up but someone who worked out a lot. She got a better look at him than at the woman; they went right by. Nothing from the databases on either of them, by the way, but look at this."

His fingers moved on the screen, and the two images slid until they were superimposed. Then he tapped a function box.

"Okay, the little machine thinks they're relatives," Salvador said. "*I* could have figured that out."

"But could you have said it was a ninety-three percent chance?"

"Sure. I just say: *It's a ninety-three percent chance*. Or in old-fashioned human language, *certainemente*. Okay, back up to what Mystery Woman was doing earlier. She and Tarnowski get in Tarnowski's car and drive off around five thirty, a few minutes earlier?"

"Mystery Woman was driving. Tarnowski looked shaky." Cesar consulted his notes. "Yeah, Mrs. Lopez said Tarnowski looked like she was going to fall over, maybe sick, and the other one helped her into the car."

"That's *two* people who have to be helped into cars. This smells."

"And then two and a half hours later someone runs in waving a sawed-off shotgun, while Mystery Woman's brother or cousin or whatever was standing outside ignoring everything and talking to himself in a strange language—"

"Strange language?"

"They just heard a few words. Not English, not Spanish, and not anything they recognized. He talks in the strange language, falls, goatsucker-with-the-gun gives him a hand, they drive off, and then the place just happens to burn down a few minutes later."

Salvador sighed and turned up the collar of his coat; it was dark, and cold.

"I need a drink. But get an APB out on Ellen Tarnowski and flag her name with municipal services and the hospitals statewide. Also the old gringo with the sawed-off shotgun, use the face-recognition protocol for surveillance cameras. We can get him on a reckless endangerment charge, trespassing, uttering threats, suspicion of arson, bad breath, whatever."

"*Sí*, and littering. The Mystery Woman and the Mystery Man too?"

"Yeah, why not? Let them all do a perp walk and we can apologize later."

He sat down and began doggedly prodding at the screen. First thing tomorrow he'd start tracing Tarnowski's life. So far nobody had died, and he'd like to keep it that way. The employer was a good first place.

II

One of the joys of a policeman's life, Eric Salvador thought the next day, wishing he'd taken more Tylenol with his breakfast. *You meet all kinds of people. Most of them hate you.* Asi es la vida. *At least she's not likely to try and blow me up with a fertilizer bomb.*

Giselle Demarcio was in her fifties, with a taut, dry, ageless appearance and a slight East Coast accent, dressed in a mildly funky Santa Fe look, silver jewelry and a blouse and flounced skirt.

Sort of a fashionista version of what my great-grandmother wore around the house, Salvador thought cynically; his family, the Spanish part at least, had been in Santa Fe since the seventeenth century. *Everything old gets new if you wait long enough. Rich Anglos get off the bus and live in pimped-up adobes and you end up in a double-wide on Airport Road.*

She had a white mark on her finger where a wedding ring would go, and she fit in perfectly with the airy white-on-white decor of Hans & Demarcio Galleries. He was *not,* he noticed, being invited back to her office; this was a semi-public reception room. The art on the walls was something he could understand, at least—actual pictures of actual things. Not the cowboy-pueblo-Western art a lot of the places on Canyon Road had either, mostly older-looking stuff. There was a very faint odor of woodsmoke from a piñon fire crackling in a kiva fireplace. The whole thing screamed *money.* It had been a very long time since Canyon Road attracted artists because the rents were low.

Santa Fe, the town where ten thousand people can buy the State and fifty thousand can't afford lunch, he thought.

"Would you like some coffee, Detective?" Demarcio said.

Wait a minute, Salvador thought. *She's not really hostile. She's* scared *for some reason. Not of me, but scared silly and hiding it well.*

"Thank you," he said, and took the cup. "That's nice."

It was excellent coffee, especially compared to what he drank at home or at the station, with a rich, dark, nutty taste. He enjoyed it, and waited. Most people couldn't stand silence. It wore on their nerves and eventually they blurted out something to fill it. Salvador had learned patience and silence in a very hard school.

"I'm worried about Ellen," the older woman said suddenly.

The detective made a sympathetic noise. "Ms. Tarnowski worked for you?" he said.

"Works. She's my assistant even if she didn't show up this morning; that's understandable with the fire and all. Not a secretary, she's an art history graduate from NYU and I was bringing her in on our acquisitions side. I'm . . . she's a sweet kid, but she's gotten mixed up in something, hasn't she?"

"You tell me, Ms. Demarcio," Salvador said.

"I never liked that boyfriend of hers. She met him playing tennis at the country club about a year ago and they, well, it was a whirlwind thing. He gave me this creepy feeling. And then his sister showed up—"

Salvador blinked. *The sister . . . the woman who was with Tarnowski?* "Boyfriend?" he asked.

"Adrian Brézé."

"Ah," Salvador said.

As he spoke he tapped the name into his notepad's virtual keyboard and hit the rather specialized search function. He'd long ago mastered the trick of reading a screen and paying attention to someone at the same time.

"Now, that's interesting. Do you have a picture of him?"

It was interesting because Salvador *didn't* have a picture; or much of anything else. Usually these days you drowned in data on anyone. There was nothing here but bare bones: a social security number, a passport number, and an address way, *way* out west of town. Just out of Santa Fe County, in fact. A quick Google Earth flick showed a big house on a low mountain or big hill, right in the foothills of the Sangres, nothing else for miles.

Not even a passport picture to go with the number. Someone likes his privacy, he thought, looking at the address. Then: *Hey, could you . . . nah, nobody can evade the Web.*

Demarcio hesitated, then pulled a framed picture out of a drawer. The glass was cracked, as if someone had thrown it at a wall.

"She told me she was going to break up with him. Couldn't take the emotional distance and lies anymore. Then she didn't show up to work yesterday."

"So she's missing the day before the fire," Salvador said, looking at the picture. "She didn't call in? Just nothing?"

"Nothing. That's not like her. She's the most reliable person who's ever worked for me."

The photo beneath the cracked glass showed a youngish man, though on second thought perhaps Salvador's own age. Or maybe somewhere between twenty-five and thirty-five. Dark hair worn a little longer than was fashionable these days, a vaguely Mediterranean-looking face. Handsome, perhaps a little too much so.

Androgynous, that's the word. But there's something dangerous looking about him too.

"He's . . ." Demarcio frowned. "You know, I met him a dozen times and I listened to *her* talk about him a *lot* and I really can't tell you much. He's wealthy . . . very wealthy, I think. Some sort of old money, but that's an impression, not knowledge. He wouldn't tell Ellen anything about that either, just some vague bullshit about 'investments.' American born, but he has a slight accent, French I think, which would fit with the name. I know he speaks French and Italian and Spanish . . . and yes, German too. I couldn't tell you where his money comes from, or where he went to university, or, well, anything."

Salvador looked at the photo. Unobtrusively, he brought up the composite picture on the notepad. The resemblance to the reconstruction of the man the Lopez family had seen standing motionless outside their house just before the fire was unmistakable. He scanned the picture into the notepad, and the program came up with a solid positive when it did its comparison.

"Would you say this is Adrian Brézé?" he said and showed her the screen.

"Absolutely," she said.

"And this is his sister?" he said, changing to the composite of the woman the Lopezes had seen with Ellen Tarnowski earlier.

"Well . . ." The picture wasn't quite as definite; they'd only glimpsed the face in passing and through a window. "Yes, I'd say so. It's a striking resemblance, isn't it? Like twins, only they'd have to be fraternal."

"Have you seen *this* man?"

The composite this time was the older man with the gun who'd frightened the Lopezes out of their home . . . and probably saved their lives, considering how fast the building had gone up.

"No, I can't say I have. That is, it's similar to any number of people I've seen but it doesn't bring anyone immediately to mind."

Salvador grunted; it was a rather generic Anglo countenance, in fact. Offhand he'd have said Texan or Southern of some sort; there was something about the cheekbones that brought Scots-Irish hillbilly to mind, and the long face on a long skull, but even that was just an educated guess. The Corps was lousy with that type.

"Do you think Mr. Brézé is capable of, mmm, violent actions?"

She paused for a long moment, looking down at her fingers. When she met his eyes again, his alarm bells rang once more.

"I think he's capable of anything. Anything at all."

"Had a temper?"

She shook her head. "No. He was always a perfect gentleman. But I could *feel* it."

Which would be a big *help in court.*

"Now, you saw Ms. Tarnowski later that evening?"

Now Demarcio flushed. "Yes, with Ms. Brézé . . . Adrienne Brézé. At La Casa Sena; they were having dinner at a table near mine."

That was an expensive restaurant on Palace, just off the plaza, in an old renovated adobe that had started out as a *hacendado*'s townhouse. Not the most expensive in town by a long shot, but up there.

"You didn't speak with them?"

"No. They, umm, didn't seem to want company." Her eyes shifted upward and she blushed slightly. "They seemed sort of preoccupied."

Ah, Salvador thought. *That sort of preoccupied. Is this an arson case or a bad movie? Sister catches her on the rebound from her brother, so brother burns the house down? Where do these sorts of people* come *from? Do they step out of TV screens or do the screenwriters know them and use them for material?*

"You knew Adrienne Brézé socially?"

"No. I'd never seen her before. Didn't even know Adrian had a sister."

"Then how did you know the woman's name?" he said.

An exasperated glance. "I asked the maitre d'hotel at La Casa Sena, of course! I'm a regular there. So is Adrian."

He hid a smile. *I think Ms. Demarcio is a nice lady. She's concerned about Tarnowski. But I also think she's a gossip of the first water.*

"Thank you, Ms. Demarcio—"

"Well, aren't you going to *tell* me anything?"

He sighed. Usually you *didn't*, but he needed to develop this source.

"We're investigating the circumstances of the fire at Ms. Tarnowski's apartment, and trying to find where she is."

Her eyes narrowed slightly; that meant *We think it was torched*, without actually saying it.

"And her disappearance?"

"Ah, yes. There's no reason to suppose it's anything but a sudden move—"

"And no reason to suppose it *is*. I talked to the Lopez family, and there was a man with a *gun*."

He sighed. Santa Fe was a small town. "True. We've got Santa Fe and Albuquerque and the state police all looking. Here's my card."

He slid it across the low table. "Please let me know immediately if Ms. Tarnowski contacts you, or you get any other information."

Outside, Cesar met him, and they walked down toward the end of Canyon, then turned right across the bridge over the small and entirely dry Santa Fe river with its strip of grass and cottonwoods. That led to Palace just north of the Cathedral, the reddish sandstone bulk of it towering over the adobe and stucco of the neighboring buildings. Salvador jammed his fists into the pockets of his sheepskin jacket and scowled, pausing only to give the finger to a Mercedes that ran the yellow light and nearly hit them. Right afterward, a rusting clunker with the driver's door held on with coat-hanger wire did the same thing.

"This is screwy," he complained, after he'd filled his partner in. "But at least we've got names to go with our composites. Adrian and Adrienne Brézé."

"This is fucked up, amigo," Cesar said cheerfully. "Because the databases are *still* not giving us anything even though we've got the names. They don't have e-mail addresses, they don't have bank accounts . . . You did send them out?"

"Yeah, local, state, Fart Barf and Itch, and Homeland Insecurity, which means the spooks. It can take a while, even now they've got the whole system cross-referenced."

"It shouldn't take a while to get *something*. Everyone leaves footprints. The question is, my friend, should we be thinking of this as an arson case, or some sort of kidnapping? Scorned boyfriend revenge thing, he burns the house and snatches her?"

"A little early for that."

Cesar grinned and showed his notepad, a picture of an elderly but well-maintained Prius. "Abandoned car on Palace, ticketed and towed about an hour ago. Registered to—"

"Ellen Tarnowski."

"So maybe, it's not so early."

Salvador's notepad beeped. "Well, fuck me. Take a look."

The picture was from the security cams at Albuquerque Sunport, the airport in the larger city an hour's drive south; the face-recognition software had tagged it.

"That's Brézé and our mystery man with the gun, all right. Still in the black leather outfit. Nine thirty to San Francisco last night, just opened up and the request got it. Wait a minute—"

He tapped at the screen. "*Fuck* me."

"What's wrong?"

"They didn't have tickets. Look."

"Could be tickets under someone else's name."

"No, there were two vacant first-class seats according to the ticketing record. But look, when they cleared for takeoff they recorded *all the first-class* seats as full. But there aren't any *names* attached to these two. Which isn't supposed to be possible. Breaks three laws and twenty regulations."

Cesar made a hissing sound of frustration. "*Mierda*, for a second I thought we'd get a name on Mr. Shotgun. What about the other end?"

"Flight got into San Francisco International . . . nothing on the surveillance cam there, and it *should* have got them."

The younger man grinned. "Maybe they got out on the way, *sí*?"

"Yeah, at forty thousand feet. At least we can retire the kidnapping theory, Cesar. But Tarnowski's still missing, even if Mr. Boyfriend didn't snatch her. Or I suppose he could have a third party holding her."

"Okay, we got her last known location in Santa Fe. Here."

The building that housed La Casa Sena and several upscale shops was mainly nineteenth century, adobe-built with baked-brick trim, rising around a courtyard-patio that featured a pool and a huge cottonwood. Originally it had comprised thirty-three rooms of living-place-workroom-storeroom-quasi-fortress that presented a blank defensive wall four feet thick to the outside, intended to repel Apaches, bandits, rebels, and tax collectors whether Mexican or gringo. Now there was a wine boutique, several stores selling upscale jewelry and froofraw, and the restaurant occupying two sides of the rectangle.

Iron tables stood out under the cottonwoods, vacant this time of year; the flower beds were sere and brown as well. A glassed-in box near the entrance covered the original well that had supplied water to the complex. He glanced at the menu posted beside the door; they weren't open for lunch yet.

"Ever eaten here?" he asked.

"Twenty-five for a *ham sandwich*?" Cesar said, peering at the prices. "You loco?"

"I had dinner here once. An anniversary, the last one before Julia divorced me. The food was actually pretty damn good."

"Jesus, if lunch is like this, what's dinner for two cost?"

"About the price of a trip to Paris." Salvador grinned and read the small print: "And the ham sandwich has green chile aioli, ciabatta, aged Wisconsin Gouda—"

"It's still twenty-five dollars for a fucking ham sandwich. Okay, a ham and cheese. I don't care if the butter was made from the Virgin's milk."

"Can I help you?" a young woman in a bow-tie outfit said, opening the door. "Lunch doesn't start seating until—"

They flashed their badges. "The manager, please."

That brought quick action: "I'm Mr. Tortensen—"

After the introductions, the manager showed them through to his office, though Salvador felt as if half the contents of his wallet had vanished just stepping over the threshold of the front door into the pale Taos-style interior. Even the office was stylish. The man was worried, brown-haired, in his thirties, lean to the point of emaciation, and licking his lips.

"What can I do for you, officers?" he said.

Salvador leaned back in the chair. He knew he could be intimidating to some. People who'd led sheltered lives particularly. He didn't have to *do* anything in particular, even if they were people who'd consciously think of him as something they'd scrape off their shoe on a hot day.

"You had two guests at dinner yesterday," he said. "From a little after five thirty to seven thirty. Ellen Tarnowski and Adrienne Brézé. I'd like some details."

The man started very slightly, and then his mouth firmed. "I'm afraid our clients' confidentiality is—"

Cesar cut in smoothly: "Ms. Tarnowski's house burned down last night, and there's suspicion of arson. Her car was found and towed from a parking spot not too far from here. We have independent confirmation that she was here last night, and she's a missing person with this as her last known location."

Salvador nodded. "So we'd *really appreciate* your cooperation in this arson and possible kidnapping investigation."

The manager started; short of shouting *terrorism* it was about the best possible way of getting his attention.

"Let me make a few calls," he said, pulling out his phone.

Cesar worked on his notepad. Salvador crossed his arms on his chest and enjoyed watching the manager sweat as he tried to get back to *his* routine. People came in to talk to Mr. Tortensen about purchasing and things that probably made perfect sense. At last, a harassed-looking man in his early twenties came in; he was slimly handsome, but looked as if he really wasn't used to waking up this early. Which, with a night-shift job like waiting tables, he might not be.

"Ah, this is Joseph Morales, officer," Tortensen said. "He had A17 . . . their table . . . last night."

Maricón, Salvador thought—clinically, he wasn't bothered by them. There had been one he knew who was an artist with a Javelin launcher. *He could put a rocket right through a firing slit, which has a good dirty joke in it somewhere.*

"Pleased to meet you," Morales said to the policemen with transparent dishonesty, but he was at least trying to hide it. "How can I help you?"

The restaurant manager started to speak, and Salvador held up a hand. "We're interested in a party of two at one of your tables last night."

He held up his notepad with Tarnowski's face.

The waiter laughed—it was almost a giggle. "Oh, *them.* Yes, I remember them well. They ordered—well, Ms. Brézé ordered—"

He rattled off a list of things, most of which Salvador had never heard of. He held up a hand.

"What did that come to?"

"With the wines? About . . . twenty-five hundred."

The manager was working his desktop, and nodded confirmation. Cesar gave a smothered sound that had probably started as an agonized grunt, passed through indignation, and was finally suppressed with a tightening of the mouth.

"Tip?"

"Very generous. Seven hundred."

Outside, Cesar shook his head. "Seven hundred for the *tip*? And you *went* there?"

"I was starting to get worried about Julia, wanted to show her I thought about something besides my job. Didn't work. Three weeks later, she told me I was just as far away living here as I had been when they deployed me to Kandahar."

"Ai!"

"Yeah, sweet, eh? What's the next stop?"

"I'll try and see if anyone around saw the van that Adrian Brézé and Mystery Man in Leather were using after they left the burn site."

Salvador laughed. "And *I'll* get back and catch up on my paperwork. Don't you wish this were a TV show?"

"So we could just work one case at a time? *Sí*, the thought has crossed my mind."

III

"OKAY," CESAR SAID TWO WEEKS LATER. "GUESS WHAT? SOMETHING FUNNY on the Brézé case."

"Tell me something funny. I could use it."

Salvador sipped at a cup of sour coffee and looked out the window at a struggling piñon pine with sap dripping from its limbs; they were having another beetle infestation, which happened every decade or two. Firewood would be cheap soon; he could take his pickup out on weekends and get a load for the labor of cutting it up and hauling it away.

The prospect was a lot more fun than the case he was working on now.

Man beats up woman, woman calls cops, woman presses charges, woman changes mind, couple sues cops. Tell me again why I'm not selling insurance?

"The funny thing is the analysis on the DNA from the puke I found in the Dumpster behind Whole Foods," Cesar said.

"Ain't a policeman's life fun? Digging in Dumpsters for puke?"

"*Sí, jefe.* Nice clean white-collar job, just what my mother had in mind for her prospective kid when she waded across the river to get me born on U.S. soil. Anyway, there's blood in the puke."

"I remember you telling me that. The attendant says it was *Adrian Brézé's* puke, right?"

"Right, he saw him puking out the rear of that van, thought he was drunk. I'm pretty sure that Brézé paid him something to forget about it—he sweated pretty hard before he talked, and I had to do the kidnapping-and-arson dance. He saw the blood in it too."

"So he's got an ulcer. Even rich people get them. How does this help us?"

Cesar scratched his mustache, and Salvador consciously stopped himself from doing likewise.

"I'm not sure it does," he said. "But it's *funny*. Because the DNA from the puke is not the same as the DNA from the blood. In fact, the DNA from the blood is on the Red Cross list. One of their donors, a Shirley Whitworth, donated it at that place just off Rodeo and Camino Carlos Rey. It seems to have gone missing from their system. They clammed up about it pretty tight. We'll have to work on that."

Salvador grunted. "Let's get this straight. The *puke* is Brézé—"

"Presumably. Male chromosomes in the body fluids. But there's no Brézé in the DNA database."

"That's not so surprising; they only started it a couple of years ago, and it just means he's not a donor and hasn't been arrested or gone to a hospital or whatever. But the *blood* is definitely some Red Cross donor's?"

"*Sí*. So, funny, eh?"

"Funny as in fucking weird, not funny as in ha-ha. Because it had to be in his *stomach*, right?"

They both laughed. "Good thing we know he comes out in daylight, eh?" Cesar said.

"Yeah, and he doesn't sparkle. I'd feel fucking silly chasing a perp who looked like a walking disco ball . . . but he *did* drink it . . . maybe some sort of kink cult thing?"

"So I'm not surprised he puked," Cesar said, still chuckling. "It'd be like drinking salt water, you know? Blood *is* salt water, seawater. My mother used salt water and mustard to make you heave if you'd eaten more than you should."

Salvador could feel his brain starting to move, things connecting under the fatigue of a half-dozen cases that were never going to go anywhere. Then his phone rang. When he closed it, he was frowning.

"What's the news, *jefe*?"

"The boss wants to see us, now."

The chief's office wasn't much bigger than his; Santa Fe was a small town, still well under a hundred thousand people. It was on a corner, second story, and had bigger windows. The chief also had three stars on the collar of his uniform; he still didn't make nearly as much as, say, Giselle Demarcio. On the other hand, his money didn't come from San Francisco and L.A. and New York, either.

Cesar's breath hissed a little, and Salvador felt his eyes narrow. There were two suits waiting for them as well as the chief. *Literally* suits, natty, one woman and one man, one black and one some variety of Anglo. Both definitely from out of state; he'd have put the black woman down as FBI if he had to guess, and the younger man as some sort of spook, but not a desk man. Ex-military of some type, but not in the least retired.

Possibly from the Army of Northern Virginia, a.k.a. the Waffen-CIA.

"Sit down," the chief said.

He was as local as Salvador and more so than Cesar, and might have been Salvador's older cousin—in fact, they were distantly related. Right now, he was giving a good impression of someone who'd never met either of the detectives, his face like something carved out of wood on Canyon Road.

The male suit spoke. "You're working on a case involving the Brézé family?"

"Yes," Salvador said. "Chief, who are these people?"

"You don't need to know," the woman said neutrally; somehow she gave the *impression* of wearing sunglasses without actually doing it. More softly: "You don't *want* to know."

"They're Homeland Security," the chief said.

"Homeland Security is interested in weird love triangles?" Salvador said skeptically. "Besides, *Homeland Security* is like *person*, it's sort of generic. You people FBI, Company, NSA, what?"

"You don't need to know. You *do* need to know we're handling this," the man said.

Wait a minute, Salvador thought. *He's scared. Controlling it well, he's a complete hardcase if I ever saw one, and hell, I've* been *one. But he's scared.*

Which made him start thinking a little uncomfortably that maybe *he* should be scared. The man was someone he might have been himself, if things had gone a little differently with that IED.

"Handling it how?" Salvador said, meeting his pale stare.

"We've got some of our best people on it."

"Oh, Christ—" he began.

"Eric, *drop* it. Right now," the chief said.

He's scared too.

"Hey, Chief, no problem," Cesar cut in. "It's not like we haven't got enough work. Right, drop it, national security business, need to know, eh?"

The two suits looked at each other and then Salvador. He nodded himself.

"Okay," he said. "I wasn't born yesterday. Curiosity killed the cat, that right? And unless I want to go *meow-oh-shit* as my last words . . ."

"You have no idea," the woman said, looking past him. "None at all."

Then she turned her eyes on him. "Let's be clear. There was no fire. There is no such thing as a Brézé family. You never heard of them. You particularly haven't made any records or files of anything concerning them. That will be checked."

"Sure," he grinned. "Check what? About who?"

Salvador waited until they were back in the office before he began to swear; English, Spanish, and some Pushtu, which was about the best reviling language he'd ever come across, though some people he'd known said Arabic was better.

"Let's get some lunch," Cesar said, winking.

Yeah, Salvador thought. *Got to remember* anything *can be a bug these days.*

"Sure, I could use a burrito."

When they were outside Cesar went on: "How soon you want to start poking around, *jefe*?"

Salvador let out his breath and rolled his head, kneading at the back of his head with one spadelike hand. The muscles there felt like a mass of woven iron rods under his hand, and he pressed on the silver chain that held the crucifix around his neck.

"It's fucking Eurotrash terrorists now, eh?" he said.

"Yeah. Eurotrash *vampire* terrorists. Maybe Osama bit them?" Cesar said, still smiling.

"Or vice versa."

"What sort of shit is going on?" Cesar said, more seriously.

"Our chances of getting that from those people . . ."

". . . are nada."

Cesar looked up into the cloudless blue sky. "Maybe these Brézés are just so rich they can shitcan anything they don't like? Call me cynical . . ."

"Nah," Salvador shook his head. "You can't get that just with money. Not with those people, the spooks. You need heavy political leverage. Whoever they were, they *were* feds, and not your average cubicle slave either. They're not going to tell any of us boondockers shit. The chief didn't know any more than we did; he was just taking orders."

"You sure?"

"I've known him a long time."

"So . . ." Cesar said.

He leaned back against a wall. "How long do you want to let it cool before we start poking in violation of our solemn promise?"

"Couple of months," Salvador said. "First thing, get all the data on an SD card and make some copies and let me have one. Scrub your notebook and anything you've got at the office. None of this ever goes on anything connected to anything else."

Cesar grinned. "I like the way you think, *jefe.*"

Dream.

The sense of sick dread got worse as the flames erupted through the door and he was flung back to lie helpless. This time he could see the figure who walked through the fire.

It was a woman, young, naked, her face doll-like and pretty with slanted eyes, hair piled up on her head in an elaborate coiffure that looked Asian. If he'd seen a picture like that, he'd have gotten horny. Instead, he felt as if giant fingernails were screeching down slate everywhere in the universe, as if he should run and run and run, and there was a *stink* that wasn't physical at all, and he retched hopelessly.

"Who's been a naughty boy?" she crooned.

Then she knelt by Johnson's body, only it wasn't Johnson anymore, it was Cesar, and he was naked too. They rolled in the dust, coupling like dogs, but Cesar was screaming. When she raised her head, blood masked her mouth and dripped from her chin and poured from Cesar's throat. Yellow flecks sparkled in her dark-brown eyes.

"I just *love* brave men," she said. "They're *delicious.*"

"Christ!"

This time there were cigarettes under his searching hand. He fumbled the lighter twice. The dark coal glowed like eyes as he sucked in the smoke. Salvador fumbled for the light switch and sat with his feet on the floor. He pulled the smoke into his lungs again, coughed, inhaled again. After a while his hands stopped shaking, and he looked at the time. It was just three o'clock, which meant he'd been asleep a bit less than two hours. The air in his bedroom smelled close, despite the warm breeze that rattled the Venetian blinds against the frame of the window. Sweat cooled on his back and flanks.

He looked at the phone. "I'm not going to call. Cesar puts up with a lot, but *he's* not sleeping alone. I can't tell him I had a bad—"

The phone rang. He picked it up.

"Jefe?"

"There's anyone else at this address?"

"Get over here. I've got something you need to see."

SALVADOR KNEW SOMETHING WAS WRONG. HE COULD *FEEL* IT, A PRICKLING along the back of his neck. The house was completely dark except for the light from the streetlamp, which was very damned odd even at three thirty, since Cesar had just called him. His partner's new Chinese import was parked in the driveway; the ground between the road and the house was gravel with a few weeds poking through. The neighborhood was utterly quiet, and the stars were bright. A cat walked by, looked at him with eyes that turned into green mirrors for an instant, and then passed. Nothing else moved.

"Shit," he mouthed soundlessly, and pulled his Glock 22, his thumb moving the safety to *off.*

Then he touched the door. It swung in. He crossed the hallway, instinctively keeping the muzzle up and tucking his shoulder into the angle between the bedroom door and the wall. Then the smell hit him. He looked down. It looked black in the low light, but the tackiness under his foot was unmistakable.

"WELL, THAT'S UNIQUE," THE CHIEF SAID.

The forensics team moved around the room. Most of them had more than one hat; Santa Fe's police force didn't run to elaborate hierarchies.

Salvador felt a surge of anger, and throttled it back automatically. It wouldn't help . . . and he'd said the same sort of thing. You did, it helped you deal with what you were seeing. Usually.

Cecile was on the bed. Usually bodies didn't have much expression, but usually they weren't arched in a galvanic spasm that was never going to end. They'd have to break her bones to get her into a body bag. The look on her face was not quite like anything he'd ever seen. He licked his lips, tasting the salt of sweat.

Cesar was naked, lying on his face between the bed and the window. His pistol was in his right hand; the spent brass of fourteen shells littered the floor around him. Most of them were in the coagulating blood, turned dark red now with brown spots. In his left was clutched a knife, not a fighting knife, some sort of tableware. A wedge of glass as broad as a man's hand at its base was in his throat, the point coming out the back of his neck.

"This is a murder-suicide," the chief said quietly.

Salvador stirred. The older man didn't look at him. "That's exactly what it is, Eric."

He doesn't call me by my first name very often.

"Probably that's what the evidence will show. Sir," Salvador added.

I've seen friends die before. I didn't sit down and cry. I did my job. I can do it now.

He hadn't been this angry then, either. He'd killed every *mouj* he could while he was on the rock pile, and that had been a good round number, but he hadn't usually hated them. Sort of a sour disgust, most of the time; he hadn't thought of them as *personal* enough to hate, really.

This is extremely personal.

"Chief."

That was one of the evidence squad. He walked around the pool of blood to them. "We got something on the windowsill, going out. Sort of strange. When did you say you got here, Salvador?"

"Three thirty. Half an hour after . . . Cesar called me."

The night outside was still dark, but there was a staleness, a stillness to it, that promised dawn.

Baffled, Salvador shook his head. The man held up his notebook. The smudge he'd recorded on the ledge turned into a print. A paw print.

"You notice a dog? Or something else like that?"

"No," he said dully. "Just a cat."

"Well, that's not it." The print was too large for a house cat. "Probably just something drawn by the smell."

"Time of death?"

"Recent but hard to pin down, on a warm night like this. Everything's fully compatible with sometime between the time you got the phone call and the time you called it in."

The chief put a hand on his shoulder and urged him outside. He fumbled in the pockets of his jacket and pulled out a cigarette and lit it.

"You know you can't be on this investigation, Eric," the older man said. "Go home. Get some sleep. Crawl into a bottle and get some sleep if you have to. Take a couple of days off."

Salvador nodded, flicked the cigarette into the weedy gravel of the front yard, and walked steadily over to his car. He pulled out very, very carefully, and drove equally carefully to St. Francis, down to the intersection with Rodeo and the entrance to the I-25. Only then did he pull over into a boarded-up complex of low buildings, probably originally meant for medical offices or real estate agents, built by some crazed optimist back in the late aughts or early teens.

"Okay, Cesar, talk to me," he said aloud, and slid the data card he'd palmed into the slot on his notebook; nobody would notice, not when he'd left his shoes standing in the pool of blood. "This better not be your taxes. Tell me how to get the *cabron*."

The screen came on, only one file, and that was video. Salvador tapped his finger on it.

Vision. Three ten in the carat at the lower right corner. Cesar was sweating as he spoke, wearing a bathrobe but with his Glock sitting in front of him within range of the pickup camera; the background was his home-office-cum-TV-room, lit only by one small lamp.

"I'm recording this before you get here, *jefe*, 'cause I've got a really bad feeling about this. I was on the net tonight and I got a query from the Quantico analysis lab we sent the puke and blood to back when, you know? They said there were some *interesting anomalies* and did I want any more information on the Brézé guy, and they attached the file. It *looked* like a legit file, it was big enough."

Cesar's image licked its lips; Salvador could see that, but his mind superimposed how he'd looked with half his face lying in a pool of his own blood.

"Okay, it was stupid. I should have asked them *Who dat?* or just hit the spam blocker. We weren't getting anywhere, creeping Adrian Brézé's house is desperation stuff, so I downloaded. Here's what I got, repeated a whole lot of times."

Letters appeared, a paragraph of boldface:

—youaresofuckedyouaresofuckedyouaresofuckedyouareso—

"I—"

"Cesar!" A scream, a woman's voice, high and desperate. Then: "Don't—don't—please, don't—"

Then just screaming. Cesar snatched up the pistol and ran. Salvador heard himself screaming too, as the shots began. Then more sounds, for a long time. Then another face in the screen.

It was the woman he'd seen in the dream; he could tell, even though her face was one liquid sheet of dull red. Only the golden flecks in her eyes showed bright, and then her teeth were very white when she licked them clean.

"You are so fucked," she crooned, and the screen went black.

THE ROAD TO ADRIAN BRÉZÉ'S HOUSE WAS TEN MILES NORTH ON THE I-25 and then east. The empty highway stretched through the night, cool air flowing in through the open windows as the tires hummed. He was going to his death—but maybe he'd learn *something.* Maybe the world would make sense again.

Since when has it made sense anyway? I'm thirty-two years old, no wife, no kids, and my best friend just died because I couldn't figure out what was going on. The only thing I've ever been any good at was killing people and frightening them. Cesar had twice my brains and now he's dead and his girl's dead.

East, and then north again on a dirt road. The Sangres low on the horizon in the light of the three-quarter moon. That and the stars were the only light as the last gas station fell away, and only a few distant earthbound stars marked houses. The road turned, winding in the pitch-dark night, and then a steep drop to his left, a hundred near-vertical feet; this was the edge of the plateau. He forced himself to stop when the wheels skidded and a spray of gravel fanned out and out of sight. He clenched his hands on the wheel.

"Am I trying to kill myself?" he murmured. Then: "No. Not yet. I've got to find out what this all *means.*"

Instead, he got out and walked down the last stretch of road. The night scents were strong, the sweaty leather of chamisos, the strong resin of the bleeding pines. Gravel crunched under his feet—it was nearly six months since Adrian Brézé had vanished, and the housekeeper came in only once a month to clean. The house itself was built right into the edge of the cliff; the final dip in the road left him looking down on its fieldstone walls. The high copper-surfaced door swung open to his touch, and a few soft lights came on under the high metal ceiling.

Yeah, about what I expected, he thought.

The whole of the opposite wall was glass, right at the edge of the cliff. It fell in crags and gullies washed pale by the moon, until the rolling surface of the semidesert stretched eastward to the edge of sight. There were a couple of pictures on the walls, ancient and beautiful.

"Why did I think I could find something here?" he said aloud.

"Maybe a little bird told you."

The voice seemed to come from behind him. He wheeled. Nothing. Back again . . . and the woman was there. A spurt of dreadful joy filled him. This wasn't a dream, or pixels. That was an actual person in front of him. There was even an appendix scar.

He raised the Glock in the regulation grip, left hand under right.

Crack. Crack.

The ten-millimeter bullets punched into her belly and she folded backward.

Crack.

Two in the center of mass, one in the head; the last snapped her head around in a whirling of long black hair and a spray of blood and the bullet starred through the glass behind her. He felt his teeth begin to show as he walked toward her. The gold-flecked eyes were already beginning to glaze.

Then her head came up. "Oooooh, that *hurt*," she said. "That can be sort of hot, you know? For starters. Then I get to hurt you. You like that, lover?"

Salvador leaped backward, almost fell as he half-sprawled against a malachite-surfaced table of rough-cast glass, then wrenched himself into a crouched firing position.

Crack. Crack. Crack—

Ten shots. Five hit. Five more punched the great window behind, starring it, then collapsing it out in a shatter of milky fragments.

"Ooooo, ooooo, you're so *rough*," the thing laughed as it advanced on him, laughing.

A hand reached out toward his neck. Then jerked back as she hissed:

"We really have to do something about those silver chains. Maybe we could make people think they cause cancer?"

She dabbed at the blood on the side of her head and stuck the fingers in her mouth for a moment, tongue curling around them.

"Mmmmm, tasty! But you want to take that stupid chain off, don't you . . . that's right . . ."

The eyes grew, the yellow flecks drawing together like drops of molten gold, running into two lakes of fire. Depth, depth, drawing him into a whirling—

She screamed, pain and rage. The great ten-foot wings beat behind her as the talons slammed home and the hooked beak drove into her neck. The snow-leopard rolled over and over—

—leopard?—

its paws striking in a blur of speed and claws. The eagle dropped out of the air into a huge tawny *something* and the big cats rolled over and over shrieking and striking and lunging for each other's throats as furniture smashed and broken glass crunched under their weight. Then the man was standing with his back to Salvador, every muscle in his lean body standing out like static waves as his thumbs dug into her throat. She was making the same bestial snarling sound as she reared back with a knee braced against his chest and her hands driving up between his forearms—

CRACK!

Much louder this time. The double splash of impact and her skull started to deform under the huge kinetic energy, and then a sparkle, and she was gone. Blood fell to the floor, with a sharp, sour, iron-salt smell. The man went to one knee for a second, panting, then rose and turned.

"You're Adrian Brézé," he said, trying to make his mind function again.

The gun came up, almost of its own volition. The slim dark man pointed a finger at him.

"Don't. Just *don't.* It's been a long day."

He cast a glance over his shoulder; the first paling of the night sky showed that dawn was coming, and he winced a little.

"I'd better go corporeal. Right back, Detective Salvador."

Salvador looked down at the pistol. *Why the hell not?* he thought, and began to bring it up toward his mouth. *That's safer. Only amateurs try to shoot themselves in the head . . .*

"I wouldn't do that if I were you."

"Why don't you kill me? Why don't you kill me?" he screamed. *"Why don't you just fucking kill me?"*

"That's why don't *they* fucking kill you," the man said. "I can tell you, if you want to know."

"You're one of them."

Brézé was slight, a bit below medium height, pale olive skin and dark hair and gold-flecked brown eyes . . .

"You're *Adrian Brézé*!"

"Yes."

Salvador drew breath in, held it, let it out. "Okay, I get it: I'm supposed to believe you're a *good* monster."

"Oh, he's a *great* monster, believe me. But all mine."

Salvador jerked at the other voice, looked down at the pistol, then dropped it to the table he was sitting on. A copper box had spilled open, full of slim cigarettes. He took one out and lit it; some distant part of himself was proud of the fact that his hand didn't shake. The second voice belonged to a woman. Tall, blond, dressed in dark outdoor clothes and boots, with a knit cap over her head and a rifle cradled in her arms—he recognized it, big Brit sniper job, long scope, aircraft-alloy body.

"You're . . . Ellen Tarnowski."

"Technically, Ellen Brézé, now. No, I'm not one of them. You don't catch it from getting bit."

A sudden charming smile. "And believe me, I know! Not even from getting married to one."

"I get the feeling you've changed."

"I had to . . . ah . . . take a couple of levels in badass, let's say."

"You killed her."

His eyes went back to the puddle of blood; there wasn't a body.

"*Oh*, yes." Her eyes were large and turquoise blue; for a moment they held a hot satisfaction. "There's a body, probably a long way away, but it's empty now."

"That . . . that wasn't his sister, was it?"

"No. That was Michiko. She's a friend of his sister. Sort of a wannabe Mistress of Ultimate Darkness."

Brézé was back. Now he was dressed, in the same sort of clothes; a light jacket covered a shoulder rig with a knife worn hilt-down on one flank and a Glock on the other.

"All right," Salvador said, taking a pull on the cigarette. "Fill me in. I know I'm really somewhere under heavy meds, baying at the moon."

For some reason, that made Adrian Brézé smile. "I'm a Shadowspawn . . . that's what we call ourselves, mostly. But . . . well, I *try* not to be a monster. It's complicated. You can choose to learn, or you can choose to forget. If you forget, you can make yourself a new life. If you learn, it'll probably kill you—but at least you'll know why you're fighting, *mon ami*."

"If you offer me a blue pill and a red pill, I'll fucking kill you!"

The couple laughed. "It's actually two file cards. Take your pick."

"Knowledge—and you can try being the guerrilla. Ignorance—and long life."

Salvador looked at the butt of the cigarette. Then he tossed it accurately into the blood; it hissed into extinction.

"Like that's really a choice?"

IT'S STILL THE SAME OLD STORY

by Carrie Vaughn

Bestseller Carrie Vaughn is the author of a wildly popular series of novels detailing the adventures of Kitty Norville, a radio personality who also happens to be a werewolf, and who runs a late-night call-in radio advice show for supernatural creatures. The Kitty books include *Kitty and The Midnight Hour, Kitty Goes to Washington, Kitty Takes a Holiday, Kitty and the Silver Bullet, Kitty and the Dead Man's Hand, Kitty Raises Hell*, and *Kitty's House of Horrors*. Vaughn's short work has appeared in *Jim Baen's Universe, Asimov's Science Fiction, Subterranean, Wild Cards: Inside Straight, Realms of Fantasy, Paradox, Strange Horizons, Weird Tales, All-Star Zeppelin Adventure Stories*, and elsewhere. Her most recent books are *Steel*, her second venture into young-adult territory; *After the Golden Age*; and two new Kitty novels, *Kitty Goes to War* and *Kitty's Big Trouble*. She lives in Colorado.

Here she takes us into Kitty's world for a poignant look at how you don't abandon old friends, even if—or maybe *especially* if—you're immortal.

RICK AWOKE AT SUNSET AND FOUND A PHONE MESSAGE FROM AN OLD friend waiting for him. Helen sounded unhappy, but she didn't give details. She wouldn't even say that she was afraid and needed help, but the hushed tone of her voice made her sound like she was looking over her shoulder. He grabbed his coat, went upstairs to the back of the shop where he parked his silver BMW, and drove to see her.

The summer night was still, ordinary. Downtown Denver blazed. To his eyes, the skyscrapers seemed like glowing mushrooms; they'd sprung up so quickly, overwhelming everything that had come before. Only in the last forty years or so had Denver begun to shed its cow town image to become another typical metropolis. He sometimes missed the cow town, though he could still catch glimpses of it. Union Station still stood, the State Capitol of course, and the Victorian mansions in the surrounding neighborhoods. If he squinted, he could remember them in their glory days. Some of the fire from the mining-boom era remained. That was why Rick stayed.

Helen lived a few miles south along the grid of streets around the University of Denver, in a house not quite as old or large as those Victorian mansions, but still an antique in the context of the rest of the city. She'd lived there since the 1950s, when Rick bought her the place. Even then, Denver had been booming. The city was an ever-shifting collage, its landmarks rising and falling, the points around which he navigated subtly changing over the decades.

Points like Helen.

He parked on the street in front of her house, a single-story square cottage, pale blue with white trim, shutters framing the windows, with a front porch and hanging planters filled with multicolored petunias. The lights were off.

For a moment, he stood on the concrete walkway in front and let his more-than-human senses press outward: sight, sound, and taste. The street, the lawn, the house itself were undisturbed. The neighbors were watching television. A block away, an older man walked a large dog. It was all very normal, except that the house in front of him was silent. No one living was inside—he'd have smelled the blood, heard the heartbeat.

When he and Helen became friends, he'd known this day would come. This day always came. But the circumstances here were unnatural. He walked up the stairs to the front door, which was unlocked. Carefully, he pushed inside, stepping around the places on the hardwood floor that creaked, reaching the area rug in the living room. Nothing—furniture, photographs, bookcase, small upright piano in the corner—was out of place. The modernist coffee table, a cone-shaped lamp by a blocky armchair, silk lilies in a cut-crystal vase. They were the decorations of an old woman—out of place, out of time, seemingly preserved. But to Rick it was just Helen, the way she'd always been.

His steps muffled on the rug, he progressed to the kitchen in back. He found her there, lying on the linoleum floor. Long dead—he could tell by her cold skin and the smell of dried blood on the floor.

Standing in the doorway, he could work out what had happened. She'd been sitting at the Formica table, sipping a cup of tea. The cup and saucer were there, undisturbed, along with a bowl of sugar cubes. She must have set the cup down before she fell. When she did fall, it had been violently, knocking the chair over. She had crawled a few feet—not far. She might have broken a hip or leg in the fall—expected, at her age. Flecks of blood streaked the back of her blue silk dress, fanning out from a dark, dime-sized hole. When he took a deep breath, he could smell the fire of gunpowder. She'd been shot in the back, and she had died.

After such a life, to die like this.

So that was that. A more than sixty-year acquaintance ended. Time to say good-bye, mourn, and move on. He'd done it before—often, even. He could be philosophical about it. The natural course of events, and all that. But this was different, and he wouldn't abandon her, even now when it didn't matter. He'd do the right thing—the human thing.

He drew his cell phone from his coat pocket and dialed 911.

"Hello. I need to report a murder."

SHE WALKED THROUGH THE DOORWAY, AND EVERY MAN IN THE PLACE looked at her: the painted red smile, the blue skirt swishing around perfect legs. She didn't seem to notice, walked right up to the bar and pulled herself onto a stool.

"I'll have a scotch, double, on ice," she said.

Rick set aside the rag he'd been using to wipe down the surface and leaned in front of her. "You look like you're celebrating something."

"That's right. You going to help me out or just keep leering?"

Smiling, he found a tumbler and poured her a double and extra.

"I have to ask," Rick said, returning to the bar in front of her, enjoying the way every other man in Murray's looked at him with envy. "What's the celebration?"

"You do have to ask, don't you? I'm just not sure I should tell you."

"It's just not often I see a lady come in here all alone in a mood to celebrate."

Murray's was a working-class place, a dive by the standards of East Colfax; the neighborhood was going downhill as businesses and residents fled downtown, leaving behind everyone who didn't have anyplace to go. Rick had seen this sort of thing happen enough; he recognized the signs. Murray wasn't losing money, but he didn't have anything extra to put into the place. The varnish on the hardwood floor was scuffed off, the furniture was a decade old. Cheap beer and liquor was the norm, and he still had war bond posters up a year and a half after V-J Day. Or maybe he liked the Betty Grable pinups he'd stuck on top of some of them too much to take any of it down.

Blushing, the woman ducked her gaze, which told him something about her. The shrug she gave him was a lot shyer than the brash way she'd walked in here.

"I got a job," she said.

"Congratulations."

"You're not going to tell me that a nice girl like me should find herself a good man, get married, and settle down and make my mother proud?"

"Nope."

"Good." She smiled and bit her lip.

A newcomer in a clean suit came up to the bar, set down his hat, and tossed a couple of bills on the polished wood. Rick nodded at the woman and went to take the order. Business was steady after that, and Rick served second and third rounds to men who'd come in after work and stuck around. New patrons arrived for after-dinner nightcaps. Rick worked through it all, drawing beers and pouring liquor, smiling politely when the older men called him "son" and "kid."

He didn't need the job. He just liked being around people now and then. He'd worked at bars before—bars, saloons, taverns—here and there, for almost two hundred years.

He expected the woman to finish quickly and march right out again, but she sipped the drink as if savoring the moment, wanting to spend time with the crowd. Avoiding solitude. Rick understood.

When a thin, flushed man who'd had maybe one drink too many sidled up to the bar and crept toward her like a cat on the prowl, Rick wasn't surprised. He waited, watching for her signals. She might have been here to celebrate, but she might have been looking for more, and he wouldn't interfere. But the man spoke—asking to buy her another drink—and the woman shook her head. When he pleaded, she tilted her body, turning her back to him. Then he put a hand on her shoulder and another under the bar, on her leg. She shoved.

Then Rick stood before them both. They hesitated midaction, blinking back at him.

"Sir, you really need to be going, don't you?" Rick said.

"This isn't any of your business," the drunk said.

"If the lady wants to be left alone, you should leave her alone." He caught the man's gaze and twisted, just a bit. Put the warning in his voice, used a certain subtle tone, so that there was power in the words. If the man's gaze clouded over, most onlookers would attribute it to the liquor.

The man pointed and opened his mouth as if to speak, but Rick put a little more focus in his gaze and the drunk blinked, confused.

"Go on, now," Rick said.

The man nodded weakly, crushed his hat on his head, and stumbled to the door.

The woman watched him go, then turned back to Rick, her smile wondering. "That was amazing. How'd you do that?"

"You work behind the bar long enough, you develop a way with people."

"You've been bartending a long time, then."

Rick just smiled.

"Thanks for looking out for me," she said.

"Not a problem."

"I really didn't come here looking for a date. I really did just want the drink."

"I know."

"But I wouldn't say no. To a date. Just dinner or a picture or something. If the right guy asked."

So, Rick asked. Her name was Helen.

RICK ANSWERED THE RESPONDING OFFICER'S QUESTIONS, THEN SAT IN THE armchair in the living room to wait for the detective to arrive. It took about forty-five minutes. In the meantime, officers and investigators passed in and out of the house, which seemed less and less Helen's by the moment.

When the detective walked in, Rick stood to greet her. The woman was average height and build, and busy, always looking, taking in the scene. Her dark hair was tied in a short ponytail; she wore a dark suit and white shirt, nondescript. She dressed to blend in, but her air of authority made her stand out.

She saw him and frowned. "Oh hell. It's you."

"Detective Hardin," he answered, amused at how unhappy she was to see him.

Jessi Hardin pointed at him. "Wait here."

He sat back down and watched her continue on to the kitchen.

Half an hour later, coroners brought in a gurney, and Hardin returned to the living room. She pulled over a high-backed chair and set it across from him.

"I expected to see bite marks on her neck."

"I wouldn't have called it in if I'd done it," he said.

"But you discovered the body?"

"Yes."

"And what were you doing here?" She pulled a small notebook and pen from her coat pocket, just like on TV.

"Helen and I were old friends."

The pen paused over the page. "What's that even mean?"

He'd been thinking it would be a nice change, not having to avoid the issue, not having to come up with a reasonable explanation for why he knew what he knew, dancing around the truth that he'd known Helen almost her entire life, even though he looked only thirty years old. Hardin knew what he was. But those half-truths he'd always used to explain himself were harder to abandon than he expected.

With any other detective, he'd have said that Helen was a friend of his grandfather's whom he checked in on from time to time and helped with repairs around the house. But Detective Hardin wouldn't believe that.

"We met in 1947 and stayed friends."

Hardin narrowed a thoughtful gaze. "Just so that I'm clear on this, in 1947 she was what, twenty? Twenty-five? And you were—exactly as you are now?"

"Yes."

"And you stayed friends with her all this time."

"You say it like you think that's strange."

"It's just not what I expect from the stories."

She was no doubt building a picture in her mind: Rick and a twenty-five-year-old Helen would have made a striking couple. But Rick and the ninety-year-old Helen?

"Maybe you should stick to the standard questions," Rick said.

"All right. Tell me what you found when you got here. About what time was it?"

He told her, explaining how the lights were out and the place seemed abandoned. How he'd known right away that something was wrong, and so wasn't surprised to find her in the kitchen.

"She called me earlier today. I wasn't available but she left a message. She sounded worried but wouldn't say why. I came over as soon as I could."

"She knew something was wrong, then. She expected something to happen."

"I think so."

"Do you have any idea why someone would want to kill an old woman like this?"

"Yes," he said. "I do."

ONE NIGHT SHE CAME INTO THE BAR LATE DURING HIS SHIFT. THEY HADN'T set up a date so he was surprised, and then he was worried. Gasping for breath, her eyes pink, she ran up to him, crashing into the bar, hanging on to it as if she might fall over without the support. She'd been crying.

He took up her hands and squeezed. "What's wrong?"

"Oh, Rick! I'm in so much trouble. He's going to kill me, I'm dead, I'm—"

"Helen! Calm down. Take a breath—what's the matter?"

She gulped down a couple of breaths, steadying herself. Straightening, squeezing Rick's hands in return, she was able to speak. "I need someplace to hide. I need to get out of sight for a little while."

She could have been in any kind of trouble. Some small-town relative come to track her down and bring home the runaway. Or she could have been something far different from the fresh-faced city girl she presented herself as. He'd known from the moment he met her that she was hiding something—she never talked about her past.

"What's happened?" he asked.

"I'll tell you everything, just please help me hide."

He came around the bar, put his arm around her, and guided her into the back room. There was a storage closet filled with wooden crates, some empty and waiting to be carried out, some filled with bottles of beer and liquor. Only Rick and Murray came back here when the place was open. He found a sturdy, empty crate, tipped it upside down, dusted it off, and guided her to sit on it.

"I can close up in half an hour, then you can tell me what's wrong. All right?"

Nodding, she rubbed at her nose with a handkerchief.

"Can I get you anything?" he asked. "Bottle of soda? Shot of whiskey?"

"No, no. I'm fine, for now. Thank you."

Back out front, he let his senses expand, touching on every little noise, every scent, every source of light and the way it played around every shadow. Every heartbeat, a dozen of them, rattled in his awareness, a cacophony, like rocks tumbling in a tin can. It woke a hunger in him—a lurking knowledge that he could destroy everyone here, feed on them, sate himself on their blood before they knew what had happened.

He'd already fed this evening—he always fed before coming to work, it was the only way he could get by. It made the heartbeats that composed the background static of the world irrelevant.

No one here was anxious, worried, searching, behaving in any other manner than he would expect from people sitting in a bar half an hour before closing. Most were smiling, some were drunk, all were calm.

That changed ten minutes later when a heavyset man wearing a nondescript suit and weathered fedora came through the door and searched every face. Rick ignored him and waited. Sure enough, he came up to the bar. His heart beat fast, and sweat dampened his armpits and hairline.

"What can I get for you?" Rick asked.

"You see a girl come in here, about this tall, brown hair, wearing a blue dress?" the man said. He was carrying a pistol in a holster under his suit jacket.

Some of the patrons had turned to watch. Rick was sure they'd all seen Helen enter. They were waiting to see how he'd answer.

"No," he said. "Haven't seen her. She the kind of girl who'd come into a place like this by herself?"

"Yeah. I think she is."

"We're past last call. I doubt she'll come in this late. But you're welcome to wait."

"I'll do that."

"Can I get you something?"

"Tonic water."

Rick poured the drink and accepted his coins. The guy didn't tip.

Patrons drifted out as closing time approached, and the heavyset man continued watching the door. He kept his right hand free and his jacket open, giving ready access to the holster. And if he did see Helen walk through the door, would he shoot her then and there? Was he that crazy?

Rick wondered what Helen had done.

When they were the only two left in the bar, Rick said, "I have to close up now, sir. I'm sorry your girl isn't here."

"She's not my girl."

"Well. Whoever she is, she isn't here. You'll have to go."

The man looked at him. "What were you in the war, kid?"

"4-F," Rick said.

He was used to the look the guy gave him. 4-F—medical deferment. Rick appeared to be a fit and able-bodied man in the prime of his life. He must have pulled a fast one on the draft board to get out of the service, and that made him a cheat as well as a coward. He let the assumptions pass by; he'd outlive them all.

"If you don't mind me asking . . ." the guy prompted.

"I'm allergic to sunlight." It was the excuse he'd given throughout the war.

"Huh. Whoever heard of such a thing?" Rick shrugged in response. "You know what I was? Infantry. In Italy. I got shot twice, kid. But I gave more than I got. I'm a hell of a lot tougher than I look."

"I don't doubt it, sir."

The guy wasn't drunk—he smelled of sweat, unlaundered clothes, and aftershave, not alcohol. But he might have been a little bit crazy. He looked like he was waiting for Rick to start a fight.

"If I see this girl, you want me to tell her you're looking for her?" Rick said.

"No. I'm sure she hasn't been anywhere near here." He slid off the stool and tugged his hat more firmly on his head. "You take care, kid."

"You too, sir."

Finally, he left, and Rick locked the door.

He wouldn't have been surprised if he'd returned to the storeroom and found Helen gone—fled, for whatever reason. But she was still there, sitting on the crate in the corner, her knees pulled up to her chest, hugging herself.

"Someone was here looking for you," Rick said.

She jerked, startled—he'd entered too quietly. Even so, she looked like someone who had a man with a gun looking for her.

"Who was he? What'd he look like?" she asked, and Rick described him. Her gaze grew anguished, despairing. "It's Blake. I don't know what to do." She sniffed, wiping her nose as she started crying again. "He'll kill me if he finds me, he'll kill me."

"If you don't mind your coffee bitter, we can finish off what's in the pot and you can tell me all about it." He put persuasion into his voice, to set her at her ease. "I can't help if I don't know what's wrong."

"I don't want to get you involved, Rick."

"Then why did you come here?"

She didn't have an answer for that.

He poured a cup of coffee for her, pressed it into her hands, and waited for her to start.

"I got this job, right? It's a good job, good pay. But sometimes . . . well. I make deliveries. I'm not supposed to ask what's in the packages, I just go where they tell me to go and I don't ask any questions."

"You told me you got a job in a typing pool."

"What was I supposed to do, tell you the truth?"

"No, you're right. It wasn't any of my business. Go on."

"There's a garage out east on Champa—"

"Rough neighborhood."

"I've never had any trouble. Usually I just walk in, set the bag on the shelf, and walk right back out. Today I heard gunshots. I turned around and there's Blake, he'd just shot Mikey—the guy from the garage who picks up the drops—and two other guys with him. He's holding this gun, it's still smoking. He shot them. I didn't know what else to do; there's a back door, so I ran for it, and he saw me, I know he saw me—"

He crouched beside her, took the coffee cup away, and pressed her hands together; they were icy. He didn't have much of his own heat to help warm her with.

"Now he wants to tie off the loose ends," Rick said.

"Of all the stupid timing; if I'd been five minutes earlier I'd have been fine, I wouldn't have seen anything."

Rick might argue that—she'd still be working as a runner for some kind of crime syndicate.

"Have you thought about going to the police? They could probably protect you. If they can lock Blake up you won't have anything to worry about."

"You think it really works like that? I can't go to the cops. They'd arrest me just as fast as they'd arrest him."

"So leave town," Rick said.

"And go where? Do what? With what money?"

"I can give you money," Rick said.

"On a bartender's salary? That'll get me to where, Colorado Springs? No, Rick, I'm not going to ask you for money."

He ducked to hide a smile. Poor kid, thinking she was the only one with big secrets. "But you'll ask me for a place to hide."

"I'm sorry. It's just I didn't know where to go, I don't have any other friends here. And now I've dragged you into it and if Blake finds out he'll go after you, too."

"Helen, don't worry. We'll figure it out." He squeezed her hands, trying to impart some calm. She didn't have any other friends here—that he believed.

"You probably hate me now."

He shrugged. "Not much point to that."

She tilted her head, a gesture of curiosity. "You're different, you know that?"

"Yeah. I do. Look, I know a place where Blake absolutely won't find you. You can stay there for a couple of days. Maybe this'll blow over. Maybe they'll catch Blake. In the meantime, you can make plans. How does that sound?"

"Thanks, Rick. Thanks."

"It's no trouble at all."

ONE OF THE UNIFORMED OFFICERS CAME INTO THE LIVING ROOM TO HAND Hardin a paper cup of coffee. Rick declined the offer of a cup for him.

"So she had a criminal background," Hardin said. "Did she do any time?"

"No," Rick said. "She was a runner, a messenger. Never anything more serious than that."

"Prostitution?"

"No, I don't think so." He was pretty sure he would have known if she had. But he couldn't honestly say what she'd done before he met her. "I know she saw a lot that she probably wasn't supposed to see. She testified in a murder trial."

"You said that was over sixty years ago. Surely anybody who wanted to get rid of a witness is long gone," the detective said.

"You only asked if I knew why someone would want to kill her. That's all I can think of. She didn't have much property, and no family to leave it to even if she did. But I do know that sixty years ago, a few people did have a reason to want her dead."

"Only a vampire would think it reasonable to look into sixty-year-old motives for murder."

He hadn't really thought of it like that, but she was right.

"Do you have any other questions, Detective?"

"What did she do since then? I take it she wasn't still working as a runner."

"She went straight. Worked retail. Retired fifteen years ago or so. She led a very quiet life."

"And you said she doesn't have any family? She never married, had kids?"

"No, she didn't. I think her will has me listed as executor. I can start making arrangements."

She rested her pen again. "Do you think she was lonely?"

"I don't know, Detective. She never told me." He thought she probably was, at least some of the time.

"Well, I'll dig up what I can in the police records, but I'm not sure we even have anything going that far back. You remember anything about that murder trial she testified in?"

"1947," he said. "The man she testified against was Charles Blake. He got a life sentence."

She shook her head. "That still blows my mind. And I suppose you'll tell me you remember it like it was yesterday?"

Rick shook his head. "No. Even I know that was a long time ago."

In fact, he had to think a moment to remember what the Helen of that time had looked like—young, frivolous, hair in curls, dresses hugging her frame. When he thought of Helen, he saw the old woman she had become. He didn't even have any strong feelings about the change—it was just what happened. His mortal friends grew old and died. He preferred that to when they died first.

Many of his kind didn't bother, but Rick still liked being in the world, moving as part of it. Meeting people like Helen. Even if it meant saying good-bye more often.

Hardin's gaze turned thoughtful. "If I were immortal, I'd go see the world. I'd finally learn French."

Rick chuckled; he'd never learned French. "And yet vampires tend to stay in one place. Watch the world change around them."

"So you've been here for five hundred years?"

"Not here in Denver, but here in the West? Yes. And I've seen some amazing things."

"A lot of murders?" she asked.

"A few," he said.

She considered him a long time, pondering more questions, no doubt. In the end, she just shook her head. "I'll call you if I need any more information."

"Of course you will."

She smirked at that.

The police were in the process of sealing the house as a crime scene. Yellow evidence tags were going up, marking spots in the kitchen—the teacup, the table, spots on the floor, the counter. Yellow tape, fluttering in a light breeze, decorated the front porch. Time for Rick to leave, then. Now and forever. He paused for a last look around the living room. Then he was done.

He drove, at first aimlessly, just wanting to think. Then he headed toward the old neighborhoods, the bar on Colfax and the garage on Champa. The shadows of the way they'd been were visible—the outline of a façade, painted over a dozen times in the succeeding years. Half a century's worth of skyscrapers, office complexes, and high-end lofts had risen and fallen around them. The streets had widened, the pavement had improved, the signs had changed. The cars had changed, the clothing people wore had changed, though at this hour he only saw a few young men smoking cigarettes outside a club. None of them wore hats.

If Charles Blake was even alive, he'd still be in prison. Did he have relatives? An accomplice he'd hatched a plan of revenge with? Rick could call the Department of Corrections, talk them into releasing any information about Blake. Just to tie off that loose end and finish Helen's story in his own mind.

Or he could let Detective Hardin do her job. Hardin was right, and Helen's sixty-year-old criminal life probably had nothing to do with her death. It might have been an accidental shooting. Some gang misfiring on a drive-by. Anything was possible, absolutely anything. Hardin didn't need his help to find out what.

Time to let Helen go.

He brought her to Arturo's.

Arturo was the master vampire of Denver, which meant he made the rules, and any vampire who wanted to live in his territory had to live by those rules. And Rick did, mostly. What he didn't agree to was living under Arturo's roof as one of his dozen or so minions. Instead, Rick kept to himself, lived how he wanted, didn't draw attention, and didn't challenge Arturo's authority outright, so Arturo let him have his autonomy. A lot of the other vampires thought Rick was eccentric—even for a vampire—and he was all right with that. In the meantime, Arturo's was the one place in the city Blake would never find Helen.

Arturo owned a squat brick building east of downtown. The ground floor housed a furniture dealer who did sporadic business, but his real work was deflecting attention from the basement. Underground, away from windows and sunlight, the city's vampires lived and ran their little empire.

He walked Helen the dozen blocks from Murray's bar to the furniture store, his arm protectively across her shoulder. She huddled against his body, glancing outward fearfully. Blake would never find them, not the way he moved, casting shadows, pulling her into his influence. But she didn't know that.

In the back of the furniture shop, a concrete staircase led down, below the street level, to a nondescript door. Rick knocked.

"Blake won't find you here," he said.

"I trust you," she said. She was still looking up the stairs, as if she expected Blake to appear, gun in hand.

What he really ought to do was put her on a train back to whatever town she came from. Tell her to find a good husband and settle down. Instead, he was bringing her here, and she trusted him.

The door opened, and Rick faced the current gatekeeper, a young woman in a straight silk dress ten years out of date, not that she would notice. Estelle hadn't been above ground during most of that time.

Helen stared. To her, Estelle would look like a girl dressing up in her mother's cast-off clothes, the skirt too long and the neckline too high.

"Hello, Estelle. I just need a room for a couple of nights."

"Is Arturo expecting you?" she said, looking Helen up and down, probably drawing conclusions.

"No. But I don't think he'll mind. Do you?"

Pouting, she opened the door and let them in.

The hallway within was carpeted and dimly lit with a pair of shaded bulbs.

"Is he in his usual spot?" Rick asked over his shoulder.

"Sure. He's even in a good mood."

Helen looked to him for an explanation. He just guided her on, through the doorway at the end of the corridor and into a wide room.

The place had the atmosphere of a turn-of-the-century lounge, close and warm, dense with subdued colors and rich fabrics, Persian rugs, and velvet wall hangings. One of Arturo's dozen minions, Angelo, a young hothead, was smoking, purposefully drawing breath into his lungs and blowing it out again—breathing for no other reason than to smoke. It wasn't as if the tobacco had any effect on him. Maybe he liked watching the smoke. Or maybe it was just habit. He was only a century old.

Most of Arturo's vampires were young to Rick's eyes. Then again, just about everyone was.

Sated with the human blood that kept them alive, they'd most likely been discussing the evening's exploits. Their latest mode of hunting involved finding a dinner party, inviting themselves over, mesmerizing the whole group, and then having a taste of everyone. They didn't kill or turn anyone, which would draw too much attention, and the group would wake up in the morning thinking they'd had a marvelous—if strange—evening. Rick sometimes suggested to Arturo that he should open a restaurant or club and let the party come to him.

Arturo—by all accounts dashing, with golden hair swept back from a square face—lay in a wingback armchair, legs draped over one of its arms. He looked at Rick and raised his brows in surprise. "What have you brought for us, Ricardo?"

The dozen vampires, men and women, straightened, perking up to look at Helen like a pack of wolves.

"She needs a place to stay," Rick said. "She's under my protection."

"Ricardo?" Helen whispered to him, and he hushed her.

"I'd just like to use the spare room for a couple of nights, if that's all right."

The young man—he looked to be in his midtwenties, a little younger than Rick appeared—considered, tapping a finger against a chin. "Certainly. Why not?"

"Thanks."

His arm still around her shoulders, he turned Helen back to the hallway, where he opened the first door on the right and guided her inside.

"Rick? What is this place, some kind of boardinghouse?"

"Sort of."

"Who are all those people?"

The room was absolutely dark. Helen gasped when he closed the door behind her. "Rick?"

He didn't need to see to find the floor lamp in the corner and turn it on.

The room had a double bed with a mass of pillows and a quilted satin comforter, an oak dresser, the lamp, and not much else. The place was for sleeping out the day and storing clothing. A rug on the hardwood floor muffled footsteps.

Helen stared. "It's a brothel. You've brought me to a brothel."

If he argued with her, he'd have to explain, which he wanted to avoid.

"Do you mind?" he said. "I could find somewhere else."

She hesitated before shaking her head and saying, "No. It's okay. As long as it isn't one of Blake's."

"It's not."

She squared her shoulders a little more firmly, as if steeling herself. "I think maybe I'm ready for that drink you offered earlier."

"I'll have to go back to the parlor for it. You mind waiting here?"

"I'll be fine," she said, wearing a brave smile.

He left the room, and Arturo was waiting in the hallway, leaning against the wall, his arms crossed.

"Ricardo."

"Arturo," he answered.

"You brought her here because you want to hide her. Why?"

"She's in trouble."

"What kind of trouble?"

"The straightforward kind. In over her head with the wrong people."

"Small-town girl trying to make it in the city?"

"Something like that."

"Hmm. Quaint. Well, I'm always happy to do a good deed for a pretty girl. But you owe me a favor now, yes?"

Rick ducked his gaze to hide a smile. He handled Arturo by letting him think he was in charge. "That's how it usually works, yes."

"Excellent."

"I assume the alcohol cabinet is included in the favor?"

"What? You're having to get your girls drunk first now?" Arturo said in mock astonishment.

"Thank you, Arturo." Rick slipped around him and into the parlor.

He returned to the room with a tumbler of ice and a bottle of whiskey. Helen was on the bed. Her jacket was off and lying on the dresser, her shoes were tossed in a corner, and she was peeling off her stockings. Rick started to apologize and back out of the room again, when she called him over.

"I'm sorry, I just wanted to get comfortable since I'm going to be here awhile," she said.

He set the tumbler on the dresser and poured a finger.

"Ricardo, is it?" she said. "Are you Mexican? Because you don't look Mexican."

"Spanish," he said. "At least, if you go back far enough."

"Spanish, hm? That's romantic."

He handed her the whiskey, which she sipped, smiling at him over the glass. "You only brought one glass. Don't you want any?"

"I'm fine," he said.

"Will you sit here with me?"

This was a turning point. He'd been in enough situations like it to recognize it. "Helen, I didn't bring you here to take advantage."

"Despite the bed and this being a brothel?" Her smile turned wry.

"You really will be safe here," he said, though his protestations were starting to sound weak. Truth be told, he wanted to sit by her, and his lips grew flush from wanting to press against her skin.

She'd touched up her lipstick while he was gone. The top button of her blouse was undone, the hem of her skirt lay around her knees, and her legs were bare. She thought she was seducing him. But as soon as he sat on that bed, she wouldn't be in control of the situation. She didn't know that. And if he played it right, she never would know. So. What was the right thing to do, really?

She drained the whiskey and patted the bed next to her—right next to her—and he sat. He laid his arm across the headboard behind her, and she pressed herself against him.

"I don't meet a lot of nice guys, working the way I do. You're a nice guy, Rick."

"If you say so."

"Yeah, I do."

Pressing her hand to his cheek, she drew him close and kissed him on the mouth. She was eager, insistent. Who was he to deny her? She tasted of whiskey and heat, alive and lovely. He drew the tumbler from her hand and set it on the floor, then returned to kissing her, wrapping his arms around her, trapping her. She scratched at the buttons on his shirt.

The fire that rose up in him in response wasn't sexual. It was hunger. A visceral, primal, gnawing hunger, as if he hadn't eaten in centuries. His only nourishment, his only possible release, lay under her skin. If he let that monster go, he would tear into her, spilling her over the bed, swimming in her innards to better feed on her blood.

There was a better way.

He worked slowly, carefully, kissing across her mouth and jaw, sucking at her ear as she gasped, then moving down her neck, tracing a collarbone, unfastening her blouse button by button, pulling aside her brassiere to gain access to a perfect handful of breast. She wriggled, reaching back to unfasten the whole contraption. When he'd first encountered the modern brassiere, he'd thought it was so much easier than a corset. But the undergarment had its own idiosyncrasies. And like undoing corsets always did, it gave them both a chance to giggle.

She sat up enough to yank at his shirt, and he let her pull it off and throw it aside. Then, once again, he pressed her to the bed and took control, peeling away her clothing—the girdle and garters were more pieces of modern clothing he was still coming to terms with—and running his cool hands over every burning inch of her, kissing as he went. Only after she came for him did he take what he needed, from a small and careful bite at her throat.

Her blood was ecstasy.

Her heart, aroused and racing, pumped a strong flow for him. He could have drained her in moments, but took in only a few mouthfuls. Not enough to completely satisfy, but enough to keep him alive for a couple more days. Vampires had learned this long ago—how much more efficient to keep them alive and producing. And how much richer to coax it from them, instead of spilling it.

He licked the wound, encouraging the blood to clot. She'd gone limp, and her breathing had settled. Propping himself over her, he turned her face so that he was looking straight down at her. Her eyes were wide, pupils dilated. Her brow was furrowed, her expression both amazed and confused. Maybe even hurt. Holding her gaze, he focused on her, *into* her, and spoke softly.

"You won't remember this. You'll remember the bliss and nothing else. I'm just a man, just a lover, and you won't remember anything else. Isn't that right?" Slowly, she nodded. Her worried expression, the wrinkles around her eyes, faded. "Good, Helen. Remember the good, let the rest go. Now, sleep. Sleep until I wake you up again."

Her eyes closed, and she let out a sigh.

Dawn had nearly arrived. The room had no windows, but he could feel it. The warm and sated glow that came after feeding joined with the lethargy of daylight. He was safe and calm, so he let the morning pull him under until he fell unconscious, still holding her hand.

THE NEXT NIGHT, RICK HAD A MESSAGE FROM DETECTIVE HARDIN WAITING for him. He called back immediately.

"Hello, Rick?" she said. "Do you even have a last name?"

"Have you found something, Detective?" he said.

"Yeah. Charles Blake? I looked him up. Not only is he still alive, he got out on parole four months ago."

The air seemed to go still for a moment, and sounds faded as he pulled his awareness to a tiny space around him—the phone, what Hardin had just told him, how that made him feel. Cold, tight, hands clenching, a predator's snarl tugging at his lips.

He drew a couple of calm breaths to steady himself, and to be able to speak to the detective. "You think he killed her?"

"I think he hired someone to do it for him. He might have collected favors in prison and called them in when he got out. Guy was a real peach, from what I gather. I can't go into too many details, but the crime scene is pretty slim on evidence, which speaks to someone with experience. The back door was unlocked. We think he might have come to see her earlier in the day. That must have been when she called you."

How small, how petty, to carry a grudge over such a length of time. How like a vampire. And yet, how human as well. That grudge might very well have kept Blake alive all this time.

"How are you doing?" she asked. "This must come as a shock to you."

It sounded like something she said to any victim's family. He smiled to think she'd next offer to refer him to grief counseling. "I'm all right, Detective. It wasn't a shock. I've been expecting this for sixty years. About Blake—do you know where he is? Have you arrested him?"

"I'm afraid I can't discuss an ongoing investigation any further. I just thought you'd want to know about Blake."

"Thank you. I appreciate it."

They both hung up, and he considered. He could find Blake. He'd be an old man now, ancient. Not much to live for, after spending most of his life in prison. He'd exacted his revenge, and Rick didn't think he'd spend a lot of time trying to get out of town or hide. And this was Rick's city, now.

Detective Hardin hadn't arrested Blake yet because she was building her case, searching for evidence, obtaining warrants. Rick had every confidence that she'd do her job to the utmost of her ability and that through her, justice would be served.

In this case, he wasn't interested in waiting.

After killing Arturo and replacing him as master of Denver, Rick had transformed the lair. The parlor was now an office, with functional sofas and a coffee table, and a desk and bookshelves for work. He paced around the desk and considered. Blake would have a parole officer who would know where he was. The man might even be living in some kind of halfway house for ex-cons. After so long in prison, it was doubtful he had any family or friends left. He had no place else to go. And if he was right about Blake's state of mind, the man wouldn't even be hiding.

He flipped through a ledger and found a name, recently entered. A woman who'd run a prostitution ring in the seventies—with blackmail on the side. She'd served her time, she knew the system, and she owed him a favor.

"Hello, Carol. It's Rick. I need to know who the parole officer is for a recently released felon."

NIGHT FELL, AND RICK WOKE.

Helen had turned over on her side and curled up, pressing against him, her hands on his arm. She looked sweet and vulnerable.

He leaned over and breathed against her ear. "Wake up, Helen."

Her eyes opened. Pulling away from him, she sat up, looking dazed, as if trying to remember where she was and how she'd gotten here. Her clothes were hanging off her, loose, and her hair was in tangles.

"You all right?" he asked.

She glared. "Did you put something in my drink?"

"No."

She looked herself over, retrieving her clothes, fastening buttons, and running fingers through her hair. Wryly, she said, "You never even took your trousers off, did you?"

He answered her smile. "Never mind. As long as you're all right."

"Yeah, I'm fine. More than fine. You're something else, Rick, you know that?"

"There's a washroom across the hall."

"What time is it?"

"Nightfall," he said. "I'm about to head to Murray's to see if Blake shows up. You should stay here."

She closed up at the mention of Blake, slouching and hugging herself. He smoothed her hair back and left a gentle kiss on her forehead.

"I'll be safe here?" she asked.

"Yes. I promise."

"What happens if Blake does show up? What can you possibly do? Rick, if he hurts you because of me—"

"It'll be fine, Helen."

He washed up, found a clean shirt, ran a comb through his hair, and left the lair.

Blake did, in fact, show up at the bar that night. Rick kept his place behind the taps and watched him scan the room before choosing a seat near the bar.

"Bourbon," he muttered. Rick poured and pushed the tumbler over.

Scowling, Blake drained the liquor in one go. After some time, when it was clear Helen wasn't going to appear, he set his stare on Rick, who didn't have any trouble pretending not to notice. Leaning on his elbow, Blake pushed back his jacket to show off his gun in its shoulder holster.

"So. Did she ever show up?" the man said.

"Who? The girl?"

"You know who I'm talking about."

"Can I ask why you're looking for her?"

"I just want to talk to her. We can work something out. You know where she's hiding, don't you?"

"Sir, I really can't help you."

Blake narrowed his gaze, looking him up and down—sizing him up, and Rick knew what he was thinking. He was thinking he was looking at a wimp, a coward, a young guy who'd sat out the war, who'd be easy to take down in a fight. Blake was thinking all he'd have to do was wave the gun around, break his nose, and he'd take him right to Helen because no broad was worth sticking up for like that.

Rick smiled, knowing it would make him crazy. Blake scowled and walked out.

Rick had the rest of the night mapped out. He knew what would happen next, how it would all play, a bit of urban theater, predictable yet somehow satisfying. Last call came and went; he offered to close up. After locking the doors, he set chairs upside down on tables, gave the floor a quick sweeping and the bar a wipe down, turned out all the lights, and went out the back, where Blake was waiting for him.

Blake lunged from the shadows with a right hook, obviously intending to take Rick out in a second and keep him from gaining his bearings.

Rick sidestepped out of the way. Blake stumbled, and Rick pivoted, grabbing Blake's shirt, yanking him further off balance, then swinging him headfirst into the wall. The man slid to the ground, limbs flailing for purchase, scrabbling at Rick, the wall, anything. The sequence took less than a second—Blake wouldn't have had a chance to realize his right hook had missed. He must have thought the world turned upside down.

Wrenching Blake's arm back, Rick dragged him a dozen feet along the pavement in the back alley. The shoulder joint popped; Blake hollered. With a flick of the same injured arm, Rick flipped Blake faceup—bloody scrapes covered his cheek and jaw. Jumping on him, Rick pinned him, holding him with strength rather than weight—Blake was the larger man. He brought his face close to smell the rich, sweet fluid leaking from him. Rick could drain the man dead.

A floodlight filled the alley, blinding even Rick, who shaded his eyes with a raised arm. Squinting, he needed a moment to make out the scene: a police car had pulled into the alley.

"You two! Break it up!" a man shouted from the driver's-side window.

Climbing to his feet, Rick held up his hands. Next to him, Blake was still scrambling to recover, scratching at the cut on his face, shaking his head like a cave creature emerging into the open.

The cop had a partner, who stormed out of the passenger side and came at them, nightstick in hand. He shoved Rick face first to the brick wall and patted him down. "What's this? A couple of drunks duking it out?"

Rick didn't speak and didn't react. He could have fought free, stunned the officer, and disappeared into the shadows. But he waited, curious.

"What have you got there?" the driver asked.

"A couple of drunks. Should we bring 'em in?"

"Wait a minute—that guy on the ground. Is that Charles Blake?"

The cop grabbed Blake by the collar and dragged him into the light.

"That's it, bring 'em both in."

Rick rode in the back of the squad car next to Blake, trying to decide if he should be amused or concerned. Dawn was still a few hours away. He had time to watch this play out. Blake was hunched over, breathing wetly, glancing at Rick every now and then to glare at him.

Within the hour, Rick was sitting in a bare, dank interrogation room, talking to a plainclothes detective, a guy named Simpson. He lit a cigarette and offered one to Rick, who declined.

He said, "You were picked up fighting with Charles Blake behind Murray's."

"That's right," Rick answered.

"You want to tell me why?"

Rick leaned back and crossed his arms. "I expected to be thrown in the drunk tank when I got here, but you're interested in Blake. Can I ask why?"

"What do you know about him?"

"He's been bothering a girl I know."

"Your girl?" Rick shrugged, and the detective flicked ashes on the floor. "That's why you were beating on him? I don't suppose I can blame you for that."

"Is Blake dangerous?"

"Do you think he is?"

"Yes," Rick said.

The detective studied him, but Rick didn't give much away. If he needed to, he could catch the man's eye and talk him into letting Rick go. It would certainly come to that if he was still here close to dawn.

Finally, the detective said, "You're right. He's the primary suspect in a murder case. You have anything else about him you want to share?"

This gave Rick an idea. "I might know someone who can help you."

"*If* I let you go—I know how that works."

"I'm the bartender at Murray's—I won't disappear on you."

"And how good is this information of yours?"

"Worth the wait, I think."

"You know what? You're a little too cagey for a bartender. Is that all you do?"

Rick chuckled. "Right now it is."

"I need evidence to lay on Blake if we're going to keep him locked up—and keep him away from your girlfriend. Can you help me out?"

"Stop by Murray's tomorrow night and I'll have an answer."

The detective let him go.

Rick knew he'd be followed—for a time, at least. He returned to Arturo's by a roundabout route and managed to vanish, at least from his tail's point of view.

Helen was waiting for him in the parlor, sitting with Arturo on a burgundy velvet settee. Rick calmed himself a moment and didn't instantly leap forward to put himself between them. She was smiling, and Arturo wasn't doing anything but talking.

"Ricardo! I was hoping you wouldn't return, and that you'd left Helen here with us."

Helen giggled—she held an empty tumbler. They'd probably been at this for hours.

"Thanks for entertaining her for me," Rick said.

"My pleasure. Really."

"Helen, we need to talk," Rick said, gesturing to the doorway.

"Your friend's a charmer, Rick," she said.

"Yes, he is. Let's go."

She pushed herself from the seat. Glancing over her shoulder, she waved fingers at him, and Arturo answered with an indulgent smile. Rick put an arm over her shoulder and guided her into the safe room.

"Don't be angry," she said. "I needed to ask him if there was a phone."

"Who did you need to call?"

"The police," she said, and ducked her gaze. "I didn't want you to get hurt, so I called the police and told them there might be trouble at Murray's."

And there was trouble, and the police had shown up.

"I'd almost taken care of Blake when the police arrived," he said. He didn't say, *You should have trusted me.*

She paled. "What happened?"

"He's in jail now, but he's not going to stay there unless they get some proof that he committed those murders. They know he did it, they just don't have evidence."

She paced back and forth along the foot of the bed. Her shoulders tightened, and she hugged herself.

"I think you should go talk to them, Helen. You can testify, Blake will go to prison, and he won't bother you again. You'll be safe."

"I can't do that, Rick. I can't say anything. He'll kill me, he'll—"

"Not if he's in prison."

"But what if he gets out? The first thing he'll do is come after me."

"I'll kill him first," Rick said.

"Rick, no. I don't want you to get in trouble over me. I don't even know why you're looking out for me, you barely know me—"

"I'm doing it because I can," he said. "But if you go to the police, they'll take care of Blake."

She moved close, pressing herself to him, wrapping her arms around him, and resting her head on his chest. This again. She was so close, he could hear blood pouring through her veins, near the surface. She was flushed and so warm. He rubbed his face along her hair, gathering that warmth to him.

"Helen," he said with something like despair.

"What's the matter?" she said.

"I'm not . . . right for you. This is dangerous—"

"Why?" She stepped away. "What's up with you? You're so nice, but you're not afraid of Blake, and you keep talking like I ought to be afraid of you. What aren't you telling me?"

Such a large answer to that question. He shifted her, so that he could see her face, trace the soft skin of her jaw, then drop to trace the pulse on her neck. He should send her to sleep and make her forget all this. He never should have taken her on that first date. And life was too long for that kind of regret. It didn't matter how immortal you were, you still needed friends.

"Have you ever read *Dracula*?" he said.

"What, like Bela Lugosi?"

"Not quite like. But yes."

"Yeah, ages ago. I like the movie better."

"Vampires exist. They're real."

She chuckled. "Sorry?"

He took her hand and placed it on his chest, where his dead heart lay still. "What do you feel?"

Her smile fell. She moved her hand, pressing it flat to his chest, his ribs digging into her palm. She stared at him. "What am I supposed to say? Tell you you're crazy?"

"Lie still," he said.

"What?"

He sat her on the bed, stacked up the pillows, and forced her back so that she reclined against them. He kissed her, and she kissed back, enthusiastic if confused. Taking in her scent, her warmth, and the feel of her blood, he let the appetite grow in him.

Planting a final kiss on her neck, he held her hand and drew her arm straight before him. No hypnotism this time, no shrouding her memory. Let her see what he was. He put his lips to her elbow—more kisses, slow and tender, tracing her veins with his tongue. She let out a moan.

He sucked on her wrist, drawing blood to the surface.

"Rick? What are you doing? Rick?"

"I said lie still." He pushed her back to the pillow and returned his attention to her wrist.

Finally, he bit, and she gasped. But she lay still.

Her blood was not as sweet as it might have been—she was too wary. But it was still sweet, and she didn't panic, and when he licked the wound closed and glanced at her, her gaze was clear. Uncertain, but clear. He was relieved. He folded her arms across her belly, wrapping her in an embrace, her head pillowed on his shoulder. She melted against him.

"I don't understand," she whispered.

"I don't expect you to. But do you trust me to look after you if Blake goes free?"

She nodded. He kissed her hair and waited for her to fall asleep.

Rick brought her to Murray's the next night, and Detective Simpson was waiting for them. Her hands were trembling, but Rick stayed close to her, and she stood tall and spoke clearly. Simpson promised she wouldn't be charged with any of the petty crimes she'd committed, in exchange for her testimony. The case against Blake went to trial, and Helen was the prosecution's star witness. Blake was convicted and sent away for a long, long time. Rick was sure he'd never see the guy again.

He only needed a little digging—a visit to a parole office, some obfuscation and inveigling, a deep look into an informant's eyes—to learn which halfway house Blake was staying at, east of downtown. He drove there with a single-minded intensity. He wasn't often wrong these days, but he'd been wrong about Blake, and he'd failed Helen. Petty revenge wouldn't make that right. But it might help tip the scales back in the right direction.

The house was back from the street, run-down and lit up, and gave no outward sign of what it was. Rick wondered if the neighbors knew. He parked his car on the curb, stuck his hands in his pockets, and headed to the front door.

The house pressed outward against him; his steps slowed. The place was protected—he wasn't sure it would be, given its nature, and the fact that people were always moving in and out. Did that make it a public institution, or a home? But here was his answer—this was a home. He couldn't enter without invitation. By the time he reached the front door, the force was a wall, invisible; he could almost press his hands against it—but not through it.

Well. He'd have to try normal, mundane bluffing, wouldn't he?

He knocked on the door. A shadow passed over the peephole, and a voice called, "Who is it? What do you want?"

"My name is Rick. I'm an old friend of Charles Blake, and I heard he was here. Can I see him?"

"Do you know what time it is?"

"Yes—sorry about that. I just got off work. Bartender."

"Just a minute. I'll get him."

"Mind if I wait inside?"

After a brief, wary moment of waiting, the deadbolt clicked back, and the door opened. A gruff man in his forties stood aside and held the door. "Come on in."

Rick did.

The living room was worn and sad, with threadbare furniture and carpets, stained walls, a musty air. A bulletin board listed rules, notices, want ads, warnings. The atmosphere was institutional, but this might have been the first real home some of these men had known. Halfway house, indeed.

"Stay right here," the man said, and walked to a back hallway.

Rick waited, hands in pockets.

The doorman returned after a long wait, what would have been many beats of his heart, if it still beat. Behind him came a very old man, pulling a small oxygen tank on a cart behind him. Tubes led from it to his nose, and his every breath wheezed. Other than that, he had faded. He was smaller than the last time Rick had seen him, withered and sunken, skin like putty hanging off a stooped frame. Wearing a T-shirt and ratty, faded jeans, he looked sad, beaten. The scowl remained—Rick recognized that part of him.

The old man saw him and stopped. They were two ghosts staring at each other across the room.

"Hello, Blake," Rick said.

"Who are you? You his grandson?"

Rick turned to the middle-aged doorman and stared until he caught the man's gaze. "Would you mind leaving us alone for a minute?" He put quiet force into the suggestion. The man walked back into the hallway.

"Bill—Bill! Come back!" Blake's sandpaper voice broke into coughing.

"I'm not his grandson," Rick said.

"What is this?"

"Tell me about Helen, Blake."

He coughed a laugh, as if he thought this was a joke. Rick just stared at him. He didn't have to put any power in it. His standing there was enough. Blake's jaw trembled.

"What about her? Huh? What about her!"

Rick grabbed the tube hanging at Blake's chest and yanked, pulling it off his face. Blake stumbled back, his mouth open to show badly fitted dentures coming loose. Wrapping both hands in Blake's shirt, Rick marched him into the wall, slamming him, slamming again, listening for the crack of breaking bone.

"You thought no one would know," Rick whispered at him, face to face. "You thought no one would remember." Blake sputtered, flailing weakly, ineffectually.

The front door crashed open. "Stop!"

Rick recognized the footfalls, voices, and the sounds of their breathing. Detective Hardin pounded in, flanked by two uniformed officers. Rick glanced over his shoulder—she was pointing a gun at him. Not that it mattered. He shoved his fists against Blake's throat.

Blake was dying under his grip. Rick wouldn't have to flex a muscle to kill him. He didn't even feel an urge to take the man's blood—it would be cool, sluggish, unappetizing. Rick would spit it back out in the man's face.

He could do it all with Hardin watching, because what could the detective really do in the end?

"Rick! Back away from him!"

Hardin fumbled in her jacket pocket and drew out a cross, a simple version, two bars of unadorned silver soldered together. Proof against vampires. Rick smiled.

Blake had to have known he wouldn't get away with murdering Helen. What had he been thinking? What had he wanted, really? Rick looked at him: the wide, yellowing eyes, the sagging face, pockmarked and splashed with broken capillaries. He expected to see a death wish there, a determined fatalism. But Blake was afraid. Rick terrified him. The man, his body failing around him, didn't want to die.

This made Rick want to strangle him even more. To justify the man's terror. But he let Blake go and backed away, leaving him to Hardin's care.

The old man sank to his knees, knocking over the oxygen canister. He held his hands before him, clawed and trembling.

"He's dead! Dead! He has to be dead! He has to be!" He was sobbing.

Maybe leaving him on his knees and crying before the police was revenge enough.

Rick, hands raised, backed out of the line of fire. "I could have saved you some paperwork, Detective."

"You'd just have forced me into a whole other set of paperwork. What the hell did you think you were doing?"

The uniforms had to pick up Blake and practically drag him away. They didn't bother with cuffs. Blake didn't seem to know what was happening. His mouth worked, his breaths wheezed, his legs stumbled.

"I take it you got your evidence," Rick said.

"We found the shooter, and he talked. Blake hired him."

He certainly didn't look like he'd pulled any triggers in a good long time.

"So that's it?"

"What else do you want?"

"I wanted to get here five minutes earlier," he said. Not that any of it really mattered. It all faded from the memories around him.

"I need to ask you to depart the premises," she said. She wasn't aiming the gun at him, but she hadn't put it away. "Don't think I won't arrest you for something, because I will. I'll come up with something."

Rick nodded. "Have a good night, Detective."

He returned to his car and left the scene, marking the end of yet another chapter.

RICK HADN'T BEEN ABLE TO ATTEND THE TRIAL, BUT HE'D MET WITH HELEN every night to discuss the proceedings. She came to Murray's, tearing up with relief and rubbing her eyes with her handkerchief, to report the guilty verdict. He quit his shift early and took her back to his place, a basement apartment on Capitol Hill. With Blake locked up, he felt safe bringing her here. He owned the building, rented out the upper portion through an agency, and could block off the windows in the basement without drawing attention. The décor was simple—a bed, an armchair, a chest of drawers, a radio, and a kitchen that went unused.

They lay together on the bed, his arm around her, holding her close, while she nestled against him. They talked about the future, which was always an odd topic for him. Helen had decided to look for an old-fashioned kind of job and aim for a normal life this time.

"But I don't know what to do about you," she said, craning her neck to look up at him.

He'd been here before, lying with a woman he liked, who with a little thought and nudging he could perhaps be in love with, except that what they had would never be entirely mutual, or equitable. And he still didn't know what to say. *I could take from you for the rest of your life, and you'd end with . . . nothing.*

He said, "If you'd like, I can vanish, and you'll never see me again. It might be better that way."

"I don't want that. But I wish . . ." Her face puckered, brow furrowed in thought. "But you're not ever going to take me on a trip, or stay up to watch the sunrise with me, or ask me to marry you, or anything, are you?"

He shook his head. "I've already given you everything I can."

Except for one thing. But he hadn't told her that he could infect her, make her like him, that she too could live forever and never see a sunrise. And he wouldn't.

"It's enough," she said, hugging him. "At least for now, it's enough."

THE LADY IS A SCREAMER

by Conn Iggulden

Historical novelist Conn Iggulden is the author of the bestselling Emperor series—*The Gates of Rome*, *The Death of Kings*, *The Field of Swords*, and *The Gods of War*—detailing the life of Julius Caesar, as well as the Conqueror series—*Wolf of the Plains*, *Lords of the Bow*, *Bones of the Hills*, and *Empire of Silver*—exploring the life of Genghis Khan. He is also the coauthor of the bestselling nonfiction books *The Dangerous Book for Boys* and *The Dangerous Book of Heroes*, as well as *Tollins: Explosive Tales for Children*. His most recent book, written with Lizzy Duncan, is *Tollins 2: Dynamite Tales*.

In the flamboyant story that follows, he takes us on the road with a raffish con man who discovers a new profession—ghostbuster—but who learns that *some* ghosts are harder to bust than others.

I SUPPOSE I THINK OF MYSELF AS RUNNING A SMALL BUSINESS, PROVIDING a necessary service. I'm just one of a hundred million guys, paying the bills with the talents God gave them. I don't have a fancy name for what I do. I'm not a stage magician and to be honest, the kind of clients I get aren't impressed by that sort of thing. If I called myself Afterlife Inc., or something, well, it wouldn't get my car there any faster. Not that car. I'm part of the backbone of America, my friend. Anyway, out of the four of us I'm the only one drawing a salary, so my costs are pretty low.

I started this to make a record of a few odd years, but I'm not really interested in passing on my pearls of wisdom. Not so someone else can wade through this kind of crap on a daily basis. If I had kids, I wouldn't recommend it as a line of work, you know? It was all right in the beginning, when it was just checking the obits and knocking on doors. Everyone wants to say a few last words to the recently departed. If you're interested, the number one choice was "Sorry," closely followed by second prize: "I should have told you I loved you more often," and my personal favorite, which was always some variation on "Are you happy?" No, my dear grieving widow with the sprayed hair still up from the funeral, he's *dead*, of course he's not happy. I'll admit I hadn't the first idea back then whether he was happy or not. I know a bit more these days, but I'll get to that. I just used to assure her that poor Brian was just fine, that he missed her and he was looking forward to seeing her in heaven. If I handled it right, I'd also get a couple of juicy hits. Sure, as I'm already talking, I'll tell you. Hits are when you get a detail right that they think you couldn't possibly know. "He says he remembers that time in the Maldives, does that mean anything to you?" It's a golden moment and you never get tired of watching the last trace of cynicism drain away from them. All it takes is a couple of Barnum statements and a little research.

Maybe I do have a little knowledge worth passing on, at that. P. T. Barnum made them famous, but it all started with a lecturer named Forer, back in the forties. I can start the list from memory, so here it is:

"You have a great need for others to like and admire you. You have a tendency to be critical of yourself. While you have some personality weaknesses, you are generally able to compensate for them. At times you have serious doubts as to whether you have made the right decision or done the right thing." And so on. You get it? They apply to everyone. Couple a few of those to some personal research and you have a cold reading they'll remember forever.

They never think I could do some actual work before turning up at the door. The Internet is good for that, though my favorite was the old microfiches they had in libraries. Newspaper records were useful, but the gold was often in court records and voting rolls. It's all public. These days, half the people I read about are still the Google and microfiche crowd—too old to have heard of Facebook. The rest are low-hanging fruit. Facebook don't dump a page for about a week after a death and their privacy policy is, well, the difference between me scoring and not, most of the time. You'd be amazed what you can find out in ten minutes.

You only need one proper hit and it's all they remember when you're gone. You're in their house and you're reading like crazy, taking in every tiny detail. With the old ladies, you ask to go to the bathroom and you check the meds. I had a lovely one at the beginning when I found a collection of insulin bottles and needle packets. I checked her name on the unopened boxes, then all I had to say was, "John says to remember your injections," and she was a goner, full-blown tears like it would never stop. When it was over, I'd made a sweet two hundred for an hour, including the drive. I think it was then I realized I didn't really need to go back to work. I could do it full-time.

It didn't work out exactly the way I wanted, not at first. That day's pay was more than I saw again in a month of trying, but I had to learn the trade and I made enough to keep me going. I could do the research in local libraries, which cost me nothing.

Well, this story isn't going the way I thought it would. As I seem to be passing on my years of wisdom after all, I'm going to tell you the best bit and let you judge if your job is anywhere near as much fun. Are you ready? This is the good part. If you work for a sandwich shop, you'll never starve. If you visit widows, you get a surprising amount of postfuneral sex. There is no greater aphrodisiac than grief. From experience, I can tell you Day Three is the winner, just when all the relatives have finally asked each other to let her mourn in peace, meaning they really want to get back to their own lives.

I can tell the best ones almost as soon as they open the door, sometimes just by reading the obituary. Big, strong husband gone too soon, sons who live in a different state. Those girls are like pressure cookers, all that raw emotion just waiting to blow. I'm telling you, just seeing the word *cancer* gave me a rush of blood after a while. Nothing gets the juices going like a long dry spell. Bless their hearts for trying, but cancer guys aren't up to much in the sack.

It all went wrong, or went right, or changed my world, however the hell you want to say it, when I met the Lady. I still don't know her name, and if she can talk, she never does to me. It's usually my curse that I have to deal with women every day. They're the ones who don't mind finding a fifty in the purse for a few words and my best soft voice. I can't say I don't understand them, like some rummy guy in a bar you might meet. I do understand them. I just don't like them all that much. They don't think like us, you know? If it wasn't for money and sex, I don't think I'd talk to them at all. Crazy, every last one of them. I grew up with a strict mom, and maybe she turned me against them all, I don't know. A man might write poetry to them or send flowers, but that doesn't last for long once he's cleared the bases, does it? Marriage is just making sure it's still there when you get the itch and maybe making a warm nest for your kids. You'll hate yourself for nodding along with me, but you know old Jack Garner speaks the truth. And, no, of course it isn't my real name. Well, I've had it all my life, but it isn't the one I was born with.

With the Lady, all I get is her blowing in my ears, like the wind. As it happens, that has turned out to be surprisingly useful, but I'll get to that too. Look, you have to let me tell the story in my own damn way.

In those days, I used to advertise. I still do sometimes, though the rates have gone way up and, frankly, there's a lot of competition. If the stock markets go down, my business goes up, I don't know why. Oh, you could probably make some change about sharks feeding on grim times, but the way I see it, I spread a lot of goodwill when people really need it. I'm a philanthropist and, yes, I know what it means. I usually left them smiling. Crying too, but smiling through the tears, mostly.

My method of starting with a local paper and checking the deaths kept me in gas and jackets and paid for the cell phone. But every now and then, maybe if I was starting in a new area, I'd put a couple of ads in the locals. There just isn't any point buying space in a specialist magazine, so let me save you a few dollars. They're full of fakes—well, obviously—but the customers you want don't get *Spirit World* delivered to their nice mailboxes, you know?

I had the kind of call that still gives me a thrill. I couldn't tell her age from the phone and there was some kind of accent, I couldn't tell which. I thought it was maybe Dutch, so I was imagining some big apple-strudel type, maybe with blond braids, just amusing myself with pictures in my head while we talked. I got out my maps and put the phone against my chest while I grinned. Penacook, New Hampshire, some godforsaken place in the middle of Merrimack County. Nice names and not a part of the world I knew that well. I told her it was four hundred miles and that I'd have to default on another job to reach her. I was sounding her out on the money, you know? But she was a good one, for all her funny vowels. I named a price and she just paused a moment, then agreed. No negotiation, which was exactly the sort of client I liked best.

After that, it all went a bit odd. I asked her who she wanted me to reach on the other side and she said, no, she wanted me to get rid of a spirit. She said she wasn't the slightest bit interested in hearing what it had to say, she just wanted it out of her house.

I nearly told her to call Ghostbusters and put the phone down. I swear, if she hadn't already agreed to a rate for gas mileage that was just ridiculous, I might have done it. Perhaps I was a bit short that week, I don't remember, but I told her I'd be there in two days and she clicked her tongue and huffed and then agreed, as if she wasn't the one who'd come calling. They don't think like us. They don't do logical. I had the idea even then that there wasn't going to be much weeping on my shoulder from that one. I was right too, but then I *am* a bona fide psychic. I should be right every now and then. Did you notice the Latin? Self-educated, but I could still kick your ass.

Penacook is one of those pretty mill towns, couple hundred years old and proud of it. There's a river, a few churches with high steeples, and a nice old Civil War memorial, like a thousand other places. I don't go near the churches, though you'd think we're in the same basic business, wouldn't you? It's all about giving a little hope. I found the address on Fisher Street and took a room at the cheapest hotel I could find to put on the black suit and kill a few hours. What I do doesn't go so well in bright sunshine. Evening is best, with the shadows growing longer. It makes them just that bit more suggestible, in my experience.

I can tell you I was disappointed when Mrs. Weathers opened the door. She was tall, taller than me even, but there was no sign of blond braids and she was thin and kind of bony. Her hair was near white and she had it scraped back so tight it must have taken years off her face. She took a look up and down the street like she was embarrassed to be seen opening the door to me, then hustled me into the house.

This isn't even the meat of my story, you know, not really. I always get caught up in the details when I'm thinking about the time I first met the Lady. I can still remember the way the door shut and I still wonder what sort of airlock door Mrs. Weathers had, because the silence was intense. It felt like I'd been wrapped in wool, like the thick carpets soaked up all the noise until I wanted to speak just to be sure it would come out. I recall there was an antique clock as tall as the old girl, but the pendulum didn't move then or any other time. I guess you would call it tasteful, but I call it rich and my money gland began to squeeze a little.

She made tea and I don't even need to tell you it was in fine china, right? Cups so delicate I thought I'd break one just by holding it. I was reading everything, getting ready for the spiel, but she didn't look like my usual customer. No red eyes, no trembling hands, nothing but that flat, blue stare as she watched me sip a cup of imported Assam.

Seems Mrs. Weathers had been in the house for only two months. I already knew she'd been a teacher. I'd seen the framed photo, with a younger version of her in a long skirt, adults at the front, smiling kids behind. It's the kind of detail I notice, but I let her tell me she had retired from all that and she lived alone. She seemed reluctant to bring up the reason for my being there, so I pushed a bit, laying a hand on her arm in a brief touch as I asked. Funny how often that works. It's like some sort of trigger.

I was busy revising my fee in my head when she finally got around to telling me about the spirit she wanted gone. I nodded when she talked about dreams of screaming, like we all had them. It was almost like she'd read *Spirit World* after all, like she had a copy on her dresser with a checklist for ghosts. Cold breezes in a closed room—check. Whispers in her ear—check. Nameless feelings of dread—check. I was beginning to think she lacked imagination, you know? When she said it was strongest in the basement, I stood up like I was excited and asked to see. I figured it would take me about an hour to tap walls down there, maybe burn a few feathers and chant my powerful old Arapahoe spirit call: "Eyelie Miggeymou, Miggeymou, Miggeymou. Eyelie Miggeymou, Plutotoo." Or "I like Mickey Mouse and Pluto too," if you really know your plains chant. I'd declare the place clean, washed of evil spirits, collect . . . maybe four hundred dollars on top of the expenses and go on my way. The funny thing is that I believed it would work. It's not difficult to banish something that exists only in someone's imagination, as long as they believe in you. I truly had no idea back then that there were any kind of spirits at all.

I've guessed since that the Lady wanted to leave that house. God alone knows why she took an interest in me. All she had to do was sit tight while I went through some routine, and then I'd have been gone, out of their lives forever.

It wasn't dark down there at all. It was a nice, modern basement, all painted white, with a bit of water damage in one of the corners. I remember a faint smell of damp in the air and I thought of spores. There wasn't much else to do, with Mrs. Weathers watching me. Apart from a jumble of old furniture, a reel of hosepipe, and a few boxes, it was just about as unhaunted a place as you can ever imagine, more like an abandoned office space than a door to the other side.

Even so, I take good green dollars as seriously as the next man. I spent the best part of an hour touching each wall, noting the new plaster, running my fingers along every crack. These things just come to me sometimes. You have to give them some kind of ritual, I've found. You can't just stand in the middle and mumble.

I nearly had a heart attack when the Lady blew in my ear that first time. The basement was closed off, with just a slit of a window at ground level, too small even for neighborhood boys to get through. There was no chance of a breeze and this wasn't some gentle breath I could tell myself I'd imagined. This was exactly like someone blowing hard into my ear and making me jump. I have to say I yelped a bit, but when I turned to Mrs. Weathers, she was way over on the other side, just smiling in that sour way she had.

"That's the sort of thing I have to live with, Mr. Garner," she said, all kind of triumphant. "So I'll be pleased if you'll cease your tomfoolery and just turn the thing out of my house. That's if you can."

I held back from saying she should be damned pleased if anyone wanted to blow in her ear at her age. I was that upset by what had happened.

"Six hundred, with expenses," I said at last. Best part of a thousand dollars was more than I'd ever asked before. She curled her lip at me, so that I could see yellow teeth.

"Very well, Mr. Garner, but I want results."

"And I'll need some privacy. You'll get what you want, don't worry about it." That was me stalling for time. It didn't help that I felt another blow in my ear as I spoke. I rubbed it and that old bitch gave me a look like she knew exactly what was going on. Which she probably did. I watched her head back up the stairs and found myself alone in that cheery, not-at-all frightening, nicely lit basement.

"Okay," I said. I remember my heart was tapping away and I felt more than a bit foolish. "If there's anyone in here, if I'm not just wasting a perfectly good evening, blow in my goddamn ear again, I double dare you."

Well, she did and I nearly peed my pants. You weren't there, so don't tell me it wasn't scary. I sort of lunged in the same direction and took a couple of steps. She blew in my right ear and I lunged that way, arms flailing like I was in a swarm of hornets. It wouldn't have looked too dignified, but there was no one watching me.

I found myself close to the far wall and whenever I turned back to the room, I felt the tickle, like she wanted me to stay where I was. I don't know exactly when I started calling her the Lady, by the way. My first wife used to blow in my ears, and maybe it reminded me of that.

I stood there facing the paint and plaster for a time, chest heaving like I'd been running. You just can't realize what a *surprise* the whole thing was. Oh, I'd been talking to the dead for years by then, nodding wisely and passing on whatever vague message of goodwill the client wanted to hear. Actually feeling one, no, interacting with one, well, it was a bit of a shaker and I don't mean the cabinets with the tiny handles.

I did move about the room, of course. I didn't just stand where she wanted me to. But she herded me back each time to the same spot, turning me left and right, or blowing on the back of my head to move me forward. I got kind of lost in the game for a time, and if you don't believe me it's only because you don't know how exciting it all was. Over and over, I ended up back at the same piece of painted plaster, new and shining. I could feel the slight pressure on my hair pushing me on, like she wanted me to walk through the damn wall.

"Can't do it," I said aloud. "Can you even see there's a wall there?" I remember thinking about secret passages, maybe an old dungeon where I'd find her bones walled up. I've read a bit about the subject, as you can see. I confess I started to get interested, but I had an idea Mrs. Weathers might refuse to pay if I cut a big hole in her wall, so I called her back down.

I was all business again, solemn and troubled.

"I'm feeling her most strongly in this wall," I said, running my hands along it. "Is there anything behind it? Like another room?"

Weathers shrugged, but for the first time, she looked troubled.

"I don't know. The previous owners might have bricked something up," she said. I could see she'd read some of the same thrillers. She brushed at her hair then, exactly as if she'd felt a fly land on her. For the first time, I felt sorry for the old bitch.

"I'm going to need a ball-peen hammer, the biggest you have," I said. She bit her lip in worry, but at last she nodded and went away to fetch one. I could feel the steady pressure on my head as I faced the wall, and I began to realize how damn irritating it would be to live with something like that. Not six hundred dollars irritating, not to me, but Weathers looked like she could spare it without much lost sleep.

When she came back with the hammer, I went at it like a teamster, walloping that drywall until it fell away and then really getting going on the bricks behind it. It's funny, I would have done a lot less damage if I'd been using my eyes a bit more. It took me a while to see there were two bricks that didn't match the rest. I'd been thinking of secret rooms, Al Capone's treasure, who knows what else. It was only when I found plastic sheeting and raw earth behind my hole that I stood back, sweating. Damp-proofing is not that sinister, and I had a nasty feeling I had just worked myself out of a fee. I took a better look at those bricks then. With all the hammering, they were already loose enough to pull out.

I noticed that Weathers still stood on the stairs, like she was afraid to come into the room. I could feel her staring as I worked the bricks out and put them on the floor. I still don't know what I was hoping to find, but in the end it was almost a disappointment. There wasn't even much of a space, just about enough to get a hand in. It was the sort of secret hiding place a child might find and then forget. I used to have something similar in my mom's house underneath the old floorboards.

In the gap, there was a lock of brown hair bound in a ring, tied with a red ribbon that looked as if some insect had been eating it. I pulled it into the light and the air changed all around me. It's hard to describe, but it felt a little bit like a plane coming down to an airport. Your ears block and suddenly you can't hear as well. As I stood there staring at the ring of hair, I pinched my nostrils and blew, but it didn't make any difference. I just knew that I'd found the real thing, that the spirit was bound to the hair.

"This is a relic," I said to Weathers, behind me. My voice sounded peculiar, still muffled like we were on the approach to O'Hare and dropping fast. I pinched my nose again, blowing hard to clear my head. It still didn't work and I began to feel a bit choked. Well, there was a way out of that.

I reached into my pants pocket and pulled out my lighter. As I'm writing my own story, I guess I could tell you it was a really cool Zippo, but the truth is it was the cheapest butane lighter you can buy. I remember my hand shook as I thumbed the wheel, and as it sparked and the flame lit, the air changed again, popped almost so that it left me gasping. There was no wind, but suddenly we weren't dropping into Chicago through a thick fog, we were just standing in a basement, staring at a cigarette lighter.

I raised the flame to the lock of hair and without any warning, it went out. I'd felt the breath on my fingers, but I lit it again anyway, just to see it happen. The flame stood up and then it vanished as the Lady blew it out.

I stood there for a time, thinking a bit more deeply than usual. She had wanted me to find the ring of hair with its sad little ribbon, but she didn't want to be set free. Like I said before, I don't know exactly why she chose me, but I've always had the Garner charm; at least my mom used to tell me I had. She never meant it in a good way, though.

I carried that thing out of the house like it was a live grenade, stopping only to accept the cash payment old Weathers took from a tin in her kitchen. Hell, I'd earned the money. I didn't even put the ring of hair in a pocket, just carried it out in front of me until my arm grew stiff. I didn't feel any breath on the back of my neck then, not until I was out on Fisher Street and walking away.

I can't explain exactly why I did the things I did that day. It would have been easy enough to throw the lock of hair down a drain, or better still into the river so it could be carried out to sea. Maybe if I'd been scared I would have done it, but you have to realize that this was my life's work. Finally I had proof I wasn't completely wasting my time. I never claimed to be a good man, but I never wanted to be a complete fake either. It felt like I'd found my Rosetta stone, the key that would unlock it all for me. It was true too, in a way.

I stayed in Penacook for a couple more days and I bought myself the box I carry today. It's a small brass thing, inlaid with mother-of-pearl, about as big as a pack of cards. The ring of hair went with me and from then on, well, I guess I was haunted.

The Lady was quiet for a few days after. I'll spare you the details of how

I tried to get her to perform—once for a newspaper guy and once in a bar when I'd had too many shots. She stayed in the box and then, just to rile me, blew in my ears all the way home until I was swatting my own head in frustration. I had enough money to live and I spent that time thinking. What if every ghost had its link to the world, like the Lady's lock of hair? It took me a while, but after about a week, I found myself in Franklin County, Massachusetts. I stopped again to put new ads in all the local papers. For the first time in years, I changed the copy and sold my services as a *Ghost Hunter—Satisfaction or Your Money Back*. It didn't hurt that I'd made more money from Mrs. Weathers than my previous six jobs combined. I didn't even grumble at the rates per word they quoted. There was gold in them thar hills.

The first few months were a bit of a nightmare, I don't mind telling you. It wasn't that I didn't get any calls; I did. I even thought I'd have to get another cell for work, it was so busy. The trouble was that of the houses I visited, not one of them had anything more supernatural than mice behind the walls. Even so, I learned the skills and I put a toolbox together that a carpenter might have approved. I could strip a room in an hour, and I guess the good builders and painters of Massachusetts must have thought it was Christmas with all the extra work I left for them. I found grumbling old pipes, rat nests, a bird trapped in a chimney, all sorts, but the Lady kept quiet. Outside, she would still tickle my head at times, just to show me she was there, but in the houses, she was quiet as the grave probably should be.

The money ran out and for a time I was forced to go back to the old work, just to keep the main ads running and pay for gas. She didn't like that. I could feel her breath on my face, pushing me away whenever I went to do my readings, until I had to leave the box in the motel room.

It all changed that winter, after a heavy snowfall. I had a live call from my Hunter ads, though it meant driving to a town named Montague, about forty miles from where I was. I couldn't afford chains and it was hard going, maybe four hours of creeping along with the wipers going and the lights lost in a blizzard. All those big trucks kept whooshing by as well, making me nervous.

I had my tools and the Lady's box with me and maybe I imagined it, but there was a feeling of excitement as I pressed the bell of a huge old house on Treadle Road, to the south of Main Street. A young Asian woman opened the door and I smiled at her, thinking that servants were a good sign for a payday. I felt that slight pressure at the back of my head as well, pushing me into the house after her.

I'd been wrong before, but not that time. I was taken to a proper library, filled with books from floor to ceiling. The man who finally came to see me was young to own a place like that. I wondered if he'd inherited it, or whether he was some high-powered broker or something. He looked uncomfortable the whole time he talked to me, and I couldn't read him that well. Turns out it was his wife who had called me, but she was out of town. You could see he would rather have thrown me out, but the snow was still falling and I assume his wife was not the sort of woman you cross lightly. I've met a few like that.

He took me upstairs, fidgeting the whole time, like he couldn't keep his hands still. He didn't offer me a drink or anything, and I could see he was going to stand over me to be sure I didn't steal anything. I didn't mind, though, because the Lady was pushing me the whole way, like she knew there was something good up those stairs.

The stairs opened up onto a landing with six or seven doors. To my surprise and mounting interest, he had to unlock one of them before I could go in. He saw my look and made a grimace.

"It's always cold in here, even with the boiler going. I don't think it was properly insulated when the house was built." I just smiled politely and he made his face again and led me in.

It was cold. Not freezing, but chilly after the rest of the house. Straight away I could feel the Lady blowing on me, but I didn't want to make it look easy.

"My usual fee is six hundred dollars for this kind of work," I said. He looked as if he'd bitten into a lemon when I said that, but I just stared him down.

"You should know I don't believe any of this," he said, like he was scoring a point. I waited for him to think of his wife and how angry she'd be if he said he'd sent me away. Thing was, though, I'd have done it for free at that moment, just to see how it should work. Still, I waited until he nodded.

"Cash," I added. He almost sneered at me.

"Of course," he said.

I left him alone. Time was I'd have taken pains to annoy a man like that, maybe even broken him up a little, but I was eager to get on and I could feel the Lady pressing me farther into the room.

It took about five minutes, maybe less. I've learned since not to do it so quickly. The Lady guided me to the right place, and I used a handsaw to cut a floorboard and a claw hammer to yank up the right part. I found a piece of bone lying in the dust there, black with soot.

"Have you ever had a fire here?" I called over my shoulder. He was looking kind of horrified at the damage I'd done, but he nodded.

"My grandfather's time, yes," he said. It would have been a good hit, just the sort of thing they don't expect you to know, even though it would have been in all the local papers at the time.

"And someone died in that fire, in this room," I said. It wasn't even a question, and he just gaped at me as I brought the bone out into the air. It was only a piece and I couldn't tell which part it had come from. Maybe an ankle, I don't know. It was enough to keep the spirit in the same place, though. I could feel the temperature dropping, though there was nothing special, like frost patterns on the window. This wasn't a powerful spirit. I'd meet those later.

I took the bone out of his house and he paid me in cash, with all his sneers and fine attitudes neatly cut out of his manner. He had a look of awe in his eyes when he went up to check the room and found it warm. I had the bone in my pocket and it felt like there was winter all round me. I saw the man flinch as he took my hand and pumped it.

"I'll destroy it," I promised. I did too. I wasn't ready then to take in another boarder, and a spirit who just made you cold was no use to me.

I don't know what he said to his wife, but that girl had connections and there are a lot of old houses in Massachusetts. I stayed there for another six months and work came flooding in. There were the usual blanks, of course, but the Lady helped me with two real ones and I was off and running. I put my rates up for the big houses and for the first time in my life, I made some real money, enough to change out the transmission on the car. I even thought of renting a house for a time, but I'm happier moving on, always have been. Of course in the past, there's always been bad memories to run from. I passed my fiftieth birthday in a motel and I even bought myself a goddamn cake and a candle. The Lady blew it out and I drank a fifth of good whiskey.

I found Geronimo halfway through my second year. Now I know what you're going to say and I agree with you. Why would that old Apache medicine man haunt an abandoned mansion in North Carolina? My honest guess is that whoever he really was, he just likes to call himself something different. I don't know whether he was a New York broker who leaped out of a window, or just some cattle driver from the thirties. I do know he's powerful, and that's what matters. That's what dragged me two hundred miles south when I heard about that old house, falling down with neglect and no one daring to live in it for half a century.

He has enough strength to speak to me. Maybe working with the Lady made me sensitive, I don't know, but I can hear the old man as a whisper and understand maybe about a quarter of it. The Lady and I found his relic in the usual way, but that was all that was usual. I'd grown accustomed to thinking of spirits as weak things—a slightly chilly room isn't *The Shining*, if you know what I mean. Geronimo could call up a storm, and we found his relics while there were books and dust swirling around us. I had to use an old door from the basement to cover my head while we dug out his bones. I guess he was probably murdered, as they don't let you bury your loved ones in the garden, even in North Carolina.

I dug them all out and took them down to the furnace in the basement. It took me half a day to get it going again, with four trips to a hardware store for supplies, but you need a high temperature to reduce bone to ash. You can't just throw gas on it and stand back. I had the last bit in my hands, a piece of broken yellow bone, when the Lady blew on my face. The house had gone very quiet since I started the burning and I could feel the tension, the way air feels before a storm.

I'd grown to trust the Lady and I put that old bone in my little box and took it away with me. Maybe she talked to him. Maybe she told him about the exciting life on the road and he went along. Hell, maybe a ghost in an abandoned house gets lonely, I don't know. I didn't really need him, or so I thought at the time. The Lady was my finder and I was getting a name for myself. I'd even had TV companies sniffing around me, but I don't want my face shown around the country. There are a few people who would be *very* pleased to see it, and I don't want to meet them again, not ever.

I did say there were four of us, when I started this record. The last to join my little family was about as muscular as Geronimo. He could throw things around like you wouldn't believe. It was an old place in Georgia where I found him, overgrown with so much green crap that it looked like it was about to sink into the marshy ground. I nearly fell through the floor more than once. There was graffiti on the walls and beer cans all over the ground floor, even some marks from fires, where kids had tried to light the old place. It was too damp to burn, I think.

I'd gone looking for his relic and he'd come at me in a dust devil, blowing the filth of a century of neglect into my face. I was blind for a while, and only the Lady guiding me got me out into the sunshine. However, I'm a professional and it wasn't so hard to buy goggles and overalls for the second trip. As it happens, I didn't need them. I reached the old kitchen and as the wind started up, I opened my little box.

"Meet the kids," I said. Well, that wind just died on the spot. I imagined them all sniffing each other like dogs.

"I can take you to places you'd never see otherwise," I said aloud. That was how I added an old gold locket with a lover's lock to my box. I never could hear him, but Geronimo told me his name was Thomas, so I always called him that.

Together, we toured the country for maybe three years. I never found another like Tom or Geronimo and if I had the slightest trouble, I'd just open the box and the air would get real heavy while they slugged it out. I don't know exactly how they could give a ghost a beating, but those boys seemed to love it when we had the chance. I might have gone on like that forever, until the fall of '04, when I finally met Erwin Trommler. He's sort of the reason I started this record, so if you've been drifting while I gave you my valuable wisdom, it might be time to sit up and gulp the cold coffee.

I'd worked the East Coast for a few years and I'd been thinking of heading farther west, maybe to Memphis. I'd gotten the idea that someone with my talents should visit Graceland, you know? If you don't understand right away, you never will, so don't worry about it.

Before I went, I had a live one call me to Long Branch, New Jersey, right on the coast. *Ms.* Gorski, she called herself, so I knew she was going to be an ugly one. Not that I did that anymore. Taking out the ghost trash doesn't seem to get them hanging off you the way speaking to the dead does. I worked out the distances and thought, yes, I could do that job and then swing west to reach Graceland in the fall.

She was standing on the step waiting for me when I swung into her road. In fact, she wasn't too bad looking. She was dark-haired and sort of formal in her manners, maybe a little plumper than I like to see in a woman, but not too far gone. I spotted her and pulled up, taking my box from the front seat. I know they could travel in the trunk, but it seemed disrespectful somehow.

When we were all inside, I took a look around, pleased to see the signs of serious money. I have a pretty good eye for antiques and there were some nice pieces in there. Good neighborhood too. It's not that I won't help poor people, it's more like I have to make a living too and poor people don't pay so well. So I was relaxing a bit as I sat there on a sofa that must have cost more than my car.

"Tell me about your father," I said. I had a routine by then, mainly to give them a sense of value for money. I could feel the Lady breathing on my neck, so I knew it was a real one. Talking to the clients didn't help me find relics any faster, but if I didn't, I think I'd have been the loneliest man alive.

Now you have to understand that her father, Erwin, had died just a few days before. If it had been a different kind of call and if she'd been more to look at, it could have been a fun afternoon for me. Like I said, I don't do that anymore, but I didn't see any grief in her. She just sat there and talked, but all the time I had the feeling she was giving me nothing. Hell, maybe I am psychic. She told me his name and that he'd come through Ellis Island a long time ago. He'd been about ninety when he died. I could see she didn't like talking about him at all. So I pushed for more details, with my bump of curiosity itching away like crazy.

"I feel his spirit in the house," she said. "Things move and there are noises, not just bad dreams. If you come back tonight, you'll feel it too. No one can live here until he's gone. That's all you need to know."

"Ma'am, you shouldn't tell me my business," I said. "If I tell you I need to know more, it's because I do. Now I can just leave and maybe you'll find some other fool, I don't know. But I'm telling you, there's no one else who can do what I can. If you truly want him gone, you'll be honest with me."

She looked at me for a long time and I felt a kind of thrill, like I was on the edge of something.

"I was born here, Mr. Garner. But my father was originally from Germany."

"Well, folks have to come from someplace," I said. My own grandmother came through Ellis, bringing her little daughter with her. I wondered for a moment if they would have stood in line with the young Erwin Gorski.

"He arrived in 1944. His real name was Erwin Trommler, before. He claimed to be Polish and he spoke the language fluently. He hid himself in America." She hesitated again and I had a sort of premonition, not so much a psychic thing as a sick feeling in my stomach.

"Tell it all then," I said softly, reaching out to touch her arm. "I need to know." There were tears in her eyes, just a glimmer, like I was seeing her heart torn out.

"He worked in Bergen-Belsen for three years, Mr. Garner. I don't know exactly what he did there, but he earned enough money to get false papers and get out before the end."

Belsen. I knew more about that than she did. The British found thousands of dead bodies in that place, left to rot on the ground. The ones they found alive made some of the most harrowing pictures you'll ever see. Walking skeletons, with dead eyes, the ones who lived. Babies, women, piles of children. If there's one thing that God will hold up to humanity, one thing to shame us on the day of judgment, it will be the Belsen concentration camp.

"My father was a cold man, Mr. Garner. He never talked about his past. It was only after his death that I went through his papers." She shuddered and I thought to myself that I didn't want to see what she had found. Not then, not ever. Some things burn themselves so deeply into your mind that you can't ever tear them out.

"Will you come back tonight, Mr. Garner? I haven't slept in here since he died, but I can still feel him. I want him gone. I want him properly dead."

I nodded, thinking I was going to have to make some plans for this one.

"You stay out of the house," I said. "I'll come back when it's dark." To her credit, she didn't flinch at the idea of giving me a key to a house full of antiques. I guess she'd seen something in my eyes as I'd listened. She trusted me, and I'd almost forgotten how good that could feel.

I stood before that old place as the sun went down and I felt a little bit like an exterminator come to kill roaches. I had my tools, a pair of goggles, and some overalls. I suppose I looked like an exterminator as well. I also had my little brass box, with the Lady, Geronimo, and Tom. The Lady was pushing me in, with that breath on the back of my neck that wouldn't let up, so I knew she was as keen as I was.

I opened the door and closed it softly behind me. I'd been in enough homes over the years to know this one was real angry. Well, that was just fine with me. I was pretty damn angry myself.

I stood inside that entrance hall in the moonlight and smiled to myself as I felt the air move and grow solid. I know the Lady's touch, and that wasn't it. Maybe I should have been freaked out by the feeling of cold fingers touching my face, but I wasn't. I really wanted him to be in there. I wanted him to fight me.

"I'm calling you out, Erwin Trommler," I said out loud. "Come to me and see what I have for you."

Now I thought Geronimo and Tom were strong, but nothing prepared me for the feeling of fingers tightening on my throat. Throwing things is almost random, but this one had control and power. I began to choke and though I waved my hands in front of my face, there was nothing to grab.

I opened the box. I don't really need to, I guess, but it works for me and for them. I think they like jumping out on some spirit who thinks he's a badass. The choking stopped in an instant and I coughed and wheezed, rubbing my throat.

"Sic 'im," I said.

It was like standing at the center of an explosion. Every damn thing in that house crashed like it had been struck by an earthquake and the air was filled with sharp pieces. If it hadn't been for the goggles, I think I'd have been blinded. I tell you now I'd never seen a fight like it, and for the first time I wondered if Geronimo and old Tom could handle this one.

They battered each other through walls, so that I could see great holes appear from nothing. The noise was incredible and I spared a moment to wonder if I'd be seeing flashing lights outside before it was over. The house was set apart from the others in the street, but I had no idea how I'd explain all this to the cops if they showed up. Plaster rained down from the ceiling, and even the lights were ripped out. I staggered after them, and sometimes I could see dim shapes and shadows grunting and struggling in the dust. My three had him down for a time, but he got up and slammed Geronimo across the room. The air was thick, winds blowing like we were standing on a cliff.

I began to worry that he was too strong for all of us, but in the moonlight, I caught sight of the Lady. She was no more than a wisp, like a piece of cloth dragged this way and that, but she closed on him when Geronimo went down and then I heard her scream for the first time. I didn't even know she could. God, I don't ever want to hear it again.

I fell to my knees, the pain was that bad. My teeth vibrated and my skull buzzed and I thought I was going to puke. I just hoped it was worse for Erwin goddamn Trommler. As it went on, I let my lunch go all over the carpet, though you couldn't even see it then, with the dust that coated everything. I was still dry-heaving when the noise stopped and the silence was so complete I thought I'd gone deaf. Then I heard a car passing outside and I got to my feet. I was a bit shaky, but I was grinning. The Lady was a screamer, who knew? She'd battered that old spirit into a corner and I could feel Geronimo and Tom standing over him, like they were daring him to get up and try it again.

I looked around at the devastation and I felt a pang for his daughter, but not too much. I still had work to do and I almost sobbed when I felt the Lady breathing on my neck once again. Erwin Trommler didn't dare stir while we searched for his relic. I was expecting hair or something. Instead, she helped me find some old teeth in a box in the attic. They had gold in them and I guess he'd kept them for that, when they came out. It made me think of the gold teeth the Nazis pulled out of Jews in the camps, and I spent a little time weeping before I came down. I'm not ashamed of it.

It was about midnight by then, and I still had work to do. I could have burned the teeth, but I'd had a few hours to think it through and buy a few things. I didn't want his relic destroyed. I wanted it to last for a thousand years, about as long as he'd once thought his Third Reich would. So I filled a little plastic jar with clear resin and put them in. I smoked a few cigarettes while it set, looking like some prehistoric thing trapped in amber, you know?

After that, I took a thin sheet of lead and I wrapped it all over, bending the metal with my thumbs. It wasn't pretty, but it felt good and solid in my hand.

I felt foolish locking that door behind me, after all the damage we'd done.

The house would need to be stripped back and every room rebuilt on that floor, but I was satisfied. The moon was bright as I drove to the ocean. I had chartered a little boat that afternoon, and though I don't know the first damn thing about boats, I figured it wouldn't be so hard to take it out into deep water and drop that lead block overboard, where it could sink into a darkness that went on forever. I wanted him to choke on eternity.

I did say I wasn't born with this name. My mother was a hard woman, but maybe that was because she'd seen things no one should ever see. I still remember the faded blue numbers on her arm. She hadn't talked about them and it was years before I knew what they were and why she wouldn't wear short sleeves even in summer. When I was still a baby, she'd changed my name from Jacob Grossman to Jack Garner. Like many before her, she started a new life in the New World. She left a lot behind, but those blue marks never did come off.

I stood in that little boat, holding the lead box over the deep waters. Even out there, with the town lights twinkling in the distance, I could feel the struggle they had to keep him still. Oh, he fought, of course he did. I hope they hurt him as they kept him down. I dropped the relic and it disappeared into the blackness. I felt like a weight had been lifted from me, one I hadn't even known I was carrying. It was a good feeling and I stayed out there to watch the sun come up.

I'd like to say I retired after that, but I didn't. I just went to Memphis.

HELLBENDER

by Laurie R. King

Here's a riveting look at a not-too-distant future where, unfortunately, intolerance is *not* a thing of the past . . .

New York Times bestseller and Edgar® Award winner Laurie R. King is the author of the eleven-volume Mary Russell mystery series of novels, one of the most successful modern Sherlock Holmes homages, detailing the adventures of a young woman who meets a retired Sherlock Holmes in his role as a Sussex beekeeper; she becomes his apprentice, then partner, and, eventually, wife. The Mary Russell novels include *The Beekeeper's Apprentice*, *A Monstrous Regiment of Women*, *The Game*, *The Language of Bees*, and seven others. In addition, King is the author of the five-book Kate Martinelli series of modern-day detective novels, consisting of *A Grave Talent*, *To Play the Fool*, *With Child*, *Night Work*, and *The Art of Detection*, and of the stand-alone novels *A Darker Place*, *Keeping Watch*, *Califia's Daughters*, *Touchstone*, and Macavity Award winner *Folly*. Her most recent book is a Mary Russell novel, *Pirate King*.

I LOOKED ACROSS MY DESK AT MY NEW CLIENT, WONDERING WHAT SHE'D say if I fished out the bottle and offered her a drink.

Might be a little early in the morning, I decided. Might be a little strait-laced.

"Miss Savoy, I—"

"Ms." The pretty sniff she gave didn't really go along with the sharpness of the correction, but I let it pass, and turned my eyes to the sheet of paper. On it were eight names. Next to each was a date, stretching back eight months. The first seven lines were typed, a printout. The last one and its date, two weeks past, were handwritten.

"Ms. Savoy, I have to say, I'm not really sure what you're asking me to do. Which of these people do you want me to find?"

"All of them!"

At that, I raised my eyes to hers. They were big and blue and welling with just enough tears to get the message across, but not enough to threaten her makeup. The color had to be some kind of an implant, I thought—although you'd swear her hair was a natural blond.

Interesting fact: People of her kind just weren't born blond.

"I don't do class-action suits, Ms. Savoy, and this many names will keep me busy for weeks. How about we start with one of them, and see how far we get?" I could see from her clothes that she didn't have the sort of money we were talking about here—her shoes and coat had once cost her something, but that was a whole lot of cleanings ago.

"Well, that would be Harry. He's the last one to go—the last one I know of—but I've known him the longest."

And, she might have said, he was the one that mattered most.

"Okay, start with him."

"Well, he disappeared two weeks ago. I was supposed—"

"Tell me a little about Harry, to begin with. How long have you known him?"

"Pretty much my whole life," she said, sounding surprised. "Harry's my brother. Harry Savoy."

"Uh-huh," I said, a noise that I tried to make noncommittal, but that came out a little disbelieving.

"No, really. We were both adopted, a year apart."

I made the noise again, although this time it may have had a little more understanding in it. I knew the kind of people who adopt more than one of this woman's kind: You probably do, too. And call them well-meaning or saints or just delusional, they're usually very religious. Which is funny, considering that those who'd rather stamp her kind out altogether call themselves religious, too.

Anyway.

"I was two and a half when I was adopted, but Harry was almost five. I never knew exactly what his early life was like, except that it was hard. For one thing, he was more . . . that is to say, you can tell that I'm . . . ?"

"Yeah." Although it was true, a lot of people might not've known with her, and certainly not right off. Still, I could tell the second she walked in. Makeup and surgery might hide the surface, but there's a kind of all-over flexibility that just shouts out when you know what you're looking at. And when you don't know—well, let's just say that a lot of this girl's type make a good living out of how they move.

"Harry was more obvious than me. He even had little lines where his gills almost came up. And because he lived in a rough neighborhood, he came in for a lot of grief."

I nodded, keeping my face straight.

"A social worker took him away from his family after his second broken arm. Mom and Dad heard about him, and first fostered him, then adopted him. So Harry was my big brother from the time I was three.

"Harry's bright—really bright—but he decided early that he wasn't going to take any more crap, from anyone. When he was a teenager he got into a lot of fights, although after he got big, the kids stopped trying to pick on him quite so much. But he refused to make any concessions, never had any treatments, wouldn't even do The Surgery.

"Oh," she said, with a pretty trace of blush rising across her cheeks. "I didn't mean, that is, I didn't intend—I'd never criticize what others choose to do."

That drink was looking better. Might help with the room, which was suddenly feeling a little cold.

"Who would?" I agreed, giving a little shrug to show how disinterested I was.

A little frown line came into being between those pretty eyes. "But . . . I mean, surely you're one, too?"

"One what?" A stupid thing to say, but she'd taken me by surprise. It'd been a long time since someone made me that fast. Most people took me for a young guy with a slight skin condition. I'd even perfected a stiff walk that made my heels jar all the way up to my neck and gave me a backache, but helped me pass.

"One of *us*. A . . . SalaMan."

I WAS BORN IN THE SECOND DECADE OF THE MILLENNIUM. OH, I SPENT A few years in a freezer first, then a lot more years in legal limbo before the case finally wound its way through the courts to give me a birth certificate, but conception took place when that oh-so-clever shit-bastard of a grad student stirred up some DNA to see what would happen, and I figure conception is when I began.

When Elizabeth Savoy came to my office that Tuesday morning, I'd been breathing for thirty-one years, although I only looked twenty. And sometimes felt fifty.

Interesting fact: People don't know just how many of us there are. Oh, you may think you do, and you can bet Uncle Sam does, but it didn't take very many bombings and riots before even the government could see that playing things down might be a smart idea. Once the Supremes turned in their decision regarding our human status, the feds were ready, and pretty much everything about us went away: numbers, characteristics, identities. There's even the occasional Web rumor that says we're nothing but a myth, which is fine with me.

As far as the government is concerned, the only time we're the least bit different from any other citizen is when we want to be. From the start, they swore up and down that they'd set up the records so even they didn't know who we were unless we chose to come to them. Which was hard to believe, but at least they kept their hands off us. We've all been counseled; we all know that it's a good idea to take any medical problem to one of their specialists rather than wonder if our local GP knows what he's looking at; we're all aware of the standing offer of money, shelter, and a lifetime of protection if that's ever what we want. And if we don't, well, we got a handshake and a wish for good luck, which is more than most of our fellow citizens get.

I had to wonder how my client had found me. I didn't exactly have a shingle out saying "SalaMan Investigations."

About a quarter of my own genes come from a species called Hellbender, a big guy that's about as ugly as most of his kind (although at least the name was cool—what if our DNA came from mud puppies or—God help us—"seepage" salamanders?). That lunatic grad student Joey Handle had to've been a genius, because he tweaked and balanced and played God with the stuff of *Cryptobranchus alleganiensis* and *Homo sapiens* to make himself a race of Others, in a way no one else has yet.

Or anyway, did so enough to prove to himself that he could. No one knows if he ever intended to warm up all his frozen embryos and see if we twitched, or just flush us all down the drain. I suspect the latter. But before the boy genius could decide, Reverend Tommy Bostitch's mad followers took over the lab, not really knowing what was there other than it was something sinful. That's where they found us, and before you know it, they'd gotten it into their well-meaning little brains that what God wanted them to do was give us life.

Reverend Tommy's men were bad enough, but the women who fell for his spiel? I mean really: How nutso do you have to be to volunteer your womb to grow what for all you know will turn out to be a monster? Religious nuts just get my goat. Even though I owe them my existence.

Mom was one of the lucky ones, sort of. First off, I lived, which most of Handle's Children didn't. Then, she wasn't one of Reverend Tommy's direct followers, so she didn't die with the others in the raid a few years later. And to top it off, I looked enough like a human baby that people didn't shriek and run when they saw me. But she volunteered to be implanted only the one time. And she had to've blamed me for the divorce. In any case, hers and mine wasn't exactly a cuddly relationship. I'd guess it's hard for a pure mammal to feel all maternal toward a baby that feels a little bit cool and maybe a touch slimy—as my client said, some of us were more blatant than others.

But for some reason, the first round of implants didn't put a complete halt to the birthing program. If it had, we'd be a lot fewer of us, and we'd all be the same age.

About a year after the embryo theft, the first of us were born. About a month after that, the government caught on that something weird was going on. And from there . . . well, by the time I was eighteen, the courts had decided that I was a citizen.

Once I'd had some work done, I could pass. I could even sleep with women without them freaking out, since I'd had what my client delicately called The Surgery (although I was still sterile, like all the others). And in the eight years I'd had my PI shingle out, I'd had only one SalaMan client, and he came in my door by accident.

So as you can guess, I wasn't exactly happy about Ms. Savoy.

I JERKED OPEN MY DESK DRAWER AND TOOK OUT THE BOTTLE AND TWO shot glasses, filling both to the top. I tossed mine down and filled it up again. To my surprise, Ms. Savoy picked hers up and swallowed half of it without a blink.

Maybe she wasn't quite as prim as she looked.

"Okay, so your brother Harry's gone missing," I said, bringing us back to the subject at hand. "Have you filed a missing-person report?"

"Yes, although the police really weren't interested."

"They told you that he's a grown man, he can go away if he wants, I know." My license meant that I had to pay attention to the rules of what a PI could and couldn't do. I had a buddy in the department, but I didn't like to ask Frank for too many favors. "You say your brother's a guy who's not at all interested in passing. You think that's related to his disappearance?"

"One has to wonder," she said. I had to agree, "one" did—every year or so there'd be another set of headlines about a SalaMan who pushed a Salaphobe's buttons and got himself beat up, or worse.

"Yeah, activism can be a dangerous hobby. What was he into when he disappeared?"

"He had a friend, a woman, who—"

"A friend, or a good friend?" I interrupted.

"I think they were serious, but I'm not certain. I only met Eileen a couple of times, but he liked her a lot. And then about six weeks ago she just up and vanished. She texted him—not even a phone call—to say she couldn't take it and she was going home. When he went to her apartment, most of her stuff was there but she wasn't. He was convinced something happened to her. He's been trying to find her—that's her name on the list, right above his. And now he's missing, too."

Harry's was the handwritten name at the bottom of the printed list.

"Who are the others?"

"I'm not altogether certain, but I think they're all people like us." I wished she'd stop putting it that way. "I found that piece of paper in Harry's desk drawer two days ago. It was on the top, so I thought it might be something he was working on, a meeting or an article or something. And I recognized two of the names—other than Eileen's, of course. Imogen and Barbara were girls I'd been to college with. So I tried to find them, to see if Harry had been in touch. But they were missing, too. Both of them."

I had to agree, the odds of coincidence here were pretty thin.

So I took her check, and I got to work.

Brother Harry had a third-floor apartment in a tired part of town near the water, which address alone would've made me wonder about him. And when I walked in, using the key his sister had given me, I'd have known for sure: The air was so moist the paint was coming off the walls, and you could smell the mildew despite the scrubbers. Which told me Harry had the kind of skin that needed to be damp. Humidity was one reason so many of his kind—okay, *my* kind—lived in San Francisco. (That, and the city's hey-it's-your-business attitude.) Which in turn was one reason I lived in Oakland where, being dryer and hotter, people didn't automatically wonder if you were One of Them.

I stood in the neat little two-bedroom, listening to the low hum of the two opposing machines—one to make the air wet, the other to battle the effects of damp—and waited for the place to tell me about Harry. He was a tidy guy, I could see that. He liked bare floors and simple furniture, and color on the walls. Not too many books, but then, books didn't like humidity, so that was hardly unusual.

More interesting, the place had been searched. So carefully that, unless you'd done a lot of cautious searches yourself, you wouldn't have noticed it. And even I might not've caught on if the sun hadn't been out, or if Harry liked sunlight a little less.

It gave me pause, for a minute. But in the end, I was here with the permission of the owner's sister, and anyway, my presence was sure to be on a camera somewhere in the neighborhood. So I went ahead with my search, keeping an eye out for bugs, but either the guy who'd searched the place was sharper when it came to planting surveillance than he was at putting back the vases on dusty surfaces, or there weren't any.

My client's brother liked damp, but he also liked light, which was unusual, considering the sensitivity of most SalaMan eyes. His walls were painted a bright white, the bulbs in his lamps were full strength, and the thin curtains over the windows were designed to keep out eyes rather than glare. Moving to the kitchen, I could see he was a cook, with a bunch of Asian-style pans and spices, more knives than I'd seen outside a French bistro, and an espresso machine the size of a small car. His refrigerator's sell-by dates didn't narrow down his departure a whole lot, although I didn't spot anything that was actually expired.

And his willingness to embrace the amphibious side of his heritage stopped well short of his palate—you wouldn't believe the things some of his—of *our*—kind tried putting on their plates.

Or maybe you would.

His closet had a suitcase in it. His bathroom had a toothbrush, electric razor, and zip-up traveling bag in a drawer. The little closet near the front door had an overcoat, a raincoat, and a leather jacket, and its only bare hangers were half-hidden by occupied ones. All of which suggested that when Harry went out, he didn't expect to be gone long.

I pressed a couple of buttons on the espresso machine, took the cup of black sludge that resulted over to Harry's desk, and settled down to the drawers.

The first thing I saw was a box of bullets. It was sitting next to a tin of oil and a cleaning rag. The box was half empty. I got up and went to look for all the likely places to hide a handgun: bedside table, behind the toilet, in the flour canister. No gun.

I had to wonder if he had a carry permit for it. Permits aren't easy to get, here in California.

My tablespoon of espresso had gone cold, so I pressed the buttons again and let the powerful syrup dribble into the cup, then returned to the desk.

Four cups later, my nerves were singing and I knew a few more things about Harry Savoy. His sister had told me he was a kind of graphic artist specializing in architectural drawings, who worked from home. The room he used as an office was drier than the rest, probably because of the equipment—I'd gone there when I'd squeezed what I could from his desk, and found a desktop computer with a state-of-the-art drawing pad, a giant wall-mounted screen, and a printer fitted with paper three feet wide. Most of the stuff I didn't touch, although I did turn on the desktop long enough to see that pretty much all the files were password protected. Which put it beyond my personal skill set, although I had a friend who could help me, if need be.

His paper files told me he made good money, and invested some. His machinery suggested that most of his friends existed online, through WeWeb, although he also had a Facebook page. I shut the computer down without logging on to either, and sat for a minute looking at the half-dozen framed pictures on the wall over the desk.

Harry was good-looking. My client hadn't mentioned that, not a thing a sister would notice maybe, but the group photos had one person in common, a guy with a dark and intense look about him I figured would win him a lot of attention, even without the litheness he was sure to have when he moved. Gun, looks, money: maybe I didn't have to look any further than old Harry's personal life for a motivation.

But I would. If nothing else, I had to earn the check in my pocket. I made notes of his phone numbers from the bills on file, and made copies of the last few months' statements on the credit cards he used. He had an address book, a tattered old thing that functioned as a backup to whatever phone he carried, but I wrote down a few of the addresses that looked more recent.

I didn't find a laptop, or a pad, or the phone.

I did make one very interesting discovery, hidden in a place so clever I nearly missed it myself—inside the heater vent, under a false side that looked exactly like the other three. I pulled it out, and sat on the floor to look at it: a nine-by-twelve envelope of printouts and clippings, nineteen of them, that made my brain whir around for a while until a little voice told me it might be a good time to leave. Taking the envelope with me.

Maybe I needed to take a look at the other names on that list, after all.

WHEN I FINALLY SLIPPED BACK THROUGH MY OWN FRONT DOOR, LATE THAT night, I stood in the dark for the longest time, straining to hear over the pounding in my heart. Stupid, to leave my gun in the safe. Stupid, stupid, to let the habits of paranoia go rusty.

After the longest time, my eyes showed no motion. No intruder shot, stabbed, or bludgeoned me, and I heard nothing outside my own skin. When I forced my hand to flip on the light, the only thing that looked back at me was my wild-eyed reflection in the mirror—good thing I didn't have a gun in my hand, I told myself, or I'd have blown a hole in the wall.

But just because there was no one waiting for me (and no one in the bathroom or in the closet) didn't mean I was safe. In ninety seconds I had my gun, my hat, my go-bag of cash, and a clean shirt, and I was out the door.

I left my car where I'd parked it, and went away on foot.

Which took care of my own safety; now for that of my client. It always looks bad when a PI loses a client. And anyway, she was probably going to owe me plenty by the time I'd finished.

She was asleep, of course, since it was just shy of two in the morning. Anyway, I hoped she was only asleep. Her small house up in Sausalito (another place with damp air and tolerant attitudes) was dark, like all of its neighbors, so I fiddled with the lock on her front door and let myself in—if I knocked loud enough to wake her, I'd wake the neighbors as well, to say nothing of giving warning to any unfriendlies who might be listening. Her cat nearly gave me a heart attack, a flash of near-ultraviolet motion followed by a slapping noise from the next room, and I came maybe half a micron from squeezing the trigger into action before my brain translated the motion and screamed at me to lay off. I eased back the pressure, feeling a little shaky: lucky she didn't have a Rottweiler.

I breathed in the air for a while, sniffing for any trace of death and blood and terror, but the house smelled good, like cooking and flowers. Like her, in fact. And only like her, which suggested that she lived alone.

So I cleared my throat and started talking in a low voice. "Ms. Savoy? Elizabeth? This is Mike Heller, the investigator you hired. Elizabeth, please, if you're here I need you to wake up. This is Mike Heller, and I found out some things that make me think you're not safe here. Sorry about breaking in like this, I sort of needed to. Um, Ms. Savoy? You there? This is Mike—"

The lights went on abruptly, dazzling my dark-adapted eyes. My right hand jerked again, and I blinked hard.

"Mr. Heller? What are you doing here?"

I blew out a breath. I was going to have to go someplace nice and quiet at the end of this damn case. Assuming I was still alive, of course. I let my gun drop to my side, although I didn't put it away.

"Ms. Savoy, I'm afraid you may be in danger. I need you to throw a few things in a bag and come with me."

"What, now? What time is it, anyway?"

"Time to go, if you want to live."

Motion in the dark doorway resolved into a figure, dressed in slinky pajamas. Her hair was every which way, her face was bare of makeup, and she had a red pillow line across one cheek. She was absolutely gorgeous.

"It's Harry, isn't it? What did you find?"

"I'm leaving here in two minutes, with or without you. I can tell you about Harry later, once I'm sure we're safe. You coming or not?"

"I can't . . . How do you . . . You broke into my house!"

"I couldn't be sure you weren't being watched. Still can't be sure."

"Get out!"

I took a step back toward the door. "If that's what you want, I'll leave. But I won't be able to keep you safe if you're not with me."

"I can't just leave. And anyway, I have to be at work in a few hours!"

"Call in sick. Ms. Savoy, I really wish you would trust me on this. I swear, you're honestly not safe here." I could feel the seconds ticking away on the clock, but what could I do? Knock her out and carry her away? All I could do was try to look honest, and wait for her to make up her mind.

The way she did it shook me more than anything that had yet happened in that already busy twenty-four hours. She glanced at the gun dangling at the end of my arm, then undulated across the room in those slinky pajamas to stand in front of me, studying my face with her human-looking eyes. Then she reached up both hands to pull my face to hers, and kissed me.

Interesting fact: What's unpredictable about genetic splicing is the distribution of each side's characteristics. Salamanders have a whole lot of DNA packed into their cells—probably the reason they combine readily with others—but very few of us came out of our foster wombs looking like lizards (very few who lived, anyway). And only a handful of us have tails, or spots, or four fingers instead of five. And although I have heard of the occasional poor bastard whose tail insists on regenerating after that particular surgery, I've never believed that any of us actually shoot out our tongues or ooze poison from our skin.

But there's no doubt, many of us do things differently from your average *Homo sapiens.*

Now, a major side effect of that Supreme Court victory was that we had as much right as anyone else to keep out of the hands of scientists (which is the reason you sometimes see ads on WeWeb and Facebook, begging for SalaMan volunteers). Science eyes us with a longing that verges on lust. It offers us considerable sums to participate in studies, then gleefully writes learned papers about our every oddity from pheromones and internal sex organs (science being as fascinated by our pre-Surgery organs as the tabloids are) to the ability to stretch the visible realm into the ultraviolet. Any of us who can prove that we've lost a scar or regenerated a finger, and don't mind spending the rest of our lives under a microscope, would never have to work another day.

But one thing I've never read about in the literature, probably because the scientists never thought to ask about it, is the odd uses of some SalaMan mucous membranes.

Elizabeth Savoy was not kissing me, she was tasting the truth on me. She took her time about it, and for sure both of us enjoyed it, but we both knew what she was doing. And we both knew what she tasted.

Without a word, she walked back into the bedroom. I heard a drawer open.

I turned off the overhead light that she'd switched on with some kind of remote, and went into the room where the cat had disappeared. A neighbor's outdoor light gave shape to kitchen cabinets, and I opened them until I found a bag of kibble, which I set on the floor with the top open. I took a big bowl and filled it with water, setting it next to the bag. My client's feline responsibilities taken care of, I pressed my face to the windows, studying the possibilities. Wondering if what I'd found at Eileen Jacobs's house was just brother Harry's coffee having its way with my nerves. But I didn't think so.

It was more than the two minutes I'd given her, but less than three, when I heard the toilet flush and feet wearing shoes coming across the room. My client fished a jacket out of the front-door closet, put it on, and picked up the small bag.

"Did you bring whatever cash you have?" I asked her. "Necessary pills, glasses, your ID?"

"Cash, a bit of jewelry, and my license and passport. No pills or glasses."

"Turn off your cell phone. Better yet, take out the battery."

She took out a pricey-looking slip of plastic, thumbing open the back and dropping the battery and the now-inert machine back into the bag's pocket.

We went out her back door, around the tiny garden, through the gate, and up the winding stairway leading away from the water, to the place I had left the motorcycle I'd borrowed from an unwitting friend in Berkeley. On two wheels, and later four, I took my client out of the Bay Area, doubling back, going as invisibly as I knew how, spending all my attention on the rearview mirror and giving out just enough information to keep her with me. Finally, late that afternoon we went to ground in a middle-of-the-road motel in Sacramento, registering as a husband and wife, in a room with two beds.

She turned on me the instant the door was shut. "Okay, all day you've been putting me off about this because you needed to concentrate on our backs. So are we now, finally, safe enough that you can answer one or two damn questions?"

"Yes," I said, "but—"

"Oh, Christ!"

"Look, Elizabeth. I'm tired and I'm cranky. Even you look like you could stomp a puppy. You go take a shower, I'll rustle up some food, we'll have a drink, and after that we'll talk as long as you like."

She wavered, but she was honest enough with herself that the call of the shower overcame her impatience.

I phoned a nearby Chinese place that delivered, and told the guy I'd add a hefty tip if he'd pick up a cold six-pack and something chocolate and girly on his way. The food and drink arrived as my client was finishing her long, steamy shower; I paid him cash, keeping my head a bit down in case someone out there flashed around a picture of my face. When she came out of the bathroom, I went in; as I closed the door, I heard the sound of a beer cap coming off.

I'll admit it: I spend most of my life pretending I don't feel the tightness of my skin and the sandpaper dryness of the air, but sometimes I can't help reveling in the luxury of water. This was one of those.

I was only half dry when I heard her call my name, in a voice that had me out of there with the gun in one hand and the corners of the towel in the other.

She was staring at the television, tuned to the six o'clock news. The young reporter stood in front of a place I did not at first recognize, and only partly because I'd just seen it at night. The main reason was, the house that had been there, wasn't.

". . . called 911, but by the time the vehicles could get up the narrow hills of this community of artists and bohemians, the house was already engulfed with flames. Neighbor Alison Stanford describes the scene."

Neighbor Alison Stanford was a petite Japanese woman of about sixty wearing artistic clothing and a thrilled expression. She earnestly described waking to sirens, seeing the leap of flames (she actually used the phrase) from the street, and was now waiting to see if the nice woman who lived there had survived. "I found her cat in my backyard," said Ms. Stanford. "It took a while before it would let me come near, but I picked it up and took it inside. I hope the owner's all right."

Ms. Stanford seemed more excited at the brush with fame than she was worried at her neighbor's safety. I stepped back inside the bathroom to exchange the towel for my trousers and add the clean shirt, then came out and took the remote control from my client's grip, pressing the power button. Silence fell.

Elizabeth drew a shaky breath, then lifted her eyes to mine. "Harry's dead, isn't he?"

"I don't know yet. Finding that out comes second on my list of things to do. First is keeping you alive."

"But why would anyone want to kill me?"

"Your brother's place was searched. So was Eileen's." I handed her the envelope of printouts. "Harry hid these, really well."

She pulled the pages out, fourteen printouts and three actual newspaper clippings, all news articles from across the country. It didn't take long for her to get the gist of them, since all the stories followed the same lines: Someone died, or someone disappeared, or someone disappeared and was later found dead.

Four of the names had been on the list my client had given me in my office the previous morning.

The stories ranged from two column inches to half the front page of a small-town paper. She read three, then read sections of the next five, and after that she just skimmed them. At the end, she folded them together and looked up at me. She looked lost—and scared. Which was good.

"They're all . . . us, aren't they?"

"SalaMen? Hard to be sure, but I'd guess so."

Only two of the stories said it openly, but three others described the victim as "private" (meaning: nervous about inviting people home) and five of them had quotes about the missing or dead person's unconventional beauty: that sinuous appeal doing its subliminal work.

"But, so many? How could the police not know?"

That was the real question. The cops, I could understand not catching it, since any database of crimes needs some point of similarity to send up a warning flag, and these were just eight unrelated people, from all over the country, who'd disappeared. The only thing that linked them was—if Harry and his sister were right—their genetic makeup. And if the feds raised that flag themselves, they were admitting that their hands-off policy toward the SalaMan community wasn't quite as complete as they said.

It wouldn't be the first time a governmental agency had chosen cold-blooded self-protection over humanitarian concerns. Especially when a lot of the population wouldn't exactly consider us human.

My client sniffed. I looked over and saw her staring down at her beer bottle, one tear snaking down her cheek. "At least my cat is okay," she said.

With that, I realized that I was holding the neck of my beer bottle so hard my fingers were going numb. I was mad, madder than I'd been in a lot of years. If the feds could've stopped this and didn't—if the feds sat back while Elizabeth Savoy went onto some Salaphobe's dirty little list . . .

I put down the bottle and handed my client a box of the takeaway and a pair of chopsticks. "Eat," I ordered, and sat down to do the same.

When we had both slowed down a little, I said, "Okay. Tell me again how you know the people on Harry's list."

"As I said, I only know Eileen and Harry. Two of the others, Imogen and Barbara, I went to college with, although I haven't seen them for years. And now I think about it, the guy named Hal Andrews? Imogen dated a guy named Hal for a while, and his name might have been Andrews, although I'm not sure. And the guy named Benny? Well, I vaguely remember Harry mentioning someone with that name from when he lived in L.A. The others don't ring any bells."

"You kept in touch with people from college, but didn't see them?"

"Oh, we lost track of each other a long time ago, but then they joined Harry's group on WeWeb, and we reconnected."

"Tell me about Harry's WeWeb group."

"If you're thinking that some hate group is targeting us through that, I don't think so. Harry was—is—very careful. Anyone who applies for membership has to wait until they have a face-to-face meeting. He has to be sure. No, it would be really tough to crash that party."

I pinched up a few more bites of cold kung pao beef, reflecting that, no, crashing a party wasn't precisely what I had in mind.

I could feel in my pocket the two printouts I'd removed from Harry's envelope before handing it to his sister.

They were both page captures from the social networking site WeWeb. One of those belonged to Eileen Jacobs and followed a discussion about a movie she'd been working on, doing set design. The other belonged to a guy named Bill Mayer, who posted mostly about a kids' baseball team that I guessed he coached.

But the reason I'd taken them out of the envelope before handing it to my client, and the reason I thought they were in Harry's secret collection to begin with, was not the brief chats the two WeWeb members had posted. It was the advertisements in the two sidebars. The first one, from Bill Mayer's page dated the previous fall, read:

SALAMAN? $500 AN HOUR FOR YOUR PARTICIPATION IN A STUDY. EASY, QUICK, UNOBTRUSIVE, PRIVATE, YOU CAN HELP OTHERS AND EARN HARD CASH FAST.

The ad ended with a linked contact address. The second page, taken from Eileen's page two months ago, had the same wording except for one thing.

The payment offered had gone up tenfold, to $5,000.

I FED MY CLIENT ANOTHER BEER, THEN THE CHOCOLATE. BEFORE LONG HER eyelids drooped into the relief of sleep. I pulled the covers over her, dropped the empty boxes into the wastebasket, and stretched out on the adjacent bed.

"Thank you, Mike," she said, her voice drowsy.

"Sure, honey. Hey, tell me something?"

"Hmm?"

"How'd you find me? When you came to my office?"

"Saw you in a bar, about six months ago. Someone I was with pointed you out, said you were a private investigator. One look, and I knew."

"Took you all that time to come up with an excuse to hire me, huh?"

"Hmm," she mumbled, and a minute later she was snoring into her pillow.

The kiss she'd given me had nothing to do with romance. I knew that. Still, I couldn't help the memory of it on my mouth as I lay there, staring up at the ceiling, six chaste feet away from her.

THE NEXT DAY, MY FIRST ORDER OF BUSINESS WAS TO STASH MY CLIENT someplace safe. It took me twenty minutes driving in circles before I found that endangered species, a pay phone, but once I'd made a call, it was only a matter of a few hours before one of the two guys I'd trust with my life showed up and took her away. She didn't want to go, but in the end, she did.

Step two, a public computer.

I'm a big fan of libraries: information, comfort, and safety, all in one place. And over the years, library associations have fought hard for privacy rights, which makes them more secure from snoops than any cyber café. This library even had a coffee bar attached to it, which was good because what I was doing wasn't going to be quick.

But before the place shut down that night, a targeted ad had popped up on the side of the shiny new WeWeb page for my made-up SalaMan, Julio Rogers. Julio was new to WeWeb for undisclosed but hinted-at reasons ("I been away, if you know what I mean . . .") and had lousy writing skills, some ill-disguised anger, and a considerable interest in SalaMan rights.

The targeting algorithm had caught Julio's SalaMan references and sent him an offer for QUICK, UNOBTRUSIVE, PRIVATE cash.

Julio's offer had gone up to $7,500. Which could mean they had come into serious funding, or that they were getting desperate. Either way was fine with me. It was fine, too, with Julio, who shot off an e-mail to the address.

I slept in a different motel that night, and had a dream about blue eyes.

The next morning I went to another library, logged on to Julio's page, and sat back with a smile on my face.

> Thank you for your interest in SalaMan Research Enterprises (SRE). If you hold SalaMan heritage, welcome! Our researchers are affiliated with the University of California, Stanford, Yale, and other medical schools, and are thoroughly trained in the protection of privacy rights. Our project is aimed at helping the particular health needs of the SalaMan community, and in the preliminary stages requires only a fifteen-minute questionnaire and a simple blood test. If you are interested in hearing about our work and how you can help us, we have public meetings across the country, for which you will be paid to attend, without making a commitment to participate further.
>
> (PLEASE NOTE: Applicants' DNA will be tested immediately on arrival, before any payment is made. False applicants will be reported to WeWeb.)

The form e-mail was signed by a man with a lot of letters sprinkled after his name, and the list of public meetings included—surprise, surprise—one at two o'clock Saturday afternoon, the day after tomorrow, at a big conference hotel less than thirty miles from the library Julio had been working at.

Julio sent his acceptance of the offer, then logged off and left that library in a hurry, never to return.

I spent the rest of that day and most of Friday moving from one library to another, putting on a lot of miles between each one, as I tried to duplicate Harry's research about the people whose names ended up in his envelope.

Saturday afternoon I was at the conference hotel, looking forward to that SRE information meeting, wondering whether they intended to pull a gun first, or just go with the tranquilizers.

I HADN'T BEEN ABLE TO GET A CAMERA INSIDE THE MEETING ROOM ITSELF, but the one I'd tucked behind the hallway flower arrangement worked fine. At half past one on Saturday, three men came down the hallway, their faces nice and clear in the camera, their heights marked by a tick I'd put in a picture frame on the wall. Two of them were clearly muscle, one a boss type. One of the big guys carried a notice board with a tripod, which he set up facing the other way, although I'd seen when he was moving around that it was the sort of corporate intro you'd expect to see when you came toward a public meeting room. The other big guy was carrying a carton, no doubt filled with the kind of meaningless forms and equipment that would reassure a sucker and get him inside the doors.

That day's only sucker, it would appear, was Julio. Whose last act on this earth was to send an e-mail at 2:04 to say that he was sorry, he'd changed his mind, maybe in the future . . .

At 2:12, the three men came out, looking considerably less friendly than they had going in. One carried the carton, now jammed every which way with stuff. They walked away from my viewpoint, and then the boss man jerked his thumb back and the other big guy whirled around and went back for the tripod sign. If I'd been standing behind the flowers instead of my camera, he'd have smashed the sign over my head.

At 2:14, the three men came out of the hotel's side doors, dumped their armloads into the trunk of a shiny black car, and drove away. I hit the send button on the laptop I'd been watching all this on, tossed it onto the passenger seat, and put my own car into gear.

Interesting fact: Cops pay attention when you send them traceable evidence of what you claim is a crime in progress. Phone calls can be about anything, post office letters can disappear, but when you tell them you're sending them an electronic file, and then you send it, that makes a trail they hesitate to ignore entirely.

The e-mail with the video attachment was to Frank, my cop . . . well, maybe not *friend*, but we'd worked together a couple times, and drunk together a few more times. I liked Frank fine, and I knew he was honest, but I also wanted a little insurance. No cop wants to go into a courtroom against a lawyer who has evidence of a murder the police could have prevented.

Mine, for example.

I followed, keeping well back thanks to the little blip on the GPS screen. While they were waiting for Julio, I'd had plenty of time to press a bug under the fender. Ain't technology great?

But not so great when the people you're following change cars, and leave your clever blip standing at the same point until the transmitter's battery runs down. Which was what I thought was happening when they went five miles and pulled into a coffeehouse.

But I lucked out. The two goons did take their equipment from the trunk and got into a second car, but my shiny black target pulled immediately out of the parking lot, signaled for a right, and in two minutes was on the freeway north.

After two hours, we'd left the freeway far behind, traffic on the smaller road was so thin I didn't dare come closer than half a mile, and it looked like the guy was planning to drive up the backside of Nevada without even a coffee break. I, on the other hand, was yawning fit to break my jaw, my bladder had gone past uncomfortable to the brink of needing attention, and the pink blip on my screen had hypnotized me into stupidity.

I only noticed it had stopped moving when I was already too close to do anything but barrel on by.

The driver—still wearing both the jacket and tie—was just getting back into the car after unlocking a gate at the side of the road. He glanced at me, seeing only a dusty car whose bored driver was rubbing his eye. In the rearview mirror I saw him pull ahead into the side road, then get out to go back and close the gate. My foot didn't move on the pedal until he had disappeared around a curve, at which time I swerved to the side and killed the engine.

I grabbed the knapsack from the seat and forced my stiff legs and screaming bladder up the nearby rise until the dust plume from the once-shiny car came into view. I kept a naked eye on it for a couple of minutes and then, when my hands were free and my bladder happy, I took a pair of binoculars from the knapsack. Just in time to see the car vanish behind some low hills.

This far from civilization, I did not expect to find a connection, and I was right. However, I wrote an e-mail on the laptop, hit send, then closed its lid and locked the thing in the trunk. If I failed to make it back, someone would eventually find it, and when it was fired up, Frank would learn where I had last been.

I pushed some things I thought I might need into the knapsack, then walked across the road in the direction of the black car.

For a dirt road in the middle of nowhere, it had a surprising amount of traffic. By the time darkness fell, I had seen three vehicles go past: a white van, delivering some cartons and full grocery sacks, then leaving; a small red Jeep, driven at speed by a thin man with white hair; and an hour later, at dusk, the black car on its way out.

Their goal was a wide, single-story building made of poured concrete with a faded blue steel roof. The only windows were on either side of the front door, although when I circled the place, I found two other doors, one on the back and the other on the western side. All three doors were steel, and solid looking. I wouldn't know if their locks were as good until I got my hands on them.

The two windows were covered from within, by slatted blinds on the left and curtains on the right. The blinds went dark about ten o'clock; the curtains snapped out of sight around half past eleven.

At one in the morning, I slipped out from the trees facing the western door. I couldn't see any security cameras, and although the light over the door was on, a quick poke with a branch changed that.

It took me a while, even with my illegal-to-own, cutting-edge cracksman tool. When the lock finally gave, I vowed to write the guy who'd invented the thing a personal letter of thanks.

I took out my gun and moved forward. Before I was fully inside, I knew: there were SalaMen inside. The air was damp, and carried on it the stink of fear and suffering.

I let the door whisper shut and went in search of them. Went in search of—okay, damn it—of my people.

Hellbender isn't a salamander that spends its life underground, so its eyes aren't as sensitive as some. Still, I had no trouble making out the shapes of the hallway and the doors, some of which were standing open. And I wasn't too surprised to find one leading to stairs, since I'd figured there might be as much of this building underground as there was above.

It wasn't a new building, although sometime in the last year or so the walls got a coat of paint and the linoleum was scrubbed. I couldn't tell what the place had been in a previous life—out here, it probably wasn't anything legal.

It wasn't now, either. That ad in WeWeb promised easy money, but what the SalaMen who answered it got wasn't money, and there was nothing easy about it. My recent library crawl, hunting down Harry's names, had given me some things they had in common beyond their genetic structure.

For one thing, an awful lot of them were strapped for cash. A couple had lost their jobs, others had mortgage problems or a divorce or kids to support (adopted kids, but still family). And as near as I could tell without going into Harry's home computer, they'd all belonged to Harry's WeWeb group. Every one of them was on WeWeb—which meant nothing in itself, most of the country was on WeWeb—but every one of Harry's names had a page where portions were blocked from view.

If his sister was right, it would be tough to infiltrate the group. However, I had no doubt that a clever and patient person could come up with an ad targeting customers of a brand of lotion soothing to SalaMan skin, or supporters of certain political candidates, or any of a hundred other possible arrows and send them the ad.

And when the poor bastards responded to it, they'd ended up here.

A research facility.

At the bottom of a flight of metal stairs was a door. It was closed, although the stink that came around it made my eyes water. I took a deep breath and went through it.

Another long corridor, with steel doors on both sides. Every door had a small barred window in it. Eyes glistened from behind some of the bars.

I took care of the camera above the door, then eased forward to the first door and breathed, "Are there any guards down here?"

"Who . . . who are you?" A man's voice, hesitant.

"Answer me!"

"Guards? No, but there's a camer—"

"Where are the keys?"

"Keys?" He was either confused or frightened by the question. It occurred to me that his captors might have played games with him, and he was afraid this might be one of them. But I didn't have time to pat his head.

"I came to get you all out of here, but you've got to help. Harry's sister sent me," I tried.

"Lizzie?"

I might as well have said Jesus and the Virgin Mary for all his astonishment. "The keys, man!"

"One key for all, on a ring near the door," he shot back.

I leaped for the door, found the simple key, and stabbed it into his door. I thought I might have to drag him out, but he came willingly enough. I shoved the key at him. "Let the others out," I started to say, but the key fell to the floor. I snatched it up, cursing his clumsiness. Then he held up his hands for me to look at.

His hands looked strange in the dim light, more like stubs. And in growing horror I saw that they were stubs. He had no fingers. No fingers at all.

"Regeneration experiment," he said, in a voice so tight, it didn't sound human.

My skin suddenly felt a size too small. I swallowed, and turned to open the next door.

There were eleven prisoners in that cellar. All of them were missing something. One woman had fingers about an inch long; God knows how many months she'd been down there. Another woman had a face that even in the near dark I could see was beautiful, but for her ruined eyes—

A thin man whose beard was either blond or gray shoved past me to embrace the blind woman, who jerked away and then cried "Bill!" and flung herself at him.

"Quiet!" I ordered, and to Bill I whispered, "Take her over to the door, we'll all go up at once."

I got the last two cages open, but one of the prisoners did not emerge. When I stepped in, I could see why.

I don't know how long I stood there, torn between abandoning a person who was going to slow us down dangerously, and the impossibility of leaving anyone in this terrible place. But eventually I became aware of someone standing next to me. It was the first man I'd freed.

I said, "You're Harry?"

"That's right. You?"

"Mike Heller. Your sister hired me. Did you find your girl here? Eileen?"

"She died."

"Ah. I'm sorry."

"Before I got here. Do you want me to carry her?" he asked, gesturing at the girl on the cot.

"Can you?"

"I'll sure as hell try."

He'd been down here only a couple of weeks, which gave him a lot more reserves than some of the others. I helped lift her onto his back, and although he let out a sound when his hand brushed her knee, he clamped his arms against her legs and turned to the door.

Eleven of them—no: twelve, of *us*—gathered at the door. I lifted the gun, and whispered, "There's stairs up and then a hallway. Go down it to the left about thirty feet, and the outside door's at the end. Keep to one side in the hallway so I have a clear line of sight. If you head out the door at the angle of two o'clock you'll be in the trees quickest. Up the hill and down, my car's on the road with a key in a lockbox near the driver's tire. If we're discovered, I'll keep these bastards in place and you move as fast as you can. Don't worry about me, just go.

"And when you get closer to town, take my laptop out of the trunk and turn it on. The last e-mail it sends will give you a safe contact in the police department. Tell him to get someone here, fast. Now, ready?"

At least six of them started talking, with questions or protests, but Harry interrupted them. "There's no time for this. We'll do as he says."

And they did. My gun leading the way, I crept up the steps, wincing at all the creaks and groans the crew behind me made. At the top, I had them all stand very still and got the door open, again sticking the gun out first, then my nose.

No one there.

I went into the hallway, and they came after me, limping and stumbling. I kept to the right, trying to look both ways at once, my heart in my throat. I mean, I've been in tight places before, even been shot at, but with eleven innocents on my back? That was a whole different ball game.

The damned door creaked as I opened it. Why, I don't know, it hadn't on my way in, but maybe I was a little more impatient this time. Anyway, it creaked, and then they were pouring past me into the darkness, little cries of disbelief and pleasure, surprise that it was dark, shuddering gasps of clean, night-scented air.

And then the lights went on.

"Go!" I said. Harry was last, with the woman on his back, and he hesitated. "Go, get her out of here!" I shoved him into the night, and then reached forward to slam the door shut, closing him out. Closing me in.

I jumped for the nearest side door, which was closed but not locked. An office of some kind, windowless of course, nice and dark. I left the door open a crack, pressing my ear to it, and about three seconds later I heard voices.

"—like the outside door." A man, his voice high, by nature or with tension.

"I'll check it." This man sounded big, his voice deeper and slower; younger, maybe. I heard footsteps approaching; they sounded heavy; my hand got ready on the gun.

"Not the door," snapped the first one. "Downstairs first, so we know if any of them are loose."

The footsteps paused; a door opened and I heard a pair of feet descending the metal stairs. The older man stayed at the top, but the voice that rang up from below was perfectly clear:

"They're gone! All of them!"

The older man's curses retreated down the corridor until they were drowned out by the racket his partner made, pounding up the steel stairs. When he reached the top, he shouted, "You want me to go after them?"

"Get a shotgun, and wake up Andrew and Mannie. Christ," he said in a lower voice, "I knew we should have a dog."

I was glad about the dog, not so happy about the shotgun. I shifted to put my eye to the crack, and eased it slightly wider until I could see a large back going away from me. My legs twitched with wanting to dive for the door, but I stayed put.

If I was on the outside, I couldn't know how many of them there were.

Outside, I could keep them from coming out that one door, but there were two others, and in no time at all, they'd circle around me. Outside, I'd be safer, but the others wouldn't.

Oh hell, admit it: I'd shut the door to force Harry and the rest to run.

I'd shut the door because I wanted to climb down the throats of these animals and tear them apart from within.

In fact, although I hadn't exactly been thinking clearly when I made my choice, it wasn't altogether idiotic. There was a good chance these guys would all make a dash for the door at once, allowing me to pick them off, or at least pin them down. I'd brought enough bullets to keep things hot for a while.

And for a minute, it looked like it would be okay. A clot of men appeared at the far end of the corridor, milling around and shouting at each other. Then they started in my direction.

I waited, counting heads: four. It was hard to tell exactly where they were in relation to the building's front door, but I could see enough to know when they passed the door to the prison stairs. I gave it a few seconds, then opened the door wide enough to fit my gun arm through.

I'd hoped the older voice, the guy in charge, would be first, but I figured he was probably the man I'd seen drive up in the red Jeep, and sure enough, the head of white hair was barely visible past various shoulders. The big guy whose back I'd seen was at the front, carrying a shotgun. The two other guys, both with that rumpled look of being dragged out of bed, seemed like people who spent their days in a lab torturing mice, more at home with scalpels and microscopes than with the weapons they carried.

Didn't matter: They were all targets.

I opened fire. The big guy saw me a split second before my finger went down and dove through a doorway—I thought I winged him, but it was one of the scientists behind him who fell. The white-haired guy and the skinny assistant on the left vanished into other doorways.

A shotgun went off, spattering the hallway but not making it through my wooden door. There was a lot of shouting and cursing, and finally a sharp order from that first voice I'd heard. Silence. Then: "Who is there?"

"Guess," I called.

"Which one of you is that?"

"Oh, I'm a whole new nightmare for you."

Silence again.

"I don't know what you want, young man, but—"

"What do I want? I want you to die, in a whole lot of pain."

Silence, longer this time.

"Well," he said at last. "You can probably understand that we don't wish to oblige you."

"Tough."

"Apart from our deaths, why did you come?"

"Because you're a monster, and monsters need to be slain." I don't know why I said that. Probably because it didn't matter what I said: The longer he talked, the farther his lab rats could scurry.

"And you are our modern-day hero, rescuing the creatures?"

"They're people. Unlike you."

"They're valuable resources, whose unique heritage could save countless lives. Think of all the soldiers whose limbs might be regrown, the blind who might see, the—"

"Yeah, and because Hitler's doctors and dentists learned things in the concentration camps, that justifies Dachau and Buchenwald? What say we put you in a lab and pull you apart, see if we can find a cure for evil?"

Jesus, I thought; stay here any longer and I'd start singing "Kumbaya."

He answered, his voice all sad and patronizing. "I can see your mind is made up. Although I'm sorry your little friends have abandoned you here."

"My choice."

"And now you're trapped."

"Is that what you think?"

"Oh, very well. Andrew, you get ready to shoot our visitor when he puts his head around that doorway. Jonah, you're on his blind side of the hallway: when I give the word—"

My gun went off, six times. The first tore up the floor next to the nose of Andrew's gun and made it jerk back; the rest of them took out the four lights overhead, leaving a couple down at the far end.

I slapped in another clip and risked putting my eye to the crack, but nobody was moving.

"There," I said. "Now it's nice and dark, like creatures prefer."

"Um, boss?" Andrew said. "What do we do now?"

"Oh, for heaven's sake," said the boss man. He sounded annoyed, more than anything, which made me nervous. I strained to hear, but I couldn't tell what he was up to—until his voice came again, talking. On a phone.

"Manny? Dr. Curtis here. We have an intruder, with a gun. He's in the office just inside the west door, the first room to the left. If you open the door, you and Jack can stand back in the darkness and blaze away, you can't possibly miss him. But make sure you take care, we're right down the hallway. How long? Okay. Yes, we're not going anywhere, but then, neither is our intruder."

That put a whole different picture on the situation.

I sighed, and reached for the knapsack.

When I was ready, I watched Andrew's doorway. I didn't figure him for a patient man, and indeed, after a minute the end of his shotgun eased around the frame. I let it come four inches, and then fired, at his door and at the other two for good measure. And once they had all ducked back in their holes, I stepped into the hallway, and threw.

Andrew's curses almost hid the first sound of breaking glass. But my second bottle, aimed ten feet farther down the hallway, made an unmistakable noise, and the third one as well.

Dr. Curtis figured out what it meant first. I could feel him staring at the dim hallway, looking at the liquid and smashed glass, and then he must have smelled it.

He waited just long enough to see that the bottles had all landed on the far side of his door, long enough to figure out what I had in mind, long enough to make his choice between a chancy bullet and a sure burning to death. The old guy came out of his doorway so fast I almost wasn't ready.

Almost.

The lighter in my hand snapped into life, the rag in the top of my last bottle flared, and I backhanded it into the corridor. Before the bottle hit the wall, the corridor exploded into a wall of flame.

The doc screamed as he ran, and he might have gotten the door open if I hadn't managed to get off a couple of shots in that direction. A slightly more solid shape among the flames went down, and although I had to slam my own door shut then, I could hear him screaming for a while before he went still. A few minutes later, the others stopped, too.

And some time later, so did I.

EXCEPT . . .

If I died, who is telling this story?

Interesting fact—a last one: Some of the myths about salamanders are more or less true.

The room burned around me, my hair and clothing crinkled and burned, the beams overhead groaned and burned. The fire department got there, snaked their hoses into the inferno, and found five dead people. Or so they thought.

Then one of them moved.

Myth has it that a salamander can extinguish fire with the cold dampness of its body. Aristotle believed it, and some of the other old Greeks. Nonsense, of course, as even Pliny pointed out—but strangely enough, not entirely.

I lost my fingers, three toes, my voice, and most of my skin. A normal man would have died. They kept me in a coma for weeks. My looks disturbed hardened nurses for months.

But that was a year ago.

By the time I was in any shape to be questioned, there were really no questions left. They sent Frank to do the interview, even though he'd had nothing to do with the case other than passing on what I sent him. I don't know, maybe I made them nervous.

Anyway, Frank told me a lot more than he asked me.

I knew about the scandals and the headlines, of course—when you're in the hospital, they leave the television on a lot. So I'd sort of vaguely heard about the police raids and the government shake-ups; I'd heard the outraged speeches and the wild rumors and the dueling news stations. Even wrapped in my blanket of pain and drugs, I was aware of the shift of public opinion that made every SalaMan into a hero.

WeWeb closed down, after nine out of ten users canceled their pages, even though WeWeb did nothing but sell the ads.

A bill went in front of Congress to ban targeted ads, although no one thought it would pass.

What was expected to pass was a slew of bills reforming how science was done. Labs across the country were shut down or raided because of the links Dr. Curtis had formed with organized crime—nothing glues people to headlines like a modern-day Mengele: high-ranking scientist hires thugs to kidnap the raw material for his experiments; thugs go on to search the victims' houses for more raw material; thugs set fires to discourage snoops.

And there's nothing that makes the lawyers drool like a case linking universities and government agencies and organized crime and weird, mostly beautiful people like the SalaMen. It's going to make the Nuremberg Trials look like squirrel food.

And you want to know the thing that astonishes me most, in all this? That Uncle Sam had in fact done exactly what it said it would: lock the door on the SalaMan files and make sure no one knew who we were. Which would've been a good and fair thing, except it meant that when we started disappearing, the FBI didn't notice, since there was no reason to tie the disappearances together. The police didn't notice, because the victims were so spread out. The media didn't catch it, because even if they'd heard, who would believe it? Nobody noticed but Harry Savoy, and Harry was too paranoid to trust the FBI, the police, or the media.

Me? I kept out of everything. I had to shut my office, although I could've been busy a thousand hours a week if I'd been in any shape to work. I'm thinking that when I open again, I may actually call myself SalaMan Investigations. I might even try just working for my own people for a while.

But when might that be? Well, last night, while Lizzie and I were . . . well, as we were occupied with things that married people do, she said "Ow!" and sat up, rubbing her ribs. When she pulled her hand away, we both saw the red welt, up the side of her pale skin. I held the stubs of my fingers under the light, and studied them.

Sure enough, there among the scar tissue was a tiny rough protuberance. It looked for all the world like a baby's fingernail.

SHADOW THIEVES

A Garrett, P.I., Story

by Glen Cook

Glen Cook is the bestselling author of more than forty books. He's perhaps best known for the Black Company books, which include *The Black Company*, *Shadows Linger*, *The White Rose*, *The Silver Spike*, *Shadow Games*, *Dreams of Steel*, *Bleak Seasons*, *She Is the Darkness*, *Water Sleeps*, and *Soldiers Live*, detailing the adventures of a band of hard-bitten mercenaries in a gritty fantasy world, but he is also the author of the long-running Garrett, P.I., series, including *Sweet Silver Blues*, *Bitter Gold Hearts*, *Cold Copper Tears*, and ten others, a mixed fantasy/mystery series relating the strange cases of a private investigator who works mean streets on both sides of the divide between our world and the supernatural world. The prolific Cook is also the author of the science fiction Starfishers series, as well as the eight-volume Dread Empire series, the three-volume Darkwar series, and the recent Instrumentalities of the Night series, as well as nine stand-alone novels such as *The Heirs of Babylon* and *The Dragon Never Sleeps*. His most recent books are *Passage at Arms*, a new Starfishers novel; *A Fortress in Shadow*, a new Dread Empire novel; *Surrender to the Will of the Night*, a new Instrumentalities of the Night novel; and two new Garrett, P.I., novels, *Cruel Zinc Melodies* and *Gilded Latten Bones*. Cook lives in St. Louis, Missouri.

In the action-packed tale that follows, Garrett learns that when trouble comes knocking at your door, sometimes it's better not to answer.

I WAS HALF ASLEEP IN THE BROOM CLOSET I CALL AN OFFICE. SOMEBODY hammered on the front door. Odd that they should. I wasn't home much anymore.

This time I was hiding out from the craziness that comes down on the newly engaged. My future in-laws dished me make-crazy stuff relentlessly.

I began disentangling myself from my desk and chair.

Old Dean, my cook and housekeeper, trundled past my doorway. He was long, lean, slightly bent, gray, and almost eighty, but spry. "I'll get it, Mr. Garrett. I'm expecting a delivery."

That was one impatient deliveryman. He was yelling. He was pounding. I couldn't understand a word. That door was fortress grade.

Dean did not use the peephole. He assumed the noise came from whoever he was expecting. He opened up.

All kinds of tumult rolled on in. Dean shrieked. A deeper, distressed voice bellowed something about getting the frickin' frackin' hell out of the way!

I started moving, snagging an oak nightstick as I went. That gem had two pounds of lead in its kissing end.

More demanding voices joined the confused mix.

I hit the hall fast but my ratgirl assistant, Pular Singe, was out of her office faster. At five feet Singe was tall for her tribe. Her fine brown fur gleamed. She slumped a bit more than usual. Her tail lashed like an angry cat's but she emptied a one-hand crossbow as calm as sniping at the practice range. Her bolt hit the forehead of a thing whose ancestors all married ugly. It was a repugnant shade of olive green, wide like a troll, and wore an ogre's charming face. It smelled worse than it looked. It filled half the hallway. Its forehead looked troll solid but Singe's quarrel was unimpressed.

What kind of toy had she found herself now?

She stepped out of my way, whiskers dancing.

Big Ugly finished collapsing. Two of his friends clamored right behind him. One tried to get hold of a very large, equally ugly human being who was down and squashing Dean because Singe's victim had fallen forward onto him. The guy was still breathing but wouldn't stick with it long. He had several serious leaks.

I laid into the hands trying to drag him. Bones crunched. Somewhere beneath it all Dean groaned piteously. I gave the final villain a solid bop between snakish yellow eyes. He took a knee after gifting me with a straight jab that flung me two-thirds of the way back toward the door to Dean's kitchen kingdom. From her office Singe called, "I was counting on you to last a little longer."

Females.

I glanced in as I headed back for more. Singe was cranking a device that would span her little crossbow, which apparently had the pull to drive steel quarrels through brick walls.

One ugly was just plain determined to take the big man home with him.

The other scrabbled after a wooden box said fellow must have dropped. I made sure my feet were solidly arranged on my downhill end and waded in.

I gagged. The guy on top of Dean, though breathing, had begun to rot.

My partner quit daydreaming and got into the game at last.

One ugly responded by voiding his bowels. He grabbed Singe's victim by an ankle and headed out. I whapped his pal till he gave up on the box, then stomped on the ally his buddy had given up dragging as he went through the doorway. Despite the bolt in his forehead, that one retained the ability to groan.

With generous assistance from a wall I launched my pursuit, but ended it leaning on the rail of the stoop.

Singe bustled out beside me, anger smoking off her. She pointed her weapon. Her bolt ripped right through one creature's shoulder. The impact spun him and knocked him down. "Whoa! This sumbitch has some kick! I think I just sprained my wrist." She watched the uglies trundle up Macunado Street. "I will go reload, then we can get after them."

Besides her genius for figures and finance, Pular Singe is the best damned tracker in TunFaire.

"The Dead Man couldn't control those guys."

"You are correct. That is not good." Singe eyed the fetid mess blanketing Dean. The big man had ceased to resemble a human being. His sailor's rags had begun to drift out of the mess.

Nothing mortal ought to decay that fast.

"I'm sure the Dead Man will tell us all about it." Which was a subtle test to see if my partner was paying attention.

A little blonde watched us from across the street, so motionless she didn't seem to be breathing. She clutched the string handles of a small yellow bag in front of her. She wore a floppy blue hat somewhere between a beret and a chef's cap. Her hair hung to just above her shoulders, cut evenly all the way round. A wisp of bang peeped out from under the hat. She wore an unseasonably heavy coat made up of sizable patches in various shades of red, gold, and brown. Its hem hovered at her knees. Quite daring, that, as her legs were bare. Her eyes were big, blue, and solemn. She met my gaze briefly, then turned and walked uphill slowly, goose-stepping, never moving her hands. I guessed her to be in the age range large nine to small eleven.

Singe said, "She has no scent."

Nor any presence except in the eyes of you two. Most unnatural.

That was my partner, the Dead Man.

A sleepy voice said, "I see her, too. I'll follow her."

Penny Dreadful, human, girl, teenager (a terrible combination), the Dead Man's pet, and the final member of this strange household, had decided to drag herself out of bed and see what the racket was all about.

As Penny pushed in between us, Singe turned a blank face my way that was all too expressive. I was in no position to grumble about anyone lying in bed since it usually takes divine intervention to roust me out before the crack of noon.

Penny is fourteen, shy around me but brash toward everyone else. She used to be the last priestess of a screwball rural cult. She lives with us because we stashed her once for her protection and she never got around to leaving. The Dead Man is fond of her inquiring mind.

"Let's deal with this mess before we do anything else. Penny, get the field cot set up in my office. We'll put Dean in there."

She grumbled. That's what teens do when they're told to do something. All life is an imposition. But she went. She liked Dean.

Singe said, "Let us shut the door before the second wave shows up."

She helped drag the injured raider. The door needed no major repairs. The damage was all cosmetic. I was pleased.

Dean and Singe's victim were less encouraging. Dean was unconscious and covered with yuck. I worried that he had internal injuries. "I'll get Dr. Harmer in a few minutes."

No need, my partner sent. *The solution to several problems is at hand.*

I stood up, bemused, though this was not the first time my stoop had hosted a raft of violent idiots. I was bemused because my telepathic sidekick was bemused. He was bemused because he had been unable to get past the surface thoughts of the raiders.

The door resounded to a tap.

Singe's head whipped round. She pushed me out of her way, cracked the peephole for form's sake, then opened up for her half-brother, the ratman gangster John Stretch. Behind him loomed his lieutenant, Dollar Dan Justice, the biggest ratman in town. All five feet three of him. More henchrat types lurked in the street.

John Stretch said, "We heard there was trouble." His whiskers wiggled as he sniffed out the story. He was a colorful dresser, wearing a yellow shirt, striped red-and-white trousers, and high-top black boots. Dollar Dan, though, was clad plain as dirt.

Singe babbled.

John Stretch patted her shoulder. "Two of them? With poisoned bolts? No? Too bad. What can we do?"

The Dead Man asked for someone to hustle a message to Dr. Harmer. And could someone please track the ones that got away? The wounded one had left a generous blood trail. I said, "I could use some help moving Dean. And some cleaning specialists to clear the mess." Meaning the rotting remains.

John Stretch said, "I hope my women can stand that."

Which said a lot about the pong. Ratfolks find most smells I don't like to be lovely fragrances.

Dollar Dan got busy lieutenanting while his boss and I chewed the fat. The crowd in the street broke up. One ratman headed downhill to get the doctor. The nastiest bunch headed the other direction, never asking what they should do if they caught up. Two more sniffed around the spot whence the blonde had watched. They couldn't find a scent.

Singe said, "I will take that once we finish here."

Her brother didn't argue so I didn't. He said, "I will ask Dollar Dan to go along. No one will look out for you better, Singe," he added when she gave him the fisheye. "So let me be selfish."

Garrett. Please bring that box in to me.

"Box?" What box?

The box that may be the reason for all the excitement.

"Oh. That box."

That bit of art in cherrywood, coated with mush, lay snuggled up to the wall beside the umbrella stand.

"It's all nasty."

Limit your contact with the filth.

"Crap. Not good. We might have to redo the floor." I scooted into the kitchen, filled a bucket with water, rounded up some cleaning rags, got back out into the hall. I found brother and sister rat people in a heated debate about Dollar Dan.

I said, "Singe, let them look out for you. It won't hurt. It's not a sign of weakness. And it'll keep your brother and Dan and me all happy."

She gave me an exasperated look but abandoned the argument.

Do not be an idiot, Garrett!

"What?" I have an old reputation as a master of repartee.

Do not open the box!

Oh. Yeah. Might be demons were willing to kill for it. It must contain something special. Maybe something dangerous.

"Right. I was distracted. Wondering why we haven't heard from the tin whistles yet."

An excellent question.

The red tops, the tin whistles, the Civil Guard, jump onto any excitement like a cat onto a herd of mice.

Be confident we will hear from them soon. Meantime, please bring the box so that I may make a more intimate examination.

Singe said, "Put it where they won't think that it might have something to do with the attack."

Yes. Of course.

"I should start my track before they get here. Otherwise, it could be tomorrow before I can get away."

Good point. The red tops, with the Specials even worse, can be intrusive and obstructive.

John Stretch said, "Hide your weapon. They see that, they will lock everyone up."

For sure. Our protectors don't want us able to fight back.

SINGE AND DOLLAR DAN, WITH PENNY TAGGING ALONG, DID GET GONE before the Civil Guard arrived. I wasn't thrilled about Penny going, but the Dead Man backed her up. I couldn't argue with that.

John Stretch and I made tea, hovered over Dean, and waited. I asked, "How come you turned up so fast?"

"We keep an eye on the place."

"You do?"

"Dollar Dan does, mostly. But there is always someone."

"He's wasting the emotion."

"You know. I know. Even Dan knows. But I will not stick my nose in."

"Probably best we don't."

"So Dan was watching when you showed up, which was a sure sign that something was about to happen."

"Hey!"

"Does anything happen when you are not here?"

"Purely circumstantial."

"No. Purely Singe. She sensibly sticks to high-margin, nontoxic projects like looking for lost pets and missing wives, and forensic accounting. She does not get tangled up with the undead, mad gods, or crazed sorcerers until you come around."

He might have some basis for his argument. But it's not like I go looking for weird. Bizarro comes looking for me.

The Guard are here and Doctor Harmer is approaching.

"And there you go," the ratman said. "You picked a family physician named Harmer."

"I did not. Singe did because he'll treat rat people, too."

"I will wait in the kitchen while you handle the Guard."

"Thank you."

The minions of the law would be excessively intrigued by the presence of a senior crime boss.

Be polite.

I was headed for the door. "I'm always polite."

You are always confrontational.

"They start it."

I do not deal well with authority. The Civil Guard is self-righteously authoritarian in the extreme.

I will spank you if you are rude.

Wow! He sounded like my mother when I was eight.

THERE WERE TWO TIN WHISTLES ON THE STOOP AND A PLATOON IN THE street. John Stretch's henchrats had turned invisible.

Dr. Harmer was just dismounting from his pretty little buggy. His driver, his gorgeous half-elf wife, stuck with the rig in case somebody tried to kype it among all the red tops.

"Lieutenant Scithe. How are you? How's the missus? Have you lost weight?"

"I *was* living a good, boring life in a tame district. Then you swooped down off the Hill."

Scithe was a tall, thin man in a big, bad mood and an ill-fitting blue uniform to match. He didn't talk about his wife. He didn't ask about my fiancée.

My whole damned life works this way. Anything happens, whatever it is, it gets blamed on Ma Garrett's oldest boy.

My partner gave me a mental head slap before my mouth started running.

Dr. Harmer shoved through the press, a thin, dark character with merry brown eyes, unnaturally white teeth, and a devilish goatee. "Show me what you've got."

"Dean is in my office. He got smushed under this thing and a guy even bigger who turned into that pile of goop."

That pile was getting smaller. Some was evaporating. Some was seeping through the floor, where it could lie in the cellar and make the house stink forever.

The doctor snorted. "I'll look at Dean first." He eased along the hallway, stepping carefully.

Scithe said, "We should have been here sooner. If we'd known you were back we'd have had somebody watching. And I had to ask the Al-Khar about special instructions." The Al-Khar being Guard headquarters.

The Dead Man laid a mental hand on my shoulder.

"The Director said we didn't need the Specials."

Oh, good. The secret police would let me skate. For now. They're so nice.

"How thoughtful."

The Dead Man squeezed, just hard enough.

Scithe asked, "So what's the story?"

"Same old, same old."

"Meaning you'll claim you don't know a thing."

"Not quite." I told it like it happened, every detail, forgetting only the cherrywood box, Singe's artillery, and John Stretch, who was probably devouring everything in my larder while he waited.

Scithe squatted beside the thing with the bolt in its forehead. "Still breathing, here." He tapped the nock of the quarrel. "I could use a better light."

The tin whistle who had come in with him said, "The wagon just rolled up, boss. I'll get a lantern."

A big brown box had pulled in behind the doctor's rig. It had crowns, keys, nooses, and whatnots painted on to proclaim it a property of the Civil Guard supported by a royal subsidy.

Scithe asked, "Any theories, Garrett?"

"Only what's obvious. He probably wanted to see the Dead Man. Somebody didn't think he should."

"They got their wish. What does the Dead Man think?"

The Dead Man is frustrated. He could not penetrate the minds of any of the attackers. Not even that one who is wounded and unconscious. Yet. That is a him, is it not?

I replied, "More or less." Mostly a whole lot more.

Scithe said, "I see ogre and troll and bits of other races."

"Trolls and ogres don't mix."

Scithe shrugged. "I see what I see. Which is that somebody with a huge ugly stick whaled on all his ancestors for five generations back. Then he fell in a barrel of ugly and drank his way back to the top."

Trolls will cross with pygmy giants on occasion. However, a more likely explanation would involve rogue researchers and illegal experiments.

The three strains of rat people exist because of old-time experimental sorcery.

That stuff is worse than murder. You can get away with murder if you make a good case for the son of a bitch needing killing.

Scithe's man came back. His lantern flung out a blinding blue-white light. Scithe got busy. He used chopsticks to poke, prod, probe, and dig into pockets. Nothing useful surfaced. He moved on to the stench pile. "Check this out."

He held up what looked like a two-inch lead slug three-eighths of an inch in diameter, pointed at one end. It had four lengthwise channels beginning just behind the ogive. The channels contained traces of brown.

"A missile?"

"Maybe. Definitely poisonous. But delivered how?" By whom, and why, were out there floating, too.

Dean's delivery has arrived.

I stepped outside.

Jerry the beer guy had pulled up in front of the doctor's rig. He was making conversation with the delectable Mrs. Harmer. He noticed me, said something to a couple red tops hating him for knowing the beautiful lady well enough to gossip with, and got them to volunteer to show off by helping carry kegs.

They brought in three ponies of froufrou girlie beers. Jerry indicated the crowd outside and the mess in the hallway. "You're back."

"What does that mean? Never mind. Just drop those by the kitchen door." I didn't want anyone to see John Stretch.

"They keep better if they stay cool."

"Put them in with the Dead Man, then."

Jerry and his helpers tiptoed around the mess and entered the demesne of the Dead Man.

I said, "Anywhere out of the way." I glanced at the cherrywood box, on a shelf with mementos from old cases. "What're they for, anyway?"

"Dean wanted to test some varietals for your reception."

"Well. That sneaky old fart."

A tin whistle pointed. "Is that him?" He'd gone as pale as paper.

My partner is a quarter ton of defunct nonhuman permanently established in a custom-built oak chair. First thing you notice, after his sheer bulk, is his resemblance to a baby mammoth with a midget trunk only a quarter the length you might expect.

Most visitors don't look close. They're petrified by the fact that he can read minds.

One red top fingered the whistle on the cord around his neck. The talisman didn't help. "Too cold in here, brothers." He beat a retreat. His pal trampled on his heels.

Jerry didn't get left behind.

The Dead Man is a Loghyr. They are exceedingly rare and exceedingly deliberate about giving up the ghost. This one has been procrastinating since he was murdered more than four hundred years ago.

Dr. Harmer tried smelling salts. The character in the hallway didn't respond. Scithe finally had a flatbed haul him off to Guard headquarters after Harmer slapped a patch on his forehead leak. The bolt stayed where it was.

Scithe left us a promise to share information, worth the paper he never wrote it on. Jerry left a real receipt. I found it a home on Singe's desk, snuggled up with Dr. Harmer's bill.

The doctor went away, too, leaving Dean in a drugged sleep.

I let John Stretch know it was safe to come out.

Ratwomen cleaning specialists turned up fast. They had been waiting on the tin whistles. They had nothing flattering to say about the mess. They wrapped their faces with damp cloth and misted the fetid air with something that smelled like the spice in hot peppers. They used garden tools to scoop goop into pails they covered securely before sending them to be chunked in the river. They avoided contact with the goop.

John Stretch and I visited the Dead Man.

"Too cold in here," the ratman complained.

"Singe's fault. She claims the colder we keep him the longer he'll last. And he don't feel it."

"I am sure she knows what she is talking about."

"She knows everything about everything. So, what's in the precious box?"

Air.

"Excuse me? Nothing? A guy died. Two more got hurt."

It is a red herring. The real box is somewhere else.

"You came up with that, how?"

With great effort and stubborn determination, reasoned out from what little I retrieved from the creature Lieutenant Scithe took away.

The Dead Man likes his strokes. "That was some good work, then."

The ladies are returning. It would appear that they enjoyed a limited success.

I let them in. Penny scooted past me and the cleaning women. Singe joined me in the chill.

"I hear you got lucky." I flipped a thumb at the Dead Man.

"The gods smiled. Just barely. There was no trail for the girl. That means sorcery. We followed the wounded creature. Those things were not with her. We were tracking them when we saw her come out of the Benbow." The Benbow is a staid old inn in the shadow of the Hill, used by out-of-towners who have business with the sorcerers infesting that neighborhood. "I sent Penny in. She oozed some girl charm and found out that she had just missed her pal Kelly, who calls herself Eliza now. Eliza shares a third-floor suite with her aunt, Miss Grünstrasse. They arrived in TunFaire yesterday."

Penny joined us. "I had to check on Dean."

"Doctor says he'll be fine. Anything to add?"

"The manager is a little guy who looks like a squirrel. I put on some cute. He let me talk to people. Eliza came from Liefmold. There's something not right about her. She doesn't talk. Her aunt has a fierce accent. That's when the squirrel got that I wasn't really their friend. He sent somebody upstairs, probably with a warning, so I cleared out."

The Dead Man touched me lightly to let me know I had no need to know about how she had charmed the Benbow staff. He didn't want me going all dad.

"I pretended I didn't know Singe or Dollar Dan when I left so they could see if anybody followed me."

"Good thinking."

Singe said, "A kitchen boy tried. Dollar Dan scared him so bad he wet himself."

"He's not useless after all."

Singe glowered. She wasn't ready to concede that. And Penny . . .

Aha! The kitchen boy's interest hadn't been his employer's idea.

Come here. All of you.

The Dead Man can tease out memories you don't know you have. He'll put his several minds to work sniffing along several distinct trails and tie everything together in startling ways.

There is nothing beyond the obvious. Our victim, Recide Skedrin, interested at least two parties enough to involve them in murder. It is likely that he was a red herring himself.

How did he know all that, suddenly?

Penny, please stand in for Dean while he recovers. Garrett and Singe will assist where necessary.

Someone had forgotten who was senior executive.

Go open the door, Garrett.

THE MAN ON THE STOOP WAS SHORT, FLABBY, AND NERVOUS. HE HAD LARGE, wet, brown doggie eyes. He felt like a guy who had lived a life of sorrow. His clothing was threadbare and dated, twenty-years-ago chic. My appearance startled him.

He had been trying to decide whether to knock. He squeaked, "Who are you?" He had a lazy, girly voice and an accent so heavy you needed a machete to cut through it.

To Singe's office, please.

The newbie did not know about the Dead Man, who reeked of wicked glee. This twitch must be an easy read.

"How come you're camped on my stoop, little fellow?"

"Uh . . ."

He would be the source of the Dead Man's unexpected knowledge.

He invested a few seconds in wondering if he should go with the lies he had rehearsed. While he strategized, Singe arranged papers so she could take notes. She was amused.

I don't care if they lie. The Dead Man can burgle their minds while they're exercising their capacity for invention.

Our visitor asked, "With whom am I speaking?"

He came without knowing? "Name's Garrett. The most handsome blue-eyed ex-Marine you're ever likely to meet. This is my place. You sure you got the right one?"

He is, in the sense that he believes this is where he may find the object of his quest.

"Mr. Garrett, I represent the Council of Ryzna." He spoke Karentine like he had a mouth full of pudding and acorns. Lucky me, I had a partner who could pass on not only what the man wanted me to know but also what he was thinking.

He realized recently that he is mostly under his own supervision. He has developed personal ambitions as a consequence.

Little man clicked his heels and bowed slightly, a habit they have in his part of the world. "Rock Truck, Rose Purple, at your command, sir," is what I heard. I shrugged. I'd heard stranger names. He made sure I knew his father was a player back in the old country. His family had been exploiting the masses for centuries.

I listened. If the silence lasted long enough he might fill it with something interesting.

"Recide Skedrin came to see you." He pronounced it *Ray-see-day Skay-drene*. Very Venageti.

The one who died.

I knew that. I am a trained observer. "I don't know that name."

"That does not surprise me. He was no one. Mate on a tramp freight carrier trafficking between TunFaire and Liefmold. A wicked young woman, Ingra Mah, recently deceased, seduced him and persuaded him to smuggle a Ryznan national treasure from Liefmold here for her. She hoped to auction the item on your Hill."

Well. That would make it a sorcerer's toy, likely with major oomph. People wouldn't be dying, elsewise.

He is telling the truth and your reasoning is sound. However, the full story also has a political aspect. The Dead Man added some visuals he had shoplifted.

I'd have to work out the man's name later. They don't put them together our way, down south. It sounded like he had done some translating. There might be a job title in there, too.

Little man produced a dagger. He said, "I am going to search . . ."

Singe said, "Really, Mr. Rock. Such bad manners."

He seemed startled to see her. The Dead Man had blinded him.

I took his dagger, careful not to touch the blade. That bore streaks in several colors, none obviously dried blood.

It went briskly. The Dead Man did not reveal himself. Singe did not leave her desk. Rock squeaked when I put him in a chair. He pouted and massaged his twisted wrist. He had extra water in his eyes.

"We'll have no more of that. Why are you haunting us?"

"I am here, at the behest of the Council, to recover the Shadow."

"The Shadow." You could pick up the capital without a hint from the Dead Man.

"What do you know about Ryzna, Mr. Garrett?"

"It's a town in Venageta with a nasty reputation."

"Sir! Ryzna is Venageti by compulsion, only because someone let besiegers into the city under cover of a bright, cloudless noonday sun, whilst all men of substance were . . ." He burbled history more than a century old.

His ancestors were the traitors. The Venageti failed to reward them to their satisfaction. They see an opportunity to turn the tables in the theft of this Shadow.

All right. I never let the fact that I don't know what's going on get in the way of getting on with getting on. "What's this Shadow gimcrack? And why look for it here?"

Any chance there was something in that box after all?

No. This would be something so powerful that any of us would have sensed it. The genuine box is lined with iron, lead, and silver. The Shadow is an aggregation of the souls of Ryzna's departed sorcerers. Their powers combined, without the personalities. Its importance to Ryzna and Mr. Rock is narrowly envisioned. The universal ambition there is to use it to control Ryzna. The deceased thief, however, realized that it could be a potent tool useful to any sorcerer anywhere.

She must have lacked wizardly talents herself. She would be busy trying to take over the world if she had some.

Exactly. Mr. Rock sees the Shadow as something abidingly dark and strong. He is in love with the potential.

So. To review. A freelance socialist decided to redistribute the wealth by purloining the Shadow of Ryzna. Rock got conscripted to bring it back because he was considered too dumb to see the personal opportunities. He'd been sandbagging. He'd decided that no one deserved to use that toy more than sweet old Rock Truck, Rose Purple, his own self.

Rock wasn't my kind of guy but he was, for sure, a type I run into a lot.

"The Shadow is . . . No. To you what it is matters not. What does matter is that it belongs to the people of Ryzna and we must have it back. I am prepared to pay four thousand silver nobles for its return."

That got my attention. And Singe would have grinned if rat people had something to grin with.

I said, "That's good." Four thousand would make me a nice dowry.

"That is very good." Then he went stupid, like I might have forgotten the original thief's reason for sending her plunder to TunFaire. "The Shadow is no good to anyone outside the Ryzna Council."

Not even true in Ryzna. The Venageti held Ryzna down with the Shadow until a sloppy guard too young to think with his head let the Ingra woman get to it.

Ingra Mah sounded like a talent. Too bad she let somebody get behind her.

"Let us be exact, Mr. Rock. What do you want? We don't have your Shadow. But we could look for it. That's what we do here."

"Recide brought you a box."

"It was empty. And he didn't live long enough to explain."

The creatures pursuing Mr. Recide were associated with Mr. Rock. There were five, assigned by the Ryzna Council to assist Mr. Rock and to keep him walking the line. They were not responsible for Mr. Recide's death.

Five. Two hurt. One of those in the hoosegow. Rock's keepers as well as consorts. Good to know. And the original thief? Was she really dead? Had she been slick enough to break her trail by faking her own demise?

"Oddly enough, I believe you, Mr. Garrett."

At the same time, Old Bones sent, *He believes she is dead.* He sent a picture from the little man's mind.

Ingra Mah had gone the way of Recide Skedrin. Rock had arrived on scene soon after the process began. The Dead Man assured me that, though Rock was a thorough villain and fully capable, he was not responsible.

Truck continued, "Recide and his ship's master moonlighted as transporters of questionable goods."

"They were smugglers."

"Bluntly put, yes."

"Why come to my house?"

"I can only guess, Mr. Garrett. Either he was directed to do so before he left Liefmold or he made inquiries on arriving and thought you met his requirements. My inquiries suggest that you have important contacts on the Hill. On the other hand—and this is the way I see it—he may just have wanted to lay down a false trail while his ship's master delivered the actual Shadow elsewhere."

"Say I find your gimcrack. How do I collect my four thousand?"

"I have taken rooms at the Falcon's Roost. You may contact me there."

Ugh. The Roost is a downscale sleaze pit not far from the Benbow. You don't have to fight off the hookers and grifters to get in or out, but its main clientele are ticks on the belly of society who perform unsavory services for those who shine from the Hill.

A man with more than four thousand nobles would be able to afford better.

Rock indicated his dagger, now resident on the edge of Singe's desk. "May I?"

"Knock yourself out."

He collected the blade, moved past me as though to leave, then turned and said, "I am going to search . . ."

Penny hit him from behind with a pot. "Supper's ready, guys."

I told her, "Keep your wrists a little looser. You don't want to end up with a serious sprain."

She gave me the fisheye but joined Singe in helping me go through Rock's pockets. We didn't find anything, so we chunked him out on the stoop, minus one deadly knife.

That became a trophy on the same shelf as the cherrywood box.

Then we convened in the kitchen.

I SETTLED AT THE TABLE AGAIN. SINGE ASKED, "WHO WAS AT THE DOOR?"

"Scithe. He thought we should know the prisoner died without talking. And wondered a lot about how a home invader ended up with a quarrel in his forehead."

"A good man. Has a sense of justice. Are you surprised about that thing dying?"

"He was lucky to hang on as long as he did."

Penny asked, "What next? How about we go back to the Benbow? After Dan scared Bottle . . ."

"You got his name?"

"He was cute."

"Don't I have worries enough?"

Singe snickered. Penny ignored all annoying parentish behavior. "How's the soup, old man?"

A little spicy. "Excellent. You paid attention when Dean showed you how."

"Thank you." She managed to sound surly while looking pleased.

Singe said, "My turn," and pushed back from the table.

Penny grumbled, "That's just sick spooky, the way she hears and smells stuff."

Singe came back with a folded letter closed with wax and a Benbow seal. "That was the blond child. Still with very little scent."

Nor any detectable presence. Though I felt unsettled. Vertiginous. Almost nauseated.

The letter was addressed to **Mr. Garrett** in a bold hand. "What did she say?"

"Nothing. She handed that over and walked. She can't be human."

I chewed some air, thinking. "Was there a clay smell? Anything like that?"

"No. But I will consider the implications."

"What is it?" Penny asked, being the only one who couldn't read over my shoulder.

"A request that I join a Miss Grünstrasse for a late dinner and a bottle of TunFaire Gold." Which is the city's finest vintage.

Penny asked, "Do I have time to clean up?"

I didn't get to explain that the invitation was just for me.

Penny, this is one of those times when you should have Garrett and Singe assist you.

There was going to be a revolution around here. Or maybe a counter-revolution.

SAILOR RECIDE SKEDRIN HAD BEEN A JUNIOR PARTNER IN A VESSEL RUMORED to be a smuggler. His ship and crew deserved a look. But, "I was too honest with Scithe. He'll have Specials poking every shadow on the waterfront."

Your appointment at the Benbow is of more immediate import. Lieutenant Scithe will begin making rounds of the public houses soon.

We were about to go, even Penny surreptitiously armed. She suddenly decided to head upstairs.

Singe dealt with the waterfront angle already.

She said, "My brother let me send Dollar Dan. Dan won't be noticed down there."

A rat on the wharves? Not hardly. He wouldn't draw a second glance.

"We set? Penny! Come on!"

Do find out why people feel free to commit murder inside our house.

"Gah! I just came here to relax!"

Singe swung the door open but didn't step out.

It was raining. Hard.

Penny thundered downstairs with umbrellas, hats, and canvas coats.

THE BENBOW HAS BEEN THERE FOR AGES. IT PUT ME IN MIND OF A CHERRY-cheeked, dumpy little grandmother of a sort I'd once had myself. It was warm, smelled of hardwood smoke and ages of cookery in which somebody particularly favored garlic. It had settled comfortably into itself. It was a good place occasionally disgraced by the custom of a bad person.

The right side, coming in from the street, was a dining area, not large, empty now. Most guests preferred taking their meals in their rooms. To the left stood a fleet of saggy, comfortable old chairs and divans escorted by shopworn side tables. Three old men took up space on three sides of a table there, two playing chess while the third grunted unwanted advice. There was no bar. Management preferred not to draw custom from the street.

The stair to the guest rooms lay straight ahead, guarded by a persnickety-looking little man with rodentlike front teeth. His hair had migrated to the sides of his head. His appearance begged for him to be called Bunny or Squirrel.

He rose from beside a small, cluttered table, gulping when Penny took off through the dining area.

His voice proved to be a high squeak.

Penny paid no attention.

Bunny sputtered. Then he recognized Singe for what she was. His sputter went liquid.

I presented my invitation.

"Oh. Of course. I didn't actually expect you." He threw a despairing glance after Penny, then another at Singe. It pained him to say, "Please come with me." There is a lot of prejudice against ratfolk.

Miss Grünstrasse occupied a suite taking up the west half of the third floor. I huffed and puffed and wondered if I was too old to start exercising. Bunny got his workout by knocking.

The blonde opened up. She stepped aside. For all the warmth she showed she could have been baked from clay. Her eyes seemed infinitely empty.

Singe went first. I followed. The door shut in Bunny's face. The girl threw the bolt, moved to the left side of the sitting room. She stood at parade rest, but with hands folded in front. She wore a different outfit without the coat. Her sense of style had not changed.

"Ah. Mr. Garrett. I was not sure you would respond. I do appreciate the courtesy. Indeed, I do."

I did a double take.

"Sir? Is something wrong?" Fury smoldered in the glance she cast Singe's way.

"Sorry. Just startled." In low light she resembled my prospective grand-mother-in-law, one of the most unpleasant women alive.

This one was huge and ugly and smelled bad, too.

The smell was a result of diet and questionable personal habits.

Her accent was heavier than Rock's, with a different meter.

"Come, Mr. Garrett. Be comfortable. Let us chat while Squattle prepares dinner." She spoke slowly. Each word, though individually mangled, could be understood from context.

I sat. Singe remained standing. There were no suitable chairs. Neither did she shed her coat, which was psychological warfare directed at the niece. The blonde adjusted her position after I settled.

"Now, then, Mr. Garrett. The Rock Truck, Rose Purple, visited you today. He was, without doubt, a fount of fabrication. He will have laid his own crimes off on others."

Rock was my client, in his own mind. I volunteered nothing.

"So. Very well, then, sir. Very well. Eliza and I have come to your marvel-ous city to reclaim a precious relic."

"The Shadow."

"Indeed. Exactly. The Rose Purple did not misinform you completely, then. Remarkable. Yes. The Shadow. Of negligible intrinsic worth, it nevertheless has substantial moral value among folk of a certain sort. We are here, at the behest of the Venageti Crown, to recover the royal property." She studied me from narrowed, piggy eyes, vast and truly ugly. "That would not be a problem, would it, sir? You won't judge me simply for being Venageti?"

"No. We won the war."

"Excellent. Excellent. I endured my own sorrows during those bleak seasons, I assure you. As did we all. Well, sir. Can I count upon you, then?"

I frowned. That didn't make sense. I confessed, "I don't get what you're asking."

"In the spirit of the new friendship between our peoples, you will return the Shadow to me, the Hand of Begbeg."

All Venageti rulers have Beg in their name. The one who quit fighting called himself Begbeg, which means King of Kings or King of the World.

"I don't have your doohickey. I don't know where it is. I don't know what it is. I wouldn't recognize it if it bit me on the ankle. And I don't much care."

"Sir!"

"I do know that somebody tried to bust into my place, somebody else made him dead, and one of those somebodies got dead himself, later on. Cutie-pie there watched everything from across the street. You probably know more than I do."

"But Recide brought you a box."

"He did? Singe, did you see a box?"

"I did not." She was distracted. Beyond Miss Grünstrasse's pong, the suite was replete with unusual odors.

"Really, Mr. Garrett. You dissemble. Eliza saw the box."

I looked at the blonde, as still and perfect as ornamental porcelain. Had she, indeed? Unlikely. Why say so, then? "She has magic eyes, she could see inside my place from where she was standing."

"You waste your time trying to provoke her."

Little bits was not my target.

Someone thumped the door with grand enthusiasm.

BUNNY LED THE DINNER DELIVERY. HE WAS IN A BLACK MOOD. HIS PRINCIPAL assistants were a boy and girl in their early teens. Penny was the girl. The boy, presumably Bottle, was more damned dangerously good-looking than she had hinted. He was blessed with way too damned much self-confidence, too.

Two more staffers brought folding tables, one at which to dine and another whence the kids could serve.

A sad old frail who might be Bunny's mate bustled in. "Found it!" She unfolded a chair designed to fit someone equipped with a tail.

The crew set four places atop clean linen. Eliza sat down but did not seem pleased.

We ate, mostly in silence, duck and some other stuff, none of it memorable. Neither was the wine, though it was a TunFaire Gold. Singe was the only one who knew what to do with the arsenal of tools.

Eliza ate just enough to claim participation. She never spoke. Her eyes were not shy, however.

Finally, over the bones, Miss Grünstrasse observed, "I will miss the food here. So. Mr. Garrett. You hope to gain some advantage from holding out on the Shadow. How can I change your mind?"

"You can't. I don't have the damned thing."

The woman laughed. Tremors surged through her flab. "Very well, then. Very well. What will it take to encourage you to find it?"

"I don't know what to look for. But Rock offered four thousand silver nobles for it."

Miss Grünstrasse began to quake all over. "The Rose Purple? Four thousand? That prince of liars! That latest in an endless procession of thieves! He will abscond on his account, wherever he is staying."

Odd thing to say. Silence followed. Eliza seemed especially interested.

Miss Grünstrasse changed approach. "You have barely touched your wine, Mr. Garrett. Is there a problem? The publican assured me that it is the finest vintage TunFaire offers."

"He would be correct, too, but I'm a beer snob." The modern obsession with spoiled grape juice is inexplicable. As someone once observed, beer is proof that the gods don't always get off on tormenting us.

"Beer, sir? I understand that TunFaire is famed for the variety and quality of its brews. Have you a favorite?"

Why not be difficult? "Weider Wheat with a blackberry finish."

"Eliza, see what Squattle has available."

The blonde inclined her head, rose, and left the suite as though driven by clockwork. I asked, "What's the story with her? Is she even human?"

"Oh, yes. She is, sir. Yes, indeed. Just quite serious. My niece. My intern, as well. Completing her elementary training. A remarkable child. Brilliant beyond her years. She will become one of the greats." Aside, "What is this, girl?"

Penny had set a plate in front of her. "A pumpkin spice turnover, ma'am. Specialty of the Benbow." She served me and Singe. Bottle followed with a cloth bag from which he squeezed a rum-based syrup.

Penny asked, "Should we ready one for the young miss, ma'am?"

Miss Grünstrasse was disgruntled. She was not accustomed to being a common "ma'am." "Keep it in the warmer. She may not want it. She doesn't eat many sweets."

I asked about Ryzna, Venageta, and the Shadow. Miss Grünstrasse evaded or tried to sell me on the sheer marvel of helping reclaim her missing gimcrack.

"Do we have an understanding, Mr. Garrett?"

"I haven't heard a word about potential benefits to me and mine. Other than this fine dinner."

She was not pleased. That was not the response that was her due. "Very well, sir. Very well. I do have to remember that I am outside that realm where my wishes have the weight of law. Very well. Bring me the Shadow and I will pay you an eight-hundred-noble finder's fee." She raised a hand to forestall the remark she expected. "Genuine Full Harbor trade nobles, not the fairy gold of the Rose Purple's will-o'-the-wisp promise."

I remained unconvinced. I looked unconvinced.

"Come with me, then, sir. Come with me." She got up, beckoned like someone Eliza's age eager to show a friend a secret.

I followed reluctantly, and got more reluctant when she headed into an unlighted bedroom. A light did come up momentarily, though. I glanced back. Boy, girl, and ratwoman looked puzzled but alert.

"Come along, Mr. Garrett. I promise not to test your virtue."

She had a sense of humor?

I relaxed a little.

"Do close the door, though. In case my niece returns. I would rather she remained unaware of this."

"Does she speak or understand Karentine?" Lacking a knowledge of the language might explain her disinterest in communication.

"Not that I am aware of, sir. But the child is full of surprises. Lend a hand, will you?"

She wanted a trunk dragged out from under the unmade bed. The bedding smelled like Miss Grünstrasse, only worse. I couldn't help wondering if she wasn't suffering from something malignant.

We swung the trunk onto the bed. She said, "Step away while I work the combination."

The latch of the trunk glimmered with a tangle of lethal spells.

I wondered if those who mattered knew we had a foreign heavyweight among us. A Venageti heavyweight who, likely, had survived our Hill folk in the Cantard.

"The war is over, Mr. Garrett. And my mission now is more important than any vengeance." She opened the trunk and removed a tray filling two-thirds of the trunk's depth. Beneath lay silver coins, rank against rank, side to side, standing on edge. Hundreds and hundreds. There was gold, too, but she hadn't offered me gold.

Eight hundred nobles is a lot of money. And this was the real magilla.

"Take a coin. Any coin. Test it."

"I can see they're real." They had the Full Harbor reeding that discourages counterfeiters.

"Even so, take one. Have it examined." She waited while I helped myself. "Eight hundred nobles, Mr. Garrett, and the rest for expenses and a shopping spree before we go back to the gloom of Venageta."

I hate it when bespoke villains show a human side.

"Come, Mr. Garrett. Let us return to the sitting room before your assistant loses her composure . . . First, though, assist me with the chest." She reinstalled the tray. She reset the locking spells, which smelled of death. I helped swing the trunk down. She positioned it with exact care.

Being in front, I missed the smug look she swept across Singe, Penny, and Bottle.

We settled at the table.

Miss Grünstrasse began to frown and fret and smell worse, which troubled Singe. The woman started muttering. "Where *is* that girl? Why does she *do* this?"

I'd picked up enough Venageti in the war zone to puzzle that out. Miss Grünstrasse was not pleased with her wonder apprentice.

She said, "I apologize, Mr. Garrett. Eliza gets distracted."

Eliza finally did turn up, carrying a tray with eight mugs aboard, in precise formation. She set the tray beside me. I said, "You are a treasure, Eliza."

I might have been furniture.

I noted moisture on her shoes. Singe's nostrils and whiskers twitched. She smelled something that hadn't been there before.

I sniffed the beers, evidently one each of what Bunny had available. Two I passed to Singe.

Penny delivered Eliza's pumpkin turnover. Bottle did the sauce. The girl fiddled, frowned, sniffed, tasted, then damned near smiled. She devoured the whole thing, taking dainty bites. Miss Grünstrasse was impressed. "We'll be seeing more of those."

Penny and Bottle began clearing away. Penny sensed a change and wanted to get a head start.

Singe began complimenting the house's selection of drafts, pretending to get tipsy. Foreigners wouldn't know that some ratfolk can suck it down by the barrel.

Once the kids were away, Singe began babbling about needing to get back to the house fast. We had a garderobe that a ratgirl could use. She didn't want to embarrass herself.

Miss Grünstrasse smiled indulgently. "Please consider my offer, Mr. Garrett."

"That's guaranteed. I'm getting married. I could use the cash."

"I'll be here till the Shadow turns up."

"I'll have a confab with my partners as soon as we get back to the house."

That sparked a big smile. Then, "I will be here."

Something was happening in an alley just yards from the Benbow. Senior Lieutenant Scithe was there, up late buzzing like the mother of all flies.

I stuck my nose in. That cost us a half hour spent answering pointless questions about how Singe, Penny, and I could possibly be found in the same city as a spanking new double homicide.

The victims were creatures like those who had invaded my house. The thing that had gotten Recide Skedrin got them, but they were melting slower. Similar lead pieces had gone in where the rot began.

Singe pointed with her folded umbrella.

I asked, "Lieutenant, might that busted box have something to do with this?" Said box was a ringer for the one recently added to the Dead Man's collection, but lined with layers of metal. It had been ripped open.

"It's got a weird feel. We'll let the forensics wonks have a sniff."

Singe got a sniff of her own.

Scithe turned us loose. Out of earshot, Singe said, "It stopped raining while we were inside, but the pavement is still wet. The girl smelled damp when she brought the beer."

"And that box was dry inside."

"She said nothing to her aunt."

"She didn't. I feel like running all the way home."

Singe and I were rattled, but Penny had other things on her mind. She said she would catch up at the house. She and Bottle were going to meet up for an egg cream.

Singe wouldn't let me get stupid.

"Here." I fished out the coin the fat woman made me take. "I want to see some change. And be careful."

Penny laughed, waved the noble in the air, and then dashed away.

Singe promised, "She will not spend it all."

THE DEAD MAN SENSED OUR AGITATION WHILE WE WERE GETTING THE door unlocked. *Come straight to me. Dean is fine.*

He asked no questions. He dived straight into our minds, slithered through the muck. He expressed no concern about Penny.

I asked, "Am I off? Or is that Eliza kid a killer?"

Given what you brought, what I got from Rock Truck, and subject to what I may get from Penny, yes. She is not what she seems. Give me a minute to digest.

He took five.

Why did the woman send the child out? Being distracted enough to have done so in Karentine?

I had overlooked that.

The answer might be implied from her lack of scent, her absence of presence, and the deep nausea I felt when she came to the door.

"Grünstrasse wanted her out because she interferes with mind stuff."

Excellent.

"And she wanted a peek inside my head."

Which she got. Clearly, though, her talent holds no candle to mine. She could not discern details or specific thoughts but did see that you truly do not have the Shadow. She saw that Penny was with you. She may have been alerted to my existence.

That might not be a bad thing. She would want to stay away.

Did she develop suspicions of the girl? Did she note the evidence you did when the child returned? If Eliza fails to volunteer a satisfactory explanation, the aunt should become extremely nervous. If she learns of the incident outside, she might suspect a sudden alliance between Eliza and Rock Truck.

I do wish I could have her in for a consultation.

I wasn't sure how he might connect Rock and Eliza but wouldn't bet against it. He conjures correct answers from gossamer and fairy dust, drawing on centuries of observing how human bad behavior takes shape.

Proof of that hypothesis will be Mr. Rock returning here.

"You think he'll panic and come to us because he doesn't know anyone else."

Yes.

"He's lethally stupid."

That was obvious from the beginning.

"What was in the box in that alley?"

Singe opined, "The same thing that was in our box here."

Air. Yes. Almost certainly. Somewhere a ship's master lies dead, murdered for nothing. Rock Truck and Miss Grünstrasse are chasing a phantom. The Shadow never came to TunFaire.

"Is Ingra Mah dead?"

Whether she tricked the child into killing someone in her place or she was killed herself after being robbed by a third party does not matter here. I do, however, fear that dreadful times will soon commence somewhere between Ryzna and Liefmold. Someone will try to use the Shadow and it will begin using him. Or her.

YOU MAY TURN IN, GARRETT. WE ARE DONE FOR THE DAY.

"Not till Penny gets home, we aren't."

Diffuse amusement.

The Dead Man began to commune with Singe. I visited Dean. That old boy was sleeping normally. He had a magnificent shiner but looked likely to be back in the saddle tomorrow.

PENNY TURNED UP SOONER THAN I EXPECTED. SHE WAS LIVID. "I WANT YOU to stomp that Bottle into meat jam!" she snarled. "That . . . ! That . . . !" Her language failed the gentility test.

"What happened?"

"We got to the place he wanted to go, and suddenly he didn't have no money! Suddenly he did have four hungry friends, one of them a bimbo named Tami."

"Life's a bitch."

"You think it's funny."

I did. But she wouldn't get the joke. Hell, I wouldn't hear the real punch line for eight more hours.

"Go see the Dead Man."

"He already sucked everything out of my head. I'm gonna go cry myself to sleep."

ROCK TRUCK TURNED UP SO EARLY THAT NOBODY BUT SINGE AND THE DEAD Man were awake. The Rose Purple was on the run. He was wet, filthy, terrified, and exhausted. Singe let him in, planted him in a chair, and told him, "Don't move." She went back to the front door, went outside, and waved.

Dollar Dan wasn't there but another ratman did ooze out of a shadow. She gave him instructions. Then she came upstairs to roust me, like the whole thing couldn't wait till a civilized hour.

While she was charging back and forth, up and down, Rock from Ryzna learned that her word was law. Hard as he tried, he could not get out of that chair.

Singe had heavy black tea steeping when I got to the kitchen, still cross-eyed sleepy. "Not ready, Garrett. My office. See the man. I'll bring it."

I was still trundling those hallway miles when the Dead Man sent, *Answer the door.* Disconcerted.

The knock happened as I freed the first bolt. I opened. Scithe boggled. I said, "You got here fast."

"Huh?"

He did not get our message.

"Serendipity?"

Scithe stepped back. Big word. Might be dangerous.

"Singe sent a runner. We caught a bad guy."

That just baffled him more. I stepped aside. Scithe and his henchman entered. Singe came out of the kitchen with a tray, half a dozen cups and tea still steeping. Scithe said, "We came about . . ." His eyes glazed.

I got a message myself, as did Singe, who nearly fumbled her tray.

Scithe closed in on Rock and rested a hand on his right shoulder. "This is the devil? Four counts of murder? He don't look the type." He bent down to whisper, "You're in the shit deep, sweetheart."

Rock squirmed. His big brown eyes ached with appeal.

I said, "Bad news, Rock. It was all for naught. The Shadow never came to TunFaire."

The Rose Purple made noises like a man trying to shout with a gag in his mouth. I think he was upset.

Scithe asked, "He's not going anywhere, is he?"

"Only if the other villains rescue him."

Chuckles all around. The other villains were about to have troubles of their own.

Scithe said, "I got to get moving on this. Ah!"

Penny had come down. She looked grimmer than I usually feel at such an absurd hour. She grabbed a cup. Singe poured. Penny added lots of sugar. "'S goin' on? Cha' wan' me for?"

Scithe said, "You were in Torah's Sweetness last night. Got rowdy."

"So? Wanna make sumpin' of it?"

"I do."

I said, "He does, Penny. Everybody there ended up a drooling moron after you left."

"Huh? Crap. You ain't gonna put that on me."

Her eyes glazed.

She settled on the nearest chair afterward. "There must've been twenty kids in there. They didn't have nothing to do with any of this. Why would somebody do something like that?"

"She wasn't after them. She expected me to bring that coin home. When her curse homed in on it, Old Bones and I would stop being the threat we turned into when she found out that we didn't have the Shadow."

"She would've got Singe and Dean and me, too."

"Yes."

"Aren't you glad you didn't get all hard-ass about me going with Bottle?"

Her heart wasn't in that, though.

"I am. That worked out nicely." Neither I nor the Dead Man chalked that up to luck, though. We believe in intuition. Something down deep had moved me to shed that coin.

I could have done a better job than I did, though.

Scithe asked, "You coming with, Garrett?"

"You inviting?"

"If you don't get underfoot and don't run your mouth."

"I agree for him," Singe said. "I will smack him if he gets out of line."

Scithe considered her with eyebrow arched.

"I'm coming, too."

"Me three," Penny added.

Scithe sighed. Civilians.

We got started after the Specials arrived. Three took charge of Rock Truck. The rest went to the Benbow with us.

Bunny was unhappy. Miss Grünstrasse had decamped during the night. Her tab was not in arrears but she had left her suite a wreck. It looked like a fight had taken place.

Singe reported, “The fat woman had words with her niece.”

I asked, “Can you track her?”

“Under water. She was extremely distressed. It did not go well for her.”

The trail led first to where the fat woman had intercepted the Specials taking Rock to headquarters. That resulted in a kidnapping, not a rescue. Witnesses said she made it quick and ugly, with no assistance from children. Her trail ran on to the waterfront, ended on an empty wharf. The ship that had been tied up there was out of sight, current carrying it out of the Guard’s legal jurisdiction.

It began to rain again.

“They get away too often.” Scithe hunched to keep the drizzle from running down his neck.

“They’ll cut each other’s throats.” Unless the Specials caught up first. They recognize no limitations in times of murder.

“Maybe.”

“My first platoon sergeant used to say, some days you eat the croc and some days the croc eats you.”

“Yeah.” He smiled grimly. “The bitch left the kid to face the music. Let’s go find her and play a few bars.”

NO MYSTERY, NO MIRACLE

by Melinda M. Snodgrass

The problem with opening a crack in the world is that you never know *what's* going to crawl through it. Which can be dangerous if it's your job to close that crack back up again . . .

A writer whose work crosses several mediums and genres, Melinda M. Snodgrass has written scripts for multiple television shows, including *Star Trek: The Next Generation* (for which she was also a story editor for several years). She was a writer/producer on *Profiler.* She has written a number of popular science fiction novels, and was one of the cocreators of the long-running Wild Cards series, for which she has also written and edited. Her novels include *Circuit, Circuit Breaker, Final Circuit, The Edge of Reason, Runespear* (with Victor Milán), *High Stakes, Santa Fe,* and *Queen's Gambit Declined.* Her most recent novel is *The Edge of Ruin,* the sequel to *The Edge of Reason.* Her media novels include the Wild Cards novel *Double Solitaire* and the Star Trek novel *The Tears of the Singers.* She's also the editor of the anthology *A Very Large Array.* She lives in New Mexico.

THE RACKET OF THE WHEELS OVER THE TRACKS WAS HYPNOTIC. MOONlight trickled through the slats of the boxcar, and, inside, a kerosene lantern lit the faces of the men reclining on their bindles. The warm golden light gave the illusion of health to sallow, stubbled skin. The lantern's presence would have raised the ire and the fists of any passing bull, but fortunately none of the railroad police had checked the train at the past two stations. Cross leaned against the back of the car and listened to the basso drone of male voices, and watched the magic that sang in their blood coruscate around them.

He had left New York City three months ago, looking for the origin point of a mysterious hobo symbol. Usually such symbols were simple affairs—a code that hobos left for other 'bos to guide them as they crissed and crossed a desperate country. An empty circle meant there was nothing for you here. A triangle with two lines thrust out like arms, and four smaller lines like fingers meant that a man with a gun lived there. A cat meant a kind old lady, and a cross meant if you listened to some religious talk you'd get a free meal. This one had a cross, but it also had a serpent. The head of the snake nestled in the angle between the upright and the cross's arms; its mouth was open, showing fangs, and there was something about the eyes that Cross found eerily familiar and disturbing.

His boss, owner of Unique Investigations, suspected that it marked the place of an incursion from another universe, and after loading up the money belt with cash, Conoscenza had sent Cross out to find it. Cross had spent weeks in hobo jungles, walking the roads, riding the rails, talking with hobos and being attacked, but he thought he saw an end to the journey. What the old man had told him in St. Louis sounded promising.

The old man had seen the mark in Buford Fork, a small town near Tulsa, Oklahoma. They would be coming up on it soon, and Cross would jump and go in search of the tear in reality and the creature that had made it. It was a warm June night, but still Cross shivered and pulled his suit jacket closer around him. He had come up against one of his own kind in West Virginia and it had shattered him. He'd lost days piecing himself back together, and he was still fragile as hell. He sensed that he could shatter at any moment, so he feared the coming confrontation.

Cross unlimbered his hip flask and gulped down a mouthful of brandy. Prohibition added to the woes of a desperate country, but Conoscenza had it smuggled in from Canada, and it was quality. After it was gone, Cross would have to find a speakeasy and buy whatever crap they were selling. Unlike a human, Cross wouldn't go blind from bad bootleg.

"It wasn't my fault." The adenoidal tones of Ed Bloom came drifting back to Cross. "My management principles were fine . . . no, better than fine, they were great. But the owner couldn't see that, and he closed the store. The employees had no cause to blame me."

It was the nineteenth time Bloom had told this story since Cross had jumped aboard the side-door Pullman back in St. Louis. It made Cross wish he'd dipped into his supply of cash and bought a seat in a passenger car, but after what had happened in West Virginia, he feared to try. If he were to splinter in a freight car among a gang of hobos, no one would listen to them. No authority figure would heed a wild story from lost and forgotten men about a man who had shattered into hundreds of slivers of multicolored light and flown away in all directions. But if it happened in front of respectable citizens—no, he couldn't risk it.

The train slowed. Cross gathered up his bindle, stuffed his fedora into the pocket of his suit coat, moved to the door, and slid it open a few feet. The spikes at the ends of the railroad ties flashed like a code. The train slowed again, the wheels giving a metallic squeal, and Cross jumped. He lost his footing but managed to get his shoulder down to take the brunt of the fall. The cinders next to the track crackled and sent up the smell of coal soot. Regaining his feet, Cross walked away.

NIGHT HAD FLUNG ITSELF OVER THE SMALL OKLAHOMA TOWN OF BUFORD Fork in a way that reminded Cross of a vast maw snapping shut. It also reminded him why he hated rural towns. He loved the glow of big cities, with electricity to hold the darkness at bay. He looked longingly at the glow of Tulsa on the horizon, but turned his back and continued down the main drag of Buford Fork. Up ahead he saw an oasis of public lighting, four gas lamps that lit the front of City Hall.

Across the street was a diner, but it was closed up tight, probably because there wasn't enough custom to make it worth the effort of opening. A handwritten menu in the window touted chicken fried steak with cream gravy and hush puppies. Cross realized the flesh he wore was hungry. He pressed a hand against his belly and felt the bulge of the money belt. Did he continue to play the hobo or offer some homeowner money for food?

He passed a movie theater. Ironically, the marquee read *City Lights, Starring Charlie Chaplin*. There was a Ford Model A truck, the black cab coated with dust, parked out front. The whitewall tires were like the flash of a smile in the dark. There were two ancient Model Ts, and several bicycles leaned up against the wall. Cross considered going inside. He liked movies, but there was no ticket seller in the kiosk.

He moved on and saw the black silhouette of a cross against the sky. It perched incongruously on the roof of a house. A mission, then. He walked up to the gate in the faded white picket fence. A hand-lettered sign read *The Blood of the Lamb Mission*. Shadows near the bottom of the gate's upright caught his attention. He bent, flicked on his lighter, and froze. The old man in St. Louis had been right. The symbol he'd been following across the depression-wracked country was carved deep into the wood. The drawing had been disturbing; the original was terrifying.

Now he regretted that he had been flippant in Conoscenza's Harlem office. The big man had skated the drawing across the polished surface of the desk.

Cross had studied the cross and the snake, met the dark gaze of the man who offered him a chance for oblivion, and asked, “I’m guessing this doesn’t mean there’s a doctor in the joint.”

Conoscenza stood, an impressive sight, because he was at least six foot six and three-hundred-plus pounds. He paced to the window and clasped his hands behind his back. The sunlight shone on his ebony skin. Cross joined him and they looked down on the throngs of humans bustling along the sidewalk. “It’s a bad time,” Conoscenza said. “Could be there’s enough desperation out there to finally allow them to tear open the membranes between the dimensions and return.”

The *them* referred to Cross’s kind, creatures that masqueraded as gods and preyed on the inhabitants of this world. Just as Cross now masqueraded as human, though he no longer fed on the hapless monkeys of Earth.

“We’ve seen worse,” was Cross’s laconic reply. “Economic depression and drought can’t really stack up against the Black Death, Genghis Khan, or the Albigensian Crusade. If this generation of humans is going to embrace the Old Ones over this, then they’re pussies.”

Now, confronted by the symbol, he was scared. Their opponents had found enough death, violence, and pain to shatter Cross. It was only because of hundreds of tiny acts of kindness that he had been able to paste himself back together. Despite being devastated by economic collapse, many people were actually worshiping the loving version of God embodied by the mythical Jesus. They were applying the principles that Conoscenza had grafted onto the previously murderous cult of a war god.

Some of this kindness was intrinsic to man—evolution tended to cultivate empathy—but some of it was due to Conoscenza’s meddling. The Old Ones might have afflicted humankind with religion, but Conoscenza had tried to guide it and shape it into something that could potentially do good. And Cross had joined him in this effort because, in the distant past, Eolas, as Conoscenza had then been called, had found Cross, created by human compassion and weakened by human cruelty, and Eolas/Conoscenza had offered Cross a bargain. Cross would help against the alien creatures, and, in exchange, Eolas/Conoscenza would help Cross die. They just never seemed to get around to the dying part. For an instant, existence lay on Cross’s shoulders like a crushing weight.

He lifted his head and faced the building. There was a flutter in his gut that had nothing to do with hunger. If this was a point of contact between the Old Ones and this world, Cross would have to handle the situation, and he was weak, so weak. Once again, he wished that they had a paladin, a human who could use the ancient weapon and kill an Old One. Instead, he had to match his strength against his own kind. He sucked in a steadying breath and pushed through the gate. Dead grass, blasted by years of drought, crackled beneath his feet. He walked up the stairs onto the wide, screened porch, complete with a swing, and knocked on the front door. He hoped the obligatory service would be over, and that no one currently in residence was actually religious. When people started praying and testifying and calling on Jesus, it made it damn hard for him to keep his hair short and his face beardless. His physical form tended to reflect the vision of the believers.

A woman answered. Thirties, pretty, brown hair piled on her head, and built like a brick shithouse. She wore a skirt and white blouse and a pair of perky open-toed red shoes. She stared at Cross for a long moment, and then a smile clicked on. He allowed a sliver of his power to flick out and touch her. Magic flared around her, and there was something very wrong with the large amber ring on her right hand. He studied the band formed of braided hair, and the undulating black shadows that flowed into it. Something was trapped and he feared it might be her.

"Evening, ma'am," Cross said. "Am I right in thinking this is a mission?"

"Yes . . . yes, it is. Welcome, do come in. I'm Sister Sharon." She stepped back and Cross stepped across the threshold. The oily taint of his kind permeated the walls and hung in the curtains. Cross's muscles tensed in preparation for an assault, but then he realized that it was faint and muted; the Old One was clearly no longer present.

"You're our only guest tonight. Most people seem to be riding on through." She had a good voice, clear and vibrant. She took his bindle and set it by the door. "If you're hungry, there's stew on the stove and I baked bread this morning."

"Yes, ma'am, I could eat."

She led him into the living room, which had been transformed into a mess hall with trestle tables and benches. Cross settled onto a bench; she disappeared through a door. Cross jumped up and hurried back to the entryway. He had the power to see magic, and the tear between the dimensions should be like a flare. He swung his head from side to side, trying to locate it, but the ring was a constant buzz, interfering with his ability. He moved toward a set of double doors and had his hand on the knob when he was startled by a sharp voice.

"Here, now, what are you doing snoopin' around?"

Cross turned and met the irate gaze of a short, rotund man. Standing behind the bristling fat man was a heavyset youth in his twenties. The flat facial features betrayed his mongolism. He smiled at Cross and bobbed his head happily.

"Sorry, just getting my bearings," Cross said.

"Looking to rob us, no doubt," the man huffed. He reached up and grabbed Cross by the ear, and tugged. "We'll see what Sister Sharon has to say." Now the idiot was looking concerned, catching the anger in the fat man's words.

"If you don't let go, you're going to lose that hand," Cross said in a conversational tone. The man met his gaze and yanked his hand back. Cross walked into the mess hall. Sharon was just emerging from another door with a bowl of stew in one hand and a loaf of bread in the other.

"Sister, I found him slinkin' around." The words were infused with the kind of self-importance only heard in palace eunuchs or majordomos. The mongoloid hung back at the door, shifted nervously from foot to foot, and cast glances at Sharon.

"I'm sure he meant no harm," Sharon said soothingly.

Cross sat down on a bench, and Sharon deposited the food in front of him. He gave the stew an experimental stir. It was thick with chunks of meat, and even held a few green beans among the carrots and potatoes. This was far better fare than was found at most missions. Sharon sat across from him. The little man stood behind her and glared.

"My husband, Marshall, and stepson are on a crusade," Sharon said. "They do the preaching, so I haven't been encouraging folks to come since there aren't services right now."

"You're just as fine a preacher as Brother Hanlin," the man said. "The spirit fills you, Sister Sharon." She smiled up at him, and he puffed out his chest. Cross stared at the darkness circling the ring and wondered what else might fill her.

"You're too kind, Stanley."

"The lack of a parson is probably an attraction for most people," Cross said as he slurped up a spoonful of stew.

"I take it you're not a godly man, Mr. . . ."

The irony nearly made him choke. He gave a short laugh. "Cross," he said, supplying the name. "And I'm more godly than you can imagine. I just know it's all snake oil and wishful thinking."

"You don't think people need the comfort? Especially in hard times?" Sharon asked.

"I'm all for comfort. If they would just leave it at that, but they never do. People always decide that everybody else has to get some comfort too, and it better be *their* version of comfort. And if it's not, they generally make their point on the sharp end of a sword or the business end of a gun."

Sharon jumped to her feet, her agitation evident in her writhing fingers as she clasped and unclasped her hands. "Perhaps we could take a walk in the night air and continue our talk, Mr. Cross."

"All right."

Cross tore off a hunk of bread and carried it with him as he escorted her to the front door. The retarded man scuttled out of the way. Behind him, the majordomo emitted gargling sounds that never fully resolved into words.

SHE LED HIM BEHIND THE HOUSE AND DOWN A PATH THAT FOLLOWED THE barbed-wire fence. The warm night air was filled with the soft lowing of cattle, and the smell of cow shit and dust. He began to mind where he stepped. Fireflies danced through the brown blades of grass like lost stars. The half moon had nearly set behind the hills.

Ahead, a sinuous line of trees marked a stream's meandering path. They broke through into a clearing where a wooden footbridge crossed the slow-flowing water. The wind shifted and Cross smelled the smoke of a campfire. There was a hobo jungle nearby. Sharon stared in that direction for a long time, then sank down on the edge of the bridge, legs swinging free, and stared down at the silver-tipped ripples passing beneath her.

Finally, she asked, "What do you do, sir? What's your business?"

"I'm currently a private detective, ma'am," he said.

She studied him for a long time. "So that means you help people." Her voice was so soft he had to lean in to hear her. Her breath puffed softly against his cheek.

"Do you need help?"

She didn't answer but turned her face away to contemplate the sky. "My husband is on his way to Chicago for the convention."

Cross didn't need to ask which convention. The Democrats had gathered to select a presidential candidate. The Republicans were sticking with the hapless Hoover, so it was critical that the Democrats pick wisely. *Not fucking likely* was Cross's estimation.

"Marshall's an alternate delegate, and he took Sean so he could see his government in action," she continued. That gave Cross a twinge of unease. A preacher with an official position and the taint of an Old One could be a toxic brew.

"I stayed behind to mind the mission." Sharon continued. She gave the ring a nervous twist. The shadow tentacles writhed. She sat silent for a moment, then turned to face him. "The Lord has given me the gift of Sight, and I can see that you are a good man. I think you were sent here to help me."

"I couldn't speak to the first part, ma'am, but if you're in trouble I could probably help," Cross said.

She presented him with her profile. "You're going to think I'm crazy."

"Why's that?"

She thrust out her hand. "This ring," she whispered. "My husband gave it to me, but I can't take it off."

"Let me see." He extended his hand, and she laid her hand in his.

Power throbbed through the ring like a heartbeat. He gathered his own power, took a grip on the ring, and gave an experimental tug. There was a flare of violet light, something seemed to kick him in the chest, and the world went black.

The first impression was that he was wet. Then Sharon was there, pulling his head into her lap and stroking his forehead.

"Mr. Cross. Mr. Cross. Are you all right?"

He forced apart his eyelids. Even the faint moonlight felt like a spike being driven into his head. He was lying with the lower half of his body in the creek. The assault from the ring had knocked him clean off the footbridge.

The bonds that supported his human form were vibrating like a struck tuning fork. He swallowed bile, closed his eyes, and took slow, deep breaths. *Don't shatter. Don't shatter. Not here. Not now. Not so soon after the last time.* Slowly, he gained control over the body.

"Do you think you can walk?"

He nodded. A mistake, so he settled for a moan and hoped it sounded enough like *yes* to get across his meaning. He struggled, trying to regain his feet. Sharon helped, supporting him under one arm.

They limped back to the mission. "I'm going to put you to bed in Sean's room. And get out of those wet clothes. If I hang them now they'll be dry by morning."

She took him upstairs to a narrow room with an equally narrow bed against one wall. There was a bookcase with schoolbooks and religious tracts. On top of the case was a collection of rocks, a crawfish in a tank, a football. A typical boy's room. She left. Cross emptied his pockets and took off the gun rig. He stripped out of his clothes, and, half-opening the door, handed out the soggy bundle.

He had the presence of mind to remove the money belt and shove it beneath the pillow. He then eyed the bed and fell naked on top of the covers.

It was the westering sun, hot on his eyelids, that brought him awake. Cross found his clothes in a neatly folded stack on the foot of the bed. The incongruity puzzled him. Little Miss Goody Two Shoes had entered the bedroom of a naked man not her husband. He checked his wristwatch. The dark power in that ring had knocked him out for twenty-one hours. Cross shuddered; something had come through the veils between the dimensions here, and it appeared to be a shitload more powerful than he was.

None of his possessions had been molested, not even the Webley. Dressed, he took a moment to quickly open the doors of the two other rooms on the upper floor. One was a study, the other a bedroom with a double bed covered with a patchwork quilt and redolent with the smell of perfume. And he found what he'd sought. Not the actual opening between the dimensions, but proof that an Old One had been resident in this house. The mirror on the dresser was gray and occluded, the result of contact with an Old One.

He sat down on the edge of the bed and considered. One of his kind had entered the world here. Which meant that there was a hole in reality. He couldn't deal with the tear; only a paladin using the weapon could close it. He needed to inform his boss and warn him it had moved on, probably to Chicago. He should head for Chicago too. Fight the Old One and maybe win. Even considering the coming battle had him shaking. On the other hand, Conoscenza had only told him to locate the source. Cross had done that. He could use the money in his belt, buy a ticket on the first train heading east, and make his report in person.

Cross went to the top of the stairs and heard the rumble of male voices from the mess hall. This evening, the Blood of the Lamb Mission had customers. Entering the converted living room, he studied the situation. Stubble adorned all the faces because razors and soap were expensive. Most of the men wore coveralls. A few, like Cross, sported suits, the material worn down to a poverty shine. The room smelled of hash, scrambled eggs, freshly baked bread, and coffee cut heavily with chicory. Beneath the good smells was the stink of body odor, halitosis, and stale cigarette smoke.

Sharon moved through the crowd doling out plates. The mongoloid staggered along behind her, carrying the plate-stacked tray. Usually the people afflicted with the condition were happy, loving people. This one was working his mouth and kept casting nervous glances at Sharon. *And he'd nearly run the night before when Sharon had approached him.* Maybe he sensed the dark presence lurking in the heart of her ring. Something clearly had him spooked.

The strutting buffoon was at her shoulder. Cross wondered, why did such a beautiful woman keep such men on a string?

Cross settled onto the end of a bench. The man next to him grunted a greeting. "Big crowd," Cross remarked.

"Yeah, we were camped down by the grain elevator. The twist came over and rounded us up." The man gave Cross a grin that revealed too much gum and too few teeth. "Guess she was lonely."

Sharon reached his table. She gave him her flashing smile and deposited a plate in front of him. "How are you feeling? Better?" she asked.

"Yeah. How do you afford a spread like this?"

She gave him a pouting smile and placed a finger against her lips. "The Lord doth provide."

"Not in my experience."

She patted him on the shoulder. She then plucked a strand of her long brown hair off his shoulder and wrapped it around her finger. "Well, perhaps I'll make a believer of you yet."

"Oh, I believe," Cross said. "Never doubt that I believe."

She moved on, and he ate. The texture and flavors of food was one human experience he really enjoyed. He mopped up the dregs of the hash with a piece of bread, slurped down the last of the coffee, gusted a sigh, and pulled out a package of Lucky Strikes. The men at the table with him gazed at the green box with the name in its red bull's-eye with avaricious eyes. Cross had barely gotten the fag between his lips when the self-important little man rushed over, wagging a forefinger.

"Sister Sharon don't hold with smoking. Take it outside."

It wasn't worth a fight; Cross shrugged and headed out onto the screened porch. Wood bees, as big as the end of his thumb, droned around the eaves, and the breathless heat of the dying day had his shirt clinging wetly to his back. That was a human experience he didn't enjoy. He adjusted the body and the sweat vanished. As he watched, the sun, bloated and red, sank beneath the horizon.

Behind him, the screen door slammed shut. Cross glanced around. A group of men, led by a hard-faced man with a knife scar across the back of his hand, had joined him. One man took a battered, partially smoked cigarette from his pocket, lit it with a match, and passed it from hand to hand.

"Harry says you had a pack of cigs." There was an angry buzz on the edge of the words.

The man with the knife scar was right behind him. Cross studied him; the light in the man's eyes screamed out his desire for a fight. Cross decided to try appeasement. He took out the pack of Lucky Strikes and offered it around. The scarred man put his cigarette in his shirt pocket. Cross pulled out his Unique lighter and lit his smoke. The men stared at the silver Dunhill lighter in amazement.

"So, who the hell are you? Daddy Warbucks?" Knife Scar asked. "And what else you got, *friend*, that you might be willing to *share*?" His eyes held all the warmth of a chip of flint.

Cross leaned his shoulders against a support post. Around him mosquitoes whined like an angry wife. He took a slow drag, blew smoke, and said softly, "You don't want to be going there, *friend*. It'll turn out badly for you."

The other men, sensing a fight, formed a circle. Their excitement and barely suppressed violence licked at the edges of Cross's consciousness. He pushed away the intoxicating brew, studied his opponent, and considered how best to handle the situation. He was still weak from being shattered and what had happened on the bridge last night. There had also been an Old One in this locale very recently. Cross didn't want to be playing with his powers, lest it draw the attention of one of his brethren.

His opponent shifted his weight from foot to foot and brought up his fists. Cross continued to lean while he finished his cigarette. He then dropped it and ground it out under his toe. The man rightly read Cross's casualness as contempt, and his anger flared. It showed as jagged lines of red and sickening yellow erupting from his body. The watchers' excitement flared in answer.

The man telegraphed the coming swing. Cross had lived a long time, much of it in human form, and he'd acquired a wide variety of fighting skills. He opted for one he'd learned in China fifty years before. He stepped into the roundhouse, blocked the punch with his forearm, then spun and delivered a kick to the side of the man's knee. The man went down screaming.

Cross bent down and twitched the cigarette out of the man's pocket. "And that's the problem with going for more, friend. You can end up with nothing." He straightened and scanned the crowd. The circle of spectators dissolved like ink floating away on a current.

The screen door flew open, crashing against the wall, and Sharon rushed out with her factotum right behind her. Planting her hands on her hips she said, "There is no fighting in this place of peace." She pointed at Cross. "You! Just get out! Go on, get!"

Cross shrugged and headed down the porch steps while the other men filed back into the mission. Sharon got her shoulder under Knife Scar's shoulder and supported him through the door.

"I'm going to put you to bed in Sean's room," he heard her say to the limping man. "You'll be right as rain by morning." The screen door fell shut, and then the heavy wooden front door was firmly closed.

Cross stood in the deepening twilight looking at that closed door and reflecting on what he had seen as the fight started. Sharon, shielded by the screen, watching with hunger in her eyes.

HE NEEDED A PHONE. NEEDED TO CALL CONOSCENZA. THIS COULDN'T WAIT for Cross to return to New York. Once his boss heard his report, Conoscenza would head for Chicago. Which meant that Cross had to go there too. Which was the last thing he wanted to do. The power in that ring had him spooked.

It was nearly eight at night. The post office had closed hours before. So he needed a house with a kind homeowner and the wherewithal to own a telephone. He moved off the main street and into a residential area, scanning the fences and gates for the bird symbol that indicated *free phone*. It took a while, but he found one. The name on the mailbox was *Dr. Adam Grossman*. It made sense a doctor would have a telephone.

There was a Ford Model A parked out front, and it had been carefully washed and waxed. Cross paused behind it and took money from his belt. He then pushed open the gate and walked up to the front door. His knock was answered by a sharp-featured young man with slicked-back black hair. The distinctive scent of Murray's Superior Pomade floated to Cross's nostrils. He wore the smart new style of cuffed trousers and plucked at the pants crease with nicotine-stained fingers, while with the other hand he pushed his wire-rim glasses higher onto the bridge of his nose. Cross's image of the white-haired, heavyset country doctor went up in a pop.

"Dr. Grossman?"

"Yes? Is somebody sick?"

"No. I need to use your telephone," Cross said, and he offered a folded double sawbuck, which he had pinched between his fingers.

The doctor's eyes widened at the sight of twenty dollars. "I generally let people use the phone for free."

"I know."

Grossman frowned. "How?"

"There's a sign on your gate." The doctor peered out the door toward the white picket fence and gate. Cross laughed. "Hobo symbol."

"Well, I'll be damned." Grossman opened the door wide. "Come on in. That explains a lot."

Cross stepped across the threshold into a ruthlessly neat front room. Books were squared up on a small table next to an armchair. Throw pillows on the sofa were lined up like portly soldiers. There was no hint of a softening female presence. The room cried out *ex-military*, and a package of Army Club The Front-Line Cigarette cemented the impression into certainty. Returning doughboys had smoked the English cigarette during the Great War. Memory flickered and touched the senses. For an instant, Cross smelled rank water, unwashed bodies, and cordite, remembered the slip of mud beneath his boot soles.

"The phone's in the hall," Grossman said, breaking the hold of the past. Cross held out the bill. Grossman held up a negating hand. "Keep your money."

"I don't need it, really. Take it. Use it to buy medicine or pay yourself for treating someone for free," Cross said. Grossman hesitated, then shrugged and took the bill.

The telephone was nestled in a niche in the wall, and a wooden chair was placed in front. Cross lifted the receiver. A few seconds later, the operator came on the line. He gave her the telephone exchange for Conoscenza's penthouse. It took a while for the call to route through, but eventually it started ringing and his boss's familiar basso rumble filled his ear.

"Conoscenza."

"Hey, it's me. I found it. It originated in Oklahoma. And you were right, it was an incursion, an Old One came through."

"Can you deal with it?"

"Nope, because it blew out of town, heading for Chicago and riding on a bush-league Bible thumper who happens to be an alternate delegate to the convention."

"What's his name?" Conoscenza asked.

"Hanlin."

There was silence for a few minutes and Cross heard the soft shush of turning pages. "He's not getting any national ink. What do you know about him? Is he a rabble-rouser stoking populist anger?"

"Couldn't say." Cross paused, then asked, "Do you think this is aimed at you? A way to block your plans for FDR?"

"Perhaps, but whether it is or not we can't take the risk. I'd best head to Chicago."

"Not that you're going to get on the floor," Cross said sourly.

"There are a few Negro alternates," Conoscenza said. The great rafter-shaking laugh filled Cross's ear and seemed to echo in the hall. "And as far as the Democrat party bosses are concerned, my skin is green. I'll get into the smoke-filled rooms, at least. You're going to have to be my eyes on the floor."

Cold coiled down Cross's back. *Then the other one will see me, and I have no strength to withstand an attack.* It was absurd, but he found himself remembering the advertising for Army Club. *This is the cigarette for the fellow with a full-sized man's job to do. When you're feeling all "hit up," it steadies the nerves.* Cross wondered if he could hit up the doctor for a few.

"Cross? Are you still there?"

He shook off the exhaustion. "Yeah, I'm here. The Old One and the preacher laid some kind of powerful whammy on a ring and left it on his wife's finger. I need to get it off before I blow town. I'll see you in Chicago."

Cross hung up the phone and found the doctor standing quietly in the hall. "What the hell was that about? Are you an anarchist?"

"No, quite the opposite," Cross said.

"And what's this Old One, and a ring—"

Standing, Cross held up a hand. "I really don't have time to explain, and, with some things, it's just better to live in ignorance."

Grossman followed him to the front door. "You seem to be making accusations against Marshall Hanlin," Grossman said. "Let me tell you, even though I'm a member of a different tribe, Marshall Hanlin is a good man."

"I'll have to take your word on that, Doc. I just know there's been some bad shit going on in his mission." Cross pulled open the door. "Thanks for the phone." Cross opened a button on his shirt, reached into the money belt and extracted a fifty.

Grossman stared at it. "I can't . . ."

"Yeah. You can." He pressed the bill into the doctor's hand and pulled open the screen door. The fireflies were back, darting through the grass.

"Who are you? Really?" The man's voice followed him into the darkness.

Cross looked back. "That goes back to your earlier question, and like that one, it's complicated. Too complicated in the time we have." Cross touched fingers to brow in a brief salute. "Take care, Doc."

He was walking down the road when a wave of terror and pain washed over him. It was so unexpected that it shattered his control and he gorged on the torrent of raw emotions. He sensed another feeder also sucking at the feast. He regained control, stopped feeding, and lost all sense of the other. He kicked into a run, dust from the road spiraling up around him, came around a final turn in the road, and saw the mission on fire. There were desperate cries from the men trapped inside.

Heavy storm shutters had been closed across the windows. A large board barred the front door. Cross lifted it out of the brackets and flung it aside. He threw open the door, and a blast of heat scorched his face, singeing his mustache and hair. In the distance, he heard the hectic ringing of the bell on the fire truck. *They'll be too late,* he thought. Power pulsed through him. He tried never to use it, so as not to fray and bend this world's reality. But someone or something was feeding on this conflagration. If he could save the men trapped inside, he would deny his enemy power.

He stretched out his power, and now he sensed the tear in the world, felt the call and pull of the other multiverse. Cross ignored the siren call and instead summoned the fire. It rushed to him like an obedient dog. It filled the hall, and he formed it into a ball, keeping its heat and destructive power from the wooden walls. He walked into the charred hallway, stepping over a burned body. Not everyone would be saved. The fire followed him, a glowing balloon. Cross pushed open the set of double doors to reveal a makeshift chapel. Rows of chairs, a raised stage that held a podium and an old upright piano, a wooden cross hung high on the wall.

The rip was on the back wall. It was small; the Old One was no longer holding it fully open. Cross pushed his fingers into the wood of the wall, opened the gap a bit wider, and thrust the fire into the other dimension. *Eat that,* he thought, with some satisfaction.

THE BUTCHER'S BILL WASN'T TOO BAD. THERE HAD BEEN THIRTY MEN IN THE mission. Four had died; two more would not survive their burns. The rest would recover. Cross spent a tense six hours at the jail telling and retelling his carefully edited story. His New York PI license was no help, and probably a detriment, but eventually the cops decided that he couldn't be charged with arson.

Cross hung around after he was released and managed to talk to a few of the ambulatory survivors. All had been sleeping and only a few had wakened when the fire took hold. *Drugged,* Cross thought, and was glad his inhuman metabolism didn't respond to most earthly agents.

It was clearly arson. The building reeked of gasoline, and the closed storm shutters and the bar on the back door and the one Cross had removed from the front left no doubt. Now the police just needed a suspect. With Cross alibied by the doctor, the bulls cast about, and another suspect came easily to hand—the mongoloid who worked at the mission and was found sleeping in the tool shed, surrounded by empty gas cans. Of Sister Sharon and her strutting factotum, there was no sign.

Cross tried to point out that this seemed very convenient. What kind of arsonist set a fire and then went to sleep at the site of his crime? But the bulls dismissed his arguments. The suspect was retarded. Of course he'd behave stupidly. Besides, this was easy and clean. The idiot was going to fry.

Cross tried to just shrug, find a train schedule, and head to Chicago, but the prayers, beliefs, and actions that had split him off from the creature that had become Jaweh and Allah, and the Jesus of the Crusades and the Inquisition, left him unable to walk away. Do-gooding was a damn nuisance, but it was burned into his deepest fibers, and it couldn't be resisted.

He went back to the smoking ruins of the mission and searched the shed. The gas cans had been removed, and the dirt floor was scuffed with the prints of the cops' shoes, and drag marks where they had rousted the mongoloid. Various tools were suspended from hooks set into the gray wood walls. There was a small table with smaller hand tools and jars filled with nails, screws, and nuts.

On a bench beneath the table, Cross discovered a mug still half-filled with a dark liquid capped with a lighter skein. He sniffed. Cocoa. It looked like the idiot had been saving half for later. He searched further and found another footprint that hadn't been obliterated by the bulls. Squatting down, he studied the toe print, and the divot left by a high heel.

He pulled out the bench, sat down, and contemplated the situation. Sharon had encouraged him to touch the ring. She had gone to the hobo jungle and brought the men back to the mission. *Needing bodies for the sacrifice?* She had sent Cross away even though she knew full well he hadn't started that fight. And she had been in the tool shed. To deliver the cocoa? And the men sleeping in the mission had been drugged. Why not the mongoloid too?

Cross had assumed that Sharon was a victim of her husband's sorcery. Now a new, darker theory arose—that Sharon had summoned the Old One. To prove that, Cross needed to find the woman, and he had a pretty good idea where she was headed. But first he had to clear the idiot. Only one question remained; had the cocoa also been laced? He knew a doctor who could provide the answer.

Dr. Grossman came through. The cocoa had been doctored with a sedative. Enough to "put down a horse," in Grossman's words. The word of the doctor was enough to get the mongoloid released. Knowing that the man-sized child would starve without care, Cross gave the doctor a couple of hundred dollars and asked him to "hire" the man. Then he bought a train ticket in Tulsa and headed for Chicago. He had considered finding an airfield and chartering a plane, but the train took longer, giving him more time to rest and prepare for the coming battle.

The blasted fields of Kansas rolled past the train's windows. They should have been high with wheat, but years of drought had reduced once-verdant farmland to a desert. Cross watched windblown dust heading east, as dark as storm clouds. The dust engulfed the train, turning the sun into a red cinder and day into eerie twilight.

It was a good thing he didn't believe in omens.

CHICAGO WAS FILLED WITH POLITICIANS, WHICH MEANT IT WAS FILLED with hookers. Barely disguised speakeasies did a riotous business, and jazz and dance music filled the night. Cross walked down Madison Street toward the Chicago Stadium. It was the largest indoor arena in the world, and the massive redbrick structure reminded Cross of a glowering toad squatting on the landscape. Delegates streamed toward the doors, ready to hear another round of speeches in support of the three leading candidates—Al Smith, John Garner, and Franklin Roosevelt.

The people glittered from the magic that flowed in their veins, but he had yet to spot the Roman fountain that marked Sharon Hanlin. He had come straight from the station to the stadium, thinking that he might just spot her in the crowd and do . . .

What?

Remove the ring, for starters. Figure out what it trapped, because it sure as hell wasn't her.

And how are you gonna do that? It knocked you on your ass the one time you tried.

He decided to abandon the haphazard search and report to Conoscenza. Cross waved down a taxi and told the driver to take him to the Palmer House. He wasn't sure how Conoscenza had managed it, but he had booked a room in the ritzy hotel. The lobby was cavernous and dominated by a ceiling mural depicting scenes from Greek mythology. Cross glanced up and found himself staring at Zeus. A real son of a bitch, that one. It wasn't until he had met Conoscenza that Cross discovered what had happened to the Old One. A paladin recruited by Prometheus (yet another of Conoscenza's identities) had taken down the god.

A self-effacing Negro porter asked if he had luggage. Cross shook his head. The elevator operator was an elderly Negro with grizzled hair. As Cross stepped off the elevator, a Negro maid pushing a cleaning cart quickly effaced herself against the wall, trying to become invisible.

Cross lifted a hand to knock, but the door opened to reveal Conoscenza and the heavy-jowled face and bald pate of Jim Farley, Roosevelt's campaign manager. Conoscenza grinned, deepening the hint of the epicanthic fold around his dark eyes, and said, "Ah, my man Cross, with impeccable timing as always. Jim, will you see to it he gets onto the floor?"

"Glad to oblige. And thanks again." The man patted his breast pocket and headed for the elevators. Conoscenza beckoned Cross into the suite.

Gold cufflinks flashed at his wrists, and a gold watch chain stretched across his powerful chest. The little maid stared in shock. Conoscenza gave her a wide smile and held out a ten-dollar bill.

"Thank you for taking such care with my room."

"Yes, sir. Thank you, sir." She gave a bobbing little curtsy. Conoscenza closed the door.

"Don't you feel strange?" Cross asked.

The massive shoulders rose and fell in a shrug. "It wouldn't be any different in a hotel on the South Side. The staff would still be Negro. This way I both make a statement and offer the possibility of a different future."

"You just like to make trouble," Cross said. He moved to the sofa and sat down.

"That too."

"Gimme that room service menu."

"There wasn't a dining car on the train?" Conoscenza asked.

"Yeah, but that was hours ago, and there was grit in my food." Cross perused the menu and ordered a porterhouse steak with all the trimmings. "So, what have you learned about Hanlin?"

"Well, he's no longer an alternate. An Oklahoma delegate became ill, and he's replaced him," Conoscenza said.

"Well, isn't that convenient." Cross stood and paced. "The wife arranged for a little auto-da-fé in Oklahoma. Maybe to provide the power to sicken the delegate. I think they're working as a team."

"When he's not on the floor, he spends his time preaching to ever-increasing crowds. I attended once, and he is very charismatic. Now that his wife has joined him, the crowd last night doubled, and today there were murmurs about drafting Mr. Hanlin as a potential vice presidential candidate."

"Well, that's fucking scary, because you know if this guy gets on the ticket in the second slot, he won't stay there. He'll end up president."

"Then you'll have to see to it that doesn't happen," Conoscenza said.

There was a knock at the door. Once the bellman was tipped, Cross settled at the coffee table and tucked in. Mouth full, he asked, "How is the convention going?"

"Roosevelt hasn't gotten enough ballots. Some of us are working on Garner, trying to get him to drop out."

"In exchange for what?" Cross asked.

"So cynical." Conoscenza sighed and studied his buffed and manicured fingertips. "You must find a way to neutralize Hanlin."

"That doesn't involve murder?" He tried to make it a joke, but Conoscenza gave him an implacable look. "You never make this easy for me," Cross mumbled, and finished his dinner.

THE PROBLEM, CROSS REFLECTED AS HE MADE HIS WAY TOWARD THE BANKrupt theater that Hanlin had appropriated, was that the kind of people who actually worshiped the loving God didn't tend to lead crusades against unbelievers, start wars, stone whores, or behead adulterers. Which put Cross at a decided disadvantage, because what fed Old Ones was a frisson of both hate *and* fear. His brethren fed off the murderer *and* the victim, the torturer *and* the tortured, while Cross could only sup on charity and love and there just weren't that many good people in the world. It wasn't the humans' fault. They hadn't been out of the trees for all that long.

All of which was an interesting mental exercise, but it didn't solve Cross's problem of what to do about Hanlin and Sharon. His vague plan was to show up, see if somebody made a mistake, and hope that somebody wasn't him. He supposed that he could embrace the full-on Jesus, but that wasn't a trick he liked to use too often, and it had worked better back in 1300. Edison's little invention had images moving on a white screen. The Wright Brothers had ensured that humans could fly, not just birds and angels, and scientists were starting to unlock the secrets of matter itself. Humanity had become less credulous, but still filled with enough irrational beliefs and reactions to be dangerous.

He joined the throng heading into the building. People clutched Bibles and crosses. *If I had actually been crucified on one of those things, do they actually think I'd ever want to see one again?* He quashed the errant and foolish thought. He was coming up against one of his own kind, and he was in no shape to face it. He needed all his focus and concentration.

The set up was similar to Oklahoma. Upright piano, the fat factotum playing a hymn. A podium. Sharon wearing a white choir robe and those incongruous red shoes, seated in a chair by the podium. An older man in a black robe pacing the stage in a manner that reminded Cross of big cats in the zoo. The predator physicality was completely at odds with his looks, since he was balding, a bit stoop-shouldered, and starting to grow a paunch. People stood just inside the doors, handing out pamphlets. The flyers appeared to have been hurriedly mimeographed, as the ink was smudged in places. The title declared:

A CHRISTIAN LEADER FOR AMERICA

Cross studied this Christian leader, and what Cross read was baffling. The flesh held little trace of magical ability, yet power shimmered all around the man. Cross looked to Sharon. The ring flashed under the lights; Sharon glittered with power, and the shadows circled. Things clicked into place. It was a team effort. As a woman, Sharon couldn't be the candidate, but she could use her power to propel her husband to high office. There was the oil-slick taste of Old One on his tongue, but Cross couldn't pinpoint its location. He shivered.

There was a gentle touch at Cross's elbow. "Sir, you need to sit down. The service is about to begin."

Cross turned and looked down at a boy on the cusp of manhood. The boy's eyes were rimmed with white, and tension hunched his shoulders. Cross also saw the physical similarity with the man on the stage.

"You must be Sean," Cross said, and was taken aback when the boy gasped, fell back a step, and dropped to his knees.

"God be praised! You've come! My prayers—"

Cross grabbed him roughly under the arm and pulled him to his feet. "Jesus, kid, cut it the hell out," he muttered out of the corner of his mouth. The boy looked confused.

"But . . . Aren't—"

"No . . ."

"But you knew my name . . ."

"Yeah . . . because . . . never mind. Ankle it." He pulled the teenager toward the doors. The music stopped.

Cross glanced back at the stage and saw Sharon frowning out over the congregation. She spotted him and stiffened. Hanlin froze, looked directly at Cross, and then Cross realized that the human skin didn't contain a human. An Old One had crawled inside. Terror choked him. He hustled the boy out of the theater.

Outside, he spotted his reflection in the glass doors and quickly made adjustments. He hated going into churches. With the beard removed and the hair shortened, he turned back to Sean. "Okay, kid, what were you praying about?"

"Shouldn't you know—"

"Pretend I don't." Dropping an arm over the teen's shoulder, Cross hustled him down the street. Behind him the door banged open and the fat man came rushing out.

Cross hurriedly flagged down a cab and thrust the kid inside. "Step on it," he ordered the driver. Cross glanced out the back window at the receding figure of the factotum.

"Where to?" the cabbie asked.

Cross looked over at the kid. "You hungry? Of course you're hungry. Kids your age are always hungry."

SILVERWARE CLATTERED AGAINST PLATES; THE WAITRESS AND THE COOK sang out a call-and-response *Blue plate, Order up.* Cross indulged in a piece of cherry pie à la mode, a slice of devil's-food cake, and a cup of coffee while the kid wolfed down the pot roast, slurped a Coca-Cola, and poured out his story.

"Ma died two years ago. Pa was really sad. Then Sharon came to the mission, and they started walking out together. They got married seven months ago."

Cross's attention drifted. He was focused on that damn thing wearing the people suit. Wondering how to fight it. Wondering if he could win. Wondering if it would end with him splintered and weakened yet again.

". . . make me brush her hair." Cross's focus snapped back to the boy, who was red-faced and looking embarrassed, which made the smattering of pimples on his cheeks stand out all the brighter. "In their bedroom, when Pa would be downstairs reading."

"Were you really brushing her hair, or is that a euphemism?"

"Pardon?"

"Another way to say *fuck*," Cross said.

The boy went white, then red again, and took a large gulp of pop. "N . . . no," he stammered. "I only touched her hair."

"Tell me about that ring."

"She had the stone in that silver setting when she showed up . . ."

My husband gave it to me. Cross flashed back to the conversation on the footbridge. *No, not a twofer. Hanlin's a dupe. It was Sharon and the Old One just finding a convenient meat puppet,* he thought.

"And she made the band out of her and Pa's hair." The boy's words seemed etched in the air.

Another memory surfaced—*Sharon carefully removing her hair from his shoulder.* "What did she do with the hair in the brush?"

Sean looked startled by both the question and the intensity with which it was asked. "She'd take it all out, and roll it up and keep it in this little box. She even made me pick up any hairs that fell on the floor."

"Has she got the box with her?" Sean nodded. Cross leaned back and lit a cigarette. It was classic hair-and-skin magic. Cross was pretty sure he knew what was trapped in that ring. He tossed a few bills down on the table.

"You're using money?"

"I got a news flash for you, kid; that whole loaves and fishes thing . . . complete bullshit. And another thing. I knew your name because your stepmother told me. No mystery. No miracle."

Sean stopped dead and stared at Cross suspiciously. "You're not my savior."

"Actually, kid, I probably am. Look, I know that thing on stage is not your dad. It's something else wearing his skin."

The boy let out an explosive sob and dissolved. No longer on the cusp of manhood, Sean was a child again. Cross handed him his handkerchief. After a few minutes, the boy regained control. He mopped at his streaming eyes.

"I couldn't tell anybody. They would have thought I was crazy, and she . . . she was my stepmom."

"Yeah, kid, I know. It's a bitch when a cliché turns out to be true. Now take me to where you're staying."

SEAN DIDN'T HAVE A KEY. "KEEP A LOOK OUT," CROSS ORDERED AS HE PULLED out a lock-pick kit and knelt down in front of the door. The hotel was a modest affair a few blocks from the lake.

"You're going to break in?"

"No, I'm going to pick the lock. Breaking in would be noisy."

Sean tittered, betraying his nervousness. "You're not nothin' like what I expected."

"Anything," Cross corrected automatically as the delicate tools caught the mechanism and the lock clicked open. "You sound like a hick, you're going to end up a hick, and I think you're brighter than that."

"You do?"

"Yeah, I do." Cross slipped the tools back into their case, returned the case to his pocket, and stood up. He pushed open the door, and he and the kid entered the room.

A carpetbag sat on the floor beneath a luggage stand that held an open suitcase. An iron bedstead was against one wall, and a flimsy chest of drawers against another. There was a mirror over the dresser, and the glass was occluded because of the Old One. A folded trundle bed filled the remaining space in the small room.

The top of the dresser held the various mysterious potions that constituted a woman's war paint. Cross didn't see a box. Maybe she kept it with her. That would make things harder.

"What does the box look like?" Cross asked.

"Metal, but it had holes, kind of like a net."

Cross searched through the drawers. No box. Cross turned to face the room and studied the sparse furnishings. Cross checked under the mattress, inside the carpetbag, and in the suitcase. Sean watched him intently. Finally Cross moved to the trundle bed and thrust a hand into the folded mattress. Felt metal. He pulled out the box. Opened it and inspected the chocolate-colored hair inside.

He snapped shut the box and held it tightly in his hand. Considered what he knew. The Old One had inhabited a human body. Interesting that it hadn't just built one the way Cross had. But that might indicate that it had limited power, which was one small bright spot in a giant shitstorm. At the mission, Cross had sensed that something was trapped. He had thought, mistakenly, that it was Sharon, but now he guessed that it was the electrical impulses that formed the essence of Marshall Hanlin.

So, all he had to do was force out the Old One. Restore the husband to his body. And deal with the Old One and Sharon.

Easy as pie.

Yeah, right.

"So, what do we do now?" Sean asked.

Cross swallowed the cold lump that had invaded his throat. "We go find your wicked stepmother."

The theater was empty. A few pamphlets flapped sadly in the gutter as a breeze off the lake kicked down the street. Cross cursed. Having brought himself to the sticking point, he wanted to get it over with. Match his strength against the other Old One. End this nightmare for the boy at his side.

Sean looked at him with a combination of awe and trepidation. "Are those *all* cuss words?"

"Yeah, now forget you ever heard them. Where would they have gone?"

"Probably to the convention. Sharon wanted to see all the famous, rich people," Sean replied.

"Okay. You want to see some famous, rich people?"

The kid shrugged. "Pa took me the first day we got here. They just looked like regular people, only in fancier clothes."

Cross reached out and ruffled the boy's hair. "You'll do, kid."

Farley had done as promised. Cross was on the list to enter the stadium. He told them Sean was his son. The statement had the kid turning red, then white, then red again.

"What the hell's wrong?"

"I can't be your son! It's sacrilege."

"No, it's just lying."

"You still shouldn't say it. And lying is wrong."

Cross gave up. "You're right. Now can we please go find them?"

It was hot in the stadium, the air heavy with competing scents—sweat, aftershave, and hair pomade. Men huddled in clumps speaking in low, urgent tones. Ties had been loosened, shirt collars were limp. Up in the bleachers sat the women, fanning themselves, their white gloves flashing like signal flags. They looked like a flock of birds in their feather-adorned hats.

Cross scanned them, searching for Sharon. Sean tugged on his sleeve. "There's my pa," he said, and pointed. The Old One in a people suit was talking with Farley.

"Sharon's the key. Help me find her. Try the other side of the stadium." The boy headed off with one last look of longing at his father's carcass.

Cross hoped that extracting the Old One wouldn't kill the human vessel. Sean was a nice kid and deserved a happy ending. Pity they came along so rarely. Because in truth, no universe gave a shit about the lives of the creatures crawling around inside it.

Cross headed off in the opposite direction, and then he saw her. Or rather, he recognized the swaying hips and the shapely calves, and those perky red shoes climbing the stairs. Cross vaulted the railing and climbed. She turned, speaking to the women to either side of her, and started to sit down. Then she spotted Cross, stiffened, and remained standing.

Cross reached into his pocket and took out the box. Fury and alarm warred across her features. Slowly he reached into his other pocket, pulled out his Unique lighter, and slid his thumb across the roll bar. The horizontal flint struck and a steady flame burned. Panic washed across her face. Awkward in her haste, Sharon started to run down the stairs toward him.

"No! No. Don't!"

He had the box open. Even though she was still ten feet away her hands stretched out to him as if she could somehow snatch back the box. Cross laid the flame against the hair. He had witnessed many battles and many autos-da-fé in his long existence. It wasn't so much the smell of roasting human meat that he remembered as the sweet/harsh scent of burning hair. The smell killed any chance that he would feel pity for her. She had made compacts with creatures bent on causing human suffering and death.

Sharon let out a scream of terror and pain. The glove on her right hand was charring. The material fell away, and Cross saw flames licking up around the amber ring as the braided band burned like the hair in the box. Sharon ripped off the ring and threw it to the floor. The last of the hair turned to ash. The metal box was hot in Cross's hand, and the cheap metal had softened. He crushed it and dropped it.

Sharon let out a keening cry, knelt on a step, and gathered the amber piece in its silver setting in her hand. Cross reached out with his power. The shadows that had swirled around the ring and around her were gone. The inside of the ring glittered as if it held captured fireflies.

There was a stir on the floor of the stadium. He heard Sean's voice, shrill with fear, crying, "Pa! Pa!"

Cross leaped up the stairs and snatched the gem away from Sharon. He then ran for Sean and the man who lay on the floor, choking in his son's arms. The Old One was exacting revenge and feeding off the son's grief and fear, and growing stronger with each psychic gulp.

In the face of such power, Cross felt helpless. He couldn't fight the other. He would fail and be shattered. It would be a disaster for Conoscenza if that happened in such a public venue. And he didn't think that he could face the pain. He started to back away. The boy looked up at him, tears clouding his eyes, but his expression showed total trust and confidence.

Cross stopped his retreat, reached out, and touched the boy's feelings about his father. He drank deeply of those more complicated emotions—respect, love, admiration. He delved into the ring and sensed the electrical impulses that made up the man. Felt his emotions—worry for the son, sorrow that he wouldn't see him grow to manhood.

Cross summoned every ounce of power. He gripped the other Old One, and it felt like icy talons gripped back. But the boy's father began to breathe again as the Old One turned its attention to Cross. Next, Cross reached into the ring and secured the man. Cross felt the bonds that held his body together weakening as he struggled to make the switch. The Old One was fighting wildly. It was going to be a near thing.

Then Cross staggered as he was struck by a bolt of power. Glancing over his shoulder, he saw Sharon, swaying drunkenly, coming onto the floor. It was taking all his energy to hold both the Old One and Marshall Hanlin, and keep himself together. He had nothing left for speech. Cross rolled an eye at Sean, who knelt on the floor holding his father in his arms. The boy looked from Cross to Sharon and down at his father.

He gently laid his father down and stood. *Hurry!* Cross said mentally. Sean ran at Sharon and slapped her hard. Her assault on Cross frayed and died. He took a tighter hold, gathered his strength, and made the switch. To his eyes, which could see beyond the normal dimensions, it looked as if Marshall Hanlin's body was washed with a net of electricity. And the inside of the amber was no longer clear. It roiled with shadows.

Slowly, Hanlin sat up and placed a hand against his forehead. "Sean?" he said weakly.

"Pa!" The boy was fighting back tears, trying to be a man. He ran to his father and embraced him.

Cross sank down on one knee and panted. *Sharon!* He forced himself back to his feet and looked for her. But like any grifter, she had good survival instincts. During the confusion, she had slipped away.

TWO DAYS LATER, FRANKLIN DELANO ROOSEVELT SECURED THE DEMOcratic nomination for president, but he did it without the vote of the alternate from Oklahoma. The original delegate had recovered and returned to the convention. Hanlin hadn't seemed too upset to learn that the mission had burned. He and Sean had decided to head for California and a new life. "Preferably one with no preaching," Cross had told Sean.

Late that night, Cross and Conoscenza stood at the edge of Lake Michigan, watching wavelets run up onto the rock beach. Cigar smoke wreathed them like gray halos.

"Are you pleased?" Cross asked.

"I'll be pleased when he wins the election," was the reply. "So, what are you going to do with that thing?" Conoscenza added, with a nod at the amber.

"Damned if I know." Cross regarded the sullen gem. "Drop it in the lake?"

"Things have a way of getting fished up. I'll take it, put it in a safe-deposit box."

"And banks don't fail?" Cross asked.

"Not my banks. And once you locate a new paladin, it'll be destroyed."

"You need to add that tear in Oklahoma to the to-do list," Cross said.

"Noted, but its priority is low. The news out of Germany is . . . disturbing. I'm sending you to Europe."

"Unh-unh, not right now."

"Why? You have something more pressing?"

"I've gotta find Sharon."

"And do what?" Conoscenza asked. "Without a paladin, we can't remove her ability for magic. And you're not going to kill her."

"I could."

"But you won't, or our deal is off."

Cross sighed, took a final drag on his cigar, and tossed it into the water. "Guess I better go pack my lederhosen."

THE DIFFERENCE BETWEEN A PUZZLE AND A MYSTERY

by M. L. N. Hanover

Big-city police detectives have to get used to dealing with killers and junkies and whores. Dealing with demons, however, is definitely raising the bar . . .

New writer M. L. N. Hanover is the author of *Unclean Spirits* and *Darker Angels*, the first two books in the Black Sun's Daughter sequence. Hanover's most recent book is *Vicious Grace*. An International Horror Guild Award winner, Hanover lives in the American Southwest.

THE GUY WASN'T WHAT DETECTIVE MASON EXPECTED. GIVEN EVERYthing about the case, he'd figured on someone with a big black trench coat, maybe a priest's collar. An air of mystery anyway. Instead, he got this chubby guy in his forties, balding, with an uncertain expression that he'd worn so long it was etched in his skin. His button-down shirt had fit him about fifteen pounds ago. The knot in his tie was so tight, it had probably been there for years, lifted over his head and put back on without ever being remade. When the desk sergeant brought him back, the guy had bumped into Winehart's desk hard enough to splash coffee out of her mug, then apologized like he was afraid she'd mace him. Now he sat down across from Mason at Anderson's empty desk, put his hands between his knees like a kid in school, and smiled nervously.

"You're Detective Mason, then?"

"Am. And you're the exorcist."

The man bared his teeth and shook his head.

"No, not really. I wouldn't put it that way. Richard Scarrey. Like the children's writer, but with an extra *e*."

"The who?"

"Children's writer. Illustrator too. He wrote the Busytown books? Pigs in lederhosen, things like that? He spelled it with the double *r*, but I also have an *e*. Still pronounce it 'scary,' though."

"Okay," Mason said. "I'm Detective Mason. Chief told you about me?"

"A little. He said you'd arrested a man, and that he thought I might be of some assistance."

"Nothing more than that?"

Scarrey shook his head again, more firmly that time. Mason leaned back in his chair and laced his fingers behind his head. Winehart's phone rang, and she took it out of her pocket and walked away with one hand over her free ear.

"So five months ago, this girl Sarah Osterman goes missing," Mason said. "College age. Had a fight with her boyfriend, stormed out of the house, never came back. He's freaked out, but it just looks like a bad breakup. No one pays a lot of attention. About a month ago, her body shows up in a warehouse down by the rail yards. She's been dead about a week, but she wasn't having any fun before that."

"I'm sorry, Detective," Scarrey said, and the way he used the words made it seem like he really was sorry. "I appreciate your professional reserve, but I will need the details. Had she been tortured?"

"Yeah."

"Um. Assaulted?"

"Raped, you mean? I've got the coroner's report. Chief said you might want it."

"Thank you then, yes. That's fine. Go on."

"The scene had some elements that made us suspect there was an occult angle. Writing on the walls. Wax from a black candle. And there was some blood spatter, and the forensics guys said there was a clean spot in it where maybe someone had an inverted cross, then took it away again after."

Scarrey was nodding with every detail, his head almost vibrating, but his eyes were flickering now, moving across the air like he was reading. It was what Mason saw people do when they were trying to remember something. When they were making things up, their eyes were stable.

"How old was the girl?" Scarrey asked.

"Twenty-three."

"Was she pregnant?"

"No."

"On her period?"

"What?"

"Was she menstruating when she died?"

"I don't know. Maybe it's in the report."

"We can ask if it isn't. I'm sorry. Didn't mean to interrupt."

"We start investigating. Turns out the girl's been seen with this scumbag, Maury Sobinski, so we find out where he is. We lean on him. He's one of those assholes who's read a book about cops and thinks he knows everything. Acts like he's practically on the force himself."

"Talks too much?"

"You know that whole give-a-man-enough-rope-and-he'll-hang-himself thing? This son of a bitch would have strung himself up on dental floss. He screws up everything. Practically makes our case for us, doesn't even know he's doing it."

"But not a confession."

"No. Just stupid things. Saying he wasn't with the girl on a particular day when we hadn't asked him yet. Talking a lot of shit about how some people invite bad things happening. Hanging out big neon I-did-it signs. We ask for a DNA sample for elimination purposes, he finally figures out that we're not just there because we enjoy his company, he stops talking. Can't remember anything. Hears his mommy calling. Like that."

Winehart came back to her desk, her expression sour. He tried to catch her eye, but she wouldn't look at him. Mason felt a pang of anxiety. Had it been Anderson? Or, worse yet, the assholes from Internal Affairs?

"And then?"

"What? Oh, yeah, we get a warrant, go through his house. He's got all her stuff there. We know he knows her, but there's nothing conclusive. No witnesses, no forensics that we can take to a jury. We know he did it, and we need a confession. So we bring him in."

"And he lawyers up?"

"Lawyers up," Mason said, pointing a finger at Scarrey. "That's good. That was the kind of term he'd throw in too. Show us he knew how it all works."

Scarrey blushed and tittered.

"It's just something I picked up. Television or . . ."

"He doesn't, though," Mason said. "Ask for a lawyer, I mean. He starts talking funny. Starts moving weird. We've got a camera on him, and he's not just doing it when he knows we're watching. Does it all the time. Calls himself Beleth, the King of Hell. Every now and then, he stops doing the whole voodoo thing, sounds like himself again, and he says he's the victim of a huge satanic conspiracy. Asks us to help him. Begs, cries, shits himself. Then Beleth shows back up, and . . ."

"Ah."

"Chief saw the act, told me to expect you. Said you might be able to help, and that I ought to cooperate with you, but maybe we don't document anything. Keep it informal."

"And you said?"

"I said 'Yes, Chief.' "

Winehart, at her desk, turned around. Whatever that call had been, she had her composure back. She looked her question at the back of Scarrey's head. Mason coughed a little to hide his nod. *Yeah, that's the one.* Winehart wiggled her fingers, faking spooky. Scarrey sighed, just as Mason realized the guy could probably see her reflection in the window glass. The guy didn't say anything about it, though.

"May I speak with the prisoner?"

"You don't have to talk with me," Scarrey said. "It's not required. I'm not a policeman or a psychiatrist or anything like that."

In addition to bars, the holding cell had a thick metal mesh too narrow to fit even a finger through. The floor was concrete, the three walls were brick painted with high-gloss cream-colored paint that came clean with a little Windex and a paper towel no matter what was smeared on it. The cot was a metal shelf bolted to the far wall with the small steel toilet beside it. The whole thing wasn't more than six feet by eight, and most days it would have three or four people in it.

Sobinski sat on the floor, legs crossed, glaring out. His eyes were rimmed red, his mouth slack. Hanks of greasy hair hung down over his face, but there was an awareness in his eyes. He wasn't zoned out. He was watching them both. Mason stood a step back, letting the expert do whatever he was going to do. Scarrey waited a long moment, then sat down himself, just outside the cage, looking in at Sobinski with their heads on a level.

"I was hoping I could talk to you about why you're here," Scarrey said. "About what happened."

Sobinski's elbows moved out to his sides with a sudden jerk. His head seemed to shift at the neck, putting his face at an angle that left him looking like someone had snapped something important in his spine. His voice was thick and greasy. The syllables ran into one another, sliding and slipping. Scarrey made a small, embarrassed noise in the back of his throat.

"Yes, I'm sorry," Scarrey said. "I wanted to speak with Maury, please."

"There is no Maury," Sobinski said, his voice sounding like something forced out through raw meat. It was too big for the body. Too big for the space. It made Mason's flesh crawl. "I am Beleth, King of Hell. This body is my property, ceded me by right."

"I understand," Scarrey said. "And with all respect, Your Majesty, I've come to speak with Maury, please."

Sobinski's jaw opened so wide it seemed in danger of coming unhinged. His tongue spilled out, lolling down toward his crossed legs.

"You want little Mo to come out and play?" the voice said again, each syllable wet and angry. The tone was mocking.

"Yes, please," Scarrey said.

The prisoner chuckled. His shoulders shifted back into place, his face lost its expression of malefic glee, and the broken-necked angle of his head slithered back to true. Sobinski looked around like he was seeing them both for the first time.

"Maury?" Scarrey asked.

The prisoner nodded uncertainly.

"My name's Rich," Scarrey said, smiling. "I wanted to talk to you for a minute about why you're in here. Will that be all right?"

"Are you a psychiatrist?"

"No," Scarrey said. "I'm not anybody in particular. I understand you've been possessed by a demon?"

Sobinski looked from Scarrey up to Mason and back. His skin was pale and fragile looking. He swallowed and nodded. When he spoke, it was barely more than a whisper.

"They don't believe me."

"I know," Scarrey said.

"I didn't kill Sarah. I'd never kill Sarah. I'd never kill anybody."

"All right."

"The demons. They're everywhere. They take people over and ride their bodies around. You can't tell. No one can tell until they let you see them, and then it's too late. They control everything. The president? The pope? You don't know. You have to believe me."

"I do believe you. I do. How did Beleth get into you, Maury? Can you tell me what happened?"

Sobinski rose to his feet. He looked like someone getting out of a hospital bed for the first time after surgery. Every movement was uncertain, every step tentative. Like he was waiting to see how far he could bend before it hurt again. Scarrey stayed sitting on the floor.

"It was maybe five years ago?" Sobinski said, rubbing the back of his neck with his hand. "I was working at this place in Detroit. Chop shop. They sold some drugs too, but I was strictly on the car side of things, right? There was this black guy. Jamaican. They called him John Zombie."

"John Zombie," Scarrey repeated, nodding.

"He was crazy. Into all kinds of weird shit. I didn't believe any of it. Figured he was just trying to look like a badass, you know? Scare people."

"Did he ever mention Carrefour? Marinette?"

"He did. He used those names. But I can't—" Sobinski said, and then without warning he leaped at Scarrey, screaming. The prisoner's body clanged against the metal, his shriek like a saw going through meat. Mason found his hand on the butt of his pistol and made himself relax.

Sobinski was yelling the same strange syllables he had before. His spine humped up and his arms shifted in repulsive jerks. Flecks of spit wetted the mesh cage. When Sobinski beat his fists against it, the metal rang. Mason stepped forward.

"Okay, asshole, you can stop that now," he said.

Scarrey rose, wiping spit from his nose and cheek.

"I think we're done here for now, Detective. I may want to come back later."

"I know you, little man," Sobinski said in his deep, demonic voice. "I know your heart. I will find you in your sleep."

"You can come back if you want to," Mason said with a shrug. "It goes like this pretty much all the time."

Scarrey nodded politely to the screaming man, and Mason led him away. With the holding cells behind them, Mason led the man to the break room and poured him a cup of coffee.

"Well?" he asked as Scarrey poured cream and sugar into his mug.

"I'll want to look through the reports. I may also need to see the crime scene? If you can take me there? As to the man himself, it's early to say. But there are some points of interest. This John Zombie he talks about may be worth remembering, but . . ."

"What about that nonsense he keeps babbling?"

"Hmm? Oh, yes. It's Aramaic."

"Yeah? How's his accent?" Mason asked.

Scarrey looked up, confused. Then, catching the joke, smiled.

"Terrible."

SCARREY ADJUSTED ANDERSON'S CHAIR FIVE OR SIX TIMES WHILE MASON brought over the reports. It had everything from the original missing-person report the ex-boyfriend had filed through the medical examiner's write-up through the report Mason had written covering the arrest. Scarrey looked it over like he was trying to make up his mind where to start on the buffet line.

"You need anything else?" Mason asked.

"Could I have a few sheets of paper? Just printer paper would be fine. For notes."

"Sure," Mason said.

"And a pen?"

Once the guy was settled in, going over the paperwork with his face squinched into a comic mask of concentration, Mason headed for the break room. Having someone else at his partner's desk felt too weird, and he could use a little caffeine anyway. He was still there, drinking the last black dregs, when the chief found him.

He wasn't old, but he'd seen a lot, and he wore it in the angle of his shoulders and the way he held his back straight. He nodded to Mason when he came in and poured himself a cup of coffee.

"He's here?"

"He is, sir," Mason said. "I gave him the files. Full access. Just like you said."

"Good. That's good."

"Sir? About Anderson—"

"I'm not going to talk about that," the chief said, stirring nondairy creamer into the black.

"He's a good cop," Mason said. "I've worked with him for six years now, and he's the sharpest guy we have on this team. We lose him over this, and it means bad people walking."

"I'm not talking about it, Mason. And neither are you. When the Internal Affairs review is finished up, we can—"

"It was a couple hundred dollars," Mason said. "This department goes through more than that in free cappuccinos every week."

The chief put his cup down, leaned against the counter, and crossed his arms. His expression was the empty calm that meant Mason had come close enough to see the line, but he hadn't crossed it yet.

"I respect your concern for your partner," the chief said. "I share your high opinion of Detective Anderson. Speaking as a professional law enforcement officer and as your superior, I'm telling you right now that we are going to toe the line on this. Whatever IA wants to know, you tell them. Whatever they want to see, you show."

"Yes, sir."

"When Detective Anderson is exonerated of all wrongdoing, I don't want anyone thinking it was on some kind of technicality, or that we pulled one over on IA."

"No, sir."

"And speaking as myself, don't worry. I'm taking care of it."

Mason fought not to grin.

"Thank you, sir."

"I don't need gratitude. I need a confession out of Sobinski."

"All right, then."

The chief took his coffee, nodded, and walked away.

Back at his desk, Mason glanced over at the expert, who was still frowning over the details of the dead girl, sighed to himself, and started filling out the death investigation reports for a homeless man who'd either walked off an apartment building or else been pushed. An hour later, Scarrey appeared at his shoulder, clearing his throat as an apology.

"Find what you need?" Mason asked.

"No, no. Only what I expected. I was hoping we might stop by the crime scene? Possibly Sobinski's apartment?"

"Okay. But you understand that the crime scene's not going to be like it was. After the forensics guys are done, we release it. Let people start using the place again. They usually get the cleanup guys in pretty fast."

"What a world it would be otherwise," Scarrey said, and then, seeing Mason's blank look, "I was just thinking what it would be like if we froze a room every time someone died in it. We'd run out of places to eat and sleep. Store food. We'd have to find some way to clean the space. Start time moving again. But then, I suppose we do that when the forensics team leaves, don't we? Try to take a room or alleyway or whatever out of the world while they go about their work, and when they make their mark, put it back in."

"Sure," Mason said. "I guess."

"The power of ritual," Scarrey said, pleased by the thought. "Well. Would you like to drive, or shall I?"

THE WAREHOUSE WHERE SARAH OSTERMAN HAD DIED WAS ONE OF HUNDREDS like it squatting in the rough triangle where the river and the railroad intersected. The morning sun pressed the shadows out of the concrete and steel. The only pedestrians were the homeless, and the traffic was all big-rig trucks and clunkers. Mason liked the district for its authenticity. That was about all it had to offer.

In the passenger seat, Scarrey hummed to himself and leaned out, peering at the addresses they passed. His thick, stubby fingers tapped on the seat beside him, almost but not quite keeping time with the humming. On the one hand, Mason could turn on the radio, try to drown the guy out. On the other, if he did, the guy might try to sing along.

They parked in front of the manager's office. A block of tall buildings with rolling garage doors and loading docks stretched off to the south. Three big rigs stood parked at the docks, but nothing was moving in or out of the warehouses. The manager, a painfully thin woman with a nasal cannula running down to her portable oxygen supply, gave him the access code and universal key. As Mason walked down the loading docks, Scarrey trotted beside him.

"The company that was renting the warehouse legitimately," Scarrey said. "Have they reported anything odd about the space since?"

"Nope. Nothing going bump in the night. At least nothing they've told me about."

"Hm."

"Expecting something?"

"Well, you'd expect people to be nervous at least, wouldn't you?" Scarrey said. "Something terrible like that happens, and people draw back or they lean forward. It's very rare that they can remain unaffected. Of course, it would have to be something significant to deserve official mention."

"Sounds like you don't think our boy was really trying to call up the devil."

"Oh, I didn't say that," Scarrey said.

Mason stopped at the door. M-15 in black on flaking yellow paint. He keyed the passcode into the button pad beside the door, put in the manager's key, and, with a loud clank, the warehouse door began to rise. Scarrey ducked under it, hurrying inside. Mason waited until he could walk in standing straight.

The place looked innocuous. Simple. Innocent. The boxes and shelving that Sobinski had moved aside were back where they belonged. The air smelled like car exhaust and WD-40, not incense and blood. The chalked words and diagrams had been washed off the floor and walls. Mason pulled back his shoulders, stretching until something in his spine cracked. Scarrey was walking around the place like a tourist in Times Square, blinking and craning his neck. He walked once around the whole place, fingertips trailing on the wall, touching the boxes of cheap DVD players and third-rate audio equipment, his eyes squinting up into the blue-white fluorescents.

"Did you see her?"

"I did," Mason said.

"What did it feel like?"

"Excuse me?"

"Well, that's the problem with reports, isn't it? They never tell you the really important parts. I know she was here," Scarrey said, standing as near to the right place as the shelving would let him and raising his arms as if the chains and hooks had been in his own flesh. "And I'm thinking suspended from that rafter and the pipe over there, yes?"

"That's right."

"That's the kind of thing reports tell you. They never say what it felt like. When you saw her, did it make you happy?"

"She was a *kid*," Mason said. "She was tortured and killed by a sick asshole, and we were too late to help her. What do you think?"

"I don't know, but it's important. Did seeing her body here make you happy?"

"No."

"Sexually aroused?"

"Yeah," Mason deadpanned. "Absolutely. Boner you could drive nails with."

"Don't do that," Scarrey said. His voice was low now, and very serious. "Don't joke about this. I can't tell what you're joking to cover. Did the body arouse you sexually?"

"Fuck no, it didn't," Mason said.

"Good. Good good good."

"What about you?"

"Me?"

"Did what happened here make *you* happy?"

"Lots of things have happened here," Scarrey said. "Some of them were terrible. Meaning what happened with that girl. Some of them were quite pleasant."

"Like?"

"Like me finding what I expected to find."

"Which is?"

Scarrey grinned and spread his arms, gesturing at the walls, the boxes, the light.

"A warehouse," he said.

"Yeah," Mason said. "Well, glad we got that solved. What's next?"

"Lunch, I'd expect. Would you like some lunch? I'll pay."

It wasn't the sort of restaurant Mason usually went for. Given his options, he usually went for a good local Mexican place or else a steakhouse. If it looked like the kind of place where he might have to wait for a table, he'd discount it out of hand. When they walked through the glass-and-chrome doors, Mason expected the woman at the maitre d' station to ask if they'd like a reservation for next month, but instead, she'd shown them back to a little cream-colored alcove with an art deco halogen lamp suspended from wires above the table. So maybe Scarrey knew something.

"What's good here?" Mason asked, looking over the menu. Fourteen-dollar BLT. Forty-dollar lamb shank.

"I usually get the salad with feta on the side," Scarrey said.

"Right," Mason said.

"There's a coffee-crusted steak that's good too. You could try that."

Mason tried to figure out if the guy was joking, and almost decided he wasn't. And if he was, it would serve him right for making the offer.

"All right. I'll give it a shot."

Scarrey waved the waiter over, and they ordered. Their drinks arrived before they'd finished. Scarrey got a European lager. Mason stuck to iced tea, and for iced tea, it wasn't bad.

"So," Mason said. "You believe all this stuff. Beleth, King of Hell. Demonic conspiracies. Like that?"

"Absolutely, I do," Scarrey said. "I've seen it. I take it you don't believe it?"

"I've seen a lot of things," Mason said. "I'm just the cop, though. You want judgment, you want a judge."

"I'm not sure being on the bench necessarily gives someone a deeper spiritual insight."

"Amen," Mason said, and Scarrey caught the joke immediately that time. The maitre d' looked over at the sound of his laughter, smiled, and turned away.

"I didn't always believe it," Scarrey said. "But I hoped. I always hoped."

"Hoped? That there was a global satanic conspiracy controlling the government and the police so it can sacrifice babies and worship the devil?"

"Well, not when you put it *that* way. But I hoped that there was a world more magical than my physical, obvious, mundane life. I was like that when I was young. Always looking for something miraculous. A visitation from God. Or a UFO abduction. I wanted to be a vampire all through middle school. Used to stand by my window every night and invite any vampires who happened to be around to come in. They can't come in unless you invite them, you know. I was a bit ahead of the times on that. I wasn't picky, though. I just wanted something to turn the world on its head."

"Sounds like you needed a girlfriend," Mason said.

"Oh, I did," Scarrey said. "No, I stumbled into riders because I hoped to."

"Riders?"

"It's what people in the trade call them. The things that live just outside the world, trying to get in."

"Why not just demons?"

Scarrey took a long drink of his lager, his frown drawing lines in his forehead. He smacked his lips.

"What's the difference between an angel and a demon?" he asked.

"One's good, the other's evil."

"What's *good*, though? What's evil? I mean, yes, you and I agree, I'm sure about almost everything. Hurting people who don't deserve it is bad, being compassionate is good, and so on and so on. We likely even agree on particular cases. But even if every man and woman and child straight out of the womb agreed that something was a wrong thing to do, does that make it true or absolute? I doubt you'll find anyone who approves of tuberculosis qua tuberculosis, but we haven't asked the bacilli's opinions."

"So Beleth the King of Hell's an angel?" Mason said.

"If you agree with him, why not?" Scarrey said. "If he destroys the things that you think should be destroyed and protects the things you want protected. Read the Old Testament; you'll see that angels are terrible, frightening things. But they work in the service of God, and since you're reading the Bible, you likely believe that God is good, and so . . . The difference between an angel and a demon is whether you both vote Republican."

"And how would you agree with something like . . . what we've got locked up?"

Scarrey's face lit up. For a moment, all the ingrained uncertainty and apology and awkwardness were gone. Mason felt like he was seeing someone different from the man who'd come in to see the prisoner.

"That's the mystery, isn't it? The *mystery*, not the puzzle. What kind of man would invite that into himself? One who hates women. One who enjoys sadism, or . . . or finds it reassuring somehow. One who is driven to it by fear."

"Or is a fucking nutcase," Mason said.

"Oh, Detective," Scarrey said, chuckling, "if you don't like my ideas about good and evil, you aren't going to be satisfied with my opinions on sanity."

The food arrived. The steak was black as a lump of coal, with a thick crust that bubbled and sizzled. Steamed carrots and broccoli florets adorned the side of the plate, alternating with the regularity of soldiers in formation. The dab of mashed potatoes smelled of hazelnuts and butter. Mason took a bite of the steak, and his eyes went wide. The forty-dollar price tag made more sense. The waiter put Scarrey's salad in front of him, and a carved crystal plate with crumbled feta beside it.

"Gentlemen," the waiter said, "the manager wanted me to tell you that all of this will be complimentary today. If there's anything else I can get for you, just let me know."

Scarrey made a little clicking noise with his tongue and teeth and shook his head.

"Tell her that she's really entirely too kind."

"Yes, sir," the waiter said, and backed away with professional and well-practiced grace.

Mason reevaluated the man across the table from him, but he kept coming back to the same place. Even now, on his home territory, he kept his elbows in at his sides, and he smiled unconsciously, nervously. But the chief could ask favors of him, and fancy restaurants downtown fed him for free. It didn't fit. Scarrey sensed the attention and fidgeted.

"The manager and I go to the same church," he said around a mouthful of lettuce. "Your chief attends services there too."

"Really?" Mason said. "I wouldn't have made him for the pious type."

"Unitarian. Do you like the steak?"

Mason took another bite. The burned taste of the coffee crust, the salt and juice of the meat. The blood.

"It's great."

SOBINSKI'S APARTMENT WAS THE UPPER LEFT QUARTER OF A FOURPLEX. THE neighborhood was a mix of lower middle class and the wealthiest ranks of the poor. Dogs ran loose on the street in a ragged pack that watched Mason and Scarrey with the wariness of locals for outsiders. As they walked up the battered steel stairway, footsteps chiming, the smell of cooking sausage wafted up at them from the downstairs apartment. After the steak, it was a little nauseating.

Mason cut the seal, unlocked the door, and let Scarrey through. The place looked the same as it had the first time Mason had seen it. Tiny kitchen. The stovetop hadn't seen much use, and the door of the microwave was spotted with splatters of brown. Narrow living room with a big flatscreen TV that was the only high-end appliance in the place, a beige carpet that couldn't hide the drips and stains, and a floral couch with a rip at the side that leaked yellow-white stuffing. Scarrey walked around the rooms slowly, his hands in his pockets. Mason wondered whether it looked different to him, and if it did, how.

"Did you arrest him here?"

"Yeah," Mason said. "I think he knew it was coming."

"And he tried to run?"

"Out the back window. Fire escape. We caught him in the alley."

"Mmm."

Scarrey went down the two steps' worth of hall to the bedroom. Single bed, unmade. Dresser with a pile of junk mail and bills. Socks on the floor. Scarrey squatted on the floor, looking under the bed.

"This was where you found the box of occult things?"

"The robe," Mason said. "A bunch of fucked-up DVDs. Some books. They're all back in evidence if you want to look at them."

"That's all right. There are other boxes down here, though."

"Yeah. Crap storage."

Scarrey went down on his hands and knees, fishing the white cardboard out into the room. Old clothes in wads. A book on how to pick up girls. A stack of pornographic magazines. Two old bricks. A pile of yellowing paperbacks held together with a wide rubber band. A collection of DVDs teaching magic, juggling, unicycle riding. Scarrey ran his fingers over everything like he was flipping pages in a book. He paused, eyes narrowing.

"Missing," he said.

"What?"

"The circus training disks. One's missing," Scarrey said. He picked up the one on juggling. On the box, a guy in clown-face makeup was grinning, a cartoon circle of blue dots and streaks standing in for actual juggling balls. Scarrey read through the text on the back, his lips moving. He made a satisfied grunt.

"Something?"

"Nothing unexpected," he said. "Contortion."

Scarrey dropped the disk back into the box and picked up the pile of paperbacks.

"Contortion?" Mason said.

"Bending," Scarrey said. "It's when someone—"

"Yeah, I know what it is."

"More to the point, it's the one he lost. Or got rid of. I don't know whether he intentionally removed it, or if it was just something he had out often enough to misplace, but it hardly matters. And these, ah look. From a church library. *Chariot of the Gods. Releasing Your Inner Light. Satan Among Us.* Ah! Look. *The True Meaning of the New Testament*, by Reverend J. Linklesser. As if there were only one meaning! But . . ."

The rubber band came off with a snap, and Scarrey let the book fall open. Mason saw underlined passages flicker by.

"Aramaic?" Mason said.

"If English was good enough for our Lord and Savior . . . except, of course, it wasn't."

"It's crap then," Mason said. "All that shit Sobinski's pulling. He's not possessed."

Scarrey looked up from the floor, baffled.

"Of course not. I mean, I had to check the site of the sacrifice to be totally certain, but really. John Zombie?" Scarrey grimaced and shook his head. "Semitic languages like Aramaic are Afro-Asiatic, not Afro-Caribbean. And Mait Carrefour and Marinette are very specific loa, neither one associated particularly with Jacob's Ladder. You were quite right about the man, he really isn't very good. Not that he's evil. I mean he *is* evil, he killed that poor girl, but he isn't very good at what he does."

"Wait a minute, you knew he wasn't possessed?"

"Of course."

"Then, excuse my saying it, but what the fuck are we doing here?"

"Oh," Scarrey said. "I'm sorry, Detective. I'm not here to find whether he's possessed. I'm here to find why he's pretending to be."

"Insanity plea," Mason said.

"No, that won't do. For one thing, in practice that defense never works. Even if it did, life in prison isn't appreciably different from indefinite detention in a mental institution, except that the prison is more pleasant. Now, given how badly he's done everything else, your man Sobinski *might* not have realized that."

"Straight-up insanity."

"He could have had some kind of psychotic break. Not to the degree that he couldn't plan and carry out a complex crime. And he didn't seem to have any signs of Beleth the King of Hell before he was arrested. Possibly being caught induced psychosis as a way to distance himself from responsibility, but . . ."

"But?"

"Well, there are some problems with it," Scarrey said, softly. "I have a hard time saying that a man who did what he did is *well*, mentally, but I think, I *think*, I know what he was looking for."

"I've already told the police what I know."

The sausage cooker downstairs was a thick-boned Korean woman in her late forties named Anna. Her kitchen was exactly the same layout as Sobinski's, but with less light and more cooking. She stood at the stovetop, stirring a pan of sizzling meat. The smell of hot gristle and salt hadn't gotten less repulsive by being closer. Scarrey didn't seemed bothered by it.

"I'm not a policeman. Did he seem to have many friends?"

She scowled at Scarrey, then up at Mason, then at the food cooking before her.

"He didn't have any for very long. He was one of those people who knows someone really well for a little while, then moves on. Drank too much. He was always . . ."

She shook her head. Scarrey looked at his own clasped hands. For a moment, he could almost have been praying.

"Frightened," he said.

Anna glanced at him, then nodded.

"Could put it like that. He was always talking about how the liberals were going to take away our rights, or how George Bush was really working with the Saudis. He was pretty evenhanded about his politics. Give him that. Hated everybody."

"Did you know him well?"

"For a little while."

"Did he frighten you?" Scarrey asked.

"No, never."

"Does *that* frighten you, considering what he did?"

"Yeah," she said, turning off the burner under her pan. "Yeah, it does."

She turned to the refrigerator and took out a round loaf of uncut bread. The place was so small, she didn't have to shift her feet.

"How did the two of you end your acquaintance?" Scarrey asked. Mason shifted his weight to his left foot. Anna took a knife from its stand and slit the loaf of bread down the side. She was quiet for long enough that Mason started to wonder if she'd heard the question, and, if she had, whether she'd answer it.

"He didn't hit me," she said. "He didn't even get mean. He just drifted off. Didn't come down for dinner anymore, and so, after a while, I stopped cooking for him."

She pushed a lock of hair back over her ear, put down the knife, and bent the opened bread, the crust cracking under her fingers, and the soft white tissue of the loaf blooming out.

"I was going to cuss him out," she said. "But I never got around to it. I wonder. If I had . . ."

"Did he take up with another woman?" Scarrey asked.

"No. He was in a band. Teaching himself guitar. Only lasted about a month. Then there were a bunch of Jesus freaks he had over for a while, until they stopped coming. I stopped paying much attention after that. I don't think he was the kind of man that ever knew much peace."

"Would you call him depressed?"

She opened the refrigerator again and took out a tub of fake butter and used the same knife she'd cut with to spread it.

"No," she said. "He wasn't happy, but he wasn't depressed. He was . . . hungry? Scared? Shit, I don't know what you want to call it. He was messed up. Bad childhood or something. He was always looking for something, always had a scheme for how it was all going to be okay this time. Only it never was."

She was still scowling, but the angle of her shoulders had changed. Her guard was coming down. Mason tried to keep his own expression soft and unintimidating. He wasn't much in practice for that.

"You guys want some food?" she asked.

Jesus no, thought Mason.

"Please," Scarrey said. "That would be lovely."

"None for me," Mason said. "Just ate."

She brought a plate over to the small, peeling-laminate table. The meat was gray with flecks of brown, surrounded by a haphazard fall of half-cooked onion. The bread and fake butter perched on the side.

"All I got's water," she said.

"Water would be lovely," Scarrey said with a big, goofy grin. "Most important nutrient there is. Hydration."

As she got a glass from the tap, Scarrey tucked into the meat as if it were the best thing he'd seen all day. Mason made a point of not noticing that Anna had wiped the water glass clean before she filled it. When she handed it to him, Scarrey nodded his thanks. Anna sat across from him, her lips pressed thin, as if offering them food had exposed her weak spots and she regretted it now.

"I know it's an odd question," Scarrey said around a mouthful of sausage and onion, "given everything you said about him, but I have to ask. With all the fear and the reaching out and letting go, all the brief attachments to people and causes and so on, did he strike you as *hopeful*?"

Anna furrowed her brow.

"Yeah," she said. "That's a weird way to put it, but . . . Yeah."

"Ah," Scarrey said, and his smile left him looking satisfied.

"WHAT DID YOU MEAN, THE MYSTERY, NOT THE PUZZLE?" MASON ASKED. They were driving down Central toward the university. The afternoon traffic was starting to thicken, the distant early warning of rush-hour gridlock.

"Have you ever considered the difference between them?"

"Can't say I have," Mason said.

"You should. It's important, given what you do."

"Solve mysteries?"

"Sometimes," Scarrey said. "But more often, I think, puzzles."

"Okay, I'll bite. What's the difference?"

A van moved up beside them, gunned its engine, and tried to pass. Mason sped up just a little to stop it, and the van slowed back.

"Puzzles have *solutions*," Scarrey said. "Do you have a napkin? My fingers are . . ."

"There's some wet wipes in the glove box," Mason said.

"Thank you. Puzzles have solutions. The lock opens. The wine bottle comes free."

"You figure out whodunit," Mason said. "I get that."

"Mysteries aren't like that. With them, there's an element of judgment. Guesswork. Not just to reach the solution, but within the solution itself."

"That sounds really deep," Mason said, "but I don't know what the fuck it means."

"Which makes it a mystery," Scarrey said. Mason laughed.

Back in the office, Anderson was at his desk, grinning and high-fiving everyone who passed by. His wide-set face and too-handsome looks didn't have the haunted look they'd acquired in the past few weeks. Mason grinned.

"Good to see you finally showing up for work, slacker," Mason said.

"Smoked all my dope," Anderson said, returning the joke. "Figured I'd better come in, hit up the evidence locker, eh?"

From across the room, Diaz growled.

"Take it outside. I'm trying to work here."

Mason lifted his eyebrows, but Anderson shook his head and pointed to the door. They paused in the hallway, Scarrey looking from one to the other in confusion.

"What's up?"

"The perp on Miawashi? Yeah, he's gone. Not at his mom's place. Not with his girlfriend."

"Knows we're looking at him," Mason said. "Well. He's got to be somewhere."

"Makes it a puzzle," Scarrey said, cheerfully. Anderson met Mason's eyes with an empty expression. He didn't get the joke.

"Internal Affairs finished chewing you over?"

"I'm not getting a written apology or anything, but yeah. That's done," he said. "What about you two? Good day?"

"Possibly excellent," Scarrey said.

"Track down the global satanic conspiracy?"

"Wouldn't go that far," Mason said. "Pretty well established that Sobinski's full of shit, though."

"Even with the . . ." Anderson moved his arms back into an awkward pose, mimicking the prisoner.

"Even with," Mason agreed. "I'm thinking we get some of the stuff we found, and we can use it pretrial if his lawyer tries to get him declared incompetent. Still no confession, but . . ."

"Well," Anderson said, nodding slowly. Maybe impressed, maybe pretending to be impressed. "Go with God."

"Yes," Scarrey said. "I was hoping I could see the prisoner one last time, though. If that's not too much trouble?"

"Fine with me," Mason said.

"Um," Scarrey said, looking pained and embarrassed.

Mason hoisted his eyebrows.

"Yes, I was wondering if I might speak with him alone."

THE INTERROGATION ROOM WASN'T BUILT FOR COMFORT. A SINGLE METAL table, bolted to the floor. A plastic chair for the perp, light enough that even if he threw it at someone, it wouldn't do any real damage. The walls were a dim, unhealthy green. The CCTV camera sat in the corner, so that the image on the monitor was tilted like something in a funhouse mirror. Maury Sobinski looked up into the camera sometimes, like he was trying to decide whether it was on or not. Mason had disabled the red light-emitting diode on the side months ago. Sobinski's wrists were in cuffs, his ankles hobbled, and a chain ran around the bolted desk. If Scarrey got himself hurt in there, it wouldn't be because Mason hadn't tried to keep him safe.

"This is a bad idea, partner," Anderson said.

"If I leave them in lockup, someone might overhear, right?" Mason said. "Interrogation rooms are soundproof. No one goes in or out without making enough noise to know they're coming. Chief's guest wants privacy, I give him privacy."

"Except for the part where you put him where you can snoop on him."

"Yeah, except for that."

"This is a bad idea."

"Shh. Here he comes."

At the table, Sobinski sat up a little straighter. Mason turned up the monitor's volume a little. Scarrey's footsteps came before the little man walked into the frame. The relative positions of Scarrey and the camera meant that Mason could only see the back of his head, and that from the top. Perfect angle to see how much the guy was balding. Sobinski's head shifted in the weird almost-broken way he had. His voice through the monitor was perfectly clear. What had seemed creepy and ominous before came across as theatrical and pretentious now.

"You return, little man. You've come for Maury, but you cannot have him."

"That isn't entirely true," Scarrey said. "You can stop. It's all right. I understand."

Sobinski's laughter rattled his chains and scooted his chair across the floor.

"You will bow before the King of Hell," Sobinski said. "Beleth will eat your heart, little man. Only open up. Let him in. Everything will end for you."

"Maury, you should stop this. It's undignified."

"I am the angel at the gate!" Sobinski screamed, his shoulders twisting in ways that looked unlikely and painful. "I am the archon of the last days!"

"You're Maury Sobinski. And you're a very bad person. I've come here to fix that."

Anderson leaned forward, his hand on Mason's shoulder.

"Mason?" he said. "What's he mean, *fix that*?"

But Sobinski was already lost in a peal of maniacal laughter. On the screen, Scarrey shrugged. His voice was quiet, almost gentle, but it carried over the prisoner's pandemonium.

"Really. Stop."

They were standing five feet apart, maybe six. But Sobinski coughed, choked like someone had him by the throat. His eyes were on Scarrey, and the fake demon show was gone.

"I don't know what happened to you," Scarrey said. His hands were in the pockets of his slacks. "You were bullied when you were a boy? Abused, maybe? That's how it is with some people. Or you just never found a place in the world. It was like that for me."

"What's he talking about?" Anderson asked. He was whispering now, even though there was no way Scarrey could hear him. Without thinking, Mason whispered back.

"Fuck if I know."

"Vampires. Did you ever want to be a vampire? God, *I* did. The interesting thing about them is that they have to be *invited*," Scarrey said. "I think you were like I was. Never comfortable in your skin. You can't keep friends very long. You can't keep your mind focused. The chances are very, very good that you're mentally ill and undiagnosed. But it doesn't matter. Here's what *does*. You killed that girl because you wanted something. You wanted to let go, am I right? You wanted someone else to take over the hard parts. You wanted to be safe from the world?"

"What do you want?" Sobinski asked.

"Nothing you wouldn't be willing to part with. What do you say? Only open up? You'll go to prison, of course, but it will be much, much easier with our help. And afterward, we can take care of things for you. Keep you from hurting anybody unintentionally. Keep you from being lost. And we'll be there, *with* you. It's what you've been looking for. And the price is very, very small. Considering."

"Who are you?"

"We're legion," Scarrey said, almost apologetically. "But we have to be invited."

"Come in," Sobinski said. Scarrey nodded.

"This is going to hurt, but it won't last long."

"What game is he playing?" Anderson whispered, and Sobinski screamed, bent backward, and collapsed. Mason was halfway to the interrogation room before he knew that he was going. The door was open when he reached it. Scarrey's wide back was retreating down the hall, his hands in his pockets, his stride casual and at ease.

"Hey!" Mason called.

Scarrey turned to look over his shoulder, grinned, and waved like a man seeing an old friend. He didn't stop. Mason leaned into the interrogation room. Sobinski sat on the floor; his chair had skittered away. He looked dazed. Mason went to him, his belly tight. If he'd let a civilian hurt a suspect in custody, there would be hell to pay. But already he didn't think that was what had happened.

"You okay?" Mason said.

"Hey, Detective," the prisoner said. He sounded winded, like he was trying to catch his breath. "Good you're here."

"You need a glass of water or something?"

"No, no," Sobinski said, with an odd, lopsided grin. "It's cool. What I wanted to say is, I killed Osterman. It was a dick move, but y'know. Anyway, it was me that did it. On the record. D'you know what I have to do to plead guilty?"

"You're confessing?"

"Sure," Sobinski said.

"Why?"

"Because I did it."

When the man smiled, he looked like Scarrey.

MASON SAT AT HIS DESK. THE WEEKEND HAD BEEN BUSY. TWO CORPSES AT a hotel down by the river in what might have been a bad drug deal or else a queer love affair gone badly wrong. A dead six-year-old in Presbyterian Hospital with head wounds that didn't match the story his dad told. A woman living down by the country club who had gotten her head caved in by burglars, except that she'd just filed for divorce. Plus which, the perp in the Miawashi vehicular homicide was still hiding out.

The week was going to be hell.

"Hey," Winehart said. "Diaz and Roper are taking the hotel gig. You and Anderson want the kid or the rich bitch?"

Before Mason could answer, the chief stepped in. He looked old. He looked tired. He looked human. Mason figured he looked just the way he wanted to look. Their eyes met for a moment, each daring the other to look away. They both knew that Mason had seen something he wasn't supposed to see. Knew something he wasn't supposed to know. The question was, what were they both going to do about it?

"How's it going, Detective?" the chief asked, carefully.

"Just another day doing the work of angels, sir," Mason said. Winehart seemed confused when the chief chuckled. She didn't get the joke.

THE CURIOUS AFFAIR OF THE DEODAND

by Lisa Tuttle

Lisa Tuttle made her first sale in 1972 to the anthology *Clarion II*, after attending the Clarion workshop, and by 1974 she had won the John W. Campbell Award for Best New Writer of the Year. She has gone on to become one of the most respected writers of her generation, winning the Nebula Award in 1981—which, in a still-controversial move, she refused to accept—the British Science Fiction Award in 1987, and the International Horror Guild Award in 2007, all for short stories. Her books include a collaboration with George R. R. Martin, *Windhaven*; the solo novels *Familiar Spirit*, *Gabriel*, *The Pillow Friend*, *Lost Futures*, *The Mysteries*, and *The Silver Bough*; as well as several books for children, the nonfiction works *Heroines* and *Encyclopaedia of Feminism*, and, as editor, *Skin of the Soul: New Horror Stories by Women*. Her short work has been collected in *A Nest of Nightmares*, *A Spaceship Built of Stone*, *Memories of the Body: Tales of Desire and Transformation*, *Ghosts and Other Lovers*, and *My Pathology*. Born in Texas, she moved to Great Britain in 1980, and now lives with her family in Scotland.

Here she introduces us to a proper young nineteenth-century gentlewoman who is about to try out a new role, that of "Watson" to an eccentric Sherlock Holmes-like figure—and who will discover a surprising aptitude for that role before their first case is through.

ONCE IT HAD BECOME PAINFULLY CLEAR THAT I COULD NO LONGER CONtinue to work in association with Miss G— F—, I departed Scotland and returned to London, where I hoped I would quickly find employment. I had no bank account, no property, nothing of any value to pawn or sell, and, after I had paid my train fare, little more than twelve shillings to my name.

Although I had friends in London who would open their homes to me, I had imposed before, and was determined not to be a burden. It was therefore a matter of the utmost urgency that I should obtain a position: I emphasize this point to account for what might appear a precipitous decision.

Arriving so early in the morning at King's Cross, it seemed logical enough to set off at once, on foot, for the ladies' employment bureau in Oxford Street.

The bag that had seemed light enough when I took it down from the train grew heavier with every step, so that I was often obliged to stop and set it down for a few moments. One such rest took place outside a newsagent's shop, and while I caught my breath and rubbed my aching arm I glanced at the notices on display in the window. One, among the descriptions of lost pets and offers of rooms to let, caught my attention.

> CONSULTING DETECTIVE
> REQUIRES ASSISTANT
> MUST BE LITERATE, BRAVE, CONGENIAL, WITH A GOOD MEMORY, &
> WILLING TO WORK ALL HOURS.
> APPLY IN PERSON TO
> J. JESPERSON,
> 203-A GOWER STREET

Even as my heart leapt, I scolded myself for being a silly girl. Certainly, I was sharp and brave, blessed with good health and a strong constitution, but when you came right down to it, I was a woman, small and weak. What detective would take on such a liability?

But the card said nothing about weapons or physical strength. I read it again, and then glanced up from the number on the card—203A—to the number painted above the shop premises: 203.

There were two doors. One, to the left, led into the little shop, but the other, painted glistening black, bore a brass plate inscribed *Jesperson.*

My knock was answered by a lady in early middle age, too genteel in dress and appearance to be mistaken for a servant.

"Mrs. Jesperson?" I asked.

"Yes?"

I told her I had come in response to the advertisement, and she let me in. There was a lingering smell of fried bacon and toasted bread that reminded me I'd had nothing to eat since the previous afternoon.

"Jasper," she said, opening another door and beckoning me on. "Your notice has already borne fruit! Here is a lady . . . Miss . . . ?"

"I am Miss Lane," I said, going in.

I entered a warm, crowded, busy, comfortable, cheerful place. I relaxed, the general atmosphere, with the familiar scent of books, tobacco, toast, and ink that imbued it, making me feel at home even before I'd had a chance to look around. The room obviously combined an office and living room in one. The floor-to-ceiling bookshelves, crammed with volumes, gave it the look of a study, as did the very large, very cluttered desk piled with papers and journals. But there were also armchairs near the fireplace—the hearth cold on this warm June morning; the mantelpiece so laden with such a variety of objects I simply could not take them in at a glance—and a table bearing the remains of breakfast for two. This quick impression was all I had time to absorb before the man, springing up from his place at the table, commanded my attention.

I say *man*, yet the first word that came to mind was *boy*, for despite his size—he was, I later learned, six feet four inches tall—the smooth, pale, lightly freckled face beneath a crown of red-gold curls was that of an angelic child.

He fixed penetrating blue eyes upon me. "How do you do, Miss Lane? So, you fancy yourself a detective?" His voice at any rate was a man's; deep and well modulated.

"I would not say so. But you advertised for an assistant, someone literate, brave, congenial, with a good memory, and willing to work all hours. I believe I possess all those qualities, and I am in search of . . . *interesting* employment."

Something sparked between us. It was not that romantic passion that poets and sentimental novelists consider the only connection worth writing about between a man and a woman. It was, rather, a *liking*, a recognition of congeniality of mind and spirit.

Mr. Jesperson nodded his head and rubbed his hands together, the mannerisms of an older man. "Well, very well," he murmured to himself, before fixing me again with his piercing gaze.

"You have worked before, of course, in some capacity requiring sharp perceptions, careful observation, and a bold spirit, yet you are now cut adrift—"

"Jasper, please," Mrs. Jesperson interrupted. "Show the lady common courtesy, at least." Laying one hand gently on my arm, she invited me to sit, indicating a chair, and offered tea.

"I'd love some, thank you. But that's your chair, surely?"

"Oh, no, I won't intrude any further." As she spoke, she lifted the fine white china teapot, assessing the weight of the contents with a practiced turn of her wrist. "I'll leave the two of you to your interview while I fetch more tea. Would you like bread and butter, or anything else?"

A lady always refuses food when she hasn't been invited to a meal—but I was too hungry for good manners. "That would be most welcome, thank you."

"I'll have more toast, if you please, and jam would be nice, too, Mother."

She raised her eyes heavenward and sighed as she went away.

He'd already returned his attention to me. "You have been in the Highlands, in the country home of one of our titled families. You were expecting to be there for the rest of the summer, until an unfortunate . . . occurrence . . . led to an abrupt termination of your visit, and you were forced to leave at once, taking the first train to London where you have . . . a sister? No, nothing closer than an aunt or a cousin, I think. And you were on your way there when, pausing to rest, you spotted my notice." He stopped, watching me expectantly.

I shook my head to chide him.

He gaped, crestfallen. "I'm wrong?"

"Only about a few things, but anyone with eyes might guess I'd been in Scotland, considering the time of day, and the fact that I've had no breakfast, but there are no foreign stickers on my portmanteau."

"And the abrupt departure?"

"I was on foot, alone, there not having been time for a letter to inform my friends—there is no aunt or cousin—of my arrival."

"The job is yours," he said suddenly. "Don't worry about references—*you* are your own best reference. The job is yours—if you still want it."

"I should like to know more about it, first," I replied, thinking I should at least appear to be cautious. "What would be my duties?"

"*Duties* seems to me the wrong word. Your *role*, if you like, would be that of an associate, helping me to solve crimes, assisting in deduction, and, well, whatever is required. You've read the Sherlock Holmes stories?"

"Of course. I should point out that, unlike Dr. Watson, I'd be no good in a fight. I have a few basic nursing skills, so I could bind your wounds, but don't expect me to recognize the symptoms of dengue fever, or—or—"

He laughed. "I don't ask for any of that. My mother's the nurse. I'm a crack shot, and I've also mastered certain skills imported from the Orient which give me an advantage in unarmed combat. I cannot promise to keep you out of danger entirely, but if danger does not frighten you—" He took the answer from my face and gave me a broad smile. "Very well, then. We're agreed?"

How I longed to return that smile, and take the hand he offered to shake on it! But with no home, and only twelve shillings in my purse, I needed more.

"What's the matter?"

"This is awkward," I said. "Unlike Dr. Watson, I don't have a medical practice to provide me with an income . . ."

"Oh, money!" he exclaimed, with that careless intonation possible only to people who've never had to worry about the lack of it. "Why, of course, I mean for you to get something more than the thrill of the chase out of this business. A man's got to live! A woman, too. How are you at writing? Nothing fancy, just setting down events in proper order, in a way that anyone might understand. Ever tried your hand at such a narrative?"

"I've written a few articles; most recently, reports for the Society for Psychical Research, which were published, although not above my own name."

His eyes widened when I mentioned the S.P.R., and he burst out excitedly, "C— House! By Jove, is that where you've been? Are you 'Miss X'?"

I must have looked pained, for he quickly apologized.

I didn't like to explain how hearing her name—one of her silly pseudonyms—when I was feeling so far from her, so safe and comfortable, had unsettled me, so I only remarked that I'd been startled by his swift, accurate deduction. " 'Miss X' *was* the name assigned in authorship to my reports, but in actual fact I was her . . . her assistant, until yesterday, when a disagreement about some events in C— House led to my sudden departure. But how do you know of it? The investigation is incomplete, and no report has yet been published."

Without taking his eyes from my face—and what secrets he read there, I didn't want to know!—Jesperson waved one long-fingered hand toward the desk piled with papers and journals. "Although not myself a member of the S.P.R., I take a keen interest in their findings. I have read the correspondence; I knew there was an investigation of the house planned for this summer.

"I am a thoroughly rational, modern man," he went on. "If I worship anything, it must be the god we call Reason. I'm a materialist who has no truck with superstition, but in my studies, I've come across a great many things that science cannot explain. I do not sneer at those who attend séances or hunt for ghosts; I think it would be foolish to ignore the unexplained as unworthy of investigation. *Everything* should be questioned and explored. It's not belief that is important, but *facts*."

"I agree," I said quietly.

He leaned toward me across the uncleared table, his gaze frank and curious. "Have you ever seen a ghost, Miss Lane?"

"No."

But he had noticed some small hesitation. "You're not certain? You've had experiences that can't be explained in rational terms?"

"Many people have had such experiences."

"Yes," he drawled, and leaned back, a faraway look in his eyes. But only for a moment. "Tell me: do you possess any of those odd talents or senses that are generally called *psychic*?"

Despite the many times I'd been asked that question, I still had a struggle with my reply. "I am aware, at times, of *atmospheres* to which others seem immune, and occasionally receive impressions . . . sometimes I possess knowledge of things without being able to explain how I know. But I make no claims; I do not discount the effects of a vivid imagination allied with sharp perceptions and a good memory. Almost every so-called psychic medium I have ever met could achieve their results through looking, listening, and remembering, with no need for 'spirit guides.' "

He nodded in thoughtful agreement. "I have performed mind-reading tricks myself. If I didn't feel obliged to explain how it was done, I suppose I could make money at it. So how do you explain ghosts? Aren't they spirits?"

"I don't know. I subscribe to the idea that the ghosts people see or sense are afterimages, akin to photographs or some form of recorded memory. Strong emotions seem to leave an impression behind, in certain places more powerfully than in others. Objects also have their memories, if I may put it like that. Occasionally, an inanimate object will give off vibrations—of ill will, or despair—so it seems to project a kind of mental image of the person who owned it."

He gazed at me in fascination, which I found a novel experience. Even quite elderly gentlemen in the S.P.R. had not found me so interesting, but of course I tended to meet them in company with "Miss X," who was used to being the center of attention.

I decided it was time to get back to business, and reminded him of his original question: "You asked me if I wrote. I presume you were thinking that I could write up your cases with a view to publish?"

"Certainly the more interesting ones. Publication would have two useful ends. On the one hand, it would bring my name to public attention, and attract new clients. On the other, it would provide you with income."

My heart sank. I had friends who survived by the pen, so was well aware of how much time and toil it required to scrape a bare living in Grub Street. Even if Mr. Jesperson solved an interesting, exciting case every week (which seemed unlikely), and I sold every story I wrote . . . I was still struggling to work out how much I'd have to write, at thruppence a line, to earn enough to pay for room and board in a dingy lodging house, when he said something that cheered me:

"Of course, I realize not every case would be suitable for publication. I only mention it so you wouldn't think you'd have to live solely on your percentage."

"What percentage?"

"That would depend on the extent of your contribution. It could be anything from ten to fifty percent of whatever the client pays me."

Mrs. Jesperson had entered the room while he was speaking, and I heard her sharp intake of breath just before she set the tray she carried down on the table. "Jasper?" she said in a voice of doom.

"I can hardly ask Miss Lane to work unpaid, Mother."

"You can't afford to pay an assistant."

Despite my discomfort, I intervened. "Please. Let's not argue over money. I must admit, it's still unclear what Mr. Jesperson would be paying me *for*, apart from the sort of intellectual support and companionship any *friend* would freely give. And I should like to be that friend."

Now I had their rapt attention. "As you deduced, Mr. Jesperson, I left my last situation rather abruptly, without being paid for my work. I came to London to seek, not my fortune, but simply honest work to support myself."

I paused to draw breath, rather hoping one of them would say something, and I took a quick glance around the room to remind myself that even if Mrs. Jesperson felt they could not afford to pay an assistant, they nevertheless had all this—the fine china, the silver, the leather-bound books and substantial furniture, a whole houseful of things—by contrast with the contents of my single, well-worn bag.

"If I could afford it, I should propose an unpaid trial period, perhaps a month to discover the value of my contribution to your work. Unfortunately, I can't even afford to rent a room—"

"But you'll stay here!" exclaimed Mrs. Jesperson. She frowned at her son. "Didn't you explain?"

Mr. Jesperson was now serenely pouring tea. "I thought you might have deduced it, from the wording of my advertisement. The part about working all hours. Of course my assistant must be here, ready for any eventuality. It's no good if I have to write you a letter every time I want your opinion, or send a messenger halfway across London and await your reply."

"There's a room upstairs, well furnished and waiting," said Mrs. Jesperson, handing me a plate of white bread, thinly sliced and thickly buttered, and then a little glass bowl heaped with raspberry jam. I saw that her tray also contained a plate of buttered toast, and a pot of honey. "And three meals a day."

THE ROOM UPSTAIRS WAS INDEED VERY NICE, SPACIOUS ENOUGH TO SERVE as both bedroom and sitting room, and far more pleasantly decorated than any accommodation I'd ever paid for in London. Not a single Landseer reproduction or indifferent engraving hung upon the wall, yet there was an attractive watercolor landscape and some odd, interesting carvings from a culture I did not recognize. The furnishings were basic, but cushions and brightly patterned swaths of fabric made it more attractive, and I felt at home there at once, soothed and inspired by the surroundings, just as in the large, cluttered room downstairs.

I spent some time unpacking and arranging my few things, and writing letters informing friends of my new address, before I lay down to rest. I hadn't slept much on the train, but now established in my new position—even if it was nearly as problematic, in terms of remuneration, as my last—I felt comfortable enough to fall into a deep and refreshing slumber.

Dinner was a delicious vegetable curry prepared by Mrs. Jesperson herself. They could not afford a cook, although they did have a "daily" for the heavier housework. That evening, as we sat together, I learned a little of their recent history, without being terribly forthcoming about my own.

Jasper Jesperson was twenty-one years old, and an only child. Barely fifteen when his father died, he'd accompanied his mother to India, where she had a brother. But they had been in India for only a year before going to China, and, later, the South Sea islands. An intriguing offer brought them back to London more than a year previously, but it had not turned out as expected (he said he would tell me the whole story another time) and subsequently he decided that the best use of his abilities and interests would be to establish himself as a consulting detective.

He'd concluded three successful commissions so far. Two had been rather easily dealt with and would not make interesting stories; the third was quite different, and I shall write about that another time. It was after that case which had so tested his abilities that he decided to advertise for an assistant.

His fourth case, and my first, was to begin the next morning, with the arrival of a new client.

"Read his letter, and you may know as much about the affair as I," said Jesperson, handing a folded page across his desk to me.

The sheet was headed with the name of a gentlemen's club in Mayfair, and signed William Randall. Although some overhasty pen strokes and blotches might suggest the author was in the grip of strong emotion, it might also be that he was more accustomed to dictating his correspondence.

Dear Mr. Jesperson:

Your name was given to me by a friend in the Foreign Office with the suggestion that if anyone could solve a murder that still baffles the police, it is you.

Someone close to me believes I am at risk of a murderous attack from the same, unknown killer to whose victim she was at the time engaged to be married.

I will explain all when we meet. If I may, I will call on you at ten o'clock Wednesday morning. If that is inconvenient, please reply by return of post with a more suitable time.

Yours sincerely, etc.

I folded the letter and handed it back to Jesperson, who was gazing at me, bright-eyed and expectant.

He prompted. "Any questions?"

"The Foreign Office?"

"Never mind about that. It's only my uncle, trying to keep me in work. Don't you want to know what I've deduced about the writer of this letter? What unsolved crime affects this man so nearly? I believe I have it."

"I think I'd rather wait and hear what Mr. Randall has to say, first. If you're right, well and good, but if you're wrong, you'll only confuse me."

He looked a bit crestfallen, making me think of a little boy who hadn't been allowed to show off his cleverness, and I said, "You can tell me afterward, if you were right."

"But you might not believe me. Oh, well, it doesn't matter."

I heard his mother murmur, "Party tricks." But if he heard, at least he gave no sign, and let me change the subject, and the rest of the evening passed quite pleasantly.

Mr. William Randall arrived promptly as the carriage clock on the (recently dusted) mantelpiece was striking ten. He was a dapper young man with a drooping moustache, his regular features lifted from mere good looks into something striking by a pair of large, dark eyes that anyone more romantic than I would call soulful.

He refused any refreshment, took a seat, and began his story after the brief, hesitant disclaimer that "it was probably a load of nonsense," but his fiancée was worried.

"The lady I intend to make my wife is Miss Flora Bellamy, of Harrow." Her name meant nothing to me, but we both saw Jesperson straighten up.

"Yes, I thought you might make the connection. She was, of course, engaged to Mr. Archibald Adcocks, the prominent financier, at the time of his terrible death."

"So she thinks his death was connected to the fact of their engagement? And that you are now in danger?"

"She does."

"How curious! What are her reasons?"

He sighed and held up his empty hands. "'The heart has its reasons, that reason knows not.' Women, you know, think more with their hearts than their heads. It is all too circumstantial to convince me, a matter of mere coincidence, and yet . . . she is so *certain*."

Listening to them was frustrating, so I was forced to interrupt. "Excuse me, but would you mind telling me the facts of Mr. Adcocks's death?"

Jesperson turned to me with a smile of secret triumph. *I could have told you last night!* said his expression, but he only remarked, "It was in all the papers, a year ago."

"Fifteen months," Randall corrected him. "He was attacked on his way to the railway station, not long after saying good night to Flora at her door. She wanted him to take a cab, because he had recently injured his foot, but he insisted that he could manage the short walk easily with the aid of a stick." He hesitated, then said, "He borrowed a walking stick from the stand beside the door."

"The injury must have been very recent," I suggested, and Randall gave me a nod.

"Not long after dinner, that same evening. He tripped in the hall and struck his foot, but although it was quite painful, he insisted it was too minor to make a fuss about."

"Not a man to make a fuss."

"He was no weakling. And quite well able to look after himself. Something of an amateur pugilist."

"Yet someone attacked him, unprovoked."

"So we must assume. He was found lying sprawled on the path, his head bloody from a terrible blow. He was barely alive, unable to speak, and died from his injury that same night, without being able to indicate what had happened. It may be that he didn't know, that the cowardly assault had come from behind."

"No one was ever arrested," Jesperson told me. "There were no suspects."

I frowned. "Could anyone suggest a motive?"

"It was usually assumed to have been an impulsive crime, not planned, since the murder weapon was his own walking stick."

"Not his own," Mr. Randall objected. "Borrowed from Flora's house."

"Even so. It may be he was attacked by a gang of thugs who thought him an easy target because he limped. Yet, if they were intent on robbery, no one could explain why they did not take his wallet, stuffed with pound notes, or his gold watch, or anything else. He was found not long after he fell, lying in the open, near a streetlamp, and there were no obvious hiding places nearby. Although one witness reported hearing a cry, no one was seen running away or otherwise behaving in a suspicious manner."

"Did Mr. Adcocks have enemies?" I asked.

"He seems to have been well liked by all who knew him, including those who did business with him. No one obviously benefited by his death."

"Who inherited his property?"

"His mother."

Before I could say anything more, Jesperson resumed. "Mr. Randall, you've suggested that Miss Bellamy believed his death was as a result of, or at least connected to, their engagement."

"No one else thought so."

"How did her family feel about it?"

He sighed and shook his head. "She has no family. Since being orphaned at an early age, Miss Bellamy has lived in the house of her guardian, a man by the name of Rupert Harcourt."

Although the even tenor of his voice did not change, when he pronounced this name, I shivered, and knew we had come to the heart of the matter.

"Her parents named this man as her guardian?" Jesperson enquired.

Mr. Randall shook his head. "They did not know him. He had no connection to the family at all. When Mr. Bellamy died, the infant Flora was all alone in the world. A total stranger, reading of her situation in a newspaper, was so struck with pity that he offered her a home."

"You find that strange," I said, remarking his tone.

His eyes, for all their languid soulfulness, could still deliver a piercing look. "It is surely unusual for an unmarried, childless man of thirty-plus to go out of his way to adopt an unwanted infant. In fact, he never *did* adopt

Flora, but set up some sort of legal arrangement to last until she married, or reached the age of twenty-one—a date still eight months in the future."

"She has money?"

"Very little. To give him credit, Harcourt never touched her small inheritance, yet she never lacked for anything; toys and sweetmeats, clothes and meals, books and music lessons were all paid for from his own pocket. The money from her father was left to gain interest. I suppose it may be near one thousand pounds."

It sounded a lot to me, being used to managing on less than thirty pounds a year, but it was not the sort of fortune to inspire a devious double-murder plot.

"Has any attempt been made on your life?" Jesperson asked suddenly, and I saw Mr. Randall wince and raise his hand to his head before he replied, "Oh, no, hardly—no, not at all."

Jesperson responded testily to this prevarication. "Oh, come now! Something happened to frighten your fiancée, whatever you may make of it. Don't try to hide it."

With a sigh, Randall lifted the lock of dark hair that half-hid his forehead and bowed his head to reveal a bruised gash, obviously quite recent, at the hairline.

He explained that a few days earlier he had been to dine with Flora and her guardian. After the meal, the two men had adjourned to Harcourt's study, a large room at the front of the house, with cigars and brandy snifters, and there Randall had asked permission to wed Miss Bellamy.

"It was a formality, really, since she had agreed, but as the man was still her legal guardian, it seemed the right thing to do."

"His response?"

"He said, rather roughly, that young ladies always made their own decisions, but he had no objections. Then he asked if I knew she'd been engaged once before. I said that I did, and he gave an unpleasant laugh and asked me if that hadn't made me think twice. I didn't know what he meant to imply, but it seemed meant to be offensive. Trying not to take offense, I told him that I loved Flora, and that since she had been good enough to accept me, nothing short of death would induce me to part from her. And it was at that dramatic moment that a book fell off a shelf high above my head."

He winced. "It looked worse than it was—scalp wounds bleed profusely—but it was quite painful. I had never imagined a book as a lethal weapon."

"Where was Harcourt when this occurred?"

"He was facing me, standing farther away from the bookshelves. Before you ask, I could see him clearly, and while I suppose he might have contrived it, I was not aware of him doing anything that could have triggered the fall. In any case, he seemed completely shocked, and almost as worried about his book as my head. I should probably say *more*. If he'd meant to harm me, I don't think it would have been at any risk to any part of his collection."

"He's a book collector?"

"Nothing so benign," he replied. "In fact, it was because of the collection that Flora rarely set foot inside that room. She found the morbid atmosphere more unpleasant than the scent of our cigars."

"R. M. Harcourt, of Harrow," Jesperson said.

"You know of him?"

"I had not made the connection until this moment. He has written of his collection—at least, certain recent acquisitions, in a journal to which I subscribe."

Turning to me, Jesperson explained that Mr. Harcourt took a particular interest in murder, and had, over the years, managed to acquire a goodly number of weapons—knives, guns, and a variety of sharp or heavy instruments that had caused the loss of human life: a lady's hat pin, a piece of brick, a Japanese sword, an ordinary-looking iron poker. In addition, he had amassed a library on the subject of the crime, as well as what might be described as mementos of murder, odds and ends that were connected in some way with any famous—or infamous—crime: hair from the heads of murderers or their victims, bloodstained clothing, photographs of crime scenes, incriminating letters. He possessed poison rings, flasks, phials, bottles, and even the very cup in which Mrs. Maybrick had mixed the arsenic powder with which she'd killed her husband.

"He's very proud of it," Randall said. "Occasionally, people call at the house to see the collection, or to offer new items they hope he'll buy. I was polite, but, frankly, I will never understand the appeal of such gruesome objects.

"After the accident, Flora became hysterical, and made me promise I'd never enter that room again. Then she decided that was not enough, and that I must not return to the house. She also suggested that we not announce our engagement, and wait until she's twenty-one to marry."

"She suspects her guardian?" Jesperson asked quietly.

Mr. Randall hesitated, then shook his head. "She *says* she does not. But she feels I am in danger, through my attachment to her, and if she's right about that, who else could it be?"

"Forgive me, but . . . are there no rejected suitors?"

"Flora told me she received but two marriage proposals in her life, and she's never mentioned anyone, I've never heard of any other man, who might harbor such strong feelings for her," he replied. "But, in any case, she is wrong. Adcocks's murder, quite naturally, affected her nerves. She sees danger, an unknown assassin, lurking everywhere; an evil force behind every accident." He paused to take a deep breath.

"Shortly after the injury in the study, I chanced to stumble over an object in the hall—and I might have fallen and struck my head a second time if Flora hadn't been there to catch me. This was the same object that Adcocks had bruised his foot on, and this coincidence was too much. Her nerves are not strong. How can they be? She's suffered so much, has lost everyone she has ever loved—that's when she insisted I leave at once, and not come back. She imagined danger where there was none."

"And yet, whether or not *you* are in danger, someone killed Mr. Adcocks," Jesperson said with heavy emphasis.

"Precisely. And if you can solve that crime, I hope her fears may be put to rest."

AFTER MR. RANDALL HAD DEPARTED, JESPERSON DASHED OFF A LETTER TO Mr. Harcourt.

"I think it best that Harcourt has no reason to connect us with his ward or her fiancé," he told me. "Therefore, I shall present myself to him as a fellow aficionado of murder. And as he shows me his collection, it may be that, if he does know something of Adcocks's death, he'll give himself away."

"Won't he wonder how you've heard of it?"

"Not at all. It is quite well-known in certain circles." He scarcely paused in his writing as he replied, stretching out his other hand and running it down the spines of a stack of journals on the desk beside him, as if he were one of those blind folk who read with their fingertips.

Abstracting one issue, he paused to flip through the pages until he found the one he wanted me to see.

It was a page of letters, with the headline *More Solutions to the Ripper Murders*. The letter indicated by his finger was signed *R. M. Harcourt, The Pines, Harrow*. Another, finishing in the next column, bore the name of J. Jesperson, Gower Street.

"So he may know who you are?"

"As you'll see by the date, this issue is a year old. I was still a mere student of crime and detection then, unknown to the public." Finished, he sealed the envelope and held it out to me. "Take this to the post office—" He stopped, with a look of chagrin. "Forgive me."

"For what? I am your assistant."

"My manner was too peremptory. I should have—"

I cut him off. "If we're going to work together, you must stop thinking of me as a female who'll be mortally offended if you forget to say *please*."

"It's not that."

I waited.

"I advertised for an assistant, not a servant. I hope we can work together as equals."

"Understood," I said, not revealing how pleased I felt. "Also understood is that when time is of the essence, politeness can go hang. And the only reason I am still standing here with this letter in my hand, rather than half-way to the nearest post office, is that I don't know where that is."

MR. HARCOURT REPLIED WITH AN INVITATION BY RETURN OF POST, SO THE next day found us on the train rattling through the northwestern suburbs of London, at one time a familiar journey to me. Although I had not been in Harrow for more than ten years, it was the scene of my youth, my father having been a classics master at Harrow School until his untimely death.

However, we had lived in the village on the hill, whereas Mr. Harcourt's house was almost a mile away, in one of the newer developments that had grown up following the extension of the Metropolitan Line.

Jesperson had said nothing in his letter about a companion, and we had decided my role would be that of Inconvenient Female Relative. Naturally, I would have no interest in the collection—indeed, if I knew what it was, I might well be shocked—so while the men were closeted together, I'd be free to conduct my own investigation. Randall had told Miss Bellamy to expect me.

The Pines was a mock-Tudor affair shielded from the road by the two namesakes that gave it a somewhat secretive and gloomy air. But that was nothing compared to the interior of the house. As I stepped across the threshold, I was gripped by panic. I am sensitive to atmospheres, no matter how much I try to blame it on imagination, and what I felt in that hallway was as bad as any haunted house. But it is difficult to describe to someone who has never experienced such things. If I were describing a smell, I could compare it to a tannery, a slaughterhouse, or a sewer. Only someone with no sense of smell could bear to live there.

Fighting the panic, I looked around for distraction. A large, attractive Chinese vase, green and yellow, had been put into service as a stand for umbrellas and walking sticks. Among the curving wooden handles clustering above the open top, the silver-capped walking stick stood out, commanding attention not simply by its different appearance, but by the grim air of menace it exuded, like a low and deadly hiss.

Of course, I knew at once what it was, and felt appalled. How could they have kept it? Why hadn't it been broken and destroyed, the wood burnt to ash, the silver head melted down to be remade into something new?

Tearing my horrified gaze away, I spotted the hideous stone gargoyle crouching like a demon near the foot of the stairs, and shuddered at its baleful look before my partner's light touch on my arm recalled me to the present as he introduced me to the owner of these things.

Mr. Harcourt was a portly, balding man with a luxuriant and well-tended moustache, and—for me, at any rate—a cold and fishlike stare. There was more warmth, and a twitch of a smile, in the greeting he gave Jesperson, leaving me in no doubt that my presence was unwelcome.

Relief came swiftly in the form of a young lady descending the stair. Slender and dark-haired, with a face that was handsome rather than pretty, she was dressed like a shop assistant or office worker in a crisp, white shirtfront and plain dark skirt. Even smiling warmly in welcome, she had a serious look, her eyes haunted by worry.

"Flora! Exquisite timing, as ever. Although if you had known to expect company you would have worn one of your pretty dresses, I hope," said Harcourt. He performed hasty introductions and rapidly withdrew with Jesperson behind a solid oak door, leaving us alone in the hall with its sinister atmosphere.

"Perhaps you'd like to see the garden," said Miss Bellamy, touching my elbow to guide me along a corridor toward the back of the house. As I passed through the door, leaving the house, the taste of open air was almost intoxicating.

"You are sensitive," she remarked, leading away from the cold back wall of the house, through an arbor, along a path, into a sheltered rose garden.

"I claim no special powers," I said, "but the atmosphere in that house is . . . extraordinary. I have to wonder how you can live there."

She nodded slightly. "And yet, you know, most people feel nothing. Mr. Adcocks never did. Mr. Randall's mood alters when he visits, and I am aware of his unease, yet he will not admit it."

Although I had not said so to Jesperson, I had toyed with the idea that Miss Bellamy herself might be the killer we sought. The manner of Mr. Adcocks's death seemed to indicate an attack by a strong and brutal man, an action impossible by most women; nevertheless, I had found that men tended to underestimate the female sex quite as much as they idealized it, and I could imagine a grieving fiancée who was in truth a coldhearted murderer.

But that idea vanished to nothing as soon as I set eyes on her, a slip of a girl, and as we sat down, side by side, on a curving bench in a sunny green spot, the scent of roses and the warm hum of bees filling the air around us, I was utterly certain that this gentle, soft-spoken woman, so concerned about the feelings of others, was incapable of killing another human being, by any means.

"How can you bear to live in that house?" I asked her.

"Don't forget, I've lived there nearly all my life," she said. "People can get used to almost anything. Imagine someone who must work in a slaughterhouse every day."

"I imagine such a person would be brutalized and degraded by his work," I replied. "If the comparison were to someone who must *live* in a slaughterhouse . . . well, I can't imagine many who would stick it for long. I'm surprised you never ran away. What was it like when you first came here? Were you terrified?"

She looked thoughtful. "I can't remember anything before I came here. I was not yet two years old. And back then, Mr. Harcourt's collection was only small. It grew along with me. Over the years, as he added items, he told me the story of each one. So I became accustomed to tales of violent death and human wickedness from an early age. I was not at all attracted to those things, but I accepted their existence. Imagine a child growing up in a madhouse or a prison. Even the strangest situations become normal if one knows nothing else."

"But now, at last, you can escape," I said. "Have you set a date for your wedding?"

She stared at me. "Surely William told you? I think it's best we don't even speak of an engagement until after I'm of age, and can leave here."

"You believe your guardian doesn't wish you to marry?"

She gave a short, humorless laugh. "Oh, I believe he would like to see me married! A wife and a widow in the same day would please him very much!"

There was no point in beating about the bush. "Do you think he killed Mr. Adcocks?"

She did not flinch. "No. Despite his fascination with the subject, Mr. Harcourt is no murderer."

"Do you suspect someone else?"

She did not reply. I thought I saw something cornered and furtive in her look. "Miss Bellamy," I said gently, "however painful this is, we can't help unless you tell me what it is you suspect, or fear, no matter how slight or strange. Were you there, did you see anything, when Mr. Adcocks was attacked?"

She shook her head. "I bid him good night and went up to my room. I thought he was safe . . ."

"And your guardian?"

"He was shut into his room, as usual."

I looked toward the house, but the ground floor was shielded from my view by shrubs and foliage. "Is there another exit? From his room?"

"No. And I would not have missed the sounds if he'd left the house."

"Who murdered Mr. Adcocks?" I asked suddenly.

"No one."

"And yet he is dead."

"He was killed by a powerful blow to his head. The blow came from a walking stick. Can it be called murder, is it even a crime, without human intervention?"

I had seen objects levitate, hover, move about, even shoot through the air as if hurled with great force although no one was near. Usually, there was trickery involved; but not always. I had seen what I believed to be the effect of mind over matter, and also witnessed what was called *poltergeist*—the German for "noisy spirit"—activity. Yet I was deeply suspicious of everything attributed to the action of "spirits." I had yet to encounter anything that was not better explained by the power of the human mind.

"What are you saying?" I asked her gently. "You believe that the stick, an inanimate object, moved, and killed a man, of its own volition?" Yet even as I asked, the memory of the malignant power I had sensed in that very stick, only a few minutes earlier, made me much less certain that I was right.

"Have you ever heard of a deodand?"

"I'm not familiar with the word."

"It's a term from old English law: *deo*, to God, *dandum*, that which must be given. It referred to any possession which was the immediate cause of a person's accidental death. The object was then forfeit to the Crown, to be put to some pious use."

I couldn't think of anything to say to that, and she smiled. "That walking stick was a deodand. Not officially; it's hardly that old. But it was the proximate cause of death to a young man almost seventy years ago—so my guardian told me.

"And the unpleasant stone gargoyle beside the stair? It fell off the tower where it had been placed many centuries before, and killed a mother and child.

"My guardian collects such things, along with his morbid keepsakes from actual murders.

"He gave Archie that stick, knowing what it was, and suspecting what it would do." She stopped and passed a hand across her brow. "What am I saying? Of course he didn't suspect. Why should he? None of them had ever hurt him, or me. Not even when I was a child who played with whatever took my fancy—he wouldn't let me touch anything dangerous, of course, nothing sharp or breakable. I whispered secrets in the gargoyle's ear, even used to kiss it, and it was that gargoyle—" She stopped, her hand to her mouth.

I waited for her to go on.

"It was in the wrong place, too near the stair. I thought perhaps, when the maid washed the floor, she'd pushed it out, but she insisted she never did. Yet it was not where it usually was, and that's why Archie stumbled against it, and wrenched his ankle.

"It happened again, just a few days ago, to Will. He fell over it, and if I hadn't caught him, he might have struck his head, might have been killed, just like Archie!"

"Someone moved it," I said, trying to inject a note of reason. "If not the maid, then your guardian, or a mysterious stranger. And if Mr. Randall's stumble had resulted in a serious injury, even death, that would have been an accident; no one could possibly call it murder, even if someone moved the gargoyle.

"But that stick . . . I really can't imagine that a stick, in Mr. Adcocks's possession, could have caused his death without the intervention of another person. If you think your guardian was controlling it, willing it to strike—"

"No! Why would he do that? Even if he had the ability, why would he want to kill my fiancé when he was looking forward to seeing how *I* would cause his death?"

She had gone white except for two hectic splashes of red in her cheeks. I shook my head. "I don't understand."

"Of course not. Because you don't understand that I, too, am a deodand. I am the gem of his collection. My early history explains why he took me in. I killed my entire family before I was two years of age."

I gripped her hands. "Miss Bellamy—"

"I am utterly sane," she said calmly. "I am not hysterical. These are the facts. Being born, I brought about the death of my mother."

"That's hardly—"

"Unique? I know. Listen. Nine months later, my father was taking his motherless children on holiday when we were involved in a railway accident. In the crash, my brother, a child of two, was thrown to the floor, as was I. I landed directly on top of him, a fact which may have saved *me* from injury, but caused his death. I have never known whether he died of suffocation, or if my weight broke his neck."

"No one could call that your fault," I said, trying not to dwell on the image.

"I know that," she said, pulling her hands away. "Believe me, I am not such a fool as to think it was anything other than extremely bad luck. I have had many years to come to terms with my past. I do not require your pity. I tell you this so you may understand Mr. Harcourt's interest in me.

"My father was injured in the accident. Some months later he was still in an invalid chair, needing a nurse to help him in and out and wheel him about. We'd gone out for a walk—when I say 'we' I mean my father in his chair pushed by his nurse, a young man, and I in my pram, pushed by mine, a pretty young woman. We stopped at a local beauty spot to admire the view. My nurse put me down on a blanket on the grass, near to my father, who was dozing in the sun, and then I suppose they must have stopped paying much attention to anything but each other as they fell to flirting. I hadn't yet learned to walk, but I was getting better at standing up, and as I hauled myself to my feet, using my father's chair as support, somehow I must have let off the brake—maybe the nurse hadn't properly set it—and as he rolled away, I just watched him go, picking up speed, until I saw the chair carrying my last living relative go over the edge of the cliff, and carry him to his death on the rocks below."

I made no more efforts to comfort. "So Mr. Harcourt considers you some sort of loaded weapon in his possession? Ready to go off when you are loved?"

"He has never said as much, but that's what I've understood by a gleam in his eye, and a quickening of interest, once I became of marriageable age. It was he who contrived to introduce me to a number of wealthy young men, until Archibald Adcocks took the bait. And he pressed me to accept, although I was inclined to wait."

"Regardless of what Mr. Harcourt believes—"

"I know. And you're right, I don't believe it of myself. Mr. Harcourt imagines, because he kept himself so coldly distant, repelling my natural affection, and sent me to day school rather than risk my becoming too close to a kind governess, that I never was loved, and never loved anyone, since my father died.

"But there was a girl at school . . . My guardian may have no idea how passionately girls can love each other, but I'm sure *you* will," she said, with a look that should have made me blush. Instead, it made me smile.

We looked at each other like conspirators. "I take it your friend remains alive and well?"

"Indeed, and still my dearest friend, although we're now more temperate in our emotions . . . or, at least, the expression of them. So, you see, I *know* my affection is not dangerous."

"And yet you seem to think that by becoming engaged to marry you, Mr. Adcocks signed his own death warrant. And that Mr. Randall is under threat for the same reason."

"Yes . . ." She looked thoughtful. "But not because of my feelings for him, or his for me. It's something else. Marriage to anyone would take me away from this house, would remove me from my guardian's collection. That's it," she said, and stood up.

"What is it?"

"He thinks marriage is the only way he might lose me. He's never imagined I might simply decide to leave."

I stood up, too, to face her. "I don't understand."

"Mr. Harcourt is scarcely sane when it comes to his collection. He cannot bear the thought of losing a single piece of it. He is happiest when gloating over it alone, and whenever he has a chance to add something new. Although he admits potential buyers, he only wants their envy and admiration as they view his objects—he will never agree to sell an item, no matter how much money he is offered.

"And while he has been talking about my marriage since I was sixteen, and began pushing me at eligible bachelors on my eighteenth birthday, driven by thoughts of what he thinks will happen when I am once more part of a family, greedily imagining how his collection will grow after the violent, accidental death of my husband, he knows this will be possible only if he lets me go. In his twisted mind, *I* am part of his collection, and the thought of losing me, even only temporarily, and in aid of gaining more, is terrible to him."

"His mind is divided?"

"I am sorry, Miss Lane. You should not have been brought into this. There was no need for William to enlist the aid of a detective. I should have realized that I am the only one who can end this madness."

She started back to the house and I followed. Although I had no idea what she intended, I felt that we were approaching crisis.

She raised her fist to rap on the heavy oak, but at the very first blow, the door swung open.

Harcourt was at the far end of the room, by the window, displaying something in a flat wooden box to Jesperson. They both looked around sharply as we entered, Harcourt startled and annoyed. Clearly, he had not expected us, and I could only assume that he had neglected to shut the door properly.

"What's the meaning of this disturbance?" he demanded, hastily shutting up the box.

"I must speak with you."

"Let it wait. We have company."

"I am happy to have witnesses." She took a breath. "I shall not marry."

I had tensed myself against the negative atmosphere upon entering the house, and had been particularly reluctant to enter Harcourt's study, expecting it to be the epicenter, yet as I followed more slowly into that room, I found that what had been unpleasant and discordant was now harmonious. Using the metaphor of smell, consider bonfire smoke. A great waft in the face is horrible, but at the right distance, the scent of burning leaves and wood is pleasant.

"You've rushed in here to say that? I am at a loss to understand why," Harcourt replied coldly. "Your change of heart is of no interest to *me*. I suggest you write to Mr. Randall."

"You don't understand. I mean I shall never marry."

His eyes bulged. "Are you insane?" Suddenly, he turned on me. "What have you been saying? What sort of mad rubbish, to turn her mind?"

"Miss Lane had nothing to do with it," Flora said swiftly. "I have been thinking matters over for the past several days, and only now decided to tell you—"

"Oh, very likely!" He had been casting a venomous glare on me, but now stared coldly at Jesperson. "I'm afraid I must ask you to take this female person away, immediately."

I could see that my partner was at a loss: Should he leap to my defense, invent excuses, or pretend to a masculine solidarity that might leave the door open for future visits? Although I didn't want to leave Flora alone with Harcourt, I didn't know what we would achieve by trying to stay, so I left the room, just as Flora was demanding, "Am I not allowed to have my own friends?"

"As long as I'm your guardian, Flora, you will do as I say. You'll have nothing more to do with that female, and you will not break off your engagement. We'll forget you ever said anything about it. Mr. Jesperson, if you please!"

As they emerged, with Flora in the lead, I was surprised to see the hint of a smile on her face. She winked at me before turning on her guardian again.

"So, I am to be your *object* and meekly allow *your* will to prevail in everything, until my twenty-first birthday changes everything?"

"That will change nothing," he said scornfully. "You don't imagine you'll be anything different than you are now? Than you've always been?"

She flinched, but held steady. "In the eyes of the law."

"The law." He snorted. "The law is an ass. It has nothing to say about *you*. It has no idea what you are." His gaze on her was horrible.

"I may as well go now," she said quietly.

"Go? What are you talking about?"

"You are right that a few months will change nothing. *You* are pleased with the situation; I am not. So I shall leave."

She looked from me to Jesperson, saying, "If it's not too much trouble . . ."

He was swift to take her meaning. "Of course, come with us. Any help we can give—"

I heard the rattle, and saw that the Chinese vase was rocking violently back and forth, until it tilted too far and fell, shattering against the hard floor, and spilling its burden of umbrellas and walking sticks.

Only one of the sticks did not come to rest with everything else on the floor, but shot through the air, straight at Jesperson.

If it had struck where it aimed, against his throat, I have no doubt it would have killed him, but he was quick. Almost as if he'd expected the attack, he stepped lightly aside, his arm rising, fluid and graceful, to catch the stick.

Unlike an ordinary thrown object, the stick continued to move after it was caught, writhing and pulling to escape, while he gripped it more firmly, frowning as he looked for a thread or wire and tried to work out the trick of it.

Certain there would be no invisible thread, I looked instead at Harcourt. His expression was nothing like those I'd seen on the faces of mediums or mentalists; he looked utterly astonished, and thrilled. If he had caused the stick's activity, it was through a power hidden from his conscious mind, something he did not suspect and could not control.

Then another movement, glimpsed from the corner of my eye, caught my attention, and as I turned to look, I heard the terrible grating, grinding noise made by the stone gargoyle as it ponderously rocked itself across the floor. Although no one was near enough to be at risk if it fell over, I nevertheless called out a warning.

Flora took one look and shouted: "Stop it! Stop it right now!"

The gargoyle stopped moving, and so did the stick, although Jesperson still kept a tight hold and a wary eye on it.

Harcourt took a hesitant step forward, his eyes still fixed upon the stick.

"Give—give it to me, if you please, Mr. Jesperson," he said. "That—that is the weapon that killed poor Mr. Adcocks; and before that, a young man in Plymouth. If not for your exceptionally quick reflexes, you would have been its third victim."

After a reluctant pause, Jesperson handed over the stick, saying, "You expected this might happen?"

"Never," the man gasped, staring at the stick in his hands with an unhealthy mixture of lust and fear. "Who would imagine that the instinct to kill would be inherent?"

"You imagined it inherent in *me*," said Flora. "A mindless, killing force so powerful that it could use me—a living, intelligent being—without regard for my own free will?"

"No, no, certainly not," he said, without conviction. "You were a mere infant, with no ability to think or act for yourself, when fate used you to terminate the lives of three innocent souls. It is quite different now." He had been looking at her, but the lure of the object in his hands proved too much, and he soon returned to staring at it like a besotted lover.

"You've always thought of me as another piece in your collection," Flora said bitterly. "A mindless, soulless thing, and not even your favorite."

"Dear Flora, don't be absurd. I know you are no 'thing.' You have been like a daughter to me. Have I not always cared for you as best I could? Bought you whatever your heart desired? My only concern has ever been to see you safely and happily married to the man of your choice, when the time came."

While my sympathies were entirely with Flora, I recognized that to an outside observer, she would seem hysterical, and Harcourt the sane one.

"Yet you must have wondered," Jesperson said, as if idly. "Eh, Harcourt? You surely wondered if your ward was intended by Fate for family happiness. Perhaps you saw her first engagement as a scientific experiment. The result was not as you *hoped*, but perhaps as you feared . . . ?"

They exchanged a look, man to man, and although Harcourt shook his head ruefully, I saw the smug satisfaction beneath the solemn look.

"You're vile," Flora murmured. She cleared her throat and announced, "I can never marry. I won't put another life at risk."

This time, Harcourt did not protest. He shrugged and sighed, and said, "I would never force you to go against your will, no matter how foolish it seems to me."

"That's not all. I'm leaving your collection today, Mr. Harcourt—"

"Oh, come now. Don't be childish. You can't blame me for what you are!"

"Not for what I am; only for what you've tried to make me. The atmosphere in this house is hideous, not because of the objects, but because of your gloating fascination with murder and violent death. I'm going. I won't set foot in this house again as long as you are alive."

Having stated her intention, she made straight for the door.

I felt the shudder that ran through the house even before her hand touched the door handle; it was a sensation so subtle yet so profound that I thought at first I might be ill.

Harcourt yelled. His nose was bleeding; the walking stick had come to life again in his hand and seemed determined to beat him to death. He managed to remove it to arm's length, and struggled to keep it under control. The gargoyle, too, was shuddering back to life, and, from the variety of creaks and groans and fluttering sounds I heard coming from the next room, so were other bits of the collection.

"Move," said Jesperson urgently, propelling me forward. "Get out of the house! Is there anyone else?" Hearing the shouts, the little maid who'd let us in reappeared, and, although looking utterly bewildered, she allowed him to usher her outside as well.

We met Flora at the front gate and turned back to look at the house.

"Where's Harcourt?" Jesperson demanded. "He was right behind me."

"He won't leave his collection," said Flora. "He'll have gone back for it. He used to worry aloud about what he should save first, if the house were on fire."

"But it's the collection itself that's the threat!"

On my own, I might have left Harcourt to his fate, but when my partner ran back inside, I felt it my duty to follow. Mounting the front steps, I was able to see through the window into the study, and what I saw brought me to a standstill.

Pale and portly Mr. Harcourt was leaping and whirling like a dervish, holding the silver-headed stick away from his body like a magic staff, as he struggled to avoid a flurry of small objects from striking him. Occasionally in his efforts he unconsciously pulled his arm in closer to his body, allowing the stick to give him a sharp crack on his leg or shoulder, and then he would shriek in pain or anger.

Books and other things continued to tumble from the shelves. Many simply fell, but others seemed hurled with force directly at him, and these struck a variety of glancing blows against his body, head, and limbs. A glass-fronted display case shook fiercely, as if caught in an earthquake, until it burst open, releasing everything inside. A great malignant swarm composed of small bottles, jars, needles, pins, razors, and many more things I could not recognize now enveloped the man, whose cries turned to a constant, terrified howling as they attacked him.

Feeling sick, I turned aside and went indoors to my partner, who was throwing himself bodily against the solid oak door, as if he imagined he could force it open. Seeing me, he stopped and rubbed his shoulder, looking a little sheepish.

I gave him one of my hairpins, assuming he would know how to use it.

As he fiddled with the lock, I listened to the horrible sounds that accompanied the violence on the other side: thuds and thumps, shrieks and wails and groans, and then a shocking, liquid hissing, followed by a gurgle, and then the heaviest thud of all, and then silence.

By the time Jesperson managed to get the door open, it was all over. Harcourt was dead. His bloody, battered corpse lay on the carpet, surrounded by the remnants of his murderous collection. Whatever life had possessed them had expired with his. There was a sharp, acrid stench in the room—I guess from the contents of various broken bottles—but nothing so foul as the atmosphere it replaced.

"Vitriol," said Jesperson. "Don't look."

But I had already seen what was left of the face, and it was no more shocking than the sounds had led me to imagine.

As I went out to give Flora Bellamy the news, and to send the maid to fetch the police, I already knew that this had not turned out to be a case I could write about for publication.

And, as it developed, it got worse.

It was fortunate indeed that Jasper Jesperson had some influential relatives who moved in the circles of power, for otherwise I think the local police would have been pleased to charge him with murder, in the absence of more likely suspects, and if he hadn't done it, I was their next choice.

Even though we might argue we had saved his life, our client was so far from pleased with the outcome of our investigations that he refused to pay us anything. It was not Harcourt's death that bothered him so much as Miss Bellamy's insistence on releasing him from their engagement. She would give him no better reason for her change of heart than to say that she was reconsidering how she might best spend her life, and that she was inclined to seek some form of employment by which to support herself "like Miss Lane."

Flora Bellamy never set foot inside The Pines again. Even though her guardian was dead, she had decided to take no chances, and hired others to empty the house before selling it. In his will, Harcourt left everything to his ward, with only one caveat: Although she could decide whether to keep or dispose of "the collection," she must do so as a whole, and not break it up.

This stipulation she decided to ignore.

"Perhaps I'm wrong," she said to me, the last time I saw her, "but I believe it could be dangerous. Individual objects are only things, but when gathered together, they became something more—first in Mr. Harcourt's imagination, and then in reality.

"The concept in law of the deodand was that something which had once done evil could be remade into something useful, even holy, by good works. That was not allowed to anything in Mr. Harcourt's collection—his use of those things was opposed to good; it venerated the evil deed."

Her way of redemption was to donate everything that remained in the house to a good cause. Being extra cautious, she chose one so far away that she would not have to fear an accidental encounter with her former possessions, and had everything sent to a leper colony on the other side of the world.

I took it as a positive sign that she did not feel obliged to sacrifice herself in a similar way.

She decided to share a flat with her school friend, and embarked on a course of training in bookkeeping and office management.

Jesperson and I, naturally, discussed the details of this case—which began with one unsolved murder, and concluded with two—at great length when we were alone together, and also with Mrs. Jesperson, but we were never able to agree upon how to assign the blame for the killings. We all agreed that both Adcocks and Harcourt were murdered, yet we also agreed that if there was no murderer, murder could not have been done.

I hope our next case will be less of a curiosity.

LORD JOHN AND THE PLAGUE OF ZOMBIES

by Diana Gabaldon

New York Times bestselling author Diana Gabaldon is a winner of the Quill Award and of the Corine International Prize for Fiction. She's the author of the hugely popular Outlander series, international bestsellers that include *Outlander* (published as *Cross Stitch* in the UK), *Dragonfly in Amber*, *Voyager*, *Drums of Autumn*, *The Fiery Cross*, *A Breath of Snow and Ashes*, and *An Echo in the Bone*, plus a graphic novel, *The Exile*, based on *Outlander*. The Lord John Grey novels are a subset of the Outlander series, being part of the whole but focused on the character of Lord John and structured (more or less) as historical mystery. The Lord John series includes the novels *Lord John and the Private Matter*, *Lord John and the Brotherhood of the Blade*, and *Lord John and the Scottish Prisoner* (to be published Fall 2011), and a collection of Lord John novellas, *Lord John and the Hand of Devils* (including "Lord John and the Hellfire Club," "Lord John and the Succubus," and "Lord John and the Haunted Soldier"). She has also written *The Outlandish Companion*, a nonfiction volume, providing background, trivia, and resources, as well as articles on the writing and research of the series.

Here Lord John brings an armed force to the beautiful but faintly sinister island paradise of Jamaica, where he is ordered to suppress an incipient slave rebellion. The uprising is the least of his problems, what with murder, cannibalism, spiders, snakes, and other deadly creatures. Including, of course, zombies.

There was a snake on the drawing room table. A small snake, but still. Lord John Grey wondered whether to say anything about it.

The governor picked up a cut-crystal decanter that stood not six inches from the coiled reptile, appearing quite oblivious. Perhaps it was a pet, or perhaps the residents of Jamaica were accustomed to keep a tame snake in residence, to kill rats. Judging from the number of rats he'd seen since leaving the ship, this seemed sensible—though this particular snake didn't appear large enough to take on even your average mouse.

The wine was decent, but served at body heat, and it seemed to pass directly through Grey's gullet and into his blood. He'd had nothing to eat since before dawn, and felt the muscles of his lower back begin to tingle and relax. He put the glass down; he wanted a clear head.

"I cannot tell you, sir, how happy I am to receive you," said the governor, putting down his own glass, empty. "The position is acute."

"So you said in your letter to Lord North. The situation has not changed appreciably since then?" It had been nearly three months since that letter was written; a lot could change in three months.

He thought Governor Warren shuddered, despite the temperature in the room.

"It has become worse," the governor said, picking up the decanter. "Much worse."

Grey felt his shoulders tense, but spoke calmly.

"In what way? Have there been more—" He hesitated, searching for the right word. "More demonstrations?" It was a mild word to describe the burning of cane fields, the looting of plantations, and the wholesale liberation of slaves.

Warren gave a hollow laugh. His handsome face was beading with sweat. There was a crumpled handkerchief on the arm of his chair, and he picked it up to mop at his skin. He hadn't shaved this morning—or, quite possibly, yesterday; Grey could hear the faint rasp of his dark whiskers on the cloth.

"Yes. More destruction. They burnt a sugar press last month, though still in the remoter parts of the island. Now, though . . ." He paused, licking dry lips as he poured more wine. He made a cursory motion toward Grey's glass, but Grey shook his head.

"They've begun to move toward King's Town," Warren said. "It's deliberate, you can see it. One plantation after another, in a line coming straight down the mountain." He sighed. "I shouldn't say straight. Nothing in this bloody place is straight, starting with the landscape."

That was true enough; Grey had admired the vivid green peaks that soared up from the center of the island, a rough backdrop for the amazingly blue water and the white sand shore.

"People are terrified," Warren went on, seeming to get a grip on himself, though his face was once again slimy with sweat, and his hand shook on the decanter. It occurred to Grey, with a slight shock, that the governor himself was terrified. "I have merchants—and their wives—in my office every day, begging, demanding protection from the blacks."

"Well, you may assure them that protection will be provided them," Grey said, sounding as reassuring as possible. He had half a battalion with him—three hundred infantry troops, and a company of artillery, equipped with small cannon. Enough to defend King's Town, if necessary. But his brief from Lord North was not merely to defend and reassure the merchants and shipping of King's Town and Spanish Town—nor even to provide protection to the larger sugar plantations. He was charged with putting down the slave rebellion entirely. Rounding up the ringleaders and putting a stop to the violence altogether.

The snake on the table moved suddenly, uncoiling itself in a languid manner. It startled Grey, who had begun to think it was a decorative sculpture. It was exquisite: only seven or eight inches long, and a beautiful pale yellow marked with brown, a faint iridescence in its scales like the glow of good Rhenish wine.

"It's gone further now, though," Warren was going on. "It's not just burning and property destruction. Now it's come to murder."

That brought Grey back with a jerk.

"Who has been murdered?" he demanded.

"A planter named Abernathy. Murdered in his own house, last week. His throat cut."

"Was the house burnt?"

"No, it wasn't. The maroons ransacked it, but were driven off by Abernathy's own slaves before they could set fire to the place. His wife survived by submerging herself in a spring behind the house, concealed by a patch of reeds."

"I see." He could imagine the scene all too well. "Where is the plantation?"

"About ten miles out of King's Town. Rose Hall, it's called. Why?" A bloodshot eye swiveled in Grey's direction, and he realized that the glass of wine the governor had invited him to share had not been his first of the day. Nor, likely, his fifth.

Was the man a natural sot? he wondered. Or was it only the pressure of the current situation that had caused him to take to the bottle in such a blatant manner? He surveyed the governor covertly; the man was perhaps in his late thirties, and while plainly drunk at the moment, showed none of the signs of habitual indulgence. He was well built and attractive; no bloat, no soft belly straining at his silk waistcoat, no broken veins in cheeks or nose . . .

"Have you a map of the district?" Surely it hadn't escaped Warren that if indeed the maroons were burning their way straight toward King's Town, it should be possible to predict where their next target lay and await them with several companies of armed infantry?

Warren drained the glass and sat panting gently for a moment, eyes fixed on the tablecloth, then seemed to pull himself together.

"Map," he repeated. "Yes, of course. Dawes . . . my secretary . . . he'll—he'll find you one."

Motion caught Grey's eye. Rather to his surprise, the tiny snake, after casting to and fro, tongue tasting the air, had started across the table in what seemed a purposeful, if undulant, manner, headed straight for him. By reflex, he put up a hand to catch the little thing, lest it plunge to the floor.

The governor saw it, uttered a loud shriek, and flung himself back from the table. Grey looked at him in astonishment, the tiny snake curling over his fingers.

"It's not venomous," he said, as mildly as he could. At least he didn't *think* so. His friend Oliver Gwynne was a natural philosopher and mad for snakes; Gwynne had shown him all the prizes of his collection during the course of one hair-raising afternoon, and he seemed to recall Gwynne telling him that there were no venomous reptiles at all on the island of Jamaica. Besides, the nasty ones all had triangular heads, while the harmless kinds were blunt, like this little fellow.

Warren was indisposed to listen to a lecture on the physiognomy of snakes. Shaking with terror, he backed against the wall.

"Where?" he gasped. "Where did it come from?"

"It's been sitting on the table since I came in. I . . . um . . . thought it was . . ." Well, plainly it wasn't a pet, let alone an intended part of the table décor. He coughed, and got up, meaning to put the snake outside through the French doors that led onto the terrace.

Warren mistook his intent, though, and seeing him come closer, snake writhing through his fingers, burst through the French doors himself, crossed the terrace in a mad leap, and pelted down the flagstoned walk, coattails flying as though the devil himself were in pursuit.

Grey was still staring after him in disbelief when a discreet cough from the inner door made him turn.

"Gideon Dawes, sir." The governor's secretary was a short, tubby man with a round, pink face that probably was rather jolly by nature. At the moment, it bore a look of profound wariness. "You are Lieutenant Colonel Grey?"

Grey thought it unlikely that there was a plethora of men wearing the uniform and insignia of a lieutenant colonel on the premises of King's House at that very moment, but nonetheless bowed, murmuring, "Your servant, Mr. Dawes. I'm afraid Mr. Warren has been taken . . . er . . ." He nodded toward the open French doors. "Perhaps someone should go after him?"

Mr. Dawes closed his eyes with a look of pain, then sighed and opened them again, shaking his head.

"He'll be all right," he said, though his tone lacked any real conviction. "I've just been discussing commissary and billeting requirements with your Major Fettes; he wishes you to know that all the arrangements are quite in hand."

"Oh. Thank you, Mr. Dawes." In spite of the unnerving nature of the governor's departure, he felt a sense of pleasure. He'd been a major himself for years; it was astonishing how pleasant it was to know that someone else was now burdened with the physical management of troops. All *he* had to do was give orders.

That being so, he gave one, though it was phrased as a courteous request, and Mr. Dawes promptly led him through the corridors of the rambling house to a small clerk's hole near the governor's office, where maps were made available to him.

He could see at once that Warren had been right regarding both the devious nature of the terrain and the trail of attacks. One of the maps was marked with the names of plantations, and small notes indicated where maroon raids had taken place. It was far from being a straight line, but nonetheless, a distinct sense of direction was obvious.

The room was warm, and he could feel sweat trickling down his back. Still, a cold finger touched the base of his neck lightly when he saw the name *Twelvetrees* on the map.

"Who owns this plantation?" he asked, keeping his voice level as he pointed at the paper.

"What?" Dawes had fallen into a sort of dreamy trance, looking out the window into the green of the jungle, but blinked and pushed his spectacles up, bending to peer at the map. "Oh, Twelvetrees. It's owned by Philip Twelvetrees—a young man, inherited the place from a cousin only recently. Killed in a duel, they say—the cousin, I mean," he amplified helpfully.

"Ah. Too bad." Grey's chest tightened unpleasantly. He could have done without *that* complication. If— "The cousin—was he named Edward Twelvetrees, by chance?"

Dawes looked mildly surprised.

"I do believe that was the name. I didn't know him, though—no one here did. He was an absentee owner; ran the place through an overseer."

"I see." He wanted to ask whether Philip Twelvetrees had come from London to take possession of his inheritance, but didn't. He didn't want to draw any attention by seeming to single out the Twelvetrees family. Time enough for that.

He asked a few more questions regarding the timing of the raids, which Mr. Dawes answered promptly, but when it came to an explanation of the inciting causes of the rebellion, the secretary proved suddenly unhelpful—which Grey thought interesting.

"Really, sir, I know almost nothing of such matters," Mr. Dawes protested, when pressed on the subject. "You would be best advised to speak with Captain Cresswell. He's the superintendent in charge of the maroons."

Grey was surprised at this.

"Escaped slaves? They have a superintendent?"

"Oh. No, sir." Dawes seemed relieved to have a more straightforward question with which to deal. "The maroons are not escaped slaves. Or rather," he corrected himself, "they are *technically* escaped slaves, but it is a pointless distinction. These maroons are the descendants of slaves who escaped during the last century and took to the mountain uplands. They have settlements up there. But as there is no way of identifying any current owner . . ." And as the government lacked any means of finding them and dragging them back, the Crown had wisely settled for installing a white superintendent, as was usual for dealing with native populations. The superintendent's business was to be in contact with the maroons, and deal with any matter that might arise pertaining to them.

Which raised the question, Grey thought: Why had this Captain Cresswell not been brought to meet him at once? He had sent word of his arrival as soon as the ship docked at daylight, not wishing to take Derwent Warren unawares.

"Where is Captain Cresswell presently?" he asked, still polite. Mr. Dawes looked unhappy.

"I, um, am afraid I don't know, sir," he said, casting down his gaze behind his spectacles. There was a momentary silence, in which Grey could hear the calling of some bird from the jungle nearby.

"Where is he, *normally*?" Grey asked, with slightly less politesse.

Dawes blinked.

"I don't know, sir. I believe he has a house near the base of Guthrie's Defile—there is a small village there. But he would of course go up into the maroon settlements from time to time, to meet with the . . ." He waved a small, fat hand, unable to find a suitable word. "The headmen. He did buy a new hat in Spanish Town earlier this month," Dawes added, in the tones of someone offering a helpful observation.

"A *hat*?"

"Yes. Oh—but of course you would not know. It is customary among the maroons, when some agreement of importance is made, that the persons making the agreement shall exchange hats. So you see . . ."

"Yes, I do," Grey said, trying not to let annoyance show in his voice. "Will you be so kind, Mr. Dawes, as to send to Guthrie's Defile, then—and to any other place in which you think Captain Cresswell might be discovered? Plainly I must speak with him, and as soon as possible."

Dawes nodded vigorously, but before he could speak, the rich sound of a small gong came from somewhere in the house below. As though it had been a signal, Grey's stomach emitted a loud gurgle.

"Dinner in half an hour," Mr. Dawes said, looking happier than Grey had yet seen him. He almost scurried out the door, Grey in his wake.

"Mr. Dawes," he said, catching up at the head of the stair. "Governor Warren. Do you think—"

"Oh, he will be present at dinner," Dawes assured him. "I'm sure he is quite recovered now; these small fits of excitement never last very long."

"What causes them?" A savory smell, rich with currants, onion, and spice, wafted up the stair, making Grey hasten his step.

"Oh . . ." Dawes, hastening along with him, glanced sideways at him. "It is nothing. Only that His Excellency has a, um, somewhat morbid fancy concerning reptiles. Did he see a snake in the drawing room, or hear something concerning one?"

"He did, yes—though a remarkably small and harmless one." Vaguely, Grey wondered what had happened to the little yellow snake. He thought he must have dropped it in the excitement of the governor's abrupt exit, and hoped it hadn't been injured.

Mr. Dawes looked troubled, and murmured something that sounded like, "Oh, dear, oh, dear . . ." but he merely shook his head and sighed.

GREY MADE HIS WAY TO HIS ROOM, MEANING TO FRESHEN HIMSELF BEFORE dinner; the day was warm, and he smelled strongly of ship's reek—this composed in equal parts of sweat, seasickness, and sewage, well marinated in salt water—and horse, having ridden up from the harbor to Spanish Town. With any luck, his valet would have clean linen aired for him by now.

King's House, as all Royal Governors' residences were known, was a shambling old wreck of a mansion, perched on a high spot of ground on the edge of Spanish Town. Plans were afoot for an immense new Palladian building, to be erected in the town's center, but it would be another year at least before construction could commence. In the meantime, efforts had been made to uphold His Majesty's dignity by means of beeswax polish, silver, and immaculate linen, but the dingy printed wallpaper peeled from the corners of the rooms, and the dark-stained wood beneath exhaled a moldy breath that made Grey want to hold his own whenever he walked inside.

One good feature of the house, though, was that it was surrounded on all four sides by a broad terrace, and overhung by large, spreading trees that cast lacy shadows on the flagstones. A number of the rooms opened directly onto this terrace—Grey's did—and it was therefore possible to step outside and draw a clean breath, scented by the distant sea or the equally distant upland jungles. There was no sign of his valet, but there *was* a clean shirt on the bed. He shucked his coat, changed his shirt, and then threw the French doors open wide.

He stood for a moment in the center of the room, midafternoon sun spilling through the open doors, enjoying the sense of a solid surface under his feet after seven weeks at sea and seven hours on horseback. Enjoying even more the transitory sense of being alone. Command had its prices, and one of those was a nearly complete loss of solitude. He therefore seized it when he found it, knowing it wouldn't last for more than a few moments, but valuing it all the more for that.

Sure enough, it didn't last more than two minutes this time. He called out, "Come," at a rap on the door frame, and turning, was struck by a visceral sense of attraction such as he had not experienced in months.

The man was young, perhaps twenty, and slender in his blue and gold livery, but with a breadth of shoulder that spoke of strength, and a head and neck that would have graced a Greek sculpture. Perhaps because of the heat, he wore no wig, and his tight-curled hair was clipped so close that the finest modeling of his skull was apparent.

"Your servant, sah," he said to Grey, bowing respectfully. "The governor's compliments, and dinner will be served in ten minutes. May I see you to the dining room?"

"You may," Grey said, reaching hastily for his coat. He didn't doubt that he could find the dining room unassisted, but the chance to watch this young man walk . . .

"You *may*," Tom Byrd corrected, entering with his hands full of grooming implements, "once I've put his lordship's hair to rights." He fixed Grey with a minatory eye. "You're not a-going in to dinner like that, me lord, and don't you think it. You sit down there." He pointed sternly to a stool, and Lieutenant Colonel Grey, commander of His Majesty's forces in Jamaica, meekly obeyed the dictates of his nineteen-year-old valet. He didn't *always* allow Tom free rein, but in the current circumstance, he was just as pleased to have an excuse to sit still in the company of the young black servant.

Tom laid out all his implements neatly on the dressing table—a pair of silver hairbrushes, a box of powder, a pair of curling tongs—with the care and attention of a surgeon arraying his knives and saws. Selecting a hairbrush, he leaned closer, peering at Grey's head, then gasped. "Me lord! There's a big huge spider—walking right up your temple!"

Grey smacked his temple by reflex, and the spider in question—a clearly visible brown thing nearly a half inch long—shot off into the air, striking the looking glass with an audible tap before dropping to the surface of the dressing table and racing for its life.

Tom and the black servant uttered identical cries of horror and lunged for the creature, colliding in front of the dressing table and falling over in a thrashing heap. Grey, strangling an almost irresistible urge to laugh, stepped over them and dispatched the fleeing spider neatly with the back of his other hairbrush.

He pulled Tom to his feet and dusted him off, allowing the black servant to scramble up by himself. He brushed off all apologies as well, but asked whether the spider had been a deadly one?

"Oh, yes, sah," the servant assured him fervently. "Should one of those bite you, sah, you would suffer excruciating pain at once. The flesh around the wound would putrefy, you would commence to be fevered within an hour, and in all likelihood, you would not live until dawn."

"Oh, I see," Grey said mildly, his flesh creeping briskly. "Well, then. Perhaps you would not mind looking about the room while Tom is at his work? In case such spiders go about in company?"

Grey sat and let Tom brush and plait his hair, watching the young man as he assiduously searched under the bed and dressing table, pulled out Grey's trunk, and pulled up the trailing curtains and shook them.

"What is your name?" he asked the young man, noting that Tom's fingers were trembling badly, and hoping to distract him from thoughts of the hostile wildlife with which Jamaica undoubtedly teemed. Tom was fearless in the streets of London, and perfectly willing to face down ferocious dogs or foaming horses. Spiders, though, were quite another matter.

"Rodrigo, sah," said the young man, pausing in his curtain-shaking to bow. "Your servant, sah."

He seemed quite at ease in company and conversed with them about the town, the weather—he confidently predicted rain in the evening, at about ten o'clock—leading Grey to think that he had likely been employed as a servant in good families for some time. Was the man a slave, he wondered, or a free black?

His admiration for Rodrigo was, he assured himself, the same that he might have for a marvelous piece of sculpture, an elegant painting. And one of his friends did in fact possess a collection of Greek amphorae decorated with scenes that gave him quite the same sort of feeling. He shifted slightly in his seat, crossing his legs. He would be going in to dinner soon. He resolved to think of large, hairy spiders, and was making some progress with this subject when something huge and black dropped down the chimney and rushed out of the disused hearth.

All three men shouted and leapt to their feet, stamping madly. This time it was Rodrigo who felled the intruder, crushing it under one sturdy shoe.

"What the devil was that?" Grey asked, bending over to peer at the thing, which was a good three inches long, gleamingly black, and roughly ovoid, with ghastly long, twitching antennae.

"Only a cockroach, sah," Rodrigo assured him, wiping a hand across a sweating ebon brow. "They will not harm you, but they *are* most disagreeable. If they come into your bed, they feed upon your eyebrows."

Tom uttered a small strangled cry. The cockroach, far from being destroyed, had merely been inconvenienced by Rodrigo's shoe. It now extended thorny legs, heaved itself up, and was proceeding about its business, though at a somewhat slower pace. Grey, the hairs prickling on his arms, seized the ash shovel from among the fireplace implements and, scooping up the insect on its blade, jerked open the door and flung the nasty creature as far as he could—which, given his state of mind, was some considerable distance.

Tom was pale as custard when Grey came back in, but picked up his employer's coat with trembling hands. He dropped it, though, and with a mumbled apology, bent to pick it up again, only to utter a strangled shriek, drop it again, and run backward, slamming so hard against the wall that Grey heard a crack of laths and plaster.

"What the devil?" He bent, reaching gingerly for the fallen coat.

"Don't touch it, me lord!" Tom cried, but Grey had seen what the trouble was; a tiny yellow snake slithered out of the crimson folds, head moving to and fro in slow curiosity.

"Well, hallo, there." He reached out a hand, and as before, the little snake tasted his skin with a flickering tongue, then wove its way up into the palm of his hand. He stood up, cradling it carefully.

Tom and Rodrigo were standing like men turned to stone, staring at him.

"It's quite harmless," he assured them. "At least I think so. It must have fallen into my pocket earlier."

Rodrigo was regaining a little of his nerve. He came forward and looked at the snake, but declined an offer to touch it, putting both hands firmly behind his back.

"That snake likes you, sah," he said, glancing curiously from the snake to Grey's face, as though trying to distinguish a reason for such odd particularity.

"Possibly." The snake had made its way upward and was now wrapped round two of Grey's fingers, squeezing with remarkable strength. "On the other hand, I believe he may be attempting to kill and eat me. Do you know what his natural food might be?"

Rodrigo laughed at that, displaying very beautiful white teeth, and Grey had such a vision of those teeth, those soft mulberry lips, applied to—he coughed, hard, and looked away.

"He would eat anything that did not try to eat him first, sah," Rodrigo assured him. "It was probably the sound of the cockroach that made him come out. He would hunt those."

"What a very admirable sort of snake. Could we find him something to eat, do you think? To encourage him to stay, I mean."

Tom's face suggested strongly that if the snake was staying, he was not. On the other hand . . . He glanced toward the door, whence the cockroach had made its exit, and shuddered. With great reluctance, he reached into his pocket and extracted a rather squashed bread roll, containing ham and pickle.

This object being placed on the floor before it, the snake inspected it gingerly, ignored bread and pickle, but twining itself carefully about a chunk of ham, squeezed it fiercely into limp submission, then, opening its jaw to an amazing extent, engulfed its prey, to general cheers. Even Tom clapped his hands, and—if not ecstatic at Grey's suggestion that the snake might be accommodated in the dark space beneath the bed for the sake of preserving Grey's eyebrows, uttered no objections to this plan, either. The snake being ceremoniously installed and left to digest its meal, Grey was about to ask Rodrigo further questions regarding the natural fauna of the island, but was forestalled by the faint sound of a distant gong.

"Dinner!" he exclaimed, reaching for his now snakeless coat.

"Me lord! Your hair's not even powdered!" He refused to wear a wig, to

Tom's ongoing dismay, but was obliged in the present instance to submit to powder. This toiletry accomplished in haste, he shrugged into his coat and fled, before Tom could suggest any further refinements to his appearance.

THE GOVERNOR APPEARED, AS MR. DAWES HAD PREDICTED, CALM AND dignified at the dinner table. All trace of sweat, hysteria, and drunkenness had vanished, and beyond a brief word of apology for his abrupt disappearance, no reference was made to his earlier departure.

Major Fettes and Grey's adjutant, Captain Cherry, also appeared at table. A quick glance at them assured Grey that all was well with the troops. Fettes and Cherry couldn't be more diverse physically, the latter resembling a ferret and the former a block of wood—but both were extremely competent, and well liked by the men.

There was little conversation to begin with; the three soldiers had been eating ship's biscuit and salt beef for weeks. They settled down to the feast before them with the single-minded attention of ants presented with a loaf of bread; the magnitude of the challenge had no effect upon their earnest willingness. As the courses gradually slowed, though, Grey began to instigate conversation—his prerogative, as senior guest and commanding officer.

"Mr. Dawes explained to me the position of superintendent," he said, keeping his attitude superficially pleasant. "How long has Captain Cresswell held this position, sir?"

"For approximately six months, Colonel," the governor replied, wiping crumbs from his lips with a linen serviette. The governor was quite composed, but Grey had Dawes in the corner of his eye, and thought the secretary stiffened a little. That was interesting; he must get Dawes alone again, and go into this matter of superintendents more thoroughly.

"And was there a superintendent before Captain Cresswell?"

"Yes . . . In fact, there were two of them, were there not, Mr. Dawes?"

"Yes, sir. Captain Ludgate and Captain Perriman." Dawes was assiduously not meeting Grey's eye.

"I should like very much to speak with those gentlemen," Grey said pleasantly.

Dawes jerked as though someone had run a hat pin into his buttock. The governor finished chewing a grape, swallowed, and said, "I'm so sorry, Colonel. Both Ludgate and Perriman have left King's Town."

"Why?" John Fettes asked bluntly. The governor hadn't been expecting that, and blinked.

"I expect Major Fettes wishes to know whether they were replaced in their offices because of some peculation or corrupt practice," Bob Cherry put in chummily. "And if that be the case—were they allowed to leave the island rather than face prosecution? And if so—"

"Why?" Fettes put in neatly. Grey repressed a smile. Should peace break out on a wide scale and an army career fail them, Fettes and Cherry could easily make a living as a music-hall knockabout cross-talk act. As interrogators, they could reduce almost any suspect to incoherence, confusion, and confession in nothing flat.

Governor Warren, though, appeared to be made of tougher stuff than the usual regimental miscreant. Either that, or he had nothing to hide, Grey thought, watching him explain with tired patience that Ludgate had retired because of ill health, and that Perriman had inherited money and gone back to England.

No, he thought, watching the governor's hand twitch and hover indecisively over the fruit bowl. *He's got something to hide. And so does Dawes. Is it the same thing, though? And has it got anything to do with the present trouble?*

The governor could easily be hiding some peculation or corruption of his own—and likely was, Grey thought dispassionately, taking in the lavish display of silver on the sideboard. Such corruption was—within limits—considered more or less a perquisite of office. But if that was the case, it was not Grey's concern—unless it was in some way connected to the maroons and their rebellion.

Entertaining as it was to watch Fettes and Cherry at their work, he cut them off with a brief nod and turned the conversation firmly back to the rebellion.

"What communications have you had from the rebels, sir?" he asked the governor. "For I think in these cases, rebellion arises usually from some distinct source of grievance. What is it?"

Warren looked at him, jaw agape. He closed his mouth, slowly, and thought for a moment before replying. Grey rather thought he was considering how much Grey might discover from other avenues of inquiry.

Everything I bloody can, Grey thought, assuming an expression of neutral interest.

"Why, as to that, sir . . .the incident that began the . . . um . . . the difficulties . . . was the arrest of two young maroons, accused of stealing from a warehouse in King's Town." The two had been whipped in the town square and committed to prison, after which—

"Following a trial?" Grey interrupted. The governor's gaze rested on him, red-rimmed but cool.

"No, Colonel. They had no right to a trial."

"You had them whipped and imprisoned on the word of . . . whom? The affronted merchant?"

Warren drew himself up a little and lifted his chin. Grey saw that he had been shaved, but a patch of black whisker had been overlooked; it showed in the hollow of his cheek like a blemish, a hairy mole.

"*I* did not, no, sir," he said, coldly. "The sentence was imposed by the magistrate in King's Town."

"Who is?"

Dawes had closed his eyes with a small grimace.

"Judge Samuel Peters."

Grey nodded thanks.

"Captain Cherry will visit Mr. Judge Peters tomorrow," he said pleasantly. "And the prisoners, as well. I take it they are still in custody?"

"No, they aren't," Mr. Dawes put in, suddenly emerging from his impersonation of a dormouse. "They escaped, within a week of their capture."

The governor shot a brief, irritated glance at his secretary, but nodded reluctantly. With further prodding, it was admitted that the maroons had sent a protest at the treatment of the prisoners, via Captain Cresswell. The prisoners having escaped before the protest was received, though, it had not seemed necessary to do anything about it.

Grey wondered briefly whose patronage had got Warren his position, but dismissed the thought in favor of further explorations. The first violence had come without warning, he was told, with the burning of cane fields on a remote plantation. Word of it had reached Spanish Town several days later, by which time, another plantation had suffered similar depredation.

"Captain Cresswell rode at once to investigate the matter, of course," Warren said, lips tight.

"And?"

"He didn't return. The maroons have not demanded ransom for him, nor have they sent word that he is dead. He may be with them; he may not. We simply don't know."

Grey could not help looking at Dawes, who looked unhappy, but gave the ghost of a shrug. It wasn't his place to tell more than the governor wanted told, was it?

"Let me understand you, sir," Grey said, not bothering to hide the edge in his voice. "You have had *no* communication with the rebels since their initial protest? And you have taken no action to achieve any?"

Warren seemed to swell slightly, but replied in an even tone.

"In fact, Colonel, I have. I sent for you." He smiled, very slightly, and reached for the decanter.

THE EVENING AIR HUNG DAMP AND VISCID, TREMBLING WITH DISTANT thunder. Unable to bear the stifling confines of his uniform any longer, Grey flung it off, not waiting for Tom's ministrations, and stood naked in the middle of the room, eyes closed, enjoying the touch of air from the terrace on his bare skin.

There was something remarkable about the air. Warm as it was, and even indoors, it had a silken touch that spoke of the sea and clear blue water. He couldn't see the water from his room; even had it been visible from Spanish Town, his room faced a hillside covered with jungle. He could feel it, though, and had a sudden longing to wade out through surf and immerse himself in the clean coolness of the ocean. The sun had nearly set now, and the cries of parrots and other birds were growing intermittent.

He peered underneath the bed, but didn't see the snake. Perhaps it was far back in the shadows; perhaps it had gone off in search of more ham. He straightened, stretched luxuriously, then shook himself and stood blinking, feeling stupid from too much wine and food, and lack of sleep—he had slept barely three hours out of the preceding four-and-twenty, what with the arrival, disembarkation, and the journey to King's House.

His mind appeared to have taken French leave for the moment; no matter, it would be back shortly. Meanwhile, though, its abdication had left his body in charge; not at all a responsible course of action.

He felt exhausted, but restless, and scratched idly at his chest. The wounds there were solidly healed, slightly raised pink weals under his fingers, crisscrossing through the blond hair. One had passed within an inch of his left nipple; he'd been lucky not to lose it.

An immense pile of gauze cloth lay upon his bed. This must be the mosquito netting described to him by Mr. Dawes at dinner—a draped contraption meant to enclose the entire bed, thus protecting its occupant from the depredations of bloodthirsty insects.

He'd spent some time with Fettes and Cherry after dinner, laying plans for the morrow. Cherry would call upon Mr. Judge Peters and obtain details of the maroons who had been captured. Fettes would send men into King's Town in a search for the location of the retired Mr. Ludgate, erstwhile superintendent; if he could be found, Grey would like to know this gentleman's opinion of his successor. As for that successor—if Dawes did not manage to unearth Captain Cresswell by the end of tomorrow . . . Grey yawned involuntarily, then shook his head, blinking. Enough.

The troops would all be billeted by now, some granted their first liberty in months. He spared a glance at the small sheaf of maps and reports he had extracted from Mr. Dawes earlier, but those could wait 'til morning, and better light. He'd think better after a good night's sleep.

He leaned against the frame of the open door, after a quick glance down the terrace showed him that the rooms nearby seemed unoccupied. Clouds were beginning to drift in from the sea, and he remembered what Rodrigo had said about the rain at night. He thought perhaps he could feel a slight coolness in the air, whether from rain or oncoming night, and the hair on his body prickled and rose.

From here, he could see nothing but the deep green of a jungle-clad hill, glowing like a somber emerald in the twilight. From the other side of the house, though, as he left dinner, he'd seen the sprawl of Spanish Town below, a puzzle of narrow, aromatic streets. The taverns and the brothels would be doing a remarkable business tonight, he thought.

The thought brought with it a rare feeling of something that wasn't quite resentment. Any one of the soldiers he'd brought, from lowliest private soldier to Fettes himself, could walk into any brothel in Spanish Town—and there were a good many, Cherry had told him—and relieve the stresses caused by a long voyage without the slightest comment, or even the slightest attention. Not him.

His hand had dropped lower as he watched the light fade, idly kneading his flesh. There were accommodations for men such as himself in London, but it had been many years since he'd had recourse to such a place.

He had lost one lover to death, another to betrayal. The third . . . his lips tightened. Could you call a man your lover, who would never touch you—would recoil from the very thought of touching you? No. But at the same time, what would you call a man whose *mind* touched yours, whose prickly friendship was a gift, whose character, whose very existence, helped to define your own?

Not for the first time—and surely not for the last—he wished briefly that Jamie Fraser were dead. It was an automatic wish, though, at once dismissed from mind. The color of the jungle had died to ash, and insects were beginning to whine past his ears.

He went in, and began to worry the folds of the gauze on his bed, until Tom came in to take it away from him, hang the mosquito netting, and ready him for the night.

He couldn't sleep. Whether it was the heavy meal, the unaccustomed place, or simply the worry of his new and so-far-unknown command, his mind refused to settle, and so did his body. He didn't waste time in useless thrashing, though; he'd brought several books. Reading a bit of *The Story of Tom Jones, A Foundling* would distract his mind, and let sleep steal in upon him.

The French doors were covered with sheer muslin curtains, but the moon was nearly full, and there was enough light by which to find his tinderbox, striker, and candlestick. The candle was good beeswax, and the flame rose pure and bright—and instantly attracted a small cloud of inquisitive gnats, mosquitoes, and tiny moths. He picked it up, intending to take it to bed with him, but then thought better.

Was it preferable to be gnawed by mosquitoes, or incinerated? Grey debated the point for all of three seconds, then set the lit candlestick back on the desk. The gauze netting would go up in a flash if the candle fell over in bed.

Still, he needn't face death by bloodletting or be covered in itching bumps, simply because his valet didn't like the smell of bear grease. He wouldn't get it on his clothes, in any case.

He flung off his nightshirt and knelt to rummage in his trunk, with a guilty look over his shoulder. Tom, though, was safely tucked up somewhere amid the attics or outbuildings of King's House, and almost certainly sound asleep. Tom had suffered badly with seasickness, and the voyage had been hard on him.

The heat of the Indies hadn't done the battered tin of bear grease any good, either; the rancid fat nearly overpowered the scent of the peppermint and other herbs mixed into it. Still, he reasoned, if it repelled him, how much more a mosquito? and rubbed it into as much of his flesh as he could reach. Despite the stink, he found it not unpleasant. There was enough of the original smell left as to remind him of his usage of the stuff in Canada. Enough to remind him of Manoke, who had given it to him. Anointed him with it, in a cool blue evening on a deserted sandy isle in the St. Lawrence River.

Finished, he put down the tin and touched his rising prick. He didn't suppose he'd ever see Manoke again. But he did remember. Vividly.

A little later, he lay gasping on the bed under his netting, heart thumping slowly in counterpoint to the echoes of his flesh. He opened his eyes, feeling pleasantly relaxed, his head finally clear. The room was close; the servants had shut the windows, of course, to keep out the dangerous night air, and sweat misted his body. He felt too slack to get up and open the French doors onto the terrace, though; in a moment would do.

He closed his eyes again—then opened them abruptly and leapt out of bed, reaching for the dagger he'd laid on the table. The servant called Rodrigo stood pressed against the door, the whites of his eyes showing in his black face.

"What do you want?" Grey put the dagger down but kept his hand on it, his heart still racing.

"I have a message for you, sah," the young man said. He swallowed audibly.

"Yes? Come into the light, where I can see you." Grey reached for his banyan and slid into it, still keeping an eye on the man.

Rodrigo peeled himself off the door with evident reluctance, but he'd come to say something, and say it he would. He advanced into the dim circle of candlelight, hands at his sides, nervously clutching air.

"Do you know, sah, what an Obeah-man is?"

"No."

That disconcerted Rodrigo visibly. He blinked, and twisted his lips, obviously at a loss as how to describe this entity. Finally, he shrugged his shoulders helplessly and gave up.

"He says to you, beware."

"Does he?" Grey said dryly. "Of anything specific?"

That seemed to help; Rodrigo nodded vigorously.

"You don't be close to the governor. Stay right away, as far as you can. He's going to—I mean . . . something bad might happen. Soon. He—" The servant broke off suddenly, apparently realizing that he could be dismissed—if not worse—for talking about the governor in this loose fashion. Grey was more than curious, though, and sat down, motioning to Rodrigo to take the stool, which he did with obvious reluctance.

Whatever an Obeah-man was, Grey thought, he clearly had considerable power, to force Rodrigo to do something he so plainly didn't want to do. The young man's face shone with sweat and his hands clenched mindlessly on the fabric of his coat.

"Tell me what the Obeah-man said," Grey said, leaning forward, intent. "I promise you, I will tell no one."

Rodrigo gulped, but nodded. He bent his head, looking at the table as though he might find the right words written in the grain of the wood.

"Zombie," he muttered, almost inaudibly. "The zombie come for him. For the governor."

Grey had no notion what a zombie might be, but the word was spoken in such a tone as to make a chill flicker over his skin, sudden as distant lightning.

"Zombie," he said carefully. Mindful of the governor's reaction earlier, he asked, "Is a zombie perhaps a snake of some kind?"

Rodrigo gasped, but then seemed to relax a little.

"No, sah," he said seriously. "Zombie are dead people." He stood up then, bowed abruptly, and left, his message delivered.

NOT SURPRISINGLY, GREY DID NOT FALL ASLEEP IMMEDIATELY IN THE WAKE of this visit.

Having encountered German night hags and Indian ghosts, and having spent a year or two in the Scottish Highlands, he had more acquaintance than most with picturesque superstition. Though he wasn't inclined to give instant credence to local custom and belief, neither was he inclined to discount such belief out of hand. Belief made people do things that they otherwise wouldn't—and whether the belief had substance or not, the consequent actions certainly did.

Obeah-men and zombies notwithstanding, plainly there was some threat to Governor Warren—and he rather thought the governor knew what it was.

How exigent was the threat, though? He pinched out the candle flame and sat in darkness for a moment, letting his eyes adjust themselves, then rose and went soft-footed to the French doors through which Rodrigo had vanished.

The guest bedchambers of King's House were merely a string of boxes, all facing onto the long terrace, and each opening directly onto it through a pair of French doors. These had been curtained for the night, long pale drapes of cotton calico drawn across them. He paused for a moment, hand on the drape; if anyone was watching his room, they would see the curtain being drawn aside.

Instead, he turned and went to the inner door of the room. This opened onto a narrow service corridor, completely dark at the moment—and completely empty, if his senses could be trusted. He closed the door quietly. It was interesting, he thought, that Rodrigo had come to the front door, so to speak, when he could have approached Grey unseen.

But he'd said the Obeah-man had sent him. Plainly he wanted it to be seen that he had obeyed his order. Which in turn meant that someone was likely watching to see that he had.

The logical conclusion would be that the same someone—or someones—was watching to see what Grey might do next.

His body had reached its own conclusions already, and was reaching for breeches and shirt before he had quite decided that if something was about to happen to Warren, it was clearly his duty to stop it, zombies or not. He stepped out of the French doors onto the terrace, moving quite openly.

There was an infantryman posted at either end of the terrace, as he'd expected; Robert Cherry was nothing if not meticulous. On the other hand, the bloody sentries had plainly not seen Rodrigo entering his room, and he wasn't at all pleased about that. Recriminations could wait, though; the nearer sentry saw *him* and challenged him with a sharp, "Who goes there?"

"It's me," Grey said briefly, and, without ceremony, dispatched the sentry with orders to alert the other soldiers posted around the house, then send two men into the house, where they should wait in the hall until summoned.

Grey himself then went back into his room, through the inner door, and down the dark service corridor. He found a dozing black servant behind a door at the end of it, minding the fire under the row of huge coppers that supplied hot water to the household.

The man blinked and stared when shaken awake, but eventually nodded in response to Grey's demand to be taken to the governor's bedchamber, and led him into the main part of the house and up a darkened stair lit only by the moonlight streaming through the tall casements. Everything was quiet on the upper floor, save for slow, regular snoring coming from what the slave said was the governor's room.

The man was swaying with weariness; Grey dismissed him, with orders to let in the soldiers who should by now be at the door, and send them up. The man yawned hugely, and Grey watched him stumble down the stairs into the murk of the hall below, hoping he would not fall and break his neck. The house was very quiet. He was beginning to feel somewhat foolish. And yet . . .

The house seemed to breathe around him, almost as though it were a sentient thing, and aware of him. He found the fancy unsettling.

Ought he to wake Warren? he wondered. Warn him? Question him? No, he decided. There was no point in disturbing the man's rest. Questions could wait for the morning.

The sound of feet coming up the stair dispelled his sense of uneasiness, and he gave his orders quietly. The sentries were to keep guard on this door until relieved in the morning; at any sound of disturbance within, they were to enter at once. Otherwise—

"Stay alert. If you see or hear *anything*, I wish to know about it."

He paused, but Warren continued to snore, so he shrugged and made his way downstairs, out into the silken night, and back to his own room.

He smelled it first. For an instant, he thought he had left the tin of bear grease ointment uncovered—and then the reek of sweet decay took him by the throat, followed instantly by a pair of hands that came out of the dark and fastened on said throat.

He fought back in blind panic, striking and kicking wildly, but the grip on his windpipe didn't loosen, and bright lights began to flicker at the corners of what would have been his vision if he'd had any. With a tremendous effort of will, he made himself go limp. The sudden weight surprised his assailant, and jerked Grey free of the throttling grasp as he fell. He hit the floor and rolled.

Bloody hell, where was the man? If it was a man. For even as his mind reasserted its claim to reason, his more visceral faculties were recalling Rodrigo's parting statement: *Zombie are dead people, sah.* And whatever was here in the dark with him seemed to have been dead for several days, judging from its smell.

He could hear the rustling of something moving quietly toward him. Was it breathing? He couldn't tell, for the rasp of his own breath, harsh in his throat, and the blood-thick hammering of his heart in his ears.

He was lying at the foot of a wall, his legs half under the dressing table's bench. There was light in the room, now that his eyes were accustomed; the French doors were pale rectangles in the dark, and he could make out the shape of the thing that was hunting him. It was man-shaped, but oddly hunched, and swung its head and shoulders from side to side, almost as though it meant to smell him out. Which wouldn't take it more than two more seconds, at most.

He sat up abruptly, seized the small padded bench, and threw it as hard as he could at the thing's legs. It made a startled *Oof!* noise that was undeniably human and staggered, waving its arms to keep its balance. The noise reassured him, and he rolled up onto one knee and launched himself at the creature, bellowing incoherent abuse.

He butted it around chest height, felt it fall backward, then lunged for the pool of shadow where he thought the table was. It was there, and, feeling frantically over the surface, he found his dagger, still where he'd left it. He snatched it up and turned just in time to face the thing, which closed with him at once, reeking and making a disagreeable gobbling noise. He slashed at it and felt his knife skitter down the creature's forearm, bouncing off bone. It screamed, releasing a blast of foul breath directly into his face, then turned and rushed for the French doors, bursting them open in a shower of glass and flying cotton.

Grey charged after it, onto the terrace, shouting for the sentries. But the sentries, as he recalled belatedly, were in the main house, keeping watch over the governor, lest that worthy's rest be disturbed by . . . whatever sort of thing this was. Zombie?

Whatever it was, it was gone.

He sat down abruptly on the stones of the terrace, shaking with reaction. No one had come out in response to the noise. Surely no one could have slept through that; perhaps no one else was housed on this side of the mansion.

He felt ill and breathless, and rested his head for a moment on his knees, before jerking it up to look round, lest something else be stealing up on him. But the night was still and balmy. The only noise was an agitated rustling of leaves in a nearby tree, which he thought for a shocked moment might be the creature, climbing from branch to branch in search of refuge. Then he heard soft chitterings and hissing squeaks. *Bats,* said the calmly rational part of his mind—what was left of it.

He gulped and breathed, trying to get clean air into his lungs, to replace the disgusting stench of the creature. He'd been a soldier most of his life; he'd seen the dead on battlefields, and smelled them, too. Had buried fallen comrades in trenches and burned the bodies of his enemies. He knew what graves smelled like, and rotting flesh. And the thing that had had its hands round his throat had almost certainly come from a recent grave.

He was shivering violently, despite the warmth of the night. He rubbed a hand over his left arm, aching from the struggle; he had been badly wounded three years before, at Crefeld, and had nearly lost the arm. It worked, but was still a good deal weaker than he liked. Glancing at it, though, he was startled. Dark smears befouled the pale sleeve of his shirt and turning over his right hand, he found it wet and sticky.

"Jesus," he murmured, and brought it gingerly to his nose. No mistaking *that* smell, even overlaid as it was by grave-reek and the incongruous scent of night-blooming jasmine from the vines that grew in tubs by the terrace. Rain was beginning to fall, pungent and sweet—but even that could not obliterate the smell.

Blood. Fresh blood. Not his, either.

He rubbed the rest of the blood from his hand with the hem of his shirt and the cold horror of the last few minutes faded into a glowing coal of anger, hot in the pit of his stomach.

He'd been a soldier most of his life; he'd killed. He'd seen the dead on battlefields. And one thing he knew for a fact. Dead men don't bleed.

FETTES AND CHERRY HAD TO KNOW, OF COURSE. SO DID TOM, AS THE WRECKage of his room couldn't be explained as the result of nightmare. The four of them gathered in Grey's room, conferring by candlelight as Tom went about tidying the damage, white to the lips.

"You've never heard of zombie—or zombies? I have no idea whether the term is plural or not." Heads were shaken all round. A large square bottle of excellent Scotch whisky had survived the rigors of the voyage in the bottom of his trunk, and he poured generous tots of this, including Tom in the distribution.

"Tom—will you ask among the servants tomorrow? Carefully, of course. Drink that, it will do you good."

"Oh, I'll be careful, me lord," Tom assured him fervently. He took an obedient gulp of the whisky before Grey could warn him. His eyes bulged and he made a noise like a bull that has sat on a bumblebee, but managed somehow to swallow the mouthful, after which he stood still, opening and closing his mouth in a stunned sort of way.

Bob Cherry's mouth twitched, but Fettes maintained his usual stolid imperturbability.

"Why the attack upon you, sir, do you suppose?"

"If the servant who warned me about the Obeah-man was correct, I can only suppose that it was a consequence of my posting sentries to keep guard upon the governor. But you're right—" He nodded at Fettes's implication. "That means that whoever was responsible for this"—he waved a hand to indicate the disorder of his chamber, which still smelled of its recent intruder, despite the rain-scented wind that came through the shattered doors and the burnt-honey smell of the whisky—"either was watching the house closely, or—"

"Or lives here," Fettes said, and took a meditative sip. "Dawes, perhaps?"

Grey's eyebrows rose. That small, tubby, genial man? And yet he'd known a number of small, wicked men.

"Well," he said slowly, "it was not he who attacked me; I can tell you that much. Whoever it was, was taller than I am, and of a very lean build—not corpulent at all."

Tom made a hesitant noise, indicating that he had had a thought, and Grey nodded at him, giving permission to speak.

"You're quite sure, me lord, as the man who went for you . . . er . . . *wasn't* dead? Because by the smell of him, he's been buried for a week, at least."

A reflexive shudder went through all of them, but Grey shook his head.

"I am positive," he said, as firmly as he could. "It was a live man—though certainly a peculiar one," he added, frowning.

"Ought we to search the house, sir?" Cherry suggested.

Grey shook his head, reluctantly.

"He—or it—came from the garden, and went away in the same direction. He left discernible foot marks." He did not add that there had been sufficient time for the servants—if they were involved—to hide any traces of the creature by now. If there was involvement there, he thought the servant Rodrigo was his best avenue of inquiry—and it would not serve his purposes to alarm the house and focus attention on the young man ahead of time.

"Tom," he said, turning to his valet. "Does Rodrigo appear to be approachable?"

"Oh, yes, me lord. He was friendly to me over supper," Tom assured him, brush in hand. "D'ye want me to talk to him?"

"Yes, if you will. Beyond that—" He rubbed a hand over his face, feeling the sprouting beard stubble on his jaw. "I think we will proceed with the plans for tomorrow. But Major Cherry—will you also find time to question Mr. Dawes? You may tell him what transpired here tonight; I should find his response to that most interesting."

"Yes, sir." Cherry sat up and finished his whisky, coughed and sat blinking for a moment, then cleared his throat. "The, um, the governor, sir . . . ?"

"I'll speak to him myself," Grey said. "And then I propose to ride up into the hills, to pay a visit to a couple of plantations, with an eye to defensive postings. For we must be seen to be taking prompt and decisive action. If there's offensive action to be taken against the maroons, it will wait until we see what we're up against." Fettes and Cherry nodded; lifelong soldiers, they had no urgent desire to rush into combat.

The meeting dismissed, Grey sat down with a fresh glass of whisky, sipping it as Tom finished his work in silence.

"You're sure as you want to sleep in this room tonight, me lord?" he said, putting the dressing table bench neatly back in its place. "I could find you another place, I'm sure."

Grey smiled at him with affection.

"I'm sure you could, Tom. But so could our recent friend, I expect. No, Major Cherry will post a double guard on the terrace, as well as in the main house. It will be perfectly safe." And even if it wasn't, the thought of hiding, skulking away from whatever the thing was that had visited him . . . no. He wouldn't allow them—whoever they were—to think they had shaken his nerve.

Tom sighed and shook his head, but reached into his shirt and drew out a small cross, woven of wheat stalks and somewhat battered, suspended on a bit of leather string.

"All right, me lord. But you'll wear this, at least."

"What is it?"

"A charm, me lord. That Ilsa gave it to me, in Germany. She said it would protect me against evil—and so it has."

"Oh, no, Tom—surely you must keep—"

Mouth set in an expression of obstinacy that Grey knew well, Tom leaned forward and put the leather string over Grey's head. The mouth relaxed.

"There, me lord. Now *I* can sleep, at least."

GREY'S PLAN TO SPEAK TO THE GOVERNOR AT BREAKFAST WAS FOILED, AS that gentleman sent word that he was indisposed. Grey, Cherry, and Fettes all exchanged looks across the breakfast table, but Grey said merely, "Fettes? *And* you, Major Cherry, please." They nodded, a look of subdued satisfaction passing between them. He hid a smile; they loved questioning people.

The secretary, Dawes, was present at breakfast, but said little, giving all his attention to the eggs and toast on his plate. Grey inspected him carefully, but he showed no sign, either of nocturnal excursions or of clandestine knowledge. Grey gave Cherry an eye. Both Fettes and Cherry brightened perceptibly.

For the moment, though, Grey's own path lay clear. He needed to make a public appearance, as soon as possible, and to take such action as would make it apparent to the public that the situation was under control—and would make it apparent to the maroons that attention was being paid and that their destructive activities would no longer be allowed to pass unchallenged.

He summoned one of his other captains after breakfast and arranged for an escort. Twelve men should make enough of a show, he decided.

"And where will you be going, sir?" Captain Lossey asked, squinting as he made mental calculations regarding horses, pack mules, and supplies.

Grey took a deep breath and grasped the nettle.

"A plantation called Twelvetrees," he said. "Twenty miles or so into the uplands above King's Town."

PHILIP TWELVETREES WAS YOUNG, PERHAPS IN HIS MIDTWENTIES, AND good-looking in a sturdy sort of way. He didn't stir Grey personally, but nonetheless Grey felt a tightness through his body as he shook hands with the man, studying his face carefully for any sign that Twelvetrees recognized his name, or attributed any importance to his presence beyond the present political situation.

Not a flicker of unease or suspicion crossed Twelvetrees's face, and Grey relaxed a little, accepting the offer of a cooling drink. This turned out to be a mixture of fruit juices and wine, tart but refreshing.

"It's called sangria," Twelvetrees remarked, holding up his glass so the soft light fell glowing through it. "Blood, it means. In Spanish."

Grey did not speak much Spanish, but did know that. However, blood seemed as good a point d'appui as any, concerning his business.

"So you think we might be next?" Twelvetrees paled noticeably beneath his tan. He hastily swallowed a gulp of sangria and straightened his shoulders, though. "No, no. I'm sure we'll be all right. Our slaves are loyal, I'd swear to that."

"How many have you? And do you trust them with arms?"

"One hundred and sixteen," Twelvetrees replied, automatically. Plainly he was contemplating the expense and danger of arming some fifty men—for at least half his slaves must be women or children—and setting them essentially at liberty upon his property. And the vision of an unknown number of maroons, also armed, coming suddenly out of the night with torches. He drank a little more sangria.

"Perhaps . . . what did you have in mind?" he asked abruptly, setting down his glass.

Grey had just finished laying out his suggested plans, which called for the posting of two companies of infantry at the plantation, when a flutter of muslin at the door made him lift his eyes.

"Oh, Nan!" Philip put a hand over the papers Grey had spread out on the table, and shot Grey a quick warning look. "Here's Colonel Grey come to call. Colonel, my sister Nancy."

"Miss Twelvetrees." Grey had risen at once, and now took two or three steps toward her, bowing over her hand. Behind him, he heard the rustle as Twelvetrees hastily shuffled maps and diagrams together.

Nancy Twelvetrees shared her brother's genial sturdiness. Not pretty in the least, she had intelligent dark eyes—and these sharpened noticeably at her brother's introduction.

"Colonel Grey," she said, waving him gracefully back to his seat as she took her own. "Would you be connected with the Greys of Ilford, in Sussex? Or perhaps your family are from the London branch . . . ?"

"My brother has an estate in Sussex, yes," he said hastily. Forbearing to add that it was his half-brother Paul, who was not in fact a Grey, having been born of his mother's first marriage. Forbearing also to mention that his elder full brother was the Duke of Pardloe, and the man who had shot one Nathaniel Twelvetrees twenty years before. Which would logically expose the fact that Grey himself . . .

Philip Twelvetrees rather obviously did not want his sister alarmed by any mention of the present situation. Grey gave him the faintest of nods in acknowledgment, and Twelvetrees relaxed visibly, settling down to exchange polite social conversation.

"And what it is that brings you to Jamaica, Colonel Grey?" Miss Twelvetrees asked eventually. Knowing this was coming, Grey had devised an answer of careful vagueness, having to do with the Crown's concern for shipping. Halfway through this taradiddle, though, Miss Twelvetrees gave him a very direct look and demanded, "Are you here because of the governor?"

"Nan!" said her brother, shocked.

"Are you?" she repeated, ignoring her brother. Her eyes were very bright, and her cheeks flushed.

Grey smiled at her.

"What makes you think that that might be the case, may I ask, ma'am?"

"Because if you haven't come to remove Derwent Warren from his office, then *someone* should!"

"Nancy!" Philip was nearly as flushed as his sister. He leaned forward, grasping her wrist. "Nancy, please!"

She made as though to pull away, but then, seeing his pleading face, contented herself with a simple, "Hmph!" and sat back in her chair, mouth set in a thin line.

Grey would dearly have liked to know what lay behind Miss Twelvetrees's animosity for the governor, but he couldn't well inquire directly, and instead guided the conversation smoothly away, inquiring of Philip regarding the operations of the plantation, and of Miss Twelvetrees regarding the natural history of Jamaica, for which she seemed to have some feeling, judging by the rather good watercolors of plants and animals that hung about the room, all neatly signed *N.T.*

Gradually, the sense of tension in the room relaxed, and Grey became aware that Miss Twelvetrees was focusing her attentions upon him. Not quite flirting; she was not built for flirtation. But definitely going out of her way to make him aware of her as a woman. He didn't quite know what she had in mind—he was presentable enough, but didn't think she was truly attracted to him. Still, he made no move to stop her; if Philip should leave them alone together, he might be able to find out why she had said that about Governor Warren.

A quarter hour later, a mulatto man in a well-made suit put his head in at the door to the drawing room and asked if he might speak with Philip. He cast a curious eye toward Grey, but Twelvetrees made no move to introduce them, instead excusing himself and taking the visitor—who, Grey conceived, must be an overseer of some kind—to the far end of the large, airy room, where they conferred in low voices.

He at once seized the opportunity to fix his attention on Miss Nancy, in hopes of turning the conversation to his own ends.

"I collect you are acquainted with the governor, Miss Twelvetrees?" he asked, to which she gave a short laugh.

"Better than I might wish, sir."

"Really?" he said, in as inviting a tone as possible.

"Really," she said, and smiled unpleasantly. "But let us not waste time in discussing a . . . a person of such low character." The smile altered, and she leaned toward him, touching his hand, which surprised him. "Tell me, Colonel, does your wife accompany you? Or does she remain in London, from fear of fevers and slave uprisings?"

"Alas, I am unmarried, ma'am," he said, thinking that she likely knew a good deal more than her brother wished her to.

"Really," she said again, in an altogether different tone.

Her touch lingered on his hand, a fraction of a moment too long. Not long enough to be blatant, but long enough for a normal man to perceive it—and Grey's reflexes in such matters were much better developed than a normal man's, from necessity.

He barely thought consciously, but smiled at her, then glanced at her brother, then back, with the tiniest of regretful shrugs. He forbore to add the lingering smile that would have said, "Later."

She sucked her lower lip in for a moment, then released it, wet and reddened, and gave him a look under lowered lids that said "Later," and a good deal more. He coughed, and out of the sheer need to say *something* completely free of suggestion, asked abruptly, "Do you by chance know what an Obeah-man is, Miss Twelvetrees?"

Her eyes sprang wide, and she lifted her hand from his arm. He managed to move out of her easy reach without actually appearing to shove his chair backward, and thought she didn't notice; she was still looking at him with great attention, but the nature of that attention had changed. The sharp vertical lines between her brows deepened into a harsh eleven.

"Where did you encounter that term, Colonel, may I ask?" Her voice was quite normal, her tone light—but she also glanced at her brother's turned back, and she spoke quietly.

"One of the governor's servants mentioned it. I see you are familiar with the term—I collect it is to do with Africans?"

"Yes." Now she was biting her upper lip, but the intent was not sexual. "The Koromantyn slaves—you know what those are?"

"No."

"Negroes from the Gold Coast," she said, and, putting her hand once more on his sleeve, pulled him up and drew him a little away, toward the far end of the room. "Most planters want them, because they're big and strong, and usually very well formed." Was it—no, he decided, it was *not* his imagination; the tip of her tongue had darted out and touched her lip in the fraction of an instant before she'd said "well formed." He thought Philip Twelvetrees had best find his sister a husband, and quickly.

"Do you have Koromantyn slaves here?"

"A few. The thing is, Koromantyns tend to be intractable. Very aggressive, and hard to control."

"Not a desirable trait in a slave, I collect," he said, making an effort to keep any edge out of his tone.

"Well, it can be," she said, surprising him. She smiled briefly. "If your slaves are loyal—and ours are, I'd swear it—then you don't mind them being a bit bloody-minded toward . . . anyone who might want to come and cause trouble."

He was sufficiently shocked at her language that it took him a moment to absorb her meaning. The tongue tip flickered out again, and had she had dimples, she would certainly have employed them.

"I see," he said carefully. "But you were about to tell me what an Obeah-man is. Some figure of authority, I take it, among the Koromantyns?"

The flirtatiousness vanished abruptly, and she frowned again.

"Yes. *Obi* is what they call their . . . religion, I suppose one must call it. Though from what little I know of it, no minister or priest would allow it that name."

Loud screams came from the garden below, and he glanced out to see a flock of small, brightly colored parrots swooping in and out of a big, lacy tree with reddish fruit. Like clockwork, two small black children, naked as eggs, shot out of the shrubbery and aimed slingshots at the birds. Rocks spattered harmlessly among the branches, but the birds rose in a feathery vortex of agitation and flapped off, shrieking their complaints.

Miss Twelvetrees ignored the interruption, resuming her explanation directly the noise subsided.

"An Obeah-man talks to the spirits. He—or she, there are Obeah-women, too—is the person to whom one goes to—arrange things."

"What sorts of things?"

A faint hint of her former flirtatiousness reappeared.

"Oh . . . to make someone fall in love with you. To get with child. To get *without* child"—and here she looked to see whether she had shocked him again, but he merely nodded—"or to curse someone. To cause them ill luck, or ill health. Or death."

This was promising.

"And how is this done, may I ask? Causing illness or death?"

Here, however, she shook her head.

"I don't know. It's really not safe to ask," she added, lowering her voice still further, and now her eyes were serious. "Tell me—the servant who spoke to you; what did he say?"

Aware of just how quickly gossip spreads in rural places, Grey wasn't about to reveal that threats had been made against Governor Warren. Instead he asked, "Have you ever heard of zombies?"

She went quite white.

"No," she said abruptly. It was a risk, but he took her hand to keep her from turning away.

"I cannot tell you why I need to know," he said, very low-voiced, "but please believe me, Miss Twelvetrees—Nancy"—callously, he pressed her hand—"it's extremely important. Any help that you can give me would be—well, I should appreciate it extremely." Her hand was warm; the fingers moved a little in his, and not in an effort to pull away. Her color was coming back.

"I truly don't know much," she said, equally low-voiced. "Only that zombies are dead people who have been raised by magic to do the bidding of the person who made them."

"The person who made them—this would be an Obeah-man?"

"Oh! No," she said, surprised. "The Koromantyns don't make zombies—in fact, they think it quite an unclean practice."

"I'm entirely of one mind with them," he assured her. "Who *does* make zombies?"

"Nancy!" Philip had concluded his conversation with the overseer and was coming toward them, a hospitable smile on his broad, perspiring face. "I say, can we not have something to eat? I'm sure the Colonel must be famished, and I'm most extraordinarily clemmed myself."

"Yes, of course," Miss Twelvetrees said, with a quick warning glance at Grey. "I'll tell Cook." Grey tightened his grip momentarily on her fingers, and she smiled at him.

"As I was saying, Colonel, you must call on Mrs. Abernathy at Rose Hall. She would be the person best equipped to inform you."

"Inform you?" Twelvetrees, curse him, chose this moment to become inquisitive. "About what?"

"Customs and beliefs among the Ashanti, my dear," his sister said blandly. "Colonel Grey has a particular interest in such things."

Twelvetrees snorted briefly.

"Ashanti, my left foot! Ibo, Fulani, Koromantyn . . . baptize 'em all proper Christians and let's hear no more about what heathen beliefs they may have brought with 'em. From the little *I* know, you don't want to hear about that sort of thing, Colonel. Though if you *do*, of course," he added hastily, recalling that it was not his place to tell the Lieutenant Colonel who would be protecting Twelvetrees's life and property his business, "then my sister's quite right—Mrs. Abernathy would be best placed to advise you. Almost all her slaves are Ashanti. She . . . er . . . she's said to . . . um . . . take an interest."

To Grey's own interest, Twelvetrees's face went a deep red, and he hastily changed the subject, asking Grey fussy questions about the exact disposition of his troops. Grey evaded direct answers beyond assuring Twelvetrees that two companies of infantry would be dispatched to his plantation as soon as word could be sent to Spanish Town.

He wished to leave at once, for various reasons, but was obliged to remain for tea, an uncomfortable meal of heavy, stodgy food, eaten under the heated gaze of Miss Twelvetrees. For the most part, he thought he had handled her with tact and delicacy—but toward the end of the meal she began to give him little pursed-mouth jabs. Nothing one could—or should—overtly notice, but he saw Philip blink at her once or twice in frowning bewilderment.

"Of course, I could not pose as an authority regarding any aspect of life on Jamaica," she said, fixing him with an unreadable look. "We have lived here barely six months."

"Indeed," he said politely, a wodge of undigested Savoy cake settling heavily in his stomach. "You seem very much at home—and a very lovely home it is, Miss Twelvetrees. I perceive your most harmonious touch throughout."

This belated attempt at flattery was met with the scorn it deserved; the eleven was back, hardening her brow.

"My brother inherited the plantation from our cousin, Edward Twelvetrees. Edward lived in London himself." She leveled a look like the barrel of a musket at him. "Did you know him, Colonel?"

And just what would the bloody woman do if he told her the truth? he wondered. Clearly, she thought she knew something, but . . . no, he thought, watching her closely. She couldn't know the truth, but had heard some rumor. So this poking at him was an attempt—and a clumsy one—to get him to say more.

"I know several Twelvetreeses casually," he said, very amiably. "But if I met your cousin, I do not think I had the pleasure of speaking with him at any great length." *"You bloody murderer!"* and *"Fucking sodomite!"* not really constituting conversation, if you asked Grey.

Miss Twelvetrees blinked at him, surprised, and he realized what he should have seen much earlier. She was drunk. He had found the sangria light, refreshing—but had drunk only one glass himself. He had not noticed her refill her own, and yet the pitcher stood nearly empty.

"My dear," said Philip, very kindly. "It is warm, is it not? You look a trifle pale and indisposed." In fact, she was flushed, her hair beginning to come down behind her rather large ears—but she did indeed look indisposed. Philip rang the bell, rising to his feet, and nodded to the black maid who came in.

"I am not indisposed," Nancy Twelvetrees said, with some dignity. "I'm—I simply—that is—" But the black maid, evidently used to this office, was already hauling Miss Twelvetrees toward the door, though with sufficient skill as to make it look as though she merely assisted her mistress.

Grey rose himself, perforce, and took Miss Nancy's hand, bowing over it.

"Your servant, Miss Twelvetrees," he said. "I hope—"

"We know," she said, staring at him from large, suddenly tear-filled eyes. "Do you hear me? *We know.*" Then she was gone, the sound of her unsteady steps a ragged drumbeat on the parquet floor.

There was a brief, awkward silence between the two men. Grey cleared his throat just as Philip Twelvetrees coughed.

"Didn't really like cousin Edward," he said.

"Oh," said Grey.

They walked together to the yard where Grey's horse browsed under a tree, its sides streaked with parrot-droppings.

"Don't mind Nancy, will you?" Twelvetrees said quietly, not looking at him. "She had . . . a disappointment, in London. I thought she might get over it more easily here, but—well, I made a mistake, and it's not easy to unmake."

He sighed, and Grey had a sudden strong urge to pat him sympathetically on the back.

Instead, he made an indeterminate noise in his throat, nodded, and mounted.

"The troops will be here day after tomorrow, sir," he said. "You have my word upon it."

GREY HAD INTENDED TO RETURN TO SPANISH TOWN, BUT INSTEAD PAUSED on the road, pulled out the chart Dawes had given him, and calculated the distance to Rose Hall. It would mean camping on the mountain overnight, but they were prepared for that—and beyond the desirability of hearing firsthand the details of a maroon attack, he was now more than curious to speak with Mrs. Abernathy regarding zombies.

He called his aide, wrote out instructions for the dispatch of troops to Twelvetrees, then sent two men back to Spanish Town with the message, and two more on before, to discover a good campsite. They reached this as the sun was beginning to sink, glowing like a flaming pearl in a soft pink sky.

"What is that?" he asked, looking up abruptly from the cup of gunpowder tea Corporal Sansom had handed him. Sansom looked startled, too, and looked up the slope where the sound had come from.

"Don't know, sir," he said. "It sounds like a horn of some kind."

It did. Not a trumpet, or anything of a standard military nature. Definitely a sound of human origin, though. The men stood quiet, waiting. A moment or two, and the sound came again.

"That's a different one," Sansom said, sounding alarmed. "It came from over there"—pointing up the slope—"didn't it?"

"Yes, it did," Grey said absently. "Hush!"

The first horn sounded again, a plaintive bleat almost lost in the noises of the birds settling for the night, and then fell silent.

Grey's skin tingled, his senses alert. They were not alone in the jungle. Someone—some*ones*—were out there in the oncoming night, signaling to each other. Quietly, he gave orders for the building of a hasty fortification, and the camp fell at once to the work of organizing defense. The men with him were mostly veterans, and while wary, not at all panicked. Within a very short time, a redoubt of stone and brush had been thrown up, sentries had been posted in pairs around camp, and every man's weapon was loaded and primed, ready for an attack.

Nothing came, though, and though the men lay on their arms all night, there was no further sign of human presence. Such presence was there, though; Grey could feel it. Them. Watching.

He ate his supper and sat with his back against an outcrop of rock, dagger in his belt and loaded musket to hand. Waiting.

But nothing happened, and the sun rose. They broke camp in an orderly fashion, and if horns sounded in the jungle, the sound was lost in the shriek and chatter of the birds.

HE HAD NEVER BEEN IN THE PRESENCE OF ANYONE WHO REPELLED HIM SO acutely. He wondered why that was; there was nothing overtly ill-favored or ugly about her. If anything, she was a handsome Scotchwoman of middle age, fair-haired and buxom. And yet the widow Abernathy chilled him, despite the warmth of the air on the terrace where she had chosen to receive him at Rose Hall.

She was not dressed in mourning, he saw, nor did she make any obvious acknowledgment of the recent death of her husband. She wore white muslin, embroidered in blue about the hems and sleeves.

"I understand that I must congratulate you upon your survival, madam," he said, taking the seat to which she gestured him. It was a somewhat callous thing to say, but she looked hard as nails; he didn't think it would upset her, and he was right.

"Thank you," she said, leaning back in her own wicker chair and looking him frankly up and down in a way that he found unsettling. "It was bloody cold in that spring, I'll tell ye that for nothing. Like to died myself, frozen right through."

He inclined his head courteously.

"I trust you suffered no lingering ill effects from the experience? Beyond, of course, the lamentable death of your husband," he hurried to add.

She laughed coarsely.

"Glad to get shot o' the wicked sod."

At a loss how to reply to this, Grey coughed and changed the subject.

"I am told, madam, that you have an interest in some of the rituals practiced by slaves."

Her somewhat bleared green glance sharpened at that.

"Who told you that?"

"Miss Nancy Twelvetrees." There was no reason to keep the identity of his informant secret, after all.

"Oh, wee Nancy, was it?" She seemed amused by that, and shot him a sideways look. "I expect she liked *you*, no?"

He couldn't see what Miss Twelvetrees's opinion of him might have to do with the matter, and said so, politely. Mrs. Abernathy merely smirked at that, waving a hand.

"Aye, well. What is it ye want to know, then?"

"I want to know how zombies are made."

Shock wiped the smirk off her face, and she blinked at him stupidly for a moment before picking up her glass and draining it.

"Zombies," she said, and looked at him with a certain wary interest. "Why?"

He told her. From careless amusement, her attitude changed, interest sharpening. She made him repeat the story of his encounter with the thing in his room, asking sharp questions regarding its smell, particularly.

"Decayed flesh," she said. "Ye'd ken what that smells like, would ye?"

It must have been her accent that brought back the battlefield at Culloden, and the stench of burning corpses. He shuddered, unable to stop himself.

"Yes," he said abruptly. "Why?"

She pursed her lips in thought.

"There are different ways to go about it, aye? One way is to give the *afile* powder to the person, wait until they drop, and then bury them atop a recent corpse. Ye just spread the earth lightly over them," she explained, catching his look. "And make sure to put leaves and sticks over the face afore sprinkling the earth, so as the person can still breathe. When the poison dissipates enough for them to move again, and sense things, they see they're buried, they smell the reek, and so they ken they must be dead." She spoke as matter-of-factly as though she had been telling him her private receipt for apple pandowdy or treacle cake. Weirdly enough, that steadied him, and he was able to speak past his revulsion, calmly.

"Poison. That would be the *afile* powder? What sort of poison is it, do you know?"

Seeing the spark in her eye, he thanked the impulse that had led him to add, "Do you know?" to that question—for if not for pride, he thought she might not have told him. As it was, she shrugged and answered offhand.

"Oh . . . herbs. Ground bones—bits o' other things. But the main thing, the one thing ye *must* have, is the liver of a fugu fish."

He shook his head, not recognizing the name. "Describe it, if you please." She did; from her description, he thought it must be one of the odd puffer fish that blew themselves up like bladders if disturbed. He made a silent resolve never to eat one. In the course of the conversation, though, something was becoming apparent to him.

"But what you are telling me—your pardon, madam—is that in fact a zombie is *not* a dead person at all? That they are merely drugged?"

Her lips curved; they were still plump and red, he saw, younger than her face would suggest.

"What good would a dead person be to anyone?"

"But plainly the widespread belief is that zombies *are* dead."

"Aye, of course. The zombies think they're dead, and so does everyone else. It's not true, but it's effective. Scares folk rigid. As for 'merely drugged,' though"—she shook her head—"they don't come back from it, ye ken. The poison damages their brains, and their nervous systems. They can follow simple instructions, but they've no real capacity for thought anymore—and they mostly move stiff and slow."

"Do they?" he murmured. The creature—well, the man, he was now sure of that—who had attacked him had not been stiff and slow, by any means. Ergo . . .

"I'm told, madam, that most of your slaves are Ashanti. Would any of them know more about this process?"

"No," she said abruptly, sitting up a little. "I learnt what I ken from a *houngan*—that would be a sort of . . . practitioner, I suppose ye'd say. He wasna one of my slaves, though."

"A practitioner of *what*, exactly?"

Her tongue passed slowly over the tips of her sharp teeth, yellowed, but still sound.

"Of magic," she said, and laughed softly, as though to herself. "Aye, magic. African magic. Slave magic."

"You believe in magic?" He asked it as much from curiosity as anything else.

"Don't you?" Her brows rose, but he shook his head.

"I do not. And in fact, from what you have just told me yourself, the process of creating—if that's the word—a zombie is *not* in fact magic, but merely the administration of poison over a period of time, added to the power of suggestion." Another thought struck him. "Can a person recover from such poisoning? You say it does not kill them."

She shook her head.

"The poison doesn't, no. But they always die. They starve, for one thing. They lose all notion of will, and canna do anything save what the *houngan* tells them to do. Gradually, they waste away to nothing, and . . ." Her fingers snapped silently.

"Even were they to survive," she went on practically, "the people would kill them. Once a person's been made a zombie, there's nay way back."

Throughout the conversation, Grey had been becoming aware that Mrs. Abernathy spoke from what seemed a much closer acquaintance with the notion than one might acquire from an idle interest in natural philosophy. He wanted to get away from her but obliged himself to sit still and ask one more question.

"Do you know of any particular significance attributed to snakes, madam? In African magic, I mean."

She blinked, somewhat taken aback by that.

"Snakes," she repeated slowly. "Aye. Well . . . snakes ha' wisdom, they say. And some o' the *loas* are snakes."

"Loas?"

She rubbed absently at her forehead, and he saw, with a small prickle of revulsion, the faint stippling of a rash. He'd seen that before; the sign of advanced syphilitic infection.

"I suppose ye'd call them spirits," she said, and eyed him appraisingly. "D'ye see snakes in your dreams, Colonel?"

"Do I—no. I don't." He didn't, but the suggestion was unspeakably disturbing. She smiled.

"A *loa* rides a person, aye? Speaks through them. And I see a great huge snake, lyin' on your shoulders, Colonel." She heaved herself abruptly to her feet. "I'd be careful what ye eat, Colonel Grey."

THEY RETURNED TO SPANISH TOWN TWO DAYS LATER. THE RIDE BACK GAVE Grey time for thought, from which he drew certain conclusions. Among these conclusions was the conviction that maroons had not, in fact, attacked Rose Hall. He had spoken to Mrs. Abernathy's overseer, who seemed reluctant and shifty, very vague on the details of the presumed attack. And later . . .

After his conversations with the overseer and several slaves, he had gone back to the house to take formal leave of Mrs. Abernathy. No one had answered his knock, and he had walked round the house in search of a servant. What he had found instead was a path leading downward from the house, with a glimpse of water at the bottom.

Out of curiosity, he had followed this path, and found the infamous spring in which Mrs. Abernathy had presumably sought refuge from the murdering intruders. Mrs. Abernathy was in the spring, naked, swimming with slow composure from one side to the other, white-streaked fair hair streaming out behind her.

The water was crystalline; he could see the fleshy pumping of her buttocks, moving like a bellows that propelled her movements—and glimpse the purplish hollow of her sex, exposed by the flexion. There were no banks of concealing reeds or other vegetation; no one could have failed to see the woman if she'd been in the spring—and plainly, the temperature of the water was no dissuasion to her.

So she'd lied about the maroons. He had a cold certainty that Mrs. Abernathy had murdered her husband, or arranged it—but there was little he was equipped to do with that conclusion. Arrest her? There were no witnesses—or none who could legally testify against her, even if they wanted to. And he rather thought that none of her slaves would want to; those he had spoken with had displayed extreme reticence with regard to their mistress. Whether that was the result of loyalty or fear, the effect would be the same.

What the conclusion *did* mean to him was that the maroons were in fact likely not guilty of murder, and that was important. So far, all reports of mischief involved only property damage—and that, only to fields and equipment. No houses had been burnt, and while several plantation owners had claimed that their slaves had been taken, there was no proof of this; the slaves in question might simply have taken advantage of the chaos of an attack to run.

This spoke to him of a certain amount of care on the part of whoever led the maroons. Who did? he wondered. What sort of man? The impression he was gaining was not that of a rebellion—there had been no declaration, and he would have expected that—but of the boiling over of a long-simmering frustration. He *had* to speak with Captain Cresswell. And he hoped that bloody secretary had managed to find the superintendent by the time he reached King's House.

In the event, he reached King's House long after dark, and was informed by the governor's butler—appearing like a black ghost in his nightshirt—that the household was asleep.

"All right," he said wearily. "Call my valet, if you will. And tell the governor's servant in the morning that I will require to speak to His Excellency after breakfast, no matter what his state of health may be."

Tom was sufficiently pleased to see Grey in one piece as to make no protest at being awakened, and had him washed, nightshirted, and tucked up beneath his mosquito netting before the church bells of Spanish Town tolled midnight. The doors of his room had been repaired, but Grey made Tom leave the window open, and fell asleep with a silken wind caressing his cheeks and no thought of what the morning might bring.

He was roused from an unusually vivid erotic dream by an agitated banging. He pulled his head out from under the pillow, the feel of rasping red hairs still rough on his lips, and shook his head violently, trying to reorient himself in space and time. Bang, bang, bang, bang, *bang!* Bloody hell . . . ? Oh. Door.

"What? Come in, for God's sake! What the devil—oh. Wait a moment, then." He struggled out of the tangle of bedclothes and discarded nightshirt—good Christ, had he really been doing what he'd been dreaming about doing?—and flung his banyan over his rapidly detumescing flesh.

"What?" he demanded, finally getting the door open. To his surprise, Tom stood there, saucer-eyed and trembling, next to Major Fettes.

"Are you all right, me lord?" Tom burst out, cutting off Major Fettes's first words.

"Do I appear to be spurting blood or missing any necessary appendages?" Grey demanded, rather irritably. "What's happened, Fettes?"

Now that he'd got his eyes properly open, he saw that Fettes looked almost as disturbed as Tom. The major—veteran of a dozen major campaigns, decorated for valor, and known for his coolness—swallowed visibly and braced his shoulders.

"It's the governor, sir. I think you'd best come and see."

"WHERE ARE THE MEN WHO WERE ASSIGNED TO GUARD HIM?" GREY ASKED calmly, stepping out of the governor's bedroom and closing the door gently behind him. The doorknob slid out of his fingers, slick under his hand. He knew the slickness was his own sweat, and not blood, but his stomach gave a lurch and he rubbed his fingers convulsively against the thigh of his breeches.

"They're gone, sir." Fettes had got his voice, if not quite his face, back under control. "I've sent men to search the grounds."

"Good. Would you please call the servants together? I'll need to question them."

Fettes took a deep breath.

"They're gone, too."

"What? All of them?"

"Yes, sir."

He took a deep breath himself—and let it out again, fast. Even outside the room, the stench was gagging. He could feel the smell, thick on his skin, and rubbed his fingers on his breeches once again, hard. He swallowed and, holding his breath, jerked his head to Fettes—and Cherry, who had joined them, shaking his head mutely in answer to Grey's raised brow. No sign of the vanished sentries, then. Goddamn it; a search would have to be made for their bodies. The thought made him cold, despite the growing warmth of the morning.

He went down the stairs, his officers only too glad to follow. By the time he reached the foot, he had decided where to begin, at least. He stopped and turned to Fettes and Cherry.

"Right. The island is under military law as of this moment. Notify the officers, but tell them there is to be no public announcement yet. And *don't* tell them why." Given the flight of the servants, it was more than likely that news of the governor's death would reach the inhabitants of Spanish Town within hours—if it hadn't already. But if there was the slightest chance that the populace might remain in ignorance of the fact that Governor Warren had been killed and partially devoured in his own residence, while under the guard of His Majesty's army . . . Grey was taking it.

"What about the secretary?" he asked abruptly, suddenly remembering. "Dawes. Is he gone, too? Or dead?"

Fettes and Cherry exchanged a guilty look.

"Don't know, sir," Cherry said gruffly. "I'll go and look."

"Do that, if you please."

He nodded in return to their salutes and went outside, shuddering in relief at the touch of the sun on his face, the warmth of it through the thin linen of his shirt. He walked slowly toward his room, where Tom had doubtless already managed to assemble and clean his uniform.

Now what? Dawes, if the man was still alive—and he hoped to God he was . . . A sudden surge of saliva choked him, and he spat several times on the terrace, unable to swallow for the memory of that throat-clenching smell.

"Tom," he said urgently, coming into the room. "Did you have an opportunity to speak to the other servants? To Rodrigo?"

"Yes, me lord." Tom waved him onto the stool and knelt to put his stockings on. "They all knew about zombies—said they were dead people, just like Rodrigo said. A *houngan*—that's a . . . well, I don't quite know, but folk are right scared of 'em. Anyway, one of those who takes against somebody—or what's paid to do so, I reckon—will take the somebody, and kill them, then raise 'em up again, to be his servant, and that's a zombie. They were all dead scared of the notion, me lord," he said earnestly, looking up.

"I don't blame them in the slightest. Did any of them know about my visitor?"

Tom shook his head.

"They said not—I think they did, me lord, but they weren't a-going to say. I got Rodrigo off by himself, though; he admitted he knew about it, but he said he didn't think it was a zombie what came after you, because I told him how you fought it, and what a mess it made of your room." He narrowed his eyes at the dressing table, with its cracked mirror.

"Really? What did he think it was?"

"He wouldn't really say, but I pestered him a bit, and he finally let on as it might have been a *houngan*, just pretending to be a zombie."

Grey digested that possibility for a moment. Had the creature who attacked him meant to kill him? If so—why? But if not . . . the attack might only have been meant to pave the way for what had now happened, by making it seem that there were zombies lurking about King's House in some profusion. That made a certain amount of sense, save for the fact . . .

"But I'm told that zombies are slow and stiff in their movements. Could one of them have done what . . . was done to the governor?" he swallowed.

"I dunno, me lord. Never met one." Tom grinned briefly at him, rising from fastening his knee buckles. It was a nervous grin, but Grey smiled back, heartened by it.

"I suppose I will have to go and look at the body again," he said, rising. "Will you come with me, Tom?" His valet was young, but very observant, especially in matters pertaining to the body, and had been of help to him before in interpreting postmortem phenomena.

Tom paled noticeably, but gulped and nodded, and squaring his shoulders, followed Lord John out onto the terrace.

On their way to the governor's room, they met Major Fettes, gloomily eating a slice of pineapple scavenged from the kitchen.

"Come with me, Major," Grey ordered. "You can tell me what discoveries you and Cherry have made in my absence."

"I can tell you one such, sir," Fettes said, putting down the pineapple and wiping his hands on his waistcoat. "Judge Peters has gone to Eleuthera."

"What the devil for?" That was a nuisance; he'd been hoping to discover more about the original incident that had incited the rebellion, and as he was obviously not going to learn anything from Warren . . . He waved a hand at Fettes; it hardly mattered why Peters had gone.

"Right. Well, then—" Breathing through his mouth as much as possible, Grey pushed open the door. Tom, behind him, made an involuntary sound, but then stepped carefully up and squatted beside the body.

Grey squatted beside him. He could hear thickened breathing behind him.

"Major," he said, without turning round. "If Captain Cherry has found Mr. Dawes, would you be so kind as to fetch him in here?"

THEY WERE HARD AT IT WHEN DAWES CAME IN, ACCOMPANIED BY BOTH Fettes and Cherry, and Grey ignored all of them.

"The bite marks *are* human?" he asked, carefully turning one of Warren's lower legs toward the light from the window. Tom nodded, wiping the back of his hand across his mouth.

"Sure of it, me lord. I been bitten by dogs—nothing like this. Besides—" He inserted his forearm into his mouth and bit down fiercely, then displayed the results to Grey. "See, me lord? The teeth go in a circle, like."

"No doubt of it." Grey straightened and turned to Dawes, who was sagging at the knees to such an extent that Captain Cherry was obliged to hold him up. "Do sit down, please, Mr. Dawes, and give me your opinion of matters here."

Dawes's round face was blotched, his lips pale. He shook his head and tried to back away but was prevented by Cherry's grip on his arm.

"I know nothing, sir," he gasped. "Nothing at all. Please, may I go? I—I . . . really, sir, I grow faint!"

"That's all right," Grey said pleasantly. "You may lie down on the bed if you can't stand up."

Dawes glanced at the bed, went white, and sat down heavily on the floor. Saw what was on the floor beside him and scrambled hurriedly to his feet, where he stood swaying and gulping.

Grey nodded at a stool, and Cherry propelled the little secretary, not ungently, onto it.

"What's he told you, Fettes?" Grey asked, turning back toward the bed. "Tom, we're going to wrap Mr. Warren up in the spread, then lay him on the floor and roll him up in the carpet. To prevent leakage."

"Right, me lord." Tom and Captain Cherry set gingerly about this process, while Grey walked over and stood looking down at Dawes.

"Pled ignorance, for the most part," Fettes said, joining Grey and giving Dawes a speculative look. "He did tell us that Derwent Warren had seduced a woman called Nancy Twelvetrees in London. Threw her over, though, and married the heiress to the Atherton fortune."

"Who had better sense than to accompany her husband to the West Indies, I take it? Yes. Did he know that Miss Twelvetrees and her brother had inherited a plantation on Jamaica, and were proposing to emigrate here?"

"No, sir." It was the first time Dawes had spoken, and his voice was little more than a croak. He cleared his throat and spoke more firmly. "He was entirely surprised to meet the Twelvetreeses at his first assembly."

"I daresay. Was the surprise mutual?"

"It was. Miss Twelvetrees went white, then red, then removed her shoe and set about the governor with the heel of it."

"I wish I'd seen that," Grey said, with real regret. "Right. Well, as you can see, the governor is no longer in need of your discretion. I, on the other hand, am in need of your loquacity. You can start by telling me why he was afraid of snakes."

"Oh." Dawes gnawed his lower lip. "I cannot be sure, you understand—"

"Speak up, you lump," growled Fettes, leaning menacingly over Dawes, who recoiled.

"I—I—" he stammered. "Truly, I don't know the details. But it—it had to do with a young woman. A young black woman. He—the governor, that is—women were something of a weakness for him . . ."

"And?" Grey prodded.

The young woman, it appeared, was a slave in the household. And not disposed to accept the governor's attentions. The governor was not accustomed to take no for an answer—and didn't. The young woman had vanished the next day, run away, and had not been recaptured as yet. But the day after, a black man in a turban and loincloth had come to King's House and had requested audience.

"He wasn't admitted, of course. But he wouldn't go away, either." Dawes shrugged. "Just squatted at the foot of the front steps and waited."

When Warren had at length emerged, the man had risen, stepped forward, and in formal tones, informed the governor that he was herewith cursed.

"Cursed?" said Grey, interested. "How?"

"Well, now, there my knowledge reaches its limits, sir," Dawes replied. He had recovered some of his self-confidence by now, and sat up a little. "For having pronounced the fact, he then proceeded to speak in an unfamiliar tongue—though I think some of it may have been Spanish, it wasn't all like that. I must suppose that he was, er, administering the curse, so to speak?"

"I'm sure I don't know." By now, Tom and Captain Cherry had completed their disagreeable task, and the governor reposed in an innocuous cocoon of carpeting. "I'm sorry, gentlemen, but there are no servants to assist us. We're going to take him down to the garden shed. Come, Mr. Dawes; you can be assistant pallbearer. And tell us on the way where the snakes come into it."

Panting and groaning, with the occasional near-slip, they manhandled the unwieldy bundle down the stairs. Mr. Dawes, making ineffectual grabs at the carpeting, was prodded by Captain Cherry into further discourse.

"Well, I *thought* that I caught the word 'snake' in the man's tirade," he said. "*Vivora*. That's the Spanish for 'viper.' And then . . . the snakes began to come."

Small snakes, large snakes. A snake was found in the governor's bath. Another appeared under the dining table—to the horror of a merchant's lady who was dining with the governor, and who had hysterics all over the dining room before fainting heavily across the table. Mr. Dawes appeared to find something amusing in this, and Grey, perspiring heavily, gave him a glare that returned him more soberly to his account.

"Every day, it seemed, and in different places. We had the house searched, repeatedly. But no one could—or would, perhaps—detect the source of the reptiles. And while no one was bitten, still the nervous strain of not knowing whether you would turn back your coverlet to discover something writhing amongst your bedding . . ."

"Quite. Ugh!" They paused and set down their burden. Grey wiped his forehead on his sleeve. "And how did you make the connection, Mr. Dawes, between this plague of snakes and Mr. Warren's mistreatment of the slave girl?"

Dawes looked surprised and pushed his spectacles back up his sweating nose.

"Oh, did I not say? The man—I was told later that he was an Obeah-man, whatever that may be—spoke her name, in the midst of his denunciation. Azeel, it was."

"I see. All right—ready? One, two, three—up!"

Dawes had given up any pretense of helping, but scampered down the garden path ahead of them to open the shed door. He had quite lost any lingering reticence and seemed anxious to provide any information he could.

"He did not tell me directly, but I believe he had begun to dream of snakes—and of the girl."

"How do—you know?" Grey grunted. "That's my foot, Major!"

"I heard him . . . er . . . speaking to himself. He had begun to drink rather heavily, you see. Quite understandable, under the circumstances, don't you think?"

Grey wished he could drink heavily, but had no breath left with which to say so.

There was a sudden cry of startlement from Tom, who had gone in to clear space in the shed, and all three officers dropped the carpet with a thump, reaching for nonexistent weapons.

"Me lord, me lord! Look who I found, a-hiding in the shed!" Tom was leaping up the path toward him, face abeam with happiness, the youth Rodrigo coming warily behind him. Grey's heart leapt at the sight, and he felt a most unaccustomed smile touch his face.

"Your servant, sah." Rodrigo, very timid, made a deep bow.

"I'm very pleased to see you, Rodrigo. Tell me—did you see anything of what passed here last night?"

The young man shuddered and turned his face away.

"No, sah," he said, so low-voiced Grey could barely hear him. "It was zombies. They . . . eat people. I heard them, but I know better than to look. I ran down into the garden and hid myself."

"You heard them?" Grey said sharply. "What did you hear, exactly?"

Rodrigo swallowed, and if it had been possible for a green tinge to show on skin such as his, he would undoubtedly have turned the shade of a sea turtle.

"Feet, sah," he said. "Bare feet. But they don't walk, step-step, like a person. They only shuffle, *sh-sh, sh-sh.*" He made small pushing motions with his hands in illustration, and Grey felt a slight lifting of the hairs on the back of his neck.

"Could you tell how many . . . men . . . there were?"

Rodrigo shook his head.

"More than two, from the sound."

Tom pushed a little forward, round face intent.

"Was there anybody else with 'em, d'you think? Somebody with a regular step, I mean?"

Rodrigo looked startled, and then horrified.

"You mean a *houngan*? I don't know." He shrugged. "Maybe. I didn't hear shoes. But . . ."

"Oh. Because—" Tom stopped abruptly, glanced at Grey, and coughed. "Oh."

Despite more questions, this was all that Rodrigo could contribute, and so the carpet was picked up again—this time, with the servant helping—and bestowed in its temporary resting place. Fettes and Cherry chipped away a bit more at Dawes, but the secretary was unable to offer any further information regarding the governor's activities, let alone speculate as to what malign force had brought about his demise.

"Have you heard of zombies before, Mr. Dawes?" Grey inquired, mopping his face with the remains of his handkerchief.

"Er . . . yes," the secretary replied cautiously. "But surely you don't believe what the servant . . . oh, surely not!" He cast an appalled glance at the shed.

"Are zombies in fact reputed to devour human flesh?"

Dawes resumed his sickly pallor.

"Well, yes. But . . . oh, dear!"

"Sums it up nicely," muttered Cherry, under his breath. "I take it you don't mean to make a public announcement of the governor's demise, then, sir?"

"You are correct, Captain. I don't want public panic over a plague of zombies at large in Spanish Town, whether that is actually the case or not. Mr. Dawes, I believe we need trouble you no more for the moment; you are excused." He watched the secretary stumble off before beckoning his officers closer. Tom moved a little away, discreet as always, and took Rodrigo with him.

"Have you discovered anything else that might have bearing on the present circumstance?"

They glanced at each other, and Fettes nodded to Cherry, wheezing gently. Cherry strongly resembled that eponymous fruit, but being younger and more slender than Fettes, had more breath.

"Yes, sir. I went looking for Ludgate, the old superintendent. Didn't find him—he's buggered off to Canada, they said—but I got a right earful concerning the present superintendent."

Grey groped for a moment for the name.

"Cresswell?"

"That's him."

"Corruption and peculations" appeared to sum up the subject of Captain Cresswell's tenure as superintendent very well, according to Cherry's informants in Spanish Town and King's Town. Amongst other abuses, he had arranged trade between the maroons on the uplands and the merchants below, in the form of bird skins, snakeskins, and other exotica; timber from the upland forests; and so on—but had, by report, accepted payment on behalf of the maroons but failed to deliver it.

"Had he any part in the arrest of the two young maroons accused of theft?"

Cherry's teeth flashed in a grin.

"Odd you should ask, sir. Yes, they said—well, some of them did—that the two young men had come down to complain about Cresswell's behavior, but the governor wouldn't see them. They were heard to declare they would take back their goods by force—so when a substantial chunk of the contents of one warehouse went missing, it was assumed that was what they'd done. They—the maroons—insisted they hadn't touched the stuff, but Cresswell seized the opportunity and had them arrested for theft."

Grey closed his eyes, enjoying the momentary coolness of a breeze from the sea.

"The governor wouldn't see the young men, you said. Is there any suggestion of an improper connection between the governor and Captain Cresswell?"

"Oh, yes," said Fettes, rolling his eyes. "No proof yet—but we haven't been looking long, either."

"I see. And we still do not know the whereabouts of Captain Cresswell?"

Cherry and Fettes shook their heads in unison.

"The general conclusion is that Accompong scragged him," Cherry said.

"Who?"

"Oh. Sorry, sir," Cherry apologized. "That's the name of the maroons' headman, so they say. *Captain* Accompong, he calls himself, if you please." Cherry's lips twisted a little.

Grey sighed.

"All right. No reports of any further depredations by the maroons, by whatever name?"

"Not unless you count murdering the governor," said Fettes.

"Actually," Grey said slowly, "I don't think that the maroons are responsible for this particular death." He was somewhat surprised to hear himself say so, in truth—and yet he found that he *did* think it.

Fettes blinked, this being as close to an expression of astonishment as he ever got, and Cherry looked openly skeptical. Grey did not choose to go into the matter of Mrs. Abernathy, nor yet to explain his conclusions about the maroons' disinclination for violence. Strange, he thought. He had heard Captain Accompong's name only moments before, but with that name, his thoughts began to coalesce around a shadowy figure. Suddenly, there was a mind out there, someone with whom he might engage.

In battle, the personality and temperament of the commanding officer was nearly as important as the number of troops he commanded. So. He needed to know more about Captain Accompong, but that could wait for the moment.

He nodded to Tom, who approached respectfully, Rodrigo behind him.

"Tell them what you discovered, Tom."

Tom cleared his throat and folded his hands at his waist.

"Well, we . . . er . . . disrobed the governor"—Fettes flinched, and Tom cleared his throat again before going on—"and had a close look. And the long and the short of it, sir—and sir—" he added, with a nod to Cherry, "—is that Governor Warren was stabbed in the back."

Both officers looked blank.

"But—the place is covered with blood and filth and nastiness," Cherry protested. "It smells like that place where they put the bloaters they drag out of the Thames!"

"Footprints," Fettes said, giving Tom a faintly accusing look. "There were footprints. Big, bloody, *bare* footprints."

"I do not deny that something objectionable was present in that room," Grey said dryly. "But whoever—or whatever—gnawed the governor probably did not kill him. He was almost certainly dead when the . . . er . . . subsequent damage occurred."

Rodrigo's eyes were huge. Fettes was heard to observe under his breath that he would be damned, but both Fettes and Cherry were good men, and did not argue with Grey's conclusions, any more than they had taken issue with his order to hide Warren's body—they could plainly perceive the desirability of suppressing rumor of a plague of zombies.

"The point, gentlemen, is that after several months of incident, there has been nothing for the last month. Perhaps Mr. Warren's death is meant to be incitement—but if it was not the work of the maroons, then the question is—what are the maroons waiting for?"

Tom lifted his head, eyes wide.

"Why, me lord, I'd say—they're waiting for *you*. What else?"

WHAT ELSE, INDEED. WHY HAD HE NOT SEEN THAT AT ONCE? OF COURSE Tom was right. The maroons' protest had gone unanswered, their complaint unremedied. So they had set out to attract attention in the most noticeable—if not the best—way open to them. Time had passed, nothing was done in response—and then they had heard that soldiers were coming. Lieutenant Colonel Grey had now appeared. Naturally, they were waiting to see what he would do.

What had he done so far? Sent troops to guard the plantations that were the most likely targets of a fresh attack. That was not likely to encourage the maroons to abandon their present plan of action, though it might cause them to direct their efforts elsewhere.

He walked to and fro in the wilderness of the King's House garden, thinking, but there were few alternatives.

He summoned Fettes and informed him that he, Fettes, was, until further notice, acting governor of the island of Jamaica.

Fettes looked more like a block of wood than usual.

"Yes, sir," he said. "If I might ask, sir . . . where are you going?"

"I'm going to talk to Captain Accompong."

"ALONE, SIR?" FETTES WAS APPALLED. "SURELY YOU CANNOT MEAN TO GO up there *alone*!"

"I won't be," Grey assured him. "I'm taking my valet, and the servant boy. I'll need someone who can translate for me, if necessary."

Seeing the mulish cast settling upon Fettes's brow, he sighed.

"To go there in force, Major, is to invite battle, and that is not what I want."

"No, sir," Fettes said dubiously, "but surely—a proper escort . . . !"

"No, Major." Grey was courteous, but firm. "I wish to make it clear that I am coming to *speak* with Captain Accompong, and nothing more. I go alone."

"Yes, sir." Fettes was beginning to look like a block of wood that someone had set about with a hammer and chisel.

"As you wish, sir."

Grey nodded and turned to go into the house, but then paused and turned back.

"Oh, there is one thing that you might do for me, Major."

Fettes brightened slightly.

"Yes, sir?"

"Find me a particularly excellent hat, would you? With gold lace, if possible."

THEY RODE FOR NEARLY TWO DAYS BEFORE THEY HEARD THE FIRST OF THE horns. A high, melancholy sound in the twilight, it seemed far away, and only a sort of metallic note made Grey sure that it was not in fact the cry of some large, exotic bird.

"Maroons," Rodrigo said under his breath, and crouched a little, as though trying to avoid notice, even in the saddle. "That's how they talk to each other. Every group has a horn; they all sound different."

Another long, mournful falling note. Was it the same horn? Grey wondered. Or a second, answering the first?

"Talk to each other, you say. Can you tell what they're saying?"

Rodrigo had straightened up a little in his saddle, putting a hand automatically behind him to steady the leather box that held the most ostentatious hat available in Spanish Town.

"Yes, sah. They're telling each other we're here."

Tom muttered something under his own breath that sounded like, "Could have told you that meself for free," but declined to repeat or expand upon his sentiment when invited to do so.

They camped for the night under the shelter of a tree, so tired that they merely sat in silence as they ate, watching the nightly rainstorm come in over the sea, then crawled into the canvas tent Grey had brought. The young men fell asleep instantly to the pattering of rain above them.

Grey lay awake for a little, fighting tiredness, his mind reaching upward. He had worn uniform, though not full dress, so that his identity would be apparent. And his gambit so far had been accepted; they had not been challenged, let alone attacked. Apparently Captain Accompong would receive him.

Then what? He wasn't sure. He did hope that he might recover his men—the two sentries who had disappeared on the night of Governor Warren's murder. Their bodies had not been discovered, nor had any of their uniform or equipment turned up—and Captain Cherry had had the whole of Spanish Town *and* King's Town turned over in the search. If they had been taken alive, though, that reinforced his impression of Accompong—and gave him some hope that this rebellion might be resolved in some manner not involving a prolonged military campaign fought through jungles and rocks, and ending in chains and executions. But if . . . sleep overcame him, and he lapsed into incongruous dreams of bright birds, whose feathers brushed his cheeks as they flew silently past.

Grey woke in the morning to the feel of sun on his face. He blinked for a moment, confused, and then sat up. He was alone. Truly alone.

He scrambled to his feet, heart thumping, reaching for his dagger. It was there in his belt, but that was the only thing still where it should be. His horse—all the horses—were gone. So was his tent. So was the pack mule and its panniers. And so were Tom and Rodrigo.

He saw this at once—the blankets in which they'd lain the night before were still there, tumbled into the bushes—but he called for them anyway, again and again, until his throat was raw with shouting.

From somewhere high above him, he heard one of the horns, a long drawn-out hoot that sounded mocking to his ears.

He understood the present message instantly. *You took two of ours; we have taken two of yours.*

"And you don't think I'll come and get them?" he shouted upward into the dizzying sea of swaying green. "Tell Captain Accompong I'm coming! I'll have my young men back, and back *safe*—or I'll have his head!"

Blood rose in his face, and he thought he might burst, but had better sense than to punch something, which was his very strong urge. He was alone; he couldn't afford to damage himself. He had to arrive among the maroons with everything that still remained to him, if he meant to rescue Tom and resolve the rebellion—and he did mean to rescue Tom, no matter what. It didn't matter that this might be a trap; he was going.

He calmed himself with an effort of will, stamping round in a circle in his stockinged feet until he had worked off most of his anger. That was when he saw them, sitting neatly side by side under a thorny bush.

They'd left him his boots. They did expect him to come.

HE WALKED FOR THREE DAYS. HE DIDN'T BOTHER TRYING TO FOLLOW A trail; he wasn't a particularly skilled tracker, and finding any trace among the rocks and dense growth was a vain hope in any case. He simply climbed, finding passage where he could, and listened for the horns.

The maroons hadn't left him any supplies, but that didn't matter. There were numerous small streams and pools, and while he was hungry, he didn't starve. Here and there he found trees of the sort he had seen at Twelvetrees, festooned with small reddish fruits. If the parrots ate them, he reasoned, the fruits must be at least minimally comestible. They were mouth-puckeringly sour, but they didn't poison him.

The horns had increased in frequency since dawn. There were now three or four of them, signaling back and forth. Clearly, he was getting close. To what, he didn't know, but close.

He paused, looking upward. The ground had begun to level out here; there were open spots in the jungle, and in one of these small clearings he saw what were plainly crops: mounds of curling vines that might be yams, beanpoles, the big yellow flowers of squash or gourds. At the far edge of the field, a tiny curl of smoke rose against the green. Close.

He took off the crude hat he had woven from palm leaves against the strong sun, and wiped his face on the tail of his shirt. That was as much preparation as it was possible to make. The gaudy, gold-laced hat he'd brought was presumably still in its box—wherever that was. He put his palm-leaf hat back on and limped toward the curl of smoke.

As he walked, he became aware of people, fading slowly into view. Dark-skinned people, dressed in ragged clothing, coming out of the jungle to watch him with big, curious eyes. He'd found the maroons.

A SMALL GROUP OF MEN TOOK HIM FARTHER UPWARD. IT WAS JUST BEFORE sunset, and the sunlight slanted gold and lavender through the trees, when they led him into a large clearing, where there was a compound consisting of a number of huts. One of the men accompanying Grey shouted, and from the largest hut emerged a man who announced himself with no particular ceremony as Captain Accompong.

Captain Accompong was a surprise. He was very short, very fat, and hunchbacked, his body so distorted that he did not so much walk as proceed by a sort of sideways lurching. He was attired in the remnants of a splendid coat, now buttonless, and with its gold lace half missing, the cuffs filthy with wear.

He peered from under the drooping brim of a ragged felt hat, eyes bright in its shadow. His face was round and much creased, lacking a good many teeth—but giving the impression of great shrewdness, and perhaps good humor. Grey hoped so.

"Who are you?" Accompong asked, peering up at Grey like a toad under a rock.

Everyone in the clearing very plainly knew his identity; they shifted from foot to foot and nudged each other, grinning. He paid no attention to them, though, and bowed very correctly to Accompong.

"I am the man responsible for the two young men who were taken on the mountain. I have come to get them back—along with my soldiers."

A certain amount of scornful hooting ensued, and Accompong let it go on for a few moments before lifting his hand.

"You say so? Why you think I have anything to do with these young men?"

"I do not say that you do. But I know a great leader when I see one—and I know that you can help me to find my young men. If you will."

"Phu!" Accompong's face creased into a gap-toothed smile. "You think you flatter me, and I help?"

Grey could feel some of the smaller children stealing up behind him; he heard muffled giggles, but didn't turn round.

"I ask for your help. But I do not offer you only my good opinion in return."

A small hand reached under his coat and rudely tweaked his buttock. There was an explosion of laughter, and mad scampering behind him. He didn't move.

Accompong chewed slowly at something in the back of his capacious mouth, one eye narrowed.

"Yes? What do you offer, then? Gold?" One corner of his thick lips turned up.

"Do you have any need of gold?" Grey asked. The children were whispering and giggling again behind him, but he also heard shushing noises from some of the women—they were getting interested. Maybe.

Accompong thought for a moment, then shook his head.

"No. What else you offer?"

"What do you want?" Grey parried.

"Captain Cresswell's head!" said a woman's voice, very clearly. There was a shuffle and smack, a man's voice rebuking in Spanish, a heated crackle of women's voices in return. Accompong let it go on for a minute or two, then raised one hand. Silence fell abruptly.

It lengthened. Grey could feel the pulse beating in his temples, slow and laboring. Ought he to speak? He came as a supplicant already; to speak now would be to lose face, as the Chinese put it. He waited.

"The governor is dead?" Accompong asked at last.

"Yes. How do you know of it?"

"You mean, did I kill him?" The bulbous yellowed eyes creased.

"No," Grey said patiently. "I mean—do you know how he died?"

"The zombies kill him." The answer came readily—and seriously. There was no hint of humor in those eyes now.

"Do you know who made the zombies?"

A most extraordinary shudder ran through Accompong, from his ragged hat to the horny soles of his bare feet.

"You do know," Grey said softly, raising a hand to prevent the automatic denial. "But it wasn't you, was it? Tell me."

The Captain shifted uneasily from one buttock to the other, but didn't reply. His eyes darted toward one of the huts, and after a moment, he raised his voice, calling something in the maroons' patois, wherein Grey thought he caught the word *Azeel*. He was puzzled momentarily, finding the word familiar, but not knowing why. Then the young woman emerged from the hut, ducking under the low doorway, and he remembered.

Azeel. The young slave woman whom the governor had taken and misused, whose flight from King's House had presaged the plague of serpents.

Seeing her as she came forward, he couldn't help but see what had inspired the governor's lust, though it was not a beauty that spoke to him. She was small, but not inconsequential. Perfectly proportioned, she stood like a queen, and her eyes burned as she turned her face to Grey. There was anger in her face—but also something like a terrible despair.

"Captain Accompong says that I will tell you what I know—what happened."

Grey bowed to her.

"I should be most grateful to hear it, madam."

She looked hard at him, obviously suspecting mockery, but he'd meant it, and she saw that. She gave a brief, nearly imperceptible nod.

"Well, then. You know that beast"—she spat neatly on the ground—"forced me? And I left his house?"

"Yes. Whereupon you sought out an Obeah-man, who invoked a curse of snakes upon Governor Warren, am I correct?"

She glared at him, and gave a short nod. "The snake is wisdom, and that man had none. None!"

"I think you're quite right about that. But the zombies?" There was a general intake of breath among the crowd. Fear, distaste—and something else. The girl's lips pressed together, and tears glimmered in her large dark eyes.

"Rodrigo," she said, and choked on the name. "He—and I—" Her jaw clamped hard; she couldn't speak without weeping, and would not weep in front of him. He cast down his gaze to the ground, to give her what privacy he could. He could hear her breathing through her nose, a soft, snuffling noise. Finally, she heaved a deep breath.

"He was not satisfied. He went to a *houngan*. The Obeah-man warned him, but—" Her entire face contorted with the effort to hold in her feelings. "The *houngan*. He had zombies. Rodrigo paid him to kill the beast."

Grey felt as though he had been punched in the chest. Rodrigo. Rodrigo, hiding in the garden shed at the sound of shuffling bare feet in the night—or Rodrigo, warning his fellow servants to leave, then unbolting the doors, following a silent horde of ruined men in clotted rags up the stairs . . . or running up before them, in apparent alarm, summoning the sentries, drawing them outside, where they could be taken.

"And where is Rodrigo now?" Grey asked sharply. There was a deep silence in the clearing. None of the people even glanced at each other; every eye was fixed on the ground. He took a step toward Accompong. "Captain?"

Accompong stirred. He raised his misshapen face to Grey, and a hand toward one of the huts.

"We do not like zombies, Colonel," he said. "They are unclean. And to kill a man using them . . . this is a great wrong. You understand this?"

"I do, yes."

"This man, Rodrigo—" Accompong hesitated, searching out words. "He is not one of us. He comes from Hispaniola. They . . . do such things there."

"Such things as make zombies? But presumably it happens here as well." Grey spoke automatically; his mind was working furiously in light of these revelations. The thing that had attacked him in his room—it would be no great trick for a man to smear himself with grave dirt and wear rotted clothing . . .

"Not among us," Accompong said, very firmly. "Before I say more, my

Colonel—do you believe what you have heard so far? Do you believe that we—that *I*—had nothing to do with the death of your governor?"

Grey considered that one for a moment. There was no evidence; only the story of the slave girl. Still . . . he did have evidence. The evidence of his own observations and conclusions regarding the nature of the man who sat before him.

"Yes," he said abruptly. "So?"

"Will your king believe it?"

Well, not as baldly stated, no, Grey thought. The matter would need a little tactful handling . . . Accompong snorted faintly, seeing the thoughts cross his face.

"This man, Rodrigo. He has done us great harm by taking his private revenge in a way that . . . that . . ." He groped for the word.

"That incriminates you," Grey finished for him. "Yes, I see that. What have you done with him?"

"I cannot give this man to you," Accompong said at last. His thick lips pressed together briefly, but he met Grey's eye. "He is dead."

The shock hit Grey like a musket ball. A thump that knocked him off balance, and the sickening knowledge of irrevocable damage done.

"How?" he said, short and sharp. "What happened to him?"

The clearing was still silent. Accompong stared at the ground in front of him. After a long moment, a sigh, a whisper, drifted from the crowd.

"*Zombie.*"

"Where?" he barked. "Where is he? Bring him to me. Now!"

The crowd shrank away from the hut, and a sort of moan ran through them. Women snatched up their children, pushed back so hastily that they stepped on the feet of their companions. The door opened.

"*Anda!*" said a voice from inside. "Walk," it meant, in Spanish. Grey's numbed mind had barely registered this when the darkness inside the hut changed, and a form appeared at the door.

It was Rodrigo. But then again—it wasn't. The glowing skin had gone pale and muddy, almost waxen. The firm, soft mouth hung loose, and the eyes—oh, God, the eyes! They were sunken, glassy, and showed no comprehension, no movement, not the least sense of awareness. They were a dead man's eyes. And yet . . . he walked.

This was the worst of all. Gone was every trace of Rodrigo's springy grace, his elegance. This creature moved stiffly, shambling, feet dragging, almost lurching from foot to foot. Its clothing hung upon its bones like a scarecrow's rags, smeared with clay and stained with dreadful liquids. The odor of putrefaction reached Grey's nostrils, and he gagged.

"Alto," said the voice, softly, and Rodrigo stopped abruptly, arms hanging like a marionette's. Grey looked up, then, at the hut. A tall, dark man stood in the doorway, burning eyes fixed on Grey.

The sun was all but down; the clearing lay in deep shadow, and Grey felt a convulsive shiver go through him. He lifted his chin and, ignoring the horrid thing standing stiff before him, addressed the tall man.

"Who are you, sir?"

"Call me Ishmael," said the man, in an odd, lilting accent. He stepped out of the hut, and Grey was conscious of a general shrinking, everyone pulling away from the man, as though he suffered from some deadly contagion. Grey wanted to step back, too, but didn't.

"You did . . . this?" Grey asked, flicking a hand at the remnant of Rodrigo.

"I was paid to do it, yes." Ishmael's eyes flicked toward Accompong, then back to Grey.

"And Governor Warren—you were paid to kill him as well, were you? By this man?" A brief nod at Rodrigo; he could not bear to look directly at him.

The zombies think they're dead, and so does everyone else.

A frown drew Ishmael's brows together, and with the change of expression, Grey noticed that the man's face was scarred, with apparent deliberation, long channels cut in cheeks and forehead. He shook his head.

"No. This"—he nodded at Rodrigo—"paid me to bring my zombies. He says to me that he wishes to terrify a man. And zombies will do that," he added, with a wolfish smile. "But when I brought them into the room and the *buckra* turned to flee, this one"—the flick of a hand toward Rodrigo—"he sprang upon him and stabbed him. The man fell dead, and Rodrigo then *ordered* me"—his tone of voice made it clear what he thought of anyone ordering him to do anything—"to make my zombies feed upon him." He shrugged. "Why not? He was dead."

Grey swung round to Captain Accompong, who had sat silently through this testimony.

"And then you paid this—this—"

"Houngan," Ishmael put in helpfully.

"—to do *that*?!" He pointed at Rodrigo, and his voice shook with outraged horror.

"Justice," said Accompong, with simple dignity. "Don't you think so?"

Grey found himself temporarily bereft of speech. While he groped for something possible to say, the headman turned to a lieutenant and said, "Bring the other one."

"The *other—*" Grey began, but before he could speak further, there was another stir among the crowd, and from one of the huts, a maroon emerged, leading another man by a rope around his neck. The man was wild-eyed and filthy, his hands bound behind him, but his clothes had originally been very fine. Grey shook his head, trying to dispel the remnants of horror that clung to his mind.

"Captain Cresswell, I presume?" he said.

"Save me!" the man panted, and collapsed on his knees at Grey's feet. "I beg you, sir—whoever you are—save me!"

Grey rubbed a hand wearily over his face and looked down at the erstwhile superintendent, then at Accompong.

"Does he need saving?" he asked. "I don't want to—I know what he's done—but it *is* my duty."

Accompong pursed his lips, thinking.

"You know what he is, you say. If I give him to you—what would you do with him?"

At least there was an answer to that one.

"Charge him with his crimes, and send him to England for trial. If he is convicted, he would be imprisoned—or possibly hang. What would happen to him here?" he asked curiously.

Accompong turned his head, looking thoughtfully at the *houngan*, who grinned unpleasantly.

"No!" gasped Cresswell. "No, please! Don't let him take me! I can't—I can't—oh, GOD!" He glanced, appalled, at the stiff figure of Rodrigo, then fell face first onto the ground at Grey's feet, weeping convulsively.

Numbed with shock, Grey thought for an instant that it *would* probably resolve the rebellion . . . but no. Cresswell couldn't, and neither could he.

"Right," said Grey, and swallowed before turning to Accompong. "He *is* an Englishman, and as I said, it's my duty to see that he's subject to English laws. I must therefore ask that you give him into my custody—and take my word that I will see he receives justice. Our sort of justice," he added, giving the evil look back to the *houngan*.

"And if I don't?" Accompong asked, blinking genially at him.

"Well, I suppose I'll have to fight you for him," Grey said. "But I'm bloody tired and I really don't want to." Accompong laughed at this, and Grey followed swiftly up with, "I will, of course, appoint a new superintendent—and given the importance of the office, I will bring the new superintendent here, so that you may meet him and approve of him."

"If I don't approve?"

"There are a bloody lot of Englishmen on Jamaica," Grey said, impatient. "You're bound to like *one* of them."

Accompong laughed out loud, his little round belly jiggling under his coat.

"I like you, Colonel," he said. "You want to be superintendent?"

Grey suppressed the natural answer to this and instead said, "Alas, I have a duty to the army which prevents my accepting the offer, amazingly generous though it is." He coughed. "You have my word that I will find you a suitable candidate, though."

The tall lieutenant who stood behind Captain Accompong lifted his voice and said something skeptical in a patois that Grey didn't understand—but from the man's attitude, his glance at Cresswell, and the murmur of agreement that greeted his remark, he had no trouble in deducing what had been said.

What is the word of an Englishman worth?

Grey gave Cresswell, groveling and sniveling at his feet, a look of profound disfavor. It would serve the man right if—then he caught the faint reek of corruption wafting from Rodrigo's still form, and shuddered. No, nobody deserved *that.*

Putting aside the question of Cresswell's fate for the moment, Grey turned to the question that had been in the forefront of his mind since he'd come in sight of that first curl of smoke.

"My men," he said. "I want to see my men. Bring them out to me, please. At once." He didn't raise his voice, but he knew how to make a command sound like one.

Accompong tilted his head a little to one side, as though considering, but then waved a hand, casually. There was a stirring in the crowd, an expectation. A turning of heads, then bodies, and Grey looked toward the rocks where their focus lay. An explosion of shouts, catcalls, and laughter, and the two soldiers and Tom Byrd came out of the defile. They were roped together by the necks, their ankles hobbled and hands tied, and they shuffled awkwardly, bumping into one another, turning their heads to and fro like chickens, in a vain effort to avoid the spitting and the small clods of earth thrown at them.

Grey's outrage at this treatment was overwhelmed by his relief at seeing Tom and his young soldiers, all plainly scared, but uninjured. He stepped forward at once, so they could see him, and his heart was wrung by the pathetic relief that lighted their faces.

"Now, then," he said, smiling. "You didn't think I would leave you, surely?"

"*I* didn't, me lord," Tom said stoutly, already yanking at the rope about his neck. "I told 'em you'd be right along, the minute you got your boots on!" He glared at the little boys, naked but for shirts, who were dancing round him and the soldiers, shouting, *"Buckra! Buckra!"* and making not-quite-pretend jabs at the men's genitals with sticks. "Can you make 'em leave off that filthy row, me lord? They been at it ever since we got here."

Grey looked at Accompong and politely raised his brows. The headman barked a few words of something not quite Spanish, and the boys reluctantly fell back, though they continued to make faces and rude arm-pumping gestures.

Captain Accompong put out a hand to his lieutenant, who hauled the fat little headman to his feet. He dusted fastidiously at the skirts of his coat, then walked slowly around the little group of prisoners, stopping at Cresswell. He contemplated the man, who had now curled himself into a ball, then looked up at Grey.

"Do you know what a *loa* is, my Colonel?" he asked quietly.

"I do, yes," Grey replied warily. "Why?"

"There is a spring, quite close. It comes from deep in the earth, where the *loas* live, and sometimes they will come forth and speak. If you will have back your men—I ask you to go there, and speak with whatever *loa* may find you. Thus we will have truth, and I can decide."

Grey stood for a moment, looking back and forth among the fat old man; Cresswell, his back heaving with silent sobs; and the young girl Azeel, who had turned her head to hide the hot tears coursing down her cheeks. He didn't look at Tom. There didn't seem much choice.

"All right," he said, turning back to Accompong. "Let me go now, then."

Accompong shook his head.

"In the morning," he said. "You do not want to go there at night."

"Yes, I do," Grey said. "Now."

"QUITE CLOSE" WAS A RELATIVE TERM, APPARENTLY. GREY THOUGHT IT must be near midnight by the time they arrived at the spring—Grey, the *houngan* Ishmael, and four maroons bearing torches and armed with the long cane knives called machetes.

Accompong hadn't told him it was a *hot* spring. There was a rocky overhang, and what looked like a cavern beneath it, from which steam drifted out like dragon's breath. His attendants—or guards, as one chose to look at it—halted as one, a safe distance away. He glanced at them for instruction, but they were silent.

He'd been wondering what the *houngan*'s role in this peculiar undertaking was. The man was carrying a battered canteen; now he uncorked this and handed it to Grey. It smelled hot, though the tin of the heavy canteen was cool in his hands. Raw rum, he thought, from the sweetly searing smell of it—and doubtless a few other things.

. . . Herbs. Ground bones—bits o' other things. But the main thing, the one thing ye must have, is the liver of a fugu fish . . . They don't come back from it, ye ken. The poison damages their brains . . .

"Now we drink," Ishmael said. "And we enter the cave."

"Both of us?"

"Yes. I will summon the *loa*. I am a priest of Damballa." The man spoke seriously, with none of the hostility or smirking he had displayed earlier. Grey noticed, though, that their escort kept a safe distance from the *houngan*, and a wary eye upon him.

"I see," said Grey, though he didn't. "This . . . Damballa. He—or she—?"

"Damballa is the great serpent," Ishmael said, and smiled, teeth flashing briefly in the torchlight. "I am told that snakes speak to you." He nodded at the canteen. "Drink."

Repressing the urge to say "You first," Grey raised the canteen to his lips and drank, slowly. It was *very* raw rum, with a strange taste, sweetly acrid, rather like the taste of fruit ripened to the edge of rot. He tried to keep any thought of Mrs. Abernathy's casual description of *afile* powder out of mind—she hadn't, after all, mentioned how the stuff might taste. And surely Ishmael wouldn't simply poison him . . . ? He hoped not.

He sipped the liquid until a slight shift of the *houngan*'s posture told him it was enough, then handed the canteen to Ishmael, who drank from it without hesitation. He supposed he should find this comforting, but his head was beginning to swim in an unpleasant manner, his heartbeat throbbing audibly in his ears, and something odd was happening to his vision; it went intermittently dark, then returned with a brief flash of light, and when he looked at one of the torches, it had a halo of colored rings around it.

He barely heard the *clunk* of the canteen, dropped on the ground, and watched, blinking, as the *houngan*'s white-clad back wavered before him. A dark blur of face as Ishmael turned to him.

"Come." The man disappeared into the veil of water.

"Right," he muttered. "Well, then . . ." He removed his boots, unbuckled the knee bands of his breeches, and peeled off his stockings. Then he shucked his coat and stepped cautiously into the steaming water.

It was hot enough to make him gasp, but within a few moments he had got used to the temperature and made his way across a shallow, steaming pool toward the mouth of the cavern, shifting gravel hard under his bare feet. He heard whispering from his guards, but no one offered any alternate suggestions.

Water poured from the overhang, but not in the manner of a true waterfall; slender streams, like jagged teeth. The guards had pegged the torches into the ground at the edge of the spring; the flames danced like rainbows in the drizzle of the falling water as he passed beneath the overhang.

The hot, wet air pressed his lungs and made it hard to breathe. After a few moments, he couldn't feel any difference between his skin and the moist air through which he walked; it was as though he had melted into the darkness of the cavern.

And it *was* dark. Completely. A faint glow came from behind him, but he could see nothing at all before him, and was obliged to feel his way, one hand on the rough rock wall. The sound of falling water grew fainter, replaced by the heavy thump of his own heartbeat, struggling against the pressure on his chest. Once he stopped and pressed his fingers against his eyelids, taking comfort in the colored patterns that appeared there; he wasn't blind, then. When he opened his eyes again, though, the darkness was still complete.

He thought the walls were narrowing—he could touch them on both sides by stretching out his arms—and had a nightmare moment when he seemed to *feel* them drawing in upon him. He forced himself to breathe, a deep, explosive gasp, and forced the illusion back.

"Stop there." The voice was a whisper. He stopped.

There was silence, for what seemed a long time.

"Come forward," said the whisper, seeming suddenly quite near him. "There is dry land, just before you."

He shuffled forward, felt the floor of the cave rise beneath him, and stepped out carefully onto bare rock. Walked slowly forward until again the voice bade him stop.

Silence. He thought he could make out breathing, but wasn't sure; the sound of the water was still faintly audible in the distance. *All right,* he thought. *Come along, then.*

It hadn't been precisely an invitation, but what came into his mind was

Mrs. Abernathy's intent green eyes, staring at him as she said, *"I see a great, huge snake, lyin' on your shoulders, Colonel."*

With a convulsive shudder, he realized that he felt a weight on his shoulders. Not a dead weight, but something live. It moved, just barely.

"Jesus," he whispered, and thought he heard the ghost of a laugh from somewhere in the cave. He stiffened himself and fought back against the mental image, for surely this was nothing more than imagination, fueled by rum. Sure enough, the illusion of green eyes vanished—but the weight rested on him still, though he couldn't tell whether it lay upon his shoulders or his mind.

"So," said the low voice, sounding surprised. "The *loa* has come already. The snakes *do* like you, *buckra*."

"And if they do?" he asked. He spoke in a normal tone of voice; his words echoed from the walls around him.

The voice chuckled briefly, and he felt rather than heard movement nearby, the rustle of limbs and a soft thump as something struck the floor near his right foot. His head felt immense, throbbing with rum, and waves of heat pulsed through him, though the depths of the cave were cool.

"See if this snake likes you, *buckra*," the voice invited. "Pick it up."

He couldn't see a thing, but slowly moved his foot, feeling his way over the silty floor. His toes touched something and he stopped abruptly. Whatever he had touched moved abruptly, recoiling from him. Then he felt the tiny flicker of a snake's tongue on his toe, tasting him.

Oddly, the sensation steadied him. Surely this wasn't his friend the tiny yellow constrictor—but it was a serpent much like that one in general size, so far as he could tell. Nothing to fear from that.

"Pick it up," the voice invited him. "The krait will tell us if you speak the truth."

"Will he, indeed?" Grey said dryly. "How?"

The voice laughed, and he thought he heard two or three more chuckling behind it—but perhaps it was only echoes.

"If you die . . . you lied."

He gave a small, contemptuous snort. There were no venomous snakes on Jamaica. He cupped his hand and bent at the knee, but hesitated. Venomous or not, he had an instinctive aversion to being bitten by a snake. And how did he know how the man—or men—sitting in the shadows would take it if the thing *did* bite him?

"I trust this snake," said the voice softly. "Krait comes with me from Africa. Long time now."

Grey's knees straightened abruptly. Africa! Now he placed the name, and cold sweat broke out on his face. *Krait.* A fucking *African* krait. Gwynne had had one. Small, no bigger than the circumference of a man's little finger. "Bloody deadly," Gwynne had crooned, stroking the thing's back with the tip of a goose quill—an attention to which the snake, a slender, nondescript brown thing, had seemed oblivious.

This one was squirming languorously over the top of Grey's foot; he had to restrain a strong urge to kick it away and stamp on it. What the devil was it about him that attracted *snakes*, of all ungodly things? He supposed it could be worse; it might be cockroaches . . . he instantly felt a hideous crawling sensation upon his forearms, and rubbed them hard, reflexively, seeing, yes, he bloody *saw* them, here in the dark, thorny jointed legs and wriggling, inquisitive antennae brushing his skin.

He might have cried out. Someone laughed.

If he thought at all, he couldn't do it. He stooped and snatched the thing and, rising, hurled it into the darkness. There was a yelp and a sudden scrabbling, and then a brief, shocked scream.

He stood panting and trembling from reaction, checking and rechecking his hand—but felt no pain, could find no puncture wounds. The scream had been succeeded by a low stream of unintelligible curses, punctuated by the deep gasps of a man in terror. The voice of the *houngan*—if that was who it was—came urgently, followed by another voice, doubtful, fearful. Behind him, before him? He had no sense of direction anymore.

Something brushed past him, the heaviness of a body, and he fell against the wall of the cave, scraping his arm. He welcomed the pain; it was something to cling to, something real.

More urgency in the depths of the cave, sudden silence. And then a swishing *thunk!* as something struck hard into flesh, and the sheared-copper smell of fresh blood came strong over the scent of hot rock and rushing water. No further sound.

He was sitting on the muddy floor of the cave; he could feel the cool dirt under him. He pressed his hands flat against it, getting his bearings. After a moment, he heaved himself to his feet and stood, swaying and dizzy.

"I don't lie," he said, into the dark. "And I *will* have my men."

Dripping with sweat and water, he turned back, toward the rainbows.

THE SUN HAD BARELY RISEN WHEN HE CAME BACK INTO THE MOUNTAIN compound. The smoke of cooking fires hung among the huts, and the smell of food made his stomach clench painfully, but all that could wait. He strode as well as he might—his feet were so badly blistered that he hadn't been able to get his boots back on, and had walked back barefoot, over rocks and thorns—to the largest hut, where Captain Accompong sat placidly waiting for him.

Tom and the soldiers were there, too; no longer roped together, but still bound, kneeling by the fire. And Cresswell, a little way apart, looking wretched, but at least upright.

Accompong looked at one of his lieutenants, who stepped forward with a big cane knife and cut the prisoners' bonds with a series of casual but fortunately accurate swipes.

"Your men, my Colonel," he said magnanimously, flipping one fat hand in their direction. "I give them back to you."

"I am deeply obliged to you, sir." Grey bowed. "There is one missing, though. Where is Rodrigo?"

There was a sudden silence. Even the shouting children hushed instantly, melting back behind their mothers. Grey could hear the trickling of water down the distant rock face, and the pulse beating in his ears.

"The zombie?" Accompong said at last. He spoke mildly, but Grey sensed some unease in his voice. "He is not yours."

"Yes," Grey said firmly. "He is. He came to the mountain under my protection—and he will leave the same way. It is my duty."

The squatty headman's expression was hard to interpret. None of the crowd moved, or murmured, though Grey caught a glimpse from the corner of his eyes of the faint turning of heads, as folk asked silent questions of one another.

"It is my duty," Grey repeated. "I cannot go without him." Carefully omitting any suggestion that it might not be his choice whether to go or not. Still, why would Accompong return the white men to him, if he planned to kill or imprison Grey?

The headman pursed fleshy lips, then turned his head and said something questioning. Movement, in the hut where Ishmael had emerged the night before. There was a considerable pause, but once more, the *houngan* came out.

His face was pale, and one of his feet was wrapped in a bloodstained wad of fabric, bound tightly. Amputation, Grey thought with interest, recalling the metallic *thunk* that had seemed to echo through his own flesh in the cave. It was the only sure way to keep a snake's venom from spreading through the body.

"Ah," said Grey, voice light. "So the krait liked me better, did he?"

He thought Accompong laughed under his breath, but didn't really pay attention. The *houngan*'s eyes flashed hate at him, and he regretted his wit, fearing that it might cost Rodrigo more than had already been taken from him.

Despite his shock and horror, though, he clung to what Mrs. Abernathy had told him. The young man was *not* truly dead. He swallowed. Could Rodrigo perhaps be restored? The Scotchwoman had said not—but perhaps she was wrong. Clearly Rodrigo had not been a zombie for more than a few days. And she did say that the drug dissipated over time . . . perhaps . . .

Accompong spoke sharply, and the *houngan* lowered his head.

"Anda," he said sullenly. There was stumbling movement in the hut, and he stepped aside, half-pushing Rodrigo out into the light, where he came to a stop, staring vacantly at the ground, mouth open.

"You want this?" Accompong waved a hand at Rodrigo. "What for? He's no good to you, surely? Unless you want to take him to bed—he won't say no to you!"

Everyone thought that very funny; the clearing rocked with laughter. Grey waited it out. From the corner of his eye, he saw the girl Azeel, watching him with something like a fearful hope in her eyes.

"He is under my protection," he repeated. "Yes, I want him."

Accompong nodded and took a deep breath, sniffing appreciatively at the mingled scents of cassava porridge, fried plantain, and frying pig meat.

"Sit down, Colonel," he said, "and eat with me."

Grey sank slowly down beside him, weariness throbbing through his legs. Looking round, he saw Cresswell dragged roughly off, but left sitting on the ground against a hut, unmolested. Tom and the two soldiers, looking dazed, were being fed at one of the cook fires. Then he saw Rodrigo, still standing like a scarecrow, and struggled to his feet.

He took the young man's tattered sleeve and said, "Come with me." Rather to his surprise, Rodrigo did, turning like an automaton. He led the young man through the staring crowd to the girl Azeel, and said, "Stop." He lifted Rodrigo's hand and offered it to the girl, who, after a moment's hesitation, took firm hold of it.

"Look after him, please," Grey said to her. Only as he turned away did it register upon him that the arm he had held was wrapped with a bandage. Ah. Dead men don't bleed.

Returning to Accompong's fire, he found a wooden platter of steaming food awaiting him. He sank down gratefully upon the ground again and closed his eyes—then opened them, startled, as he felt something descend upon his head, and found himself peering out from under the drooping felt brim of the headman's ragged hat.

"Oh," he said. "Thank you." He hesitated, looking round, either for the leather hatbox or for his ragged palm-frond hat, but didn't see either one.

"Never mind," said Accompong, and leaning forward, slid his hands carefully over Grey's shoulders, palm up, as though lifting something heavy. "I will take your snake, instead. You have carried him long enough, I think."

BEWARE THE SNAKE

An SPQR Story

by John Maddox Roberts

John Maddox Roberts is best known for his acclaimed twelve-volume SPQR series of historical mysteries, detailing the adventures of a young Roman aristocrat who keeps getting entangled with murder and other nefarious doings in the dark underworld of Ancient Rome. The SPQR series consists of *The King's Gambit*, *The Catiline Conspiracy*, *The Temple of the Muses*, *The River God's Vengeance*, and eight other novels. In addition to the SPQR books, the prolific Maddox has written fantasy series such as the five-volume Stormlands sequence (consisting of *The Islander*, *The Black Shields*, and three others), science fiction series such as the two-volume Spacer sequence (*Space Angel*, *Window of the Mind*), and the three-volume Cingulum series (*The Cingulum*, *Cloak of Illusion*, *The Sword, the Jewel, and the Mirror*); contemporary detective novels (*A Typical American Town*, *The Ghosts of Saigon*, *Desperate Highways*); eight Conan novels; a Dragonlance novel; novels in collaboration with Eric Kotani and under the name Mark Ramsay; and stand-alones such as *Cestus Dei*, *The Strayed Sheep of Charun*, *Hannibal's Children*, and *King of the Wood*. His latest novel is *The Year of Confusion*, the new SPQR mystery.

Everyone knows that some snakes can be deadly. As Decius Caecilius learns in the SPQR story that follows, sometimes the problem is *knowing* one when you see it.

YOUNG HEROD ONCE TOLD ME THAT HIS PEOPLE ABHOR SERPENTS. IT seems to have something to do with his people's fall from a sort of Golden Age, in which the serpent is mysteriously implicated. This is the sort of primitive superstition one must expect from barbarians. Civilized people, by contrast, think the world of snakes. We revere and esteem them. Snakes enhance the prophecies of oracles and facilitate contact with the gods of the underworld. It is difficult to imagine civilized life without snakes. Egyptian kings had cobras on their crowns, while Mercury and Aesculapius bear serpent-wound staffs. The very spirit of a place is symbolized by a pillar with a snake coiled around it.

To be sure, one occasionally encounters the odd asp, adder, or cobra, which carry deadly venom, but that is just the gods' way of reminding us that their gifts are often double-edged. It keeps mortals on their toes and prevents them from growing too complacent.

It is true that certain people carry this reverence for serpents too far. Some families, including very respectable ones, keep a family snake and consult with it on all matters of importance. Personally, I consider this a rather un-Roman practice. It's more like something Greeks would do. But nobody in Italy is as mad about snakes as the Marsi, the mountain people who live around Lake Fucinus, east of Rome.

Which brings us to the day the Marsian priest came calling.

"We have reason to believe that our snake is in Rome." The man wore a saffron-colored toga and a ribbon of the same color around his brow.

"I see. I don't suppose it crawled here on its own?"

"Of course not! She was stolen and we want her back!"

So the gender of the snake was established. We were making progress already. I glanced down at the letter of introduction the priest had brought. Its message was characteristically bald and laconic.

Decius Caecilius, the bearer of this letter is Lucius Pompaedius Pollux, high priest of the temple of Angitia. He is my client and he has a problem and I can think of no man more fit than you to solve it for him. Below the brief text was appended, instead of a seal, the signature *Caesar, Pontifex Maximus.* Since he invoked his office as *pontifex*, this was to be treated as a religious matter.

"Has there been a ransom demand?" I asked.

"Ransom?" Pompaedius looked scandalized. "You think this is some sort of kidnapping?"

"I don't see why not. Distinguished personages are often held for ransom. People have been doing it since Homer. No reason why the same can't be done with a beloved snake."

"Senator, the Serpent of Angitia is a sacred being of the utmost religious importance, not some sort of—of *animal*!"

"And I would never suggest such a thing," I assured him. "It is simply that I can assist you better if I can establish some sort of motive for this unique theft. The motive for theft is usually profit of one sort or another. If not money, then what?"

He pondered this for a moment. "Power."

"What?" I said, brightly.

"What is it you Romans say about the Marsi?" he asked.

I could think of several sayings we had said about the Marsi, all of them uncomplimentary, but I knew the one he meant. "That we have never triumphed over you, and have never triumphed without you."

"Precisely." He seemed to think he had answered something.

In the old days, we had fought several wars with the Marsi, and they had made us regret it. A very tough, disciplined, military people, to be sure. We much preferred to have them as allies. They had stood fast with us against the incursions of the Gauls and had not wavered when Hannibal all but destroyed Rome. Our last fight against the Marsi had been a generation before this time, when they had joined with the rebelling allied cities of Italy in demanding their citizenship rights. The war had been bloody, but once the rebels knew they could not win, the Senate had acknowledged the justice of their demands and granted them citizenship. I thought of the Marsian soldiers I had seen with our legions. They wore distinctive helmets, usually crested with serpents in fanciful coils and loops, often in threes.

"Are you telling me that this serpent embodies the martial valor of your people?" I hazarded.

"Very much so. When the Marsi first became a people and founded Marruvium on the lake, they prayed and sacrificed to Angitia, asking her to grant them a token of her approval and her patronage of our city and our people. On the tenth day of the rites, a great serpent emerged from the lake. The people built a temple to Angitia on that spot and built a sanctuary for the serpent in its crypt. The serpent is the protector of the people. As long as she is in her sanctuary and healthy, Marruvium is safe and the Marsi will be victorious. Should word get out that she is *gone* . . ."

"You mean the Marruvians and the Marsi in general are unaware that their snake has been purloined?" I asked.

"Yes," he said. "If her disappearance should become common knowledge, I fear there could be widespread panic. In these unsettled times, with so many of our men serving in the armies, there could be disaster. Thus far, only the priesthood of the temple know."

"Of what breed is she? What does she look like?"

"The sacred serpent of Angitia belongs to a breed known only near the lake, called a swamp adder. They are black on the head and back, with a white belly. Of course our serpent is an especially magnificent specimen, about five feet long and as big around as your arm."

"An adder? Then she is poisonous?"

"Decidedly. The swamp adder is deadlier than any Egyptian cobra or asp."

"A brave thief, then."

He shrugged. "Venomous serpents are easily handled, if one has the skills."

"And why do you think that your sacred snake is in Rome?"

"When the theft was discovered, I pledged all of the personnel of the temple to silence and secrecy, and then I sought an omen from the goddess."

"I am guessing that this involved snakes," I said.

"What else?" he said, seemingly astonished.

"What else, indeed? And how did the goddess answer your entreaty?"

"First, we gathered several score of wild snakes from the lands adjacent to the temple, all of them belonging to lines known to us for generations."

"One wouldn't want to consult with foreign snakes," I concurred.

"Of course not. After fasting for a day and a night, we performed all the proper sacrifices and sang the prayers in the original Marsian language, which has not been spoken for many generations. Then—"

I know all too well the tedium of hearing a man expound upon his favorite subject, which is of no interest to oneself, so I interrupted. "And what omen did you receive?"

"Oh. Well, at the moment the rite was finished, all kept silence in anticipation, and immediately there came a loud clap of thunder from the west. Clearly, the goddess wanted us to search to the west to find our serpent, and Rome lies to the west of Marruvium."

"Couldn't be clearer," I agreed. "Yet there remains the matter of who snatched your snake and precisely why. What were the circumstances surrounding her disappearance? In what sort of confinement was she kept? I presume she was not permitted to just slither freely about the grounds?"

Again he looked pained. "She has a sanctuary beneath the altar."

"What is it like? How large is it?"

He seemed puzzled at these questions. People often do when I interrogate them. My method of gathering evidence in small increments from as many sources as possible in order to get at the essence of what really happened left most people utterly mystified. The more charitable opined that I had invented a new school of philosophy. Those of a magical disposition think it is some sort of sorcery. I just consider it good sense, but I can convince few of my peers that this is the case.

"It is circular, earth-floored, naturally, but strewn with fragrant cedar bark. There are a number of statues of the present serpent's revered ancestors, on small pedestals."

I was tempted to ask him how each new holy snake was chosen, since snakes do not have offspring one at a time, but I was afraid that he would answer. "And how is the sanctuary accessed?"

"By a single passageway, quite narrow, that descends from a doorway pierced through the stairway ascending to the portico and altar."

"And this is the only ingress or egress available to either human or serpent?"

"It is."

"And is the access by way of a stairway, or by an inclined ramp?"

"It is a slanted floor. There are no stairs. Is this somehow significant?" He was getting impatient. I was used to that.

"It is indeed. A snake might have trouble ascending a stair, but not a ramp. Might it not have simply wandered off on its own? It must get dreadfully boring down there. One can only spend so much time contemplating the images of one's ancestors. I know this. In my own atrium are the death masks of dozens of my Metellan ancestors, and a more sour-faced pack of patriotic villains is difficult to imagine. If I had to look at them all the time—"

"Senator!" Pompaedius hissed, rather like his missing reptile. "We need to find the sacred Serpent of Angitia! I do not think you appreciate the gravity of the situation."

Sometimes if I needle someone sufficiently I can trick him into saying something intemperate, something more revealing than he had intended. Not this time, it seemed.

"Lucius Pompaedius, I will find your snake. I fully appreciate how crucial this is, not because of the importance of the Marsi, or because of their goddess and her reptilian consort, but because I have been instructed to do so by Caius Julius Caesar, and keeping Caesar happy is of utmost importance to all sane Romans."

That evening, I consulted with my own household authority on religion, my wife, Julia.

"Angitia?" she said. "She's the one to sacrifice to if you've been bitten by a snake."

"If you can make it from Rome to her temple on the lake," I observed, "you will have recovered anyway."

"She has a shrine here in Rome," Julia said. She pondered the business for a while as she picked at dinner. "I think we should have a household snake. Some of the best families have them. The Claudians have always kept snakes."

"The Claudians," I observed, "are a family of insane hereditary criminals."

"Appius Claudius the Censor wasn't insane or a criminal," she objected.

"A single, outstanding exception to an otherwise inflexible rule," I said. The estimable Appius had been brother to my old enemy Clodius, who had been both criminal and insane, and that was only the start of it. "No snakes for us. Neither the Caecilians nor the Julians have been serpent fanciers. In any case, I think it is unfitting for holy icons to crawl out of a swamp. Sacred tokens should fall from the heavens, like the Palladium and the sacred shields of Mars."

"Only one of the sacred shields fell from the sky," Julia pointed out. "The rest are counterfeits to fool thieves and jealous gods."

"We are getting away from the problem here," I said. My head was beginning to hurt. "Your uncle Caius Julius wants me to find a snake. Rome is a rather large city, and it seems to me a snake must be fairly easy to hide. Any long, narrow space or container would do. Snakes can arrange themselves in compact coils, so a basket or jar would suffice. Where to begin?"

"A good place might be the snake market," Julia suggested.

"Now why didn't I think of that?" I wondered.

So the next morning Julia and I, accompanied by one of her girls and my freedman Hermes, set out for this exotic destination. Since Julia was going along, we had to have a litter, of course, instead of walking on our own perfectly good feet. Well, my feet had fallen somewhat short of perfection by that time. In fact, just getting about the city was enough effort for me.

The snake market was just off the Forum Boarium, not far from the northern end of the Circus Maximus. The old forum was bustling with livestock. Everywhere you looked there were pens for cattle, horses, pigs, sheep, goats, and donkeys and hutches full of rabbits. There were beautiful specimens for sacrifice and others, less attractive, for eating, some of these specially fattened on olive pulp. There was a section for poultry: peacocks, chickens, cages of songbirds. One area was devoted to exotics: monkeys, gazelles, Egyptian ibises, cheetahs, and so forth. It was fashionable for the wealthy to adorn their estates with such creatures. It was noisy and smelly, and I was grateful that our house was on the other side of the city.

"I think it's down this street somewhere," I said, directing the litter slaves. I knew my native city intimately, but there were still a few parts of it I had never visited, and the snake market was one of them. This was because I had never been in the market for a snake.

"Ah, here we are." We had come to a large shop with a striped awning above its portico. Spelled out in mosaic on the doorstep was the legend *Sergius Poplicola, Purveyor of Fine Snakes.*

The possessor of this imposing name greeted us at the door, his eyes going wide at the sight of our fine carriage and my senatorial insignia. "Welcome, Senator! Welcome, my lady!"

I took both of his hands in a hearty politician's handshake. "My friend Sergius, I am here to see you about a snake."

"Of course, of course, please come inside." He bustled within, clapping his hands and calling for his slaves to step lively. The interior was spacious and cool, with open skylights. Here and there about the floor were small pits, their bottoms strewn with cedar shavings. Over all hung the scent of fragrant cedar, but beneath it there was a slight but disagreeable musky odor. Snakes, no doubt. While the slaves set up chairs and a table and loaded it with refreshments, I examined a large clay pot from which came a rustling noise. I peered within and saw that it was half full of grain, barley, and wheat by the look of it, and it swarmed with mice.

I took one of the chairs and accepted a cup of wine. It turned out to be an unusually fine Cretan, powerful enough to put anyone into a buying mood. "I am looking for a very particular snake," I began.

"But naturally," said Sergius. "Whether you need a snake for divination, for communication with the chthonian gods, for keeping the pantry free of mice, for eating, for whatever purpose, rest assured I have just the snake for you, and as many of them as you may require."

"For eating?" Julia said.

"Certain of our African snakes are esteemed as delicacies," he assured her.

"Oh, we've been to Egyptian banquets," I told him. "It's just not what one expects to see in Rome."

"Rome is a very cosmopolitan city," he reminded me.

"So it is. No, snakes for the table are not on my agenda today, nor for the pantry, but a snake for the altar, that is different. Do you happen to have a swamp adder on the premises?"

"A swamp adder?" He seemed taken aback. "Are you sure you wouldn't rather have a cobra? We have plenty of those, of several varieties, in fact."

"Who buys cobras?" Julia asked, seemingly intrigued.

"The Isis cult is growing quite popular in Roman territory, my lady. Cobras are an absolute necessity for the rituals of Isis. If you have visited Egypt you have observed that the cobra, along with the vulture, is prominently featured on the uraeus crown of the pharaohs, since adopted by the

Ptolemys. The cobra goddess, Wadjet, has been the patroness of the royal family since earliest antiquity."

Here was another man about to launch into an oration on his favorite subject, so I took quick action to forestall him. "Is there some sort of problem with the swamp adder? It is, after all, native to Italy, not some exotic foreign breed. Rather prolific around Lake Fucinus, I hear."

"Decidedly so. There is a reason the Marsi need a goddess of their own just for snakebite. Do you know much about venomous serpents, Senator?"

"Only that I don't like them much."

"Well, people think that cobras and asps and such are terribly deadly creatures. In truth, they are fairly easy to avoid, and their venom, while quite dangerous, will seldom kill a healthy adult. Their victims are usually the very young, the very old, and the infirm. Often, snakebitten people simply frighten themselves to death because they believe all snakes to be deadly."

"Really?" I said. This was fascinating.

"Absolutely, Senator. I know of many cases in which people have died after being bitten by perfectly harmless snakes. For this reason, the common ratsnake that farmers keep in their barns for vermin control have probably killed more people than all the cobras in Egypt."

"I see. But the swamp adder actually lives up to its reputation?"

"Beyond question. Its venom is more than powerful enough to kill a man in a few moments. In fact, the Marsi have an annual ritual in which a bull is sacrificed by placing it in a pit with a large swamp adder. It is a rather small pit, so it doesn't take long for the bull to annoy the adder and be bitten. The priests of Angitia draw a great many omens for the coming year according to where the bite or bites are located on the bull, whether it staggers for a while, or has violent convulsions, or just drops down dead. The best omen is if the bull falls down dead instantly from a single bite."

"What does this signify?" Julia asked.

"That nothing much will happen in the coming year. The Marsi consider this a good forecast."

"As should we all," I affirmed. "Is the serpent used in this rite the sacred specimen kept in Angitia's temple?"

"Oh, no. There is too much danger of the snake being injured or killed, as sometimes happens when the bull falls. That is a portentous event in itself, meaning disaster to come. No, an adder is captured wild in the swamp by a team specially trained for this hazardous activity. If it lives, it is released back into the swamp, bearing the prayers of the people along with messages for their dead."

"I see. So I take it you don't have a swamp adder?" I said.

He shook his head. "Neither I nor my staff are that brave. You are aware, I take it, that almost all of the snake charmers you see in the markets and at festivals are Marsian? They never use swamp adders for their performances. They would never touch one except for religious purposes. You aren't really looking to buy one, are you, Senator?"

"No, I just need to learn about them. Matters of state between Rome and the Marsi, as it were."

"Actually," Julia said, "I am quite interested in purchasing a house snake, one for family consultation, although I suppose it would do no harm if it catches mice as well. Could you show us your stock?"

Needless to say, we went home with a snake, a small, green creature of no great distinction that I could see. It came with a supply of cedar shavings and careful instructions as to its care and feeding, housed in an Egyptian basket artistically plaited from papyrus fiber. Julia seemed almost as delighted with the basket as with the snake.

"Have we learned anything?" Hermes said as we wended our way back toward the Subura.

"Other than that I am an indulgent husband?"

"We already knew that, dear," Julia said, gloating over her purchase.

"I am a bit puzzled," I said, running a few things through my mind. "Pompaedius acted as if the handling of venomous serpents is a simple business, yet Poplicola told us that it takes a specially trained team of Marsi just to catch one for the bull sacrifice."

"Maybe it's catching one in the swamp that's the tricky part," Hermes said. "Maybe they live in packs out there. The sacred snake sounds domesticated."

"Pompaedius," I mused. "Wasn't that the name of the man who led the Marsi in the Social War?"

"Quintus Pompaedius Silo," Julia said. "He is said to have held Cato out of a high window by his heels, when Cato was about ten years old."

"Should've dropped the little bugger on his head," I observed. "I remember the story now. He was in Rome drumming up support for Marsian citizenship rights, and little Cato refused to take his oath or some such. I always thought it was something Cato's supporters made up to make him sound patriotic instead of just an insufferably rude little twit."

"Do you think it's significant?" Hermes asked. "For all I know, Pompaedius is as common a name in Marsian territory as Cornelius is in Rome."

"Probably nothing," I said. But in truth I was not so sanguine. Religion and politics are inseparable, which is why the founders of the Republic wisely made priesthood and omen-taking a part of public office. That way it can be kept under control, after a fashion. But Caesar himself had decided that this silly business was worth pursuing. Of course, he was obliged by ancient custom to aid a client who was in Rome with a problem. "How did a Marsian named Pompaedius become Caesar's client?" I wondered aloud.

"If I recall correctly," Julia said, "most of the Marsi were clients of Livius Drusus. But then he was murdered."

"He championed the Italian allies in the Senate, didn't he?" It was coming back to me. Drusus had tried to get citizenship for all our Italian allies, but word got out, whether truthfully or not, that they had all secretly pledged to enter his clientele if he was successful in making them citizens. That would have made him too powerful, and his enemies had him assassinated. Typical politics for that generation. For any generation, if truth be told.

"That's right," Julia said, "but in the Social War, his brother was killed leading a Roman army against the Marsi, and the Livii repudiated their patronage." Julia's knowledge of the great families was far more comprehensive than my own. "After all the fuss died down and they were citizens, the Marsi took clientage under the Pompeius family, and when Pompey Magnus was killed, Caesar offered them patronage. His support in that part of Italy was weak, so he courted the Marsi. With them in his clientele, the other people of the central mountain district followed."

"That sounds like Caesar," I said. "They sent a good many young men to serve in his legions. I wonder what he promised them in return?"

"Nothing but the proper mutual obligations of patron and client, I am sure," Julia said. She probably believed it.

Hermes spoke up. "Didn't you say Angitia had a shrine in Rome?"

I had completely forgotten it. "Where is it, Julia? We ought to see if anyone there knows anything."

"It's just a tiny place near the grain market," she said. "I don't know if it even has a permanent staff. There is some sort of ceremony at the time of the Martialis, and people leave offerings there to protect them from snakebite. That's as much as I know."

The Martialis is a harvest festival and signifies the close of the agricultural year. A good time to ask the favor of a snake goddess to protect the granaries from mice. It made sense. I told the litter slaves to carry us to the grain market, and they complied with sour looks. Litter slaves always think that every direction is uphill.

We passed by the great plaza of the grain merchants with its spectacular statue of Apollo and turned down a tiny side street. Other than a small fountain at its entrance, there was nothing to distinguish it from Rome's thousands of other little streets.

"How did you know of this place?" I asked Julia.

"My grandmother brought me here when I was a little girl. It was when Caesar departed for Syria. Aurelia believed that the entire Orient is carpeted with venomous serpents and she came here to sacrifice for his protection."

"She was a pious woman," I agreed. "When I was with Caesar in Gaul, she used to write him long letters detailing the sacrifices she had provided to protect him from enemies, from drowning, from accident, from scurrilous gossip and slander, and on and on. Caesar said she was single-handedly supporting all the animal sellers and priests in Rome."

"That's an exaggeration," Julia protested.

"Not by much. I used to read those letters to him. He complained that he was ruining his vision with all the writing he did, so he had none to spare for his mother's letters. She had incredibly tiny handwriting. Lavish though she was with sacrifices, she was stingy with paper, and crowded as much as she could onto a single sheet. To this day, it pains my eyes to think about those letters."

"You never run out of things to complain about," she observed.

"I've lived a tragic life," I told her as the litter slaves set us down, gasping and puffing abundantly, despite the paltriness of the effort they had expended.

The shrine was at the very end of the street, which in turn wasn't much more than an alley between two grain warehouses. The few doors of the flanking buildings looked as if they hadn't been opened in years. The door to the shrine was flanked by low-relief pilasters wound with sculpted snakes. The paint was faded and flaking away. The door itself stood open. In the usual fashion of Italian temples and shrines, the portico sat atop a dozen or so narrow, steep steps.

"It looked better than this when I came here with Aurelia," Julia said.

"We all looked better thirty years ago," I told her. I was about to step inside when Hermes placed a hand on my arm and turned to Julia.

"What's on the other side of this door?" he asked. I knew I was getting old. This was an elementary precaution I should have taken without conscious thought. When I was younger and my wits sharper, I would have sent Hermes through first.

"I didn't go inside," she said. "I stayed out here with some slave women while Grandmother went in. I don't know if there was a priest inside or if she just made her sacrifice and came back out."

Blood sacrifices are usually made on an altar before a temple, not inside. But there was no altar before the entrance. Sometimes food offerings were left at the feet of the deity's image, incense burned, that sort of thing. "Is anyone here?" I shouted. There was silence from within. I looked at Hermes and jerked my head toward the doorway. He put a hand on the hilt of the sword he wore concealed beneath his clothes and strode through the doorway. Hearing no sounds of violence, I followed. Something about that open door bothered me. Thieves would not hesitate to rob the sanctuary of a foreign goddess.

Inside it was very quiet and smelled as temples usually smell—of many years of incense and the smoke of lamps, torches, and candles. No fires were burning at this time, but there were other scents beneath that of the smoke and incense. Julia's shadow fell across the doorway.

"Don't come in yet!" I urged her. "Do you smell that?"

"Something's dead in here," Hermes noted.

"And I smell cedar," Julia said.

"Right, "I said. "There's a snake in here somewhere and if it's one of those damned swamp adders, we have a problem. Julia, what sort of sacrifice did Aurelia bring that day?"

I could hear the frown in her voice. "It was a long time ago. She had a small cage or basket of some sort."

"She was bringing mice," I said. "That's how you sacrifice to Angitia. You feed her snake. It should have a pit or crypt of some sort here, like the one in the big temple at Lake Fucinus. The sacred snake got out of that one. This one may have as well."

"Something's dead," Hermes persisted. "Maybe it's a dead snake."

"We can always hope." My eyes were growing accustomed to the gloom. I moved my feet very carefully. Even a torpid and inoffensive snake will whip around and bite if something touches it unexpectedly. The shrine was little more than a long, narrow room. At its far end was a statue of a benevolent-looking woman, her shoulders draped with snakes, more snakes wound about her feet. The statue was slightly smaller than life size. Smaller than life size for a mortal woman, anyway. You never know about goddesses.

"The smell is coming from there," Hermes said, pointing toward a gaping square opening in the floor before the statue. With great trepidation, I made my way to the edge of this ominous aperture. It was perhaps ten feet on a side, its rim slightly raised. The gloom made its bottom all but totally obscure. I could make out some sort of shapeless mass on its floor, five or six feet down.

"Hermes," I said, "go fetch torches. Be careful. That snake could be anywhere."

"You don't have to tell me," Hermes said with great sincerity. He edged his way back to the doorway, shuffling his feet as if he could shoo the swamp adder away. Once he was at the door, I heard the patter of his sandals as he ran to find us some sort of illumination.

"What's down there?" Julia said.

"We're about to find out. I didn't want you to come in. That snake could be anywhere."

"The priest said there was a ramp leading down to the sacred serpent's crypt," she pointed out. "I don't see any such ramp here. The sides look quite sheer."

"What has that to do with anything?" I said, exasperated. "I didn't want you to come in! Is that too much to ask?"

"Yes, it is," she said. Well, she was a Caesar.

Hermes returned with commendable alacrity, accompanied by a pair of linkboys. These juvenile torchbearers usually slept through the day in order to spend their nights illuminating the way of citizens through Rome's benighted streets. Hermes didn't caution them to watch out for the snake. Any snake biting a linkboy wasn't biting him, I suppose.

"This is better," Julia said. With a bit of light, the little shrine was much more cheerful. The walls were covered with old, smoke-smudged frescoes of scenes from, I presumed, the myths of Angitia and her fellow Marsian deities. Needless to say, snakes featured prominently.

I gestured to the boys. "Come over here. Hold your torches over this pit and be very, very careful."

Mystified, they did as I ordered. When their light flooded the pit one of the boys gasped and would have dropped his torch had I not grasped his hand. "Steady. It's just a dead man. You've seen plenty of those."

"Not like that one!" said the other boy, a bit older. Roman street boys were a hard lot to shock, but I was forced to acknowledge that this was a bit more than the usual alley corpse.

Julia turned away and gagged, and she was as unflappable as the rest of her family. When she had her composure back, she asked, "Is that the priest who came to you about the snake?"

"The yellow toga and headband are the same," I said. "Otherwise it's hard to tell."

"I think of saffron as more of an orange than a yellow," she replied, now fully in control of herself.

The dead man who lay on the carpet of cedar bark and shavings was bloated and almost purple. His skin was covered with giant blisters like fist-sized, semitransparent bubbles. Yet the unmistakable scent of death was rather faint.

"Hasn't been dead long, though he's looking rather poorly," I remarked.

"Should I fetch Asklepiodes?" Hermes asked, understandably eager to be away.

"I think not," I said. "His specialty is wounds and death caused by weapons. Poisons and venoms are not in his realm of expertise."

"Poplicola, then?" he said, hopefully.

"He'd just try to sell Julia another snake. Let's review what we have here. A priest of Angitia came from the Marsian country to ask me to find his snake. Today, in the shrine of Angitia, we find a priest of Angitia, possibly the same man, dead from what looks like the bite of a serpent that fully lives up to its reputation." I pondered a moment. "Correct that: We have a corpse in the clothing of a priest of Angitia. It could be almost anybody."

"You're very tiresome when you get this way, dear," Julia reminded me.

"We are in a holy shrine," I said, "dealing with a goddess and sacred snakes. This is a religious matter. Hermes, go find Caesar and ask him if he would be so good as to come here on a matter of some urgency. Tell him I require his expertise as *pontifex maximus*. He is probably in the Domus Publica."

"Do you think Caesar will be able to help?" Julia said when Hermes had dashed off.

"Probably not, but I want him to see this. It's not every day we see a murder as unique as this one in Rome."

"Murder? Surely this was an accident."

"Then where is the snake?" I asked her. "It didn't crawl out of there unaided after biting the unfortunate priest or whoever he was." I looked around me. Between the small torches and my eyes adjusting to the gloom, I could see tolerably well. It was quite a small space, only a single room with no access save the narrow doorway. The floor was completely bare and the walls featureless except for some faded paintings that depicted what I presumed to be scenes from the cult of Angitia. I was unfamiliar with the myths but there was a woman resembling the statue, a bull, and a great many snakes.

"It could be under the body," Julia pointed out. "Poplicola said the bull sometimes falls on the snake."

"Foretelling disaster," I noted. "I wonder if being crushed by a falling priest is a similarly dire omen. And if so, is it just for the Marsi or for anyone in the vicinity?"

We were but a short distance from the Domus Publica in the Forum, so it was not long before we heard the tramp of twenty-four lictors preceding the Dictator in great pomp. We went to the doorway and saw that the great man had indeed arrived, followed by a mob of gawking Forum layabouts (some of them my fellow senators). Crowds always followed Caesar around in those days, just to see if anything should happen, I suppose. He wore his pontifical regalia along with his usual gilded laurel wreath and triumphator's robe. Hermes stood behind Caesar, but the man to his right caused Julia to gasp.

"It's Pompaedius!" she whispered. "He's alive!"

I was not entirely surprised. "I am sorry to have interrupted your day, Caesar, but matters here require your presence."

"Nonsense, Decius Caecilius," Caesar said jovially. "You always find the most bizarre murders for our entertainment. What is it this time?"

"If you will come inside, Caesar and Pompaedius, but please, no others. It is already quite cramped enough."

Caesar entered. "And how is my favorite niece today?" he said to Julia, as always the soul of courtesy.

"A bit upset, I'm afraid. The dead priest is in the most deplorable condition."

"Priest?" Caesar said, leaning over the pit. The linkboys gaped at the Dictator's splendor. They were certainly getting an eyeful that day.

"Well, we think he was a priest," Julia said. "He's in the robes of Angitia's priesthood, anyhow. In fact, we thought it was Lucius Pompaedius here. I see now that we were mistaken."

Caesar straightened. "May I know the meaning of this?"

"It is precisely that meaning that I have been trying to ascertain," I told him. "Perhaps your client Pompaedius can enlighten us."

"This man has died from the bite of a swamp adder," the priest said. "That much is clear. It must have been he who purloined the sacred serpent. You all bear witness to how the goddess has punished him for the sacrilege."

"And his identity?" I asked.

"Just some imposter," Pompaedius said. "All the priests of Angitia wear the saffron toga, but only I, the high priest, am entitled to this." He touched the yellow fillet encircling his brow.

"I see." Caesar turned to me. "Decius, as you should know, in my office of *pontifex maximus* I pronounce judgment on all matters pertaining to the state religion. Bring me a problem involving Jupiter, Juno, Saturn, Mars, and I can sort it out for you. Quirinus and Janus fall within my realm of authority. I do not pronounce on matters concerning foreign deities. For that, one usually consults with the *quinquidecemviri* and they in turn consult the

Sybilline Books. Typically, this is done when the fate of the state is involved, and I fail to see such a matter here." Caesar could lay on the sarcasm when he wanted to.

"Actually, Caesar, I am afraid that I stooped to a subterfuge," I admitted. "Your presence here is required in your capacity as the supreme magistrate."

Caesar looked annoyed and began to reply when Julia said, "Everyone be very still."

"Eh?" I said with my usual quick wit.

Very slowly Julia raised her arm and pointed toward the statue's feet. "One of those snakes is alive."

"By Jupiter, so it is," I said, eyeing the slowly wriggling form with horrified fascination. "The light in here is too uncertain to determine coloration, but I am willing to hazard a guess that this is a swamp adder."

"Somebody kill that thing," Caesar said with distaste in his voice. He never did like snakes.

"Caesar, you cannot!" Pompaedius protested. "That is the sacred Serpent of Angitia!"

"That does present us with a problem," Caesar said. "I wouldn't want my Marsian troops to hold me responsible for killing their holy snake."

"Please, there is no danger," Pompaedius said complacently. With great solemnity he walked around the pit and stood a pace from the statue, to which he bowed and muttered something while holding his hands forth, palms down. This told me that Angitia was worshipped as an underworld deity. I was getting quite an education in religious matters that day.

His devotions completed, Pompaedius turned his attention to the snake. He extended his arms toward it and began wiggling his fingers rhythmically, edging closer with tiny steps. The snake stared at his hands and seemed enthralled. I watched with a mixture of fascination and revulsion. It always makes me uncomfortable to see someone performing magic.

Very slowly, the fingers of his right hand slowed and then stopped their wriggling. His left continued the spell-casting. Then he moved his right hand gradually toward the snake's head until it was behind the flaring base of the wedge-shaped skull. Julia gasped when he grasped the thing by the neck. At least I'm pretty sure it was Julia. I don't think it was me.

Pompaedius straightened. The snake, which was indeed a huge, fat specimen, tried to wrap itself around him, but he somehow arranged it in graceful loops draped from his shoulders with a terminal coil around his waist. He cooed into the place where a snake doesn't have an ear and the thing seemed to relax.

"And I thought draping a toga properly was an exacting task," I observed.

"You see?" Pompaedius said, ignoring me. "All is well. Divine justice has been served. I will take the sacred serpent back to her home by the lake, and the luck of the Marsi will be restored."

"With quite a bit of prestige accruing to you," I observed.

"Well," he said modestly, "it will certainly do me no harm. I must thank you, Senator, for locating her so conscientiously. I am in your debt, as are all the Marsi. And to you, Caesar—"

"Caesar," I said, "I wish to arrest this man."

"What!" cried Pompaedius. "What is this outrage?"

"This man is the imposter. That's Lucius Pompaedius in the pit there." Caesar looked at the repulsive corpse bemusedly.

"But I am Lucius Pompaedius!"

"So you are," I agreed.

"Decius Caecilius," Caesar said, "philosophical paradoxes have never been your style. Can you not speak plainly?"

I took Caesar's letter from the place in my toga where I stash things and unrolled it. "Caesar, yesterday when this man came to me I was struck by his name."

"Pompaedius?" the priest said. "My ancestor was indeed a leader of the uprising against Rome, but we have been loyal citizens for many years, and loyal supporters of Caesar as well."

"Not your family name, but the appended name, Pollux."

His eyes shifted ever so briefly toward the doorway. "The *dioscuri* are patrons of Rome, and my parents gave me the name in token of our loyalty."

"Commendable," I said. "But it is also customary to name twin boys Castor and Pollux. Pollux is always given to the senior twin, as Pollux was the immortal brother of the two, fathered by Zeus upon Leda, with Castor fathered by Tyndareus and therefore mortal."

"That's one version of the myth," Caesar said. "There are others." Sometimes Caesar strayed into pedantry.

"I do not speak of the myth but of the naming custom. The dead man down there is Lucius Pompaedius Pollux, firstborn of the twins. This man who has assumed that name is Lucius Pompaedius Castor."

"But why?" Julia wanted to know.

"He said it when he called on me yesterday," I told her. "Power. Prestige. He planned to return to Marruvium as a veritable triumphator. By now his priests have spread the word that the sacred serpent has been stolen, and the whole Marsian countryside will be in a fine lather over it. He will return on horseback with the snake draped over him like Caesar's purple robe and take his brother's place, no doubt with a bloodcurdling story about how his jealous brother Castor tried to betray the Marsi by stealing their snake, only to have Angitia, aided no doubt by himself, strike the criminal down for his sacrilege."

"How did he lure his brother here in order to kill him?" Julia said.

"He didn't. He killed him in the sanctuary of Angitia at the lake. Easy enough to do for a man as expert with venomous snakes as this one. All he had to do was distract his brother, get him to look in the wrong direction, then jam the serpent's head into some vulnerable spot. Quite ingenious, really. Pompaedius, did you actually use the sacred snake for this purpose, or did you catch a scaly accomplice in the marshes?" I was rather curious about this. Novel methods of homicide have always fascinated me.

"However it was done," I went on, "he loaded the rapidly bloating corpse onto a wagon and brought it to Rome. The distance isn't all that great. This shrine and its alley are so obscure that he could easily unload the corpse at night, without being seen. He left the snake there among its sculpted fellows, knowing that as long as it wasn't hungry, it would not leave its cool, dark sanctuary with its familiar scent of cedar. That way he knew he could impress his highly placed Roman friends with his snake-charming skill. And indeed we were all impressed. With this done, he paid his call on Caesar, who sent him to me."

"He is mad!" Pompaedius hissed. "What proof is there?"

"I don't need proof," I told him. "The question is, have I convinced Caesar?"

"He is correct," said Caesar. "You will not be tried before a jury. I am Dictator and I can have you executed right here, should I choose to do so. Arrest him, Decius Caecilius."

I reached for the priest without thinking and began the old formula, "Lucius Pompaedius Castor, come with me to—" Then he thrust the snake's head at me.

Julia later told me that I leapt backward with a cry like a frightened girl, but I remember no such thing. Pompaedius began backing away, hissing in his reptilian fashion, holding the deadly head at arm's length, threatening whoever stepped close.

"Lictors!" Caesar shouted. Instantly the doorway filled with his attendants, holding their *fasces* like weapons.

"Look out!" Julia cried. "He has a snake! And he'll use it!" The lictors flattened themselves against the walls, eyes gone wide.

Pompaedius made a dash for the door. Just as he stepped through it a foot stuck out, catching his ankle. With a whoop, the priest went tumbling. I saw the soles of his sandals for an instant, and then he was gone. There came a meaty crash, then a howl of horrified agony.

"Nasty tumble, that," I remarked. "Those steps are steep."

"I don't think the fall made him bellow like that," Caesar said. "Let's go see."

We went to the doorway and then out to the portico. Hermes was nursing a sore ankle. "Haven't done that since I was a boy," he said, "but it still works."

Pompaedius was still convulsing and flopping about, but he was probably already dead. His flesh was swelling and darkening, the skin beginning to sport huge blisters. The people who had been gawking panicked and jammed the alley with their bodies, trying to flee. They thought this might be some new and horrible disease, and they wanted no part of it. Several were trampled, but I think none fatally.

For a while we watched bemusedly. We could see about half of the snake protruding from beneath the body, wriggling weakly. Then it was still.

"It's always about power, isn't it, Caesar?" I said. "Whether you get it with politics, legions, money, or snakes, power is power."

Hermes borrowed a lictor's *fasces* and levered the body over. "The snake's dead. He crushed it when he fell."

"Bad luck for the Marsi," I observed.

"I'll have a lustrum performed and endow Angitia's temple," Caesar said. "That will satisfy them that the curse is lifted."

"But their sacred snake is dead," Julia said.

Caesar shrugged. "They'll find another. There are always other snakes in the swamp."

These things happened on two days of the year 709 of the City of Rome, during the third Dictatorship of Caius Julius Caesar.

IN RED, WITH PEARLS

by Patricia Briggs

New York Times bestseller Patricia Briggs is perhaps best known for the Mercy Thompson series, detailing the paranormal adventures of a coyote-shapeshifting car mechanic embroiled in the world of vampires, werewolves, and gremlins, and the related Alpha and Omega series, but she has also written traditional fantasy series such as the four-volume Sianim sequence (*Masques, Wolfsbane, Steal the Dragon, When Demons Walk*), the two-volume Hurog series (*Dragon Bones, Dragon Blood*), and the Raven duology (*Raven's Shadow, Raven's Strike*), as well as the stand-alone novel *The Hob's Bargain*. Her most recent book is *River Marked*, a new Mercy Thompson novel.

In the thriller that follows, we accompany werewolf private investigator Warren Smith, who will be familiar to readers of the Mercy Thompson series, as he races to crack a case involving zombies, witches, and lawyers. Just another day at the office.

I'M REAL GOOD AT WAITING. I RECKON IT'S ALL THE TIME I SPENT HERDING cows when I was a boy. Kyle says it's the werewolf in me, that predators have to be patient. But Kyle knows squat about herding cows. I'd say he knows squat about predators, too, but he's a lawyer.

I stretched out my legs and put the heels of my boots on the desk of Angelina the Receptionist and Dictator of All Things Proper at Brooks, Gordon, and Howe, Attorneys at Law. Angelina would have thrown a fit if she'd seen my feet propped up where anyone could just walk in and see me.

"Image, *hijo*," she'd said to me when I started working for the firm. I kinda liked it when she called me *hijo*. Though I was a lot older than any son of hers could possibly be—she didn't know that.

She'd given me a disapproving look. "It is all about image. Your appearance must be just so to get the clients to spend their money, Warren. They like expensive offices, lawyers in suits, and private detectives in fedoras and ties—it tells them that we are successful, that we have the skills to help them."

I'd told her I'd wear a fedora when the cows came home wearing muumuus and feather boas. I consented, however, to wearing ties to work and to play nicely during office hours, and she was mostly happy with that.

Office hours had been officially over for a good while, the tie was in my back pocket, and Angelina was gone for the day. I'd have been gone for the day, too, but one of Kyle's clients had come bursting in all upset and he'd taken her into his office and was talking her down.

Kyle was usually the last one out of the office. This time it was a sobbing client who suddenly decided that the jerk who'd slept with her best friend was actually the love of her life and she didn't really want to divorce him, just teach him a lesson. Tomorrow it would be a mound of paperwork that would only take him a few minutes to straighten up and a few minutes would stretch into a few hours. He tended toward workaholism.

I didn't mind. Kyle was worth waiting a bit for. And, like I said, I'm pretty good at waiting anyhow.

A noise out in the hall had me pulling my feet off the desk just before the outer door opened and a young woman in a sleek red dress with a big string of pearls around her throat entered the office in a wave of Chanel No. 5; she was stunning.

"Hey," she said with a big smile and a dark breathy voice. "Are you Kyle Brooks?" Her ears had pearls in them, too. Her hands were bare, though I could see that she'd recently been wearing a wedding ring. Dating a divorce attorney makes me notice things like that.

"No, ma'am," I told her. "After hours here. Best you try him tomorrow."

She leaned over Angelina's desk and the low-cut dress did what sleek little dresses are built to do in such circumstances. If I ran that way, I might have counted it a treat for the eyes. "I have to find Kyle Brooks."

She was close enough that the feel of her breath brushed my face. Mostly mint toothpaste. Mostly.

"Well now," I said, standing up slowly and sauntering around the desk as if I found her all sorts of interesting. Which I all-of-a-sudden surely did. "Just what do you want with Kyle, darlin'?"

Her smile died and she looked worried. "I have to find him. I have to. Can you help me?"

Kyle's office was down the hall and in the back. I could hear the woman he was with talking at him as she had been for the past half hour.

"Think I can," I said, and led her the opposite direction, to the big conference room at the other end of the offices. "Stay right here for a couple of minutes," I told her. "He'll be right in."

She'd followed me docilely and stopped where I told her to. I shut the door on her and hightailed it back to Kyle's office.

I opened the door without knocking and ignored Kyle's frown. "Would you do me a favor?" I asked tossing him my cell phone. "Call Elizaveta—her number is under *w*." Under *witch*; he'd figure it out, he was a smart man. "Tell her we have an incident, a *her* kinda incident, we'd like some help with. 'Scuse me, ma'am." I tipped my nonexistent hat to his indignant client before turning back to Kyle. "Might be the kind of thing we should clear the offices for."

"Your kind of thing?" Kyle asked obliquely. Something supernatural, he meant.

"That's right." I ducked out of his office and ran back to the conference room.

"One minute seventeen," the beautiful woman was saying when I rejoined her.

She stopped counting when the door opened, her body tense. When she saw me, she frowned. "I need Kyle," she said.

"I know you do," I told her. "He'll be right here." Hopefully not until after he got his client out safely and called Elizaveta Arkadyevna, my wolf pack's contractual witch.

I heard the front door of the office close and thought that I should have done something to make Kyle leave, too. But I hadn't known how long our guest would have stayed put—probably exactly "a couple of minutes" from the sounds of it. Not enough time to get Kyle to do anything except call Elizaveta—which he'd done because I heard Elizaveta's cranky voice; my cell phone distorted it just enough that with the door between us, I couldn't tell what she was saying.

I wasn't the only one who heard it. The zombie turned its head to the door.

My first clue about what the woman was had been that her breath had come out smelling fresh and oxygen-rich instead of dulled like someone's who was really breathing would have. A vampire's did the same thing, but she didn't smell like a vampire, not even under the rich scent of the Chanel. The second was the way she'd obeyed what I'd told her. Zombies are supposed to be really cooperative as long as what you tell them doesn't contradict what their master tells them to do.

"Yes," Kyle said from the hallway, closing in on the conference room. "This is Kyle Brooks. We're at my offices. Fine, thank you." The door popped open. "What's—"

The zombie launched itself at him.

I knew it was going to do it as soon as Kyle named himself. I was ready when he opened the door. I'm damned fast and I thought I had a handle on it, but that thing was faster than I'd thought it would be. I grabbed its shoulders and yanked it back, so it missed its target. Instead of nailing Kyle's throat, it latched onto his collarbone.

"Sh—" he cried out, jerking back.

"Stay still," I told him sharply, and he froze, his eyes on me and not on the zombie gnawing on him.

I don't often use that tone of voice on anyone, and I hadn't been sure it would work on a human. But if he tried to pull himself away, he was just going to do more damage to himself.

I tried not to think about the blood staining his shirt because I didn't know if the witch needed the zombie still up and moving to tell who sent it after Kyle.

And I was damned sure going to get whoever had sent it after Kyle.

If I couldn't tear the zombie apart, I had to avoid looking at Kyle's blood. He helped. He didn't look like a man in pain; he looked thoroughly ticked.

"Get her off," he gritted, while trying to do it himself. He may be slightly built, but he's tough, is Kyle. But it had locked its jaw good and tight, and Kyle couldn't budge it.

I'd always assumed that taking on a zombie would pretty much be like fighting a human—one that was relentless and didn't react to pain—but basically a human. When it moved on Kyle, it was moving a lot faster than I'd seen any mundane human move and now it was proving stronger, too.

It didn't so much try to get away from me as it did to get to Kyle. I'd have thought that would make it easier to subdue. Finally I got an arm wrapped all the way around its shoulders, pulling it tight against me. Then I could put my other hand to work on prying her teeth apart. *Its* teeth. Its jaw broke in the process—and I got my thumb gnawed on a little.

Kyle staggered back, white to the bone, but he stripped off his shirt and wadded it against the hole she'd dug in him. "What is she?" he asked. "Why isn't she bleeding more?"

He was looking at it in quick glances. I understood. It wasn't pretty anymore with its jaw hanging half off.

"Zombie," I told him a little breathlessly. It was now trying to get away from me, and that did make things a bit more difficult, but at least I wasn't trying to pry it off Kyle.

"Your business, then?" he said.

Usually I'd agree; not even shark-sharp lawyers like Kyle were so exotic as to call for assassination by zombie—it was too flamboyant, too blatant. The witches and supernatural-priest types who could create zombies had never been hidden the way the werewolves used to be, but they lived among the psychics, Wiccans, and New Agers where the con artists and the self-deluded provided ample cover for a few real magic practitioners. They didn't give up that cover lightly. Somebody would have had to have paid a lot for a zombie assassination.

I shook my head. "Don't know. Seems awfully set on you, either way." The zombie hadn't managed to get a limb free for the past few seconds, so I chanced turning my attention to Kyle. His wound worried me.

"You get out Howard's good malt," I told him. "He keeps the key behind the third book on the top left shelf. Clean that wound out with it. It's liable to have all sorts of stuff in its mouth." I didn't know much about zombies, but I knew about the Komodo dragon, which doesn't need poison to kill its prey because the bacteria in its mouth do the job just fine.

Kyle didn't argue, and took himself out of the conference room. As soon as he was out of sight, the zombie started crying out something. Might have been Kyle's name, but it was hard to tell what with its jaw so badly mangled.

I held on to it—by now I'd gotten a hold that prevented it from hitting me effectively or wiggling loose. That gave me the leisure to be concerned with other things. Kyle had shut the door gently behind him. I tried not to speculate about Kyle's reaction, tried to wrap up the panic and bury it where it could do no harm. He'd seen weird things before, even if none of them had drawn blood.

I could have destroyed the zombie and left it in the conference room for later retrieval with no one the wiser; could have hidden all of this from my lover as I used to do. But it had been different with Kyle from the beginning. The lies I'd told to him about who and what I was, lies that necessity dictated and time had made familiar, had tasted foul on my tongue when spoken to him. Now he knew my truths and I wouldn't hide from him again. If he couldn't live with who and what I was, so be it.

But none of that was useful, so I forced my attention to the matter at hand. Who would send a zombie to kill Kyle? Was it something directed at me? The zombie was pretty strong evidence that it was someone from my world, my world of the things that live in the dark corners, and not Kyle's; he was as human as it got.

Still, I couldn't think of anyone I'd offended so much that I'd made Kyle into a target. Nor, with the possible exception of Elizaveta herself—who was, as Winston Churchill said of her mother Russia, "a riddle wrapped in a mystery inside an enigma"—could I think of who could even create a zombie in the Tri-Cities. Eastern Washington State was not a hotbed of hoodoo or voodoo.

Maybe someone had hired it done? Hired an assassin, and the assassin had chosen the manner of death?

Kyle had a lot more enemies than I did. When he chose to use it, his special gift was to make the opposing parties in a courtroom look either like violent criminals, or like complete idiots—and sometimes both. Some of them had quite a bit of money, enough to hire a killer, certainly.

Maybe it wasn't my fault.

A zombie hit, though, screamed expensive, a lot more expensive than someone like Kyle would normally command. Which meant it was probably my fault.

I heard Elizaveta arrive and stride down the hall to the conference room. The lack of talking led me to believe that Kyle was still cleaning up.

Elizaveta opened the conference room door and entered like the *Queen Mary* coming to port in a wave of herbs and menthol instead of salt water, but with the same regal dominance, a regality accompanied by enough fabric and colors to do justice to a gypsy in midwinter—and it was hotter than sin outside.

I'd always thought that she must have been beautiful when she was young. Not a conventional beauty, something much more powerful than that. Now her nose looked hawkish and her eyes were too hard, but the power was still there.

"Warren, my little cinnamon bun, what have you found?" She never spoke to me in Russian as she did Adam, who understood it; instead she translated the endearments that peppered her speech—probably because they made me squirm. Why would you compare a grown man to a sweet roll?

I responded to her overblown presentation as I usually did, dipping down into my childhood accent—added to a bit by Hollywood Westerns. "Ah reckon it's a zombie, ma'am, but I thought you oughta take a good look first."

She smiled. "What was it doing when you found it?"

"It found me, ma'am. Lookin' for Kyle."

"And you relocated its jaw for that, my little Texas bunny?" she asked archly.

"No," said Kyle from the doorway. His spare shirt hung over his shoulders, folded back to avoid possible contact with the blood from the liberally splattered towel he held to his collarbone. He smelled like whiskey, but not even a zombie attack could make him unpretty or completely destroy his composure.

"He broke her jaw when he pulled her off me. You must be Elizaveta Arkadyevna Vyshnevetskaya. I'm Kyle Brooks."

She looked down at him—she is damn near as tall as I am. Her face was turned away from me, but Kyle had his lawyer face on, so I doubted her expression was friendly. The zombie's noises increased and so did its struggles. The witch turned to look at it without addressing Kyle.

"Quit playing and kill it," she told me coolly. "Breaking its neck should be enough." She'd never been happy with bringing humans into things she'd rather they be ignorant of. I guess she was trying to teach him and me a lesson.

I didn't like playing her game, but if she didn't need the zombie running around, Kyle would be safer with it dead.

I didn't look at Kyle when I popped the thing's neck. Its spine broke easily under my hand—which was what she'd wanted Kyle to see. I laid the limp body down on the conference table as carefully as I could, pulling the dress down over the dead woman's thighs.

Elizaveta turned her attention to the corpse, and I finally noticed that she wasn't alone. Nadia's gift was blending in—some of that was magic. I'd been occupied with the zombie, Kyle, and Elizaveta, but I still I should have noticed her.

"Nadia," I said, "thank you for coming." Of all Elizaveta's numerous family, I liked Nadia the best; she was quiet, competent, and smart. She also was, I understood, one of three of the family who were honest apprentices rather than dogsbodies who did Elizaveta's bidding.

The old woman's grandson, who was supposed to inherit the family business, had been found to be jump-starting his career in a manner Elizaveta found embarrassing. He'd quietly disappeared. I figure in a few hundred years someone would discover his remains in a jar in Elizaveta's basement.

I'd shed no tears for him. He'd conspired to murder Bran Cornick, the Marrok who ruled the wolves in this part of the world—the man who made being a werewolf less of a nightmare than it might have been. Elizaveta was still mad at Bran for outing the wolves—I'd always secretly wondered if she'd been a part of that mess, too, if only by being complicit.

Nadia lifted a pair of deep gray eyes to mine and smiled at me, light crow's feet dispelling the illusion of youth that her fine-pored skin and gray-free, seal-brown hair gave her. But the appearance of youth was no great loss because her smile was big and sweet.

"Warren," she said. She'd been born in the Tri-Cities and not a hint of Russian accent touched her voice. "You look . . ."

"Dressed up?" I said looking down at my slacks. "I'm working for Kyle's firm and they are a bit upscale. I got to keep the boots, though. As long as I remember to polish 'em once in a while."

She flushed a little. "I didn't mean to be rude, sorry. I didn't know you were a lawyer."

"Nah," I told her. "Kyle's the lawyer." I introduced her to him. She took the hand he held out and murmured her greeting. "I'm the gofer," I told her, answering the question she hadn't gotten around to yet.

"Private detective," corrected Kyle.

"Ink's so new it might smear," I told Nadia's raised eyebrows.

"Niece, quit flirting with the men and tell me what you see," said Elizaveta sharply, without looking up.

Nadia blushed—not because she'd been flirting, but because her great-aunt had embarrassed her—and turned her attention to the body on the table. After a steadying breath, she was all business.

"I know her face," she said in some surprise. "This woman has been in the papers. She disappeared when out for a jog last Saturday morning. I don't remember her name—"

"Toni McFetters," said Kyle. "You're right. I didn't recognize her before."

"Not unexpected under the circumstances." Nadia was clearly paying more attention to the dead body than she was to any of us; her voice was clinical. "Easiest way to get a corpse to raise is to kill her yourself."

"Are you saying that she was killed just for this?" Kyle looked cool and composed, but I could smell his agitation.

"Probably," said Nadia when her great-aunt didn't say anything. "This kind of magic works best on a fresh corpse. Hopeless to try it with one a mortuary has filled with embalming fluid, and stealing a body from a hospital morgue is tough. Too many people at a hospital." She glanced over her shoulder, saw Kyle, and clearly, from the consternation on her face, ran the past few minutes of conversation through her head. "I'm so sorry. I'm not used to discussing my work with a layman. I do know this is difficult for you. Whoever did this was willing to kill you—I'd imagine that murder doesn't bother them much."

"If it had killed Kyle," I asked, "would it have died?"

"Deanimated," said Elizaveta briskly. "It was already dead when it came here. It would be possible to give such a one a directive, and then dissipate the magic after that directive was accomplished."

"So someone would have come in here and found Kyle dead—killed by this woman who would be dead, too," I said. "Elizaveta, ma'am—" I tried to work a way around the question I wanted to ask without offending her. "Is there anyone in the Tri-Cities who knows how to animate a dead body like this?"

Elizaveta gave me a smile with teeth, so I guess she was offended. "Yes, my little bunny, I could have done it. But I am obligated to the Alpha of your pack and I am aware of your ties to the lawyer. I would not accept a commission to kill him." She examined my face and saw that wasn't enough for me. "No," she said clearly. "I did not kill this woman, nor did I turn her into a zombie and send her after your lover."

"My apologies," I told her. "But I had to ask."

"The magic keeps them warm," murmured Nadia into the tense atmosphere. I couldn't tell if she was blind to the tension between me and Elizaveta, or if she spoke to dispel it. "Almost at normal body temperature. Forensics wouldn't give an accurate time of death. It would look as though she'd died at the same time he had. A murder-suicide, perhaps. Impossible to tell without further work—but I think she was killed with an overdose of something that overworked her heart. Cocaine, perhaps. Something of that sort."

I don't know about Elizaveta, but I was distracted from her by what Nadia said. There wouldn't be a zombie to horrify the mundane public, just a mystery of why they'd killed each other. The use of the zombie as a murder weapon suddenly made more sense. No one would know about the magic—and no forensics to tie the real killer to the crime.

Nadia continued with her analysis. "In view of the fact that she was abducted while out jogging, her clothing is of some interest—no one jogs in a dress like this. The pearls are fake—good fakes, but nothing any insurance company or jewelry store would have a record of. The lipstick is of a common shade. The dress is more interesting. It isn't new. Maybe it came from a thrift store—we should be able to check it out."

"Shouldn't we call the police?" asked Kyle.

We all looked at him.

"We have a dead body of a missing person on my conference table. Someone is going to notice," he said.

"She has disappeared," said Elizaveta, speaking to him for the first time. "There is no gain in making her reappear."

Kyle's face hardened. "She has a family. Two kids and a husband. They deserve to know what happened to her."

"Can you fix her up?" I asked Elizaveta. "Repair the damages I did and then leave her somewhere she'll be found?"

"It is safer and easier to dispose of the body entirely," said Elizaveta dismissively.

"Well, yes, ma'am," I told her, making a subtle motion with my hand to stop Kyle from saying anything more. If Kyle started demanding things, we'd be up a creek without a paddle and maybe with a few more bodies besides. He saw my gesture and let me take point. Of all the humans I've ever known, Kyle is one of the best at reading body language.

"Easier and safer," I agreed with Elizaveta blandly. The witch shot me a suspicious look. "But if you *did* decide to put the body out where someone could find it—you and I both know that *you* could do it so's no one would ever associate it with you, this office, or magic of any kind. Easier if the damage I did to her, which might be tough to explain, can be repaired."

"There's no bruising around the site," said Nadia. "I could mend the flesh together, Aunt Elizaveta, so they could never tell."

The old witch stared at me, torn between resenting my manipulation and preening under my confidence in her abilities. I meant it and made sure she could hear it in my voice.

"You know that you enjoy the tough ones more," I coaxed. "Cleaning up another body is boring. This presents more of a challenge."

"*Another* body," said Kyle. But he said it real quiet and I think I was the only one who heard him. One of Elizaveta's gifts was making bodies disappear—around a werewolf pack, even a well-run pack like ours, there are going to be some bodies that need to disappear.

The corners of Elizaveta's mouth turned up, her shoulders relaxed, and I knew that I'd won.

"All right, sweet boy. You are right. Never could forensics unravel the mystery I can weave. If I wanted them to learn nothing, nothing is what they would learn. Still . . ." She smiled at me, eyes veiled with satisfaction. "It would be more challenging yet to show them evidence that doesn't exist. You, my private detective, will help to find who did this. When it is known, I will point the police in the correct direction."

"Thank you," I said, dropping my eyes from hers as was proper. As I did so, I noticed that Kyle had dropped the hand that held the towel and I didn't like what his wound looked like. I know about bite wounds; I've seen a lot of them. Bite wounds shouldn't get black edges a half hour after they've been inflicted.

I took a step closer to him and pulled the towel down so I could get a better look, and my nose wrinkled at the scent of rot that had set up far too soon.

"Ma'am?" I said. "Would you look at this, please?"

She glanced at Kyle and pursed her lips. Looking back at me she said, "Not my business. Take him to the emergency room."

I didn't growl at her, but only because my control is very, very good. The hair on the back of my neck stood up as the wolf inside decided he didn't like her answer.

"He *is*," I said, staring at her. "He is my mate and that makes him your concern."

Naming Kyle as my mate was a big step—but one my wolf and I were pleased with. I felt Kyle's attention spike and heard Nadia's indrawn breath, but kept my eyes on my target. Kyle's agreement would be needed, but not now, not for this.

"Mate implies procreation," Elizaveta said in prissy tones. "The two of you cannot have children. He is not your mate." She couldn't care less that I was gay, despite her words. I knew why she was behaving this way. I'd gotten my way with the body, and she wanted to win one of the battles tonight. She'd chosen the wrong one.

"You can discuss that with Adam," I said softly. The wolf would have torn out her throat happily—though that wouldn't have gotten Kyle fixed up. "Kyle, do you still have my cell phone?"

"I'd rather go to the emergency room," he said.

"No," I told him sharply. "No emergency room." I couldn't afford to divide the battle between them. "Elizaveta, do you want me to call Adam?"

Kyle, bless him, stopped arguing.

"I will remember this," she told me.

"That's fine." I worked at keeping my temper. "Remember that I'm only expectin' you to live up to the letter of the agreement you have with my pack." I'd won. Time to let her keep her pride if I could. A bit of flattery and a bone. "You know that the emergency doctors could do nothing with this—I can smell the gangrene. This is beyond them. If you don't take care of it, he'll die." I was afraid that was the truth and let her hear it.

"Only for you, cinnamon bun, only for you would I do this," she said. Then she reached out and pinched my cheek hard—the cheek on my face.

All business, she stepped between Kyle and me and pulled the towel farther out of the way and sniffed.

"Good whiskey," she said, dropping the thick Russian accent and exchanging it for a hint of Great Britain. "Not as good as Russian vodka, but not the worst thing you could have done. Still, neither could fix this. For this you need me."

I'd carried the body out to Elizaveta's car wrapped in a rug. I know it's a cliché, but a rug works pretty well to disguise a body because people expect it to be awkward and heavy. I used the rug from Kyle's office and told Elizaveta to keep it—which pleased her because it was an expensive rug. Kyle wouldn't want it back.

Kyle wasn't in the reception area where I'd left him. I listened and tracked him to his office. He was looking out his window at the traffic below. We were three stories up—pretty high for the Tri-Cities, which were still able to sprawl instead of climb to deal with the pressure of expansion.

I couldn't tell what he was thinking—but he didn't turn around when I came into the office, not a good sign.

"Kyle? Do you want me to take you to the emergency room?" The blackness was gone from the wound, but Elizaveta was no healer. I didn't think it would scar permanently, but it would hurt for a while yet.

"I want to find out who killed that woman," he said. "Someone killed her to get me—a woman I didn't even know."

I heard it in his voice under the anger. No one else would have, but I have very, very good hearing.

I took a chance and stepped in close to him, putting my arms around him and pulling him into me. "Not your fault," I said. "Not your fault."

"I know *that*," he snapped, but he didn't pull away. After a moment, he leaned back against me and put his hands on my arms, holding them where they were. "I know that—who better? I see it all the time. 'But maybe if I were a better cook, he wouldn't hit me' or 'If I could just have bought that car she wanted, she wouldn't have taken off with my best friend.' It is *not* my fault that someone killed her—not your fault either if it turns out to be that way."

I just held him.

"It feels like it, though," he said in a much different voice, the voice that no one else ever heard from him. He didn't let himself be vulnerable in front of anyone else.

"I'll find him," I told him, and then I leaned down and blew a teasing huff of air into his ear. "Or else Elizaveta will turn me into a toad."

We went out to eat that night. Kyle likes to cook, but he takes too long and it was way past dinner time. He didn't talk much over the food, pausing occasionally to stare into space, as he did when working on a particularly difficult case instead of dealing with getting munched on by a dead woman.

I'd lost him once, when he'd found out what I was. It says something about Kyle that it wasn't the werewolf part that bothered him, but the lies I'd told to keep the wolf from him. I hadn't had a choice about the lies—I think that was the only reason he forgave me.

I'd gotten him back and I wasn't likely to take him for granted anytime soon. The food tasted like sawdust as I waited for him to realize that he wouldn't have zombies trying to kill him if I weren't part of his life.

"Hey," he said, his gaze suddenly sharpening on my face. "You okay?"

"Fine." I smiled at him and tucked into supper with a little more effort. I wasn't going to kill the chance I'd been given by brooding over losing him before it happened.

Of course, there was a note on the door to Kyle's house when we drove into the driveway.

Kyle ripped it off and opened it. "He's objecting to your truck," he told me dryly as he read, giving me the abbreviated version. "He's sent a duplicate letter to the city. With photos to illustrate his point."

"Nothin' wrong with my truck," I said indignantly, and Kyle grinned. He lost his smile as soon as he looked back down at the note.

Three months ago, the nice family who lived next to Kyle's house had moved to Phoenix and sold their place to a retired man. We hadn't thought much about it at the time, not until the first note. Some children (three solemn-faced kids who, with their mother, were staying with us until their mother's ex-husband quit threatening them) had made too much noise in Kyle's pool after seven P.M., which was when Mr. Francis went to bed. We should make sure that all children were in their beds and silent so as not to disturb Mr. Francis if we didn't want the police called.

We'd thought it was a joke, had laughed at the way he'd referred to himself as "Mr. Francis" in his own notes.

The grapes along the solid eight-foot-tall stone fence between the backyards were growing down over Mr. Francis's side. We should trim them so he didn't have to look at them. He saw a dog in the yard (me) and hoped that it was licensed, fixed, and vaccinated. A photo of the dog had been sent to the city to ensure that this was so. And so on. When the police and the city had afforded him no satisfaction, he'd taken action on his own. I'd found poisoned meat thrown inconspicuously into the bushes in Kyle's backyard. Someone dumped a batch of red dye into the swimming pool that had stained the concrete. Fixing that had cost a mint, and we now had security cameras in the backyard. But we didn't get them in fast enough to save the grapes.

He'd been some kind of high-level CEO forcibly retired when the stress gave him ulcers and other medical problems. He came here, to the Tri-Cities, because he was a boat-racing fan. Other cities had boat races, I'm sure of it. Maybe I could recommend some for him.

"This kind of thing is supposed to happen when you live in an apartment," Kyle told me, crumpling the latest note in his hand. "Not in a four-thousand-square-foot house on three-quarters of an acre."

"We need to have a paintball game in the backyard," I told Kyle. "I could invite the pack."

"Escalation is not a solution," Kyle said, though he'd smiled at the thought. He'd seen some of our paintball games. "Right now the city is on our side. We want to keep it that way." Since Mr. Francis moved in, the folks in city hall, the police department, the zoning commission, and the building code enforcement office had all grown to know us by name.

"I know," I groused, unlocking the front door. "As long as we act like adults, there's nothing he can do to us."

Kyle followed me into the foyer. His house was the first place I'd ever lived that was big enough to have a foyer.

"I could move," he said reluctantly.

"Nah," I rubbed his head affectionately—Kyle loved his house. "You'd miss Dick and Jane."

Dick and Jane were the life-size naked statues in the foyer. The woman was currently wearing a little Bo Peep bonnet he'd found somewhere and a green silk sari that had belonged to his grandmother. Dick was still sporting the knitted winter hat with the long tail and a poof ball on his pride and joy because Kyle hadn't found anything he thought was funnier yet.

"We could move back into your apartment."

That apartment was a point of contention. He said I was keeping it because I didn't believe that he really understood he was sleeping with a werewolf. He also said I was being stupid because he was mine as long as I never lied to him again, werewolf or not. Kyle was a smart man. He was right about why I kept it—but I wasn't sure he was right about the rest. So I hadn't given up the apartment yet.

Proposing a move back to it showed that Mr. Francis was getting to him. If so, the time might have come to quit playing nice.

My cell phone rang. I pulled it out of my pocket and took a look. It wasn't a number I knew, but that wasn't unusual anymore—I was starting to get a little work from people unconnected to the law firm.

"Warren here," I said.

"This is Nadia," said the witch's niece. "Listen, Aunt Elizaveta wants me to go talk to the dead woman's husband tomorrow. I can do that, but I thought it might be useful if you came along. You can tell when someone's lying, right?"

"I can," I agreed. "But won't that arouse the wrong people's interest if you're out questioning people?" Wrong people like the police. I'd thought she intended to do a little magical forensics and leave the questioning to me.

"That's one of the things I'm good at," Nadia said. "People don't remember me asking them things if I don't want them to. If no one reminds him, he'll eventually even forget I came by."

I thought about that a moment, not entirely happy about what she said.

"I can't do it to you," she said anxiously. "Or anyone who is alert for it. It's an uncommon talent—that's why Aunt Elizaveta picked me to be one of her students."

"I was just thinking that I have a few people to question as well," I told her. "How 'bout I go out with you and then take you with me? We can have a cooperative investigation."

"Cooperative investigation," she said. "Sounds good to me."

"Let me pick you up," I told her. "If I leave my truck here another day, it's liable to be towed or have all the tires slashed."

Nadia laughed because she thought I was kidding, and we made arrangements to meet the next morning.

NADIA'S HOUSE WAS AN F HOUSE IN A SEA OF ALPHABET HOUSES IN RICHLAND. The government had done Richland a favor with all the World War II–era carbon-copy houses: kept it from looking like all the other well-heeled towns I've seen. A stranger to the Tri-Cities would be justified in thinking that it was the poorest of the cities rather than arguably the wealthiest, at least in absolute house values. The F houses were small, two-story, Federal-style houses that looked somewhat regrettably like the houses in a Monopoly game.

I wondered if Nadia chose her house because it disappeared into the woodwork the same way she did. I drove up her narrow, bumpy driveway and she ran out the door.

"Aunt Elizaveta is not happy," she informed me a little breathlessly as she fastened herself in. "I hope we find something today." She was lying about the last part, which puzzled me a little.

"What's wrong with your great-aunt?" I asked, pulling out into traffic.

"She couldn't find any magic signature on the body or the clothes the zombie was dressed in, except for mine and hers. That means there's a witch or priest out and about who is skilled enough to hide from my aunt."

There was just a hint of a smile on her face; I reckon it wouldn't be easy to be at Elizaveta's beck and call. Might be fun to see her stymied once in a while. That would explain the earlier lie.

"Where are we meeting Toni McFetters's husband?" I asked.

"At his house. He's on compassionate leave." She gave me the address. "The children are at his in-laws' house. He told me that when I called him yesterday and told him we're investigating his wife's disappearance. Our questioning should just blend in with that of the police if I can manage it right. It helps that he'll be the only one to work on."

Toni's husband's house was only a couple of blocks from Nadia's, in a newer neighborhood—no alphabet houses at all. It was a big house, not as upscale as Kyle's house, but not an inexpensive property either.

I pulled up in front and turned off the truck. "We can keep this short. All we need is to find out if he killed her or knows who did. And if he's noticed anything suspicious."

"Why don't you do the talking?" she said. "I'll work better if all I have to do is the magic."

I didn't like it, this business of messing with someone's mind, any more than I had liked lying to Kyle before he knew that I was a werewolf. But I'd lost my innocence a long time ago.

The man who let us in smelled of desperation. He matched his wife in good looks—or would have with a few more hours of sleep—but showed none of the signs of vanity that a lot of good-looking men display, men like Kyle for instance. McFetters's haircut was basic; his clothes were off the rack and fit indifferently.

Before I asked a single question, I knew that he had had nothing to do with his wife's disappearance.

"Mr. McFetters, thank you for speaking to us," I told him, refusing his offer to come in and sit down. "This won't take long."

"Call me Marc," he said. "Has anyone found out anything?"

"No," I said. It was a lie, but in a good cause. "Did anything happen in the past few weeks—before your wife disappeared—that caught your attention? Strangers in the neighborhood, someone your wife noticed when she was out jogging?"

He rubbed his hands over his head as if to jar his memory. "No," he said, sounding lost. "No. Nothing. I usually jog with her, but I got a late start that morning; we'd . . . Anyway she has an extra hour before she has to be at work. She says she can't think without her morning run."

"What was she wearing?" I asked, and listened to a detailed rundown that proved that whoever said that straight men don't pay attention to clothes was wrong.

"She was wearing a pink jogging suit we'd picked up in Vegas—it was her favorite, even though the right knee had a hole from where she fell a few weeks ago. She had size-eight Nikes—silver with purple trim. She likes her green running shoes better, but they clash with the pink. She wore the topaz studs I got her for our anniversary in her ears, and her wedding ring . . . white gold with a quarter-carat Yogo sapphire I dug up when I was eighteen and on a family vacation." There was a sort of desperate eagerness in his voice as he went on without prompting to describe their usual running route; as if he believed that somehow, if he could only manage to give enough details, it would help him find his wife.

He ran down, eventually, and, almost at random, his gaze focused on Nadia. He frowned. "I know you from somewhere, don't I? What was your name again?"

"Nadia," she said.

"Did you go to Richland High?" He rubbed his hair again and tried to find the proper social protocol.

"Along with half of Richland," she said in a gentle voice. "It's not important right now, Marc."

"Did you have anything to do with your wife's disappearance?" I asked as gently as I could, pulling him back to important things. He hadn't. I'd have bet my life on it, but for Elizaveta, I'd get absolute proof.

"No." He blinked at me, as if the thought were too strange to contemplate. He wasn't angry or offended, just bewildered. "No. I love Toni. I need to find her but I don't know where to look." Bewildered and terrified. "Where should I look?"

I SHUT THE DOOR BEHIND US AND WAITED WHILE NADIA MUTTERED A little under her breath and dropped a few herbs she had in a baggie on the steps.

"Well?" she asked after climbing in beside me.

I drove away from Toni McFetters's house before I answered her. Churning in my gut was the understanding that if I hadn't been with Kyle last night when the zombie came, I'd be in much the same state as Marc McFetters.

"We need to find who did this. That man doesn't deserve the police jumping down his throat."

"He didn't kill her," she said, but it was more of a question than a statement. I couldn't believe that she'd been in the same room I had and hadn't recognized the man's innocence. Witches don't have a wolf's nose, I suppose.

"Absolutely not."

"Good," she said. "He was right, we did go to high school together. A geeky kid, but a real sweetie." She shifted nervously in her seat as if she felt uncomfortable. "So that leaves us where?" Her question was a little fast. Maybe she'd liked Marc McFetters more than she was comfortable with me knowing. He seemed like a good man.

"We're going to have some conversations with a few people who are very unhappy with Kyle."

THERE WERE FOUR PEOPLE I WANTED TO CHECK OUT. IT MIGHT SURPRISE people who knew him that the list wasn't longer: Kyle did not make friends of the opposition in the courtroom. He was, however, fair and honest—which meant that most of the opposing lawyers got over their anger pretty fast.

I'd decided somewhere along the way that the zombie animator had been hired to assassinate Kyle. Gut instincts were always important to the detectives in the movies, but they were more so to werewolves. Mostly, gut instincts were just little bits of information floating around that resolved themselves into the most likely scenario.

That meant that we were looking for two different people. The one who did the hiring, and the one who was hired. Motive. My license might be new, but *I* was old. I'd survived because I understood what moved people, why they acted and why they did not. Old werewolves aren't that common; most of us who survive the Change die in fights with other werewolves shortly thereafter, because most werewolves don't understand body language. They also don't think. They trust their fangs and claws—even though *other* wolves have fangs and claws, too. I watched and learned.

Motive was easier to find than an assassin for hire. I'd find the man who wanted Kyle dead, and then I'd find the killer. That was why my list wasn't longer. Today we'd try the people who hated Kyle and could still afford to hire an assassin after Kyle got through with them in court. If I didn't find a likely suspect, tomorrow I'd leave Nadia at home, call in the pack, and go hunting for someone who'd hate me enough to kill the man I loved.

I'd called Sean Nyelund's office and made an appointment to see him under the name of my pack Alpha—Adam Hauptman—before I picked up Nadia that morning.

Nyelund worked in a newer office building in Kennewick, making money with other people's savings. He was good at it. Very good.

What he had not been good at was taking care of his own. He got the possession down fine, but not the concern for their welfare that should have gone along with it. His wife had sneaked out of his house in her underwear and hid in a neighbor's garage for three hours before they'd found her. It was the first time she'd been out of the house in two years. Now she lived in Tennessee with her family, a good chunk of the money her husband had made in his life, and a new husband who was good with his guns.

Nyelund hated Kyle, and he certainly had the money to hire an assassin. The only question was—had he?

Sean's receptionist was a pretty young thing not long out of high school. She had a bright smile to match the bright voice I'd talked to on the phone. Her eyes were frightened.

"Just a moment, let me announce you," she told me. Then she picked up her phone. "Mr. Hauptman to see you, sir."

A human wouldn't have heard the quiet "Send him in."

He had his back to us when we entered his office, typing rapidly on a keyboard. It was a power play that worked against him because I shut the door and used a little pack magic to keep the noise confined to this room. We wolves don't have much magic other than the shifting itself, but what we do have is good for keeping our business private.

He turned around, "Mr. Haupt—" and then he saw who I was. He stiffened subtly, his hand hidden by the desk—and then he noticed Nadia. His hands were suddenly both clearly visible on the top of his desk. "Ah, I see. Mr. Smith, using pseudonyms now? I wasn't aware you had enough money to invest. Perhaps the lady?"

Nyelund looked like a slightly overweight soft-bodied, soft-minded kind of guy, the kind who should be out saving puppies on the street corner. He had dimples and good manners. It was his eyes that gave him away, cold and assessing. If he hadn't been smart, he'd already have been in jail.

"I thought it would save some time," I said. "Did you order a hit on Kyle Brooks?"

"Would I do such a thing?" he asked, spreading his hands out. Just a good ol' boy, that was Sean Nyelund. "I don't know where you came up with that idea."

I questioned him for twenty minutes or so and couldn't get a straight answer out of him. It could mean that he'd done it. It could mean that he was thinking about doing it—or that he enjoyed the hell out of frustrating me. Hard to tell.

Finally, he said, "Go away, Mr. Smith. You bore me. Come back if you have money to invest."

"You take care, now," I said, tipping an imaginary hat. "I'd hate to see anything happen to you."

He grunted and turned back to his computer.

Nadia worked her magic under the cover of my opening the door, and then we strolled out past the receptionist.

"He pulled a gun on you," Nadia said, belting in.

"I saw it," I told her. "You saved me, darlin' girl."

She laughed. "Or reassured him that you weren't about to attack."

"Could be," I acknowledged, but thought that Nyelund would happily have shot me if he could have gotten away with it. Something to keep in mind.

"What did you learn?" she asked. "I couldn't tell anything about him."

"The jury is out on Nyelund," I told her. "He makes such a point of not answering questions, he might as well be fae."

"Does he know that you're a werewolf?" she asked. "And that werewolves can smell lies?"

I shook my head, relatively certain of my answer. The public might know about werewolves—but I wasn't taking out advertising. Kyle knew, but he was pretty much the only human who did. Using Adam's name might make Nyelund suspicious—Adam had become a celebrity once the word got out that he was the local pack Alpha. If I were Nyelund, though, I'd bet that the celebrity part was why I'd used Adam's name, not the Alpha-werewolf part. And should he think I was a werewolf anyway, he couldn't prove anything and it just might make Kyle a mite safer.

If Nyelund was smart and subtle, Phillip Dean, the next man on my list, was a different kettle of fish. He'd done some time after Kyle worked his magic in court—but only because he *was* stupid and talked his way into jail by threatening the judge. Dean was a nasty brute who'd inherited his father's money a couple of years ago. The money wasn't really enough to hire anyone—but he had the contacts, and it was only a matter of time before he killed someone. He'd almost managed to make it his ex-wife and wouldn't mind at all making Kyle Brooks his first kill.

He also, as it turned out after I made a few phone calls, was vacationing in Florida—Disney World.

"Doesn't mean it isn't him," I told Nadia. "But he's kinda a long shot anyway. Doesn't think ahead very well, though he's cunning enough when cornered."

"So? Where to now?"

"Ms. Makenzie Covington."

"A woman?"

I smiled at her. "Most of Kyle's clients are women, but he takes on cases for men, too. Ms. Covington is a real piece of work; tried to pose as the abused wife so that she could take her ex to the cleaners—she was not happy when Kyle proved that she inflicted her bruises herself. Her ex-husband's bruises were also her doing. She lost visitation rights—not that she cared about the kids, but it humiliated her in front of her friends. Two years from now, she'll be off tormenting her third or fourth husband, and wouldn't make my list. Six weeks after her divorce, though, her ire is still focused pretty hard on Kyle."

"Why not on her ex?"

I smiled a bit grimly. "By the time she got through with him, all he could say was 'Yes, dear' and look at the ground. Kyle was the one who humiliated her and protected her victim."

Makenzie Covington worked at home—which was currently a condo in South Richland. She was striking rather than beautiful. Dark hair, dark eyes, and strong features, she looked like a passionate woman who lived life to its fullest. Which was sort of true. She didn't recognize me when she answered her doorbell.

I introduced myself and Nadia.

"I've never met a private detective before," she cooed at me. "Won't you come in?"

It didn't take long to figure out that it wasn't her. If she'd ordered a hit on someone, she wouldn't have welcomed a pair of private investigators into her home and gotten all hot and bothered about it. Sometimes being a werewolf gives you interesting insights into people.

Still.

"Ma'am, you haven't ordered a hit on Kyle Brooks, have you?"

"No," she said immediately and truthfully. "But if you find someone who will, tell him I'll pay half." That was the truth, too.

"I'll do that," I told her. Then it took me about twenty minutes to extract us from her condo, by the end of which even Nadia caught on to what Ms. Covington wanted from us.

"I am really glad I brought you with me for that," I told Nadia.

Nadia giggled. She hadn't even bothered doing any magic. No need for it. "I don't think I was much help. She'd have taken both of us to bed, wouldn't she?"

"You, me, and the stray dog outside, yes, ma'am." I pulled out into traffic. Maybe I was driving a little faster than normal.

"I've never seen you disconcerted before," she said. "Usually you just talk slower and use lots of *ain't*s and *ma'am*s."

"Now I know how those sixty-year-old wives feel when their husband of forty years comes back from the doctor with a bottle full of blue pills." I wasn't as flustered as I made out, but I enjoyed Nadia's laughter. She didn't laugh as often as she ought.

HARPER SULLIVAN WAS A RETIRED DOCTOR.

Divorce is a nasty business and secrets tend to come out. The good doctor's secret was that he liked to diagnose his patients with various life-threatening diseases they didn't have. Of course, that meant they had to come in for frequent treatments. Eventually (especially when they were getting ready to get a second opinion), they were miraculously cured, all credit going to the doctor.

Kyle'd used blackmail to get a nice settlement for the doctor's ex-wife (who wasn't any great shakes herself if she'd kept quiet about what he was doing for twenty years) and to force the doctor to retire. There wasn't real proof, Kyle'd explained to me, only hearsay—enough to ruin Sullivan's reputation and get the AMA on his case, but he'd likely have kept his license. Blackmail was better because it kept more people from being harmed. Kyle can occasionally be as pragmatic as a wolf when it comes to making sure that justice is done.

Dr. Sullivan was weeding his azalea bed when we drove up. He didn't look up until I cleared my throat. It always bothered me that he looked like that doctor in that old TV show—*Marcus Welby, M.D.*

"Doctor," I said, "I'm Warren Smith. I'm a private investigator. This is my partner for the day, Nadia Popov. I'd like to ask you a few questions."

"Of course," he said, getting up and pulling off his work gloves. "It is getting hot out, though. Why don't you come in and have some iced tea?"

I'd met him a couple of times, and it was unlikely that he didn't know me. But he gave no sign of it that I could discern, even when I introduced myself.

He led us around to the back door of the big brick house—explaining that he didn't want to track dirt inside. He showed us into his living room—a big space with hardwood floors, real Persian rugs, and antique furniture, some of it even older than I was. But the thing that dominated the room was a wall of windows that looked out over the Columbia River.

We were both staring at the view when he shot me.

It wasn't silver, and a lead bullet wasn't going to kill me—but it hurt a lot. I spun and snarled, a hand to my shoulder. He wasn't a very good shot if he missed my heart at that range.

It was the second time I'd had a gun pulled on me today—I'd expected something of the sort from Nyelund, though I'd hoped that meeting him at his work would preclude actual violence. The doctor I'd picked as someone who'd hire out his dirty work. At least he wasn't a marksman.

"Oops," he said and adjusted his aim.

"*STOP,*" said Nadia.

Now a dominant can enforce his will on a lesser wolf. I'd done something of the sort with Kyle yesterday when I'd made him quit pulling against the zombie's bite. But this was something else again, 'cause not only did the doctor freeze, but so did I. And it wasn't the kind of hesitation—the loss of will to disobey that my Alpha could hit me with—my body flat-out refused to move at all.

Screw that.

I drew in a deep breath and called out the wolf—who shook off the magic like water that wanted to cling where it wasn't supposed to. He also healed up a fair bit of the damage the pistol had done. I took a step mostly to prove I could.

She didn't even notice me; she was too busy with Sullivan. "*You won't kill anyone,*" she told him in that same black-magic voice. "*You'll leave Kyle Brooks alone.*" I was really glad I'd broken her hold on me before that one. "*You won't remember this. You'll just feel as though whatever we were talking about got solved. Everything is all right.*"

"All right," muttered the doctor, and my wolf saw that something was broken inside him, something that had been whole and well when we'd come here. In an elk, it was the sign that the animal was done for; next blizzard, next predator, and it wouldn't fight to survive.

Nadia turned and seemed a little surprised to see me so close. "Your shoulder?"

"Healing," I said. "I'm fine." Sometimes things like that took a long time to heal, and once in a while they just closed right up. This was that once in a while. I looked around, but there had been surprisingly little blood; most of it had been absorbed by my clothes.

The bullet had gone right though me and through the window, leaving behind a spiderweb of cracks. The doctor appeared to have forgotten about us and shuffled off with his gun, muttering to himself, "It's all right. Everything is fine."

Nadia grabbed a damp towel from the kitchen and wiped the blood off the hardwood floor, leaving not a trace behind. Then she took the splattered towel and held it against the broken window.

The wolf felt her magic and backed away. Not frightened, just cautious. When she pulled the towel away, it was clean of my blood and the window was intact.

"Waste not, want not," she said. "I thought I'd have to supply some of my own to finish it up—but your blood is potent."

I took her arm. "Let's go before he breaks loose," I said, though I didn't think he'd really break loose. The suggestions she'd planted might fade. But she'd broken him, and my instincts said that was permanent.

That's the problem with witches; they don't really care about anyone except themselves. Their power comes from pain, blood, and sacrifice—*other people's* pain, blood, and sacrifice, when they could manage it. If they flinched away from doing harm, they wouldn't have any power. Then other witches would take advantage of that and steal what little power they had. White witches were few, and tended to be psychotically paranoid. Elizaveta and her family skirted the edge of true black magic, but they did stand on that edge and look into the abyss with open eyes.

The wolf could respect a predator like that, but neither of us were entirely comfortable with it. What she'd just done to the doctor was wrong: it would have been kinder to kill him.

"I'm sorry," she said softly as I drove back across the river into her part of Richland.

"What for?" I asked. "Saving my life?"

"You didn't like it that I stole his will," she said. "I admit I could have been more careful. But he'd shot you, and I used that, used your pain. It gave me a little more power than I'm used to. He'll be all right."

If she wanted to believe that, who was I to tell her differently? Maybe I was wrong, but I didn't think so.

"So," she said softly, "are you finished with this? Did you find out what you needed to know with Dr. Sullivan? Is it solved, then?"

I opened my mouth, thought a bit more, and said, "Yes, I suppose I am finished."

We didn't talk much more, but when she hopped out of the truck when I stopped in her driveway, she said without looking at me, "Maybe we could see each other again? I make a mean cherry pie."

I smiled. "Maybe so."

She relaxed, gave me a rare grin, and kissed her fingertips, and blew the kiss my way before she ran into her house, looking about sixteen.

Everything will be all right. I flexed my fingers on the steering wheel.

KYLE AND I ATE DINNER AT A MEXICAN RESTAURANT KITTY-CORNER FROM Kyle's offices. The music was loud enough that human ears wouldn't hear private conversations—one of the reasons I liked to eat at this place.

"You're awfully quiet," Kyle said. "Find something?"

I looked at him. He looked tired. "Yes."

"Are you going to tell me?"

I looked down at my food. "Yes. But not tonight. I have a few more things to check out—a couple of things to do."

"Illegal?"

I gave him a half grin. "Like I'd tell you ahead of time."

"You'll just make me an accessory afterward," he grumbled.

"I've a little justice to serve," I told him.

He thought about it while he ate a few bites of his fish tostada. "Toni McFetters deserves justice," he said. "Are you sure you can't go about it legally?"

"I plan on using proper channels for some of it," I said. "But there's some of it that it's not possible to do that with."

Kyle believed in the court system—one of the few traces of optimism in his cynical worldview. However—as his blackmail of Sullivan proved—he understood its limitations.

"All right," he said. "I can live with justice. Will I see you at home tonight?"

"I'll be in later," I said. "Maybe very late."

He looked at me seriously. "Don't get caught. Don't get hurt. Don't think I didn't notice that you're wearing a different shirt than you put on this morning and aren't using your right arm to eat with."

"I won't," I said earnestly. "I'll try not to. I would never try to get something like that by you."

He laughed, stood up and leaned across the narrow table, and kissed me, oblivious to the stares we got. The Tri-Cities is a pretty uptight town, and two men kissing in public is not a common sight.

A girl in the next table gave a wolf whistle and said, "Can I kiss the cowboy next?"

Okay, so maybe everyone wasn't that uptight.

Kyle gave her a cheeky grin. "Sorry. He's my cowboy, you'll have to find your own."

She sighed. "I have one. But he doesn't look like that when he blushes."

"Maybe if I kissed him, he would?" Kyle arched an eyebrow.

She laughed. And if some of the people might have made an offended scene about the kiss, she'd taken the edge off. I kissed her cheek in appreciation as I passed her table on the way out. Her cowboy might not blush, but she did.

From the office, I called Ben. A fellow pack member, Ben was also a computer geek. I can get by on the computer, but Ben makes me look like a complete Luddite. It took him the better part of an hour to run down the information I'd asked him for—it would have taken me a week or more. I put the hour to good use, pulling out the clues my instincts told me were there, running off some photocopies of sensitive files, and calling a few more people. After Ben called me back, I called George and then went out to do a little private detecting.

George, in addition to being a werewolf, was also a Pasco police officer. He was my link to the "proper channels" I'd promised Kyle.

George met me at a fast-food place a few blocks from Sean Nyelund's house in West Pasco. He drove his own car and came dressed casually, but he was on the job despite the late hour. We both ordered something to drink and sat down. It was nearly closing time and it wasn't tough to find a place where no one would overhear us.

"You said you have something on Nyelund." His tone was eager. In addition to being a police officer, he was into the BDSM scene—which kept a very low profile around here. During Nyelund's divorce, Nyelund admitted that he was into BDSM, and that tidbit made the news. George and his friends didn't appreciate that one bit. Nyelund wasn't a BDSM dom. He was a psychopathic, sadistic bastard who enjoyed breaking people.

"Right," I told George. "He's got another victim." I gave him the name of Nyelund's receptionist. "These files you don't have," I told him, giving him copies I'd made in the office. "Confidential lawyer/client/doctor stuff. They'll show you what to look for—but I promised the victim they would be for your eyes only."

I waited while he paged through Nyelund's first wife's medical files and transcripts of her therapy sessions. She'd given them to Kyle and then told him he couldn't use them. I'd called her and told her about Nyelund's little receptionist. It had taken me most of that hour I'd waited for Ben to talk her into it. She'd told me I could show George, but no one else.

He whistled through his teeth. "Poor kid," he said. But he wasn't surprised. He'd known what the case was about, but Nyelund's ex-wife's refusal to bring charges against him had tied his hands. It was the details that were new to him.

"He's got a bunker, a secret room," he said, sounding like a kid in a candy store. Secret rooms were pretty easily sniffed out if the one looking happened to have a wolf's sense of smell. "And he likes to film things. Illegal things. How helpful of him."

"Is it useful?"

"I need a reason for the search warrant."

I gave him a thumb drive. Nyelund thought his guard dogs would keep people from taking photos through his window. Guard dogs don't bark at me if I don't want them to, and Nyelund had been too occupied to notice me. His lights had been on, so I hadn't even had to use a flash. My camera had helpfully recorded the time and date.

I tapped the drive. "You'll find the photos on that good for probable cause. You can even give my name as the photographer. I'm a private detective and I was sent out to take photos of this guy's wife, only I got the address wrong. When I realized what I was taking photos of, I gave you a call."

A snake doesn't change his spots. It had been only a matter of time before Nyelund tried his tricks on a new victim. Kyle and I'd been keeping an eye on him, but we'd missed the receptionist. Ben said she'd been working for him for about two months—right after she moved to the Tri-Cities.

"She's seventeen," I told him.

George grinned at me, his eyes enraged. "Is she, now? And look at him with that camera. Wrapped up like a great big birthday present. Thanks, Warren."

"Don't mention it." I tipped my imaginary hat to him. If Nyelund hadn't been so obliging, I'd have resorted to being a credible witness, but this was better.

IT WAS VERY LATE WHEN I MADE IT TO MY NEXT STOP. THE BACK DOOR wasn't locked and let me into the kitchen. I waited a minute and listened. Only one person in the house, and that person was asleep.

I walked into the living room, toward the stairs that led to the bedrooms. I'd been thinking about this all night, and I still hadn't made up my mind what I was going to do.

Instinct was one thing; proving what I knew was an entirely different proposition.

I'd planned on a little sleuthing and then interrogation—but then the lights of a car driving past illuminated the top of a curio cabinet where there were a bunch of photos. One of them caught my eye and I went over and picked it up.

I didn't need the light to see it; one of the benefits of my condition is superb night vision. I stared at the photo of a pair of happy people for a moment, then replaced it.

I went into the bedroom and did what I had to do. Nadia didn't even wake up when I snapped her neck. It was easier than snapping the neck of the zombie she'd made of the woman she'd killed.

I searched the room and found a few things. From the bedroom, I called Nadia's great-aunt.

"You call me late, my little sticky bun. Did you find out something I can use?"

"No," I told Elizaveta. "It was Nadia."

"You are wrong," she pronounced. "Nadia does not have the skill to animate the dead." She'd always underestimated Nadia. Everyone had. Everyone but me.

"Nine thousand dollars was transferred into one of her bank accounts two weeks ago and another last week." Ten thousand or over, and the feds start to pay attention. "Last year she made a hundred and ten thousand dollars; she listed her profession as artist. From her bank records, she made four or five times that much this year."

Elizaveta would not consider Nadia's profession as an assassin an issue.

"She worked exclusively for humans," I told her. "She keeps copies of her contracts. Her employers all knew she was a witch. It was her edge." That would be an issue. Mundane folks tend to get all frightened when they figure out they have monsters in their midst, and it results in things like the Inquisition and the witch hunts that wiped out the majority of the witch bloodlines in Europe a few centuries back.

"You are at her house."

"Yes, ma'am."

"Wait there for me. Do not do anything rash."

I looked at Nadia's face. "No, ma'am. I don't do rash."

I WAITED IN THE DARK, SITTING IN THE LITTLE ROCKER IN NADIA'S ROOM, until Elizaveta came in.

She stared at her great-niece for a moment and then said in a very chilly voice, "I told you not to do anything rash."

"It was already done," I informed her.

"It was *my* business to take care of," she said.

"Folks think that your grandson is dead," I told her.

I figured he wasn't. Like I said, witches draw their power from suffering, from sacrifice, like Nadia using my blood to mend the window at Dr. Sullivan's. I wasn't providing Elizaveta anyone else to torture.

Elizaveta stared at me, gray eyes sharp as a harpy's. Witches don't have much trouble seeing in the dark either.

"She moved against what was mine," I told her. "That made stopping her my business. I'm a wolf, ma'am. Not a cat. I don't play around with my prey."

I had liked Nadia, the Nadia I thought she was anyway. It was better that I killed her quickly.

I reached out and handed her the ring I'd found in Nadia's jewelry box. "This is Toni McFetters's wedding ring. When you put out the body for the police to find, it will cause fewer questions if she's wearing that ring. The clothes she was wearing are in a paper bag in the closet—a pink running suit. Maybe she should die of natural causes. I'm sure you can figure something out."

She took it and sighed, her voice softening and the Russian accent gone. She sounded old. "You know, it is very difficult to raise a witch so that they do not self-destruct. I myself had six siblings and only two of us survived. My sister had no talent at all. The temptations are so great."

She looked at Nadia. When she looked back at me, the accent had returned. "She had a crush on you, my little Texas bunny. Otherwise she wouldn't have been so foolish as to do this where I might find her out."

"She knew that I'm gay," I told her, startled.

She laughed. "Forbidden fruit is the sweetest, Warren, my darling. She thought she could change that if you would just look at her. I imagine getting paid to kill your boyfriend was too much temptation for her to resist." She smiled sweetly at me, waiting for me to understand that this was all my fault.

She cared for Nadia, I thought, but she cared more that I'd robbed her of the opportunity to get more power. Maybe she was also ticked that I'd seen what was going on under her nose before she did.

I hate witches.

"Nadia made her choices," I said abruptly, standing up. "I need to get home."

As I walked out of the bedroom, Elizaveta said, "Tell your Alpha that Nadia has decided that she wants to explore the world. She already has tickets to France. No one will much notice when she doesn't come back."

Meaning that Elizaveta would live with my killing Nadia and wouldn't break the deal she had with the pack. When I'd called Adam to warn him what I had to do, he'd told me that was what Elizaveta would do.

I didn't slow down or reply.

DESPITE WHAT I'D TOLD ELIZAVETA, I HAD ONE MORE STOP TO MAKE. FOR this one I would be the wolf. It took me a while to shed my human form for the wolf, longer than usual. Probably because I'd been shot; physical weakness makes the transformation harder for me.

The second-story window, the bedroom window, was open, and I jumped through it from the ground. I landed with a thud, but my victim, like Nadia, didn't wake up. I needed this one awake. So I made more noise, letting my claws tick on the hardwood floor.

It wasn't hard. I was very, very angry.

"Wha—"

He turned on the light, but I was already out in the hall. Just around the corner. I made a little more noise.

He grumbled, "Damned mice."

He walked into the hallway where I waited for him.

I CRAWLED INTO BED, EXHAUSTED, WEARY TO MY SOUL.

"Warren?" He pulled me close. "Baby, you're freezing."

If he asked, I would tell him.

"Can you sleep?"

I nodded.

"Fine, tell me about it in the morning."

I took the comfort he offered gratefully.

WE WERE AWAKENED BY THE AMBULANCE.

Kyle went out to find out what he could while I showered. He came in while I was drying off.

"Mr. Francis died of a heart attack last night." He had an odd expression on his face. Hard not to feel some relief, I guessed—and harder not to feel guilty over it. "I guess we won't be getting any more notes." He frowned at me, then donned his lawyer face. "Warren?"

Among the health issues our neighbor had retired with was a weak heart. Much easier to explain a heart attack than death by wild animals. This was the twenty-first century after all, not the nineteenth.

"I'd have gotten more satisfaction if I could have sunk my teeth into him," I told Kyle, rubbing the towel over my hair with a little more force than necessary. "Apparently he decided that you'd never be a neighbor he could cow properly. He hired Nadia, Elizaveta's niece, to kill you."

"Mr. Francis?" Kyle said incredulously. I pulled the towel off my head to see him standing slack-jawed. *"Mr. Francis* hired a witch to make a zombie to kill me?" After a moment, he shook off his shock. "I thought for sure it would be Nyelund."

"Covington said she'd pay for half if we told her who hired someone to kill you," I told him. "It was Sullivan who shot me"—Kyle looked at the red mark on my shoulder that was all that was left of the wound—"but he won't be a threat to anyone anymore."

Nadia broke Sullivan—but she'd aimed that magic at me, too. I wasn't supposed to think about Kyle anymore, I was supposed to leave off the investigation with the feeling that everything would be all right. And I wasn't supposed to remember the magic she'd worked to ensure that result. She'd spent so long teaching everyone to underestimate her, she'd overestimated herself.

Kyle frowned at me. "Tell me."

So I told him about Sean Nyelund while I got dressed. I paced restlessly and told him about Nadia while he sat on the bench at the foot of the bed and watched me.

"Justice was served, Warren," he said when I finished. "I'm sorry it had to be you who served it."

"I'm not," I told him. I'd only done what I needed to protect my own. I'd do it again.

He smiled a little as if he knew something I didn't. "If you say so."

"She was right," I said.

"Who was?"

"Nadia. She said the red dress might be useful in finding out who'd killed Toni McFetters."

He reached up and caught my hand, pulling me down to sit beside him.

"You liked her," he told me.

"She had a prom photo in her house." On top of the curio cabinet. "Toni's husband had taken Nadia to her high school prom. That red dress Toni was wearing? It was Nadia's prom dress; so were the pearls and shoes, near as I could tell. He'd taken her to the prom and hardly remembered her." She'd remembered *him*, though. I'd expected to have to search her house for Toni's missing belongings or, if that hadn't worked, wake Nadia up and question her. She'd made things easy for me.

"Elizaveta only objected that she'd exposed herself as a witch to the humans," Kyle said. "If you hadn't told her that, she would have left Nadia alone. You didn't have to kill her." He put his arm around me. "Tell me that's not what you're thinking now. Tell me that's not what is bothering you."

It wasn't. Not quite. I was thinking that she had attacked Kyle and part of me would have been happier if I'd eaten her. It had taken more will than I'd thought I had not to eat the old man next door, who was even more to blame than Nadia.

I stared at Kyle. I know that the wolf must have been showing through, but he didn't flinch, didn't drop his eyes.

"She was escalating," he said. "She killed for money and learned to like it. She killed Toni because Toni and her husband jogged past her house every day and they were happy. She tried to kill me because we are happy."

He thought I was a hero. He needed to know better.

"I killed two people last night," I told him. "Premeditated murder." I swallowed, but told him the other part of it, too. "I enjoyed it."

He kissed me. When he was finished, he told me, "You're a werewolf—a predator. A skilled killer, but not an indiscriminate one. So am I. If my prey is still writhing when I'm finished, it doesn't make me any less a predator."

I looked at him and he gave me a crooked grin. "Ready to get rid of that apartment yet?"

I laughed and leaned into him.

"Maybe," I said. "Just maybe."

THE ADAKIAN EAGLE

by Bradley Denton

World Fantasy Award, John W. Campbell Memorial Award, and Theodore Sturgeon Memorial Award winner Bradley Denton was born in 1958, grew up in Kansas, and took an MA in creative writing from the University of Kansas. He sold his first story in 1984 and soon became a regular contributor to *The Magazine of Fantasy and Science Fiction*. His first novel, *Wrack and Roll*, was published in 1986, and was followed by *Buddy Holly Is Alive and Well on Ganymede*, *Blackburn*, *Lunatics*, and *Laughin' Boy*. He's perhaps best known for his series of Blackburn stories and novels about an eccentric serial killer, but he won the John W. Campbell Memorial Award for his novel *Buddy Holly Is Alive and Well on Ganymede*, and the Theodore Sturgeon Memorial Award for his novella "Sergeant Chip." His two-volume collection *A Conflagration Artist* and *The Calvin Coolidge Home for Dead Comedians* won the World Fantasy Award as the year's Best Collection, and his stories have also been collected in *One Day Closer to Death: Eight Stabs at Immortality*. He lives in Austin, Texas.

Here he takes us to the frozen, wind-blasted landscape of the Aleutians to join a group of soldiers guarding a barren rock during World War II—one of whom you might recognize—who must face sinister magic, and the even more sinister, and murderous, secrets of the human heart.

I

THE EAGLE HAD BEEN TORTURED TO DEATH.

That was what it looked like. It was staked out on the mountain on its back, wings and feet spread apart, head twisted to one side. Its beak was open wide, as if in a scream. Its open eye would have been staring up at me except that a long iron nail had been plunged into it, pinning the white head to the ground. More nails held the wings and feet in place. A few loose feathers swirled as the wind gusted.

The bird was huge, eleven or twelve feet from wingtip to wingtip. I'd seen bald eagles in the Aleutians before, but never up close. This was bigger than anything I would have guessed.

Given what had been done to it, I wondered if it might have been stretched to that size. The body had been split down the middle, and the guts had been pulled out on both sides below the wings. It wasn't stinking yet, but flies were starting to gather.

I stood staring at the eagle for maybe thirty seconds. Then I got off the mountain as fast as I could and went down to tell the colonel. He had ordered me to report anything hinky, and this was the hinkiest thing I'd seen on Adak.

That was how I wound up meeting the fifty-year-old corporal they called "Pop."

And meeting Pop was how I wound up seeing the future.

Trust me when I tell you that you don't want to do that. Especially if the future you see isn't even your own.

Because then there's not a goddamn thing you can do to change it.

II

I FOUND POP IN A RECREATION HUT. I HAD SEEN HIM AROUND, BUT HAD never had a reason to speak with him until the colonel ordered me to. When I found him, he was engrossed in playing Ping-Pong with a sweaty, bare-chested opponent who was about thirty years his junior. A kid about my age.

Pop had the kid's number. He was wearing fatigues buttoned all the way up, but there wasn't a drop of perspiration on his face. He was white-haired, brown-mustached, tall, and skinny as a stick, and he didn't look athletic. In fact, he looked a little pale and sickly. But he swatted the ball with cool, dismissive flicks of his wrist, and it shot across the table like a bullet.

This was early on a Wednesday morning, and they had the hut to themselves except for three sad sacks playing poker against the back wall. Pop was facing the door, so when I came in he looked right at me. His eyes met mine for a second, and he must have known I was there for him. But he kept on playing.

I waited until his opponent missed a shot so badly that he cussed and threw down his paddle. Then I stepped closer and said, "Excuse me, Corporal?"

Pop's eyes narrowed behind his eyeglasses. "You'll have to be more specific," he said. He had a voice that made him sound as if he'd been born with a scotch in one hand and a cigarette in the other.

"He means you, Pop," the sweaty guy said, grabbing his shirt from a chair by the curving Quonset wall. "Ain't nobody looking for me."

Pop gave him the briefest of grins. I caught a glimpse of ill-fitting false teeth below the mustache. They made Pop look even older. And he had already looked pretty old.

"Cherish the moments when no one's looking for you," Pop said. "And don't call me 'Pop.' 'Boss' will do fine."

"Aw, I like 'Pop,'" the sweaty guy said. "Makes you sound like a nice old man."

"I'm neither," Pop said.

"You're half right." The sweaty guy threw on a fatigue jacket and walked past me. "I'm gettin' breakfast. See you at the salt mines."

Pop put down his paddle. "Wait. I'll come along."

The sweaty guy looked at me, then back at Pop. "I think I'll see you later," he said, and went out into the gray Adak morning. Which, in July, wasn't much different from the slightly darker gray, four-hour Adak night.

Pop turned away from me and took a step toward the three joes playing poker.

"Corporal," I said.

He turned back and put his palms on the Ping-Pong table, looking across at me like a judge looking down from the bench. Which was something I'd seen before, so it didn't bother me.

"You're a private," he said. It wasn't a question.

"Yes, sir."

He scowled, his eyebrows pinching together in a sharp V. "Then you should know better than to call another enlisted man 'sir.' You generally shouldn't even call him by rank, unless it's 'Sarge.' We're all G.I.'s pissing into the same barrels here, son. When the wind doesn't blow it back in our faces."

"So what should I call you?" I asked.

He was still scowling. "Why should you call me anything?"

I had the feeling that he was jabbing at me with words, as if I were a thug in one of his books and he were the combative hero. But at that time I had only read a little bit of one of those books, the one about the bird statuette.

And I had only read that little bit because I was bored after evening chow one day, and one of the guys in my hut happened to have a hardback copy lying on his bunk. I wasn't much for books back then. So I didn't much care how good Pop was at jabbing with words.

"I have to call you something," I said. "The colonel sent me to take you on an errand."

Pop's scowl shifted from annoyance to disgust. "The *colonel*?" he said, his voice full of contempt. "If you mean who I think you mean, he's a living mockery of the term *intelligence officer.* And he's still wearing oak leaves. Much to his chagrin, I understand. So I suppose you mean the *lieutenant* colonel."

"That's him," I said. He was the only colonel I knew. "He wants you and me to take a drive, and he wants us to do it right now. If you haven't eaten breakfast, I have a couple of Spam sandwiches in the jeep. Stuck 'em under the seat so the ravens wouldn't get 'em."

Pop took his hands off the table, went to the chairs along the wall, and took a jacket from one of them. He put it on in abrupt, angry motions.

"You can tell him I don't have time for his nonsense," he said. "You can tell him I'm eating a hot meal, and after that, I'm starting on tomorrow's edition. I'm not interested in his editorial comments, his story ideas, or his journalistic or literary ambitions. And if he doesn't like that, he can take it up with the brigadier general."

I shook my head. "The general's not in camp. He left last night for some big powwow. Word is he might be gone a week or more. So if I tell the colonel what you just said, I'm the one who'll be eating shit."

Pop snorted. "You're in the Army and stationed in the Aleutians. You're already eating shit."

He tried to walk past me, but I stepped in front of him.

He didn't like that. "What are you going to do, son? Thrash an old man?" He was glaring down at me like a judge again, but now the judge was going to throw the book. Which was something I had also seen before, so it didn't bother me.

"I'd just as soon not," I said.

Pop glanced back at the poker players. I reckoned he thought they would step up for him. But they were all staring at their cards hard enough to fade the ink, and they didn't budge.

"Did you see the boxing matches yesterday?" I asked.

Pop looked back at me. His eyes had narrowed again.

"There was a crowd," he said. "But yes, I watched from a distance. I thought it was a fine way to celebrate the Fourth of July, beating the snot out of our own comrades in arms. I hear the Navy man in the second match was taken to the Station Hospital."

I shrugged. "He dropped his left. I had to take the opportunity."

Pop bared those bad false teeth. "Now I recognize you. You K.O.'d him. But he laid a few gloves on you first, didn't he?"

"Not so's I noticed." Thanks to the colonel, I'd had two whole weeks during which my only duty had been to train for the fight. I could take a punch.

"So you're tough," Pop said. His voice had an edge of contempt. "It seems to me that a tough fellow should be killing Japs for his country instead of running errands for an idiot. A tough fellow should—" He stopped. Then he adjusted his glasses and gave me a long look. When he spoke again, his voice was quiet. "But it occurs to me that you may have been on Attu last year. In which case you may have killed some Japs already."

I didn't like being reminded of Attu. For one thing, that was where the colonel had decided to make me his special helper. For another, it had been a frostbitten nightmare. And seven guys from my platoon hadn't made it back.

But I wasn't going to let Pop know any of that.

"A few," I said. "And if the brass asked my opinion, I'd tell them I'd be glad to go kill a few more. But the brass ain't asking my opinion."

Pop gave a weary sigh. "No. No, they never do." He dug his fingers into his thick shock of white hair. "So, what is it that the lieutenant colonel wants me to assist you with? I assume it's connected with some insipid piece of 'news' he wants me to run in *The Adakian*?"

I hesitated. "It'd be better if I could just show you."

Pop's eyebrows rose. "Oh, good," he said. His tone was sarcastic. "A mystery." He gestured toward the door. "After you, then, Private."

It felt like he was jabbing at me again. "I thought you said enlisted men shouldn't call each other by rank."

"I'm making an exception."

That was fine with me. "Then I'll call you 'Corporal.'"

A williwaw began to blow just as I opened the door, but I heard Pop's reply anyway.

"I prefer 'Boss,'" he said.

III

We made our way down the hill on mud-slicked boardwalks. On Adak, the wind almost always blew, but the most violent winds, the williwaws, could whip up in an instant and just about rip the nose off your face. The one that whipped up as Pop and I left the recreation hut wasn't that bad, but I still thought a skinny old guy like him might fly off into the muck. But he held the rail where there was a rail, and a rope where there was a rope, and he did all right.

As for me, I was short and heavy enough that the milder williwaws didn't bother me too much. But as I looked down the hill to the sloppy road we called Main Street, I saw a steel barrel bouncing along at about forty miles an hour toward Navytown. And some of the thick poles that held the miles of telephone and electrical wires that crisscrossed the camp were swaying as if they were bamboo. We wouldn't be able to take our drive until the wind let up.

So I didn't object when Pop took my elbow and pulled me into the lee of a Quonset hut. I thought he was just getting us out of the wind for a moment, but then he slipped under the lean-to that sheltered the door and went inside. I went in after him, figuring this must be where he bunked. But if my eyes hadn't been watering, I might have seen the words *THE ADAKIAN* stenciled on the door.

Inside, I wiped my eyes and saw tables, chairs, typewriters, two big plywood boxes with glass tops, a cylindrical machine with a hand crank, and dozens of reams of paper. The place had the thick smell of mimeograph ink. Two of the tables had men lying on them, dead to the world, their butts up against typewriters shoved to the wall. A third man, a slim, light-skinned Negro, was working at a drawing board. It looked like he was drawing a cartoon.

This man glanced up with a puzzled look. "What're you doing back already, Pop?" He spoke softly, so I could barely hear him over the shriek of the williwaw ripping across the hut's corrugated shell.

"I don't know how many times I have to tell you," Pop said. "I don't like 'Pop.' I prefer 'Boss.' "

"Whatever you say, Pop. They run out of scrambled eggs?"

"I wouldn't know. My breakfast has been delayed." Pop jerked a thumb at me. "The private here is taking me on an errand for the lieutenant colonel."

The cartoonist rolled his eyes. "Lucky you. Maybe you'll get to read one of his novellas."

"That's my fear," Pop said. "And I simply don't have enough whiskey on hand." He waved in a never-mind gesture. "But we've interrupted your work. Please, carry on."

The cartoonist turned back to his drawing board. "I always do."

Pop went to an almost-empty table, shoved a few stacks of paper aside, and stretched out on his back. The stack of paper closest to me had a page on top with some large print that read: HAMMETT HITS HALF-CENTURY—HALF-CENTURY CLAIMS FOUL.

"Have a seat, Private," Pop said. "Or lie down, if you can find a spot." He closed his eyes. "God himself has passed gas out there. We may be here awhile."

I looked around at the hut's dim interior. The bulb hanging over the drawing board was lit, but the only other illumination was the gray light from the small front windows. Wind noise aside, all was quiet. It was the most peaceful place I had been since joining the Army.

"This is where you make the newspaper?" I asked.

"You should be a detective," Pop said.

I looked at the two sleeping men. "It sure looks like an easy job."

Pop managed to scowl without opening his eyes. "Private, have you actually seen *The Adakian*? I suppose it's possible you haven't, since there are over twenty thousand men in camp at the moment, and we can only produce six thousand copies a day."

"I've seen it," I said. "I saw the one about the European invasion, and maybe a few others."

Pop made a noise in his throat. "All right, then. When have you seen it?"

"Guys have it at morning chow, mostly."

Now Pop opened his eyes. "That's because my staff works all night to put it out *before* morning chow. Starting at about lunchtime yesterday, they were typing up shortwave reports from our man at the radio station, writing articles and reviews, cutting and pasting, and doing everything else that was necessary to produce and mimeograph six thousand six-page newspapers before sunup. So right now most of them have collapsed into their bunks for a few hours before starting on tomorrow's edition. I don't know what these three are still doing here."

At the drawing board, the Negro cartoonist spoke without looking up. "Those two brought in beer for breakfast, so they didn't make it back out the door. As for me, I had an idea for tomorrow's cartoon and decided to draw it before I forgot."

"What's the idea?" Pop asked.

"It's about two guys who have beer for breakfast."

Pop grunted. "Very topical."

Then no one spoke. I assumed parade rest and waited. But as soon as I heard the pitch of the wind drop, I opened the door a few inches. The williwaw had diminished to a stiff breeze, no worse than a cow-tipping gust back home in Nebraska.

"We have to go, Boss," I said.

Pop didn't budge, but the cartoonist gave a whistle. "Hey, Pop! Wake up, you old Red."

Pop sat up and blinked. With his now-wild white hair, round eyeglasses, and sharp nose, he looked like an aggravated owl.

"Stop calling me 'Pop,' " he said.

Outside, as Pop and I headed down the hill again, I said, "That's something I've never seen before."

"What's that?" Pop asked, raising his voice to be heard over the wind.

"A Negro working an office detail with white soldiers."

Pop looked at me sidelong. "Does that bother you, Private? It certainly bothers the lieutenant colonel."

I thought about it. "No, it doesn't bother me. I just wonder how it happened."

"It happened," Pop said, "because I needed a damn good cartoonist, and he's a damn good cartoonist."

I understood that. "I do like the cartoons," I said.

Pop made a noise in his throat again.

"Would it be all right, Private," he said, "if we don't speak again until we absolutely have to?"

That was fine with me. We were almost to the jeep, and once I fired that up, neither of us would be able to hear the other anyway. The muffler had a hole in it, so it was almost as loud as a williwaw.

IV

Halfway up the dormant volcano called Mount Moffett, about a mile after dealing with the two jerks in the shack at the Navy checkpoint, I stopped the jeep. The road was barely a muddy track here.

"Now we have to walk," I told Pop.

Pop looked around. "Walk where? There's nothing but rocks and tundra."

It was true. Even the ravens, ubiquitous in camp and around the airfield, were absent up here. The mountainside was desolate, and I happened to like that. Or at least I'd liked it before finding the eagle. But I could see that to a man who thrived on being with people, this might be the worst place on earth.

"The Navy guys say it looks better when there's snow," I said. "They go skiing up here."

"I wondered what you were discussing with them," Pop said. "I couldn't hear a word after you stepped away from the jeep."

I decided not to repeat the Navy boys' comments about the old coot I was chauffeuring. "Well, they said they were concerned we might leave ruts that would ruin the skiing when it snows. After that, we exchanged compliments about our mothers. Then they got on the horn and talked to some ensign or petty officer or something who said he didn't care if they let the whole damn Army through."

Hunching my shoulders against the wind, I got out of the jeep and started cutting across the slope. The weather was gray, but at least it wasn't too cold. The air felt about like late autumn back home. And the tundra here wasn't as spongy as it was down closer to camp. But the rocks and hidden mud still made it a little precarious.

Pop followed me, and I guessed it had to be tough for him to keep his balance, being old and scrawny. But he didn't complain about the footing. That would have been far down his list.

"Tell me the truth, Private," he said, wheezing. "This is a punishment, correct? The lieutenant colonel stopped me on Main Street a few months ago and asked me to come to dinner and read one of his stories. But my boys were with me, so I said, 'Certainly, if I may bring these gentlemen along.' At which point the invitation evaporated. That incident blistered his ass, and that's why we're here, isn't it?"

I turned to face him but kept moving, walking backward. "I don't think so. When he sent me up here this morning, it didn't have anything to do with you. I was supposed to look for an old Aleut lodge that's around here somewhere. The colonel said it's probably about three-quarters underground, and I'd have to look hard to find it."

Pop was still wheezing. "That's called an *ulax*. Good protection from the elements. But I doubt there was ever one this far up the mountain, unless it was for some ceremonial reason. And even if there was an *ulax* up here, I can't imagine why the lieutenant colonel would send you looking for it."

"He has a report of enlisted men using it to drink booze and have relations with some of the nurses from the 179th," I said. "He wants to locate it so he can put a stop to such things."

Pop frowned. "Someone's lying. The 179th has twenty nurses here at most. Any one of them who might be open to 'such things' will have a dozen officers after her from the moment she arrives. No enlisted man has a chance. Especially if the lady would also be required to climb a mountain and lower herself into a hole in the ground."

"Doesn't matter if it's true," I said. "I didn't find no lodge anyway." I turned back around. We were almost there.

"That still leaves the question of why we're up here," Pop said.

This time I didn't answer. Although he was a corporal, Pop didn't seem to grasp the fact that an enlisted man isn't supposed to have a mind of his own. If an officer asks you to dinner, or to a latrine-painting party, you just say "Yes, sir." And if he tells you to go for a ride up a volcano, you say the same thing. There's no point in asking why, because you're going to have to do it anyway.

"Are we walking all the way around the mountain?" Pop shouted, wheezing harder. "Or is there a picnic breakfast waiting behind the next rock? If so, it had better not be another Spam sandwich."

"You didn't have to eat it," I said.

Pop started to retort, but whatever he was going to say became a coughing fit. I stopped and turned around to find him doubled over with his hands on his knees, hacking so hard that I thought he might pass out.

I considered pounding him on the back, but was afraid that might kill him. So I just watched him heave and thought that if he died there, the colonel would ream my butt.

Pop's coughing became a long, sustained ratcheting noise, and then he spat a watery black goo onto the tundra. He paused for a few seconds, breathing heavily, then heaved again, hacking out a second black glob. A third heave produced a little less, and then a fourth was almost dry.

Finally, he wiped his mouth with his sleeve and stood upright again. His face was pale, but his eyes were sharp.

"Water," he said in a rasping voice.

I ran back to the jeep, stumbling and falling once on the way, and returned with a canteen. Pop took it without a word, drank, then closed his eyes and took a deep breath.

"That's better," he said. He sounded almost like himself again. He capped the canteen and held it out without opening his eyes.

I took the canteen and fumbled to hang it from my belt. "What was that?" I asked. "What happened?" I was surprised at how shook-up my own voice sounded. God knew I'd seen worse things than what Pop had hacked up.

Pop opened his eyes. He looked amused. "'What happened?'" he said. "Well, that was what we call coughing."

I gave up on fixing the canteen to my belt and just held it clutched in one hand. "No, I mean, what was that stuff that came out?" I could still see it there on the tundra at our feet. It looked like it was pulsing.

"Just blood," Pop said.

I shook my head. "No, it ain't. I've seen blood." I had, too. Plenty. But none of it had looked this black.

Pop glanced down at it. "You haven't seen old blood," he said. "If this were red, that would mean it was fresh, and I might have a problem. But this is just old news coming up."

"Old news?" I asked.

"Tuberculosis, kid. I caught it during the *previous* war to end all wars. Don't worry, though. You can't catch it from me."

I wasn't worried about that. But I was confused. "If you were in the Great War, and you caught TB," I said, "then how could they let you into the Army again?"

Pop grinned. Those bad false teeth had black flecks on them now. "Because they can't win without me." He gestured ahead. "Let's get this over with, Private, whatever it is. I have to go back and start cracking the whip soon, or there might not be a newspaper tomorrow."

So I turned and continued across the slope. I could see the hillock I'd marked with rocks a few dozen yards ahead. I hoped Pop wouldn't go into another coughing fit once we crossed it.

V

Pop's eyebrows rose when he saw the eagle, but otherwise it didn't seem to faze him.

"Well, this is something different," he said.

I nodded. "That's what I thought, too."

Pop gave a small chuckle. "I'm sure you did, Private." He looked at me with his narrow-eyed gaze, but this time it was more quizzical than annoyed. "When I asked you what this was about, you said it would be better if you just showed me. Now you've shown me. So what the hell does the lieutenant colonel want me to do? Write this up for *The Adakian*?"

"I think that's the last thing he wants," I said. "He says this thing could hurt morale."

Pop rolled his eyes skyward. "Christ, it's probably low morale in the form of sheer boredom that did this in the first place. Human beings are capable of performing any number of deranged and pointless acts to amuse themselves. Which is precisely what we have here. The brass told us we couldn't shoot the goddamn ravens, so some frustrated boys came up here and managed to cut up a bald eagle instead. And they've expressed their personal displeasure with their military service by setting up the carcass as a perverse mockery of the Great Seal of the United States."

"The what?" I asked.

Pop pointed down at the bird. "There's no olive branch or arrows. But otherwise, that's what this looks like. The Great Seal. Aside from the evisceration, of course. But I suppose that was just boys being boys."

"You think it was more than one guy?" I asked.

Pop looked at me as if I were nuts. "How on earth would I know?"

"You said 'boys.' That means more than one."

"I was speculating. I have no idea whether this was a project for one man, or twenty."

I tossed the canteen from hand to hand. "Okay, well, do whatever you have to do to figure out who it was."

Now Pop looked at me as if I weren't only nuts, but nuts and stupid, too. "There's no way of knowing who did this. Or even why. Speculation is all that's possible. The bird might have been killed out of boredom, out of hatred, or even out of superstition. I have no idea."

None of that sounded like something I could report. "But the colonel says you used to be a detective. Before you wrote the books."

Pop took off his glasses and rubbed his eyes. "I was a Pinkerton. Not Sherlock Holmes. A Pinkerton can't look at a crime scene and deduce a culprit's name, occupation, and sock color. Usually, a Pinkerton simply shadows a subject. Then, if he's lucky, the subject misbehaves and can be caught in the act." Pop put his glasses back on and held out his empty hands. "But there's no one to shadow here, unless it's every one of the twenty thousand men down in camp. Do you have one in mind? If not, there's nothing to be done."

I looked down at the eagle. As big and magnificent as it might have been in life, it was just a dead bird now. What had happened here was strange and ugly, but it wasn't a tragedy. It wasn't as if a human being had been staked out and gutted.

But in its way, the eagle unnerved me almost as much as the things I'd seen and done on Attu. At least there had been reasons for the things on Attu. Here, there was no reason at all—unless Pop was right, and it had just been boredom. If that was the case, I didn't want to know which guys had been bored enough to do this. Because if I knew, I might get mad enough to hurt them. And then there'd be something else I'd have to see in my sleep over and over again.

"All right, Pop," I said, keeping my eyes on the eagle. "There's a can of gasoline strapped to the jeep. What if we tell the colonel that when you and I got up here, we found this thing burned up?"

Pop cleared his throat. "You'd be willing to do that, Private? Lie to the lieutenant colonel?"

I had never sidestepped an order before. The colonel had made me do some stupid things and some awful things, but this was the first time that it looked like he was making me do a pointless thing. Besides, Pop was older and smarter than the colonel—even I could see that—and if he thought the eagle was a waste of time, then it probably was.

Besides, we were enlisted men, and we had to stick together. As long as there weren't any officers around to catch us doing it.

"Sure," I said, looking up at Pop again. "I've lied before. Back home in Nebraska, I even lied to a judge."

Pop gave me a thin-lipped smile. "What did you do to wind up in front of a judge?"

I had done so much worse since then that it didn't seem like much of a fuss anymore. "I beat up a rich kid from Omaha for calling me a dumb Bohunk," I said. "Then I stole his Hudson, drove it into a pasture, and chased some cows. I might have run it through a few fences while I was at it."

Pop chuckled. "That doesn't sound too bad. Some judges might have even considered it justified."

"Well, I also socked the first deputy who tried to arrest me," I said. "But I think what really made the judge mad was when I claimed that I wasn't a dumb Bohunk, but a stupid Polack."

"Why would that make the judge angry?" Pop asked.

"Because the judge was a Polack," I said. "So he gave me thirty days, to be followed by immediate enlistment or he'd make it two years. That part was okay, since I was going to sign up anyhow. But the thirty days was bad. My old man had to do the hay mowing without me. I got a letter from my mother last week, and she says he's still planning to whip me when I get home."

I noticed then that Pop's gaze had shifted. He was staring off into the distance past my shoulder. So I turned to look, and I saw a man's head and shoulders over the top edge of another hillock about fifty yards away. The man was wearing a coat with a fur-lined hood, and his face was a deep copper color. He appeared to be staring back at us.

"Do you know him?" Pop asked.

I squinted. "I don't think so," I said. "He looks like an Eskimo."

"I believe he's an Aleut," Pop said. "And the only natives I've seen in camp have belonged to the Alaska Scouts, better known as Castner's Cutthroats. Although that may be for the alliteration. I don't know whether they've really cut any throats."

I was still staring at the distant man, who was still staring back.

"They have," I said.

"Then let's mind our own—" Pop began.

He didn't finish because of a sudden loud whistling noise from farther down the mountain. It seemed to come from everywhere below us, all at once, and it grew louder and louder every moment.

"Shit," I said. I think Pop said it, too.

We both knew what it was, and we could tell it was going to be a fierce one. And there were no buildings up here to slow it down. It was a monster williwaw whipping around the mountain, and we had just a few seconds before the wind caught up with its own sound. The jeep was hundreds of yards away, and it wouldn't have been any protection even if we could get to it. Our only option was going to be to lie down flat in the slight depression where the dead eagle was staked out. If we were lucky, the exposed skin of our hands and faces might not be flayed from our flesh. And if we were even luckier, we might manage to gulp a few breaths without having them ripped away by the wind. I had the thought that this wasn't a good time to have tuberculosis.

Then, just as I was about to gesture to Pop to drop to the ground, I saw the distant Cutthroat disappear. His head and shoulders seemed to drop straight into the earth behind the hillock. And in one of my rare moments of smart thinking, I knew where he had gone.

"Come on!" I shouted to Pop, and I dropped the canteen and started running toward the hillock. But I had only gone about twenty yards when I realized that Pop wasn't keeping up, so I ran back to grab his arm and drag him along.

He didn't care for that, and he tried to pull away from me. But I was stronger, so all he could do was cuss at me as I yanked him forward as fast as I could.

Then the williwaw hit us, and he couldn't even cuss. Our hats flew away as if they were artillery shells, and I was deafened and blinded as my ears filled with a shriek and my eyes filled with dirt and tears. The right side of my face felt as if it were being stabbed with a thousand tiny needles.

I couldn't see where we were going now, but I kept charging forward, leaning down against the wind with all my weight so it wouldn't push me off course. For all I knew, I was going off course anyway. I couldn't tell if the ground was still sloping upward, or if we were over the top of the hillock already. But if I didn't find the spot where the Cutthroat had disappeared, and find it pretty damn quick, we were going to have to drop to the ground and take our chances. Maybe we'd catch a break, and the williwaw wouldn't last long enough to kill us.

Then my foot slipped on the tundra, and I fell to my knees. I twisted to try to catch Pop so he wouldn't hit the ground headfirst, and then we both slid and fell into a dark hole in the earth.

VI

THE SOD ROOF OF THE *ULAX* WAS MOSTLY INTACT, BUT THERE WERE HOLES. So after my eyes adjusted, there was enough light to see. But Pop had landed on top of me, and at first all I could see was his mustache.

"Your breath ain't so good, Pop," I said. "Mind getting off me?"

At first I didn't think he heard me over the shriek of the williwaw. But then he grunted and wheezed and pushed himself away until he was sitting against the earthen wall. I sat up and scooted over against the wall beside him.

Pop reached up and adjusted his glasses, which had gone askew. Then he looked up at the largest hole in the roof, which I guessed was how we'd gotten inside. It was about eight feet above the dirt floor.

"Thanks for breaking my fall," he said, raising his voice to be heard over the wind. "I hope I didn't damage you. Although you might have avoided it if you'd told me what you were doing instead of dragging me."

I didn't answer. Instead, I looked around at the mostly underground room. It was maybe twenty feet long by ten feet wide. At the far end was a jumble of sod, timber, and whalebone that looked like a section of collapsed roof. But the roof above that area was actually in better shape than the rest. The rest was about evenly split between old sod and random holes. Some empty bottles and cans were scattered around the floor, and a few filthy, wadded blankets lay on earthen platforms that ran down the lengths of the two longer walls.

But there was no Cutthroat. I had watched him drop down into the same hole that Pop and I had tumbled into. I was sure that was what had happened. But I didn't see him here now.

"What happened to the Eskimo?" I asked.

Pop scanned the interior of the *ulax* and frowned. "He must have gone elsewhere."

"There isn't any elsewhere," I said, almost shouting. I pointed upward. "Listen to that. And this is the only shelter up here."

Pop shook his head. "The man we saw was a native. He may know of shelters on this old volcano that we wouldn't find if we searched for forty years. Or he may even be so used to a wind like this that he'll stand facing into it and smile."

I looked up at the big hole and saw what looked like a twenty-pound rock blow past. "I saw him jump down here. That's how I knew where to go. And I think I would have seen him climb back out. Unless he can disappear."

And then, from behind the jumble of sod and whalebone at the far end of the *ulax*, the Cutthroat emerged. His hood was down, and his dark hair shone. He was in a crouch, holding a hunting knife at his side. A big one.

"Who the fuck are you people?" the Cutthroat asked. His voice was low and rough, but still managed to cut through the howling above us. This was a man used to talking over the wind.

Pop gave a single hacking cough. Then he looked at me and said, "Well, Private, it doesn't look as if he disappeared."

Right then I wanted to punch Pop, but it was only because I was scared. I wished the Cutthroat really had disappeared. I didn't recognize his dark, scraggly-bearded face, but that didn't mean anything. I didn't remember many living faces from Attu.

But I did remember the Cutthroats as a group. I remembered how they had appeared and vanished in the frozen landscape like Arctic wolves.

And I remembered their knives.

"I asked you two a question," the Cutthroat said, pointing at us with his knife. "Are you M.P.'s? And if you're not, what are you doing here?"

Pop gave another cough. This time it wasn't a tubercular hack, but a sort of polite throat-clearing. And I realized he didn't understand what kind of man we were dealing with. But maybe that was a good thing. Because if he had ever seen the Cutthroats in action, he might have stayed stone-silent like me. And one of us needed to answer the question before the Cutthroat got mad.

"We aren't M.P.'s," Pop said. "So if you've done something you shouldn't, you needn't worry about us."

"I haven't done a fucking thing," the Cutthroat said. Even though his voice was gravelly, and even though he was cussing, his voice had a distinctive Aleut rhythm. It was almost musical. "I just came up here because a guy told me there was a dead eagle. And I thought I'd get some feathers. I'm a goddamn native, like you said."

I managed to take my eyes off the Cutthroat long enough to glance at Pop. Pop had the same expression on his face that he'd had when I'd first seen him, when he'd been whipping the strong, shirtless kid at Ping-Pong. He was calm and confident. There were even slight crinkles of happiness at the corners of his eyes and mouth, as if he were safe and snug in his own briar patch, and anybody coming in after him was gonna get scratched up.

It was the damnedest expression to have while sitting in a pit on the side of a volcano facing a man with a knife while a hundred-mile-an-hour wind screeched over your head.

"I understand completely," Pop said. "We came up to find the eagle as well, although we didn't have as good a reason. We're only here because an idiot lieutenant colonel couldn't think of another way to make us dance like puppets. It's a stupid, pointless errand from a stupid, pointless officer."

The Cutthroat blinked and then straightened from his crouch. He lowered the knife.

"Fucking brass," he said.

"You're telling us," Pop said.

The Cutthroat slipped his knife into a sheath on his hip. "Colonel Castner's not too bad. He lets us do what we know how to do. But the rest of them. Fuck me, Jesus. They didn't listen on Attu, and they ain't listened since."

I knew what he was talking about. The Cutthroats had scouted Attu ahead of our invasion, so they had told the brass how many Japs were there and what to expect from them. But they had also warned that Attu's permafrost would make wheeled vehicles almost useless, and that we'd need some serious cold-weather boots and clothing. Plus extra food. Yet we'd gone in with jeeps and trucks, and we'd been wearing standard gear. Food had been C-rations, and not much of that. It had all been a rotten mess, and it would have been a disaster if the Cutthroats hadn't taken it upon themselves to bring dried fish and extra supplies to platoon after platoon.

Not to mention the dead Jap snipers and machine gunners we regular G.I.'s found as we advanced. The ones whose heads had been almost severed.

"I cowrote the pamphlet on the Battle of the Aleutians," Pop said. "But of course it had to be approved by the brass, so we had to leave out what we knew about their mistakes. And we also weren't allowed to mention the

Alaska Scouts. The generals apparently felt that specific mention of any one outfit might be taken to suggest that other outfits weren't vital as well."

The Cutthroat made a loud spitting noise. "Some of them *weren't.*" He sat down with his back against the sod-and-whalebone rubble. "Don't matter. I was there, and I killed some Japs. Don't much care what gets said about it now."

The noise of the williwaw had dropped slightly, so when Pop spoke again his voice was startlingly loud.

"If you don't mind my asking," Pop said, "why are you on Adak? I was told the Scouts had gone back to Fort Richardson."

The Cutthroat's upper lip curled, and he pointed a finger at his right thigh. "I got a leg wound on Attu, and the fucking thing's been getting reinfected for over a year. It's better now, but it was leaking pus when the other guys had to leave. Captain said I had to stay here until it healed. But now I got to wait for an authorized ride. And while I wait, they tell me I'm an orderly at the hospital. Which ain't what I signed up for. So I tried to stow away on a boat to Dutch Harbor a couple weeks ago, and the fucking M.P.'s threw me off."

"I assume that means you're now AWOL from the hospital," Pop said. "Which explains why you thought that the Private and I might be police."

The Cutthroat shook his head. "Nah. The hospital C.O. don't really give a shit what I do. He let me put a cot in a supply hut and pretty much ignores me. I'm what you call extraneous personnel." He jerked a thumb over his shoulder. "I just thought you might be M.P.'s because of this dead guy back here. I think it's the same guy who told me about the eagle, but maybe not. You people all look alike to me."

It took me a few seconds to realize what the Cutthroat had said. When I did, I looked at Pop. Pop's eyebrows had risen slightly.

"Would you mind if I have a look?" Pop asked.

The Cutthroat shrugged his shoulders. "What do I care? He ain't *my* dead guy."

Pop stood up stiffly, and I stood up as well. With the williwaw overhead now a somewhat diminished shriek, we walked, hunched over, to where the Cutthroat sat. And now I could see that the *ulax* had a second, smaller chamber whose entrance had been partially obscured by the fallen sod and bone.

We went around the pile of debris, through the narrow entrance beside the wall, and into the second chamber. It was about ten by eight feet, and its roof was also pocked by holes that let in light. But these holes were smaller, and they changed the pitch of the wind noise. The shriek rose to a high, keening whistle.

On the floor, a stocky man lay on his back, his open eyes staring up at the holes where the wind screamed past. His hair looked dark and wet, and his face was as pale as a block of salt except for a large bruise under his left eye. His mouth was slack. He was wearing a dark Navy pea jacket, dark trousers, and mud-black boots. His bare, empty hands were curled into claws at his sides.

Pop and I stared down at him for a long moment, neither of us speaking.

At first, I didn't recognize the man because he looked so different from how he had looked the day before. But then I focused on the bruise under his eye, and I knew who he was. My gut lurched.

Right behind me, the Cutthroat said, "Back of his head's bashed in."

Startled, I spun around, fists up.

The Cutthroat's knife shot up from its sheath to within two inches of my nose.

Then Pop's hand appeared between the blade and my face.

"Easy, boys," Pop said. "I'm the camp editor. You don't want your names in the paper."

I lowered my fists.

"Sorry," I said. I was breathing hard, but trying to sound like I wasn't. "It was just a reflex."

The Cutthroat lowered his knife as well, but more slowly.

"Now I recognize you," he said, peering at me intently. "You boxed yesterday. And you were on Attu. Okay, mine was just a reflex, too."

I still didn't know him, but that still didn't mean anything. The Cutthroats hadn't stayed in any one place very long when I had seen them at all. And some of them had worn their fur-lined hoods all the time.

Pop took his hand away, and then all three of us looked down at the body. I opened my mouth to speak, but suddenly had no voice. Neither Pop nor the Cutthroat seemed to notice.

"He's Navy," Pop said. "Or merchant marine. A young man, like all the rest of you." Pop's voice, although loud enough to be heard over the wind, had a slight tremble.

"Don't worry about it, old-timer," the Cutthroat said. "He's just another dead guy now. Seen plenty of those."

Pop got down on one knee beside the body. "Not on this island," he said. "Other than sporadic casualties generated by bad bomber landings, Adak has been relatively death-free." He gingerly touched the dead man's face and tilted it to one side far enough to expose the back of the head. The skull had been crushed by a large rock that was still underneath. The dark stuff on the rock looked like what Pop had coughed up earlier.

Feeling sick, I turned away and stared at the Cutthroat. I tried to read his face, the way I might try to read an opponent's in a boxing match. I'd been told that you could tell what another fighter was about to do, and sometimes even what he was only thinking about doing, just from the expression on his face.

The Cutthroat gave me a scowl.

"Don't look at me, kid," he said. "I would've done a better job than that."

Pop opened the dead man's coat, exposing a blue Navy work shirt. I could see his hands shaking slightly as he did it. "I believe you," he said. "Whatever happened here was sloppy. It may even have been an accident." He opened the coat far enough to expose the right shoulder. "No insignia. He was just a seaman." He opened the shirt collar. "No dog tags, either."

Then he reached into the large, deep coat pockets, first the left, then the right. He came up from the right pocket clutching something.

Pop held it up in a shaft of gray light from one of the ceiling holes.

It was a huge, dark-brown feather, maybe fourteen inches long. It was bent in the middle.

"That bird," Pop said, "is turning out to be nothing but trouble."

VII

We left the body where it was and went back into the larger room. The wind was still furious overhead, so we were stuck there for the time being. Pop and I sat back down against the wall at the far end, and the Cutthroat lounged on the earthen shelf along the long wall to our right.

Pop didn't look so good. He was pale, and he coughed now and then. I think he was trying to pretend that the dead man hadn't bothered him. He had probably seen death before, but not the way the Cutthroat and I had.

Still, this was different. In battle, death is expected. Back at camp, when the battlefields have moved elsewhere, it's something else. So I was a little shook up myself.

The Cutthroat didn't seem bothered at all. His mind was already on other things.

"This goddamn williwaw might take that eagle away," he said. "If it does, I won't get my feathers. I should have come in the other way, like you guys did. I saw you there with it, but then I felt the wind coming. I didn't think you two were gonna make it here."

"Neither did we," Pop said. "But if you want an eagle feather, you can have the one I took from that young man." He reached for his jacket pocket.

The Cutthroat made a dismissive gesture. "That one's bent in the middle. It's no good to me. The power's bent now, too."

"What sort of power do you get from feathers?" I asked. I immediately regretted it.

The Cutthroat gave me a look too dark to even rise to the level of contempt. "None of your fucking business. In fact, I'm wondering what you and your damn lieutenant colonel wanted with the eagle in the first place."

Pop coughed. "The private and I wanted nothing to do with it at all. But the lieutenant colonel seems to be curious about who killed it, gutted it, and staked it out like that. He incorrectly assumed I could help him discover that information."

The Cutthroat sat up straight. "Somebody killed it on purpose?"

"That's what it looks like," Pop said. "Couldn't you see it from over here?"

The Cutthroat's brow furrowed. "I just saw you two, and the eagle's wings, and then the wind hit me before I could come any closer. You say somebody pulled out its guts?"

"Yes." Pop's color was getting better. "And staked it to the earth with nails. Does that mean anything to you?"

The Cutthroat scowled. "Yeah, it means that somebody's a fucking son of a bitch. I ain't heard of nothing like that before." He scratched his sparse beard. "Unless maybe a shaman from a mainland tribe was here, trying to do some kind of magic."

Pop leaned toward the Cutthroat. His eyes were bright. "Why would killing an eagle be magic?"

The Cutthroat's hand came down to rest on the hilt of his knife. It made me nervous.

"The people along the Yukon tell a story about eagles," the Cutthroat said. "It's the kind of story you white people like to hear us savages tell. I even told it to some officers one night on Attu. Took their minds off the fact that they were getting a lot of kids killed. Got a promise of six beers for it. They paid up, too." He gave Pop a pointed look.

Pop gave a thin smile. "I don't have any beer at hand. Will you take an IOU?"

The Cutthroat answered Pop's smile with a humorless grin. "Don't be surprised when I collect." He leaned forward. "Okay. Long ago, a pair of giant eagles made their nest at the summit of a volcano. I'm talking about eagles nine, ten times the size of the ones we got now. They'd catch full-grown whales and bring them back to feed their young. And sometimes, if they couldn't find whales, they'd swoop down on a village and take away a few human beings. This went on for many years, with the giant eagles raising a new brood of young every year. These young would go off to make nests on other volcanoes and attack other villages."

Pop took a Zippo and a pack of Camels from a jacket pocket. "So they were spreading out like the Germans and Japanese."

The Cutthroat nodded. "Yeah, I guess so. Anyway, one day, one of the original eagles, the father eagle, was out hunting and couldn't find any reindeer or whales or nothing. So the father eagle said, fuck it, the babies are hungry. And he swooped down and took a woman who was outside her house. Carried her back to the volcano, tore her limb from limb, ripped out her guts, and fed her to his giant eaglets."

The pitch of the wind outside dropped, and the Cutthroat paused and listened. Pop lit a cigarette and then offered the pack to me and the Cutthroat. The Cutthroat accepted, but I declined. I'd promised my mother I wouldn't smoke.

The wind shrieked higher again as Pop lit the Cutthroat's cigarette, and then the Cutthroat went on.

"But this poor woman happened to be the wife of the greatest hunter of the village," he said, exhaling smoke. "And when the hunter returned and was told what had happened, he went into a rage. He took his bow and his arrows, and even though everyone told him he was a fool, he climbed the volcano."

"Most truly brave men *are* fools," Pop said. He gestured toward me with his cigarette. I didn't know why.

"I wouldn't know," the Cutthroat said. "In the Scouts, we try to be sneaky instead of brave. Works out better. Anyway, when the hunter got to the eagles' nest, he found six baby eagles, each one three times the size of a full-grown eagle today. They were surrounded by broken kayaks, whale ribs, and human bones. The hunter knew that some of those bones belonged to his wife, and that these eaglets had eaten her. So he shot an arrow into each of them, through their eyes, and they fell over dead. Then he heard a loud cry in the sky, which was the giant mother eagle returning. He shot her under the wing just as she was about to grab him, and then he shot her through the eyes. She tumbled off the mountain, and that was it for her. Then there was another loud cry, which was the father eagle—"

"And of course the hunter killed the father eagle as well," Pop said.

The Cutthroat glared. "Who's telling this fucking legend, old man? No, the hunter didn't kill the goddamn father eagle. The eagle dived at him again and again, and each time the hunter put an arrow into a different part of its body.

But he never hit the father eagle in the eye. So, finally, pierced with arrows all over, and his whole family dead, the giant eagle flew away into the northern sky, and neither he nor any of his kind were ever seen again. But the eagles of today are said to be the descendants of those who had flown away in earlier times." The Cutthroat gave a loud belch. "At least, that's the story."

Pop leaned back again, looking up at the holes in the roof and blowing smoke toward them. "It's not bad," he said. "Not much suspense, though. I'm not sure it's worth six beers."

"I don't give a damn what you think it's worth," the Cutthroat said, tapping ash from his cigarette. "It ain't my story anyway. My mother heard it a long time ago from some Inuits on the mainland, and she told it to me when I was a kid. But we're Unangan. Not Eskimo."

"So you think an Eskimo might have killed this eagle, too?" Pop asked. "Staked it to the ground, gutted it?"

The Cutthroat frowned. "Like I said, I ain't heard of anything quite like that. But I ain't heard of a lot of things. Some of those shamans might still hold a grudge against eagles. People can stay mad about crap like that for five, six hundred years. Or maybe some guy just thought if he killed an eagle, he could take its power. And then he could be a better hunter, or fisherman, or warrior. I've heard of that. And you white people like stuff like that, too. I'll toss that in for free."

Pop was giving the Cutthroat a steady gaze. "But you're saying it wouldn't have been you who killed the eagle. Or anyone else Unangan."

The Cutthroat shook his head. "Doubt it. Sometimes the eagles show us where the fish are. And sometimes we toss 'em a few in return. We get along all right."

Pop nodded, sat back against the earthen wall, and closed his eyes. He took a long pull on his cigarette. "I've been all over the post, both Armytown and Navytown, many times. But I've seen very few Aleuts or Eskimos. So just from the odds, I doubt that a native is our eagle-killer."

As much as I hated saying anything at all in front of the Cutthroat, I couldn't keep my mouth shut anymore. Pop was infuriating me.

"There's a dead man over there!" I yelled, pointing at the section of collapsed roof. "Who cares about the eagle now?"

Pop opened his eyes and regarded me through a smoky haze.

"Actually, I don't care much," he said. "But because of that dead man, the eagle has become slightly more interesting."

"Why?" I asked, still furious. "Just because he had a feather in his pocket? That doesn't mean anything. He might have found it."

Pop's eyebrows rose. "I don't think so. He and the eagle have both been dead less than a day. So the coincidental timing, plus the feather in his pocket, suggests a connection. Either he killed the eagle, and then had an unfortunate accident . . ."

He fixed his gaze on the Cutthroat again.

". . . or whoever did kill the eagle, or helped him kill it, may have then killed him as well."

The Cutthroat ground out his cigarette butt. "I told you guys before. It wasn't me."

"And I still believe you," Pop said. "I'm just wondering if you might have any idea who it may have been."

"Nope," the Cutthroat said. There was no hesitation.

Pop leaned back against the wall again and looked up at the holes in the roof.

"I don't have any idea, either," Pop said. "But I think you were right about one thing."

"Huh?" the Cutthroat said. "What's that?"

"Whoever it was, he's a fucking son of a bitch."

The wind seemed to scream louder in response.

VIII

THE WILLIWAW FINALLY SLACKED OFF A LITTLE AFTER NOON, LEAVING ONLY blustery gusts. The three of us stirred ourselves on stiff joints and muscles and rose from our places in the main room of the *ulax*.

Pop and the Cutthroat had both dozed after finishing their cigarettes, but I had stayed wide awake. I knew who the dead man was. But I hadn't told Pop yet for fear that the Cutthroat would hear me.

That was because, while I didn't recognize this particular Cutthroat, I knew who he was, too. On Attu, the Alaska Scouts had saved my life and the lives of dozens of my buddies, but they hadn't done it by being kind and gentle souls. They had done it by being cruel and ruthless to our enemies.

And I knew that a man couldn't just turn that off once it wasn't needed anymore. I knew that for a cold fact.

I boosted Pop up through the hole in the roof where we'd dropped in, and then I followed by jumping from the raised earthen shelf at the side of the room, grabbing a whalebone roof support, and pulling myself through.

I joined Pop on the hillock just beside the *ulax*, blinking against the wind, and then looked back and saw the Cutthroat already standing behind me. It was as if he had levitated.

"So this thing here is not our fucking problem," the Cutthroat said, speaking over the wind. "We all agree on that."

Pop nodded. "That's the body of a Navy man. So the private and I will tell the boys at the Navy checkpoint to come have a look. And if they ask our names, or if they know who I am, I'll be able to handle them. They're twenty-year-olds who've pulled checkpoint duty at the base of an extinct volcano. So they aren't going to be the brightest minds in our war effort."

I didn't like what Pop was saying. But for the time being, I kept my mouth shut.

The Cutthroat nodded. "All right, then." He turned away and started down the slope.

"We have a jeep," Pop called after him.

The Cutthroat didn't even glance back. So Pop looked at me and shrugged, and he and I started back the way we had come. A few seconds later, when I looked down the slope again, the Cutthroat had vanished.

When we reached the spot where the dead eagle had been staked, I thought for a moment that we had headed in the wrong direction. But then I saw the rocks I'd used as markers, so I knew we were where I thought we were. The eagle was simply gone. So were the nails. So was my canteen.

"The Scout was right," Pop said. "The wind took it."

If I tried, I could make out some darkish spots on the bare patch of ground where the bird had been staked, and when I looked up the slope I thought I could see a few distant, scattered feathers. But the eagle itself was somewhere far away now. Maybe the ocean. Maybe even Attu.

"This is a good thing," Pop said, continuing on toward the jeep. "Now when you tell the lieutenant colonel that the eagle was gone, you can do so in good conscience. Or good enough. It's certainly gone now. That fact should get me back to my newspaper until he thinks of some other way to torment me."

He looked at me and smiled with those horrible false teeth, as if I should feel happy about the way things had turned out. But I wasn't feeling too happy about much of anything.

"What about the man in the lodge?" I asked.

Pop frowned. "We're going to report him to the Navy."

"I know that," I said. "But what should I tell the colonel?"

Pop stopped walking and put his hand on my shoulder.

"Listen, son," he said. His eyes were steady and serious. "I'm not joking about this. Are you listening?"

I gave a short nod.

"All right." Pop sucked in a deep breath through his mouth and let it out through his nose. "When you see the lieutenant colonel, don't mention the dead man. You brought me up here to show me the eagle, as ordered, and it was gone. That's all. Do you understand?"

I understood. But I didn't like it.

"It's not right," I said.

Pop dropped his hand and gave me a look as if I'd slapped him. "Not right? How much more 'right' would the whole truth be? For one thing, there's no way of knowing how the eagle got into the state it was in. So there's no way to give the lieutenant colonel that information. But now it's gone, which means that problem is gone as well."

"You know I don't mean the eagle," I said.

Now Pop's eyes became more than serious. They became grim.

"Yes, we discovered a dead man," he said. "And the gutted eagle nearby, plus the feather in the dead man's pocket, raise some questions. But they're questions we can't answer. The simplest explanation? The sailor's death was an accident. He came up here, either alone or with comrades, got drunk, and hit his head when he passed out. But even if it was manslaughter or murder, he was Navy, and the guilty party is probably Navy as well. So we're telling the Navy. After that, it's out of our hands. Besides, Private, what do you suppose the lieutenant colonel would do if you did tell him about it?"

I didn't answer. I just stared back at Pop's grim eyes.

"I'll tell you what he'd do," Pop said. "He'd question us repeatedly. He'd make us trek back up here with M.P.'s. He'd order us to fill out reports in triplicate. He'd force me to run a speculative and sensational story in *The Adakian*, even though it's a Navy matter and affects our boys not at all. And then he'd question us again and make us fill out more reports. And all for what? What would the upshot be?"

I knew the answer. "The upshot," I said, "would be that the man would still be dead. And it would still be a Navy matter."

Pop pointed a finger at me. "Correct. And telling the lieutenant colonel wouldn't have made any difference at all."

I glanced back toward the *ulax*.

"It's still not right," I said.

The cold grimness in Pop's eyes softened. "There's nothing about a young man's death that's right. Especially when it was for nothing. But a lot of young men have died in this war, and some of those died for nothing, too. So the only thing to do is simply what you know *must* be done, and nothing more. Because trying to do more would be adding meaninglessness to meaninglessness." He stuck his hands into his jacket pockets. "And in this case, what we must do is tell the Navy. Period."

Then he started toward the jeep again. But I didn't follow.

"That won't be the end of it," I called after him.

He turned and glared at me. His white hair whipped in the wind.

"Why not?" he shouted.

I jerked a thumb backward. "Because I gave him that bruise on his face."

Pop stood there staring at me for a long moment, his stick-thin body swaying. I didn't think he understood.

"That's the guy I whipped in the ring yesterday," I said.

Pop just stared at me for a few more seconds. Then he took his right hand from his pocket and moved as if to adjust his glasses. But he stopped when he saw that he was holding the bent eagle feather he'd found on the dead man.

I saw his thin lips move under his mustache. If he was speaking aloud, it was too quietly for me to hear him over the wind. But I saw the words.

"Nothing but trouble," he said again.

IX

This time, I stayed in the jeep while Pop talked with the Navy boys at the checkpoint. He had said things would go better if I let him handle it. I thought they might give him a bad time, since that had been their inclination with me that morning. But Pop had given a weak laugh when I'd mentioned that. He assured me it wasn't going to be a problem.

It took twenty minutes or more. But eventually Pop came back to the jeep. Through the shack's open doorway, I could see one of the Navy men get on the horn and start talking to someone.

"Let's go," Pop said.

I still didn't feel right. I had known the dead man, even if it had only been for a few minutes in a boxing ring. And although I had seen what had happened to the back of his head, and I knew that it had to have happened right there where we'd found him, I couldn't shake the notion that my clobbering him had somehow led to his death.

Pop nudged my shoulder. "I said, let's go. We may have to answer a few questions for whoever investigates, but the odds are against it. Those boys told me that the *ulax* we found is well-known to their comrades as an unapproved recreation hut. They've never even heard of Army personnel using it. So this really is a Navy matter."

I didn't respond. Instead I just started the jeep, which clattered and roared as I drove us back down to camp. I didn't try to talk to Pop on the way. I didn't even look at him.

He didn't say anything more to me, either, until I had stopped the jeep on Main Street near the base of the boardwalk that led up the hill to the *Adakian* hut. I didn't mean to shut off the engine, but it died on me anyway.

"You can go on back to work," I said, staring down Main Street at the long rows of Quonset huts interspersed with the occasional slapdash wood-frame building . . . at all the men trudging this way and that through the July mud . . . at the wires on the telephone poles as they hummed and swayed . . . and at the black ravens crisscrossing the gray air over all of it. I still wouldn't look at Pop. "I'll tell the colonel the eagle was a bust, like you said."

Pop coughed a few times. "What about the dead man?" he asked then. "Are you going to mention him, or are you going to take my advice and leave it to the Navy?"

Now, finally, I looked at him. What I saw was a scrawny, tired-looking old man. He might have been fifty, but he looked at least eighty to me. And I wanted to dislike him more than I did. I wanted to hate him.

"I'm going to tell him I found the body," I said. "But I'll leave you out of it. And I'll leave the Cutthroat out of it, too, since that's what we said we'd do. I'll just say that I spotted the lodge and went to have a look, but you were feeling sick and headed back to the jeep instead. I'll tell him I found the dead guy and told you about it, but you never saw him. And that we went down and told the Navy."

Pop's eyebrows pinched together. "Not good enough. With a story like that, he'll want to play detective. So he'll try to involve me regardless."

I shrugged. "That's the best I can do. I found a dead man while I was doing a chore for the colonel, and I have to tell him. Especially since he arranged for me to fight that same guy. So even if the Navy handles it, he'll still hear about it. And once he knows where they found him, and when, he'll ask me about it. So I have to tell him. It'll be worse later, if I don't."

Pop bit his lip, and I saw his false teeth shift when he did it. He pushed them back in place with his thumb. Then he stared off down Main Street the way I just had.

"Ever since this morning, I've been puzzled," he said in a low voice. "How is it that a lieutenant colonel is using a private as an aide, anyway? Officers over the rank of captain don't usually associate with G.I.'s lower than sergeant major. Unless the lower-ranking G.I. has other uses. As I do."

"Then I guess I have other uses, too," I said. "Besides, I'm not his aide. He has a lieutenant for that. But when we got back from Attu, he said he was getting me transferred to a maintenance platoon so I'd be available for other things. And now I run his errands. I shine his shoes. I deliver messages. I box. And when he doesn't need me, I go back to my platoon and try not to listen to the shit the other guys say about me."

Pop gave another cough. He didn't sound good at all, but I guessed he was used to it.

"You haven't really answered my question," he said then. "You've explained what you do for him. But you haven't explained how you were selected to do it. Out of all the enlisted men available, what made him notice you in particular?"

He was jabbing at me yet again. I thought about dislodging his false teeth permanently.

Instead, I told him. As much as I could stand to.

"It was on Attu," I said. My voice shook in my skull. "Right after the Japs made their banzai charge. By that time some of those little bastards didn't have nothing but bayonets tied to sticks. But they wouldn't quit coming. My squad was pushed all the way back to the support lines before we got the last ones we could see. We even captured one. He had a sword, but one of us got him in the hand, and then he didn't have nothing. So we knocked him down, sat on him, and tied his wrists behind his back with my boot laces." I glared at Pop. "Our sergeant was gone, and by then it was just me and two other guys. Once we had the Jap tied, those guys left me with him while they went to find the rest of our platoon. Then the colonel showed up. He'd lost his unit, too, and he wanted me to help him find it. But I had a prisoner. So the colonel gave me an order."

Pop looked puzzled. "And?"

"And I obeyed the order."

Pop's eyes shifted away for a second, then back again. I thought he was going to ask me to go ahead and say it.

But then he rubbed his jaw, raised his eyes skyward, and sighed.

"All right," he said. "I'll go with you to speak with the lieutenant colonel. You won't have to tell him that I didn't see the corpse. But we'll still have to leave our friend from the Alaska Scouts out of it. And I'll have to go up to

The Adakian first, to make sure the boys have started work on tomorrow's edition. There's nobody there over corporal, and they each refuse to take direction from any of the others unless I say so. I'm a corporal as well, of course, but our beloved brigadier general has given me divine authority in my own little corner of the war. He's an admirer. As were those Navy boys at Mount Moffett, as it turned out. Although I had the impression that what one of them really likes is the Bogart movie, while the other thinks I might be able to introduce him to Myrna Loy. But they were both impressed that I actually met Olivia de Havilland when she was here."

Pop liked to talk about himself a little more than suited me. But if he was going to do the right thing, I didn't care.

I got out of the jeep. "I'll go with you to the newspaper. In case you forget to come back."

Pop got out, too. "At this point, Private," he said, "I assure you that you've become unforgettable."

After a detour to the nearest latrine, we climbed up to the newspaper hut. Pop went in ahead of me, but stopped abruptly just inside the door. I almost ran into him.

"What the hell?" he said.

I looked past Pop and saw nine men standing at attention, including the three I had seen there that morning. They were all like statues, staring at the front wall. Their eyes didn't even flick toward Pop.

Someone cleared his throat to our left. I recognized the sound.

I looked toward the table where Pop had napped that morning, and I saw the colonel rise from a chair. His aide was standing at parade rest just beyond him, glaring toward the *Adakian* staff. I had the impression they were being made to stand at attention as a punishment for something.

The colonel adjusted his garrison cap, tapped its silver oak leaf with a fingernail, then hitched up his belt around his slight potbelly and stretched his back. He wasn't a large man, but the stretch made him seem taller than he was. His sharp, dark eyes seemed to spark as he gave a satisfied nod and scratched his pink, fleshy jaw.

"It's about damn time," he said in his harsh Texas accent. Then he looked back at his aide. "Everyone out except for these two. That includes you."

The aide snapped his fingers and pointed at the door.

Pop and I stepped aside as Pop's staff headed out. They all gave him quizzical looks, and a few tried to speak with him. But the colonel's aide barked at them when they did, and they moved on outside.

The aide brought up the rear and closed the door behind him, leaving just the colonel, Pop, and me in the hut. To Pop's right, on the drawing board, I saw the finished cartoon of two soldiers having beer for breakfast. One soldier was saying to the other:

"Watery barley sure beats watery eggs!"

Pop's eyebrows were pinched together. He was glaring at the colonel.

"I don't know how long you made them stand there like that," Pop said. "But I'll be taking this up with the general when he returns."

The colonel gave a smile that was almost a grimace. "We'll cross that bridge when we come to it. At the moment, we're in the middle of another. I've received a call from a Navy commander who tells me a dead sailor has been found on Mount Moffett. He says the body was discovered by you, Corporal. I play cards with the man, and he's sharp. So I believe him."

Pop sat down on the cartoonist's stool, which still kept him several inches taller than me or the colonel.

"That's right," Pop said. He was still frowning, but his voice had relaxed into its usual cool, superior tone. "At your request, the private and I were looking for the dead eagle he'd found earlier. But it had apparently blown away. Then a williwaw kicked up, so we found shelter in an old Aleut lodge. That's where we found the unfortunate sailor."

The colonel turned toward me. "I understand it was the sailor you fought yesterday."

"Yes, sir," I said. I had gone to attention automatically.

"What happened?" the colonel asked. "Did he try to take another swing at you?" He was still smiling in what I guessed he thought was a fatherly way. "Was it self-defense, Private?"

It was as if an icicle had been thrust into the back of my skull and all the way down my spine.

"Sir," I said. I don't know how I managed to keep my voice from quaking, but I did. "He was dead when we found him, sir."

The colonel's fatherly smile faded. "Are you sure about that? Or is that what the corporal said you should tell me?"

Now Pop was staring at the colonel through slitted eyelids. And now he had a slight smile of his own. But it was a grim, knowing smile.

"Son of a bitch," he said.

The colonel turned on Pop with sudden rage. His pink face went scarlet.

"I wasn't speaking to you, Corporal!" he snapped. "When I need answers from a drunken, diseased has-been who hasn't written a book in ten years, you'll be the first to know. At the moment, however, I'll take my answers from the private."

Pop nodded. "Of course you will. He's just a kid, and he doesn't have a brigadier general in his corner. So you're going to use him the way you've used him since Attu. What happened there, anyway?"

"We won," the colonel said. "No thanks to the likes of you."

Pop held up his hands. "I'd never claim otherwise. At that time I was stateside having my rotten teeth pulled, courtesy of Uncle Sam."

The colonel stepped closer to Pop, and for a second I thought he was going to slap him.

"You're nothing but a smug, privileged, Communist prick," the colonel snarled. "The general may not see that, but I do. I've read the fawning stories you print about Soviet victories. You might as well be fighting for the Japs."

Pop's eyes widened. "Colonel, I realize now that your attitude toward me is entirely my fault. In hindsight, I do wish I could have accepted your dinner invitation. However, in my defense, by that time I had seen a sample of your writing. And it was just atrocious."

The colonel's face went purple. He raised his hand.

Then, instead of slapping Pop, he reached over to the drawing board, snatched up the new cartoon, and tore it to shreds. He dropped the pieces on the floor at Pop's feet.

"No more jokes in the newspaper about beer," he said. "They undermine discipline. Especially if they're drawn by a nigger."

Then he looked at me, and his color began draining back to pink.

"Private," he said, his voice lowering, "you and I need to talk. Unfortunately, I'm about to have lunch, and then I have to meet with several captains and majors. The rest of my afternoon is quite full, as is most of my evening. So you're to report to my office at twenty-one hundred hours. No sooner, no later. Understood?"

"Yes, sir," I said.

The colonel gave a sharp nod. "Good. In the meantime, I'm restricting you to barracks. If you need chow, get it. But then go to your bunk and speak to no one. While you're there, I suggest that you think hard about what happened today, and what you're going to tell me about it. If it was self-defense, I can help you. Otherwise, you may be in trouble." He glanced at Pop, then back at me. "And stay away from the corporal."

"Yes, sir," I said.

The colonel pointed at the door, so I turned and marched out. I caught a glimpse of the colonel's aide and the newspaper staff standing up against the wall of the Quonset, and then I headed down the boardwalk toward Main Street. The wind cut through me, and I shivered. I still had to return the jeep to the motor pool. Then get some chow. Then go to my bunk. One thing at a time. Jeep, chow, bunk. Jeep, chow, bunk.

The colonel seemed to think I had killed the Navy man. And that Pop had advised me to lie about it.

Jeep, chow, bunk.

Of course, Pop *had* advised me to lie, but not about that. Because that hadn't happened.

Or had it? Could I have done something like that and then forgotten I'd done it? Why not? Hadn't I already done things just as bad?

Jeep, chow, bunk.

All I knew for sure was that the colonel hated Pop, and that I had been in trouble ever since finding the eagle.

Jeep, chow, bunk. It wasn't working.

How I wished I had never seen the eagle. Or the *ulax*.

How I wished I had never met another Cutthroat after Attu.

How I wished I could have stayed in my combat unit.

How I wished I had never met Pop.

How I wished I had never been sent to the Aleutians in the first place.

How I wished I had never punched that rich kid from Omaha, and that I had stayed home long enough to help my old man with the hay.

X

I HAD MY QUONSET HUT TO MYSELF WHILE I WAITED FOR THE AFTERNOON to creep by. I didn't know what job the rest of my bunkmates were out doing, but it didn't matter. I would have liked to find them and do some work so I wouldn't have to think. But I was under orders to stay put.

Other than the truth, I didn't know what I would tell the colonel when 2100 finally came. Even if I included every detail, including the ones Pop and I had agreed not to tell, it still wasn't going to be the story the colonel wanted to hear. And whatever story that was, I knew I wasn't smart enough to figure it out.

I hadn't gotten any chow. My stomach was a hard, hungry knot, and I knew I should have eaten. But I was also pretty sure I wouldn't have been able to keep it down.

Sure, I had been in trouble before. But back then, I had just been a dumb Bohunk kid who'd gotten in a fight, swiped a Hudson, and insulted a judge. None of that had bothered me. But none of that had been anything like this.

I wasn't even sure what "this" was. But I did know that another kid, a kid just like me except that he was Navy, had gotten his skull bashed in. And the colonel thought that maybe I was the one who'd done it.

It all went through my head over and over again, and the knot in my stomach got bigger and bigger. I lay in my bunk and closed my eyes, but I couldn't sleep. Outside, the Aleutian wind whistled and moaned, and occasional short rat-a-tats of rain drummed against the Quonset tin. Every so often, I heard planes roaring in and out of the airfield. I tried to guess what they were, since the bombing runs from Adak had pretty much ended once we'd retaken Attu and Kiska. But I had never been good at figuring out a plane from its engine noise. If an engine wasn't on a tractor or jeep, I was at a loss.

"First impressions can be so deceiving," a low, smooth voice said.

I opened my eyes. Pop was sitting on a stool beside my bunk. He was hunched over with his elbows on his knees, his hands clasped under his chin, his dark eyes regarding me over the rims of his glasses. I hadn't heard him come in.

"How'd you know where I bunk?" I asked.

Pop ignored the question. "Why, just this morning, Private," he continued, "you seemed like such a tough young man. Such a hardened fighter. Yet here we are, scarcely nine hours later, and you're flopped there like a sack of sand. Defeated. Vanquished."

"Don't those mean the same thing?"

Pop gave me that thin smile of his. "My point is, you're taking this lying down. That doesn't sound like someone who'd dare to punch a rich kid from Omaha."

I turned away from him and faced the cold metal of the Quonset wall.

"I'm under orders," I said. "And I'm not supposed to be talking to you."

Pop laughed a long, dry laugh that dissolved into his usual hacking cough. "Under orders?" he asked through the coughing. "Just how do you think you got into this confusing court-martial conundrum in the first place? You followed orders, that's how. Logically, then, the only possible way out of your current situation is to *defy* orders, just this once. It's only sixteen thirty, and the lieutenant colonel won't be looking for you until twenty-one hundred. You've already wasted more than two hours wallowing here, so I suggest you don't waste any more."

I turned back to face him.

"Just what am I supposed to do?" I asked. "My only choice is to tell him everything that happened, and the hell with our promise to the Cutthroat. So that's what I'm going to do."

Pop shook his head. "You can't tell him everything," he said, "because you don't *know* everything."

"And you do?"

"No." Pop stood and jerked his thumb toward the door. "But I know some of it, and I'm going to find out the rest. You see, unlike you, I've spent the past few hours doing something. My job is to get the news, and a large part of that involves getting people to talk. So for the past two hours, people have been talking to me and my boys a lot. But now the boys have to work on the paper. And my cartoonist has to draw a new cartoon, which has put me into a vengeful mood."

"So go get your revenge," I said. "What's it got to do with me?"

Pop leaned down and scowled. "It's your revenge, too. And I don't think I can find out the rest of what I need to know if you aren't with me."

I rose on my elbows and stared up at him. It was true that following orders hadn't really worked out for me. But I didn't see how doing what Pop said would work out any better.

"You say you know some of it already," I said. "Tell me."

Pop hesitated. Then he turned, crossed to the other side of the hut, and sat on an empty bunk.

"I know the lieutenant colonel placed a bet on your fight yesterday," Pop said. "A large one. And I know that your opponent had a reputation as a damn good boxer. He'd won eighteen fights, six by knockout. How many have you won?"

"Two," I said. "Yesterday was my second match. The first was with the guy whose bunk you're sitting on. It was a referee's decision."

Pop's eyes narrowed. "So any sane wager yesterday would have been on the Navy man. And I saw the fight, Private. He was winning. Until the third round, when he dropped his left. And as you told me this morning, you took advantage. Who wouldn't?"

I sat up on the edge of my bunk. In addition to the knot in my stomach, I now felt a throbbing at the back of my skull.

"You're saying it was fixed," I said.

"If I were betting on it, I'd say yes." Pop waved a hand in a cutting gesture. "But leave that alone for now. Instead, consider a few more things. One, we know that the *ulax* we found was used by Navy men for unofficial activities. The dead man is Navy. And the Navy boys we talked to said they didn't know of anyone but sailors having any fun up there. After all, they control access to that part of the island. Yet the lieutenant colonel sent you up because, he claimed, he had reports of Army G.I.'s entertaining nurses there. Which doesn't quite jibe with the Navy's version."

"That's odd, I guess," I said. "But that's not anything you found out in the past two hours."

Pop looked down at the floor and clasped his hands again.

"No," he said. Now I could barely hear him over the constant weather noise against the Quonset walls. "I learned two more things this afternoon. One is that the lieutenant colonel will soon be up for promotion to full colonel. Again. After being passed over at least once before. And I know he wants that promotion very badly. Badly enough, perhaps, to do all sorts of things to get it."

Pop fell silent then, and kept looking down at the floor.

I stood. My gut ached and my head hurt. And I thought I knew the answer to my next question. But I had to ask it anyway.

"You said you learned two more things," I said. "What's the second?"

Pop looked up at me. His expression was softer than it had been all day. He looked kindly. Sympathetic. I had wanted to hit him earlier, but not as much as I did now.

"It's not really something new," Pop said. "It's what you already told me. Or almost told me. But of course I know the order that the lieutenant colonel gave you on Attu."

I clenched my fists. Maybe I would hit the old man after all. Maybe I wouldn't stop hitting him for a while.

"I won't say it aloud if you don't want me to," Pop said.

I turned and started for the door. I didn't know where I was going, but I knew I was getting away from Pop.

He followed and stopped me with a hand on my shoulder, so I whirled with a roundhouse right. He leaned back just in time, and my knuckles brushed his mustache.

"Jesus Christ, son," Pop exclaimed.

I grabbed his scrawny arms and pushed him away. He staggered back, but didn't fall.

"He was a Jap," I said. I was trembling. "He was trying to kill me not five minutes before. And it was an order. It was an order from a goddamn colonel."

Pop took a deep, quaking breath and adjusted his glasses.

"It was an order," I said.

Pop nodded. "I know. And now I need you to listen to me again. Are you listening, Private?"

I glared at him.

"Here it is, then," Pop said. "No one, and I mean no one—not your chaplain, not the general, not anyone back home, and sure as hell not me—*no one* would condemn what you did. If the circumstances had been reversed, that Jap would have done the same to you, and he wouldn't have waited for an order."

I could still see him lying there, his blood staining the thin crust of snow a sudden crimson. He had been as small as a child. His uniform had looked like dirty play clothes.

He was a Jap. But he was on the ground. With his hands tied behind his back. His sword was gone.

Pop wasn't finished. "The problem isn't that you followed the order. The problem is that out of the three thousand Japs you boys fought on Attu, we took only twenty-eight prisoners. I'm not saying that killing the rest was a bad thing. But prisoners can be valuable. Especially if they're officers. And a man with a sword might have been an officer. So someone would have wanted to ask him things like, what's your rank, who are your immediate superiors, where are your maps, what were your orders, what's your troop strength on Kiska, and where does Yamamoto go to take his morning shit. That sort of thing."

Pop was talking a lot, again. It wore on my brain. And Yamamoto's plane had been shot down a month before we'd hit Attu. But at least now I had something else to think about.

"You mean we need a supply of Japs?" I said.

Now Pop smiled his thin smile. "I mean that a lieutenant colonel in the Intelligence Section did a stupid thing. He wasn't even supposed to be near the fighting. But that banzai charge came awfully close. So in rage or fear, he forgot his job and ordered you to destroy a military intelligence asset. That's an act that could negatively affect his chances for promotion." Pop pointed at me again. "If anyone happened to testify to it."

I rubbed the back of my neck, trying to make the pain at the base of my skull go away.

"I don't understand how anything you just said adds up to anything we saw today," I told him.

Now Pop pointed past me, toward the door. "That's why there's more to find out, and that's why I need you to help me with it. There was one other man on the mountain with us this morning. And since you and he were freezing and fighting on Attu while I was elsewhere, I think he might be more willing to part with any answers if you're present."

That made some sense. The Cutthroat hadn't liked me, but he might respect me more than Pop.

Still, there was one thing that I knew Pop had left out in all his talk.

"What about the eagle?" I asked.

Pop bared his false teeth.

"That's the key," he said. "That's why we have to talk with the Scout again. Remember what he said about magic and power? Well, he also said that he told those same stories to officers on Attu." He went past me to the door. "Now, will you come along?"

I turned to go with him, then hesitated.

"Wait a minute." I was still trying to clear my head. "Are you saying the colonel believes in Eskimo magic?"

Pop held up his hands. "I have no idea. But magic and religion are based on symbols, which can be powerful as hell. And I know the lieutenant colonel *does* believe in that. After all, there's one symbol that he very much wants for his own."

I was still confused by most of what Pop had said. But this one part, I suddenly understood.

A full colonel was called a "bird colonel."

Because a full colonel's insignia was an eagle.

I went with Pop.

XI

THE 179TH STATION HOSPITAL WASN'T JUST ONE BUILDING. IT WAS A COMplex of Quonset huts and frame buildings, and it even had an underground bunker. When Olivia de Havilland had come to Adak in March, she had spent an entire day there, visiting the sick and wounded. There were a few hundred patients on any given day.

But all we needed to do was find the Cutthroat. So I waited outside the main building while Pop went in and charmed whomever he needed to charm to find out what he wanted to know. I was beginning to realize that there were some things, even in the Army, that superseded rank.

When Pop came out again, his hands in his jacket pockets, he tilted his head and started walking around back. I followed him to three Quonset huts behind the main building. He stopped at the lean-to of the first hut and looked one way and then the other as I joined him. There were a few G.I.'s trudging along nearby with no apparent purpose. Maybe, I thought, they were just trying to look busy so they wouldn't be sent to the South Pacific.

"Do you see anyone you know?" Pop asked. "Anyone who might tell the lieutenant colonel we're here?"

I tried to take a good look. But the usual gray light was dimming as evening came on, making all the soldiers appear gray as well.

"I don't think so," I said. "But everyone's starting to look alike to me."

Pop gave me an annoyed glance. "You sound like the Scout," he said. He stepped away, moved quickly to the center Quonset, and slipped into its lean-to. I followed. Then he barged into the hut without knocking.

The Cutthroat was in a small open space in the center of the hut, surrounded by shelves packed with boxes and cans. He was sitting on the edge of a cot under a single lightbulb that hung from the ceiling, leaning over a battered coffeepot on a G.I. pocket stove. The smell was not only of coffee, but of old beef stew, seaweed, and mud. My still-knotted stomach lurched.

The Cutthroat looked up, and his slick dark hair gleamed. "You guys." He didn't sound surprised. "Did you bring my beers?"

Pop and I stepped farther inside, and I closed the door behind us. There were two folding stools set up on our side of the pocket stove.

"I'll bring your beers tomorrow." Pop went to the right-hand stool and sat down. "In the meantime, I want you to know that both the private and I are doing our best to live up to this morning's agreements. For one thing, we haven't mentioned your presence on Mount Moffett to anyone else."

"I believe you," the Cutthroat said.

"But we have a problem," Pop continued. "So we may not be able to keep that confidence much longer. There's a lieutenant colonel who's trying to use that Navy man's death to make our lives hell."

The Cutthroat looked back down at his brew. "Yeah, I know." He rubbed his right thigh. "Goddamn, my leg is hurting tonight. I better not climb any more mountains for a while."

I sat down on the left-hand stool. The fumes from the stuff bubbling in the coffeepot were intense.

"What do you mean, you know?" I asked. "How could you know that?"

The Cutthroat glanced up at me. "Because I wasn't sure I trusted you guys. So I followed you. You didn't drive fast. I was outside the back wall of the newspaper hut when you got your asses chewed. I couldn't hear it all, but I got most of it. He's got it in for both of you. And I recognized his voice."

Pop's eyebrows rose. "That was quite stealthy of you."

The Cutthroat snorted. "I've snuck up on Japs in machine gun nests, and they knew I was coming. Buncha desk soldiers who don't expect me ain't a challenge."

"Nevertheless," Pop said. "I respect a man who can shadow that well. Especially if I'm the one he's shadowing."

The Cutthroat reached to a shelf behind him and brought down three tin cups. "You guys want coffee before you start bothering me with more questions?"

"Is that what that is?" I asked.

The Cutthroat gave me a look almost as dark as he'd given me in the *ulax*. "You need to work on your fucking manners."

Pop and I both accepted cups, and the Cutthroat poured thick, black liquid into both of them. It was something else that reminded me of what Pop had coughed up that morning.

Then the Cutthroat poured a cup for himself and set the pot back down on the pocket stove. He took a swig and smiled.

"That's good," he said. "This stuff will help you think better."

Pop took a swig as well, and I took a tentative sip of mine. It didn't taste as bad as it smelled, so I drank a little more. There was a hint of rotted undergrowth. But at least it was hot.

"Thank you," Pop said. He took a long belt. "But now I'm going to bother you, as you suspected. How did you recognize the lieutenant colonel's voice?"

The Cutthroat blew into his cup, and steam rose up around his face. "Because I've heard it before. On Attu, he was one of the shitheads who wouldn't listen to our scouting reports. But he loved our colorful stories. Here on Adak, I've been bringing him and his officer pals booze and coffee while they play poker right here in this hut. And when they get good and drunk, they want me to tell more stories. Like I said, you people can't get enough of that noble-savage crap."

"Do those poker pals include a Navy commander?" Pop asked.

"I guess that's what he is," the Cutthroat said. "He and the lieutenant colonel set up yesterday's boxing matches. They made a bet on the Army-Navy one." He pointed at me. "The lieutenant colonel bet on this guy."

"I know," Pop said. "For a lot of money, correct?"

The Cutthroat scowled and took a long drink. "Maybe there were side bets for money. But the bet between the lieutenant colonel and the Navy officer was for something else. See, the Navy guy has friends and family in high places. Like fucking Congress. So if the Army boxer won, the commander promised to have these friends pull strings and help with a promotion."

"What if the Navy man won?" Pop asked.

The Cutthroat grinned and shook his head. "Then the commander was going to have dinner with you, Corporal. That's what the lieutenant colonel promised. You must be famous or rich or something. Gotta say, it seemed like a lopsided bet to me."

Pop drained his cup and set it on the floor. He seemed to wobble on his stool as he did.

"Very lopsided indeed," he said, "since I wouldn't do a favor for the lieutenant colonel if my life depended on it."

I had been sipping the hot coffee and listening, but now I spoke up. "What about the eagle?"

The Cutthroat fixed me with an even gaze. "I still don't know about that. Not for sure. But nobody ever knows anything for sure. No matter who you ask, or what you find out, you'll never know all of anything that's already past."

The single lightbulb began to flicker. My stomach knot had relaxed, but now I found myself feeling lightheaded. I knew I should have had some chow.

"So I'm giving you both the opportunity to know as much as the lieutenant colonel," the Cutthroat said. "I told him the legend I told you. And once, he asked me about taking power from animals. I said I couldn't really explain that, since I didn't understand it myself. But if he were to take a spirit journey or have a vision, like some shamans do, he might have a chance to know all the secrets he wanted. He might die and be reborn. He might be torn apart and remade. He might meet his totem animal and be given its strength. He might gain whatever he desired. He might even see his entire life from his birth to his death." The Cutthroat shrugged. "Or he might go crazy. Or he might just pass out and sleep it off. It all depends on the individual."

The Cutthroat stood up from the cot, and he split into five men before me. "Here," they all five said in harmony. They reached for Pop and grasped his forearms. "You take the cot. My mother got this recipe from the same people who told her the eagle story, and she always said that the most important part was to lie the fuck down. There's some mushrooms and other shit in it, and you don't want to know what I have to do to mix it right. But it hardly ever kills anyone."

The five Cutthroats put Pop on the bunk, and Pop curled up on his side. He looked like a toy made out of olive-drab pipe cleaners with a cotton-swab head. I could see his eyes behind his glasses, and they were like hard-boiled eggs.

Now the Cutthroat condensed into one man again, and he reached for me.

"You'll have to take the floor," he said. "But you're younger. It's fair."

As he grasped my wrist, I watched my tin coffee cup tumble from my numb fingers. It turned over and over, and brown droplets spun out and circled it. The cup turned into the sun.

The bright light was high above my eyes. I could see it between Pop's fingers.

"That's the best I can do for you," the Cutthroat's voice said. I couldn't see him anymore. He was far away. "Your enemy took this journey before you. But maybe you're better suited for it. I don't say that this means you'll beat him, or that you'll understand what he's done. But at least now you have the same magic. So it's a fair fight. You're welcome."

The earth shook with a deafening rumble, and the back of Pop's hand fell against my forehead.

Then, in brilliant flashes, in a cacophony of voices and noise and music, I began to see everything.

Everything.

I began to see both the past and present of every place I had ever been, every object I had ever touched, every thing I had ever done. It was as if I were a movie camera in the sky, looking down and watching it all.

Then, even as the past and present were flashing and roaring around me, I saw the future as well. And not just mine.

Pop's, too.

My advice: Never see the future.

Not anyone's.

I'm in my foxhole when the Japanese make their charge. I have to struggle for my helmet, for my weapon. When I make it out of the hole I run backward, firing as they come toward me. Some keep coming even after I hit them. One gets very close and sets off a hand grenade, trying to kill us both. But he trips and falls, his body covers it, and I'm all right. Then, to my left, I see my sergeant bayoneted. I shoot the one who did it. But it's too late.

A younger Pop, his hair not yet all white, is at a typewriter. It clacks and clatters, and the bell rings over and over again. He puts in page after page. He smokes cigarette after cigarette and drinks two bottles of whiskey dry, but he doesn't stop typing. He does this for thirty hours without a break. When he finally stops I can see his eyes. And I know he has emptied himself. There is nothing left.

The colonel points at the little man on the ground and shouts at me. I look at the little man and know he's a Jap who just tried to kill me. But now he's lying facedown, his hands behind his back. He hardly looks like a Jap now.

The colonel points and shouts again and again, louder and louder. I put the muzzle of the M1 at the base of the little man's skull and pull the trigger.

Pop, much, much younger, is wearing a uniform and walking into a hospital. He doubles over coughing as he climbs the steps. A pretty nurse rushes over and puts her arm around his shoulders.

I am much, much older, sitting in a tangle of metal and plastic. A young man is using huge steel jaws to push the metal apart and make a hole for me. You'll be okay, sir, he says. I'll get you out. I manage to take a small plastic rectangle from my pocket. It has little square buttons. I punch the buttons and call my daughter. You're right, I tell her. I shouldn't drive anymore.

The colonel is standing over the dead eagle. He is holding a knife. The sailor who fought me appears at the hillock beside the lodge, and the colonel goes to him. You'll have to trust me for an IOU, he says. It'll be a while before I can collect my winnings. But you did good. And thanks for the bird.

Pop, looking only a bit older, but wearing a nice suit, is being escorted from a bus by armed guards. They take him into prison and put him into a cell by himself. He stays in the prison for six months. He writes a lot of letters. But all his books go out of print. The radio money stops. When they let him out, he is sicker than ever and looks twenty years older. He is broke and goes to live in a tiny cottage owned by friends.

Guess I don't have any choice, the sailor says. But I know you're good for it, sir. Do I still get the date with the nurse? The blonde who swabbed my face and said I was handsome for a Navy man?

I am standing at the altar with my younger brother beside me, looking down at the far end of the aisle, when the pipe organ blares and all of the people on either side of the aisle stand up. A gorgeous woman in white appears on the arm of an older man, and they walk toward me, smiling. I can't wait for them to get here so I can find out what her name is.

You still get the date, the colonel says, holding out a bent eagle feather. Show this to her when she comes. It's dark down there, and she has to know it's you. She'll be here in a little while. Go on down and wait.

The heavy, sweating man with greasy, wormlike hair leans forward and looks down from his high, long podium. I would like to ask, he says in a thick voice. Is Mr. Budenz being truthful when he told us that you were a Communist? So now Pop leans forward, too, toward the microphones on the table where they've made him sit, and he says, I decline to answer on the grounds that an answer might tend to incriminate me. He is out of prison, and he is poor. But they won't leave him alone. They won't let him at least try to write.

The sailor goes down into the lodge, and the colonel walks away, past the eagle. Another sailor approaches. He's in there, the colonel says, pointing back toward the lodge. Down where you boys have your fun. He threw the fight. He lost your money.

I am holding a baby. Her eyes look like mine. How the hell did this happen, I wonder. How did we finally have a girl after all these years? After all the bad things I've done, how did my life turn out to be this good?

The second sailor stops and stares down at the eagle. Never mind that, the colonel says. It's just a dead bird. It's none of your business. Go talk to your friend. He threw the fight.

In the hospital bed, Pop opens his eyes and he sees the woman. There have been dozens of women. Even a wife. But this is the one. The only one, really. She's there leaning over him.

In the lodge, the two sailors argue. You sold us out, the second sailor says. The first says, no, I'm going to share the winnings with you guys. I don't have any of it yet. But I will. Joe, calm down. Joe, no.

My daughter claps her hands the first time I walk to the mailbox and back without the crutches. You are one tough old bird, she says. Yes, I say. Yes I am. Guess what kind of tough old bird. I have its feather in my room. Have I ever shown you?

The woman leaning over Pop is at once plain and beautiful. That paradox was the first thing that drew him to her. And then her frighteningly sharp mind kept him there. More than thirty years now. She is his best friend, was several times his lover, has always been his savior. But he's been hers, too, so that's only fair. She looks so frightened. Why? Pop wonders, and then he knows. That makes him frightened, too. And angry. He's sixty-six. That's not old enough for this, is it?

The two sailors fight. The first catches the second with a punch to the jaw, but then the second shoves him back into the little room behind the jumble of sod and bone. He knocks him down, then slams his head back. He does it again.

Pop is frightened and angry for only a moment. Then he sinks away, down into warm black cotton, and can only hear the woman's sobs from far, far away. It's okay, Lilishka, he tries to say. It's okay.

My little grandson and granddaughter run out and throw their arms around my legs, and I drop all the mail. So I look up at my daughter on the porch and ask her to go get her mother to help me. But she frowns and says, Dad, don't you remember?

I don't. So she begins to tell me.

XII

Then Pop was slapping my face, hard, back and forth on both cheeks.

"That's enough," he said. "That's more than enough, goddamn it. Get up. Get your ass up right now, soldier."

He grabbed my collar and tried to pull me to my feet, but he wasn't strong enough. So he let me drop back down. My head thumped on the plywood floor, and then he started slapping me again. The light hanging above us shone around his wild white hair like a halo.

I almost slipped back into the visions, but Pop wouldn't stop slapping me. Finally, I came up from limbo enough to grab his right wrist with my left hand. My right fist clenched.

"Hit me again, old man," I said, my words slurring. "Hit me again, and I'll lay you out."

Pop sat down on the edge of the cot and ran his hand back through his hair. "All right," he said. "I'd like to see that. You tried to slug me once before, and all I got was a cool breeze. I'm beginning to think you aren't actually capable of hitting anyone who hasn't been paid to take a dive."

I struggled up to my knees, tried to make it all the way to my feet, and fell back onto one of the stools. It tipped, but Pop reached out and grabbed my sleeve to keep me from going over.

I didn't say thanks. I was mad at him for smacking me around. My cheeks were burning.

Pop let go of my sleeve and then shook his head as if trying to clear it.

"That may have been the worst coffee I've ever had," he said.

My head was muzzy, and Pop was going in and out of focus. But I was in the hospital's supply hut again. I was in the here and now. I looked around the room for the Cutthroat and didn't see him anywhere.

"He was gone when I came out of it," Pop said, anticipating my question. "Then I heard you talking to people who obviously haven't been born yet. So I decided that whatever you were experiencing, you'd better not experience any more of it. You're too young for family responsibilities."

I began to feel less angry toward Pop as I looked at him and remembered what I'd just seen. His hand had been touching my forehead, and I had seen everything about him.

Including his death.

"Did you . . . hallucinate?" I asked.

Pop looked at his wristwatch and stood. "We both know those were more than hallucinations. And I believe you and I saw and heard the same things, up to the point where I snapped out of it. But now it's eighteen thirty, and I have to piss like a thoroughbred. Then I have to go into Navytown and ask around for a certain commander. I understand he's an admirer of mine. Are you all right to take yourself to your bunk, or to mess, or wherever you need to go?"

I stood, too, but I was feeling considerably wobblier than Pop looked.

"Why aren't you shook up?" I asked. "If you'd seen anything like what I saw, you'd be shook up."

Pop smiled that thin smile. "I've seen a lot of things, Private. And they've all shook me up, even when they didn't involve Aleutian magic. But the key is to realize that it's all like that. It's all magic, it's all insane. So you make sense of what little you can, and you rely on alcohol for the rest." He gestured toward the door. "And now I really must be going."

"Are you sure you don't want me to go with you, Pop?" I asked. "I don't like the thought of you dealing with those Navy goons all by yourself. And I don't have to be at the colonel's office until twenty-one hundred."

I really wanted to stick with him so I could keep my mind off that meeting. I still had no idea what I was going to say to the colonel. What could I tell him? That I'd had a vision of what he'd done? I doubted that would go over too well with him. Or with a court-martial, either.

Pop shook his head. "No, Private, I don't want you with me this time. Frankly, you don't get along as well with those Navy people as I do. But while I'm gone, I would like you to do two things for me."

"Whatever you want," I said. "Shoot."

Pop held up an index finger. "One. Do not go to the lieutenant colonel's office at twenty-one hundred. I know he ordered you to be there. But again, ask yourself how well his orders have worked out for you so far. Stay in your barracks or hide somewhere. With luck, I'll be back before twenty-one hundred anyway. And I'll take care of all of this."

He stepped past me and headed for the door.

"How, Pop?" I asked. "How are you going to do that? We don't have proof of anything. All we have are hallucinations."

Pop paused at the door and looked back at me.

"No offense, Private," he said, "but that's all *you've* got. I plan to return with considerably more." He turned away and opened the door.

"Wait," I said. "You said you wanted me to do two things. What's the second?"

He held up two fingers and answered without looking back.

"Don't call me 'Pop,'" he said. Then the door swung closed behind him.

I stepped out just a moment later and found that a thick Aleutian fog had fallen. The wind, for a change, had died.

I looked down past the third storage hut. But between the fog and the dim light, I only caught a glimpse of Pop's thin, shadowy form before he disappeared.

XIII

My squad was back at our Quonset by the time I returned, and I went with them to mess. A couple of them tried to rib me by asking about what kind of soft duty I'd pulled that day, but I wouldn't even look at them. Pretty soon they got the idea and left me alone.

I made myself eat. I don't remember what it was. Some kind of gray Adak food that matched the gray Adak fog outside. I didn't want it. But I knew I had to put something in my stomach if I didn't want to collapse. I hadn't had anything to eat since the Spam sandwich more than twelve hours earlier. Besides, I wanted something to soak up whatever remained of the Cutthroat's black sludge. Whatever it had been.

The whole platoon had the evening off, which meant that my hut would be full of talking and card games. I didn't want to have to put up with any of that, so I took off after chow and slogged northward up Main Street, toward the airfield, in the opposite direction from Navytown. Pop had made it clear that he didn't want me around. So I didn't want to be tempted to go look for him.

I hadn't even met him before that morning, but now he seemed like the only friend I had on the whole island. I had considered my old sergeant to be my friend, but he had died on Attu. The closest I had gotten to anyone since then had been to the poor Navy guy at the Fourth of July boxing match. But apparently that hadn't been an honest relationship.

Somehow, I wandered my way eastward to the rocky shore of Kuluk Bay. The iron-colored, choppy water stretched out beyond the fog, and a frigid wind blew in and numbed my face. There weren't even any ships visible, since they were all anchored to the south in Sweeper Cove. So I had the feeling that I was alone at the edge of the world, and that all I had to do was step off into the cold dark water to be swallowed up, frozen and safe.

Then I glanced at my wristwatch, which my old man had given me as I'd left for basic. It was a lousy watch and lost almost fifteen minutes a day. Right now it said that it was 8:36, which meant that the actual time was about nine minutes before twenty-one hundred hours. Which was when the colonel had ordered me to be at his office. An order Pop had said I should disobey.

I thought about it.

Then I started back the way I had come, trudging through the muck as fast as I could. Maybe Pop was right, and I was an obstacle to the colonel's promotion. Maybe he was going to blame me for the sailor's death. Maybe he was going to have me court-martialed. Or maybe he was just trying to scare me into keeping my mouth shut no matter what anyone else might ask me.

It didn't matter. Whatever was going to happen to me now, I wasn't going to count on Pop to get me out of it. I had seen that he was going to have his own problems soon enough.

And I knew my life was going to be all right. I had seen that, too. I hadn't seen every day or every detail. And I knew there would be some tough times, too. But overall, it was going to be better than what most people got. Better than I deserved.

It was going to be better than what Pop had coming, anyway.

When I reached the small frame building that housed the colonel's office and living quarters, I had to stop and stare at it from across the road. The edge of the peaked roof was lined with ravens, stock-still except for a few ominous wing flaps. Normally, they would be swooping and squawking over my head. But now they were sitting on the colonel's roof in silence. There must have been fifty of them.

A few G.I.'s walking by looked up, and one of them made a comment about "those weird birds." But otherwise, Main Street was almost empty. And that was weird, too.

I crossed the slop, went up the wooden steps, and wiped my feet on the burlap mat at the top. The real time was almost exactly twenty-one hundred. I knocked on the door and waited for the colonel's aide to let me in.

Instead, as if from a great distance, I heard the colonel's voice say, in a rough monotone, "Enter."

I opened the door and went in. The first small room was the colonel's aide's vestibule. The lamp on the desk was on, but the aide wasn't there. Beyond the desk, the door to the colonel's office was ajar. I crossed to it and hesitated.

Beyond the door, the colonel spoke again. "I said enter."

I pushed the door open just far enough and stepped into the colonel's office. The room was small and plain and lined with filing cabinets. The colonel's desk was dead center, with the overhead light shining down onto a small stack of papers between the colonel's hands. His garrison cap, its silver oak leaf shining, was flattened neatly beside the papers. The colonel's face was mostly shadowed, with just the tip of his nose glowing in the light.

I stepped smartly to within a foot of the desk, front and center, then saluted and stood at attention. It was the same thing I had done every time I had ever been summoned here.

"Thank you for coming, Private," the colonel said.

I almost laughed. He had never thanked me for coming before. But now he had thanked me as if we were equals and I had done him a favor. He had thanked me as if I weren't there because of a direct order that had been wrapped around a threat.

"Yes, sir," I said. "My pleasure, sir." I kept my eyes focused on an invisible point just over his head. But I could still see everything he did.

The colonel touched the top of the small stack of papers with his fingertips and pushed the top sheet across the desk toward me.

"I won't waste your time or mine, soldier," the colonel said. "This is a statement to the effect that this morning, 5 July 1944, you assisted your friend the corporal in a drunken escapade in which you killed an American bald eagle and then recklessly contributed to the accidental death of a Navy seaman. You are to sign at the bottom. I personally guarantee that you yourself will serve no more than one year in a stateside stockade, after which you'll receive a dishonorable discharge."

He placed a fountain pen atop the piece of paper.

I didn't even try to think. I just stayed at attention with my arms stiff at my sides and my eyes staring at that invisible spot above his head.

"Sir," I heard myself saying. "I decline to sign that statement on the grounds that signing it may tend to incriminate me."

I had heard words similar to those just a few hours before. But they wouldn't be spoken for a few years yet.

The colonel gave a growl. He picked up the pen, pushed across the next piece of paper, and put the pen down on top of it.

"Very well," he said. "This next statement is to the effect that you weren't intoxicated at all, but had an altercation with the sailor and committed manslaughter. And the corporal witnessed it."

"Sir," I heard myself saying again. "I decline to sign on the grounds that signing may tend to incriminate me."

The colonel stood, put his hands on the desk, and leaned forward into the light like a Nebraska judge. Now my eyes were focused on the top of his head. He had the same greasy, wormlike hair as the man at the high, long podium in my vision.

"Son, you'd best listen up and listen good," the colonel snarled. He pushed the remaining three pages onto the first two. "I have five confessions here, each with a slightly different version of what you and the corporal have done. You can sign any one of them. The consequences vary depending upon which one you choose. But if you don't choose one, then I'll choose one for you. And you won't like that. Nor will you like the way things go for you when both my aide and I swear that we witnessed the aftermath of your crimes as well as your signature."

I heard every word he said, and I knew what each one meant.

But what I said in reply was, "Sir, I decline to sign on the grounds—"

Then I heard the telltale sound of a hammer clicking back, and my eyes broke focus from the top of the colonel's head. I looked down and saw his .45 service automatic in his hand. It was pointing at my gut.

"Let me put this another way, Private," he said. His Texas accent slid into a self-satisfied drawl. "You can sign one of these pieces of paper, or I can tell the judge advocate that you went berserk when I confronted you with the evidence. I can tell him that you attacked a much superior officer, namely myself, and that the officer was therefore compelled to defend himself."

I stared at the muzzle of the .45 for what seemed like a long, long moment. Then I snapped my eyes back up to a point above and behind the colonel's head.

Maybe I hadn't seen the future after all. Maybe this was the future, right here. And maybe that was fair.

Maybe this would make me even again.

"Sir," I said. "I decline to sign. You already know why."

The colonel gave a disgusted groan. "That's a damn poor choice, son. But if that's the way you want it . . ."

Another hammer clicked.

This one was behind me. It was followed by a thick, hacking, tubercular cough. But that only lasted a second.

Then I heard that smooth, sophisticated voice.

"Speaking of damn poor choices," Pop said.

I looked down at the colonel again. His eyes were wide, and his face was twitching with mingled fury and fear.

But the fear won. He put his left thumb in front of the .45's hammer, let it down slowly, and then set the pistol on the stack of confessions.

"Lovely," Pop said, coming up on my right. He held up a fifth of Johnnie Walker Red with his free hand. God knows where he'd gotten it. "Now, let's have a drink."

XIV

Pop didn't even glance at me. He kept his eyes on the colonel, giving him the same thin smile I had been seeing all day. He had a .38 revolver in his right hand and the fifth of Johnnie Walker in his left.

"You can sit back down," he told the colonel. "But we'll stand."

The colonel sat down. He looked up at Pop with a mockery of Pop's thin smile. It was a repellent sneer.

"A Communist corporal holding a pistol on a lieutenant colonel," he said. "This is not going to end well for you."

Pop set the bottle of whiskey beside the stack of confessions. "Nothing ends well for anyone," he said. He picked up the .45 and dropped it into a small metal wastebasket on the floor beside the desk. "Do you have any glasses? I'd rather not pass the bottle."

The colonel nodded past my shoulder. "In the bottom drawer of the file cabinet beside the door. But don't touch my brandy."

Pop's eyes didn't move from him. "Private, would you mind?"

I took a few steps backward, bumped into the filing cabinet, and squatted down to open the drawer. There were two short glasses and a cut-glass bottle of liquor. I took out the glasses, closed the drawer, and brought the glasses to the desk.

"We need three," Pop said.

I set the glasses down beside the confessions. "I decline to drink," I said. My mother had asked me to avoid alcohol, too.

Pop still didn't take his eyes off the colonel, but he grinned. His false teeth didn't look so bad all of a sudden.

"You're an amusing young man, Private," he said.

The colonel crossed his arms. "Neither of you will be very amusing once my aide returns. You'll both be damned."

Pop shrugged. "We're damned anyway. Besides, I happen to know that your aide is at the movies with a nurse of my acquaintance. He'll be there at least another hour. I believe tonight's film is *They Died with Their Boots On*. Which isn't too surprising, since Olivia de Havilland has been popular here lately. Although the story of Custer's Last Stand might not be the most tasteful selection for an audience of G.I.'s."

The colonel glowered. "If you shoot me, it'll be heard. There'll be dozens of men converging on this building before you're out the door."

Pop finally looked at me. His eyes were bright, and he laughed out loud.

"Can you believe this joker?" he asked. "*Now* he's worried about a shot being heard."

Pop turned back toward the desk, reached out with his left hand, and unscrewed the cap from the whiskey. He dropped the cap, picked up the bottle, and poured a hefty dose into each glass. Some of the booze splashed out onto the confessions.

"I have no intention of shooting you," he told the colonel. "I only brought the gun so you wouldn't shoot *us*." He tilted his head toward me. "That's right, Private. I knew you'd be here. You've hardly listened to me all day."

"Sorry," I said. "You're not an officer."

Pop put down the bottle and picked up one of the glasses. "I'll drink to that," he said, and downed the whole thing in three swallows. Then he set it down and refilled it. "Better have yours, sir." He said *sir* with deep sarcasm. "You're falling behind."

The other glass sat where it was, untouched, the amber liquid trembling.

The colonel bared his teeth. "I don't drink that stuff."

Pop picked up his glass again. "Ah. But I know something you do drink. You had a little belt of something cooked up by one of our Alaska Scouts, didn't you? But what you didn't know is that some men can hold their mystical potions, and some men can't. You see, to take a spiritual journey, you have to have a fucking soul to begin with. Otherwise, you just suffer from delusions of grandeur. Especially if that was your inclination to begin with." He downed his second glass of Johnnie Walker.

The colonel leaned forward. "Have another, corporal," he said. His voice was almost a hiss. "I really wish you would."

Pop poured himself another.

"Uh, Pop . . ." I said.

Pop picked up his glass a third time. "Mother's milk, son," he said. "And don't call me 'Pop.' "

As Pop slammed back the drink, the colonel lunged sideways and down, reaching for the wastebasket. But Pop kicked it away with the side of his foot, simultaneously draining his glass without spilling a drop. He moved as casually and smoothly as if he were swatting a Ping-Pong ball.

The colonel fell to his hands and knees. Pop leaned down and put the barrel of the .38 against the base of his skull.

"Feel familiar?" Pop asked.

The colonel made a whimpering sound.

"Bang," Pop said. Then he straightened, set down his glass again, and stepped over to the filing cabinet where the wastebasket had come to a stop. Pop picked up the wastebasket, brought it back, and set it on the corner of the desktop.

The colonel awkwardly hauled himself into his chair again. His face was florid and sweating.

"If you aren't going to shoot me," he said, "then what do you want?"

Pop scratched his cheek with the muzzle of the .38 before turning it back toward the colonel.

"I suppose I just want to see your face as I tell you what I believe I know," Pop said. "I want to see how close I am to the truth. And then I should return this pistol to the commander. Fine fellow, by the way. He says you stink at poker."

The florid color in the colonel's face began to drain. But the sweat seemed to increase. His wormlike hair hung in wet strands before his eyes.

"While you were drinking and playing cards," Pop said, shaking the .38 as if it were an admonishing finger, "you listened to stories told by our friend the Scout, some of which he'd told you before on Attu. And you decided you wanted to try out some of what he said for yourself. Well, that was fine with him. What did he care what a stupid white man might want to do to himself? Besides, you're a lieutenant colonel. If he crossed you, you might take him out of his hut behind the hospital and put him to work digging latrines.

"So he gave you the magic, and you drank it. But as I said, you and the magic didn't mix. So your overall unpleasantness became a more specific, insane nastiness. And you decided you were tired of waiting for that promised promotion. You decided you'd do a few things to make it happen.

"You'd kill the symbol of the power you desired, thus making its strength your own. And while you were waiting for that chance, you'd befriend a Navy commander with power of a different kind. The power of political connections.

"Finally, you'd eliminate some obstacles and settle some scores. And you'd use both the dead eagle and a fixed fight to do that. You'd set up the soldier who could testify to your panicked fuckup on Attu. And you'd set up the dirty, unjustly famous Marxist corporal who'd snubbed you and your talent—and who might also cause you trouble because of his habit of talking to every G.I. in camp. Including the occasional sailor."

Pop reached down with his free hand, picked up the confessions, and dropped them into the wastebasket on top of the .45. Then he pointed the .38 at the colonel's chest.

"Are there any carbons?" Pop asked. "Tell the truth, now. I was a Pinkerton."

The colonel, pale and perspiring, shook his head.

Pop picked up the colonel's untouched glass of whiskey and poured it into the wastebasket.

"The one thing I can't figure," he said, "is how you arranged the timing and the murder. I know how you got your fall-guy sailor to show up at the *ulax* this morning—money and sex. But I don't know how you managed to have him capture an eagle for you to kill at almost the same time. And I don't know how you could be sure that the second sailor, even as angry as he was over being cheated, would go so far as to kill the boxer."

Now the colonel, still pasty and sweating, smiled. He looked happy. It was the scariest thing I'd seen since Attu.

"I saw the future," he said. His voice was as thick and dark as volcanic mud. "That's how."

Pop cocked his head. "Ah. Well, that wouldn't have made sense to me yesterday. But it's not yesterday anymore." He reached into a jacket pocket and brought out his Zippo. "So maybe you already saw this, too."

He lit the Zippo and dropped it into the wastebasket. Blue and yellow flames flashed up halfway to the ceiling, then settled to a few inches above the lip of the basket and burned steadily.

"We're going to leave now," Pop told the colonel. He picked up the bottle cap and replaced it on the Johnnie Walker. "You aren't going to bother us again. The private here isn't your slave anymore. And I don't have the time or stomach to read your stories." He picked up the bottle with his free hand and took a few steps backward toward the vestibule.

I hesitated, thinking that perhaps I should put out the fire. But neither Pop nor the colonel seemed concerned by it.

"You can't prove any of it," the colonel said. His voice was shaking and wild now. "You don't have anything you can tell anyone. You can't do a thing to me."

Pop stopped, then stepped forward again. He held out the bottle of whiskey toward me. I took it.

Then Pop uncocked the .38 and slid it into in his right jacket pocket. He stepped up to the desk again. I could see the light of the flames dancing in his eyeglasses as he nodded to the colonel.

"You're partly right," Pop said. "No one can go to a court-martial and submit visions as evidence. But I do have a few things I can use in other contexts. I have a new friend in the Navy, a great admirer of my work, who has high connections. And I gave this same friend the name of a possible murderer. A sailor named Joe. I didn't have to tell him why or how I had the name. My reputation in matters of murder, fictional though those murders may be, seemed good enough for him.

"Now, the naval investigators might not find the right Joe, and even if they do, they might not be able to prove what Joe did. Especially if he's smart enough not to confess. But the Joe in question is a bit of a hothead. So, since those Navy boys will be questioning every sailor on Adak named Joe, it's possible that an angry Joe might reveal that one of yesterday's boxing matches was fixed. And he might tell them who else knows about that, and who he saw by that dead bird this morning. And then those Navy boys might come talk to some of their colleagues in the Army. Don't you think?"

The colonel began to rise from his chair again.

"Goddamn slimy Red—" he began.

As quick as a snake striking, Pop reached into his right jacket pocket and came up with the bent eagle feather. He thrust it across the desk and held it less than an inch from the colonel's nose.

"You," Pop said. "Will not. Fuck. With us. Again."

Then Pop reached down to the desk with his left and picked up the colonel's garrison cap. He dropped it into the wastebasket.

The flames shot higher, and something inside the basket squealed.

The colonel's mouth went slack. His eyes opened wide and stared at the fire without blinking. He looked like a wax statue. Or a corpse in rigor mortis.

Pop turned and put the feather back in his pocket. Then he gave me a glance and jerked his head toward the door. I turned and went out with him.

But Pop looked back toward the colonel one last time.

"By the way," he said. "If you've ever thought about asking for a transfer, now would be an excellent time. I understand MacArthur wants to get back to the Philippines in the worst way. And I'm sure he could use the help."

Then we went out. The fog was still thick, but we could see where we were going. Even this late in the day, there was a sun shining somewhere beyond the gray veil. It was summer in the Aleutians.

I looked back and saw that the ravens were gone.

XV

THE LIGHTS WERE BURNING BRIGHT IN THE WINDOWS AT THE *ADAKIAN* HUT when Pop and I came up the hill. They were shining down through the fog in golden beams. And as we drew closer, I could hear the clatter of typewriters and the steady murmur of voices. Pop's staff was in there hard at work on the July 6 edition.

"I'm sorry your cartoonist has to draw his cartoon over again," I said as we climbed the last dozen yards.

Pop coughed. "He was upset. But between you and me, it wasn't his best work. I suspect he'll do a better one now. Unfair losses can be inspirational."

As we reached the entrance lean-to, a figure stepped out from behind it. It was the Cutthroat. Neither Pop nor I was startled.

"What took you guys so long?" the Cutthroat asked. "The colonel's shack ain't that far. I've been here five minutes already. Thought you might have died or something."

Pop and I exchanged glances.

"You were listening outside again, weren't you?" I asked.

He looked at me as if I were a moron. "What do you think? I wanted to know what you guys were gonna do. Which wasn't what I expected, but I guess it was okay. Might've been better if you'd gone ahead and shot him." He scratched his jaw. "You sure he's gonna let you be? More important, is he gonna let *me* be?"

"I suspect he'll have no choice," Pop said. "You see, I've already asked my new Navy comrade to inquire with his high-placed friends regarding a transfer for the lieutenant colonel. So whether he asks for one or not, one will soon be suggested to him. Assuming he doesn't find himself in Dutch before that happens. Because whenever the general returns, I may be having a conversation with him as well."

The Cutthroat gave a snorting laugh. "You are one strange fucking excuse for a corporal."

"That I am," Pop said. "And you brew the goddamnedest cup of coffee I ever drank. Next time, I'll make my own."

But the Cutthroat was already heading down the boardwalk. "Leave my six beers outside my shed," he called back. He glowed in the golden shafts of light from *The Adakian* for a few seconds, and then was gone.

Pop turned to me. "It was kind of you to walk back with me, Private. But unnecessary. I may seem like a frail old man. But despite my white hair and tuberculosis-ravaged lungs, I do manage to get around, don't I?"

"Yes, sir," I said.

"Jesus Christ," Pop said. He pointed at me with his bottle of Johnnie Walker. "What did I tell you about 'sir' and enlisted men?"

I held out my hand. "Well, I'm sure as hell not going to salute you."

He gave me a quick handshake. His grip was stronger than he looked.

"It's been a long and overly interesting day, Private," he said. "And I sincerely hope, you dumb Bohunk, that I only encounter you in passing from now on. No offense."

"None taken."

He turned to go inside. "Good night, Private."

But I couldn't let it go at that.

"That Navy boy is dead," I blurted. "It was the colonel's fault, and we're letting him get away with it."

Pop stopped just inside the lean-to. "Maybe so." He looked back at me. "But sometimes the best you can do is wound your enemy . . . and then let him fly away."

"Is that what happened?" I asked. "Is that what it meant when you showed him the feather?"

Pop rolled his eyes upward and grinned with those bad teeth.

"That didn't mean a thing to me," he said. "But it meant something to *him*." He checked his wristwatch. "And now I really do have a newspaper to put out. Any more silly questions?"

There was one.

"How can you do that?" I asked.

Pop frowned. "How can I do what?"

All the way back from the colonel's office, I had been struggling with the words in my head. I wasn't good with words. And Pop already thought I was stupid. So I knew I wouldn't say it right. But I had to try.

"How can you go back to what you did before?" I asked. "How can you do anything at all now that—" I closed my fist, as if I could grab what I wanted to say from the fog. "Now that you know what happens."

Pop's shoulders slumped, and his eyes drifted away from mine for a moment.

But only a moment.

Then his shoulders snapped up, and his eyes met mine again. They were fierce.

"Because I'm not dead *yet*," he said. He turned away. "And neither are you."

He opened the door with the words *The Adakian* stenciled on it. He raised the whiskey bottle, and a roar of voices greeted him. Then the door closed, and the long day was over.

I started back down the boardwalk. I thought I might go back to the bay and just watch the water all night. I'd probably get cold as hell without a coat, even in July. But as long as there wasn't a williwaw, I'd survive.

In the morning, at chow, I would tell my squad leader that I was all his.

Epilogue

THERE WAS BUZZ FOR THE NEXT SEVERAL DAYS ABOUT THE NAVY MURDER, and I eventually heard that they arrested a seaman named Joe. But no one ever questioned me, and I never heard what they did with him. And I didn't try to find out.

I saw the Cutthroat only once more, at a distance, just a few days after the fifth of July. He was boarding a ship at the dock in Sweeper Cove. It didn't look like he was sneaking on. So I think he probably made it back to Fort Richardson and finished the war with the Alaska Scouts. But I don't know.

The lieutenant colonel left Adak less than two weeks after that. I didn't hear where he had been sent. But a few years after V-J Day, my curiosity got the better of me, and I made some inquiries. I learned that he had gone to the Philippines and had died at the outset of the Battle of Leyte in October 1944. A kamikaze had hit his ship, and he had burned to death. He never received his promotion.

I never spoke with Pop again. I saw him around throughout the rest of July and the first part of August, because he was hard to miss. I even passed by him on Main Street a few times. Once he gave me a nod, and I gave him the same in return.

That was all that passed between us until Pop was transferred to the mainland. We had all heard it was happening, since he was the camp celebrity and there was a lot of debate as to whether it was a good thing or a bad thing that he was going. But no one seemed to know just when it would occur.

Then, one evening in August, I came back to my bunk after a long day of working on a new runway at the airfield. And there was a manila envelope on my pillow. Inside I found the bent eagle feather and a typed note:

> CLEARING OUT JUNK. THOUGHT YOU MIGHT WANT THIS. YOU OWE ME A ZIPPO.
>
> P.S. WHEN YOU BRAG TO YOUR CHILDREN ABOUT HAVING MET ME, DO NOT CALL ME "POP."
>
> D.H.

I have not honored his request.

Toward the end of the war, I heard that Pop had made sergeant and been reassigned back to Adak in early 1945. But by then I was gone. I had been sent south to rejoin my old combat unit and train for an invasion of the Japanese home islands.

Then came the Bomb, and I was in Nebraska by Christmas.

Now, as an old man, I take the bent eagle feather from its envelope every fifth of July. Just for a minute.

My life has been good, but not much of it has been a surprise. I saw most of it coming a long time ago.

But then Pop slapped me awake. He slapped me awake, and he kept me from seeing the end.

I've always been grateful to him for that.

I don't know whether he was a Communist. I don't know whether he subverted the Constitution, supported tyrants, lied to Congress, or did any of the other things they said he did.

But I know he wore his country's uniform in two world wars. And I know he's buried at Arlington.

Plus one more thing.

Just today, decades after I first saw that hardback copy on another guy's bunk . . .

I've finally finished reading *The Maltese Falcon*.

And you know what? I wish I could tell Pop:

It's pretty goddamn good.

ABOUT THE EDITORS

George R. R. Martin has been called "the American Tolkien," and his books, including the volumes in his landmark A Song of Ice and Fire fantasy series, have been on bestseller lists around the world and are now a series on HBO. He's won four Hugo Awards, two Nebula Awards, the World Fantasy Award, and the Bram Stoker Award. As editor, he's produced the very long-running Wild Cards original anthology series as well as the New Voices series and others. He's also worked for Hollywood and television, being part of the creative team behind such shows as *Beauty and the Beast* and the new *The Twilight Zone*.

Gardner Dozois has won fifteen Hugo Awards and twenty-eight Locus Awards for his editing work, plus two Nebula Awards and the Sidewise Award for his own writing. He was the editor of the leading science fiction magazine *Asimov's Science Fiction* for twenty years and is also the editor of the annual anthology series The Year's Best Science Fiction, now in its Twenty-Ninth Annual Collection. He is the author or editor of more than a hundred books, and was inducted into the Science Fiction Hall of Fame in 2011.

CREDITS

Printed in the United States
by Baker & Taylor Publisher Services